The Miner & the Viscount

by Richard Hoskin

The Cornish Chronicle
Publisher
Cold Spring, Kentucky

The Cornish Chronicle
Publisher
Cold Spring, Kentucky

ISBN 13: 978-1499724363
ISBN 10: 149-9724365

Dedication

This book is dedicated to my family in Cornwall and America, including my forbears who filled my veins with Celtic blood, my head with their stories, and my fingers with the itch to write them down; to my children to whom I pass on my heritage; and above all to my wife who not only inspired and supported my creative efforts but also gave me the time over several years to research and write this story while domestic details were seamlessly attended to.

Book interior and cover design by Cynthia Osborne Hoskin
St. Michael's Mount cover photograph by Michael Saunders, Cornwall

This book is available for special promotions and premiums.
Address requests to cynthiaosborne@cornishchronicle.com

What They Say

Peter Eliot, Australia

I was delighted to share my family research with Richard Hoskin and see his descriptions of the house that was formerly a priory, the great park, and the church that was once the cathedral of Cornwall. He has woven the local history of Cornwall into the history of England and tells a gripping story.

Mr. and Mrs. A.D.G. Fortescue, Boconnoc, Cornwall

We are delighted to read of the leading roles of the Pitt family at Boconnoc. We have devoted decades to restoring this great house to its former glory, and it is gratifying to read of the historic part it played. Richard's descriptions of the house and its occupants are so vivid they should tempt a filmmaker!

Maureen Fuller, Grand Bard of Cornwall (Steren Mor)

This book will be a best seller around the world. I am delighted to have helped in telling parts of the story in Kernewek, our ancient Cornish language.

Paul Holden, National Trust, Lanhydrock, Cornwall

An accuracy that can only come from experience. The author must also be congratulated on his meticulous and engaging approach to story telling and his natural ability to embrace the people and places of eighteenth-century Cornwall. I swear you can hear the sea lashing against the harbour wall as you read.

Tom Luke, Bard of the Gorsedh (Colon Hag Enefyn Bendygo), Australia

One thing we Aussies know is where to dig for precious metals, and for sure there is gold in your novel.

Margaret McEwan, Bench Films, South Africa

It's a sweeping story about fascinating characters in a beautiful place – it should be made into a movie.

Barry Raut; Author, Lecturer, USA

As a teacher of creative writing and author of historical fiction I know great work when I see it. Richard Hoskin's gift for the music of language and his passion for his boyhood home of Cornwall guarantee the reader a riveting armchair adventure for savoring with a glass of sherry by the fire.

Tom Rusch, President, Cornish American Heritage Society, USA

Richard Hoskin's historical novel is not only a grand yarn but a heart warming resource for Cousin Jacks and Jennys scattered around the world who yearn to know about "home" and where their families came from. My pride in being Cornish swells at the stories of the historic worldwide leadership of my ruggedly independent people.

The Historic Characters

ELIOT FAMILY, of Port Eliot
> **Edward Eliot** (1727-1804), created first Baron Eliot 1784
> **Catherine Elliston Eliot** (1735-1804) his wife
> **Edward James Eliot** (1758-1797) their eldest surviving son
> **John Eliot** (1761-1823) their second son, first Earl of St. Germans
> **William Eliot** (1767-1845) their third son, second Earl of St. Germans
> **John Eliot** (1742-1769) younger brother of Edward Eliot

PITT FAMILY, of Boconnoc
> **Thomas "Diamond" Pitt** (1653-1726) East India merchant, Governor of Madras
> **Robert Pitt** (1680-1727) his eldest son, married **Harriet Villiers** (c.1680-1736)
> **Thomas Pitt**, (1705-1761) elder son of Robert, former Lord Warden of the Stannaries, married **Lucy Lyttelton**
> **William Pitt, the Elder** (1708-1778) second son of Robert, married **Lady Hester Grenville** (1720-1803)
> **William Pitt, the Younger** (1759-1806) second son of William Pitt the Elder
> **Harriot Pitt** (c. 1758-1786) younger daughter of William Pitt the Elder

Ralph Allen (1693-1764) Postmaster of Bath, entrepreneur.
Thomas Bolitho, merchant, investor, man of business
Frances Boscawen (?-1805) widow of Admiral Edmund Boscawen, member of Blue Stockings Society
Hannah More, intellectual, educator, member of Blue Stockings Society
St. Piran (c. 6th century) patron saint of Cornwall and of tin miners
Joshua Reynolds, portraitist, patronized by Eliots
John Smeaton, inventor, first civil engineer, Fellow of the Royal Society
Philip Stanhope, illegitimate son of Earl of Chesterfield, MP for Liskeard and later St. Germans, diplomat
Reverend John Wesley, founder of Methodism
John Williams, captain of Poldice Mine
James Davis, Mayor of Liskeard
Edwin Ough, Town Clerk of Liskeard
Stephen Clogg, Councilman of Liskeard
Thomas Peeke, turnpike witness

The Fictional Characters

PENWARDEN FAMILY

    Addis, a tin miner in the Poldice mine; mine captain at Wheal Hykka

    Jedson, a tin miner and younger brother of Addis

    Lizzie, wife of Addis

    Jeremiah (Jemmy), his firstborn son

    Jedson, second son

    Jennifer, his infant daughter

TRENANCE FAMILY, of Lanhydrock

    Baron Trenance

    Sir James Trenance, his son; becomes **Baron Trenance** upon the death of his father; later acquires title of **Viscount Dunbargan**

    Lady Elianor, his wife

    Honorable James Trenance, their son

    Honorable Gwenifer Trenance, their daughter

Willy Bunt, valet and footman at Lanhydrock , then worker at Port Eliot

Mary Bunt, née **Abbott**, Willy Bunt's wife and former maid at Lanhydrock

Catherine Bunt, their daughter, goddaughter to Catherine Eliot

Charles Bunt, their son, godson to Charles Polkinghorne

Joseph Clymo, steward of Lanhydrock estate

Morwenna Clymo, his daughter

Tom Kegwyn, member of a mining family, ringleader at Wheal Hykka

Reverend Peter Perry, Perranporth, Methodist minister

Charles Polkinghorne, man of business for Port Eliot estate.

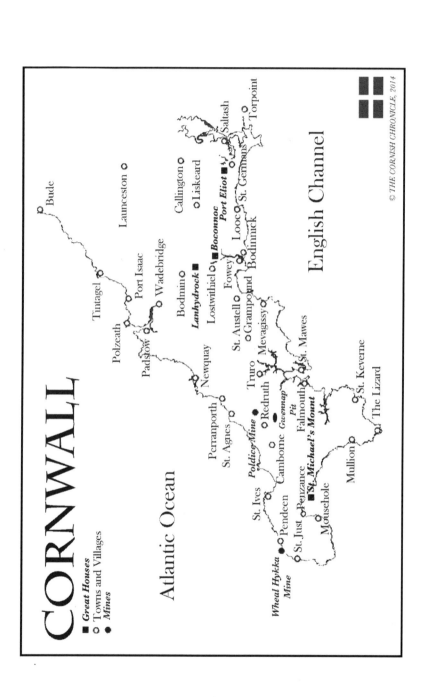

CORNWALL

■ *Great Houses*
○ Towns and Villages
● *Mines*

Atlantic Ocean

English Channel

Bude

Launceston

Tintagel

Port Isaac

Wadebridge

Polzeath

Padstow

Bodmin

Lanhydrock ■

Lostwithiel ○

Callington ○

○ Liskeard

■ *Boconnoc*

Port Eliot ■

○ St. Germans

Fowey

Looe ○

Bodinnick

Saltash

Torpoint

Newquay

St. Austell ○

Grampound

Mevagissy ○

St. Mawes ○

Perranporth

St. Agnes ○

Truro ○

Redruth ○

Poldice Mine ●

Camborne ○

Gwennap Pit

Falmouth ○

St. Keverne ○

The Lizard ○

St. Ives ○

Pendeen ○

Penzance ○

St. Just ○

St. Michael's Mount ■

Mousehole ○

Mullion ○

Wheal Hykka Mine ●

For Robert —

You didn't have to
retire just so you could
read my book!

Richard Hoskin

February 27, 2015

Prologue

He was terrified. Never had he hurt this badly. He felt as if his bones had been broken where they had beaten him with clubs. He was bruised and cold. The wind and rain from the north tore at his naked, scratched skin. No heat reached him from the huge fire that lit the darkness. The only warmth came from his blood where it oozed onto the abrasive surface of the millstone on which his body lay spread-eagled. He tried to move to ease the pain where the stone dug into his hip. But the thongs with which they had bound him were too tight. If he could move he would only hurt worse.

He was terrified. Helpless, above the scream of the wind and the crashing of the waves in the Celtic Sea below, he heard the bearded Druid order four strong men to tilt the great round millstone up onto its edge. He heard them threaten that they would roll it down the slope of the cliff top to crash on to the jagged rocks far below. He was unrepentant. He would surely crash with it. He did not want to be a martyr, but there was no escape.

In the seconds after the stone was righted and started rolling he promised the Christian God that he would serve him faithfully and perform heroic deeds if his life were spared. He had no time to reflect that it was prayers like this that had got him into trouble in the first place. Even a hundred years after the death of St. Patrick, many of the Irish had not accepted his teaching. The youthful Piran had tried to be a worthy successor as a missionary, but he had alienated more people than he had converted.

He gasped in a desperate breath as the wheel gathered speed. It bounced jarringly once or twice, and once again, before it lurched onto the rocks at the base of the cliff and threw up a cascade of spray as it plunged deep into the icy, foaming sea. The impact knocked his breath from his lungs; he shut his eyes tight. He was terrified.

Somehow, Piran was able to gasp for breath again. The millstone had surged upwards and broken through the waves to the surface far away from the rocks.

Miraculously Piran had not died, but the storm had. The rain and wind had stopped and the sea became calm. Piran glimpsed in the light of the flames at the top of the cliff behind him the faces of his tormentors, pointing and shouting in amazement at the escape of their prey. Piran exulted with relief, and breathed thanks to the God in whom his faith would be unbounded for the rest of his life.

He set to the task of making his escape and staying aboard his unlikely craft as the currents carried it southward. Had a miracle saved his life? Or was the millstone made of something like pumice, light enough to float? At least his bindings kept him from falling off. He strove to stay awake but exhaustion overcame him, and he slept until the rising sun stirred him. As he peered around he saw nothing but sea. The currents carried the millstone along for another night and another day. Thirsty, hungry and tired, he slept again, until the motion eventually slowed to a stop. The only sounds were the lapping of little waves as they rolled into a sheltered cove and the cries of seagulls soaring above in a clear sky. His millstone had come ashore on a broad sandy beach. Piran looked around. Close by was a limpet shell. Stretching his numb fingers along the sand, he was able to grasp the shell and slowly, patiently, he sawed through the thongs around his wrist and freed himself.

After a while he crawled up the beach, and drank fresh water from a stream at the base of the cliff beyond. Gaining strength, he sought out a cave for shelter and shellfish for food. He no longer feared. His soul grew calm as his body healed and circulation returned. He gathered driftwood, twigs, dry moss, then made a fire on a black hearthstone at the back of his cave. The fire grew hotter and hotter until a stream of hot white metal trickled out of the hearthstone. What Piran had discovered were deposits of tin in the rocks around what became known as Perranporth, west of Newquay on the north coast of Cornwall.

With health and confidence restored he ventured out amongst the local residents, made friends and spread his message. True to his promise to God Piran brought Christianity to Cornwall. He built a small Oratory in the sands. His first converts were a badger, a fox and a bear. With his mission, however, came the many conflicts with the old religion that he thought he had left behind in Ireland. He remained steadfast and eventually founded the Abbey of Lanpiran and became its abbot.

He also brought about the prosperity that derived from mining and smelting tin, copper, zinc, silver and wolfram and the development of the deep mines thereabouts that over the centuries played a major role in the life and history of Cornwall. Their names spoke of the Cornish and their language: Wheal Betsy, Bodannon, Cuddrabridge, Dizzard, Castle-an-Dinas, Geevor, Poldice.

After Piran's death his devoted followers built a church to his memory at the furthest corner of Perranzabuloe Parish. St. Piran's in the Sands they called it. Piran was venerated as the Patron Saint of Tin Miners becoming with time the Patron Saint of all of Cornwall. His banner is a white rectangular cross on a black ground, representing the tin flowing on the hearthstone of his hermit's cave. And on March 5th every year good Cornishmen and true celebrate St. Piran's Day and his part in their proud heritage.

Kernow bys vykken! Long live Cornwall!

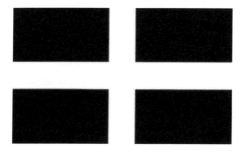

Chapter One

The Miners

Despite the dirty weather they were crowding into the hollow that Friday evening. Preacher said he would be telling about strange goings on and they should watch out. He said George II would soon be dead and a new king would rule their lives. They did not often think much about what happened up country, up London way. Real life was right here in Cornwall where they needed work to feed their children and wood to heat their cottages, or coal if they could find some. But when preacher told them that he had something special to say, they always came to hear him, always paid attention.

After work, some of them had walked to Gwennap from nearby tin and copper mines around Redruth and St. Day. Some had come from as far as St. Agnes and Truro, mostly men, because it would be men's affairs most likely. There were some wives with their husbands, some bal maidens who picked ore at the mine, and a few of the children old enough to work there, seven or eight, maybe ten years old. Farm laborers wore burlap sacks tied over their shoulders to ward off the squally rain blowing in from the Atlantic. Weather-beaten fishermen were dressed in thick, hand-knitted wool pullovers and oilskins against the weather. There were hundreds of them already, and there would be over a thousand when the meeting started.

They gathered at Gwennap Pit. It was a natural amphitheater, some fifty feet deep and two hundred feet across one way and three hundred the other, likely formed by collapse of a mine. A speaker could be heard clearly all around. It was a favorite place for the preachers who were barred from holding their meetings in the Anglican churches and whose followers were too poor to build big chapels of their own.

Preacher had driven his pony and cart from his cottage in Perranporth. He was the Reverend Peter Perry. There was about him an air, an aura that commanded attention. He often spoke about his fascination with the Celtic origins of Cornwall, its unique character, the teachings of the Druids, the stories of the saints. As a young man he was ordained a clergyman into the Church of England but later had come to embrace the principles and practices of the Methodist movement. As he took the lantern from his cart and walked to the upper side of the hollow the crowd fell silent. When he started to speak the wind and the rain fell silent. His voice carried throughout the Pit.

He prayed, without a book, for peace and health, for kindness toward each other, for comfort among the tribulations of this world and for salvation in the world to come. And some heard him call upon the goddess to bring them rain for seedtime and sun for harvest. He spoke some words that most of them understood in their own ancient language. He prayed for sustenance and forgiveness. *"Ro dhyn ni hedhyw agan bara pub-dydhyek; ha gav dhyn agan kendonow kepar dell evyn ni ynwedh dh'agan kendonoryon."* They resented the English church that was whittling away at their own language. A hundred years ago their forebears had given their lives, had rebelled against the new prayer book of the established church that made them say it differently: "Give us this day our daily bread. And forgive us our trespasses, as we forgive those who trespass against us."

Preacher asked them to listen closely to his message. He told them he had seen a comet a week ago when he walked at night across the cliffs to Penhale Point. It had been Friday, February 29th, and 1760 was a leap year. It was the third heavenly sign in three months. These were omens of changing times over a three-year span. He knew in his heart that new men were coming into positions of influence and power, and soon there would be more. George II was getting old and poorly and could not last forever. A new king would have new ministers.

"Reverend Perry, what's that got to do with we?" interrupted a belligerent voice up the slope at the back. *"Dhe'm brys, res yw dhyn kavoes agan negys agan-honan. Nyns eus travyth dhe wul adro dhodho. Ke dhe ober dres dydhyow hir ha maga agan teyluyow.* Us better moind our own business. Ain't nothin' us can do 'bout it anyways. Just got to work long days an' feed our famblies."

It was Addis Penwarden, a leader in the village of Gwennap. He was a little above medium height, wiry, broad-shouldered and powerfully built, with muscles honed by hard work and long hours. Beneath his flat cap, his hair was black and curly, his face lined and careworn, pallid from lack of sun.

Addis worked for tribute, as it was known, in the great Poldice mine that was owned by the Trenances, who lived in a big house up Bodmin way. Addis led his own team, or "pare," that worked digging out the ore and breaking it up and sorting it. Every couple of months he would bid on Setting Day for a contract from the mine captain. If he was lucky his bid was low enough to win a sett, and if he was skilled and his pare worked hard enough he would turn a profit. If he lost he worked for others if they would have him, for less money. Or else it was hardscrabble until the next sett. But he never lost. He was a hard man but fair and, by and large, respected by his workers and neighbors.

"Times are changing, Addis," replied the preacher, "and if you and yours don't change with them you'll always struggle for a bare living.

What happens up country and across the sea won't leave Cornwall out of it, you mark my words. We Cornish, Celts like the Irish, the Welsh, the Scots, the Bretons, we can be too independent, and if we don't band together, befriend each other, we'll lose what little we have."

"Aargh, them'll allus need Cornish tin and copper, preacher," retorted Addis. "Us be the best miners in the world, and we'm got the deepest mines, been tradin' our metal far across the seas forever. Right 'ere in Gwennap be the richest square mile in the 'ole world. And I'd stake my soul, me and mine, that us bring up more ore than any bloody furriner."

The crowd grunted agreement, but there seemed to be an air of discontent. Times were hard, and no one wanted them to get worse. There might be something in what the Reverend Perry said.

Just then there was a disturbance as some made way for a boy pushing through the crowd. Addis felt a tug at his hand. He looked down and saw his eleven-year-old son, Jeremiah. "What d'ye want now, Jemmy?" he asked. "Can't you see I'm busy?"

"Dad, Dad," piped up the boy, out of breath, "*An welivedhas a lever ty dhe dhos mar uskis dell yll'ta. Babyn nowydh Mamm yw yn forth.* The midwife says come quick nor you can. Mum's new baby's on the way."

"*Duwr'soenno dhis! Henn yw avar! Skon y fydh ganow aral dhe vaga,*" cried Addis. "Lor' bless 'ee! That be early! So soon there'll be another mouth to feed."

The people around him wished him good cheer, as he and Jemmy pushed through them and made their way out of the pit. But the crowd had become distracted and grew restless, stirred, some started to leave.

The preacher raised his arms, then raised his voice. "Listen to what I have to tell you," he called, "you mark my words and mark them well. Change is coming to Cornwall, big change, hard times. You must change too, or you will be the losers. The way you live is wrong, each man for himself. You win the sett, your neighbor loses; your family eats, your neighbor starves. Oh, I know some help their cousins, their friends, but nothing they can count on. The owners don't care for you, only for their comfort, their wealth. I promise that I will stand by you, help as far as I can. Pray to God and He will help you, but He needs you to help yourselves. You must band together, every family in every village in every parish.

"It is time to go to your homes. Blessings upon you all and depart in peace, but mark my words, take them in and be ready to act. Good night and peace be with you. *Oll an gwella.*"

Just before midnight a strapping black-haired boy was born into Addis' family. Addis beamed with pride as he kissed his exhausted wife Lizzie and gathered his lustily crying son into his arms. "Us'll call 'im Jedson," he pronounced, "after my brother. Just take a look at that young feller me lad. Us'll make a proper Cornish miner of 'im one of these fine days. *Res yw dhyn gul denbal kernewek gwiw anodho unn jydh teg.*"

Chapter Two

Trenance

The handsome young valet's cheerful "Good mornin' zir" as he drew back the curtains roused Sir James Trenance into full wakefulness from his dreams of possibilities that lay in the day ahead. His bias for having attractive people around the house included the tall, black-haired young Bunt. Sir James was just sorry he had not stirred and stolen a peep at pretty little Mary, the upstairs chambermaid, when she came in to rouse up the embers of the fire and put on more coal. At least when he struggled out of bed the room was warmer than it looked to be outside. He glanced out over the frost-covered park sparkling in the early light.

Sir James had slept deeply, alone on the feather mattress in the small bed in his dressing room. Perhaps he had enjoyed too much port, but he had only his own company to keep. Last evening he had been dismissed from the four-poster bed he usually shared with his pregnant young wife, Elianor. She had gone to bed early complaining of feeling queasy. He had just gone up to undress and join her for yet another frustratingly monastic night when she let out a moan.

"James, James," she cried, "I've just had an awful pain, I think the baby's coming You'd better do something, quickly." She moaned again and arched her back as she lay in the bed.

"That's a bit soon, isn't it? What do you expect me to do?" said Sir James. "It's not as if you were a mare, then I'd know how to help. Grab the foal by the feet and give it a good pull."

"Don't just stand there," said Lady Elianor breathing hard. "Get the midwife, now."

James put on his dressing gown over his nightshirt and rang for a footman. A few minutes later there was a knock on the door and an out of breath Bunt came in.

"Where the hell have you been, man?" demanded Sir James. "Her ladyship is about to have her baby. Go to the village right away and get the midwife and send a groom to Bodmin to fetch the doctor. Tell him not to dawdle, or he'll have to answer to me."

"Right away, zir," said Bunt, "Oi'm on my way."

Soon after, the midwife arrived. She had delivered Sir James and his siblings and was used to handling a birth on her own. She was a formidable woman and took charge immediately. "Now, young master, you leave her ladyship to me. Just send the housekeeper up to 'elp me and you keep out of my way."

Sir James wanted the doctor also in attendance just to make sure all was well, in case the baby was an heir, but he felt this was not quite the moment to inform the midwife of that. The doctor should be quite capable of looking after himself. James decided to take himself off downstairs to the library. He had the room to himself, his father must have already gone to bed. He was stretched out in a chair with his feet to the fire, and helped himself to a glass of his father's finest port. No point in disturbing a servant to pour it for him, and anyway his father might get to hear of it; the old man was a bit proprietary about his cellar. He thought of finding a book to read but there was not much in his father's collection that interested him so he had another glass of port instead.

He was comfortable in front of the fire and after a while he dozed off. He had no idea how much time had passed when he was awakened by a knock on the door. It was the smiling housekeeper; her face lit up as she came into the library. "Sir James," she announced, "You have a fine son with ten fingers and ten toes and by the sound of him a fine pair of lungs too!" She tactfully did not mention that two of the toes on each foot were webbed.

Sir James stirred himself and sat up. "Ah, Mrs. Trethewey, that is excellent news; son and heir. Father will be pleased. Does the little fellow take after his father?"

"Oh, he's a handsome little boy, sir," said the housekeeper. "No mistake about that. But you'd best wait 'til morning to see for yourself. Her ladyship's really tired."

"Good news, Mrs. Trethewy," he said beaming. "Congratulate her ladyship for me. Tell her I will drink a special toast to celebrate. That'll please her. Will you join me?"

"Best not, sir, thank 'ee," said the housekeeper. "I must go and see to her ladyship and the little one."

"Before you go, be sure to tell the rector the news, so he can arrange for us all to give thanks in St. Petroc's on Sunday." He smiled. "But given the date, the little fellow hardly has an advantage with which to launch his life. Twenty-ninth of February, he'll only be able to celebrate his birthday one year in four. I suppose it'll at least keep him young," he said, chuckling at his own joke. "He'll just have to make up for it in other ways."

Sir James drank deeply. He had certainly done the family proud. He had married Elianor just over a year ago on her eighteenth birthday. Sir James' father, old Baron Trenance, was ambitious for his line to be continued. Sir James had two sisters, but it was time for the next generation to include a son to carry on the family's great wealth and position. Baron

Trenance had schemed to acquire a fine wife for young James. Elianor came from good breeding stock, old Cornish gentry with generations of male heirs. She was young and would surely be fertile.

Her people were Whigs and Church of England, with the essential qualification of providing a substantial dowry. James had felt pressed to settle down sooner than he would have preferred, but he was not averse to the match, as he admired Elianor's striking beauty, her womanly comportment, her healthy skin, her green eyes, her thick hair the color of copper beech. There were disturbing rumors that on occasion she had not always been a dutiful or obedient daughter, getting into tussles with other children and taking off across country on her pony, exasperating the adults.

She also seemed to possess more intelligence than was required for fulfilling her new household responsibilities. James hoped she did not prove to be a meddler in the estate's business, which he assumed none too soon would be left entirely up to him. No doubt Elianor would settle down after entering motherhood, and he was confident that any superfluous spirit would be curbed by a sharp tug on the rein.

Well, Sir James had lost no time in keeping his side of the bargain, a fine fellow. Now his father had to be proud of him. He looked forward to giving the old man the news, but it could wait until the morning. He drank another glass of port, well deserved no doubt, and nodded off to sleep. He was not aware of Bunt the footman coming in, helping him upstairs and putting him to bed in his dressing room.

The next morning Sir James sat on the chair by the washstand as Bunt poured hot water from the ewer into the basin and wrapped a steaming towel around Sir James' head for a few moments before taking the shaving brush and lathering his face. Bunt stropped the razor before deftly scraping away the stubble. Thank God young Bunt was no cutthroat! Sir James liked the clean-shaven style. It showed off his fashionably lean face that attracted the ladies. He was good looking in a rakish way, with curly black hair, striking grey eyes and a ruddy complexion, resulting from time outdoors in the fresh air and indoors with the bounty of his father's cellar. His most distinguishing feature was a prominently beaked nose.

Bunt helped him off with his nightshirt and into his undergarments. His hunt livery of dark green coat with red velvet collar was laid out along with his white breeches and yellow waistcoat. None of those namby-pamby pinks for the Lanhydrock Hunt while he was master. Bunt helped him into his shirt. Then Sir James tilted his chin while Bunt tied the stock around his neck and inserted the gold stock pin given him by his grandfather to secure it. However, Sir James put on his knitted wool socks himself, because he did not want Bunt or anyone else to see that his second and third toes were webbed, just like his father's. Bunt pulled on Sir James' bespoke tall riding boots with boot hooks. Now he was ready to go downstairs for a quick bite.

"Sir James," said Bunt diffidently, "Mrs. Trethewy said to tell you that 'er ladyship would like to see you before you goes out this morning, to greet your new son, zir."

"Ah, Bunt, thank you. I was in a hurry to break my fast. I almost forgot." He turned back and burst through the connecting door into the great bedroom. His wife lay dressed in a beribboned nightgown, her copper ringlets spread on lace edged pillows, a breakfast tray table across her lap. Mrs. Trethewy stood at one side of the bed and the midwife at the other, a swaddled bundle in her capacious arms.

"Lady Trenance," Sir James addressed his wife. "Good morning, well done!" Turning to the midwife, he bellowed, "Show me my heir. Mrs. Trethewey. No, not too close, there's no telling what might be beneath those cloths. Well, bless my soul, fine little chap and no mistake. Can't wait to get him on a horse. Everyone doing well, eh? Must be going now, hounds won't wait." He kissed his wife on her forehead and strode out of the door and down the stairs, beaming with pride at the achievement of his virility. His father would be pleased with him.

He acknowledged the butler's greeting with a nod as he entered the morning room. Baron Trenance was already seated at the drum table, and Sir James looked forward to joining him in staving off hunger pangs with a pair of mutton chops and a tankard of home-brewed ale.

"Morning, sir," said Sir James, "and how's your liver this fine day?" He hoped to keep the conversation with his father light. He was not disposed to get into another of the harangues about tempering his ways and fitting himself to take on his responsibilities as future head of the family that the old baron delivered these days with increasing frequency.

"Morning, son," replied his father. "Lovely day for a gallop. 'Fraid I won't be joining you. Can't keep up like I used to. Have to leave it to you young 'uns, huntin', overseein' the estate, business, even the ladies. Roskilly tells me they've seen foxes prowlin' around the hen houses in the home farm, then making off to Restormel woods."

"Talking of young 'uns, father, you'll be pleased that Lady Elianor produced an heir last night," said Sir James. "I just went in to see them, looks like a fine little fellow, another James. Seems to have inherited my good looks, as far as I could tell. Make sure you pop in and see him when you go upstairs, congratulate the new mother."

"Heartiest congratulations to you too, my boy, good bloodlines. Well done, got to keep the family going, don't you know? I'll be sure to pay my respects, soon as you all set off."

At last, the baron thought. That was more like it. Had to maintain the family position, the wealth too. After all, he had private expenses that had to be met. It was expensive to keep mistresses, and especially to keep their discretion, and he was in little doubt that his son had the same tendencies in that direction.

"Now, my boy, who've you got coming back to the hunt breakfast?"

The Lanhydrock Hunt offered exceptional sport, with points as long as twenty miles without riding beyond the estate grounds. There weren't as many deer about as there used to be, so the fox had become the preferred quarry, but the old deer park provided excellent country. Roskilly, the huntsman, could field a pack of fifteen and a half couples of fit and eager hounds. The privileged members of society in the county enjoyed being invited as guests, and a few farmers were included too so that they did not complain when their crops were trampled or their hedges damaged.

"The Bolithos will be here, sir. They are promising to invest in the extension at the Poldice mine, although their participation may be in the form of a loan; you know what those partners are like. Young Eliot from St. Germans is coming, bringing his wife too, or so you said. They tell me he's an up and comer; he's been keeping an eye on their boroughs. You're expecting the Pitts aren't you, William and Lady Hester down from London? I hope Sir Thomas stays home at Boconnoc, he's never got a good word to say to anyone, shows me little enough respect. Steward Clymo is bringing his daughter Morwenna; she has a fine seat. And Vivian from the home farm and a number of the tenants will be here too."

"Yes, I've got a letter from William Pitt's secretary; they've accepted," said the baron.

"It'll be a lively meet," Sir James continued. "We'll get them off to a good start. I've ordered up some of that French brandy for the stirrup cups; should warm them up a bit. I'm sure you can get plenty more."

"You keep your hands off my cellar, my boy," said the baron. "I've been able to get some exceptional brandy over the years and lay down a wonderful vintage port. While I'm still alive the key to the cellar stays in my weskit pocket. The brandy's mine, and I will decide when and to whom I will offer it."

James rolled his eyes but softened the gesture with a smile, restraining the impulse to protest as a footman came in and whispered discreetly to the butler, who in turn announced, "Sir James, the groom has led your horse around to the front. Mr. Roskilly and the whip have brought up the hounds, and the guests are beginning to arrive."

"Well, must be off, Father," exclaimed Sir James, "can't keep the hounds waiting."

Picking up his crop and with a wave of his top hat to his father, he strode off to the front hall, where Bunt was waiting to put on his spurs for him. Then he went out of the front door into the sunny forecourt. He waved a greeting to the gathering field and got a leg up into the saddle of his hunter. His stallion stood all of sixteen hands high, eager, in tip-top condition, beautifully groomed with a plaited main and a gleaming coat, saddle and bridle polished, double reined with a harsh curb bit. The breath of the horses fogged the frosty air, and their hooves crunched on the gravel as they danced about, impatient to be off. The hounds' flags were wagging, heads up, alert for the call of the Master's horn.

As the pack moved off with Sir James in the lead, the baron appeared on the doorstep and gave a wave of his hand and shouted, "Good hunting." He went back into the house and chuckled contentedly to himself. Should make the neighbors grateful. It was another of those invigorating occasions at Lanhydrock, but they didn't grow on trees.

How did these young people think things really worked? Didn't they realize that the money came from more than investing in mines and farms and lending their money at risk? Did that smuggler over at Polzeath find the money to buy his yawl underneath his mattress? Who got the first pickings of fine wines and brandy from those Frenchmen? Did those East Indian clippers lose a few chests of their precious tea by accident as they sailed up the Channel to the Port of London?

Well, time enough to pass on some of this specialized business to the young folk. He was glad to hear that Bolitho was coming to hunt; he was a sound fellow. He'd chat with him about his concerns. Between him and Steward Clymo they could push James to pay attention to what was needed, give him wise advice, keep an eye on him. He hoped that the young fool would learn the rest in time.

Best look in on that new grandson. He went into the smoking room for a moment, anticipating the encounter with satisfaction. He went to a chest of drawers, reached in, unlocked a casket and slipped a small object into each pocket. Then as he slowly climbed the stairs, leaning heavily on the banister, Baron Trenance pondered what the future held in store. Perhaps this little lad would take the family's fortunes to greater heights, a loftier title, a place in the government. He prayed that he himself would stay alive long enough to do him some good, counteract some of the boy's father's increasingly evident lack of interest in the fundamentals that assure advancement.

He knocked on the door of his daughter-in-law's bedroom and went in. She was sitting propped up against the goose-down pillows at the head of her bed, the breakfast tray on the table beside her, the baby bundled in her arms. The old nurse was standing at the far side of the bed, beaming and watchful.

"My warmest congratulations, my dear," he said. "You have done me proud, let me take a good look at him. James, I hear?" Elianor smiled ruefully at the name but otherwise greeted the Baron affectionately.

"Father, how good of you to trouble to see me. How are your legs? Yes, James, your son insisted on 'James', and no doubt you approve. Would you like to take a close look at him?" She folded the soft woolen shawl back from the baby's face and turned him to face his grandfather. The old Baron leaned over, rested on the side of the bed with one hand and reached over with the other, a gnarled finger stroking the baby's cheek.

"He's a fine little fellow, my dear," said the baron. "I see he's got the Trenance nose already. No mistaking his ancestry; an heir to be proud of. Birth not too bad I trust, Mrs. Trethewey?"

"Not more than usual, my lord," said the nurse. "Her ladyship done us all proud, thank you kindly."

Baron Trenance put his hand in his pocket and took out a small package for Elianor to open. In it was a somewhat dented silver christening mug. "For your son, my dear; it was mine when I was a boy."

Elianor smiled delightedly as she accepted it and showed it to the baby. She looked quite girlish sometimes. The Baron reached into his other pocket and took out a long narrow velvet-lined box and put it on Elianor's lap. She handed the baby to the nurse to free her hands to press a catch and open the lid. The box contained a gold necklace set with emeralds, with matching bracelet and pendant earrings. "Oh, Father," she breathed, "Father, thank you, thank you."

Elianor was touched. She had known when she married into the family that the Trenances had reputations as hard businessmen. Perhaps the old boy had mellowed with age or had a softer spot in his heart for women than for the men he had striven against throughout his life. She smiled at him.

"They were my wife's," said the baron, "and now they are my son's wife's, with my thanks." He leaned over, took Elianor's hand and kissed her warmly on the cheek. He turned and left the room. As he walked carefully down the stairs he felt uplifted that his prayers might be answered, that things would indeed be in good hands in his family; perhaps in the near future, surely for many generations to come.

Chapter Three

The Eliots

Edward Eliot and his wife Catherine slept late this Saturday morning. The Eliots had traveled by wagon the previous Wednesday from Port Eliot, the family's country estate in St. Germans not far from the Devon border, to their town house in the nearby borough of Liskeard, leaving their son, one-and-a-half-year-old Edward James at home with his nurse. Eliot House was situated near St. Martin's church and below Castle Hill, near enough to the center of the town for conveniently conducting business.

Many Eliot interests lay in Liskeard. It was the ancient market town for the surrounding villages, farms and estates. Much of Port Eliot's agricultural produce was sold there, especially in its wool market. As a borough it had two seats in parliament, both of which Edward Eliot owned. While Edward's first love was politics, his way of life was supported by the Port Eliot estate and by wise investments and sound management in farming and business. He had come with his steward to spend two days pursuing matters of politics and business.

Customarily it was not done for women to play an active role in business and Catherine took no part in her husband's meetings. Edward, however, when they were alone at the end of each day, did tell his wife of what transpired. He appreciated her intelligence and the perspective it gave to the advice she offered. Besides, he enjoyed their companionship. Now they would continue their journey, despite its certain discomfort and possible danger, to Lanhydrock, near Bodmin. Edward explained to his wife why he felt it so important for them both to go.

"Catherine my dear, I felt I simply had to accept the invitation of the Trenances to stay with them at Lanhydrock and join their party. I realize that they do not have the best reputation socially but the Trenances are filthy rich, wealthiest family in Cornwall I've heard. And they are expecting important guests. Nothing like cultivating personal contacts my father always said, and anyway these days with all the wars one can't travel on the continent, so one might as well impose on the hospitality of one's acquaintances. I am quite looking forward to it in a way and it would be good for you to meet more of the people who matter in the county. Frankly I count on your charm showing me in the best possible light."

"Must we?" Catherine had responded. "I don't want to plead delicacy of health but one never can be sure of one's condition and I so hope to be with child. I feel I should be careful and these roads make traveling virtually unbearable."

"I do sympathize, but duty must come first," Edward said. "We must go, it's important to the future of Port Eliot. We leave in the morning."

Catherine had already presented Edward with two sons. However, the first survived only a month and now little Edward James was sickly. They agreed that is was desirable to ensure that a healthy heir came to manhood to keep the estate in the immediate family. Edward saw to it that Catherine was well provided with servants, and she in turn carefully supervised the nurse and nursery maids in taking care of their son. So far, *deo volente*, all was well and with good fortune and good care Catherine would indeed soon become with child again. As an added precaution rather than journeying on horseback they traveled in the wagon.

That morning Edward was fully awoken by a discreet knock on the door. His valet came into his dressing room and got him ready for the country in a full serge coat and worsted breeches. Edward was tall and would cut a fine figure with his wavy dark hair and finely boned aristocratic features, lit by piercing eyes. Now it was time to rouse his wife and for her to summon her maid. Edward went quietly into their bedroom and bent over his wife.

"Catherine," he whispered as he leaned over to kiss her awake, "It is time to stir our stumps. We have a long day ahead."

Catherine stretched and opened her eyes.

"Oh, Edward, I was hoping to lie a little longer. Life has been so hectic since we married that surely I'm due a few mornings of lying about. In fact, this morning I was dreaming that you might join me here." Realizing the impossibility of that prospect, she sat up. "Are you going to ride to hounds when we get there?"

"No, we shall be late for the meet, and I am glad to give it a miss. My business in Liskeard has consumed my energy. However, we must strive to get to Lanhydrock at least in time for the hunt breakfast. Baron Trenance hints that young Sir James yet lacks the experience to be a sound man of affairs, but to my mind his family and connections make him a valued ally. The baron writes that he is hoping Mr. William Pitt and Lady Hester will be there; I need to mend my fences with Pitt. And I trust you will find Lady Trenance a pleasing companion."

"You have informed me, Edward, that she is with child and quite advanced in that state, so she may be preoccupied in duties other than being a hostess. I have been thinking, by the way, when we have another son we must call him John. I know how much you admire your great ancestor."

"That is a most considerate suggestion, my dear," said Edward. "I will not forget it. Now come along, we must prepare for our journey."

"I look forward to seeing Lanhydrock and meeting these people, especially Lady Trenance. However, I trust, sir, I may not be denied listening to the conversation of the gentlemen, which I find much more interesting than that of the ladies." With a smile she added, "Perhaps you will permit me from time to time to air my own opinions."

Fully awake now, Catherine summoned her maid and made short work of dressing. She went down to the morning room with Edward where they enjoyed a good breakfast. Edward ordered his valet to summon the coachman to Eliot House's side door that opened on to Church Street, which led to Baytree Hill and thence to Moorswater. The footman had already strapped trunks with clothes for their stay to the back of the wagon. Now, as Edward and Catherine settled in the wagon, he laid the traveling rug over Catherine's lap and wrapped it over her legs to keep her warm in the frosty air.

There was one more precaution before they set off. His valet would be riding his master's hunter as escort, and Edward discreetly enquired of both servants whether they had brought pistols. One could not be too careful with the highwaymen that lurked in these parts. Only then did he order the coachman to set off for Bodmin and Lanhydrock. At the first bone-jarring jolt of the wagon, Edward mused that something would have to be done about these roads.

"Are you all right, my dear?" he asked Catherine solicitously. She smiled at him and tucked the heavy rug more tightly about her. "I am perfectly well, Edward, thank you," she said patting his knee. "Stop fussing and enjoy the ride."

In Baron Trenance's letter inviting the Eliots to stay for a day or two with several guests at his magnificent estate, Lanhydrock, near Bodmin, he explained that the occasion was a meet of the Lanhydrock hounds. They would hunt foxes since the deer park was solely ornamental these days. The baron had confided to Edward that his purpose was to ensure that his son become better acquainted with his important neighbors in the county. The time would come none too soon when his heir must assume responsibility for the Trenance family's wealth. The baron also mentioned that young Sir James Trenance had been married for a year and his wife was expecting any day now.

Edward realized that Baron Trenance not only wanted to cultivate a relationship with him and his parliamentary influence but also to seek opportunities to lend him money. Too many people had learned that Edward's father had spent a fortune in London during his extravagant sojourn in the household with the Prince of Wales. Edward had heard that the Trenances could be shrewd, and indeed unscrupulous, in their business dealings but they could be useful and he might need them. His wife would be invaluable in ensuring an alliance.

Catherine Elliston had married Edward Eliot upon reaching the age of twenty-one some three and a half years ago. Catherine brought much needed wealth into their marriage, a fortune of sixty thousand pounds inherited from her father Captain Edward Elliston, who was a member of the East India Company. Captain Elliston had made a connection with Edward Eliot's father over an investment in the India tea trade. This was in the Eliot tradition, since Edward's grandfather had also invested in India with William Pitt's grandfather, Governor Thomas Pitt. Governor Pitt had amassed great wealth in India and upon his retirement to England had purchased the Boconnoc estate in Cornwall.

Money lay heavy on Edward's mind even after he and Catherine married and her dowry came to Port Eliot. Early that Saturday morning as he lay drowsily in their bed in the Liskeard town house he mused about his marriage and their future. They were happy together and had borne the loss of their first child stoically. Catherine was as adorable as she was admirable. She loved and respected him as much as he cherished and appreciated her. His wife seemed to have settled happily into Port Eliot and no doubt as her love for the magnificent place grew she would want to improve it, modernize it, make it more suitable for their aspirations. He wanted those things too, but they all cost money.

Edward's business in Liskeard had gone well and would add to the estate's income in due course. And recently he had finally received the government place he had been seeking for years. Disappointingly, it was the least important of the royal commissions, the one that dealt with Trade and Plantations, but as a Commissioner he received £1,000 per annum and it all helped. They at least owed him that if they wanted to benefit from the influence his boroughs gave him. He would have to go up to London and pay attention to his duties one of these days, not that they would be demanding.

What he really needed was to make a lot of money, to acquire real wealth on his own account. He just needed the opportunities, more than the estate and the boroughs provided, even than the family investment in the growing India tea trade. That is why he had accepted the invitation from Baron Trenance to join his house party at Lanhydrock and spend a night or two. Edward hoped that some good would come of it; it must.

Chapter Four

Hard Rock Mining

By dawn on Saturday their cousins had walked back from their shift, the night core, at Poldice Mine to roust the Penwardens from their beds in the tiny cottage. Six hours cramped labor in poorly ventilated heat and humidity had left them worn out, sweaty and dirty. They looked forward to their share of time in the beds. But first Lizzie got up to stoke up the fire in the kitchen and get them warm milk to drink and barley bread and dripping to eat. Then the cousins climbed rickety stairs to the chilly bedroom under the roof and piled in under feather-stuffed covers still warm from the earlier occupants. That would thaw their chilled limbs, stiff and aching after trudging home across the frost covered fields. The beds were often occupied around the clock as Addis and his team of miners worked turn and turn about.

Addis Penwarden's wife Lizzie had baked pasties for them to take to the mine that day. Young Jemmy had snared a rabbit the night before, so there was meat enough. His dad had taught him to become a skilled poacher, and so far the squire's gamekeeper had not caught him. Jemmy knew to stay out of any deer park and never to kill deer. You could be hanged for that. Anyway, there were plenty of rabbits, and his dad had told him the warrens used to be common land, so it was not as if he were breaking any law blessed by God. Jemmy had skinned and gutted the rabbit and fed the scraps to the cat. He was saving up the skins so his mum could make him a warm fur weskit.

Lizzie had made the pasties just the way the men liked them, shaping the heavy, protective pastry into a crescent around the filling, then crimping the edges to seal in the gravy. She had cut salt from the block she kept by the stove and added it for a savory taste. Some spilled, so she took a pinch and threw it over her left shoulder for good luck. The Cornish used all kinds of different ingredients in pasties, the choice was up to the eater. People said that the devil wouldn't come to Cornwall because he was afraid that he would end up in a pasty.

Addis liked his pasty with turnips and onions from his garden. Lizzie had taken a knife and marked the pastry crust at one end with 'AP' so there would be no mistaking it. His younger brother Jedson liked potatoes and no onions in his; she marked it 'JP'. After the pasties were baked, Lizzie took them out of her cloam oven, wrapped them in a cloth, and put them in a box lined with hay so they would keep hot until dinnertime.

As the men got up to leave, Lizzie went to kiss her husband good-bye and give him a hug. She was staying home a week or so while the baby was little, but she would go back to work at the mine as soon as she could. With another mouth to feed they needed the money more than ever. She wasn't used to Addis going off without her or to the feeling that he might not come back. She hugged him for quite a while. "*Byth war, ow melder.* Take care of yourself, me 'andsome," Lizzie said quietly.

"*Na vrogh, ow haradow.* Don' 'e fret, my love," replied Addis, "Oi'll be back afore ye know it. Tomorrow's Sunday an' Oi'll stay 'ome with you an' the boys, or mebbe Oi moight take us to chapel an' listen to the Reverend Perry preach. Oi could 'ave a bit of a sing with the choir too."

Addis, his brother Jedson and young Jemmy set off for Poldice. It was a long walk and Addis had plenty of time to daydream. As they trudged along he reflected how some lodes nearby had been worked for over two hundred years. Poldice was an important mine these days and he was proud to work there. Its tinners made more money than most. Addis had heard tell that there were plans for Poldice to be drained by the Great County Adit. The adit had been the work of old Captain John Williams. His son was captain at Poldice now, and a good man too. Folks said they were going to drive the adit forty miles and drain fifty or more mines. It is amazing what Cornish miners could do.

Addis stopped to pick up two neighbors and their wives who were part of his pare, and then they set off together. The men all wore dirty woolen work shirts and breeches, stained red by the tin oxide. They were good workers, experienced, knew what needed to be done and how to do it. His brother Jedson was a good worker too, but had not learned his trade yet. That would just take time. He had a sweetheart and did not always keep his mind on his job. He would grow out of that. Addis would just have to keep an eye on him. He noticed that Jedson had barely touched his milk before they set off. Instead, he had taken a swig of Addis' scrumpy, his home-made rough cider. He would have to watch out that it did not become too much of a habit for Jedson. Preacher would disapprove.

The men's wives and sisters were bal maidens, women who worked at the surface of the mine, the grass as it was called, wearing the characteristic aprons and protective bonnets. Bal maidens picked through rock that had been hauled up from below by the kibble men and landers. The women sorted the ore from the waste, then would spall the ore, breaking it up with hammers into pieces each no bigger than a fist. Next the grass men placed the ore under the stamps, great iron-capped logs six in a row weighing more than a hundredweight each. Each stamp was lifted and dropped over and over by a waterwheel, crushing the ore to break out the metalliferous crystals from the rock. More bal maidens would then sort the pebbles and sand and pack the tinstuff in panniers to be carried by mule to the smelters at the blowing houses.

After arriving at Poldice, the men collected their tools and supplies from the store building and put on their tulls, hard resin-impregnated felt hats to protect their heads. Each miner strung half a pound of candles around his neck. The cost would be reckoned up by the purser and taken out of Addis' pay at the end of the month.

"Us better be movin', my dears," said Addis, "This won't earn the old woman 'er ninepence. Got everythin'?"

They left the women in the stamping shed and walked over to the entrance of the main shaft to make the descent to their working level, three levels below the grass. The shaft yawned dark and deep. It was just wide enough for the iron kibbles, the buckets that hauled the ore from the lode up to the surface, and for the ladders used by the miners.

Each ladder was five fathoms long, fastened to one side of the shaft, with a small landing at the bottom of each. There were six ladders down to their level, so they had to climb down thirty fathoms altogether, one hundred and eighty feet in the dark, with water draining at intervals down the sides of the shaft.

Addis and his mates lit one candle each and stuck it in a lump of wet clay on the brims of their hats. It was too dangerous to climb down in complete darkness. They had to watch out every step of the way. Some of the ladders had missing rungs. Addis went down first, followed by his brother. Addis shouted out the number of the level every time he got to the bottom of a ladder to make sure the others kept count. It wouldn't do to stop off at the wrong level.

Their muscles ached. The deeper they went the warmer it got. The air became stifling and sulphurous. The candle flames flickered and the gloom thickened. They climbed on down as fast as they dared. They had made it almost to the bottom when there was a clattering that echoed against the rock walls, and then a splash. "What the 'ell's goin' on?" Addis yelled. "Sorry," called Jedson, "Oi dropped me 'ammer."

"You'd drop your 'ead if 'tweren't tied to your shoulder, *ty vothenn veur*, you gurt lummox," shouted Addis. "Watch out, can't be too careful."

When they got down to their level they gathered round a puddle at the bottom and looked around. They kept looking until Jedson found his hammer by the light of their candles. Addis led the way along to the allotted pitch where they would work. The passage was tall enough in most places to stand more or less upright, six foot or so. It was about four foot wide, a bit wider at elbow height with room enough for the wheelbarrows used to bring out the ore and waste.

There were adits throughout the mine to drain the water that constantly seeped in, but in some stretches the miners splashed through puddles. They had to take care in the dim candlelight not to trip over the planks that young Captain Williams had put down in the rougher places to ease passage of the barrow wheels. That cost a bit, but the planks speeded up the work, and time after all was money. Anyroad, Addis didn't have to pay for that, the mine did. He was just glad to get the lumps of ore they had blasted out cleared out of their way so they could get on with blasting and digging out more. That is what they were paid for, not hauling the tin stuff up to the grass.

As a tributer, Addis Penwarden would bid every month on Setting Day for a pitch, or section of the mine. Addis and his pare, as his gang was called, were paid a share of the ore they got out, depending on its richness and weight. They had to work hard and efficiently to make a decent living. Addis had to buy tools, gunpowder, rope, candles and other supplies from the mine owners. He had to pay to have their tools sharpened too, and often there were fines for mistakes or missing work. That was fair enough. The young captain, John Williams, had to stop the tinners just taking off, maybe going after the spoils of a wreck out to sea. Hundreds of them, sometimes as many as a couple of thousand, would leave the mines and head for the cliffs. What was that old saying? It is an ill wind that brings no good to Cornwall!

Addis' job at Poldice was getting the ore out of the lode and out to the bottom of the shaft. Course, you learned a thing or two when you were your own man. The owners paid the tutworkers separately. Tutworkers sank the shafts and cleared the levels; winning ground, they called it. Sometimes they were paid by the day but usually by the fathom or the kibble or the hundredweight, or some other measure. But that was the mine captain's concern, nothing to do with Addis as long as the work he needed was done. And a bob or two here and there would always get a little extra help moving waste when the underground captain was somewhere else.

They eventually arrived at the pitch where they would be stoping the ore, blasting out the rock and breaking it with their poll picks and hammers to get at the mineral treasure it concealed. At setting time Addis had bid with Captain Williams to work the pitch forty-five fathoms east from the shaft at the thirty-fathom level until he reached Henry Nancarrow's pitch. Addis knew he had to look out for himself and he drove a hard but fair bargain for a return of one twelfth of the tin stuff they mined. Addis knew already that this lode was rich in cassiterite, the valuable tin-bearing ore, and he hoped they might find copper and lead and even silver as they went further in. Lodes often ran parallel to each other, so once you hit one chances were you would find others. You might do very well. Course, you might not, and that was your hard luck.

The granite, feldspar and quartz in this lode made hard work. Sometimes you would get lucky and find a layer of granite already decomposing into kaolin, which was soft enough to use as china clay. The unlucky fellow who took the pitch before him had run into a layer of elvan, quartz porphyry, so hard that it was all his pare could do to just get through rock that month. They brought out so little ore that they starved.

"All right then, lads," said Addis. "Us must finish the 'oles by the end of work today. Then us can fire 'er up right before us leave, an' let the smoke clear out while we'm out of 'ere Sunday."

"Aargh, 'tis Perrantide on the fifth, that be Wednesday," said Jedson. "Them'll give us drink money and toime off. Bain't 'ardly worth stirrin' back, that's what Oi reckon."

"Ye be a shiftless ne'er do well, Jedson," Addis said to his brother. "Just wait 'til ye wed that lass of your'n, if 'er'll 'ave 'e. Ye'll sing a different song when ye 'ave wife an' little 'uns to feed, leastwise Oi 'opes you do."

"Just a bit of fun, me 'andsome," said Jedson, "us can't be solemn all the time. Leave that to the preacher an' the old men."

"Enough of your cheek," said Addis, "you may be a big lad, but Oi can still give you a clip over the lug 'ole. Besides, St. Piran's the patron saint of tinners, and us owes 'im respect once a year. Mebbe 'e'll bless our work for the next twelvemonth. If us gets done, mebbe us can stay 'ome a day or two. Now, look lively you lot."

Previously, Addis had marked out eight locations where he wanted holes drilled in a pattern known as the pyramid cut. His pare had already sunk four holes in the lode, each one and a half inches in diameter and four foot six deep. They were driven horizontally or down into the face for underhand stoping, angled so that the blast would create a cavity in the rock. They'd made good progress, driving through an inch of granite every minute or so. Now they needed to finish drilling the next four Addis had marked for stoping, overhand towards the roof. This would be more difficult and laborious, because they would have to swing their hammers in an upward arc, and there wasn't much room.

"Right now, Jemmy, you 'old the boryer this end for me and your Uncle Jedson," said Addis. "You two finish off that one the other side of the next one, take turns 'oldin' an' 'ammerin'. When us is done, us'll move over. Oi want these a full five foot six deep, not an inch less. Oi'll be measurin', so don't think you can pull the wool over me eyes."

They lit fresh candles, gathered up their tools and got to work. The Penwardens soon got into a rhythm and made good progress. Young Jemmy had grown up strong, but he was still a little boy, and after an hour he asked for a rest, tired from turning and setting the heavy boryer. They were all hot and sweaty and had taken their shirts off. They were thirsty. Addis took pride in the rough cider he brewed from the apples he picked from the tree behind his cottage.

"Stop for a minute an' take a break," Addis said. "Oi've got a nice drop of me own cider to wet our whistles." He fetched his jug from his knapsack and passed it around. Jedson took a long swig. "Hey, not too much, mind," said Addis.

"Don't be an ol' miser," said Jedson, "you got plenty more where that lot come from."

They set to again, eager to get the job finished. Addis and Jedson took turns swinging their hammers while young Jemmy struggled with the heavy cast steel drill rod, the boryer. Addis settled into a powerful rhythm, striking the head of the drill hard and true, feeling the tip cutting into the hard rock. Lift, strike, slide his top hand under the head of the hammer, lift, slide back, strike. Addis wondered whether he would be able to save enough money by the time new baby Jedson was ten or twelve, so that the boy would not have to go to work at the mine. Perhaps he could go to school instead. If he got an education he could aspire to be a mine captain, or maybe even a mining engineer. Then he could earn enough to support his family in comfort. But it did not do to wonder too much and surely not while his mind needed to stay fixed on the job at hand.

"Watch it!" Addis yelled. His brother Jedson was not paying attention; his hammer head had slipped off the boryer. Could have crushed Jemmy's hand. "Keep your mind on what you're bloody doin'!"

Addis knew plenty about how dangerous mining was. He had heard news last week that two men had been killed when they walked back along their level, thinking the powder had not fired. Just as they got to the hole to reset the fuses the blast went off in their faces.

The Penwardens worked steadily until Addis guessed it was about noontime. He could not of course tell the time by the sun in the depths of the mine, and he did not yet possess a pocket watch. But he did feel hunger pangs.

"It be toime for dinner," he told his men. "Us'll take a break an' eat our pasties while they still be 'ot. You go fetch our croust. Find a nice dry ledge where us can bide a while." They could not waste time going up to the surface just to take a break and eat their dinner. One of the neighbor men fetched the warm hay boxes and the jug, and Addis passed around the cider.

"Toime for we to get back to 'en," announced Addis after half an hour. "Us must finish this stretch ready for blastin' afore the day be done."

"Aw, us can knock off now," said Jedson, "Oi'm wore out. They'm plenty deep."

"Oi said five foot six, an' that's what Oi meant," said Addis. "Get on with it."

They worked steadily on, moving to the last holes along the lode. Addis was looking forward to the end of the day, getting back to the cottage to see Lizzie and see how his new son was getting on. She was a good, kind wife, a firm mother, and she did not take any lip from young Jemmy. She had put on a pound or two between pregnancies and it looked good on her.

Tomorrow on Sunday he would take it easy, just working around his smallholding, although he had half promised Lizzie to take them to chapel for the morning service. It was good to keep peace with his Maker every week or so, and he should give thanks for the birth of a healthy son. He wondered what the important news was that Reverend Perry had promised them at Gwennap Pit.

Addis stopped daydreaming and checked the final holes. They passed his inspection. He nodded, well pleased. They had worked hard and with skill. "Right then, let's get 'em ready for blastin'. Where's that needle, so Oi can tamp in the powder? Jemmy, you make up some paper tubes for them overhand 'oles. Jedson, gimme the powder an' Oi'll tamp it in loose in the underhand ones."

"What powder?" Jedson asked, "Oi ain't got no powder."

"Whaddya mean, you gurt lummox?" demanded Addis. "You was supposed to bring the powder. That's always your job. You go upside right away and get some. You'm 'oldin' us up."

"But Oi never," said Jedson, "not always."

"Get on with it," Addis said, irritated, "you don't need to take no money. The count house will put the powder on tick. Us'll finish up 'ere. Go careful, moind. I saw you take that extra swig of cider after dinner. Be sharp about it. And moind that candle near the powder when you come back."

The young tinner set off along the passage, cursing under his breath, to climb the long ladders up the shaft to the top, three levels above them.

He was taking a long time, but it was a long climb. Addis began to worry. "Where's that boy got to?" he said, "Oi'd better go chivvy him up."

Suddenly there was a loud clattering, followed by an explosion and the sound of rock falling and a rush of wind through the level where they were working. Their candles were blown out, and they were in complete darkness. With shaking but practiced hands Addis found a flint in the pocket of his breeches and relit their candles. He felt that his heart had come up into his throat and was choking him.

"*Deus uskis*, come quick," he said to the others, as calmly as he could manage. "Let's see what's 'appened. Bring picks and shovels and get a rope."

They stumbled across a scene of total calamity. Through the cloud of dust and smoke at the bottom of the shaft, the candlelight picked out a pile of rubble and splinters of planking. They hurried closer. They glimpsed a shadowy, shapeless pile of clothing half buried under the rock fall. It was stained red, but different from the water from the tin. There was a broken box, with black powder spilled in the fall.

"*Byth war an polter-na*! Watch out for that powder! Mind them candles!" yelled Addis. There was no time for grief now. He knew right away what had happened. He quickly organized his little party of frightened men to clear rock away, pull on the lower rungs of the broken ladder, take the rope and secure the ladder to the post at the bottom of the shaft. Addis swept up the spilled powder into the box as best he could and set it aside where it would be safe.

"Let's go up, careful now. You take the tools, can't leave 'em, we'll need 'em another day. Oi'll follow. Oi've another load to carry. Us'll leave the blastin' 'til next week, after Perrantide."

There will be a next week, Addis thought. There always is. But he wouldn't be singing hymns in chapel tomorrow, nor saying his prayers to give thanks. He would be at home making a long box. Next time he saw preacher it would be for a funeral, to pray that his brother's soul would rest in peace. Addis vowed to do his best to make this death the last at Poldice. He would pray to keep Lizzie and their family safe and free from harm. And he would pray that little Jedson would have a better life than his namesake, the uncle he never had a chance to know. And by God, that would come to pass, sooner or later; that was a promise.

Chapter Five

Travel by Road

The Eliot wagon lumbered along, the horses managing an occasional trot on the few level parts of pitted and stony roads hardened by the early morning frost. Progressive by inclination, Eliot had instructed the wheelwright to make wheels wide enough to survive the ruts. The wagon's body was supported on leather straps to soften the worst bumps.

As the sun rose higher on this first day of March, the temperature rose with it, enough to soften to mud the thin crust of frost. The horses eased as they climbed the long hill past Dobwalls and headed towards East Taphouse. As the wagon approached the big bend near the top, Eliot's valet, riding ahead, reined in his hunter, turned in his saddle and urgently waved Eliot to stop.

The Callington to Bodmin stage wagon had gone off the road into a ditch and was tilting at a dangerous angle. There were few such conveyances in this part of the world, and the Trenances, for the convenience of their visitors, funded this one. One of the wagon's wide rear wheels had come off and the vehicle lurched dangerously. The four-horse team had been unhitched. Passengers stood about looking frightened and helpless, their trunks burst open, contents scattered on the ground.

The guard waved his coach horn in one hand and a blunderbuss in the other. "'Twas bloody 'ighwaymen! Armed to the teeth they was," he shouted. "Rode us off the road as we got to the bend. Made the passengers turn over their jewels and watches and belongin's. Couldn't get to my gun in toime to stop 'em."

"Did you recognize them, my good man?" demanded Edward. "Did you see which way they came from?"

"No sir, they came out from behind the hedge sudden like, and 'ad masks tied across their faces. And I could'n say as 'ow I took much notice at the time," replied the frightened guard.

"They should be hanged!" cried Edward. "These ruffians are a menace to decent citizens. They must be rooted out! Unfortunately we cannot stop now; we have to get on to our destination, but no doubt other travelers will be passing by and will be able to help you."

"Sir, I too must reach my destination," pleaded one of the passengers standing by the damaged vehicle. "I am Edwin Ough, and I have the honor to be the Town Clerk of Liskeard. I am traveling to

Bodmin at the request of the new mayor, Mr. James Davis, to a meeting that will be of benefit to my townspeople, and I must be on my way."

"Ah, Mr. Ough, I should have recognized you," said Edward. "I believe my agent Polkinghorne was hoping to see you in the last day or so but found you were unavailable. We will make room for you in my wagon and get you on your way." And to the distressed guard he added, "I will send my servant ahead to find a blacksmith at East Taphouse and have him come and replace your wheel on its axle, so you and your passengers can get on your way too."

Edward Eliot gave the order to his man and showed Ough to a cramped seat in the wagon. Eliot knew Edward Ough to conscientiously devote a few hours of his week to his position as Town Clerk, but most of his time was spent as a small shopkeeper dealing in groceries and herbal remedies. He had the physique of one not used to manual labor, with soft hands and an inclination to corpulence. He possessed a round head adorned by a carefully trimmed and luxuriant moustache, which was no doubt intended to distract from the thin brown hair combed over a balding pate, revealed when he removed his hat.

Eliot introduced Ough to his wife sitting opposite.

"Welcome, Mr. Ough," Catherine greeted him. "What a frightening experience for you! Had we left a little earlier," she said, remembering her reluctance to rise, "as I believe my husband secretly wished, we might have been the ones threatened and robbed. He is as always quite correct; something must be done to improve the safety of the roads."

Eliot nodded at her with a reassuring smile. When they were underway and once again clattering over the road, he asked their unexpected passenger, "Tell me, Mr. Ough, what takes you to Bodmin?"

"It's an irony given the circumstances I find myself in, but I am seeking the support of the bigger parishes in these parts to join Liskeard in a petition to Parliament to do something to deal with these highwaymen," replied Mr. Ough. "The truth is they are bad for business. People are frightened to travel, and some of the farmers have stopped coming to market. Traveling is hard enough without fearing for your life. They've got to be prevented."

"I will have a word with Polkinghorne," Eliot said in agreement. "I always encourage him to see to it that our tenants improve the yields of our farms. That will accomplish little for their income unless they can get their wool to market and their beef to the butcher. For that we all need not only safety for honest men, but also for the parish roads to be greatly improved. Parliament must be made to see the merit of providing the means."

"Tell me, Mr. Eliot, how much farther is it to Lanhydrock?" asked Catherine. "I must confess the jolting in the carriage is making me feel queasy."

"Not much longer now, my dear," responded Eliot, looking concerned, "and then we will get Mr. Ough on his way."

They soon reached the gateway in the wall protecting Lanhydrock and their wagon made its way down the long drive to the lodge. They slowed as the lodge keeper came out to greet them and direct the coachman to the main house. Just then they saw the hunt party walking across the park towards them from the direction of the deer park. The riders were mud spattered, the horses' flanks steaming, and exhausted hounds had their tongues hanging out. A single rider swerved to meet them as the wagon halted.

"My dear Eliot, and Mrs. Eliot!" boomed a ruddy faced Sir James. "Welcome to Lanhydrock. "You've missed a good run, thought you might have joined us. We found twice and we killed one of the varmints. And," he said waving his hat towards the house, "you're just in time for breakfast." Dismounting he called his groom who had approached from the stable yard.

"Here, my lad, give him a good rub down," he shouted. "And get one of the other lads to take the Eliots' horses over to be stabled and watered. Send Bunt out to see to our guests' luggage and lay their things out in their room. Look sharp!"

He lowered his voice and smiled. "Now then, Eliot, we'll get you both out of that carriage and into the house. You must meet our other guests. Who's this fellow with you?"

"Sir James, this is Mr. Ough," said Edward. "He was on his way to Bodmin in the stage when they were set upon by highwaymen and robbed. The stage wagon lost a wheel, so we gave him a ride. Perhaps you could be kind enough to help him . . . ."

"Yes, yes, my dear fellow," interrupted Sir James, pointing towards the northwest, "you may take a short cut through the park that way. Bodmin is but a brisk walk. You can't miss it."

"But Trenance," insisted Edward, "Mr. Ough is the Town Clerk of Liskeard and he informed me of needs that . . . ."

"Splendid, splendid," interrupted Sir James again. "Be on your way, fellow." Thus dismissing Mr. Ough, he eyed Catherine admiringly.

"Mrs. Eliot, you must be hungry after your journey. Come and say hello to father and the others, and there is a new member of the family you must meet. I'm sure, Eliot," he added, turning, "you will find a great deal in common with our guests. Mr. William Pitt has come down from London and already been over at Boconnoc; he and his wife, Lady Hester, have just arrived here at Lanhydrock and are settling in. Do you know the Bolithos? It might favor you to meet them. They are in money. I believe you will find much in common."

"New member, Sir James?" asked Catherine, "I gathered that you and Lady Trenance were expecting joyous news. Boy or girl may I ask?"

"Boy, yes indeed a son and heir," said Sir James, beaming.

"Congratulations, Sir James," said Edward. "You must be delighted, and a great relief to your father."

"All in a day's work, Eliot," said Trenance, "the old man assigned me the task and I performed. And thank you for your kind wishes, m'dear. Come along this way with me, we'll go on to the house." Taking Catherine by the arm, Sir James strode off as she stumbled along trying to match his pace. Eliot stayed behind and called to the Town Clerk of Liskeard who was already a distance up the hill.

"Mr. Ough," he said, "Hold hard. I can't let a man in your position go off like that." He turned to his coachman and said, "Water the draught horses and stable them. Then borrow a couple of hacks and ride with Mr. Ough to Bodmin and bring the horses back with you later. Be off with you."

"Oh, thank you, sir," said Ough, trotting breathlessly back down the hill. "I won't forget your kindness."

Eliot waved his hand and turned towards the house.

Chapter Six

Lanhydrock

Edward caught up with Sir James and Catherine, and Sir James escorted his guests through the front entrance and into the hall where the butler met them and took their hats, coats and gloves.

"Where is his lordship, in the smoking room? Yes, then come, Mr. and Mrs. Eliot, let us find father. He is expecting you and will be glad to see you," boomed Sir James. "Ah father," he continued as they entered, "there you are! Enjoying a cigar, eh? You know Mr. Eliot, and this is his wife Catherine, making her first visit to us. Mrs. Eliot, allow me to introduce Baron Trenance."

"Welcome, my dear," said his lordship, putting his cigar down on an ashtray, looking up from the pile of papers on the desk in front of him and removing his spectacles. "Delighted you could join us, wonderful to make your acquaintance. Eliot, glad to see you again," and glancing at Catherine he added, "and I must say you are a fortunate man in having such a charming wife, old chap. Excuse me a moment, I have been busy just now looking over affairs with my man here."

Joseph Clymo stepped over to take the papers from the baron's outstretched hand.

"Now Clymo, be off with you, and put these accounts back in a safe place in the business room. I appreciate your frank advice, sound as ever. I know the Trenance family will always be able to rely on you. Be sure to join us when we all sit down to breakfast."

The baron stood and turned his attention to his guests. "Speaking of family, heard our good news? Young James has done all right by the Trenance dynasty. Boy born last night. Splendid little fellow."

"I'm delighted to hear it, Baron," said Eliot, "and I'm sure my wife joins me in offering our congratulations."

"I do, indeed," said Catherine, "you must be very proud."

"I am. As an old codger I am entitled to concern about the future of everything I have accomplished, need to know it's in good hands with you young 'uns. My father made that very clear when he handed things on to me, expect yours did the same."

"Yes, of course he did," said Edward, without elaboration. He did not feel close enough to the old baron to discuss his misgivings at his own father's mishandling of what he might have inherited.

The baron addressed Catherine with enthusiasm. "Mrs. Eliot, I would be glad to show you Lanhydrock. We should have time for at least a part tour before the rest of the field gets their horses settled and comes into the house. Did you know that the house was originally a priory? St. Petroc's, after one of our ubiquitous Cornish saints, but the monks were dispatched with the Dissolution. The Crown sold it off, always needing money. Course, we're not short of churches around here; the parish church is handy to the house. We Trenances made a little money, and my ancestor bought this place in 1620."

Catherine murmured, "How interesting." She realized that learning about family history was a duty she could not shirk since moving to Cornwall, but felt that the Eliots had quite enough of their own without her having to absorb that of the Trenances as well. It is just my weariness, she told herself, and summoned gracious interest. "My husband's family did a very similar thing at Port Eliot," she said. "But those monks can't have lived in much comfort, although no doubt the venerable priors did all right for themselves."

"Well, my dear, my ancestors improved the house," said Baron Trenance, "made those monk's cells a bit more comfortable. We've got over fifty rooms, should be enough to house future generations," he added, winking at Sir James. "We're particularly proud of the Long Gallery. Just wait until you see the plasterwork ceiling, seventeenth century, really beautiful, tells the story of Genesis."

"Oh, come along father," said Sir James, "Mrs. Eliot doesn't want to hear all about what happened long before any of us were born. She came here for enjoyment."

"I would love to see it," said Catherine. "I have some ideas myself for further improvements at Port Eliot, especially the public rooms. I only have to persuade my husband of the need. I must say, my lord, I much admired the grounds as we drove in."

"Thank you, my dear. My ancestors planted the avenue of sycamores, landscaped the park. Suits me the way it is. Expect James would like something a bit more fancy now that he has a son and heir, but he'll have to see to that himself. Won't be my doing. Come along, Mrs. Eliot, let's go and take a look."

"Now Father, please," interrupted Sir James, "Mrs. Eliot won't be wanting to rush off around the place after her journey. Besides, she would rather see the young fellow upstairs. And I want her to meet Lady Trenance. I'm certain they will become great friends, and after all we must not bore our neighbors. Come, Mrs. Eliot, I'll show you upstairs."

The Baron pursed his mouth, and then with a smile said to Catherine, "Well, perhaps later, Mrs. Eliot. By all means, go see the little chap, fine-looking specimen if I do say so."

Catherine's warm smile embraced both father and son. "It will be a pleasure."

The Baron picked up his cigar and stood aside to allow the Eliots to pass through the door. Sir James invited Catherine to precede him, partly out of courtesy, but also out of a desire to appraise her figure from the rear. They walked along to the teak staircase and up to the bedroom floor. Sir James knocked on the door of her ladyship's bedroom. It was opened by the lady's maid.

"Lady Trenance, you have a visitor!" announced Sir James, striding into the room. Catherine hesitated, but he waved her in. "Permit me to introduce Mrs. Eliot. She and her husband drove here from Port Eliot by way of Liskeard where they spent a few days at Eliot House. I rescued her from Father's clutches. I'm sure she's more interested in meeting you and young James than traipsing around a draughty old house like Lanhydrock." Pointing at the baby that Elianor held and then back at Catherine, he continued, "James Trenance, born yesterday, poor little chap, February 29th. Won't have many birthdays."

"James! Yes, that's my son's name," exclaimed Lady Trenance, with more than a hint of irritation. Perhaps emboldened by the neutral presence of Catherine, she continued in this tone, "I was not consulted. My husband insisted on James."

"Now, now, my dear, we have guests, *pas devant*," responded Sir James, embarrassed by his wife's ire and unprecedented willfulness. "Trenances always choose their sons' names, and I have chosen to call my firstborn after me. I naturally assumed that you would agree and would wish to please me. As indeed you will!" he added, his anger starting as he considered the slight she had just pitched at him. He glanced at Catherine to assess her reaction, but she remained impassive. Striding to his wife's bedside and glaring down, he said softly, "Now, if you please, good lady wife, address your guest. She would like a chair. I will not require one."

Sir James exited, slamming the door behind him and leaving the women to talk alone.

"Nanny!" called Lady Trenance. When the woman appeared, she handed little James into her care, wrinkling her nose and saying, "I think he needs attention, and then kindly bring him back."

Although Elianor was sorely discomfited by her husband's highhanded manner, she decided this was neither the time nor place to discuss it with a stranger. What had got into him? He was quite solicitous during the early months of their marriage and even during the long pregnancy.

Despite an attempt not to show her feelings a smile escaped Catherine. "My dear Lady Trenance, I must observe that James has been a dignified enough name to grace several of the holders of the thrones of both England and Scotland. I might also mention that my own son was christened Edward James. And," she joked, "I see you have married one!"

"Forgive me, Mrs. Eliot, it's clear I must learn greater tact." She was warming towards her new acquaintance. Elianor had grown up in a loving family where she was never lonely. The old Baron had just shown great consideration to her, but she increasingly felt the need for female companionship. Elianor continued, "And if I may be candid, it also appears I must learn how to stand up for myself. It was not like this when I was a girl. My father stood no nonsense, but he was kind. My family was perhaps not the wealthiest in Cornwall, but we enjoyed a position of respect, one that was earned over the generations, not one that we bought with newfound wealth."

Catherine, while not wanting to be drawn into family tensions, also felt empathy for the young and quite lovely young woman as she lay on her pillows with her mass of copper hair spread about her. Catherine walked over to the window and looked out over the park. She said, "You are fortunate to live among the most beautiful surroundings, Lady Trenance. Lanhydrock offers such harmony, such tranquility."

"The outward appearances indeed have no equal, Mrs. Eliot," said Elianor.

Catherine remained at the window. "Sometimes men take their wives for granted once they have what they desire," she said. "It is clear to me that Sir James deeply wished to have a son, perhaps to please his own father; so now you have done your duty. I am a little more experienced than you, my dear, and I have learned that wives can find ways into their husbands' hearts by ensuring that there is always a little something reserved that their spouses simply must possess." She turned towards Elianor smiling but her smile was not returned.

Elianor appeared troubled, a little embarrassed. Before she could explain her feelings the nurse carried the baby back swaddled in fresh linens and laid him on the bed beside his mother. The nurse plumped up the lace-trimmed pillows on which Elianor reclined. The baby responded with a healthy bawl, his grey eyes filling with tears and his face reddening. He kicked in fury, and his wooly shawl fell away from his legs. As Catherine rose and leaned over him, wrapping the shawl again over his legs and feet, she could not help noticing that his second and third toes were webbed.

"Oi expects 'e's just 'ungry, Mum," said the nurse, "wantin' 'is feed. He'll quieten down with a nipple in 'is mouth, Oi'll be bound."

"Well, he won't have mine, no matter how loudly he complains," said Lady Trenance. "Where has that wet nurse from the village got to?"

"I b'lieve her's 'ome givin' her 'usband 'is dinner, Mum," said the nurse apologetically. "She'll be 'ere presently."

"Presently is not now," complained Lady Trenance. "Send for her immediately. Can't you see the baby is practically starving? Take him away where I cannot hear his complaints. James indeed!"

Turning to Catherine, she said, "I apologize for my servants, Mrs. Eliot. Having so many can be trying. I can see I am going to have to learn to take the household duties into my own hands. Is your life filled with similar challenges?"

"I have been the mistress of Port Eliot for some three and one half years only, Lady Trenance," replied Catherine, "and during that time, I have spent more time producing heirs than I have taking charge of properties and servants. Mr. Eliot and I suffered the misfortune of having our first son die at an early age, and our second is not as hardy as we would wish. We just pray that our young Edward James grows stronger and thrives."

"I'm saddened to hear about your first child," said Elianor, "and I wish you, your good husband and young Edward James good health as well."

"And I pray that your babe be blessed with a long and healthy life," replied Catherine. "The early weeks can be trying but I know baby James will become a great joy to you. I pray, though, since his arrival has taken place so recently, that you are not discomfited and overburdened by our visit."

Elianor shook her head. "You are kind, but please be assured that your presence with us will be no burden to me. Rather, it is a great pleasure, for in this house I lack female company," said Lady Trenance. "Perhaps we shall become friends. Our husbands spend much of their time forming alliances and it behooves us to do the same. Perhaps tomorrow you will tell me more about yourself. Now I must rest, and you must join the gentlemen at the hunt breakfast."

As Catherine rose, the door opened from the adjoining room where a welcome silence had fallen, and the nurse came in to make an announcement. "The wet nurse is here, and little Master James is feedin', Mum."

Catherine made her way downstairs and found the entrance hall filled with people milling about near the dining room. Catherine was far from fastidious, after all she now lived in the country, but it was obvious to her sense of smell that these people had come straight from the hunt. They reeked of the sweat of horses and humans as well as varieties of ordure still clinging to their boots. She ignored the odiferous assault and put a smile on her face, determined to leave it there for the duration of this important social event.

Catherine saw her husband chatting with a group of guests, and he waved his hand for her to join them. "My dear," said Eliot, wrapping his arm around her waist, "I wish you to have the pleasure of making the acquaintance of Mr. William Pitt and his wife, Lady Hester. Mr. Pitt's family seat is at Boconnoc nearby and is long connected with Cornwall."

The wives smiled and nodded at each other. Lady Hester appeared intelligent and well-bred, younger than her husband. Pitt was lean, tall, with a commanding figure. His face was dominated by a beaked nose, Roman, and hawk-like dark eyes. When he spoke his voice was resonant. People turned when they heard him.

"The pleasure is mine," responded Pitt, bowing to Catherine. "Unfortunately my duties with His Majesty's administration keep me mostly in London, but I enjoy revisiting my family's hunting grounds from time to time when I can get away from Town."

"We are delighted to have you with us in Cornwall, sir," said Edward. "I wish we could enjoy your company and learn from your wisdom more often." Pitt inclined his head towards Edward and turned back to Catherine.

"As I was mentioning to your husband, I remind myself to maintain cordial relationships with voters and those who exert influence on them. My colleagues point out that I am often at fault by neglecting my relationships as I grow preoccupied with policy. I will make amends here and now. Mr. Eliot indicates that there are matters we might profitably discuss while we are together."

"Mr. Pitt, I am flattered that you should mention such weighty matters in the presence of ladies," said Catherine with a twinkle in her eye.

"Ah, my dear," Pitt replied, "Lady Hester tells me I talk of little else than affairs of state or of business, which she does not always find amusing. In my own defense I must say that I try to pay some attention to my family since our marriage, and particularly to young William who will soon be a year old."

"He is nine months, Mr. Pitt," said Lady Hester, "and a little frail. You should pay attention if you want him to follow in your footsteps."

"Nearly a year old?" said Catherine. "Our son Edward James will be two this summer. With the new Trenance heir just now being born our sons are of an age. Perhaps they will grow up to be friends."

"Indeed, the Baron mentioned to me earlier that young James will join our son at Eton," said Lady Hester. "And yours?"

"Eton, of course," said Catherine. "It's an Eliot tradition." She smiled to her companions and noticed that William Pitt looked detached. "What is your opinion, Mr. Pitt?"

"Quite," he responded. "Fortunately, Lady Hester tolerates and, indeed, understands my preoccupation with affairs, since her own family is much embroiled in public life. Indeed, her brother George Grenville and I are colleagues from time to time. Of course, the nature of my calling determines where my primary duty lies. It is rare that I can enjoy such pleasant recreation as a visit like this." He looked up. "I see our host beckoning; we must go in to breakfast. Come along, my dear."

Lady Hester smiled understandingly at Catherine as she took her husband's arm.

As the noisy crowd moved to the dining room Edward whispered to his wife. "Mr. Pitt is the most brilliant orator I have ever heard, my dear," said Edward. "He holds the House enthralled for hours at a time. It is a privilege to be in his company."

"From time to time I have felt it might be a privilege to be a member of that House myself," whispered Catherine. "Of course, I realize that gentlemen will never permit ladies to invade their deliberations, but at times like this I wonder whether I would possess the patience to join you if you ever invited me." Edward patted her arm, put a finger to his lips and led her towards the footmen who were helping the ladies with their chairs and filling the glasses of the exuberant sportsmen with home-brewed cider and beer, or with sack or mead for special guests.

It was truly a groaning board, laden with hams, legs of mutton, a baron of beef, suet puddings and cheeses. The sound of a horn silenced the chatter, and a beaming Baron Trenance called for a toast.

"Halloo! To Reynard for providing good sport and to our good huntsman Roskilly for keeping the pack on the scent! To Miss Clymo, blooded at her first kill: Morwenna, my dear! And to all our guests, welcome and more sport in the future."

"I'll drink to that," said the vicar in a piping voice from a corner of the room, "A splendid chase!"

"To Reynard," said Sir James, "and there is one more toast to add."

"Ah yes, my boy," said the Baron, clapping his son on the back. "To the new son and heir, the Honorable James Trenance!"

Sir James beamed with uninhibited self-congratulation, raised his glass and swallowed greedily. "Just leave it to your best stallion," he chortled," when you want to be sure of good breeding, eh Pater?"

The crowd drank and ate heartily and chattered as more toasts were offered around the long table. The footmen were kept busy, and the exuberance grew noisier and more boisterous. There was nothing like a hunting crowd for enjoying itself, especially at Lanhydrock. The Trenances always saw to that.

Willy Bunt took especially good care of Morwenna Clymo and exchanged a wink with her when no one was looking. They had been playmates when they were children and got into mischief together in the woods. He had a soft spot for her and she had encouraged him that the feeling was mutual.

As he was finishing the last of his breakfast, Edward felt a tap on his shoulder. It was William Pitt, who whispered, "Come, Eliot, let us steal away to the smoking room for a quiet word. We have matters to discuss."

They were hardly noticed amid the general revelry as they made for the door.

Chapter Seven

Politics

Pitt and Eliot had the smoking room to themselves. The room was cold and drafty. They settled either side of the mantel into chairs with wings to keep the drafts from their necks, and each man's leg nearest the fire warmed up as his further leg stayed frozen.

"After all of that home-brewed rotgut, I could do with a decent bottle of port," said Pitt. "I wager old Trenance has some hidden away in his cellar." Pitt rang for a servant. A footman answered his summons. It was young Bunt, who also acted as Sir James's personal valet.

"Have the butler decant us your best port, and bring me a footstool," ordered Pitt.

"Aargh, zir," acknowledged Bunt, and placed a stool to support Pitt's foot, which was as ever painfully swollen with gout. Bunt arranged the skirts of Pitt's long coat to warm his thighs. The valet left the room and soon returned with a silver tray bearing a decanter and a pair of his master's best hand-blown glasses with fashionable air-twist stems. Knowing the baron's proprietary interest in his best port, Bunt had made the butler aware that his selection should be for the most favored guests. However, the Lanhydrock butler was an old hand and well knew the intricacies of his job.

"Butler asked me to serve you gen'lemen, since 'is lordship's got 'im occupied with breakfuss guests, zir," Bunt said as he carefully poured the rich ruby wine and proffered each a glass. "Told us 'e'd decanted it earlier this mornin' so's it be ready for this evenin', 'ad plenty of time to breathe then." He placed the decanter and tray on an elegant mahogany sofa table from Thomas Chippendale's workshop and retired from the smoking room.

The two men sipped their port; Pitt smacked his lips appreciatively. "Our host deserves his reputation as a connoisseur. Wonder where he got this?"

"Probably discreet not to ask," said Eliot, "Certainly wouldn't tell." Pitt smiled, sipped again and spoke.

"Ah yes, discretion! I trust I can rely on your confidence, Eliot, since our families have been friends and neighbors since our grandfathers' day," he began.

"You may, indeed, Mr. Pitt," responded Eliot. "I recall as a boy hearing tales of Eliot investments in the India tea trade, and Governor

Pitt's adventures in Madras. I believe it may have been my grandfather who suggested Boconnoc to the Governor as he sought to enjoy the fruits of his great success. Indeed, through the years not only commerce but also politics has often brought our families together. And, after all, we both went to Eton, and that bond is strong on its own."

Pitt nodded. "Close ties, and here we are together in Cornwall where both our families have their seats." He continued, "As to politics, my esteemed colleague the Duke of Newcastle tells me that congratulations are in order for your appointment to the Commission of Trade and Plantations."

"Thank you sir, you are kind," said Eliot. "I have hopes that one day I may aspire to a loftier place, but I trust my new position will enable me to serve my king and country to the best of my ability. Although my interests and experience lie mainly in Cornwall, I am striving to broaden both my knowledge and my efforts on the national and foreign stages on which you so skillfully tread."

"The experience will serve you well, Eliot," Pitt said, and smiled. "I will keep an eye on you and who knows what your loyal service may lead to. Meanwhile, have no doubt your influence on the Commission may serve your own interests, too. You would be quite unusual in the halls of power if that were not the case. I must add that it would serve me greatly to have the eyes and ears of one far from London, someone who is close to affairs in the country, to help guide me as I strive to lead the king's ministers. Better yet, I would welcome your support in inspiring your fellow country gentlemen to favor a nobler zeal for public affairs over their hounds and horses, preferring for once their parliamentary duty."

"You do me honor, sir," said Eliot.

Pitt shifted his leg on the stool to ease the excruciating pain in his foot and reached for his glass. "My beacon is the greater good of the English people," said Pitt. "But as a matter of practical politics, while I lead the administration in the House of Commons, I am obliged to work with the Duke of Newcastle in the Lords, which requires more tact and persistence than I would choose to deploy. But, we all know he has the ear of the king." He waved his hand in the air for emphasis. "At least His Grace revels in the work of maintaining support in Parliament and managing elections, which endeavor assures us a continuing majority."

"I perceive that His Grace takes little interest in policy," said Eliot, "thus leaving you a free hand."

"Indeed, Newcastle leaves foreign affairs largely to me," replied Pitt, "so that I may concentrate my energies on a greater, more prosperous and glorious England. I must observe, however, that he has a somewhat parsimonious hankering to restrict my actions and thus is all too ready to negotiate a premature end to the expenses of the war. It would be far more beneficial if he were simply stronger with the Treasury and raised taxes. If that proved insufficient, borrowing is an option, and if the Bank of England will not adequately support us, then he must find other moneyed men." At this, Pitt leaned forward and slapped his knee emphatically. "He must learn to think on a grander scale. The price is indeed great, but the prize is greater."

"Mr. Pitt, I must say," said Eliot, "as I sit in the House representing St. Germans and observing your leadership of the Commons, how much I admire your skill and breadth. However, it seems to me that you are torn between the Duke's desire for peace and the King's ambitions to intercede in Europe militarily."

"Your confidence and support, Mr. Eliot, mean much to me and lift me up. It is hard at times to maintain optimism," replied Pitt with a shake of his head. "However, fundamentally, the Duke needs me as long as there is a war to manage. And he, in turn, has his value to me. Some say I dwell too much on measures and not enough on men, whereas the Duke has no equal at scheming and conniving. So, while I cannot fully trust him, he suits my purposes." Pitt paused and stared into the fire for a moment. "You appreciate my dilemma, Mr. Eliot?"

"Assuredly so, Mr. Pitt," said Eliot fervently. "I admire your intellect and trust you to do what is best for England. I hope, too, that from time to time you may see opportunities to do what is best for Cornwall, as well. Tell me, how much support can you count on from the king?"

Pitt shifted uneasily in his chair again and failed to stifle a groan.

"What troubles you, Sir?" inquired Eliot.

"My damnable gout!" exclaimed Pitt, "although I confess it is but one of many troubles, including at times the king himself."

"Allow me to summon the footman and have him bring you a cushion for your foot," said Eliot. So saying he pulled on the bell and gave the order to Bunt as he came back into the smoking room.

Pitt looked over his shoulder as Bunt started to move away and said, "Pray refill our glasses while you are about it, my good fellow. Port is an excellent palliative." The footman retrieved a silk cushion from the other end of the room and put it on the footstool by Pitt's chair. He then filled their glasses and placed another log on the fire before taking his place discreetly near the door.

"We must soon rejoin our hosts," Pitt told Eliot. "But let us not interrupt our colloquy just yet. We have more to discuss. Now what was I saying? Ah, yes, the king!" He raised his glass and sipped appreciatively, holding the glass aloft and swirling the port around it while he gathered his thoughts.

"God bless him! His Majesty's influence is profound," Pitt went on. "His ultimate power lies in his ability to appoint or dismiss ministers, as well as choosing the commanders of our army and navy. The Duke manages him better and has better access than I, but when I feel I must make a stand on critically important matters, he will listen to me. I never forget that George is not only the King of England but also the Elector of Hanover, and that enormously affects our policy towards Europe. He still revels in his successes as a soldier and having personally led our army in battle on the continent. Between His Majesty and His Grace, however, they continue to rely on the old system and remain embroiled in the petty intrigues of Europe."

"England enjoyed an *annus mirabilis* last year around the world under your leadership," Eliot said, "from Germany to France, from India to the West Indies, from the American colonies to Canada. You have distracted the French from an invasion of England, Mr. Pitt. I have followed closely your speeches in the House, but tell me frankly, how we can sustain the operations of the army and the Royal Navy on such scale? Where do you place the greatest importance?"

"My greater abilities lie in administration and in thoroughness of planning and the drafting of instructions," replied Pitt. "Such details may seem trivial to some, but I have learned that they are all-important. I have surrounded myself with devoted clerks, men who assemble the information, the figures. I know, for example, precisely which of the French ports are most vital to their trade. Thus I direct our brave seamen to blockade just those whose idleness will cause the greatest hardship."

Pitt settled more comfortably in his chair; the port seemed to be alleviating his pain. Eliot judged that it was also relaxing the great man's manner. Their conversation was going well, and he judged that he could be frank.

"As you say, Mr. Pitt, your detractors claim that you pay too much attention to measures and not enough to men. From where comes this criticism?"

"There is some truth in it," admitted Pitt, "especially where cultivating support in the House is concerned. I am happy to leave that to Newcastle. But where carrying out my policies is concerned, I did learn during my youth in the army the importance of men. Sound and vigorous leaders are essential. I study the situation and take great care in making those appointments that are within my power, not only within the ministry but also in the army and navy.

"That must explain in part the successes England has enjoyed under your leadership," said Eliot.

"Yes, there is no *deus ex machina* in war," Pitt continued after breaking off for another sip of port. "Let me cite an example. We owe much to a fine Cornish seaman, Admiral Edward Boscawen. His great victory at the Battle of Lagos in Portugal last year severely crippled the invasion plans of the French. He put five large ships out of action and took two thousand prisoners. And the year before, his knowledge of American waters and his planning of the combined army and navy assault on Louisburg in Nova Scotia, together with General Amherst and young Brigadier Wolfe, effected its capture and destruction. This was despite the fact that weather delayed our arrival and allowed the French to bolster defenses. His ships landed the guns and supplies, and his sappers and pioneers assisted the siege. Their success at Louisburg widened our approaches into the heart of Canada."

"That was a splendid victory, sir," said Eliot. "I'll drink to that!" They raised their glasses and sipped more port.

"And it was Boscawen's crew of Cornish miners who volunteered to undermine the French entrenchments," Pitt added with a smile. "You know what they say, wherever there's a hole you'll find a Cornish miner at the bottom of it!"

Eliot laughed and said, "I know the Boscawen family well, Mr. Pitt. Our wives have become friends; Catherine and Frances admire each other and share an interest in the arts. My father was a friend of his father, Viscount Falmouth, and I see the Admiral when he occasionally has time at home to take his seat in the House for Truro. Do you know the portrait that Joshua Reynolds painted of him? As a native Devonian, Reynolds is deprived of the privilege of being Cornish, but he is nevertheless a fine artist. My father patronized him, and we hang his work at Port Eliot."

"My wife tells me Reynolds' work is much admired," said Pitt. "Her Ladyship urges me to have him paint my portrait, but I must disappoint her while this war commands my attention."

"Nor for much longer, I trust," responded Eliot, then returned to talk of admirable Cornishmen. "You may recall, sir, that Edward's brother Colonel George Boscawen commanded the 29th Regiment of Foot at Louisburg. I am proud of what my fellow Cornishmen have achieved for England."

"Indeed, yes!" said Pitt. "Give me enough good Cornish lads with broad backs and rebel spirits, and I will prevail every time! Cornishmen serve the king bravely on land as well as on the high seas. Your 46th Regiment of Foot fought at Ticonderoga under Amherst in '58 and has engaged the French in Canada throughout this year. You're one of them yourself, Eliot. You serve Cornwall well, as you do England."

"Thank you, sir, you do me more than justice," said Eliot. "I am grateful for my place with the Commission of Trade and Plantations, and will fulfill my duties conscientiously. I must add that we Eliots have a naval tradition too, one which my younger brother John is following. He did well at Eton, then joined the Royal Navy as a midshipman. He is posted to Plymouth Dock, close enough to Port Eliot for me to keep an eye on him, as does our mother, too, sometimes to his chagrin. Lord Edgecumbe is kind enough to be watching out for his career."

"Let me know how he progresses," said Pitt. "The navy is always in need of promising young officers. It is gratifying to observe how old families maintain the tradition of public service."

"At the same time, I also am entrusted with nurturing the Eliot family fortunes, and I endeavor to be an enlightened as well as a prosperous landowner," Eliot said. "I believe the incomes of Port Eliot will grow from helping our tenants to prosper, rather than merely racking their rents and sucking capital; money better spent by them to invest in improved stock and seed and methods. However, Mr. Pitt, I would welcome the opportunity to study your methods and apply, what I am able, to my own work both for England and for Cornwall."

"Wisely spoken, Mr. Eliot. Perhaps indeed we need to work more closely together," said Pitt. "There is, after all, much in common between commerce and government. I have profoundly studied economy and know precisely where to draw the most blood from French trade. Indeed, I have concluded that it is the underlying trade and commerce that must be at the root of our strategy."

"Sound policy, Mr. Pitt," continued Eliot, "and sound strategy."

"Beating the French is the key to England's future," said Pitt, waving his glass. "We must beat them not only in Europe but in Africa, the Indies and, above all, the Americas. The Royal Navy anchors our power, and Cornish mariners play their part. If my prayers were granted we would have more such volunteers and would not be obliged to resort to impressment."

Rising to this subject on which he held strong opinions, Eliot declared, "The press gangs are a great trouble to our Cornish mariners. It is unjust and damaging that our fishing fleets should be deprived, unpredictably, of many of their most experienced men."

"The Cornish fishermen, however temporarily displaced, will soon prosper in the waters around the new found land," said Pitt. "I am encouraged to hear from my correspondents of their confidence that New France will soon be no more, that we will seize Canada and with it the trades in timber, furs and fisheries. The Cornish are masters in mining, and

I foresee riches abounding in developing the mineral resources in North America."

Eliot was not mollified on the issue of impressment. "Yes, sir, that is possible, but think of our mariners' families. These men disappear overnight, leaving women and children behind. I do, indeed, hope we share a determination that the press gangs should be abolished. They sorely disrupt the trade of the merchants and the fishermen, so important right here in Cornwall. I would urge you to improve naval pay and conditions to encourage volunteers."

At this point, seeing that Pitt had already drained his glass, Bunt stepped forward to replenish it. He had heard his employer say that Mr. Pitt was known for consuming two bottles of port a day. That no doubt eased his pain but apparently did little to assuage his gout, let alone preserve the baron's cellar.

"Now then, Mr. Pitt," said Eliot, "you are campaigning against not only the French to the benefit of England, but also the Indians to the benefit of the colonists. You appear to hold a strong interest in America."

"I do, indeed," said Pitt. "I am drawn to the broadest possible vision of its potential for England. Of all our conquests, America has the greatest promise for future expansion. Our colonists need more land, not least to reward our soldiers. Indeed, it is our Christian duty to remove the ignorant, bloodthirsty savages and put in their place God fearing civilized men with modern methods to make better use of that land and to pay taxes to England."

"I understand that the iniquitous French have bribed the Indians to fight against us by deceiving them into false alliance," commented Eliot.

"Indeed, such conduct is deplorable and ungentlemanly," said Pitt, "something I, as an Englishman, would hesitate to countenance. Furthermore, they spring out from behind trees when they fight and do not stand firm when attacked."

"No gentleman would comport himself in such a cowardly way," snorted Eliot.

"Indulge me a moment, Eliot, if you would be so kind," said Pitt. "Allow me to tell you of an honor from America which brought me much satisfaction. The commander of our expedition to the Ohio country took Fort Duquesne from the French. He was kind enough to rename the place Pittsborough in recognition of my support and his admiration of the soundness of my grand strategy."

"Then you have gained immortality, Mr. Pitt," chuckled Eliot. "Would that be granted to us all!"

"I do no more than my duty, Mr. Eliot," said Pitt, retreating into humility once his point had been made. He drained his glass and looked around for Bunt who refilled it, emptying the decanter. "We'll need more, my good man," said Pitt. "While you're about it ask your butler where he procures this exceptional port. I would like to lay in some in my own cellar."

When they were left alone in the room Pitt turned again to Eliot. Pitt stretched his legs and laid his gouty foot in a new position on the footstool. "I am enjoying this opportunity to get to know you better, Mr. Eliot, and you are making my visit to Cornwall more pleasant and possibly more fruitful than I had anticipated when I undertook the journey from London."

"I assure you the pleasure is mine, Mr. Pitt," said Eliot, "It is a privilege to hear of your aims and achievements from your own mouth."

"We have spoken of matters large and small," said Pitt, "but I reflect that the great achievements for which I aspire for England are at the last for the benefit of her citizens, and those beneficiaries rightly include our families and our friends. It pleases me to assist you in bringing to fruition your aspirations for Cornwall and your family. There are opportunities we can seize while we are at Lanhydrock."

Eliot could hardly believe his good fortune and was absorbed in what the great man might say. "What do you have in mind, sir?"

Neither of them noticed that Bunt had slipped back into the room with a refilled decanter and stood quietly by the door ready to serve them.

"I wish to encourage the merchants at home to support foreign ventures," said Pitt. "Now I see the Bolithos are with us here at breakfast, and I hear that they seek investment. And the Trenances, perhaps they could lend their support; we should explore possibilities. They have plenty of money. I know the baron to be a sound fellow, but what of his son? He is youthful and lacks experience, certainly, but is he of reliable intelligence. Is he of sound judgment?"

"The old baron is loosening the reins, and I do not yet know how far young Sir James is to be trusted," replied Eliot. "I, too, think he lacks experience, and he appears to have more interest in skirts and the chase than in affairs of business or politics."

Pitt nodded and pressed on. "Nevertheless, young Trenance should be cultivated and may prove tractable. Both you and he have several boroughs. He may be persuaded to be of service to my administration and could further our shared goals. Indeed, there may be more places to be had." Pitt paused and sighed, and sipped again at his port. "You and I should talk with him while we are here together. I seem to have made long speeches, Eliot, but I would sincerely welcome your views."

After a moment's thought Eliot responded, "You know that I and my family are Tories, and I ensure that loyal Tories sit for my boroughs.

Above all, my supporters and I are devoted to serving what is best for England. At the same time, my prime task is to continue to build a strong foundation at Port Eliot and throughout Cornwall." He paused a moment for emphasis and then continued.

"I value your judgment and ability, Mr. Pitt, as much as I do your reputation, as did my father. In general, I support the measures that you advocate and your visionary strategy for the war. That said, like you, I value sound friends. The Cornish people in these parts look to me to forward their affairs. Now, I have heard that the Trenances are eager to expand their mining interests, including their large venture at Poldice. They are money lenders and merchants, mineral lords, as well, lessors of the land mined by the tinners.

"We should, indeed, venture together, although with due caution. One cannot entirely rely on their loyalty to their friends if advantage is to be had. There is no gainsaying that their wealth is sufficient to pursue opportunities on several continents. Nevertheless, I am concerned that Sir James may yet lack wisdom in conducting matters of business."

"That may be to our benefit, Eliot," mused Pitt. "We may conspire to manage both Sir James' wishes and his influence while enjoying his wealth and support. And now," he added standing and leaning on his cane, "it is high time that we return to the company and seek out Sir James and also Bolitho. But first, is there anything further I can do in Westminster to support your aims?"

"There is, indeed, something," replied Eliot, rising also, "which could benefit Cornwall as well as myself and my friends. On our journey here we passed over roads that were not only poor but also unsafe. We came across a stage wagon that had been forced off the road by highwaymen and into a huge rut, thus losing its wheel. The Town Clerk of Liskeard, one of my boroughs, was a victim. The prosperity of Port Eliot and, indeed, all of Cornwall depends on better and safer roads for the travel of our people and, as important, to get our goods to market. If Parliament would add a turnpike trust for Liskeard, I am sure my neighbors as well as myself would provide support and indeed be grateful."

"I understand perfectly," said Pitt. "That would be an appropriate expenditure of parliamentary time. We all remember the horse and rider drowning in a pothole on the Great North Road! Let us indeed work more closely together. There will be many opportunities when both our interests can be served. Now that you mention it, I will have a discreet word with my brother Thomas. There are reasons that he may have interest in an investment that promises a sound return. It would be a considerable favor to me. Now, while I am here I could just ask Trenance if he is with us, but perhaps I should take your advice and be discreet before offering him involvement."

"I will leave that to your excellent judgment, sir," said Eliot. "As to your brother, as an Eliot it would be a pleasure to assist a Pitt in any way." He bowed and made his way to the door. Pitt joined him and they shook hands warmly before heading back towards the dining room, where the now weary and well-fed breakfasters were taking their leave.

They took no notice of the unobtrusive footman, Bunt, standing at the end of the smoking room as they passed through the door into the hall. And they had quit the room by the time he helped himself to a large glass of port, which he drained at a swallow before pouring himself another.

Chapter Eight

Influence

Among the few breakfast stragglers was Sir James who, having watched her progress around the room, was attempting to engage Catherine in conversation. Seeing her break away from a group of women by the window, he moved forward.

"Mrs. Eliot," he beamed and bowed, "I know my father's offer to show you around Lanhydrock was poorly timed, but perhaps you would accept an invitation from a more vigorous escort, thus making shorter work of it. After a hearty breakfast I am sure we could both do with some exercise, and a brisk stroll through the park after the tour would better prepare us for the excellent prospect of dinner. For my part it would be a great pleasure."

Catherine was not easily discomfited in social situations, but she sensed, not so much in Sir James's speech as in his tone and demeanor, possible trespass of the line between polite compliments and unwanted advances.

He continued, nonetheless. "I enjoy a woman who combines intelligence and wit with great charm and beauty such as you. And I must say Lady Trenance seems to have found her confinement, and now our son, more engaging than his father. What do you say?"

"Sir James," she said firmly, "you are too kind. However, I am tired after enjoying your hospitality following our trying journey. If I am to equally enjoy your conversation and the other guests this evening, it would be prudent for me to rest. Perhaps I can find my husband to escort me to our room. Ah, there he is coming now with Mr. Pitt." She addressed her husband urgently. "Edward, I am glad to see you! Would you take me to our room? I am desirous of a rest."

"Certainly," said Edward, searching Catherine's face with concern. There was something in her tone that struck him as different from her normal open and vivacious self. "Sir James, Mr. Pitt, please excuse us. I will rejoin you later."

"Eliot, that would be desirable," said Pitt with emphasis. "Sir James, we have some things to be discussed among gentlemen. May we meet in the smoking room? And perhaps you could persuade Mr. Bolitho to join us, say in half an hour?"

"Certainly, Pitt," said Sir James. "I will arrange for port."

So saying, the Eliots went upstairs where Catherine immediately confided her misgivings about Sir James to her husband.

"I do not trust that man, Edward; I feel shivers when he gets near me. You do not encourage me to meddle in your business affairs, but I must speak out and urge you to be cautious. I realize that the baron is exceedingly rich and Sir James will inherit. But my instinct tells me that he is not only lacking in competence but also in integrity. It's my woman's instinct, if you will, and you may not feel that is much to go on, but if Mr. Pitt presses you, and you feel that you must do business with the Trenances, be sure to guard your own interests. I love you for your honesty, but sometimes I fear that it may lead you to place your trust where it is not warranted."

"My dear," responded Edward warmly, "rest assured that I am growing to value your opinion and your observations. I may not yet go so far as to ascribe your opinion to magical womanly properties, but I at least take your views into account from time to time as I go about my affairs. Now, you rest, and I will rejoin the gentlemen. With prudence!"

Meanwhile, Sir James had gone to the smoking room where Bunt was clearing the decanter and glasses and tidying the table. "Bunt, glad I caught you. Arrange port for us."

"As 'ee wish, zir," said Bunt, hesitantly.

"What's up man?" demanded Sir James. "Say what you have to."

"Well zir," said Bunt, "p'r'aps it's not my place, but oi 'eard the gen'lemen discussin' business when Oi was servin' them 'ere in the smokin' room, an' oi fears them want to take advantage of thee in some way or t'other."

"Nonsense, Bunt, they are guests in my home, friends and neighbors, more likely seeking favors from my father and myself. Besides, I am well able to take care of myself against any man."

"Well zir, oi'd moind my Ps and Qs if oi were ye. Dunno zackly what them moight 'ave in moind, but them be clever devils to be sure."

"You just mind your own Ps and Qs, Bunt; you are being impertinent. If I want your advice I will ask for it, which likely I never will. Never speak of gentlemen to me in tones like those ever again, or I will have you horse-whipped to teach you your manners. Mr. Pitt and Mr. Eliot are, like me, Old Etonians. And don't you ever, ever tell me what to do," stormed Sir James, purple in the face. "Just get about your duties."

As Bunt opened the door to leave the room, Pitt, Eliot and Bolitho were entering from the hall. Bunt stood aside and waited for orders as Sir James greeted them. Pitt observed that their host appeared out of sorts.

"Gentlemen!" Sir James said, calming himself and summoning a stiff smile. "May I offer you some port or brandy? I must say they are excellent; they come from my father's cellar."

"Eliot and I have already sampled his port," replied Pitt, "and I compliment your father on his taste. I would, indeed, enjoy some more. Might he be persuaded to share his wine merchant with me?"

"He may make an exception in your case, Mr. Pitt," said Sir James, "but he takes great pride in his cellar and guards his sources jealously. I would dearly wish the same information, but so far it has been denied me."

Bunt left and presently returned with the port, refilled the gentlemen's glasses and once again took his place quietly near the door.

"Now look here, Sir James," said Pitt authoritatively, "I do not imagine for one moment that you and your father invited me here for this visit just to enjoy your hunt, which indeed my damnable foot prevents me from doing anyway. I've asked Eliot and Bolitho to hear what you have to say; we are all ears."

"Permit me to send for my father to join us. His experience and advice will be invaluable," said Sir James, "and also Clymo, our man of business."

"Indeed, no, I insist," said Pitt firmly. "If you are to take the reins of the affairs of Lanhydrock, there is no time like the present and no better place than among friends and neighbors. You will be a wealthy man. You must take your rightful place, forward modern ideas and not be held back by old-fashioned notions. Bolitho here is astute in matters of economy, and as a good Cornishman his advice will no doubt serve us all equally on any local matters you wish to discuss."

"In that case, let me mention something that has been brought to my attention," said Sir James, striding towards the mantel and placing one arm on it as he faced his audience. He appeared not to notice Bunt's discreet cough by the door.

"The Lanhydrock land holdings are extensive, tens of thousands of acres all over Cornwall," he continued, "including areas at the coasts where the soil is poor and little fit for farming. Fortunately, according to father, deposits of tin have been discovered in a number of previously unexplored places. Many of the lodes are deep, and we have leased setts to miners to dig out the ore and crush and sort it for smelting. The mine captains have told Clymo that greater riches lie deep underground and often under the sea. But deep mining requires capital. We would consider sharing with investors the riches that await exploitation."

"Undoubtedly, you would consider sharing the risks, as well," interjected Bolitho firmly. "Too often the lodes peter out or prove to bear little tin. And those coastal workings require continual drainage and, worse yet, they can be eroded and collapsed by the tides. Many an adventurer has lost his wealth in mining and many a lender too. Before we would contemplate putting money into such a venture we would require much more knowledge, and security beyond."

"Come, Mr. Bolitho," soothed Pitt, "pray recall that nothing ventured nothing won. The formation of a joint stock company would ensure that the risks are fairly borne and a bearable burden for each adventurer. My administration encourages such for the exploitation of the riches of the colonies."

"That's as may be," responded Bolitho, little mollified, "but my partners would at least need to know the quality of cassiterite, the oxide of tin, and whether other additional metals have been discovered. Is there copper, lead, iron, silver? And what would be the substance of those who would bear the risk?"

"Mr. Bolitho," responded Sir James, moving towards a chair, "details of a technical nature would be best addressed to Mr. Clymo. They are not for me to discuss, but I am sure his answers would be favorable."

"Gentlemen," interposed Eliot, "it seems to me that such a venture would be beneficial to the Cornish people, since it would provide employment to hundreds and bring contentment by alleviating the state of poverty."

"Stuff and nonsense!" said Sir James. "It's those very needs that drive these people to work hard. Remove the needs, and you have no workers!"

"There may be something in what you say," replied Eliot blandly, "but let me suggest another consideration. There will be greater need for horses to power the mechanical devices and to transport the metal to market. However, the use of packhorses and mules is slow and costly. The horses must be arranged to draw wagons that carry more goods, of all kinds, and for that, the roads must be improved."

"That is entirely up to the parishes, Mr. Eliot," said Bolitho, "And there is nothing we can or should do."

"Now there is a subject Eliot and I have already explored and where I may be of assistance," offered Pitt. "My administration has from time to time enacted turnpike trusts that empower the erection of toll houses and collection of tolls to provide the monies to improve and maintain the roads more efficiently, a factor fundamental to the furtherance of trade."

"With respect, sir, should we further such work in Cornwall, what may you or your administration seek in return?" asked Eliot.

"Gentlemen, my duty lies with England," replied Pitt, "and what serves her serves us all. Of course, it is a matter of necessity that my colleagues and I retain the reins of power in order to serve. You, Mr. Eliot, are not known as the Lord of the Boroughs for nothing. Should you and Sir James see it in your interests to persuade your boroughs to return members to the House who see fit to support myself and the Duke of Newcastle, then doubtless my administration would thereby be better able to continue to meet the just needs of Cornwall."

"May I suggest, Trenance," said Eliot, "that you elevate the improvement of roads to a matter of great importance? Should this be accomplished, then possibly at some future date I may also consider lending support from among my acquaintances to further ventures such as the expansion of mining."

"Well, perhaps as an alternative we could," muttered Sir James.

"Does such an approach meet with your approval, Sir James?" interrupted Pitt firmly. "No doubt, Mr. Eliot would assist in petitioning Parliament for the necessary Bill. And the Eliots have long enjoyed the place of Receiver General of the Duchy of Cornwall where his influence would be inestimable. It would appear to be in your interests to agree, Sir James, and it would be beneficial if Mr. Eliot and his friends could count on the Lanhydrock estate to contribute substantially to the necessary funds. No doubt he would see to it that you have a voice in the turnpike trust."

"Since my participation is essential to the success of the project," said Sir James, failing to hide a scowl, "I will give it my deepest consideration."

"Indeed you will, sir," said Pitt, "I will count on it. Furthermore, I suggest that the involvement of my brother Thomas could be of benefit to you all. He has a great deal of experience in such matters and I will be seeking his guidance on the degree of support that my administration should consider."

Without further discussion, Pitt rose. "Having concluded our business, perhaps now we should rejoin the ladies."

"Yes, yes of course," said Sir James, pulling himself out of his chair as well, "you can count on my father and myself."

Sir James graciously led the way out of the smoking room. He was inwardly out of sorts. He was willing to agree with them for the time being, but he felt forced by Pitt to this position on the issue. Of course no man would best him; he could match wits with any of them despite their greater experience. He would make more money than his father ever had, show the old man a thing or two. Nothing to it if you were determined! And nothing like great wealth to impress the ladies.

He would play his hand with skill and daring, give nothing away. He permitted himself a small smile as Bunt opened the door for them. The footman's face was expressionless as he bowed them out.

Chapter Nine

Villainy

Sunday morning was bright and sunny by the time Sir James awoke with a headache. He rang for Bunt to dress him.

"Good mornin', zir," called pretty little Mary Abbott the upstairs maid as she answered his call and came in to draw the curtains. James had once again been relegated to sleeping in his dressing room, while Elianor commanded their marital bedroom with their always hungry and often complaining son and heir nearby.

He had called in on his wife last evening after a hearty dinner where the wine flowed freely to the apparent enjoyment of their important guests. He had indulged himself excessively as was his habit but at least had remembered to wish Elianor a good night on his way to bed, when he had been gallant enough to resist the temptation to offer to join her. He hoped that before too many weeks had passed his wife would become more companionable.

Fortunately, not all of the women of his acquaintance were unattainable, although he was not planning to visit London in the near future. Yesterday, Sir James had done no more than his duty as a host to welcome Catherine Eliot to Lanhydrock but she had rebuffed even his mildest efforts at gentlemanly warmth. Perhaps pretty little Mary would be more accommodating. But why was she drawing his curtains? That was Bunt's job, his personal valet.

"Where is Bunt, Mary?" Sir James inquired, smiling.

"'E's not feelin' hisself, zir," she replied, keeping her eyes cast down.

"That is no excuse," asserted Sir James. "His job is to do his duty to me regardless of all other considerations." He paused. "But perhaps, Mary, you could look after my personal requirements. I need help with my breeches for a start."

"Oi dunno 'bout that, zir. Oi would'n' knaw what to do. Oi best be off downstairs an' 'elp with them fires."

"I'm sure there's no hurry, Mary; just sit beside me on the bed and tell me a nice secret," wheedled Sir James, and he grabbed at her hand as she tried to slip past him. She opened her mouth in surprise and shock. Sir James pulled the girl towards him and with his other hand roughly covered her mouth. She squeaked.

"Now be quiet, you silly girl. You just be nice to me, and I will be nice to you," he said. But she struggled and squealed, and he was afraid that if he persisted she would disturb Lady Trenance in the next room.

"Well then, I will let you go. Trot off for now, and you can be specially nice to me later." As Mary turned her back on him and darted for the door, Sir James smacked her on the bottom and followed her exit with a gleam in his eyes.

After struggling to dress himself, he went downstairs to find the company in the hall dressed for the outdoors and about to leave for church.

"Finally decided to join us, me lad?" said Baron Trenance heartily. "Just in time to come and confess your sins, what? You'll have to hurry up."

"'Fraid I'm a bit short in the sin department, Father," said Sir James, avoiding his father's eye. "But I'll take a quick bite and follow along later. That communion bread isn't very filling."

The baron walked slowly to the church, led his guests to the front rows and settled into the family pew. He knelt and bowed his head, sunk in worrisome memories rather than prayer. He had seen that look in James before. There was something deceptive and untrustworthy about it, as if he had been up to something that he feared would bring punishment if he were found out.

The baron was still concerned about his son's capability to take on the responsibilities inherent in the title, the place in the Lords, and the overseeing of the business of the Lanhydrock estate. He had tried to be a good father. He had not spoiled the boy, certainly not spared the rod. But he was disappointed in the way young James was turning out.

The baron remembered sending his boy away to school to give him a good classical education, toughen him up, instill some character. The British Empire is won on the playing fields of Eton and all that, he thought. Young James should have been popular; he was a bright and attractive enough little boy. But James hated boarding school for some reason, hated going back after the school holidays, at least until he was older. Of course, the baron knew there was always bullying of the new boys, but one got over that if one had any pluck, learned to defend oneself.

He had also tried to interest James in business affairs, not those that were strictly confidential, of course; but he had encouraged Clymo to pass on his knowledge to the boy. The baron personally introduced James to the work on the home farm, showed him the volumes of the Lanhydrock Atlas where their forbears had recorded their vast land holdings, and he had even taken him down west to see the great mines. As a boy himself the baron had been fascinated with the workings, but James showed little interest; he preferred to wander off into the woods by himself. He remembered one such time when the boy had been how old? About twelve or thirteen? Something had happened, but all the baron knew was that on the way home to Lanhydrock, James had been quiet and yet somehow elated. Where was the boy anyway? He should have got to the church by now.

James never told his father what had occurred back then. He rarely confided in his father, whom he found strict and often critical. In fact, he was too ashamed ever to tell anybody about it. Looking back on it, he knew that he should have felt pleased that the baron finally was paying him some attention when he took him deep into west Cornwall with him to inspect the family's mining properties. But the old man went on and on about how cleverly the family acquired land through foreclosing on loans, how much of the land proved to be tin bearing, and endlessly explaining how the mines were worked.

James felt that baron showed no concern with his homesickness and misery at school, let alone his struggles with maturing; not that James would tell his father his innermost thoughts anyway. Nor would his father have cared. It seemed that all that mattered to the baron was getting his son to face up to his responsibilities to the family and his future role in the direction of its business interests. James was bored, bored.

One day when he was supposed to go to the great Poldice mine, James summoned up his courage to get permission from his father instead to take a few hours off on his own exploring in the nearby woods. He said he wanted to seek adventure. His by now exasperated father had allowed him to go provided he promised to be back before sunset.

Left to himself, as he walked along the leafy deer paths, James could not help dwelling on how unhappy he was at school. When he was younger he was not allowed to go to the school in Bodmin; that was just for the common children. He was kept at home and taught at first by a governess and later by a tutor. When they had tried to make him study, let alone discipline him, he went to his mother and whined, and she soon put them in their places. He knew he was a crybaby, but he found it worked well in getting his way except when his father, on the rare occasions he involved himself, insisted on his bracing up and acting like a man.

James had been poorly prepared for Eton and was overwhelmed by his studies. He had no friends from Cornwall when he first went and was lonely. He was put in the lowest form with the strictest masters who beat him to make him learn. The treatment by the masters was not as bad as that of the older boys. They delighted in bullying the "new bugs," boys who failed to abide by the arcane customs and traditions on which the school prided itself. Once, he was held down and beaten for the unforgivable sartorial error of fastening the bottom button of his waistcoat.

Worse yet, a handsome youth with a sensitive mouth and long wavy hair kept touching him and trying to persuade him to do disgusting things with him in private in the woods beyond the playing fields, under the pretext of offering James sympathy and comfort. He tried to avoid the bigger boy's persistence, and sometimes James's curiosity almost overcame his fear. Anyway, he had no friends to turn to, so he was not sure what to do. He hated Eton; he did not look forward to going back. Now, as he tramped through the sun-flecked forest, he felt miserable; he could not stop the tears that trickled down his cheeks. He was glad his father couldn't see him.

He took the left-hand fork on the path that led through a stand of beech and hazel to a thicker part of the woods. He hoped these woods did not have nasty big boys lurking. He kept a look out as he walked cautiously. The path broke into a sunny clearing and James found himself opposite a grassy bank filled with holes heaped with fresh earth at their entrances. He had stumbled across a rabbit warren. Before he could collect himself, he startled a boy of about his own age kneeling on the far edge of the bank, with a burlap sack on the ground beside him and another in his hand, its neck tied with twine. The boy was poorly dressed, ragged, his face muddy. He looked harmless enough. He started up at the sight of James.

"Wait, don't run," called James, "what are you doing? Who are you? Are you poaching?" He'd heard his father say that poachers were bad, a nuisance; they stole from the estate. They had to be severely punished or else there would be nothing stopping them from stealing all the rabbits and hares and pheasants that the gamekeepers had been protecting. If they killed deer they could be hanged. This boy, however, did not look dangerous, quite pleasant beneath the dirt on his face. James smiled at him.

"Oi don' mean no 'arm, zir," said the boy, touching his forelock. "Us was just seein' 'ow them rabbits is doin', 'ow they'm breedin' like, 'ealthy an' all. Didn' mean no 'arm."

"What've you got in those sacks then?"

The boy blushed, put the bulging one on the ground behind him, untied the twine around the neck of the other sack and showed it to James. "Look inside, but don' 'ee put your 'ands inside mind you, teeth're sharp as needles. Them's my ferrets, what Oi be trained to chase rabbits out of 'oles, so us can catch 'em for breedin' like."

James peeked inside, then pulled backed as a ferret bared its teeth and squealed at him.

"What's in the other sack?"

The boy stared back at James, looking puzzled, avoiding answering directly, then said, "Hold on, ye been cryin'? Somethin' bad the matter? What's yer name, then?"

James rubbed his eyes with his knuckles, embarrassed. "If you promise not to tell, I won't tell you've been poaching. Breeding, hah; I bet I jolly well know what's in that other sack. Dead rabbits! My father would have you punished. I'm James Trenance, the Honorable James Trenance. My father's a baron, owns the mines around here. What's your name?"

"Oi'm Addis. Me dad's a tinner, works in the mines around 'ere. Better not let 'im catch you tryin' to get me in no trouble. Them all look up to 'im; 'e's a tributer with 'is own pare an' 'is own setts; best around Poldice; Cap'n Williams says so an' 'e knows. 'Ere, what you been cryin' for? Oi promise not to tell."

James stared at him for a moment. The boy seemed to care; no one else ever did. "I've got to go away from home again soon to school and I hate it. The masters are mean and beat me if I make mistakes, and the boys are bullies. I'd like to fight back but the beaks wouldn't permit it, and the boys are too big and nasty. Anyway, I'm not much good at fighting." He rubbed his eyes with his knuckles.

"Them masters be easy to deal with," said Addis, "just be'ave, do what them say, lie low, an' keep out of their way as much as ye can. That's what Oi'd do. With boys ye got to fight back, got no choice. When you'm bigger ye can beat them. Fer now make sure to 'urt them, 'it 'em back whenever them come at you."

James looked sceptical.

"Ever seen Cornish wrasslin'?" asked Addis. James shook his head. "When a big 'un goes for a good little 'un, the little 'un just gives way and throws the big 'un off balance; lets 'im use 'is own strength to throw 'imself."

"Could you show me?" asked James.

Addis nodded. "Take yer coat off so it don't get messed up; come over to this grassy bit. Don' go 'ard at it loike, just practice."

Addis demonstrated different holds, different throws, made James try again and again until he got it right. He showed him one trick where he stood by James's side and put one forefinger at the back of his neck, pressed the other forefinger hard against his upper lip under the front of his nose, and threw him effortlessly to the ground.

Addis got James to try the same move on him and fell in turn. "You'm gettin' the 'ang of it," Addis said. "Them'll think twice about goin' after ye now."

James was sweating, puffing, ready to take a break, but he was quite enjoying himself, feeling confidence grow. "That was fun!" he said. "Now, can you show me how to poach rabbits?" He grinned.

"Sure ye c'n keep a secret? Cross your 'eart and 'ope to die?" said Addis. James nodded. "Right then." Addis reached into one of his sacks and pulled out several nets and some twigs about six or eight inches long, notched at one end and sharpened at the other. "First ye fasten them nets over all of the 'oles to them burrows 'cept one." He took a net, stretched it across the entrance to a burrow and pressed twigs into the surrounding earth so that the notches held the net down.

"Can I help?" asked James.

Addis said, "Get a flat stone and 'ammer them pegs well in so rabbits can't burst through." James did as he was told, following Addis around the warren. "What next?" he asked.

Now Oi put the ferrets in the open 'ole," said Addis.

James was enthusiastic. "Can I do that?"

"No," said Addis, "Oi'm afraid them'll bite. Them're wild little critters but them're used to me. Anyroad, first Oi've got to tie their muzzles with twine so'm can't bite the rabbits. Them got to scare the rabbits out, not eat 'em. The eatin's for me 'n' my fambly, maybe sell a few to neighbors. Ready? Stand back."

Addis muzzled two of the ferrets, picked them up and pushed them into the open hole. James watched expectantly.

There were sounds of scuffling and screaming and a rabbit appeared at the mouth of one of the other burrows, getting entangled in the net as it struggled to escape. Addis reached in under the edge of the net, grabbed the rabbit by the nape of its neck and pulled it out. With his other hand he picked up the flat rock and hit the rabbit hard at the base of its skull. It kicked once, twitched, its eyes glazed over and it lay still. Addis put it into his other sack and added to his booty of dead rabbits.

James's eyes glistened. He picked up a flat rock and crouched by the entrance of another burrow further along the bank. He swiftly caught another netted rabbit, hit it hard on the back of its neck and gave a whoop of triumph as he killed it and put it into the sack. His eyes sparkled. Between them the boys killed eight rabbits. James was elated.

It was getting cool as the sun went lower. "Oi got to go," said Addis, "me mum don't let me stay in the woods late. Don' say nothin' to nobody mind."

"Good-bye," said James, "I won't, I promise." He thought of shaking Addis's hand but it was not only muddy but covered with blood. Anyway, he would never see the boy again.

People like him could not play with tinners' sons. He had a position to keep up. He would take what he learned and move on in his own life. He would never catch rabbits again but one thing he had learned for sure. When he grew up he would be the one hitting people smaller and weaker than he, not the other way around. Now he had to get back to where he and his father were staying. He hoped the old man would not see him and ask where he had been or what he had been doing.

At the church at Lanhydrock, the baron was paying scant attention to the vicar's dreary recitation of the Sentences of Scripture. As he glanced around the family pew he observed that his guests were doing no better; James had still not joined him. Where was the boy? Hope he had not wandered off like he used to when he was a boy. Time he got here, or he would be late; poor example to show the villagers. The Order for Morning Prayer continued as the vicar droned on.

"Dearly beloved brethren, the Scripture moveth us in sundry places to acknowledge and confess our manifold sins and wickedness; and that we should not dissemble nor cloak them before the face of Almighty God our heavenly Father; but confess them with an humble, lowly, penitent, and obedient heart; to the end that we may obtain forgiveness of the same, by his infinite goodness and mercy."

The congregation shuffled and knelt and echoed the words of the General Confession with an unconvincing blend of boredom and embarrassment. The baron allowed his thoughts to wander back to the present. Perhaps these old words had meaning. Did they apply to James? Was there something he had to confess? He was a disappointing son, not an heir he could count on. He would have to have a serious conversation with James, again.

Back at the house, James had gone into the dining room and wolfed down a plate of sausages, poached eggs and fried bread served by the butler, washed down with a tankard of ale. Then, realizing he would be late and annoy his father again, he left to walk quickly to the nearby church, hoping the fresh air might clear his head.

He thought he might go for a ride after the service; he could do with the exercise. He glanced towards the stable block to see if his groom was about so that he could order him to have his horse ready. Instead. his eye caught a cloaked figure carrying a basket and stealthily scurrying into the side entrance to the stables. James quickly followed and went inside.

Standing still and listening for a moment, he heard rustling in the straw in an empty stall near the ladder to the hayloft above. He went past the partition and startled Mary as she headed for the bottom of the ladder.

"Whatever are you doing here, girl?" he demanded.

"N-nuthin', zir," Mary stammered, "Oi wuz just lookin' fer eggs fer Cook, Oi dare say, p'raps."

"Were you, indeed?" expostulated Sir James, moving towards her and grabbing her basket, opening the cloth that covered it. "So why is there bread and cheese in your basket? You know perfectly well your place is in the house. You are not permitted to wander where you like. I should have you beaten to teach you a lesson!"

"Aw, please don' do that, zir," pleaded Mary, her eyes filling with tears, "Oi'm a good girl; Oi won't do it again."

"Perhaps I should take matters into my own hands," hissed Sir James seizing her by her shoulders, all thought of church and the forgiveness of sins out of his mind. "Just be nice to me and I promise I won't hurt you."

"Oh no zir, Oi could'n' do nothin' loike that," whimpered Mary.

Her fear stirred Sir James even more. He tore off her cloak. He was powerful. He was on the scent. He pulled at her voluminous skirts. This was the kind of chase he enjoyed. He threw her down on the straw. Lady Elianor could keep her damned laces, perfumes, manners, and her maternal preoccupations with her delicate untouchability. He could not wait for the kill.

Sir James did not hear the shuffling in the loft above, nor did he see the desperation on the face of the man with a pitchfork in his hand peering down through the hatch. Aha, his terrified victim was a virgin, the biggest prize of all! After all too few moments of frenzied activity he gathered himself together, leaving Mary weeping in the straw.

"If you ever breathe a word of this to anyone, my girl," hissed Sir James through clenched teeth, "I'll see to it that you are ruined. You will be dismissed without a reference; you will never work again." Still fastening the front panel of his breeches, he strode out into the sunlight.

When the coast was clear the man climbed down the ladder.

"Oh Mary, me luv," said Bunt, for it was the missing valet. "Oi was goin' to get away from 'ere, Oi can't work for that bastard no more. Oi did'n' mean to get you in no trouble when Oi asked you to bring me food. Oi should 'ave rescued you from that bloody bastard, but Oi was afraid Oi would kill 'im if once Oi laid my 'ands on 'en. Oi would've run 'im through with the pitchfork, then they would've 'anged me, an' you too Oi 'pect."

He leaned over and helped Mary gently to her feet, and wiped the tears from her eyes.

"Oi dunno what to do," sniveled Mary. "What'll 'appen to me now? What if Oi 'ave a baby? What'll 'appen to the poor little mite?"

"That probably won't 'appen. An' if it does, Oi'll marry ye. Fact, Oi'd like to marry you anyway. Oi'll do one better. Oi'll take you away from 'ere right now with me, and neither of us ain't never comin' back to this cursed place. Us won't take no more from that Sir James. Us'll manage some'ow," said Bunt.

"Oh Willy, Willy, yes, let's go; us'll manage some'ow," said Mary, more bravely than she felt. "Let's leave before the others come out of church. Us can take the bread an' cheese an' walk to Liskeard. My big sister lives near there; St. Germans it be called. Us'll foind someone to show us the way and 'elp us once us gets there."

Mary and Willy ran to the house and gathered their few belongings and tied them in a bundle. Cook and the others were scurrying around in anticipation of the churchgoers' imminent arrival with big appetites. No one noticed the pair creep quietly in through the kitchen, pick up more food, put it in their basket and slip away.

Chapter Ten

Worship

Further west, by Addis and Lizzie Penwarden's cottage, Sunday dawned chilly and bright but later clouded over, gently soaking the landscape in the persistent drizzle typical of winter in that part of Cornwall. Addis had barely slept and was already up and about in the outhouse behind the cottage, sawing and planing planks for his younger brother's coffin. He was working hard and fast, putting his mind to it to slow his thoughts from the terrible accident down in the mine that had in an instant taken Jedson from them.

He had changed his mind about staying home this morning from chapel. He felt after all that he needed to go and pray for his brother's soul to rest in peace and perhaps find solace for his own. He was active in the chapel. He was proud to sing in the male voice choir, which he felt was at least as good as the fishermen's male voice choir in St. Ives. The music would stir him, take his mind off his grief. And he could talk to Reverend Perry. Perhaps he would have advice to give. Preacher was wise and could be comforting as well as rousing.

Addis was interrupted by a call of "Breakfas's ready!" from his wife, standing in the open doorway of the cottage, wiping her hands on her apron.

"What be ye doin' up an' dressed?" Addis asked his wife. "Lizzie my love, 'tis no time since ye gave birth to young Jedson, an' he's a strapping lad."

"Oi can manage well enough," Lizzie replied. "Oi did'n' 'ave no time to lay about for the last one. Too much to do. Family to feed, cottage to take care of. Besides, workin' around the mine makes us' strong, women an' children as well as men. An' Oi b'lieve us needs to go along to chapel and talk to preacher about the funeral an' all."

She turned to the hearth and ladled hot barley porridge from the pot hanging there into a wooden bowl, which she put on the bare homemade table in front of Addis' customary place at the head.

"You'm right there," said Addis. "Nearly finished the coffin, good pine from farmer. We owe 'im a brace of fowl an' couple of dozen eggs. You better bring Jemmy, young Jedson, too, sit at the back case he yowls."

"You put on clean shirt then, Addis, Oi put it by fire to dry. Put in a collar stud," said Lizzie, "and don't forget your good weskit. Oi'll go an' feed the baby an' change 'is nappy and brush my hair. You put on more coal an' us'll soon be ready."

Lizzie couldn't get her brother-in-law's death out of her mind. When she had spilled the salt and thrown it over her left shoulder, it had failed to keep away bad luck. They would get over it. They were strong. They had no choice. She went upstairs and tried on her Sunday dress, which she had sewn by candlelight from left over deep blue velvet curtain material that the publican's wife had given her. Lizzie was afraid she wouldn't be able to get into it so soon after giving birth. She let out all her breath and was relieved that it was only a little tight. She was ready to go to chapel with her family.

Addis went to the outhouse to fetch coal. He and his brother had walked over to the beach at Portreath after a storm and picked up two nearly full sacks of coal washed ashore after a cargo vessel had wrecked on the rocks. Coal burned longer than wood, and the fire would still be going to keep the kitchen warm after they got back from chapel.

It was a good cottage with cob walls, solidly made of stone and lime cement and whitewashed, a stone chimney, an extra room upstairs, and a roof of slate that came from up Delabole way. It sat by itself with enough garden for a few hens, a pig, an apple tree, and a patch to grow potatoes, onions and turnips for their pasties, practically a smallholding.

The mine owned the cottage, but the owners liked Addis's work and wanted to keep him, so they let him have it at a modest rent. He would see to it that one day young Jemmy and Jedson would earn enough to own their own cottages, not depend on any mine owner.

The family walked to the chapel in good time for the morning service. They felt more at home at the little Wesleyan chapel than they used to at the parish church. The windows were plain clear glass, the walls were whitewashed, and the furnishings were simple. The services were less formal, too, and there was hymn singing, which they enjoyed. Most of the congregation was made up of working folk like themselves, or small shopkeepers or artisans, so there was less dressing up. Lizzie would not look out of place in her homemade dress and second-hand coat and hat. She carried the baby in her arms as they walked and Jemmy rode on his father's shoulders; he would soon be too big for that.

Lizzie asked, "Addis, be goin' to sing with the choir then? Or p'r'aps ye could sit with me an' the boys. Oi'd loike that, today of all days, me 'andsome."

"Well, all right then, Lizzie. Oi'd loike that too. Our family will stick together."

They went through the big door at the front of the chapel and sat with the children in the back row facing the dais where the preacher would stand. A congregant played reverent music on the harpsichord. Choir members trickled in and sat in benches near the front facing the modest congregation. Then Reverend Perry entered wearing a scholar's simple black robe, and the service began with a hymn by Charles Wesley.

Love divine, all loves excelling,
Joy of heaven, to earth come down,
Fix in us thy humble dwelling,
All thy faithful mercies crown!

Despite his dark mood, Addis felt his heart lift, and he joined in with gradually improving spirits. After the hymn, preacher offered his own prayer. He rarely used the English Prayer Book in chapel. He specially asked for divine comfort in their grief for Addis and Lizzie and the Penwarden family. When it came time for the sermon, Addis was expectant, remembering the preacher's passionate words on Friday evening at Gwennap Pit.

"My brothers and sisters," boomed Reverend Perry in a voice that reverberated, "when I spoke to you at Gwennap Pit I told you that I see great things happening, and I told you that the comet that appeared a week ago in this leap year of 1760 portended great changes coming about. I told you there would be changes in London. George II will not last forever. Don't mistake that such things will not affect Cornwall, because they will. And keep in mind that those in great places do not think first about working Cornish men and women."

He continued, "Only yesterday one of our young men was taken from us, Addis Penwarden's younger brother, Jedson, killed down the mine. His funeral will be in this chapel. I ask you, what matters most to the mine owners? Winning the tin and the copper from beneath the earth, or keeping the miners safe and sound? We all know the answer to that."

Addis bowed his head, and there was a perturbed stirring in the congregation; this was a worship service and a Sunday, after all.

As if in answer to their discomfort, Reverend Perry continued, "You might ask, what has this to do with us, sitting in prayer in a house of God? Does the Church of England care about ordinary people? I'll grant you that the Church in Cornwall is more independent than most of those in England. Ever since St. Piran landed nearby at Perranporth, we Cornish have worshipped in our own ways. But how many parsons are sons of miners or sons of fishermen, or farm workers? No, they are sons of squires. Do the people appoint the bishops? No, the king and his ministers have the say."

Addis heard someone sitting a few rows in front of him gasp. This was dangerous talk indeed.

"The sons of squires go to school to be educated. Is there a proper school for the sons of plain folk in this village, or even in Redruth? How can the miner's family improve its lot without proper education? Where can fishermen look to meet the needs of their community? Will the Redruth borough council listen to you? Will even the parish council listen? You have a Member of Parliament in London. Does he ever heed us in this village? No, he does what the gentry tell him, and the gentry tell the voters whom to vote into parliament. Where does all this lead? Where it leads is to keep us in our places, toiling for the wealth of others, generation after generation."

Reverend Perry placed his hand on his breast and looked in turn into the eyes of his listeners around the room. He continued, "I have no doubt that things will change before many years are out. England will have more interests across the seas, especially in America. Different leaders will tell us what to do. Things are going to be done in different ways. But if we ordinary Cornish folk want the changes to benefit us, then we need to pull together. We must meet together to understand what is best for us, to make our voices heard. We must seek support, and we must choose leaders of our own, you mark my words. *Kernow bys vykken*! Long live Cornwall!"

Lizzie turned and looked anxiously at Addis. He reached across Jemmy and baby Jedson and patted her hand.

"Where better place to meet than in this here chapel?" Perry asked. "And I tell you something else. There's one who is coming after me, the straps of whose riding boots I am unworthy to unloose. John Wesley has been coming to Cornwall to preach his message, and he will be coming here to Gwennap, and many times more. We can learn from him, not only of the faith, but also of what goes on up country. He and his brother Charles went to America to save the Indians and they know what opportunities lie across the seas. He knows how to lead." The preacher's voice was growing hoarse, but still he pressed on passionately.

"Mark my words. Stand together, support each other, give each other strength and courage. Above all trust in the Lord and keep your faith."

Preacher raised his arms and looked heavenward as he blessed his flock: "And now I commend my words and your souls to Him who dwells above. Let us join together in singing our final hymn."

When the hymn ended, the congregation gathered themselves and their belongings to greet the preacher as they left the chapel. Some were joyful, but most were more subdued and pensive than usual.

"Them's powerful words, preacher," said Addis. "Oi dunno what to make of they. Us would'n' want to get in no trouble. But Oi tell you one thing for certain sure. If it does take trouble for my Jemmy and young Jedson to 'ave better lives nor me and my brother, may 'is soul rest in peace, then you can count on me an' mine. And Oi would'n' moind bein' the one tellin' others what to do neither. After all, that's what Oi do with my pare down the mine."

Lizzie stood aside and watched Addis as he spoke, her brow furrowed, but she squared her shoulders, raised her chin and strode purposefully beside her husband as they walked with their family through a light drizzle back to their cottage.

"You're askin' fer trouble, Addis," she said, "but thinkin' about it, it may be trouble what's needed."

He glanced at her, "And Oi forgot to talk to Preacher about funeral. Oi'll 'ave to do that bye an' bye."

Chapter Eleven

Escape

After leaving Lanhydrock stables in haste, Mary and Bunt went through the back of the house into the servants quarters to gather their few belongings. Mary laced on her sturdiest boots and put on a wool scarf she had knitted. Willy buttoned on his outdoor coat, put on his hat and pocketed the pitiful bag of coins hidden under his mattress, his life's savings. They had food in the basket and, as they left, he added to the small larder with a few apples snatched from a table by the door.

Willy Bunt and Mary Abbott set off on their long walk. As they hastened towards the Liskeard road, they went around the church and crossed the park to avoid the main drive and the lodge keeper. They wanted to escape not only the wrath of Sir James, but also the chance of being dragged back and prevented from leaving. They kept to the woods until they were well clear of the house and only then trod onto the road where they could make a better pace.

Darkness would fall early this wintry day, and they wanted to get at least to Liskeard before nightfall. They had heard tales of highwaymen in the area, so they sought to avoid them, as well as possible pursuers from the estate, by keeping well to the side of the road where they could dodge into the thick hedges for cover.

There were few travelers on this Sunday afternoon, and the only thing that slowed their progress after seven or eight miles was a blister that developed on Mary's heel. She held on to Willy's arm as he carried the basket, and they managed to limp into the outskirts of Liskeard towards sunset. They headed down Bay Tree Hill and over Church Street towards the Plymouth road. A few stragglers were on their way home from Evensong at St. Martin's church, so Willy stopped a kindly looking woman.

"Excuse me for troublin' ye, mum," he said, "but can you point us the way to St. Germans? We'm trying to get there afore the night is over."

"It's too far to go tonight, young man, and too dangerous," she said. "You should stay in Liskeard until tomorrow. I can point out an inn. The Barleysheaf is nearby right below the church."

"Us don't have enough money for no inn, ma'am," chimed in Mary. "Us was hopin' to stay with my big sister Nelly. She works for a fambly by name of Eliot."

"Nelly?" asked the woman, "Nelly Abbott with the big smile and the dark curly hair? I'm cook at Eliot House, and one of my kitchen maids has taken poorly, so our Mr. Polkinghorne sent down your Nelly from St. Germans to help me out for a few days."

"You knaw my Nell, then?" asked Mary, delighted.

"I do, indeed, and I'm right glad to have her," was the warm reply. "We're expecting Mr. and Mrs. Eliot to stay here the night on their way back to Port Eliot, and they'll be hungry when they arrive. Can you two make yourselves useful? You can both help in the kitchen, and Nelly'll give you a bed in the attic for tonight."

"We'm not married, mum," said Willy.

"That's all right, we've got more than one bedroom in the attic," said the woman. She paused and looked at Mary. "And you young lady, you're limping. What be painin' ye?"

"Aw, 'tis nothin', mum," protested Mary. "Oi just got a blister on my heel from walkin'."

"I'll soon get that taken care of," said the woman. "You two follow me; us is right nearby."

Presently they came to the side door of a large town house. "Come on inside, and I'll have Nell soak your foot in Epsom salts and hot water. You'll soon be as right as rain. Now, my name is Annie Bartlett, and you?"

"That's kindly of you, mum," said Willy. "Oi be Willy Bunt, and this 'ere's Mary Abbott, sister of Nelly."

Willy was thanking his lucky stars at such good fortune, but he hoped that it would not occur to her that he might serve in the dining room. He remembered that a Mr. and Mrs. Eliot had been guests at Lanhydrock. He had served port to Mr. Eliot in the library. It would not do to be recognized by him, nor asked too many questions.

Mrs. Bartlett took them in through the back door and into the kitchen where Nelly was helping the scullery maid prepare food for the Eliots' arrival. She turned and saw them. "Oh, my God, it be you Mary. Whatever is this about?" She wiped her flour-covered hands and the sisters warmly embraced. Mary introduced Willy to Nelly and told as much of the story of their adventure and hasty flight from Lanhydrock as she dared in front of those moving about the kitchen.

Following the cook's directions, Nelly sat Mary down in a kitchen chair, poured some hot water from a kettle on the stove into a pan and stirred in Epsom salts. Mary took off her shoe and stocking. She squealed as her blistered heel smarted in the hot salty water.

Mrs. Bartlett was about to introduce Mary and Willy to the other servants, but before she could there was a commotion at the front door and the sound of voices.

"My laws," said Mrs. Bartlett, "It's Mr. and Mrs. Eliot here already. We've got to make haste and get them something to eat and drink. They'll be hungry after their journey. You two get out of the way. Take a quick bite if you want, then get on up them back stairs and take the two attic rooms on the left. You can start helping in the morning after I have a chance to show you 'round the house."

Nelly gave Mary and Willy some bread and cheese and a mug of milk each, and they escaped up the servants' stairs without anyone in the front hall being any the wiser.

Mary and Willy stayed well out of the way as the household bustled with activity during the evening, and only after quiet descended did they venture to take a short walk outside in the brisk evening air to settle their anxiety. Then they retired to their rooms for the night, giving each other a hug and a kiss on the cheek.

As Mary pulled the blankets over her shoulders there was a light tap at her bedroom door. Who could it be? Not Willy, she hoped. She was in no mood for that kind of visit; she was sore. She said nothing, pretending to be asleep already. The door opened quietly and Mary saw the light of a candle in the hall outside. It was her sister Nelly.

"Mary," Nelly whispered, coming in, "you awake? Tell me what's goin' on, you'll get into awful trouble when they find out you've gone. They'll come after an' catch you, give you a whippin'. Why'd you ever do such a silly thing?"

Mary sat up. She reached out and hugged her sister, sobbing. "Come sit on the bed. Oi'll tell you everythin'. Oi don't know what Oi'm goin' to do, but Willy told me 'e'll 'elp me, 'e's so kind, tells me 'e'll marry me, says 'e loves me."

"Why would 'e marry you? You can't 'ardly know 'im. You've never said nothin' to me about 'im before. 'Ave you gone an' got a bun in the oven?"

"Oi dunno, mebbe. 'Twas Sir James. Grabbed me in the stable 'e did, pushed me down, tore my skirt, jumped on me. Oi tried to push 'im away, but 'e was too strong. Nasty bugger, thinks 'e 'as the right to do whatever 'e likes, doesn't care about the likes of we. Can you 'elp me? Us can't go back to Lanhydrock now."

"You poor mite," said Nelly, resting her hand on Mary's cheek. "Don't you worry, somethin'll turn up. Oi'll talk to Cook in the mornin'; you try an' get some sleep. You'll need it." She kissed her sister and went to her own room, leaving Mary alone, sobbing quietly in the dark.

Nelly was as good as her word. The next morning she got up while it was still dark and went downstairs and made a pot of tea. The cook appeared in the kitchen soon after, grateful for the cup that Nelly offered her. Tea was a luxury, but a privilege enjoyed from time to time by the Eliots' servants.

"Mrs. Bartlett," Nelly said, folding and unfolding her hands, "I've somethin' to ask you special, a secret like." She poured out the story of her sister's predicament, not revealing the name of the man responsible.

Annie Bartlett soon guessed who the culprit was. "Your Mary's got nothin' to be ashamed of," she said, hands on her ample hips. "Ain't the first time somethin' like this 'as 'appened to an innocent young girl and 'twon't be the last. You tell 'er not to fret. Oi'll tell Mrs. Eliot and us'll take care of it. Now you get on with the breakfast. Mr. Eliot has callers coming and Oi'll need to get them something so they won't go 'ungry."

Soon after, the day started for the Eliots and they came down to the dining room. It would be a busy morning. Anticipating their return from Lanhydrock to Port Eliot by way of their town house, Edward Eliot early yesterday had sent his valet ahead to deliver a message to Polkinghorne, his man of business. He had ordered Polkinghorne to come to meet him in Liskeard and also to get in touch with Mr. Ough, the Town Clerk of Liskeard, and request that he bring with him James Davis, the Mayor of Liskeard, and join them at Eliot House to discuss matters of interest.

Just before ten o'clock, Polkinghorne arrived from St. Germans. Edward met him in the morning room, leaving Catherine in the dining room where she summoned Mrs. Bartlett to discuss arrangements for meals later in the day. Shortly thereafter, the Liskeard officials were announced and shown into the morning room, where Edward Eliot greeted them.

"Gentlemen, welcome to Eliot House," he said. "Mr. Mayor, I am gratified that you could join us. Mr. Ough, I see you are returned safely from Bodmin after leaving us at Lanhydrock. No more highwaymen, I trust? I am curious as to the outcome of your meeting. Were you able to persuade the good burghers of Bodmin to join your cause? Might they append their signatures to support a petition for a turnpike?"

"They need further encouragement, Mr. Eliot, sir," replied Ough, "but I am confident they understand the importance of making the roads between the towns not only safer but also able to carry wheeled vehicles. They are concerned, though, with who will pay to improve the road in the first place, and after that who will pay to keep it in repair. Mr. Davis and I believe if others will lead they will follow."

"You have done well, Mr. Ough," replied Edward, "and therefore we have much to discuss. Tea, gentlemen? It is a refreshing drink and will keep our minds alert as we wrestle with the challenges of public policy and finance."

Eliot embroidered his invitation. "We Eliots have had an interest in the tea trade ever since my great-uncle invested in India and then in trade in the Far East. Our fellow adventurers' ships carry tea from Canton into the Port of London. It is a lengthy voyage. The captains crowd on sail, but if faster ships could be designed and built, we could get to market faster and enjoy better prices. But, I digress." Eliot rang for a servant.

Edwin Ough reflected on his host's inspired approach to business. He believed he could work with a man who was progressive, open to ideas and, most of all, willing to invest in them. Tea was a luxury that few people could afford to enjoy. He had heard that some of his neighbors were able to buy tea a little cheaper from time to time, thanks to small boats that carried away part of the cargo from ships of the Dutch East India Company as they sailed up the English Channel to Antwerp on the last leg of their voyages. The enterprising Cornish were famous for smuggling, as well as wrecking. He himself would have no truck with such dealings, but he sometimes mused that perhaps Mr. Pitt's administration would be wise not to tax such a desirable beverage as tea too harshly.

The tea was brought in and poured. Ough could not but help notice that the fine decorated china, blue and white, looked foreign. Not that he was envious, but he was curious. It would be nice to be rich and take such things for granted. The others were looking at the footman pouring the tea. Ough stole a quick peek at the bottom of his saucer. It said "Royal Worcester." H'mm, it would be good for Cornwall if some day Cornishmen could get involved in manufacturing such fine objects. He sipped from his cup and set it back in the saucer as they settled down to business.

Edward had noticed the town clerk's actions but made no comment so as not to embarrass him. He seemed to be an observant fellow, could be useful. "Mr. Ough," he said, "when we last met, the circumstances were somewhat alarming, although those wretched highwaymen did bring to our attention the vital importance of getting something done about these roads. I am happy to say that my visit to Lanhydrock turned out to be much more enjoyable than our journey, and possibly quite helpful. Don't you agree, Polkinghorne?"

"So you have informed me, Mr. Eliot," agreed Polkinghorne. "I have observed if I may say so that your negotiations seem to go particularly well when you are among friends and join them in social intercourse."

Eliot continued, "My good friend Mr. William Pitt, the king's chief minister in the House of Commons, was a fellow guest. He has the interests of England at heart, and in his wisdom wishes to see commerce flourish. And as you may know, he has many connections with Cornwall; his great-grandfather acquired the Boconnoc estate and spent considerable time in the Duchy. Mr. Pitt would also welcome our support at elections, of course, providing our candidates put the country first.

"Now then," Eliot went on, "Mr. Pitt's administration has enacted many Turnpike Trusts throughout the kingdom, and it is high time we enjoyed such legislation in Cornwall. That is how we will improve our roads."

"How would this come about, Mr. Eliot?" enquired James Davis, the mayor. "I believe the parish is not in a position to assume the responsibility for keeping a new road in repair. It is burdensome enough to provide labor or money to look after the poor roads we already have."

"Ah, Mr. Davis, that is where you and Mr. Ough come in," explained Eliot. "As Mayor and Town Clerk, you gentlemen have influence with the aldermen and councilors of the borough's corporation. Here's what you must do. Before the next meeting of the council, take your friends into your confidence and emphasize the importance to Liskeard of better roads. After all, it is a market town, and if sheep and cattle and wool and all the other goods can get to market easier and faster, then the market will prosper and so will the town.

"Further, you must persuade the town council to draw up a petition to present to parliament, praying for the enactment of a Turnpike Trust. The trust will be empowered to collect tolls from passing travelers to pay for repairs. There is a spot at the south end of the town where we can erect a toll house."

"But that will be a matter of law and lawyers, Mr. Eliot," said Davis hesitantly. "And making the road will require much labor and more money than we can lay our hands on."

"You can leave that to me, Mr. Mayor," said Eliot confidently. "My man of business will assist with drafting the petition, won't you Polkinghorne? And no doubt I can invite my good friend the High Sheriff of Cornwall to lend his name to this beneficial cause."

"That would be of great assistance, Mr. Eliot," said Davis, "but how will it be paid for? That's what I don't understand."

"As to finding ways to finance this project, I have spoken to some venturers who have already as good as given me their word," said Eliot. "Don't you worry about that; I will see that it is done."

The meeting ended, Edwin Ough bowed as he made his farewell. He felt he and the Mayor had already done a good morning's work for his fellow burghers and merchants. What they had left to accomplish should not be too burdensome now that they had friends in high places.

"Gentlemen, be sure to let me know what I can do to help," said Polkinghorne, leading the way to the front door. "I am often in Liskeard on

Mr. Eliot's business. Otherwise, you can send a message to me at Port Eliot."

As he turned to go back into the morning room, Polkinghorne caught sight of a young man just coming into the entrance hall from the service quarters. He was unfamiliar and did not belong in Eliot House. He challenged him.

"What are you doing here, my good man?" he demanded, approaching him to seize him by the shoulder.

"Nothin' zir," came the uncommunicative response.

"Nothing sir, my good man?" repeated Polkinghorne insistently, raising his voice. "Tell me immediately, unless you want to be put in the stocks; what are you doing here? Who let you in? Who are you? What's your name?"

"Well zir, my sweetheart's sister works in the kitchen, zir, and us thought . . . well, zir, my name is Bunt and Oi was a footman at Lanhydrock and Sir James Trenance's valet, zir."

At that moment Catherine Eliot came down the stairs into the entrance hall. Seeing the commotion she asked, "What exactly is going on here, Polkinghorne?"

Before he could explain, the door to the morning room opened and out came Edward Eliot. "Yes, indeed, Polkinghorne, what is going on? I won't have a disturbance in my house. Servants must keep their place. Did I hear something about Lanhydrock?"

"Yes, sir," said Polkinghorne. "This fellow's name is Bunt. He was just explaining that he was Sir James Trenance's valet. He and his apparent paramour, for some reason, have shown up at Eliot House."

"Ah, weren't you the fellow that served the port in the library while I was there with Mr. Pitt? Hung around by the door, too, eavesdropping on what was going on I dare say." Eliot turned to Polkinghorne. "Well the pair of them had better go back to Lanhydrock and explain themselves to Sir James. Tell cook to give them bread and cheese for their journey and send them on their way immediately."

"Mr. Eliot," interposed Catherine, "let us not be too hasty. Cook had a word with me while you gentlemen were meeting. The girl is our Nelly Abbott's sister. There is a reason for their precipitate departure. They deserve some understanding. It is rare that servants choose to leave their employ. I will explain to you later what occurs to me and perhaps make a suggestion."

"Of course, my dear," replied Eliot, curbing some irritation at being even courteously contradicted by his wife. "You know how I value your counsel. Send for the girl and talk to them both in the dining room."

As Catherine took her seat at the head of the dining room table, Polkinghorne ushered in the young couple. Willie Bunt and Mary Abbott stood with downcast eyes, shuffling their feet nervously.

"Thank you, Polkinghorne," said Catherine. "You may leave us." Alone with the fugitives, Catherine was firm. Servants needed discipline or they would become unmanageable. She addressed them. "Now you two, what is going on? Why did you leave Lanhydrock? Why should we not simply send you back as my husband suggests?"

"Well, your ladyship," said Bunt, embarrassed, "Us be afeared to go back, us can't, loike, cos' of what 'appened."

"Stop mumbling man, just get it out. Why are you blushing, young lady? What have you been up to? And 'your ladyship' I am not," said Catherine.

"Beggin' your pardon, mum, but the squire done wrong to my Mary," said Bunt.

"Where and when?" asked Catherine, showing less surprise than one might expect.

"In the stable 'twas, yesterday while ye were all in church. Mary was that upset, she wanted to leave that very minute."

"I see," said Catherine. "I will speak to Mr. Eliot to see what should be done. I will ask him to see to it that neither of you come to harm, but the proper thing is for you to go back where you belong."

"Us don' want no 'arm, mum. 'Cept Sir James said he would have me beaten, an' Oi was just tryin' to tell 'im that 'e should watch out fer what the other gen'lemen were plannin' loike."

"Wait in the hall while I speak to Mr. Eliot," Catherine said, puzzled at the implications of this last bit of information but not wishing to engage in a lengthy discussion with their neighbor's servant.

She went to Edward and explained what had presumably happened to Mary and of Sir James' threat to Bunt. They had confirmed what Mrs. Bartlett had hinted at. If it were all true, then Mary had indeed suffered not only pain and indignity but the possibility of continuing harassment and most probably a future pregnancy. If, however, Bunt had told Sir James of Eliot's conversation with Pitt, then there was the possibility that Trenance knew more of her husband's confidential plans and the nature of his relationships than was good for Eliot interests.

"They should return to Lanhydrock, my dear. They may be exaggerating; you know what servants are like," said Edward when he heard the story, "even though there's something about Sir James I rather distrust. But be good to them; it may be to our advantage having their gratitude. People in his house who warn us of behavior that could affect our interests could be an asset."

"Distrust is too mild a descriptive!" exclaimed Catherine. "The man is a snake. I can well believe that he did wrong to young Mary, and you don't need informers to tell you the kind of tricks he'll be up to. Just be on your guard in any and all dealings with that man. Come to think of it, the last thing these young people should be asked to bear is to go back to serve Sir James. Have Polkinghorne take them to Port Eliot. It might be better that we put them to work, treat them well, and then you can count on their loyalty to Eliots."

Edward got up from his chair and went to the window. Catherine waited, watching him twist his hands behind his back. Finally he turned and smiled at her. "Once again I believe you are right, my dear," said Edward. "We'll do as you say where the young people are concerned, but be aware that there is a definite advantage in doing business with a man of great wealth like Trenance, however unstable he might be. I must pursue the opportunity to gain his support. But I can assure you that he will not take advantage of me. Who knows what more we may learn from these young people? I'll instruct Polkinghorne to make arrangements."

"You are wise, Edward," said Catherine. "Yours is a capital idea."

"Enough of that, my dear," said Eliot, clearly aware of her turning the praise his way but also pleased. "It's time to make our way home. I need to get to work on this turnpike project. And I can't wait to breathe the pure air of Port Eliot."

Chapter Twelve

A Plan

Not many days later, primroses were peeping out of the high stone and earth hedges enclosing patchwork fields that covered the rolling hills and little valleys of verdant countryside between Liskeard and St. Germans. Daffodils and jonquils would soon burst into flower, and the hawthorn and the hazel were braving the risk of late frost and coming into bud. The meadows were fresh with bright new grass. Sheep munched contentedly, their fleeces heavy with spring mud and winter growth. The morning air was chill but bright in the sunshine of early spring, the sky blue and pocked with small downy clouds.

The St. Austell to Tor Point stage wagon was winding its way between the hedges, up and down hills on what passed for a road. One of the passengers was Edwin Ough. He had got on the stage wagon in Liskeard and paid for a ride as far as St. Germans. On his lap lay a small parcel containing a pasty.

Ough opened the window and looked out to see if he was getting close to the village. He breathed in the clear air and soaked in the beauty of the unfolding countryside, glimpsed through gaps in the hedges where gates were placed to let the animals be driven from one field to another. He reflected on stories from people in the town who were thinking of emigrating to America for a better life. Personally, he couldn't bear the thought of leaving Cornwall and its varied beauty, especially in the springtime. He loved the countryside around Liskeard, the bleak moors with their ancient Stone Age monuments north of the town, the gentle English Channel coast down by Looe, and the wooded valleys he had seen on his journey to Bodmin. One of these days he would like to see the rugged Atlantic coast and perhaps Mr. Eliot would take him to see the mining country down west.

His reveries were interrupted when the guard sounded the coach horn to announce their approach to the village. He was the only passenger to get off at this stop. The guard handed down his bag from the roof. Edwin asked directions to Port Eliot, and accordingly set off towards the River Tiddy and the Eliot home. He soon caught sight of the towers of St. Germanus church and walked through the Gate Lodge and up the long drive through the park to the house.

He knew the house had originally been a monastery and that the family, in the seventeenth century, had greatly improved it as a residence;

he had heard there were plans afoot to do more. As he drew closer, Ough stood for a moment admiring the grandeur of the house and its approaches. The church was to the right and close by, with its great west door facing him. The broad front of the house seemed to go on forever. The house was not as ornate or decorative as Lanhydrock, that he had only glimpsed briefly before that rude owner sent him on his way, but it appeared older, grander in a way.

Unbeknownst to Ough, he was following in the footsteps of Willie Bunt and Mary Abbott, whose arrival had been arranged by Polkinghorne following Catherine Eliot's directive a few weeks before. They had settled in as new servants at Port Eliot but were being kept out of the way for the day so they would not be seen by Sir James Trenance who had come over from Lanhydrock for the meeting with Eliot.

Edwin Ough announced his arrival at the entrance. He was expected as a valued guest and warmly welcomed by the butler who showed him into the salon, where Edward Eliot and Polkinghorne stood and greeted him as he entered.

"Mr. Ough, welcome to Port Eliot," said Edward. "You know my man of business, Mr. Polkinghorne, of course. We just wanted to have a word with you before we join the others." He nodded to Polkinghorne.

"No doubt, Mr. Ough, you carry with you messages of support from the Mayor and the leading townspeople," said Polkinghorne. "I am confident you will carry back promises of support from Mr. Eliot and his guests from Lanhydrock here today. These gentlemen represent great means; they are in a position to provide funds. Make sure they are persuaded that there will be many sources of traffic on the turnpike commanding tolls from which they will be remunerated."

"You can rely on me, Mr. Polkinghorne," said Ough. "His Worship has entrusted me with full authority."

"We are also relying on you to ensure as this venture moves forward that the interests of Port Eliot are recognized. Not only will Mr. Eliot see to it that proper influence is brought to bear in parliament but that his good name will ensure the probity of the management of the turnpike commission, without which no Act would be forthcoming."

"There is one other matter, Mr. Ough," said Eliot. "Be advised that Port Eliot's yarn jobbers travel far and wide in these parts, passing out wool to the spinners in their cottages, buying the finished yarn and carrying it to market. They alone will be a source of tolls for the turnpike. There are many parties in this, all of whom will contribute and benefit to their varying degrees."

"Mr. Eliot wants you to bear in mind," said Polkinghorne, "that while Port Eliot gains much from Liskeard, in business as well as politics,

Liskeard must understand that it gains much from Port Eliot, and must see to it that our interests are regarded in future dealings regardless of other parties."

"I understand, sir," said Ough.

"Then give us your hand on it, Mr. Ough," said Eliot. "Let us proceed to the library and commence our meeting."

Ough observed that there were three other gentlemen present in the dining room, one of whom he had seen before in less welcoming circumstances.

"Let me present you to Sir James Trenance and Mr. Thomas Bolitho, his family's financial adviser," said Eliot. "Sir James has come up from Lanhydrock and brought his steward with him, Mr. Joseph Clymo. Gentlemen, Mr. Ough here is the worthy Town Clerk of Liskeard."

They all shook hands and Eliot waved them to their seats.

"Gentlemen, please join me in some tea, and then let us to business." Eliot waited until the butler poured and they were all settled. "Now, I understand, Mr. Ough, you went ahead and met with Mr. Polkinghorne in Liskeard, and you have garnered the support of your town council to make a start with the petition for the turnpike."

"Yes, sir," replied Ough, "We expect to have enough support from the aldermen and councilors by the next meeting of the Quarter Sessions, and the Justices of the Peace as well. The merchants in the town are for it, especially the wool merchants, so they will append their names. They say it'll be easier for the weavers and serge makers from up country to get into the yarn market in Fore Street."

"It'll be cheaper for them to carry off the wool after they've bought it, too," said Eliot. "Who else?"

"I've talked to one or two leading farmers, though," replied Ough. "They do want the benefit of better roads to get to market, but they say they are in no position to pay higher rates."

"Mr. Ough," chuckled Eliot, "Whatever my gifts may be, they do not include prophecy. But I assure you that it doesn't take a prophet to have foretold exactly what you would have heard from the farmers! They like to hold on to their money.

"Many of them are my tenants, though," Eliot continued. "I assure you we will find it a simple task for them to contribute to the excellent advantages they will receive in ways that do not come out of their own pockets."

"Nevertheless, Mr. Eliot," interjected Bolitho, "on behalf of my partners it would be remiss of me not to make clear that we will require adequate security in the receipts from tolls before we could advance capital to finance the building of such roads as you contemplate."

"Oh come, Bolitho," said Sir James, "don't be such a stuffed shirt. It's only money after all, and you and your partners have had enough business put your way from Lanhydrock that you should consider it a privilege to arrange the entire venture."

"That's all well and good, Sir James," said Bolitho, "but we have many clients' interests to think of, in many parts of the county, not to mention our shareholders. In fact, we would be able to look on the venture more favorably if we could foresee participation from you and the baron."

"Gentlemen," interposed Eliot, "what you say is wise and right. I believe our friends in Westminster may also see the advantage of our bearing a goodly share of the burden. Furthermore, as Receiver General I have considerable influence with the Duchy of Cornwall. I have, since our previous conversation and during my recent attendance at the House of Commons, made further inquiries of Mr. Pitt. He is not in a position to promise anything just yet, but he has indicated that he would be willing to lend his not inconsiderable support to a Turnpike Act for Liskeard."

Ough was impressed at Eliot's influence. He was a valuable patron to the borough. Liskeard indeed owed much to Port Eliot.

Bolitho stroked his chin. While he and his partners profited from assisting in financing the Trenance interests, it was increasingly apparent that Eliot was an up-and-coming force to be reckoned with, someone to support. "Please continue, Mr. Eliot," he said.

"To be frank with you," said Eliot, "if I may rely on your confidence, I am given to understand that, provided I myself act as a trustee and supervise the administration of the trust, friends of the king's ministers may well provide some of the funding. I am confident that I can persuade the High Sheriff of Cornwall to join me. However, a modicum of local financial support is desirable, and that, Sir James, is where you come in."

"Exactly what do you have in mind, Eliot?" asked Sir James, "and how would our participation benefit the Lanhydrock interests?" His posture having deteriorated into a slouch, he now sat up straighter and adjusted the cuffs of his jacket. "My father will require an explanation."

Young Trenance is showing unexpected signs of business judgment and shrewdness, thought Eliot. Time to nip that in the bud before he becomes hard to control. After a moment's though he spoke. "Surely you can make a decision without consulting your father, Sir James," he said, a trifle acidly. "I had understood that the baron wishes to pass the reins along to his heir. Anyway, rest assured you would be required to do little more than lend your good name to support the project, which would only enhance your reputation in the eyes of your neighbors and, indeed, your tenants and workers."

"I have brought Clymo with me to this meeting, Eliot," said Sir James. "The Trenance family has always sought his advice and found it to be invaluable. What say you, Clymo?"

Joseph Clymo shifted in his chair, a little uncomfortable to be put on the spot in front of the representatives of such wealth. He pondered for a moment, then drew on his considerable experience. "There are many calls upon our capital, Sir James, which many think considerable," said Clymo. "With respect, we are drawing up plans to greatly expand the workings at the Poldice mine in the near future. And there are urgent improvements in drainage required at one or two of our other mines where the workings pass under the sea. These are opportunities we must seize if we are to gain full benefit from investments we have already made."

"But surely nothing would detract if you merely provide Mr. Bolitho with your general support for the turnpike project," Eliot interjected. "After all, Sir James, better roads would aid the expansion and improve the profitability of your enterprises, too. Do you not agree, Mr. Bolitho?"

"My partners would no doubt appreciate the benefits for the Lanhydrock interests," responded Bolitho, "but they usually insist on gaining comfort from hard assets being pledged to support any loan. But perhaps our notary could draft a suitable agreement backed by Sir James's word that would suffice."

"It's settled then," said Eliot cheerfully. "Mr. Ough, Polkinghorne, you may proceed with confidence with your part of the proceedings. Now, Sir James, keep in mind that Mr. Pitt may ask us both to reinforce his ability to serve Cornwall by seeing to it that our boroughs elect men who can be relied upon.

"Gentlemen, let us make some preliminary determination as to the details of our plan," Eliot continued. "I am given to understand that the initial responsibilities of the Liskeard Turnpike Trust will be to improve the Post Road between Callington and St. Austell, and also from the Tor Point Passage and the two crossings from Devon across the Tamar estuary to the port of Looe."

"There are also requests afoot," interjected Ough, "to repair the existing road from West Taphouse Lane through St. Pinnock, and from Crimble Passage to Liskeard through Hessingford and Crafthole. A Mr. Joseph Johnson has said to the justices that this is the usual way for both horses and carriages and is nearer and more level than the St. Germans Road."

"What does this Mr. Johnson know of such matters?" demanded Eliot. "What judge is he of repairing roads?"

"Well, sir, he told the justice that he used to drive a carriage," said Ough. "And a Mr. Thomas Peeke said that the militia in their march from Plymouth to Liskeard went the Hessingford Road. And the road through St. Germans cannot be amended without purchasing land."

"I'll see to whatever is needed in the way of land," said Eliot firmly. "The people of this area depend on the port on the Tiddy for much of their livelihood. Now, Polkinghorne, next time you are in Liskeard be sure you provide some good ale for these acquaintances of Mr. Ough's and his good friend the mayor. See to it that they are persuaded of the wisdom of the routes we select."

"I fail to see how improving the road through St. Germans will benefit the citizens of Bodmin and the miners employed by the Trenance mines," said Sir James petulantly.

"We cannot expect to accomplish everything at once, my good fellow," said Eliot cheerily. "You are their natural leader and must make them see the broadest perspective. Their turn will come, and eventually all of Cornwall will benefit. I am confident that they will follow you. Now, finish up your tea, gentlemen, and I will ring the bell for port so that we may celebrate the progress we have made and toast future prosperity for all of Cornwall."

Eliot reached out to the bell-pull beside the fireplace. After receiving his orders the butler returned with port and glasses, which he filled and offered to each of the men in turn, then took his place by the door. Turning to his guests Eliot said, "Now, gentlemen, let us be upstanding and drink to His Majesty, Mr. Pitt, Cornwall, progress and turnpikes!"

Sir James stood, looked from one gentleman to the next, then taking his glass, he drank deeply. He glanced at Bolitho and then at Eliot, a thoughtful look on his face.

Edward Eliot signaled to the butler to open the door and lead the guests out. "Gentlemen," he said, "I thank you for your attendance and bid you farewell. I will be sure that you are kept informed as matters progress."

As they left the room Eliot waylaid his man of business. "A word, Polkinghorne," he said, softly and urgently. "Arrange to meet Ough and his friends in Liskeard as soon as possible. We must strike while the iron is hot and before any rivals seek to outwit us. Be courteous but firm. Make it clear to the good citizens that they can depend only on Port Eliot to bring this advantageous project to a successful conclusion. Extract promises from them, no dillydallying."

"Right you are, sir," responded Polkinghorne, "I'll see to it immediately."

"And be sure to draw up a schedule of tolls so that the trustees see sufficient income to carry out their public duties. Take the new man who is assisting you, Bunt. Let him see how things are done at Port Eliot, see what he's made of."

"I'll do my best, sir."

"I know I can count on you, Polkinghorne, like your father before you."

Chapter Thirteen

Turnpike

D ays were so fully occupied at Port Eliot that it seemed no sooner had spring turned into summer than autumn was following hard on its heels. Edward Eliot was keeping Charles Polkinghorne so busy that Polkinghorne was grateful to have Willy Bunt as an assistant. He seemed a bright enough fellow, and they would see whether he could become of value to their enterprises. So, early on a cool September morning, Polkinghorne took Bunt with him to Liskeard on the mission Eliot had assigned him, to meet with the borough's leaders and pursue the new turnpike project. Bunt was too inexperienced to be of much help in the negotiations, but it would be instructive for the young man to observe how a master of the art plied his trade. Not that he would admit it to his companion, but Polkinghorne, too, was glad to have an escort for the road. You never knew whom you might run into.

They rode out of St. Germans village, past the Almshouses, onto what passed as a road and hacked towards Liskeard under a watery sun. The leaves on the hazels, beeches and oaks were donning their colors of brown, yellow, copper and red. Polkinghorne rode a hunter from the Eliot stables. Bunt, not an experienced rider, dug his knees tightly into the withers of a sound but aging cob, reins held with white knuckles beneath his knitted mittens.

Both men carried pistols. Bunt had shot for the first time at the practice target the day before.

"How do you like life at Port Eliot so far then, young fellow?" asked Polkinghorne.

"Oi loikes it right well enough, zir," replied Bunt, "and the Eliots seem kind compared with the Trenances. Oi would never in my loife go back to Lanhydrock."

"And why is that, may I ask?" said Polkinghorne.

"Well, zir, 'twas loike Oi told 'er ladyship, zir," said Bunt reddening. "Sir James was awful cruel to my Mary, and 'e treated me worse nor 'is dog. Us w'dn' go back to be treated loike that no how, no matter 'ow much Oi needed a place. Oi'd rather starve. Oi'm a loyal sort of feller, but it ain't right to be treated that way."

"I can assure you that if you are loyal to Mr. Eliot, you will not find a kinder nor more just master," said Polkinghorne smiling warmly.

"You worked at Port Eliot long, Mr. Polkinghorne?" asked Bunt. "Got a fambly?"

"Some people might say it's impertinent to ask personal questions," replied Polkinghorne frowning.

"Didn't mean no offence, zir," said Bunt, "just interested. Oi loike to know what's what, who Oi'm workin' for. That way Oi can try me best."

Probably do no harm to satisfy the young man's curiosity, thought Polkinghorne, and he was proud of his own family's association with the great Eliot family.

"Polkinghornes have been at Port Eliot for longer than I can remember, since my great-great-great-grandfather's day," he recounted. "He came from down west up to these parts to farm. Rented a smallholding with a cottage from the Mr. Eliot of those days, worked hard, his wife, too. Prospered, raised a family, needed more room, moved to a bigger farm. Had to pay more rent, but he made the farm pay and the Eliots have always been good landlords," Polkinghorne said, warming to his story.

"The family carried on like that for several generations, gradually improving their position. Some setbacks along the way, of course, when times were hard. My grandfather changed over to raising sheep when wheat prices went down."

Bunt nodded appreciatively at the prosperous progression of the Polkinghornes and asked, "You 'ave a fambly yourself, Mr. Polkinghorne?"

Polkinghorne paused then changed the subject. "We'll keep bearing up the hill to the right," he said, "towards Menheniot way. That fork down to the left takes you along the Great Post Road that crosses the Tamar by Cremyll and then takes you down to the English Channel by Looe. If you see the St. Germans Beacon, you'll know you've gone the wrong way. You mark what I say so you know the way yourself next time."

They ambled along for several minutes in an increasingly companionable silence, each with his own thoughts. Bunt called to mind Mary's whispered remark this morning when she brought the freshly baked bread into the servants hall at breakfast. It was urgent that they talk, she had said. They didn't get much chance to talk together except on Sundays when they had half days off to go to church. Mary slept in the maids quarters at the top of the big house, and his bed was over in the stable block along with the other young unmarried men who lived in. Willy would be sure to talk to Mary next Sunday, if not before. He wondered what the urgency of their discussion might be. Perhaps family matters?

Not one to remain silent long, Bunt eventually spoke, "So you never 'ad no fambly of your own, Mr. Polkinghorne?" The man was getting really old, probably in his forties already. High time to father children before it was too late.

"Not yet, Bunt," said Polkinghorne. "My job keeps me busy. No time to run around courting. Anyway, I haven't met the right young woman."

"Oi expect you will one of theses days, zir. Just a matter of toime," said Bunt, encouragingly. "So 'ow come you ain't farmin'?"

Polkinghorne was becoming inured to Bunt's persistent curiosity. And though he was not used to imparting so much information about himself, discourse did help to make the trip go faster. "My uncle was the eldest son, so he inherited the farm. My father was made steward for Port Eliot. He was fortunate; it was an important position and a nice house in the village came with it. When I left school I apprenticed to him, in a manner of speaking. He was killed in a riding accident and then the present Mr. Eliot made me his man of business. It's an interesting job, plenty of variety, always lots of projects."

"Squire must put great stock in ye, Mr. Polkinghorne," said Bunt.

Polkinghorne gave a slight smile. "Mr. Eliot trusts me with responsibility, he's a good squire. You could do well working for Port Eliot, if you keep your nose to the grindstone."

"Oi didn't get much school," observed Bunt. "Don't need it, manage all right."

"You need learning if you're to go far," said Polkinghorne. "I was fortunate. I learned enough arithmetic to get a job in the estate office keeping records, reckoning costs, collecting rents, figuring where to buy at advantage."

Bunt was unconvinced. "Aargh, but your dad got you that job," said Bunt. "My dad couldn't do nothin' for me. Drunk 'alf the toime."

"I still had to show Mr. Eliot I could do the job," said Polkinghorne, "and learn how to take on more."

The riders continued on their journey with Polkinghorne telling stories about the traditions and history at Port Eliot that underlay his own loyalty to the Eliots, and answering more questions from Bunt.

"So 'ow did Mr. Eliot get a big place like Port Eliot then?" Bunt asked.

"It used to be a priory until the Dissolution of the Monasteries," said Polkinghorne.

"What are ye talkin' about then, this diss'lution, zir?"

"It was when King Henry VIII established the Church of England so he could divorce the old Catholic queen and marry young Anne Boleyn. He sold off the old monasteries."

Bunt let go of the reins long enough to scratch his chin. Before he could open his mouth with another question, Polkinghorne continued. "Mr. Eliot's ancestors bought Port Eliot after that. They expanded the park by changing the course of the River Tiddy and then built the quay to make a port."

"Gor blimey," said Bunt, "that took a lot of doin', big job."

"Eliots do big things, Bunt," said Polkinghorne, "and you can expect to help as long as you work here."

Bunt was silent a while, impressed. His thighs were getting sore from gripping and rubbing along the saddle, but he did not want to make a bad impression by complaining. He was thankful a couple of hours later when Polkinghorne pointed out the tower of St. Martin's church, a sign that they were approaching the outskirts of the town.

"Not much further now," said Polkinghorne. "The road is fair for these parts but slow going, and it doesn't do much good for our tenants who want to get to the market in Liskeard."

"Bit dark to see much when I got 'ere with Mary," said Bunt. "Oi'd like to see more of the town. Wonder what keeps 'er folk busy?"

Polkinghorne had had enough of Bunt's inquisitiveness and they rode in silence past the church, then stopped at Eliot House to leave their horses to be fed and stabled. Bunt lumbered down and swayed a bit getting his balance as he reached the ground. They proceeded on foot over to Pike Street where the chambers of the town council were located.

Bunt's curiosity resurfaced. "Why is Mr. Eliot so interested in what goes on 'ere in Liskeard, zir??"

"Liskeard is a borough and an important market town, an important town to the Eliot family," Polkinghorne said. "It was granted its charter in 1240 by Richard, Earl of Cornwall. It's had two seats in Parliament since 1294. Mr. Eliot owns them both, as well as the two in St. Germans, and the two in Grampound attached themselves to him, as well."

"You can't own seats in Parliament in Cornwall!" scoffed Bunt. "Parliament's in London, that's where the seats are kept so the members can sit on them when they go there to argue with the king."

"Bunt, you don't know about such things. Mr. Eliot has these seats in his pocket, that's what they call it. He decides who is going to be a candidate; he's well paid for it, too. And there are only a few voters."

"Don't sound right to me," said Bunt, "not fair, 'tisn't proper."

"It's the way things work, Bunt; always have, always will. If you keep your nose clean next time there's an election Mr. Eliot may have you help. Now, we're almost at the corporation's offices."

"What's a corporation?" asked Bunt.

"You must listen, Bunt," said Polkinghorne, sighing, "I'm not going to keep telling you. Liskeard is a borough, so it's governed by a corporation. It has a mayor and aldermen and a town council. They are elected. We're going to meet with the mayor and his town clerk and some other men. Mr. Eliot has a lot of influence with the town council and he helped out the town clerk get to Bodmin after a highwayman robbed him. No, I won't tell you about that now. Here's the door to the council chambers. Let's get inside."

Going into the building, they climbed the stairs to the office the mayor used for his official meetings, Bunt stiffly aware of his aching muscles. James Davis, the Mayor, was there with Edwin Ough, the Town Clerk, who greeted them warmly.

"It is my pleasant duty to welcome you both to Liskeard," said Davis. "Mr. Ough and I received your message, Mr. Polkinghorne, and we have invited some people who may be involved with the turnpike petition to join us. I took the guidance of Mr. Eliot and have not informed our friends in Bodmin. I must say, however, I am curious as to why not."

"Mr. Eliot is a good Cornishman, gentlemen, and he has the interests of this borough and its surrounding villages at heart," Polkinghorne replied. "For the moment let me just say that he would prefer this conversation not to reach ears at Lanhydrock. I advise you to depend on Mr. Eliot to understand the workings of Parliament, where there are many competing interests and, indeed, a war to fight on four continents. As far as local affairs are concerned he understands that little priority remains. The interests of Cornwall get put below those parts of the country nearer London, and it is prudent to advance only one measure at a time. You would be well advised to leave it to him"

"Those arguments are telling, Mr. Polkinghorne," said Ough. "I did observe also during our meeting that Mr. Eliot seemed to be somewhat at odds with Sir James Trenance."

"If ye want my opinion . . ." ventured Bunt. Polkinghorne interrupted him.

"That'll do, Bunt," he said, "mind that you are here merely to escort me on the road. You may leave opinions to your betters." Bunt reddened but sat back in silence.

There was a loud knocking from the street below, followed by the sound of tramping feet climbing the stairs, and two men came into the room.

"Gentlemen, allow me to introduce Mr. Stephen Clogg, one of our council members, and Mr. Andrew Hingston, who is our Justice of the Peace," Davis said. "They will be of great assistance in drafting the petition for the turnpike."

Polkinghorne addressed the men. "The main task we need to accomplish is to determine where it would be most advantageous to site the new road," he stated. "It is imperative that it should serve the most farmers and merchants along its path. That, after all, is why Parliament is willing to assist us."

Clogg interjected: "I have a document here, sir, with a map that will make that clear. It proposes some repair and improvement to existing roads and some building of new ones. The new turnpike should pass from West Taphouse Lane through the parishes of Broad Oak, St. Pinnock, Liskeard, through Menheniot and over Butterdon Water to Comb Rise House in the parish of St. Ives, pass Sheviock, Anthony and Maker to Crimble passage on the River Tamar."

Polkinghorne replied forcefully. "I must insist that it pass near St. Germans," he said, "as there are many farmers there who take their wool to Liskeard market."

"But we have heard from a Mr. Thomas Peeke," said Hingston, "who averred that the road from St. Germans to Crafthole is hilly and bad. The military prefer the road through Hessenford to avoid St. Germans."

"I must advise you, gentlemen," stated Polkinghorne, "that parliamentary support for Liskeard is dependent on the road taking the St. Germans route. It is a matter of doing what is of benefit to the farming community."

Here they broke off their discussion for pasties and a pot of ale at The White Horse, but then continued their wrangling well into the afternoon. Polkinghorne urged that the road include Anthony and St. Germans. Those parts of the route would indeed be twisty and hilly, mused Ough, but kept his thoughts to himself. After all, the gentry would be well served, not only the Carews at Anthony, but also, most importantly, the Eliots at Port Eliot. Ough's mind meandered as much as the proposed road, but his concentration was sharply brought to heel by a peremptory question from Polkinghorne.

Polkinghorne felt it was high time to carry out Mr. Eliot's instructions and make sure that the good citizens well understood whose influence they were depending on. "And how pray will you pay for the road?" he demanded. "Does money grow on hedgerows? Or is the borough's strongbox filled with gold? If it is, it is high time that I advised Mr. Eliot to raise the rents in the parish."

The citizens of Liskeard were taken aback. For a moment they were at a loss for a response. Bunt's inquisitive mind was taking in this exchange. He wanted to learn from observing Polkinghorne in action. It appeared to him that Polkinghorne's behavior changed depending on his perception of whom he was dealing with. With his betters he was deferential; with his equals he was firm; with his inferiors, like poor Willy himself, he could be dismissive. In his experience Mr. Eliot would not speak in this way.

The pause dragged on until Councilman Clogg spoke up. "Perhaps Parliament would vote an appropriation," he offered.

"Never!" said Polkinghorne. "It is not up to Parliament to provide for local expenses. Besides, they are scouring the financiers for money to pay for the war, not only in Europe but in America. No, Parliament will merely provide the legislation to enable the way to be found through a turnpike trust. It is up to Liskeard and the surrounding parishes to find the means, until the tolls received repay the initial outlay."

"Opinion in the borough favors doing our utmost to go forward," said Hingston. "I am confident that if we can agree upon a plan, the Justices of the Peace will be supportive at the next Quarter Sessions. But there is limited gold in the corporation's coffer."

"I can perhaps trespass further upon the goodwill of Mr. Eliot who, as you know, has many connections," said Polkinghorne. "I understand Mr. Thomas Bolitho and his partners may be willing to assist, dependent on his client Sir James Trenance's participation or at least his pledge. It is a matter of providing sufficient guarantees to induce them to lend against the projected revenue from tolls."

"The townspeople understand the need to pay reasonable tolls," said Clogg, "but the farmers are always reluctant to pay more than is absolutely necessary."

"I have prepared a proposed schedule of tolls," said Polkinghorne, as he laid a document on the table. "Let me explain. The method is to assess tolls for each section of the pike according to the class of user. The customary rate is one shilling and sixpence for a carriage drawn by four horses, a penny for an un-laden horse, and ten pence for a drove of twenty cows. The first thing we must do is erect tollgates, which the toll keeper can raise upon receiving payment. Mr. Eliot has already offered to assist with a toll house for Liskeard."

"I believe the borough council could undertake to account for the collection of tolls," said Ough. "We can find a reliable man to take the tolls and look after the money for a modest remuneration."

"The administration of this project is more complex than it may appear," said Polkinghorne. "The Act of Parliament will require that a board of trustees be set up, with oversight by an experienced chairman. That chairman will wish to have a say in all appointments. Usually a member of the gentry is asked to serve in that position, for an appropriate emolument."

"In that case I can think of none better suited for chairman than Mr. Eliot," said Edwin Ough, "that is if he would be willing to accept the burden. He has shown great interest in this project."

"I am confident that he could be persuaded," said Polkinghorne. "Mr. Eliot is a gentleman with a high regard for his public duties."

The group concurred without demur in the excellence of that notion. This completed their business for the time being, and Davis, in his position as mayor, called for an adjournment. Polkinghorne and Bunt took their leave and walked back to Eliot House to remount, hoping to reach St. Germans before nightfall.

To make good time they cantered for stretches of the road that were reasonably level, although there were few enough of these. Bunt bounced along in the saddle until he finally got the rhythm and settled in. As they slowed to a walk to take the last hill before St. Germans, Bunt took the opportunity to give voice to a thought that had been running through his mind.

"Oi been thinkin', zir, Mr. Polkinghorne, that there turnpike will need an awful lot of stone if the new road is goin' to be any better than the same muddy old cow track where you slides about all over the place after a good rain and bumps uncomfortable like over the ruts after the sun dries 'em out."

"You're not paid to think, young man," said Polkinghorne, "you're paid to do." After a few minutes, he added, "The question is, what to do about it?"

"Well, zir, beggin' your pardon, but Oi was doin' an errand to one of the farms across the road from Port Eliot t'other day," said Bunt, "an' as Oi was lookin' around to see more about where Oi was livin' nowadays, Oi saw the side of an 'ill where there was an awful lot of big rocks sticking out. You couldn't miss 'em, not if you kept your eyes peeled. Oi 'spect us could dig 'em out an' break 'em up an' use 'em to make a road that you could drive a wagon over."

"H'mm," said Polkinghorne, looking at Bunt with a bit more interest as they jogged along. "I'll mention that to Mr. Eliot. It just might be worth looking into."

The travelers were relieved soon after to reach Port Eliot safely without encountering highwaymen or, indeed, wild animals as they passed the woods near Trerulefoot.

Bunt led the horses back to the stable and handed them over to the care of the groom. Polkinghorne walked over to the estate office to write out his report of the meeting. He thought he might mention the idea of quarrying road stone and adding to the revenue from the turnpike project.

As he entered the small room that served as his office, he noticed a message from Eliot lying on his desk. It read:

"Meet first thing after breakfast. Must leave for London immediately thereafter to attend Parliament. Pitt confident continued pressure will bring victory, but Newcastle is dragging for peace. Pitt needs my support. Provide details of Liskeard turnpike project before I depart."

Polkinghorne sighed, knowing he would be burning candles late. However, at least he would have the opportunity to give Mr. Eliot an account of the meeting in Liskeard that shed a favorable light on his own performance.

Eliot stayed in London for several weeks and was able to influence many Tories to support Pitt. They were persuaded by Pitt's argument to the House that "the only way to have peace is to prepare for war."

Newcastle was increasingly unwilling to raise the funds for the prosecution of the war and was jealous of his colleague and rival as a man "always fertile in schemes and projects."

Finally, however, by September, General Jeffrey Amherst had captured Montreal, and not long after that the French surrendered Canada to the British. There were other successes in India, in Africa, in the islands of the Caribbean, and in Europe. Total victory around the world was in Pitt's grasp, and his power appeared secure despite the constant nipping at his heels.

Then on the twenty-fifth of October, the king went into his water closet and there collapsed. He died before help could arrive. The cry went up, "Long live the king!" whereupon his grandson, the Prince of Wales and Duke of Cornwall, assumed the crown.

The reign of George III began, as did the treacherous influence and jealous grasp of his favorite, the Earl of Bute, the "Minister behind the Curtain."

Pitt was halted to virtual impotence.

Great change was on its way to England.

Chapter Fourteen

The Visitor

The autumn days down west brought a steady drizzle that was characteristic of the Cornish climate. It was a late September Sunday. Addis and Lizzie Penwarden were just leaving the little Wesleyan chapel at Gwennap, the baby Jedson in her arms and young Jemmy walking proudly beside his father. The Reverend Perry approached the family and spoke to Addis, his tone urgent. What he said first was not the only thing on his mind.

"Penwarden, Mrs. Penwarden, I'm glad to see you here on this Holy Day, keeping up your attendance at our little chapel regularly. Sometimes when we suffer great loss as you have, we are inclined to withdraw, to suffer our grief alone. Our healing is more complete when we share it with our friends, with our community, and even then it seems to take forever. Please know that I am here for you whenever you need the comfort of His love."

"Us be surely grateful for all you've done, Reverend," said Addis. "Ye know too whatever needs you 'ave, us'll do what us can for you. You only 'ave to ask. Now me an' Lizzie is just goin' to pay respects to my brother's grave before us go 'ome. 'Twas months since you gave 'im that there lovely funeral, the 'ole village there payin' their respects, but seems loike no toime since 'e was taken from us. After we tend 'is grave us'll be workin' in the garden or the cottage if ye need us, but not very 'ard since it's s'posed to be a day of rest."

"We'm goin' to pick some pretty branches to leave on the grave," said Lizzie. "Oi can't get 'im out of my mind, the dear of 'im. Us wants the 'ole village to remember 'im still. 'Tid'n' right that miners is allus gettin' 'urt or killed down them mines. Somethin' should be done about it, that's what Oi say."

"I understand that you feel that way," said Reverend Perry, "and it's right and proper that you should. I'm having a special meeting later at the chapel after evening worship," he said. "It's about that very thing among others, about the whole community looking after its own. I want you to come. It's important that you do. Both of you, Lizzie too. Bring the children. There'll be ladies of the church to look after them while we talk. The schoolmaster from the church school will be coming, the grocer, the butcher, and a few of the other miners, perhaps one or two of the fishermen from nearby."

"Us'll be there, eh Lizzie?" replied Addis. "What us needs to do at 'ome can wait. Anyroad, if this rain keeps up it won't be very nice workin' outside."

"Bless 'e, Addis," grinned Lizzie, "if us stopped for every little drop of drizzle us'd never get anythin' done. You'm too used to bein' sheltered down that mine."

A knot of other people leaving the chapel had gathered around them, exchanging greetings, chuckling at Lizzie's sally. "Can us come too?" asked one of the village elders. "Us likes a good ol' chin wag, give us somethin' to do of a Sunday."

"You're all welcome," said Reverend Perry. "We have a lot to discuss. Be sure to come to evening worship, too. We have an important visitor; I want you to hear what he has to say. He will help see to it that things are improved for ordinary folk. I told you there would be change coming to Cornwall."

Reverend Perry waved goodbye to the Penwarden family. He turned and called to Jonathon Turner and his wife, members of his congregation, and as arranged walked together to their cottage nearby. There, they were to meet their visitor for mid-day Sunday dinner.

The reverend had no sooner been welcomed inside and settled in to the little parlor than they heard the clopping of an approaching horse. Perry and Turner went outside again to greet the new arrival. The travel-stained rider was dressed in black from head to foot with a broad-brimmed hat and white linen bands at the front of his neck signifying that he was a clergyman. The rider dismounted somewhat stiffly. He appeared to be about sixty years of age. He was below medium height, but well proportioned and strong looking, with a clear complexion, a full head of grey hair that fell to his shoulders, and a strong nose set between bright eyes in a saintly, intellectual face.

"Mr. Wesley, how blessed we are to have you in our midst once again," said Reverend Perry heartily. "Do you remember Jonathon Turner from your last visit? He is a loyal and dependable member of our little chapel. His wife is in the kitchen putting the finishing touches to a roast chicken for our Sunday dinner, complete with his homegrown parsnips and potatoes. Jonathon, could you help the Reverend John Wesley with his horse?"

"'Twould be my pleasure, zir," said Turner. "Us 'as a little lean-to be'ind the cottage. Oi'll take 'im back for ye and unsaddle 'im, let 'im 'ave some hay and water. P'raps later on Oi could give 'im a bit of a rub down. 'Ow far have ye come today?"

"It took me six days to ride from London into Cornwall, where I made for Launceston and then Trewint, near Altarnun," said Wesley. His voice was rich and resonant, a man accustomed to addressing large crowds. "I stayed with my good friend Digory Isbell. Today, I preached early this morning in Penryn."

Jonathon Turner took the horse from Reverend Wesley and led it around the back. There was a call from inside the cottage that dinner was ready. Mrs. Turner appeared at the open door of the cottage, red-faced and flustered, wearing an apron and waving a long-handled spoon. "Welcome, gentlemen, come in and take your seats do, or my roast chicken will be spoiled." She stood aside as they took off their hats and made their way inside. Reverend Wesley returned her greeting.

"Thank you for having me to stay here for a few days, Mrs. Turner. It is good people like you and your husband who make possible the mission of me and my colleagues."

The windows of the cottage were small, and the sky outside was overcast, but nevertheless the room emanated good cheer. Jonathon Turner joined them in the parlor after putting the horse away. He showed their distinguished guest to the place of honor, such as it was. The rest sat around the humble scrubbed plank table. John Wesley asked for blessings for the wholesome meal that Mrs. Turner had prepared for them. After being served a hearty plate of chicken with bread sauce and home-grown vegetables, Wesley settled in his chair and looked up.

"I look forward to meeting with your good fellows this evening after your service, Mr. Perry. I have much to talk to them about, and we must enjoin them to spread our message and champion our work. I have others to meet in the district during my stay, and I seek all of your help to ensure that a large multitude hears my words next Sunday when I preach again at Gwennap. And after that I must head back to St. Ives."

"I trust you will have a better reception there than your brother Charles did during his first visit. When was that, some twenty years ago?" asked Reverend Perry.

"Almost, I remember it as if it was yesterday," said Wesley, "but all is forgiven. Ah, yes, back then Charles traveled to Cornwall before me in the summer of 1743. He had been called from Bristol to preach in St. Ives, where there was a small religious society of some twelve souls. He went to the church where the curate's text was 'Beware of false prophets.' The Church of England did not approve of us Methodists in their midst. They could be violent in their opposition."

"Them early days must've been quite frightenin', sir," said Jonathon Turner. "I wonder you kept up the good work with all them people carryin' on against you."

"Strangely enough we had no fear," said Wesley. "We simply trusted in our Lord. My brother Charles went out the next day to preach, and a mob formed and tried to pull him down. But he came to no harm. I remember he wrote to me, 'They had no power to touch me. My soul was calm and fearless.' That was not the only time he had similar experiences." He paused in reminiscence and looked at them each in turn with a smile lighting his face. "But only a few days later on Carnegy Downs he preached to a crowd of a thousand tinners, who received the seed into good and honest hearts."

"When did ye follow in 'is footsteps down 'ere then, Reverend?" asked Turner, his curiosity aroused about the early days of the Wesleys in Cornwall.

"It was a month or so later, in August, with another of our preachers," responded Wesley. "Neither I nor my trusty horse were up to the challenge of travel in Cornwall, and we got lost on Bodmin Moor, which is an awful place when the weather is bad. We got lost there again on our second visit that winter, but Providence led us through the wind and snow to the door of Digory Isbell in the village of Altarnun. He was inspired by the Old Testament story of the Shunammite woman who built a prophet's chamber for Elisha. Mr. Isbell was kind enough to build a preaching room onto his cottage and above it a bed chamber where I and my companions can stay."

Their hostess bustled hospitably about and proffered the platter. "Do 'ave some more of my chicken stuffin' an' gravy, Reverend. I made it for you special, all fresh from my garden."

"Thank you, just a little, Mrs. Turner," said Wesley. "If the Devil himself ever enlisted your help his temptations would be irresistible. But then, I sometimes think that the Devil is no match for you Cornish. They told me the old story, of course, that he doesn't visit Cornwall because he is afraid that like everything else he would be put into a pasty! But any people who can live among so much fog and drizzle must have great strength of character."

Reverend Perry joined in the amusement but was not to be distracted from getting the answers he was seeking from the great man. He was concerned about his own ministry, about how effective he was being in following his calling. "But how about your mission, Mr. Wesley?" he asked. "How long did it take you to save the souls of our sinful neighbors? How many setbacks? It can be a disappointing journey at times."

"Be of strong heart, my brother," said Wesley. "We must persist, and sometimes we learn that those who resist the call the longest are the strongest believers in the end."

"But how long did it take you?" persisted Perry. "How did you overcome the many obstacles? Now that you are well known and people flock to hear you preach, many assume that your task was easy. I myself experience discouragement from time to time. There are so many wrongs to be righted, so many souls to be saved."

"One must forever pray and keep faith," said Wesley. "Like my brother Charles when I first went to St. Ives that July, the mob broke into the meeting room roaring and striking those who stood in their way, throwing stones and mud at me, as though the Devil himself possessed them. I wondered then, as I often do, whether I had truly been chosen to deliver a message that shone a bright enough light.

"But I went forward with the encouragement of my friends. By September I preached to nearly three thousand people at Trezuthan Downs, and on Tuesday the twentieth, here at Gwennap, to ten thousand souls who stayed until dark and listened with the deepest attention."

They ate silently, until Reverend Perry took the opportunity to ask the honored guest another question.

"Mr. Wesley, you asked especially to meet with a small group this evening. Would you tell us more about what you have in your mind?"

"Of course, Mr. Perry," Wesley answered. "As you must know, you have for many years been one of my most effective exhorters here in west Cornwall. It is in no small part due to your efforts over the years that more and more of the ordinary folk have found salvation in Christ and become dedicated Methodists. You have inspired the great crowds to come and hear me preach. You breathe the spirit and have faith in the Word. But more than that, and more than many of my valued supporters, you deeply understand that our flocks need more than faith and spiritual enlightenment to lead fuller and happier lives on this earth."

"Yes, I was talking to one of my most faithful members after morning service, Addis Penwarden," interposed Perry. "He works in the great Poldice mine; he's a tributer, has his own pare. His younger brother was killed in the mine not long ago. He'd gone upside to fetch powder for blasting and was climbing down the ladder with it by the light of a candle. There was an explosion. Addis confessed they'd had a drop or two of cider with their pasty, so the young man's head may not have been clear."

"I have preached against the evils of drink for many years," said Wesley, "and I have seen countless thousands of families destroyed. I have concluded that nothing short of total abstinence will save people from being possessed by this devil. Some will stop at nothing to obtain spirituous liquors."

"Oi haven't touched a drop in years," said Jonathon Turner, "not since Oi took the pledge."

"You'm a lot nicer to live with since then, too," said his wife fondly.

"I'm glad to hear it, Mrs. Turner," said John Wesley. "But from what I heard of him from your preacher he has really been a good husband all along. But, Mr. Perry, as I was about to tell you, soon after I examined our newly founded society in St. Ives, I found an accursed thing among our own stewards. Well nigh one and all bought uncustomed goods. I therefore delayed speaking to them any more till I had met them all together. This I did in the evening and told them plainly either they must put this abomination away, or they would see my face no more. They severally promised me to do so, so I trust this plague is stayed. Nevertheless, smuggling remains rife in Cornwall at large, and neither the gentry nor the clergy and scarcely the magistrates have any will to end it."

"But there are many more evils that beset mankind, especially the poor and ignorant among us," said Perry. "Take Penwarden. He is capable and hard working. Compared with many he is prosperous. But his own eleven-year-old son works long hours down the mine beside him six days a week, and his wife Lizzie labors as a bal maiden picking and sorting the ore. Penwarden is blessed with native wit but has little education. His family has no prospects of improving themselves. What can such as they possibly do?"

"It is the duty of those of us who have received the Word, and those of us privileged to have received education to help our fellow men," said Wesley. "We must help in all ways that will make their lives on this earth better, as well as in the world to come. Heaven knows their employers do little or nothing, nor do the landowners, the Justices of the Peace, the Parliament, even the Church of England. They all wish to protect their privileges and expand their wealth, uncaring that it is at the expense of the common man."

"But what can us poor people do?" asked Jonathon Turner. "They don't take no notice of the likes of we."

"But I say to you," said John Wesley, smacking the flat of his hand on the table, "and I will speak about it at greater length when we meet at the chapel this Sabbath evening, the stage is set in England for great change. George III is a new king and appoints new ministers, new generals. While I detest war and pray for peace, we must acknowledge that the war will bring great prosperity to England, not just from artisans and farmers in our own land but from trade around the world and especially from America."

Wesley paused a moment before continuing. He cleared his throat and took a deep swallow from the glass of water beside his plate. He noted that the Turners appeared to keep no beer or wine in their home.

"The list of abuses is endless. The condition of the prisons is appalling. People are imprisoned for simply being poor and punished severely for minor offences, ill fed and confined in filth. Gaolers profit the more they deprive their charges. Disease is rampant. Gaols are overcrowded, and when I was in America I saw English convicts who had been transported there to make room in our prisons here at home. And there's an even worse commerce in human beings, the capture and transporting of heathens from Africa to America and the West Indies, sold into slavery, and stripped of all human dignity. The natives in America are treated worse than dogs, with little effort to convert them to Christianity. Surely all men are loved by God and are worthy of decent consideration."

Wesley paused again, and took another sip of water. His gesture seemed to be more due to mounting emotion than to thirst. The others waited for him to speak.

"Such outrages make my blood boil, Mr. Perry. There are countless wrongs to be righted. By God's grace, there will be more opportunity for the common man to live a decent life, not less. And by our preaching, our teaching, we can and will play our part to help those less fortunate to share, as is their due, in the rewards of the earth's bounty and the fruits of their labors. It is their God given right."

"Amen," said the Turners.

"Amen," echoed Reverend Perry. And the light shone in his eyes.

Chapter Fifteen

No Surprise

Sunday brought an early hint of winter to St. Germans. It was drizzling, and as the sun rose it brought a chilling wind with it. The red and orange and brown leaves of autumn were jettisoned from their branches. Willy and Mary had not managed to see much of each other in the first months after being taken in at Port Eliot. But today they had arranged to sit together when they went to church with the other servants. They really would have preferred to have found a Wesleyan chapel to attend, but the butler made it clear that all members of the Eliot household were expected to be good Anglicans and loyally attend the nearby St. Germanus church, of which the family and most of its servants were justly proud.

The service was more ornate than they were accustomed to. They struggled a bit with the responses and lessons in the prayer book and were relieved that the little choir was responsible for chanting the unfamiliar psalms and canticles.

However, as they left after the service by the west door and looked back, they remained silent. They could not help but be moved, not only by the ritual but also by the building's solid architecture that spoke of eternal truths. These were not observations that they were able to express, but rather almost spiritual feelings that they mutually experienced.

Polkinghorne had passed on to Bunt during their ride back from Liskeard much of the history of the Port Eliot estate and the church. The family felt it was important for their servants to keep in with the traditions at Port Eliot.

The church building was huge, much bigger than one would expect of a typical village church. It had not one but two towers at its west end. Their architecture was Norman at their lower parts, but the upper section of the north tower turned into an octagon, and the south tower had an external stair, the only one of its kind in Cornwall. The ornate doorway was carved from Elvan, a native variety of quartz-porphyry or "greenstone," which had been quarried nearby in Landrake. The "new" church had replaced the old Saxon building, which had until about the year 1042 been the cathedral for Cornwall, hence its size. The construction of the grander Norman church was begun in around 1161, although it took so long that it wasn't consecrated for a hundred years. It became the priory church for the Augustinians until the Dissolution of the Monasteries in

1539, when the whole estate was bought by a family who then sold it to an Eliot a couple of generations later.

After the service was over, Willy took Mary for a walk down to the quay where the River Tiddy flowed into the larger River Lynher. Lower down they formed the Lynher Estuary, where the Tiddy and the Lynher joined the River Tamar that marked the boundary between Cornwall and England. Willy and Mary found a place to sit on the quay, near where the gamekeeper caught salmon for the kitchens at Port Eliot. They chatted affectionately but soon turned serious.

"What is it 'e wanted to tell us?" asked Bunt, his tone betraying his concern.

"It's 'appened, Willy," said Mary, blushing, "just as Oi feared it would."

"What, me luv? What 'appened?"

"Oi'm 'avin' 'is baby," whimpered Mary, trying to hold back tears.

"What? Sir James's?" asked Bunt.

Mary nodded, and tears rolled down her hot cheeks.

"That nasty bugger! Oi'll 'ave 'is guts for garters if ever Oi gets my 'ands on 'im, gentry or no gentry!"

"Oi thought you would've guessed weeks ago. What am Oi to do? Oi can't tell nobody but you. They'll turf me out. Oi won't 'ave nowhere to go. Oi won't be able to take care of the baby. They'll send me to the work 'ouse. Oi'll starve, me and the baby too."

"Now don' 'e take on so, my luv. What about your sister Nelly? Why don't you ask 'er what to do? Oi wish you'd told me afore Oi went to Liskeard. Mr. Polkinghorne was in a blasted 'urry, but Oi could 'ave took a moment to talk to 'er in the circumstances loike. An' that there cook lady at Eliot 'Ouse, Mrs. Bartlett, 'er were kind, 'er might 'elp."

"Nell would only tell our dad, an' then Oi'd be in worse trouble nor ever," wailed Mary, her tears flowing faster. "Oi dunno what to do. If only Oi could just end it all."

She scrambled to her feet and ran across the quay to the river's edge. Bunt quickly chased after her to grab her before she could jump, although he had never been in the water in his life and couldn't swim. But then he saw that the tide was out and the banks of the Tiddy were just sticky, smelly mud.

"Listen, Mary, my luv. Oi said Oi would marry you if anythin' 'appened, and Oi meant it, if you'll 'ave us, that is."

"Oh Willy," said Mary, "O' course Oi will, but are you doin' it out of kindness? That wouldn't do."

"Kindness," laughed Willy. "You must know I luv you; Oi told you back then that I wanted to marry you anyway, before all this. 'Tisn't everyone would do such a thing for a woman in your condition, but us wants to, an' don't you forget it," said Bunt. "We'll 'ave the vicar call the banns an' us'll get right on with it. Us'll bring the little 'un up as if 'twere our own. There then, wipe your eyes, an' we'll go back to the church right now an' see if 'e still be there."

"Oh, Willy, I do luv you too! An' us'll 'ave our own fambly, an' p'raps they'll let us 'ave our own cottage 'ere at St. Germans."

"Oi knows they will, me luv," said Willy, more confidently than he really felt. After all, they had not been in service at Port Eliot for long. "An' Oi will work hard for Mr. Eliot, and Mrs. Eliot, an' Oi'll make good an' sure that bastard over Lanhydrock never do get the best of either of 'em, that Oi swear. Us knows 'is conscience wouldn't get the better of 'im, so 'e'd never 'elp support the poor little thing, not in a month of Sundays. But you can be sure, Mary, 'e'll be brought up as our son, and 'e'll be a Bunt through an' through."

Mary gave Willy the biggest hug she had ever given anyone in her life. As they walked together back towards the house, they saw a familiar figure waving at them. They waved back at Charles Polkinghorne and walked over to see what he wanted.

"Forgive me for interrupting your Sabbath peace, Bunt, but I have heard from Mr. Eliot and there is some news that affects you."

"What may that be, Mr. Polkinghorne?" asked Bunt expectantly.

"Mr. Eliot wants to go ahead with carrying out tests on deposits of rock in the village to determine whether they would be suitable for road building," said Polkinghorne. "If this looks feasible, he is willing to expand quarrying. But we would have to look lively. He has heard that Sir James Trenance has his eye on supplying all the stone for the new turnpike roads throughout Cornwall. You will assist me with this project, so there will be some long hours for you."

"Oh thank 'ee, zir!" said Bunt, "Oi could start today if ye want."

"Oh Willy," said Mary happily, "'tis fortune smilin' on you." She thought that their own cottage might happen sooner than they had hoped. She wanted to give Willy an even bigger hug than before but thought better of doing it in front of Mr. Polkinghorne.

Chapter Sixteen

Inheritance

On the following Saturday, in late morning, curtains were still closed in the main bedroom in the east wing of Lanhydrock. Foolhardy, given the state of his health, Baron Trenance had been determined to take his gelding and hack over to the season's first meet of the Lanhydrock hounds. He had a rather bad cold. The day was wet and windy, and the chill sliced through his riding coat and his thick wool breeches. Even the short ride exhausted him, and by the time he got back to the house he was feeling poorly.

The butler gave instructions to prepare a hot mustard bath, and the baron had been packed off to his bed under a thick feather comforter with a red flannel mustard poultice on his chest under his nightshirt. An upstairs maid stoked the fire in the bedroom, so that at least some of the cold was taken off the drafts coming in around the window frames.

Baron Trenance was wheezing, his fever alleviated intermittently by bouts of shivering. His head hurt and his throat was sore, but he had managed to swallow a cup of hot beef tea. He did not at that moment welcome his son bursting into his bedroom with a cheery greeting.

"Good morning, Father, you missed an excellent chase!" James was still wearing his hunting livery, and his face was red after a morning of exertion. Halted by the sight of his father's sallow face and the thick layers of bedding, Sir James added, "Right. Well you do look a sight, don't you? Seems you're not really up to it these days." He pulled a chair up by the bedside. "I suppose we need to be thinking about a changing of the guard. In any case, I've brought your grandson in to see you!"

Elianor was waiting by the door with the nurse who held young James in her arms. "Come along on in, Elianor, show off the fine son and heir I have produced for Lanhydrock!"

Elianor came into the room followed by the nurse carrying a well-fed and contented baby boy. He had grown plump during the last few months, with a sturdy build, thick and curly dark hair like his father, and the distinctive grey Trenance eyes set wide apart over chubby and ruddy cheeks, crowned by a strong nose.

"Shall I put 'im on the pillow beside you, zir?" the nurse asked. "Oi've just washed 'im and changed 'is nappy so he's clean and fresh."

Elianor, stepped forward, "Oh, no Nurse. The baron is ill, and we don't want young James to catch his cold!"

"I can see him quite well from here, thank you Nurse," said the baron with a scowl and gasping a little. "At least he's a lot better behaved than his father was at his age. Must be his mother's influence, eh, Elianor m'dear?"

"We do our best, father-in-law," said Lady Trenance, "but we have the influence of heredity with which to contend." She smiled at her little joke so as not to offend her father-in-law. "He is a good little boy, all things considered, and Nanny tells me he has a healthy appetite. I trust he will make a worthy heir."

"Perhaps I should consult Clymo right away," said the baron, "the lad might do better for Lanhydrock than his good-for-nothing father." He spluttered and wheezed and gasped, and it was hard to tell whether from shortage of breath or excess of paternal disappointment.

"Come Father," said Sir James, reddening, "do not distress yourself, you must rest. Lanhydrock is in good hands with me. You have prepared me well for my responsibilities."

"Not well enough, it too often seems," said the baron. "You get in too many scrapes, and you allow your betters to take advantage of you. You are too stubborn to listen to what I have to say. Now get out of here and leave me be!"

He threw his pillow feebly at James, but it fell harmlessly off the bed to the floor.

"Now Father," said Sir James, dodging, "that's the exaggeration of an old and ill man. I may have high spirits, but be assured, I have listened." He rose and patted his father on the shoulder. "We will leave you in peace to recover. You just caught a slight chill, and it has possibly affected your mind. If it gets any worse we will send for the doctor." He waved Elianor and the nurse to the door, saying to his wife, "You go down and give orders for the cook to rustle up some more warm broth. The maid here will come down with you and bring it up when it's ready."

"Wave farewell to your grandfather, James," said Elianor, "and help Nanny and me find Cook."

Elianor did not realize that this farewell would be her last while the baron was alive. Half an hour later, the maid knocked on Baron Trenance's bedroom door to bring in a tray with the fresh broth. There was no response. The old master must have nodded off. Nervously, she went into the bedroom. The maid noticed right away the pillow that the baron had thrown to the floor, which she had been intending to pick up and replace on the bed, now lay on the bed leaning against the headboard covering her master's face. She put the tray on a table and stepped to the side of the bed where the baron was lying. She picked up the pillow to plump it up, intending to help him sit up and place it under his head to make him more comfortable as he sipped the broth.

As the maid moved the pillow, she saw that the baron's head lolled awkwardly, his eyes staring, body unmoving. She started back, then regained her composure enough to speak to him, wake him up. He did not answer. She did not want to touch him. Tentatively, she held her hand under his nose. The old baron was not breathing. She put her hand to her mouth, ran outside the door and screamed.

"It's the old master, 'e ain't breathin', Lord 'elp us!" she shouted.

A footman came running. He followed her pointing finger into the bedroom. "What's goin' on? What's the matter with the master? Sir, are you all right? Say somethin'. Cor' blimey!"

The maid stayed behind the footman, leaning over the bed to look closer at the baron's still form, saying, "Do somethin', can't you see 'e needs 'elp?"

"Ain't no use, 'e's deader nor a doornail," said the footman, his face pale. "Go fetch Butler and tell 'im what's 'appened."

The maid did not move, did not speak, then sputtered, "Oi'd swear that pillow was on the floor when Oi left the room, Oi swear."

The footman grabbed her by the shoulders and shook her. "No use blatherin', girl, fetch Butler an' make 'aste about it."

The maid quickly brought the butler from his pantry below stairs. Sir James came along from his own bedroom where his valet was laying out his morning clothes. Seeing the butler rushing to his father's room, James followed him in and demanded, "What's the fuss about?"

"It's the baron," the butler whispered. "I'm not quite sure, sir, but it appears as if his lordship is unwell. He's not breathing; well, sir, it appears that we'd better call the doctor."

James was calm. He leaned over and put two fingers against his father's wrinkled neck. There was no feeling, the skin was dry and cold. "What good would the doctor do?" he asked. "He's dead. We'd be better sending for the parson. And while you're about it, tell Clymo to meet me in the smoking room. Wait, before you leave; give me the keys to the wine cellar. I'll take charge of them from now on."

"Right away, Sir James, God rest his soul," said the butler, who handed over a small bunch of keys from his waistcoat pocket, then looked away to hide a tear. James frowned, coughed peremptorily and stared at the butler. "Aren't you forgetting something?"

"Sir James?" said the butler, puzzled.

"My Lord," said James.

"Excuse me, sir," continued the butler, "that is I meant to say, I'll be off right away and fetch Mr. Clymo, My Lord. Unless there is anything else, My Lord."

The butler bowed and walked out of the bedroom backwards, bowing again to the new Baron Trenance. James stood for a moment beside his father's still body upon the bed and then strode out, leaving the maid and the footman to tidy up as best they could.

"Lady Trenance," James called as he went down the stairs into the hall, "come quickly. You have arrangements to make. The old boy has finally dropped off the perch."

Elianor's hand flew to her mouth.

"Don't look so shocked," James said. "He was old, and like the old fool he was, he made himself ill by trying to do too much. He should have left everything to me to manage years ago. You organize the servants. Be sure that young James is properly seen to. I'm going to talk to Clymo."

James paused before going into the smoking room and glanced in the looking glass hanging near the front door. He braced his shoulders and straightened the lapels of his coat. He was Baron Trenance. He pictured himself taking his seat in the House of Lords as a peer, elegantly clothed in robes and ermine and coronet. He would show them all. He was going to run Lanhydrock the way he wanted. Now, he controlled the money and he would spend it as he wanted. As lord of the manor he had rights and privileges, and everyone around him would, by damn, feel the weight of that influence. He'd take the pick of everything and everybody. He entered the smoking room and took a chair facing the door.

Elianor entered. "James," she began, her brow furrowed, "the maid just came to me and said she found the pillow your father threw at you back on the bed when she discovered him dead. How can that be?"

He scowled at her. "How the hell would I know? Maybe someone threw it back on the bed. Perhaps I did before I left the room. It's hardly important now."

"But did you?" she persisted. Seeing his look, she faltered. "Ah, yes, maybe you did. With the shock and everything, it would be hard to remember." She turned and left the room.

There was a knock on the smoking room door, and an ashen Clymo came in. James described to him what had happened. "We had just left him seeming quite on the mend, and I had ordered some broth. When the maid came back up with it, he was gone."

Clymo offered his condolences. "That is sad news, indeed, sir. The baron was a fine man and a good master. This must be a grievous loss for you and he will be greatly missed by all."

"Never mind all that now," said James, leaning forward in his chair and placing his hands upon his knees, "that can wait for the funeral. What is important for Lanhydrock at this juncture is money. There are certain expenses that are urgent to be met, and I see from the state of our counting house that you have most imprudently committed funds to ventures that may not yield a return until well into the foreseeable future. Pray explain yourself. Tell me why I should not employ a more skillful steward?"

"My Lord," stammered Clymo, flustered, but collecting himself enough to mind his manners. "Sir, I have been conscientious in carrying out the late baron's orders and, more recently, your own. Indeed, Lanhydrock has invested large amounts, especially in our tin mines. But the revenues are commensurately large and the promise is larger. Even though there are setbacks from time to time, I have always assured a supply of ready gold to meet the normal expenses of the household and, indeed, the whole estate."

"Well you should have been a bloody sight more prudent, man," said the new Baron Trenance angrily. "I have a position to keep up and it is your task to provide the wherewithal, should you wish to stay employed by me."

"May I inquire as to the source of your additional needs, so that I may better prepare in future?" asked Clymo tentatively, rubbing his chin.

"No, you may bloody not!" yelled James. "It is my job to spend the money, your job to ensure it is available."

"Indeed, Sir James, er, your lordship," said Clymo. "Perhaps I could approach Bolitho's and enquire whether they could tide you over."

"Are you insane?" demanded James. "That Bolitho fellow has no business knowing about my private affairs."

"We have been negotiating with Bolitho's to provide funding for improvements at the Poldice mine," said Clymo. "We are still using horses at our mines, for the whims, you know, 'capstans' the mariners call them, to raise the ore from the bottoms, as well as hauling. They are slow and getting more expensive to keep. They must be replaced with steam engines if we are to keep up with our rivals. The coal we bring in from south Wales is cheaper than it used to be, but we can reduce costs if we build improved unloading facilities at the ports, which will require investment. In addition, there are measures we must take to improve safety for the miners. There have been accidents and the men are getting restless."

"Safety?" said James, "for the miners? I'm damned if I'll pay a single penny for nursemaids for those bloody tinners. They can go to hell for all I care. I will only pay for more ore and more tin and copper to sell to the smelters, more diggings if I have to and, yes, steam engines, I suppose, if you are sure they will make the mines more profitable."

"What I was going to suggest, My Lord," said Clymo, "is that perhaps Bolitho's could arrange more funds than are needed at the mine. No one needs to know how the extra moneys are spent, if you take my meaning."

"Capital idea, Clymo," said James, smiling and leaning back, his arms now folded across his chest, "at last you are making some sense. Go ahead as fast as you can, and spare me the details. I need one thousand pounds within two weeks."

Clymo's jaw dropped at the enormity of the sum, but he turned away so that the new Baron Trenance would not notice.

"And while we're about it," said James, "there are some details I demand to know. Where did my father get his excellent port and brandy? I forgot to ask him, and I know he would want me to know. My friends in London have expressed a desire for a favorable supply. Is there money in that?"

"Your father, my lord, felt it important to be extremely discreet about his sources," said Clymo. "You must know that we purchased uncustomed wines and spirits. Perhaps you did not realize that Lanhydrock lends gold for expenses to both smugglers on the south coast and wreckers on the north. You surely wish that not to be widely known."

"Do you take me as a fool, man? Do you think I'm going to go blabbing to the parson or the Justice of the Peace?" asked James mockingly.

"The parson is among our best customers, my lord; indeed, he ensures that no stranger enters the crypt of St. Hydroc's until a shipment has been disposed of," said Clymo. "And Justices of the Peace have shared with us in many a venture. Sometimes reputation is risked if profit is high enough."

Ah," said James more equably, "pray tell me more. Do our customers repay in gold? What are some other sources of ready cash? Must be high time that some of our loans are due to be repaid, eh?"

"Our most profitable ones are some years off, my lord, those we have extended. If I may be frank, patience makes profit. My most important task for Lanhydrock is to ensure that our loans are secured with unbreakable mortgages on property of more than sufficient value. Often our borrowers get into difficulties and we are only too glad to accommodate them with additional sums at higher interest and sterner mortgage agreements more cunningly drafted."

James raised his eyebrows. There was more to the old man's business than he had appreciated. "I see," he said, attempting to sound wise.

"If Fortune smiles upon us," continued Clymo, "as indeed she often does, there will come a time when the borrowers cannot meet the terms. Then we regretfully explain that we have no alternative but to foreclose. The property comes into our hands, without fail worth more than the balance still due on the loan."

"Poor devils," said James, "must be embarrassing to find oneself short of a little cash."

"One can't feel sorry for them, sir," said Clymo. "They have only themselves to blame; they've either been foolish or extravagant beyond their stations. And on some enviable occasions, particularly when land has been in the hands of many generations that have not paid attention or kept up with the times, we discover reports of deposits of tin or copper. Then we are more than willing to accommodate a hard-pressed borrower a little longer. If I may speak freely, Lanhydrock has prospered by husbanding its own gold and lending to those who have managed theirs less well."

"I hope I do not misunderstand your meaning, Clymo," said James frowning, "or otherwise I might have to have you thrashed as an insolent dog."

"I meant no more, sir, than to explain how Lanhydrock acquired its profits. The old baron always said that the more the needs of others were more pressing than our own, the more we would prosper."

"Explain to me, pray, how those profits may be made available to me to spend now. Make no mistake, don't expect me to forego my needs for my great-grandson's pleasure. I need ready money. You must be able to lay our hands on some more. What about these damn smugglers? How do they pay? How soon?"

"Sometimes they pay in gold," said Clymo, "usually in kind, part of their cargo: port, brandy, rum, tea. Of course, they furnish us with additional supplies of goods that we can sell. Come to think of it one of the smugglers is seeking finance for a larger vessel, one that can sail across the Atlantic and withstand bombardment from the cannons of privateers."

"Is there a market for port in America?" asked James. "I should have thought that the taste of the colonists did not rise to such luxuries."

"Not port, my lord, laborers," replied Clymo, "laborers, mainly for the West Indies and the sugar plantations. Cheap labor that requires no wages. The Irish need work, and criminals are sent from the gaols and put to work. However, the most profit comes from furnishing savages from Africa with broad backs who can work in the hot sun. And their women who will work in the plantations as well as the great houses and who have no husbands to protect their virtue. The savages are captives and have to be shackled on the journey for the safety of the crew."

"Capturing them sounds dangerous," said James. "If it were me being captured I would resist fiercely and fight to the last breath."

"The captains and their crews do not capture them," said Clymo. "They are merely traders. They sail from home with a cargo to the coast of West Africa that they sell to the inhabitants: cloth, trinkets, guns, ammunition, beads. Then they buy from the heathen chiefs savages they have captured in warfare. The brutes are bound by the wrists and neck, so that they can offer no resistance. They are sold in auctions on the other side of the Atlantic, those that survive. Then the ships scrub down and carry sugar and molasses for the rum trade back to Bristol, and thus avoid the expense of sailing on empty bottoms."

"Sounds like an excellent arrangement. How soon can we start?" asked James, a greedy glint in his eyes. "How profitable can it be?"

"No doubt, as soon as I can talk further to Mr. Bolitho," said Clymo, "and explain that we plan extensive investment in new diggings and in expanding production of tin and copper at our mines."

James nodded, and then waved his hand in the air. "Now, there is one other matter, and that's the building of the turnpike roads," he said. "You will recall the conversations with Mr. Eliot of St. Germans. He, with Mr. Pitt's help, pressed us hard to pledge financial support, as indeed Mr. Bolitho is well aware. Just make sure that there is no warranty that in some untoward event may ever be called upon. Draw up the documents yourself; don't let Bolitho meddle in it. As backers, I feel there are many more opportunities for Lanhydrock to profit in this business than we have yet sought out. Make sure we do."

"The new turnpikes will certainly help our mining business," said Clymo, "and make it easier and cheaper for wagons to replace pack horses for carrying the goods, coal coming in, tin stuff going out. You know my daughter Morwenna a little, but perhaps not well enough to know that she is a bright lass. I do from time to time discuss business matters in her hearing, in the most complete confidence of course, and she gave me an idea that might be profitable for your lordship."

"Well, out with it man," said James, "don't keep me waiting if there are riches to be had."

"Well, sir," said Clymo, "we will be incurring cost in removing rock from the mines to sink new shafts and extend passages. Could we not crush that rock and sell it for road stone? That would be like manna from heaven. You have said that you want Lanhydrock to be the supplier for the Liskeard turnpike, but there will be others with the same idea. We'd make sure that nobody could meet our price, yet no one would need to know the profit we would make from selling waste from our mines. Bolitho would surely deem it prudent to furnish additional capital for such a venture."

"I do believe you may yet become a good steward, Clymo," said James smiling and stroking his chin. Morwenna's idea, eh? Perhaps he should seek to express his appreciation to her in person; could be amusing.

James turned his thoughts back to his steward and the business at hand. "Arrange what capital is necessary from Bolitho. Just make sure there is a little extra for me, and keep my name out of those other special ventures on the side. After the damn funeral I will leave to travel to town and see about taking my seat in the House of Lords."

With that James rose and strode out of the room. Clymo breathed a sigh of relief. He sat for a moment thinking, wringing his hands, and then, too, rose and left.

As his valet was pulling off his riding boots James, now Baron Trenance, mused that perhaps the patience of his friends in London could be stretched a little further by a hogshead or two of brandy. Of course, next time he got back to the gaming tables he could recoup everything and probably a great deal more; or perhaps the time after, or even the time after that. He would show those London dandies that just because he lived in Cornwall he was no unsophisticated farmer. Now that he had Clymo to provide adequate stakes he could play with his fellow members of the House of Lords. Perhaps he could even turn over a card with Lord Bute over what he still owed on his viscountcy, or persuade Henry Fox to allow him to win part of the fortune he had gained as His Majesty's paymaster.

At least James was now free of his father's iron hand. The old baron never guessed what James got up to when he was out of his father's reach in London. But then, now he never could impress the old fool with the glittering social success he would enjoy in London, once he became a steady winner. Perhaps he would seek instruction from someone to devise a reliable system so that he consistently won at baccarat. No one else need know. Keep himself occupied, amused, he paid a steward to manage the mundane details at Lanhydrock. And if he played his other cards right, perhaps he would be offered a lucrative place in the government.

But as for that damned maid, he needed to be sure she would hold her tongue regarding the pillow, and that pompous do-gooder Clymo must never hear of it.

Chapter Seventeen

Old Order

As soon as he could get away from the pressing business of attending to the details arising from the unexpected death of the old baron, Joseph Clymo intended to set off on a journey. He of course stayed to pay his respects at the funeral in St. Petroc's, along with the house servants, the larger tenant farmers, leading villagers, and guests invited from among the neighboring gentry and better tradespeople. The little church was crowded, but the vicar was in good voice, and even the servants and villagers standing at the back could hear every word of his loquacious eulogy in honor of the deceased, who to all appearances was as virtuous and paternalistic as he was industrious and farseeing. If the customs of the Church of England had permitted such a display of emotion, Clymo had no doubt that the congregation would have burst into applause when the vicar finally droned to a conclusion.

Clymo was privileged to sit, along with his daughter Morwenna, only six rows back behind the family pew. He observed that Mr. and Mrs. Eliot were seated in front of him, as was Mr. Bolitho, the Trenance family's trusted adviser. While the Pitts from nearby Boconnoc were there, he was observant enough to note the absence of Mr. William Pitt, who had presumably concluded that neither the importance of the late baron nor the influence of his successor were sufficient to merit the long and tiring journey from London, nor indeed the interruption of Mr. Pitt's labors in Parliament defending against the ongoing rebuttal of his persistent opposition.

Joseph Clymo was relieved that he at least had a seat and was not relegated to mingle with the rabble near the porch at the west end. After all, he had important responsibilities and a position to keep up. He was of a florid complexion and on the portly side, as could only be expected given his hearty appetites of middle age, and he was glad to save his breath for praying rather than standing.

Clymo had lost his wife in her early forties due to incurable biliousness. However, he was well looked after by their only daughter Morwenna, who despite having reached her nineteenth year, remained unmarried. Clymo was unaware of any suitors, although he was more than prepared to defend her virtue with vigor should the need arise. He was devoted to Morwenna, a pretty, intelligent, well-informed and energetic girl, with a charming figure and a mass of curly blonde hair that escaped her attempts to tame it with combs and ribbons. He often took her excellent advice but rarely acknowledged it. Despite his fatherly pride, he admitted, if only to himself, that she could be willful.

Although Clymo had been modestly educated at the church school in nearby Bodmin, he had been an outstanding student and was well aware of the advantages this afforded him. He was particularly quick with his sums, adding pounds, shillings and pence in columns of income and, more reluctantly, taking them away to record expenditures. When he left school at fourteen, the curate who had taught him recommended him to the old baron's steward. He was put to work as a clerk in the Lanhydrock counting house, where he received an income of a few shillings every quarter day. He kept his ledgers neatly and was quick and accurate, and of growing value to his employer was his ability to perceive patterns lurking behind the endless columns. His shrewd brown eyes could spot which activities brought most profit and which cost too much in relation to their slow growth. He was brought to the notice of the old baron and marked as a lad to watch as the estate's needs for careful and conscientious record keeping grew with its investments.

After several years of labor, his responsibilities increased, and he learned that cultivating personal relationships and pleasing his superiors were the skills truly essential to advancement. When the old steward's failing sight led to his retirement, it was no surprise that young Joseph was appointed to take his place. His satisfaction was complete when the comfortable furnished steward's house on the estate was turned over to him and Morwenna rent free.

His employer had entrusted him with more and more responsibilities over the years and more authority had followed. Only a week or so ago, shortly before he left this mortal coil, the old baron paid him the great compliment of asking him in strict confidence to look out for the son who had now succeeded him. Clymo was told frankly by the baron what he had already realized for himself, that James Trenance lacked experience and judgment and left on his own could jeopardize the Lanhydrock interests. Clymo promised faithfully to keep an eye on the young man and see to it that neither he nor the estate came to serious harm.

When the congregation left the church to follow the coffin to the burial plot, Clymo fell in step beside Thomas Bolitho.

"Mr. Bolitho," he said in a confidential manner, "a word with you, if you please. Perhaps after the crowd has left we could meet in the estate office."

Joseph Clymo was aware of the class difference between himself and the wealthy Mr. Bolitho, but he felt that his importance to a baronial family justified at least a modest level of familiarity. Waiting until the crowd dispersed after the burial, he headed for the estate office. Bolitho entered shortly thereafter, and they finally had privacy. The steward and the counselor settled down to discuss their shared interests and those of the new Baron Trenance, now that he had sole charge of Lanhydrock and had neither the advice nor restraints of his late father.

"Mr. Bolitho," said Clymo, "I would deem it a privilege if you would take a journey with me. His lordship is most anxious to increase the income of the estate. His tastes are lavish, his energies in the pursuit of pleasure profuse, and his needs for money far exceed those of the late baron."

"Come now, Clymo," protested Bolitho, "show more respect. You are speaking of a peer of the realm, who is now your employer."

"I beg your pardon, sir, but I feel I must be frank with you, I do not know to whom else to turn. The circumstances have changed. It is clear we must invest beyond our immediate means to meet his demands and keep our jobs. I must have support in dealing with his lordship. But I assure you there are opportunities without limit, and any loans you provide would be in sound ventures and safe hands."

"Customarily I would do business with the baron, not his steward," said Bolitho. "Nevertheless, my partners share my regard for your high ability and integrity, Mr. Clymo, especially under the new circumstances. Undoubtedly the assets of the Lanhydrock estate have values that are yet to be fully realized. But if I may be candid, the new baron is not yet practiced in affairs. We will therefore deal with you for the time being. However, when we are asked to provide money we will not be prepared to rely solely on his lordship's personal word, for reasons you are in a position to appreciate. We must require adequate security."

"I assure you that can be arranged," said Clymo. "We have many projects that will produce income and enable loans to be repaid as promised."

"You must recall," said Bolitho, wagging his forefinger, "that Lanhydrock is already committed as a guarantor to Mr. Eliot's new turnpike project for Liskeard. Bolitho's can go no further without assets being pledged, and furthermore specific assets with known qualities."

"Mr. Bolitho, that is precisely why I suggest you accompany me on a journey to Redruth and then on to the Poldice mine. I want to show you at first hand the workings where the greatest improvements can be made and the opportunities lie. The baron intends to return to London on urgent business, and I am confident he will allow us to take two good hunters from the Lanhydrock stables for our ride."

"All right, Mr. Clymo, I am convinced of your determination, and curious to see what you have to offer," said Bolitho. "Meet me in my office in Bodmin in three days time. We will arrive at Poldice for setting day on Michaelmas, when the miners bid on the work for the next three months."

Three days passed in a flurry of activity for Clymo. The new baron had many questions and many demands, and explaining to him the finer points of running a large estate was no mean chore. When he finally met with Bolitho and they set off together, the weather was fair. They made their way west, congratulating themselves that at least the journey was not as cold or uncomfortable as it might have been, and conversing as they went as to the benefits of expanding turnpike roads throughout Cornwall and various other local matters. Before darkness fell, they dined and stayed at an inn, where the ostler saw to their horses. The innkeeper provided a hearty supper, clean beds and breakfast the next morning, which provided another opportunity for a chat.

"Clymo," said Bolitho pushing his plate away and resting his elbows on the table, "if we are to work well together, we must get to know each other better. Now, when I came over to Lanhydrock for that hunt, the old baron took me to one side and into his confidence. I trust I can rely on your discretion, but you need to understand that the baron charged me with looking out for his son as he took over control of the estate. Wished there was more time for Sir James to learn, but felt his health was failing, and he might not have the luxury of time. Between us, he had doubts not only about the boy's experience but also his seriousness; feared that he was extravagant, perhaps unreliable. Now this is just between us, keep it under your hat."

"I am gratified that have confided in me, Mr. Bolitho," said Clymo. "As a matter of fact, the old baron asked me very much the same thing. I assure you that after all these years of loyalty to his lordship I hold the interests of Lanhydrock close to my heart. I will do everything in my power to support you in carrying out the charge, although I fear that from time to time the new baron will present us with challenges."

They exchanged smiles and shook hands as they rose from the table. As they continued on the rest of their way to Poldice, they rode much of the time in companionable silence, no doubt each in his own way contemplating the tasks and challenges that lay ahead. Before they left Bodmin they had sent a message to the mine captain John Williams to expect them. They had news of the important change in ownership of the mine, and wanted a discussion of business that would include planning the sinking of more shafts and more adits.

The scene that greeted them as they dismounted in front of the counting house at Poldice was not at all the orderly and busy production of tin and copper ore that they expected. A crowd of people, miners, bal maidens, even children were milling around in front of the mine captain's office demanding that he come out and meet with them. The door opened and out strode John Williams, putting on a top hat, his badge of office, as he did so. He was an imposingly tall figure, and he immediately took charge.

The crowd was no surprise to him. It was quarter day, Michaelmas Day, which always fell on the twenty-ninth day of September. And in the world of the Cornish mines it was setting day. The chance for the miners to earn a decent living for the next three months turned on the success of the bid put in by the tributer. Typically, setting day was expectant, even festive. But the gathering that Bolitho and Clymo came upon was far from joyful. It had an air of restiveness about it. The miners and their women were muttering among themselves, and the tone was discontented, angry.

"I don't like the look of this, Clymo," whispered Bolitho. "I well remember the tinners' insurrection at Penryn, hundreds of them, armed with clubs and bludgeons. Angry over the price of corn. Soldiers from Falmouth were summoned to quell the tumult, had to fire upon them, killed two. That quietened them."

One man stood out as their leader. His curly black hair showed beneath his felt helmet, his complexion was pale, his brown eyes intense, a true Cornishman. He was of medium height and muscular and appeared to be in his early thirties. They were soon to learn that this was Addis Penwarden. Another man stood on the fringe of the crowd at the back; he was dressed in black with white linen bands at his collar and a broad brimmed black hat. The crowd fell silent on the appearance of the mine captain, but the leader spoke out.

"Cap'n Williams, zir," the leader announced confidently, "there be things us needs to talk about before us gets to settin' the tribute. Us won't go down yon mine or any other mine to break our bones or kill oursel's for other men's gold. Proper measures needs to be taken for we to work safe like. Us ain't frighted, but us ain't barmy neither. Us needs to work to live, but us don't need to work bad enough to die."

"Oh come now, Penwarden," said John Williams, "we all knew mining was dangerous work when we took it on. All work has its risks. Would you rather work for the wage of a fisherman or a farm laborer? Fishermen have to go out in storms, and plenty have been swept overboard and drowned. We always hear about farm laborers being kicked by horses or gashed by a scythe, and their crops often come to naught due to bad weather or low prices."

"Now wait just a minute, Captain Williams," interposed the man in black from the back. "Addis Penwarden here lost his own brother, killed by an explosion down this very mine. You and the owners must do something to make work safer, repair broken ladders, provide more candles, pump the sea water out of the lower workings, protect the powder." This was the Reverend Peter Perry, who must have driven his pony and cart over from the nearby fishing village of Perranporth. Williams knew that he was the Methodist minister for the villages around, including Gwennap near the Poldice mine.

John Williams respected both speakers. Addis Penwarden was one of his best tributers, a good leader who always bid a fair price and saw to it that he and his pare met his targets and aimed for high-yielding ore. Reverend Perry was a follower of John Wesley. The Methodists had done good work among the tinners and fishermen in these parts. They had not only preached the gospel of salvation but also discouraged hard drink, the cause of much poverty and many a squabble and broken family, not to mention a number of mine accidents. In fact, Williams had heard that a drop too much cider had killed Penwarden's younger brother, but it was no time to bring that up now.

The mine captain had heard also that since that John Wesley's last visit the reverend was beginning to stick his nose in things that shouldn't concern him. There was talk of the chapels providing schools for the children and even offering education for the adults. Perry had always preached against smuggling, and that didn't sit too well with the gentry and others whose interest in that trade was not as secret as they liked to think. And now here he was talking about safety for the tinners.

Views such as these would not suit the mine owners whose interest was in production and profit. After all, they risked their wealth. They put up the money for the tutwork to dig the shafts and pump out the water, paid for the coal to drive the steam engines, for supplies of powder and rope and candles and tools and everything needed to keep the mine going, not to mention the stamps for crushing the ore and hiring the mules to carry the raw metal to the smelter. For sure old Baron Trenance, who owned Poldice, watched every report out of the counting house and demanded value for every guinea he put up. Captain Williams now noticed that Trenance's steward Clymo had just arrived with another gentleman. What did they want? Now was certainly not the time for trouble from the miners, nor was it any better for interference from the reverend.

The crowd was growing more restless, growling their discontent. It was time he told Penwarden and his holier-than-thou friend Perry to hold their fire and keep their men in check until he could find out what else was going on. Before taking a strong line with the men or even thinking about compromising, it was time to see what lay behind the visit from Mr. Clymo and his important-looking gentleman companion.

Williams was a man who sorted out all the facts before coming to a decision, and there seemed too much he didn't understand here. He waved a hand at the crowd, and in a loud voice said, "Take heed what I say, all of you. Go back to work now, cause no trouble, that's the best way. Leave it to me to deal with. I'm your captain, you know me, you know you can trust me. I must meet with these gentlemen now. Get back to work now, all of you."

The crowd grumbled and seethed speaking in a strange language whose words were impossible for the visitors to understand. At first they refused to move, stood in their tracks, demanding to be heard. Then under the urging of Addis Penwarden and the Reverend Perry they heeded the mine captain's words. They stood aside and did nothing to impede Clymo and Bolitho as John Williams waved the gentleman from up country to the door of the count house.

Chapter Eighteen

New Order

"Gentlemen, you had better come with me into the counting house," said John Williams, "and you, Penwarden, get back to work, and take the men with you. We'll talk about the sett later when I am ready, not now. And you, Reverend, take your preaching to your chapel and keep it out of my mine. Your business is their souls; my business is their work and making money for the venturers and the owners."

Bolitho and Clymo handed their horses' bridles over to a waiting boy and walked more boldly than they felt to stand beside Williams on the step of the counting house, but not without some obstruction and jostling as they pushed their way through the crowd. Postponing this business with the miners was not going to be as easy as Williams thought.

"Hold hard, Mr. Williams," said Penwarden loudly, "these men need to know where they stand, aye and their women and children, too. It's their livelihoods us care about, and their deaths and injury. Settin' day be as good as any; 'twon't get any better for waitin' on. Us is stayin' right 'ere 'til us gets satisfaction, make no mistake about it."

"Penwarden's right, Mr. Williams," said the Reverend Perry. "The men don't mean to make trouble, but they have rights just as much as the owners. They are not going to wait until another of them is killed or broken down the mine before seeking proper conditions. They need action now. I believe in prayer and the power of the Holy Spirit as much or more than any man, but down the mine they need safe ladders, enough lanterns, proper drainage. You can provide those a lot quicker than God. There's plenty of money being made in tin and copper, and there's no need to starve the miners to make more."

"Gentlemen, gentlemen," interposed Clymo, stepping forward, "may I have your attention? I am the agent for Lanhydrock. I am sorry to announce that the Baron Trenance, owner of Poldice, died last week, his funeral was held a few days ago."

There were murmurings among the crowd, but it was hard to tell whether in celebration of the passing of a hard man whom they did not know, beyond his reputation for shaving the last ha'penny out of the revenues of his estate, or perhaps they were expressing a general sorrow in the face of a fate that would eventually reach them all. In either case, it was certainly not personal grief for a beloved master. This was the first time John Williams had heard the news, as well.

"Gentlemen, please!" shouted Clymo, trying to make himself heard above the rumblings. "There is a new Baron Trenance, and he has instructed me to come and meet with your mine captain to make arrangements for improvements at Poldice Mine, from which you will all benefit in good time. Allow me to meet with Captain Williams undisturbed, and we will shortly have an announcement of good news." He moved closer to the mine captain.

"Williams," he continued quietly, "go inside with me and Mr. Bolitho here. Perhaps we can quiet this mob later. If not, we needs must send a message to the Lord Lieutenant to call out the militia."

The three men made their escape into the counting house, shutting and bolting the sturdy door behind them. The door was designed to thwart the most determined thief, although its resistance to a mob had not been tested. The noise of grumbling followed them into the building. There was a coal fire burning in the grate of the well-appointed office.

Clymo was red in the face. He took a large kerchief out of his pocket and mopped his brow, whether he was sweating from the sudden change in temperature from the wintry outside or from stress was not clear.

Williams motioned to them to remove their coats and hang them on the hallstand in the corner. He calmly took off his own overcoat and top hat and hung them up. "Gentlemen," said Williams, "I'm taken by surprise by the baron's death, not that it was unexpected at his advanced age. I hope his son has half his good sense, even though the old baron was a hard taskmaster."

John Williams moved to the fire and stirred it and then waving at two chairs placed on one side of a pine table, he said, "Please draw up chairs and be seated at my table. You need not fear for your personal safety. I know these men and their families well, like my father before me, God rest his soul. The tinners are hard workers, their wives and children, too. They are angry now, and frightened for their safety and their livelihood. I have always treated them firmly but fairly. They respect me, and obey me. We will deal with this difficulty." Williams sat at the table across from his visitors with his back to the fire.

"I am sorry to hear only now that your father has died," said Clymo. "He was captain at Poldice for many years before he retired and much respected by the Trenance family. With old Baron Trenance having died last week, this is indeed a changing of the guard. Sir James has, of course, succeeded to his title and his interests. We are here to pursue the new baron's demand to increase the revenues of the Lanhydrock ventures to meet his needs for funds, which he advises me are extensive and pressing."

Williams' expression was impassive. Clymo shuffled his feet. "I should introduce my companion, Mr. Thomas Bolitho, whose father knew your father well," he continued. "The Bolithos have many interests in Cornwall and have been assisting Lanhydrock with financial services. He has expressed some interest in our present task."

Williams and Bolitho shook hands across the table. They sat in silence for a moment, the rumbling outside subsiding somewhat. Williams looked at them and said, "But, gentlemen, I am remiss. Can I get either of you something to refresh you after your journey?"

"Not for me, thank you," answered Bolitho. "We'll make for the inn in due course."

Clymo started to speak again. "Mr. Williams, we must expect to do things differently now. Baron Trenance is insistent that . . . ."

"Mr. Clymo," interrupted Williams, "now is not the time to starve Poldice; it is the time for investment. The demand created by the war has strengthened prices for copper, and tin is also in greater demand."

Williams continued to make his case. "We are getting out more ore as we dig deeper shafts. The answer to greater profits is to be more efficient. And the deeper we go, the more springs bring water into the mine, so we must have more efficient pumps. We need to dig more adits. The Great County Adit was my father's bold idea, and it travels tens of miles and drains scores of mines. But our workings at Poldice have outstripped it.

"We are still using some horse whims and kibbles to bring up the ore, and ladders for the men to enter and leave the deep shafts. We are still using bal maidens to buck the ore on anvils. We must put in stamps and water wheels. Better still would be steam engines. More and more of our competitors are installing the engines that Thomas Newcomen designed. We must keep up. We lose too much time, and that produces nothing. We need better methods."

"Adits? Whims? Mr. Williams," said a puzzled Bolitho, "are you speaking a foreign language, or was that a form of Cornish with which I have yet to become familiar?"

"No, sir, it's just the way we miners are used to talking. We use shallow passages or adits to drain the lower levels or sometimes for access. Our seafaring cousins call a whim a capstan; we drive ours with horses to haul up or lower great buckets, which we call kibbles. The job of stamps is to crush the ore before smelting. Whatever you may call them, we need more of these things. Above all, we need better driving power. Up country in the coal mines they are using steam engines, and we must follow suit to make more money. No good can come of trying to squeeze more profit out of a business that is falling behind its competitors because of antiquated methods."

"How much will all this cost?" asked Clymo. "The baron will be resistant to risking more, and also we will need to offer great persuasion to new venturers or, indeed, to Mr. Bolitho and his money partners."

"In addition, Mr. Clymo," added Bolitho, "there is the need to expand the workings at Wheal Hykka. You will need not only machines and supplies but also another captain to make them productive. Mr. Williams cannot oversee it all alone, no matter how much we regard his knowledge and experience."

"I have been giving much thought to such possibilities, gentlemen," said Williams. "You may not be aware of this, but my father saved a great deal of money during his lifetime, and he has entrusted it to my care for the benefit of his family. You may recall the words of Addis Penwarden. Like the miners, I do not warm to working my life away just to make rich men richer, but I will work far harder than any man if I see my way to improving the lot of my own family. Make me a part owner of the mines I oversee."

"That is all very well," sputtered a surprised Bolitho, "but the mineral lords own these properties, as has long been the custom, and often lease the workings to reputable venturers. The position of the gentry must be preserved."

"Speak for yourself, Mr. Bolitho," said Williams. "No doubt you count yourself among the gentry, but tell us how long it has been since your grandfather was merely a tanner in Penwith? It is your good fortune that your family rose in station. All I am asking is the same opportunity for myself. And to be frank, I am not willing to continue as mine captain for the Lanhydrock estate unless I share fairly in the wealth I help create."

"Come, Williams," said Clymo, "I oversee the accounts. I know full well that you are paid generously. Places like yours do not grow on trees." He pulled his kerchief out of his pocket and mopped his reddened face, where beads of sweat had again broken out on his forehead.

"I value loyalty, Mr. Clymo, not only in myself and those that work for me, but also those that employ me," said Williams. "However, I must inform you that I have had offers of positions from Trenance rivals, although I have until now given them short shrift. Nevertheless, I am clear in my own mind that I have reached the fulcrum in my life. Allow me to join the gentry, and I will act like gentry. At this time I must place the needs of my family on the same level as the greed of my employer, even if I have to break rocks to do so."

"Mr. Williams, enough," said Bolitho, "mind your manners and mark your place!"

"Then it appears we have said all there is to say, gentlemen," said Williams, placing both hands on the table and rising. "It simply leaves you to deal with the miners outside. I doubt they will wait for an answer much longer." He went to the coat rack, reached for his overcoat and put his top hat on his head.

"Now hold hard, gentlemen," said Clymo, "I am solely responsible for the management of Lanhydrock in the absence of the young baron. I will inform him of our decisions when he returns. We can settle these matters among ourselves for the benefit of all concerned. Times are changing in England, and they must change in Cornwall, too, so that we all may prosper. Take off your hat, Mr. Williams, and hang up your coat."

"I may, Mr. Clymo, and I may not," said Williams. "It depends. I don't need assurances, I need promises. Gentlemen, will you or will you not give me the authority and provide the capital to improve the mines?"

Clymo mopped his brow and looked to Bolitho who kept his gaze on Williams and did not respond.

After a long silence Clymo spoke. "The adventurers will kick up a ruckus, but if Mr. Bolitho will support me in discussions with Baron Trenance, I will make them wait for their money. I will ensure that sufficient money is retained from earnings at the mines to pay for improvements as we go along. Naturally, you must propose an itemized plan with all details spelled out."

"That's not good enough," said Williams, slapping his hand on the table. "Fresh capital is required. We must move fast, we must get more ore to the smelters faster than our competitors. We can't plod along waiting for the mines to pay their own way. How about it, Mr. Bolitho?"

"I trust you with Mr. Clymo's guidance to make this work, Captain Williams," said Thomas Bolitho, "subject, of course, to reviewing your written proposal. Your own confidence in putting your family's savings at risk is comforting. I will have to gain the approval of my partners, but this should be only a formality." He nodded at Clymo who smiled his concurrence and, indeed, relief.

"There's another formality needed, gentlemen," said John Williams, "and that is a document confirming the terms of my ownership, and I will require the signature of the baron himself."

"I will instruct our notary upon my return, sir," said Bolitho, "and pass the document to Mr. Clymo for his approval before we present it to Baron Trenance for signature. Right, Clymo?"

"Right, Mr. Bolitho," said Clymo. "Tell me one thing before we go forward, Captain Williams. Whom would you suggest to become the captain of Wheal Hykka Mine?"

"There is no doubt in my mind," said Williams. "There is one man whose knowledge, experience, honesty and willingness to work places him head and shoulders above all the rest."

"His name?" asked Bolitho. "Where do we find him?"

"He is outside at this moment. Addis Penwarden."

"That troublemaker?" demanded Bolitho. "Why, he is a rabble rouser!"

"Penwarden is the leader of that mob!" exclaimed Clymo.

"You're right about that," said Williams, "he is the leader all right. The miners and their families look up to him and respect him, both in the mine and in Gwennap and the villages around, and in the chapel. You just ask Reverend Perry. Penwarden will be the best mine captain you have, next to me. I would stake my reputation on it, nay my life, even my fortune.

"That's settled then. I'll call him in and tell him the good news, and we'll go ahead with setting day. While I'm about it I'll tell him that other improvements have been agreed to around here, right gentlemen? That'll settle things down."

The jaws of Bolitho and Clymo dropped. Williams with an effort refrained from smiling, kept his top hat on his head, put on his overcoat, unbolted the door of the counting house and strode outside.

Chapter Nineteen

Liskeard

It was mid-November and Parliament was still in session, but Edward Eliot had heard enough. He felt he had done his duty conscientiously as a member. He had listened to debates and expressed his opinion, in the lobby if rarely on the floor of the house. On the rare occasions when ministers felt that they had not reached a consensus sufficient to take a decision and move forward on a policy or a position and that therefore a division was advisable, then Edward registered his vote in the traditional way by walking through one of the doors labeled aye or nay.

Early in his parliamentary career Edward had allied himself with the Pelham brothers, leaders of the Whig interest. While Edward was of more than average ability, something prevented him from reaching the first rank of the administration at the national level. Though loathe to acknowledge any shortcoming in himself, perhaps he did not possess the ruthless degree of drive or unswerving ambition necessary; and indeed did not at heart wish to be that kind of man. However, he aspired to more than he presently had and applied himself to achieving it.

He importuned the elder Pelham, the Duke of Newcastle, for a remunerative place in the administration. The Duke had been appointed to lead the king's administration from the House of Lords. His Grace exerted much of his influence through managing appointments and favors, while taking some advice from the king. For more than three years he held off Edward's blandishments with promises. However, Edward's persistence had been finally rewarded the year before, and the Eliot family interests and income were reinforced when he was appointed by the Crown to be a Commissioner of Trade and Plantations.

Edward realized that the commission was not the most prestigious of bodies, merely an attachment to the Privy Council. However, the duties were not onerous, he had no alternative, and it went some way to satisfying his ambitions and Catherine's, too.

As he became familiar with his duties he saw the importance of the commission growing as England gained more possessions around the world. Trade was increasing, which he felt offered opportunities for revenue, not only to the administration in the form of excise taxes and tariffs, but also to enterprising individuals in the form of investment and business opportunities. The body was charged with developing English commercial interests and, while he had a strong sense of duty, Edward relished even more the influence that his political interests afforded him and expected to take full advantage of the business opportunities that came his way. No doubt his new position would help expand his income beyond the amount of his salary, and he could, with propriety, be of more value to his friends.

In politics Eliot had been accustomed generally to supporting the Duke of Newcastle's Whigs. But though he was coming to see the value of his belated appointment, Eliot remained disappointed at what he considered his Grace's ungraceful dilatoriness in giving him a place, and then only at a lowly commission. So, during the present session Eliot had generally voted with those Tories who were persuaded by his oratory to support William Pitt, despite his more or less Whig connections. As a country gentleman, this was a perfectly acceptable position for Eliot to occupy; it was usually more beneficial to support the issue than the party. If his interests or those of Cornwall lay elsewhere, then Edward voted with whatever group he felt most closely aligned. He could usually count on favors being repaid, and that is how he had brought about the Turnpike Act for Liskeard, which he would ensure would benefit him as well as his borough.

Now it was time for Edward to leave London and return to his constituency to see to his local interests in Cornwall, business as well as politics. One must keep an eye on things if one is to prosper and keep a hold on affairs. Catherine had them packed up and, with their servants and her purchases, they traveled by sea down to Cornwall.

After the long trip, disembarking at the Port Eliot quay, and a night of rest, Eliot directed Polkinghorne and Bunt to join him and Catherine in his wagon to journey the eight miles into Liskeard. He had arranged to meet again with James Davis, the mayor, and Edwin Ough, the town clerk. He also wanted an opportunity for a confidential conversation with his lieutenants during the two or three hours the journey would take.

"Bunt, you ride inside with the rest of us; there are things I want you and Polkinghorne to hear in order to guide your work for Port Eliot."

After they set off Edward jumped right into discussing what was on his mind. "Gentlemen, we must keep the turnpike project moving. We must ensure that I control the board of trustees and that Port Eliot secures the contracts for the road stone. We have no time to lose."

"What brings about this urgency?" asked Polkinghorne. "You seem concerned, if I may say so."

"I don't want Trenance and his gang at Lanhydrock stealing a march on us. At the same time I do want his support for the venture, as

Mr. Pitt urged when we met together. We all know his actions will require constant vigilance."

"Quite so, my dear," said Catherine Eliot, "he is to be trusted no further than Bunt here could throw one of your precious road stones."

"Aargh," said Bunt, "Oi would'n' trust 'im neither, not if it were up to Oi, not after the way 'e treated me and my Mary."

"Keep your opinions to yourself, young man," Polkinghorne said, "until you're asked for them, and that won't be soon or often."

"Come now, Polkinghorne," said Catherine, "don't be too hard on Bunt. He does have eyes, ears and the ability to think."

Polkinghorne glanced at her and quickly changed the subject. "You indeed think highly of Mr. Pitt, sir," he said, leaning forward and looking at Eliot.

"Indeed," Eliot said, warming to one of his many favorite topics. "Did you know that he even had his young daughters treated with that new fangled inoculation against the smallpox, to show us all an example and overcome our fears? He is a visionary man, and England will sorely miss his wise leadership if ever his enemies persuade him to leave his post."

Eliot was about to launch into a long explanation of his mentor's virtues and policies, but the clumsy wagon lurched as it bumped and swung around the bend approaching Trerulefoot. They each grasped for support to avoid losing their balance. Catherine rapped on the roof of the wagon and called out to the coachman, "Look out, man, not so fast! You'll have us all in the ditch!"

Polkinghorne took a deep breath and was about to make another comment but Catherine, quick-minded as ever, asked the question that was on his mind before he could give it expression.

"Brave of Mr. Pitt, but what of Cornwall's future? What is happening that might be of benefit to Port Eliot?" asked Catherine, and Polkinghorne nodded his support for her subject. She had brought into her marriage a clear-eyed understanding of the need to increase the family's wealth, and with that would come the well-being of those who earned their livings on the estate. Edward Eliot's listeners appreciated that he had a wide variety of interests, but Mrs. Eliot was not slow in bringing her husband back to the point that most interested her, even in front of their servants.

Eliot responded willingly enough, while not abandoning his lofty perspective. "For one thing," he said, "Cornwall is a lot closer to America than people like you, Polkinghorne, would have us think. You must make an effort to broaden your mind, expand your outlook, if you are to serve Port Eliot to the fullest. Take myself, for example; as you know, I am now a Commissioner of Trade and Plantations. From that vantage point, I am more than ever aware from my discussions with Mr. Pitt and other gentlemen of importance of the large promise for growing trade with the Americans, although I cannot say that His Majesty's Government in its entirety perceives the vision as clearly as he."

"It's still hundreds of leagues, sir," grumbled Polkinghorne. "For the life of me, I can't see that Cornwall stands to gain much, not all that way away."

"Cornishmen have already played a part in the army and the Royal Navy," Eliot said. "And I strongly believe our tradespeople and miners and mariners must be alert to seize their opportunities, our fishermen too. There's plenty of cod off Newfoundland. We just need to drive those damn Frenchies out. Of one thing I am sure; the foundation for greater prosperity in Cornwall lies in better roads so that goods can be moved faster and cheaper. We are already on our way to ensuring that happens."

"Other than the turnpikes, where can Port Eliot play a part?" asked Polkinghorne.

"There are many opportunities for investment," said Eliot. "The fishermen in East and West Looe will need more boats. The merchants need to finance cargoes of trade goods to sell in the colonies. The mining companies need more equipment and machinery to take advantage of the new inventions. The farmers need better breeding stock, equipment, seeds."

"You are clever to paint such a broad picture, my dear," said Catherine and smiled at her husband. "Our tenants are fortunate to have you as their squire."

"I need at least to be alert," he said to her. "Where opportunity abounds, the fruits go to the quickest and best prepared. Port Eliot must be ready to lead and take its rightful place here in Cornwall. In the meantime, England must strengthen her position with all her colonies, and I am in a position to ensure that Cornwall enjoys her rightful share of the opportunities."

"Ah, sir, it will all take a great sum of money," said Polkinghorne, rubbing the side of his nose.

"Aargh, that bloody Trenance 'as what it takes," said Bunt. "Got more money than 'e knows what to do with, though 'e tries 'ard to get rid of it, Oi'll give 'im that."

"You mustn't speak disrespectfully of your betters, Bunt," said Polkinghorne. "He inherited it, and that is a method well regarded by society."

"Indeed," said Catherine, starting to smile and covering her mouth with her gloved hand, "and he may have followed the example of his ancestors and married it, too; that's what I hear."

"Enough gossip," said Edward. "The pursuit of money is a noble calling, and we should not criticize others provided their methods are above reproach."

"Or nobody let's on 'ow 'tis done," Bunt said with a grin.

"Come now, Bunt," said Catherine, "it's money that makes possible fine things. What would our Mr. Joshua Reynolds do without his rich patrons commissioning his portraits?"

"Oi dunno about that," said Bunt scratching his armpit, which caused him to jostle Polkinghorne, sitting next to him in the cramped wagon.

"There's much you don't know about," said Polkinghorne, jerking himself upright. "If you used your ears more and your trap less you might learn something."

"Oi dunno know about such things, stuck 'ere in Cornwall. Us never gets up to London town, sees the big buildings, parliament, the king, stuff like that."

"Have you lived in Cornwall all your life, Bunt?" enquired Catherine.

"Well, not yet, mum," said Bunt. He grinned. Catherine covered her mouth to hide a smile. The man is irrepressible she thought.

Polkinghorne attempted to regain his part in the conversation and restore its serious purport. "Now, Mr. Eliot," he said, "you were telling us how you would find the money for these important projects."

"I am confident we will find what is required if the need is made clear enough," said Eliot, unperturbed by the squabbling among his underlings and persistent in his own train of thought. "In that regard, important measures were announced for the country in the king's speech from the throne at the opening of Parliament earlier this month. Did you know that the king has handed all the income from the crown estates over to Parliament? In exchange, Parliament will vote him a Civil List annually to pay the costs of the army and navy, and a fixed sum of eight hundred thousand pounds to defray his personal expenses and the costs of government. So, he will have the funds to remunerate those he appoints to office."

The cumbersome wagon lurched again, interrupting Eliot as he steadied Catherine and giving Polkinghorne an opening to ask a question that was still very much on his mind. "But what of financing for projects in Cornwall?" he pressed.

"Ah yes, of course, matters here at home. I bear in mind constantly that I am a country gentleman as well as a Member of Parliament and a servant of the king. Leave it to me; I will write a letter to Bolitho. He is a useful fellow. I'll get him to draft a prospectus of some kind, get his partners and some of his wealthy friends to put up the funds, promise them attractive returns for their wise and far-seeing investment." Eliot smiled at the fine prospects he envisioned.

"Now I must turn to news of great import. There will be a parliamentary election next year. My friends tell me it will most likely be called for March. You gentlemen will be fully occupied as my agents. As you know, we have several boroughs to manage. Our candidates will not represent any party and will for the most part stand unopposed. The voters are few but influential, and you must see to it, especially with those that do not live in the boroughs, that they cast their votes for our men."

Despite his master's urgings to broaden his horizons, Polkinghorne's first concern lay close to home. He asked, "What of St. Germans, sir?"

"I have resolved to keep my seat at St. Germans," said Eliot.

"I am pleased to hear it," said Catherine. She looked at them all appreciatively. "It can at times be illuminating to ride with gentlemen of affairs. One learns things. And I have grown quite fond of our burgesses since living at Port Eliot!"

"Your approval means much," said Eliot. "Now I must tell you that I am going to ask Anthony Champion to change his seat to Liskeard and then bring Philip Stanhope from Liskeard to St. Germans where I can keep a closer eye on him. His father purchased the seat for him for £2,000 as well as obtaining diplomatic places. It is no surprise that he inherited his father's Whig ways, and I want to ensure he supports Mr. Pitt when we need him."

"I remember that his father was a friend of your father's and sat for St. Germans," said Polkinghorne, "and then later for Lostwithiel."

"That was until old Stanhope went to the upper house as the Earl of Chesterfield. He was a sturdy opponent of Walpole's you know, and back in '44 the king sent for him and Pitt and their Broad Bottom party to form an administration. Then when I was a young man, Philip Stanhope and I did the Grand Tour together. Our families go back a long way."

"Indeed they do, my dear," said Catherine, "but at least Eliots stayed on the right side of the blanket. I can't imagine what our vicar would say at the Stanhopes' goings-on."

"I have no doubt his French lady was charming," said Eliot, "and it is a shame they never married. But who are we to judge? Their son has turned out quite well, and Chesterfield has been good to him."

"It never ceases to amaze me, Mr. Eliot," said Catherine, "that these sleepy little boroughs in your Cornish backwater are represented in parliament by such high-ranking and outstanding people. One would think they would seek more important constituencies."

"English politics works quite well for all its faults, my dear," said Eliot. "It's a matter of custom and precedent, mutual accommodation. His Majesty's administration finds it quite convenient to find seats here in their Duchy of Cornwall for worthy men for whom there is not room elsewhere, and I am happy to oblige them as far as it is within my power. My boroughs, while not inexpensive, bring me some revenue and not a little influence."

Eliot was not to be distracted for long from his earlier track and resumed his reminiscences. "Do you know, young Stanhope confided to me that old Chesterfield wrote several letters to him while he was at Westminster School. Gave his son some good advice: 'An able man shows his spirit by gentle words and resolute actions.' I try to take some of it myself."

"Indeed you do, Mr. Eliot," said Polkinghorne. "I can attest to that, and I dare say your tenants would agree with me."

"Pity Oi 'ad nobody to learn me things like that," muttered Bunt.

"Never too late to learn if you put your mind to it, Bunt," said Catherine. "Ah look, Mr. Eliot, we are getting close to Liskeard. I have some housekeeping matters to attend to at Eliot House. And now that the weather is getting cold, I may go into the town to see if I can purchase some wool for the housekeeper to do some knitting and sewing."

"Thank you for reminding me, my dear" said Eliot, "it is about Liskeard that I also wished to talk to you gentlemen. As I started to say when we set out, we must keep the turnpike project progressing. I am confident of our future, save for one thing; Trenance has seized his new opportunity in the Lords to throw in his lot with Newcastle and his party. He may be in a position to make trouble for us, and we know he has ambitions for Lanhydrock."

"Hardly a man of principle, it seems," said Polkinghorne.

"'E's a dirty bastard," said Bunt.

"Now, Bunt, I don't disagree with your sentiments, and I can't help admiring your conviction, but I rebuke your expression of them," said Eliot. "You must learn to be more diplomatic if you are to succeed in my service, especially in front of Mrs. Eliot."

"Sorry, zir, us knows we 'ave a lot to learn, and Oi should listen more than Oi speak," said Bunt, "an' Oi'm willin' to do just that. But Oi can't stand the thought of that rascal, not after what 'e done to my Mary."

"Holding grudges can often lead us to rash behavior, Bunt. Baron Trenance will pay for his sins and that long before he meets his maker," said Eliot. "But no one connected with Port Eliot will ever do anything that is against the law. Understood?"

"Aargh, understood," said Bunt, lapsing into silence and staring out at the passing hills.

"My concern is that being chairman of the turnpike trustees may not be enough to ensure that Port Eliot is the sole supplier of road stone. It's an obvious enterprise on which to compete and don't imagine Clymo and Trenance haven't already thought of it. We are going to meet with the mayor and town clerk when we arrive. I would like you, Polkinghorne, to urge that I become mayor when Mr. Davis's term comes to its conclusion next year. That should keep our rivals surrounded. Even General Amherst would be proud!"

Polkinghorne and Bunt exchanged admiring glances. William Pitt may be admired as a statesman of genius, but on the Cornish stage their employer was not far behind. He marshaled his forces with skill.

The wagon lumbered on past St. Martin's church and turned down the hill to Eliot House. The footman helped them step down. They made their way into the house where James Davis, the Mayor of Liskeard, and Edwin Ough, the Town Clerk, were awaiting them in the hall. The footman took their coats and hats. Catherine greeted both gentlemen and then excused herself to go into the parlor with the housekeeper.

"It is good to see you again, Mr. Ough, and you Mr. Mayor," said Eliot, shaking each warmly by the hand. "You know Polkinghorne, of course, and this is Bunt. Let us get down to business in the library. Port, gentlemen?"

Eliot took his seat by the fire, and the others sat across from him. The butler poured port. There was a troubled expression on the faces of the town officials.

"Anything amiss?" asked Eliot.

"I am a little concerned," said Ough, shifting in his chair. "It's about the turnpike workings."

Chapter Twenty

Competition

"Out with it, Mr. Ough," said Polkinghorne. "If anything is not working according to plan we simply have to deal with it. Just tell us what is going on."

Edwin Ough laced his fingers together in his lap. His expression was somewhere between embarrassment and self-satisfaction. "Mr. Davis in his official capacity as mayor had a visit from Mr. Clymo," Ough said. "He's the steward at the Lanhydrock estate, as you know."

"Get on with it," said Eliot, "we know very well who Clymo is. What was he about? That's the question."

"He wants to make us a proposition. Lanhydrock is planning to add more diggings in their mines down west. They'll be removing large quantities of rock, so they'll have to dispose of tailings, some of it sound granite. They are prepared to crush it and, since it would otherwise be waste, sell it at low prices for the Liskeard turnpike."

"Oi'd want someone to look awful careful at that waste before Oi'd trust any bugger from Trenance country to sell rock with the right quality for turnpike stone, that's what Oi'd say," said Bunt. "Them might show you granite and sell you somethin' else. And anyroad, 'ow much would it cost to haul to Liskeard from down west? That's a fair piece, make no mistake." He lapsed into an embarrassed silence, remembering his prior rebuke.

"Bunt makes a good point," said Polkinghorne, somewhat jealous but wishing to earn credit for his protégé's growing contributions. "Once more turnpikes are built, heavy loads could be transported a long distance at reasonable cost, but not yet."

"Seems to us t'would be cheaper to send it by lugger from the quay at Port Eliot to Looe, and then up the Looe river to where us'm goin' to need the stone near the workin's loike," said Bunt, rubbing his chin. "Us could get that started in no toime, plenty of ships to hire already."

"So Port Eliot could deliver cheaper than Lanhydrock and get started while they're still thinking about it! Capital idea," said Eliot. "I do believe we have an assistant manager for the quarry company, don't you agree, Polkinghorne? It'll take us no time to put in the crushing machinery at Port Eliot, right Bunt? If we put you on it, I'd wager Port Eliot could produce and ship better road stone quicker and cheaper than anyone else in Cornwall for many years to come. What do you think of that, gentlemen? We'll go ahead right away. We'd be ready a lot sooner than Lanhydrock would."

Polkinghorne grunted an affirmative. Davis and Ough appeared overwhelmed, and Bunt's countenance emitted an unmanly blush.

"As chairman of the turnpike trust," continued Eliot, "I advise that Liskeard do everything possible to hold costs down. Mr. Davis, just keep Mr. Clymo busy. Tell him to investigate the possibilities for road stone nearer home: Bodmin, or Lostwithiel or St. Austell. Won't be needed there for some time yet, and you can't get a bill through parliament at the drop of a hat, even if one of your adventurers now sits in the House of Lords. And one still requires friends, a commodity that Trenance has had little time to cultivate. Anyway, delay won't hurt them, it'll give them time to get organized."

"I do believe the borough's corporation will support the trustees of the turnpike in this arrangement with Port Eliot as you suggest, Mr. Eliot, which seems sensible and beneficial," said Davis. "No doubt they will express their gratitude in due course." He and Ough looked relieved.

"It occurs to me, if I may be so bold," said Polkinghorne, "that when you set aside the burdens of office, Mr. Davis, the capital burgesses may find it advantageous to persuade Mr. Eliot to accept election to the responsibilities of the mayoralty of Liskeard."

There was an uncomfortable silence.

"I had originally hoped to continue," said Davis, "but now that you mention it, my wife has urged me not to linger past my present term, and one term is customary," said the mayor. "Besides, there are personal business and family issues that call for my attention. It all depends on what would lie in the best interests of the borough. What is your opinion, Mr. Ough? I value your experience in such matters."

"It would be hard to replace your dedication and integrity, your worship," said Ough, "but I can think of no one more qualified than Mr. Eliot, if he would be willing to grace us with his acceptance."

"Oi think that'd make sure the road stone were supplied by Port Eliot; that be what Oi think," said Bunt. "If Mr. Eliot be both chairman of turnpike trustees and Mayor of Liskeard, no other bugger would 'ave a chance, that's what Oi think."

There were a few moments of silence as impassive faces gazed at Bunt.

"Well, anyroad, that's what Oi think," Bunt lumbered on bravely. "And us needn't stop with Liskeard neither. Why leave Bodmin an' Lostwithiel an' them other turnpikes to that there Lanhydrock crowd?"

Polkinghorne cleared his throat. "Quite," he said, glaring at Bunt and smiling at the good burghers. "There is perhaps some possibility that if

Mr. Eliot could spare the time such an arrangement might be advantageous for Port Eliot as well for the citizens for Liskeard. On the other hand . . . ."

"There is no question, gentlemen," said Davis. "I would lend my full support. I am confident that if a busy man like Mr. Eliot could be persuaded to serve Liskeard in a mayoral capacity, then our citizenry would be well served and more than grateful."

"Ah, gratitude," said Eliot with a sardonic smile spreading over his face, "now there is an emotion that uplifts us. We are agreed then, and I am sure we will all be discreet. In that case, before you take your leave I should mention that Mrs. Eliot is a trustee for the estate of my late cousin, St. John Eliot. The young man was in delicate health, and no doubt his duties as Rector of St. Mary's in Truro taxed him greatly. But he was blessed with comfortable means, and one was able to persuade him of the needs of Liskeard for schooling. He left one fourth of the thirty-five pounds income from his holdings in Old South Sea Annuities to be applied annually towards the teaching of poor children to read."

"Wonderful news," Mr. Eliot, said James Davis. "Liskeard has much to thank the Eliot family for. As you know, we indeed prize schooling. The corporation has paid for a school since 1574, when we allotted four pounds a year; the cost since those days has gone up, and additional funds would be welcome."

"Yes, indeed, Mr. Mayor, there is always need for money to preserve and maintain one's standards," said Eliot. "I commend Liskeard on keeping that always in mind. Gentlemen, I wish you good day. We've had a tiring journey, but this has been a most productive conversation, and I'm grateful to you both. I will have the butler show you out."

Eliot told Polkinghorne and Bunt to be prepared to leave in half an hour and went into the adjoining parlor to find Catherine. Bunt took the opportunity to find Mary's sister Nellie in the kitchen and tell her that Mary's baby had still not arrived.

"Edward, I trust that your business went well?" asked Catherine, looking up from a newspaper she had on her lap.

"As well as could be expected," Edward replied. "There was a lot to talk about regarding the turnpike, and I did not interrupt that conversation to forewarn them about the parliamentary election. However, there was some discussion of local politics, and I do believe I will be asked to be mayor when Mr. Davis leaves office."

"My dear, you are always busy, always active, always planning," said Catherine.

"I do it for us, and for our family," said Eliot. "Now what have you been up to?"

"Cook has given me some sad news. Her sister in St. Germans has just lost her husband. You remember him? He was the head vegetable gardener at Port Eliot. He has been suffering ill humors for some years."

"I am sorry to hear it. He was a loyal servant. Will he be buried in the St. Germans churchyard? Perhaps we can provide a gravestone."

"I believe so. I am told that his widow will not be able to live alone. Perhaps we could find her a place at the Almshouses. She would be comfortable there, and have a place she could manage. Then their cottage in the village would be empty. Perhaps we could give that to the Bunts. Their baby is expected soon. Do you agree, and can you arrange it with Polkinghorne?"

"Indeed. A sound plan," said Edward. "The more dependent Bunt becomes on Port Eliot, the more useful he will be. He has a good grasp of many considerations, and I believe he could become a good manager of men. But if his familiarity with goings on at Lanhydrock is to be of any use to us, he is going to have to learn his manners." He reached for her hand. "Come my dear, let us be on our way. We need to get home to Port Eliot before it gets dark."

"Leave the Bunts to me," said Catherine, rising from her chair. "Turnpikes and farms, places, politics and business are your world, Edward. My world is our people, and I manage them very well."

Catherine rang for the butler to fetch their coats, and they went out into the hall to go out to the wagon and leave for Port Eliot. Polkinghorne and Bunt were already waiting. They helped the Eliots to their seats and followed them inside.

"Bunt, we have some good news for you," said Catherine as they set off. "There is a cottage in the village that will shortly be vacant, and in light of your new position, Mr. Eliot has decided to allow you and Mary to have it. I will arrange for some furniture to be loaned to you, and you will soon receive a wedding present that the estate carpenter is making for the new baby."

"That be very kindly of you, my lady," said Bunt beaming, "and Mr. Eliot too. Mary and me thank you, Oi'm sure." He was now anxious to break the good news to Mary.

"Bunt, I am not Lady Eliot," said Catherine. "I have told you that before. But I cannot get too cross with you, since I hope that one day you will prove correct, at which time I shall probably have to correct you again!"

Edward hid a smile. Really, Catherine was incorrigible. He would have to speak to her in private about not appearing too ambitious in front of servants or tenants. It was just not done. She really must grasp the small nuances that matter in the country.

"Mr. Polkinghorne advises me that he expects you to do well in your new position, Bunt," said Eliot, "and I and Mrs. Eliot are confident you will do well by Port Eliot."

"Thank 'ee, zir," said Bunt, "Oi been thinkin' loike. Mebbe I could go over to Lanhydrock one day, before Sir James . . ."

"You mean Baron Trenance, Bunt," said Catherine tapping him on the knee.

"Oh yes, mum, Oi means Baron Trenance. Anyroad, before his worship gets back from London; perhaps Oi could run into Mr. Clymo and talk to 'im loike and mebbe find out what them is really up to with that there road stone, and 'ow they was thinkin' of getting' ahold of them mine tailings and makin' them right to use for road stone, sortin' out the soft stuff, gradin' them the proper size an' all. 'Twouldn't be no good just any'ow, would them?"

"Good idea, Bunt," said Eliot. "Arrange with Mr. Polkinghorne to borrow a horse from the stables and get on your way as soon as possible."

"Don't forget that Mary is expecting the baby any day now," said Catherine. "You might allow Bunt to wait until after he sees the newborn."

"Quite right, my dear," said Eliot. "Just arrange matters with Mr. Polkinghorne, Bunt."

Charles Polkinghorne looked pensive and settled back into his seat. Perhaps young Bunt was being paid to think after all. He could turn out to be very useful, indeed. And there again, perhaps it would be as well to keep a close eye on him; it would never do for his own position to be diminished.

Chapter Twenty-one

Birth

"Good night, Willy, me 'andsome," said Mary Bunt. "Ye've to get up early in the mornin'. Twouldn't do to be late gettin' to work."

"You sleep well, too, me luv," said Willy. "'Tis lovely an' cosy 'ere, b'ain't it? An 'ere us be in our own bed in our own cottage. Us be blessed lucky, an' no mistake."

"That's because them Eliots think you be a good worker, Willy," said Mary, "so don' keep yammerin' all night, ye can't afford to oversleep. An' let me get some sleep too, if Oi can get comfy. 'Tain't easy with a big belly loike this."

"Oi 'spect the baby will come soon, luv, should be 'ere by now."

"That's what the midwife says, an' 'er should know, what with all the babies 'er's dropped in St. Germans," said Mary. "Now go to sleep, so Oi can, too, mebbe."

They both dropped off a few minutes later, tired but contented. They had been working in their spare time these last couple of days of November, cleaning and arranging their new cottage and its garden. The Port Eliot estate had allowed them a very reasonable rent after Willy got his new job as assistant manager on the road stone project, working directly with Charles Polkinghorne.

The cottage came with some meager furniture provided by the Eliots, including a four-poster bed, and they had borrowed a few second-hand pots and pans and utensils from friends in the village. There was a cradle with rockers that the estate carpenter had made, a wedding present from Mrs. Eliot in expectation of the new arrival. She had also loaned them the birthing chair that sat in the corner of the bedroom.

However, as things turned out they were not able to sleep for long.

"Willy, wake up!" whimpered Mary, "Oi'm all wet like, in the bed, an' Oi 'ad some big pains down in me tummy. You'd better go fetch the midwife; 'urry. The baby's comin'. Oi'm a bit frightened."

"You just stay right there, me luv," said Willy, "Oi'll just light the candle an' put my boots on an' a coat, an' Oi'll fetch 'er in two shakes of a cat's tail."

It seemed like an age to Mary as she stiffened with yet another pain, but the midwife and her young assistant arrived at the cottage in less than a quarter of an hour. They bustled up the narrow staircase, followed by an anxious Willy.

"Now 'ow ye be doin', m'dear?" the midwife asked, taking charge. Turning around she demanded, "What you doin' up 'ere, young man? This ain't no place fer the loikes of you. You leave this to we. You go back down them stairs an' put a stick of wood on the stove, fetch some water and put a big kettle on. Us'll need lots of boilin' water and not just for makin' tea neither."

Humbly, Willy did as he was told. Mary groaned.

"Roight then, me sweetheart," said the midwife, "let's take a look at ye." She drew back the bedclothes and examined Mary. "How often be the pains comin' now?" she asked.

"S'about toime you got 'ere," said Mary, "Where you been to? Oi 'ad another one since Willy left to get you."

"Then it'll be a good while yet," said the midwife, "You've barely started. An' judgin' by the looks o' ye, the baby's nowhere near ready. Now us be goin' to need some rags an' things." She addressed her assistant. "You go find what you can, tear up some old shirts if you 'ave to."

Mary rolled her head sideways and saw the assistant grab one of Willy's shirts. "Don' you go tearin' up that shirt! Oi just mended it so Willy could wear it a bit longer."

"You 'ush up, my girl, Oi's the one who decides what gets tore up. What your baby needs matters more than that there lummox down that kitchen," said the midwife with the firmness of one used to being obeyed. "You lie on your side now, and Oi'll rub your back. Ye'll feel easier, an' it'll bring the baby on. May take a while, first born allus takes longest."

She turned to the young woman she had brought with her. "Now you watch me careful, and then you do what Oi do, just the same. Oi've got to go down kitchen and make up some 'erb teas."

"But Oi want to come down with you, so Oi can learn that too," said the young woman.

"Don't you be impatient, missy," said the midwife, "Oi'll teach you 'erbs and medicines proper like after you 'elped me for a full seven years."

The midwife massaged Mary's back with long firm strokes, and in a few minutes Mary relaxed. She soon had another contraction, and the midwife pressed down on her back and relaxed her again. After a while the young assistant took over under her mentor's watchful eye.

"Oi'm goin' down kitchen now," said the midwife, once she was satisfied her assistant was doing it right. "Be sure an' call me if either of you need anythin', anythin' at all."

She went down the narrow stairs and asked Willy whether the kettle was boiling yet. He nodded. She got a basin and put it on the scrubbed pine table and reached into the capacious pockets of her apron and drew out little packets twisted up in paper, and vials of colorless liquids. Then she took out a pouch containing a small pestle and mortar, some different sized spoons and a sharp knife. She measured out small quantities of leaves and dried roots and began chopping up the leaves and pounding up the roots and adding them to the crock pot. She poured boiling water from the copper kettle over the mixture and let it infuse.

"What's this 'ere then?" asked Willy peering down into the mixture. "Some kind of witchcraft, Oi'll be bound."

The midwife did not take offense; she had often heard such accusations. "No witchcraft," she said, "but some b'lieve what my potions do is akin to magic. Me granny learned me 'ow to foind these plants in the woods and hedges, an' 'er granny before 'er, an' 'ow to make healin' concoctions. This 'ere is root of wound wart, full of juice, hot and biting to the taste; these yellow flowers is colewort; these leaves an' buds be common mugwort; and these seven berries I picked myself in Liskeard on Bay Tree Hill. Them expel crude and raw humors from the belly, hasten the sore travail of childbirth, and they expel the afterbirth.

"Us must take care not to use them until the woman's time is come, or she will suffer abortion. 'Twill make Mary's time easier and ease her pain."

"Oi s'pose that's all right then," said Willy doubtfully. "Oi s'pose ye know what you're about. Now what's in those bottles then?"

"This little one's got laudanum, a sip of this will help Mary through the worst of the pain if 'er 'urts really bad. T'other's got a nice drop o' gin, 'twill make 'er feel 'appy loike, instead of feelin' sad after the baby come, loike some women feel."

"Oi would'n' moind a swig o' that meself," said Willy, putting the bottle to his lips and taking a couple of big swallows. "Whoo! Tha's powerful stuff! Us needs a drink of water!"

After a few minutes, the concoction was ready, and the midwife strained the hot liquid into a pottery mug and climbed the stairs to the upper room, where Mary was groaning again. Willy started after her, lurching against the wall.

"Young man, Oi told 'ee to stay out of my way, down in that there kitchen," ordered the midwife. "What we'm about is woman's work. Anyroad you don' seem too steady on your pins; you'd be better off in that chair by the stove." She continued up the stairs. "You can stop rubbin' that poor gel's back, missy," she said as she entered the room, "you don' 'ave to push the baby out for 'er in five minutes. Oi did'n tell ye to go on all day." The girl stood back, looking crestfallen.

"Now then, Mary," the midwife went on, "Sit up a bit an' drink all of this down. Mind, slowly now, it still be 'ot from the kettle. That'll make you feel better."

Mary puckered up her lips at the bitter taste, but swallowed the liquid down as she was told. She lay back down on her side. She groaned again as another, stronger pain came on. The pains were coming more often now. The midwife examined her. "Ow," Mary yelled, her hands on her belly. "Feels 'ard as rocks."

"You be comin' along nice, 'twon't be long now. Don' be 'fraid to shout out when the pains get more, 'twill make 'e feel stronger."

Mary did as she was told, and again, and again. Time passed as the midwife continued her ministrations. Mary cried out as a deep contraction strained her body.

The midwife wiped the sweat off her forehead, then felt her belly again and reached a decision.

"Come on missy, 'er toime is gettin' near, 'elp me get 'er out of the bed an' onto that there birthing chair. You set down there, me luv, ye can squeeze onto them arms when ye need to push. Missy, get that pillow and set it under 'ere, under the openin', and that there tore up shirt."

"Oh, oh, Oi feel another big 'un comin' on, mum," panted Mary.

"All right girl," said the midwife, "You'm doin' foine, you puff an' push loike when the pain comes on. Just keep on doin' that whenever a pain come on."

Mary panted and pushed, and groaned and pushed and panted, and then a triumphant smile came over her face.

"Again!" said the midwife, and with a last big push Mary gave birth to her first born, and there was a protesting cry as a new person entered this world.

"Ye have a bonny baby girl, me love. Now you go on, missy, stop gawpin'. Ain't ye seen a newborn before? Get on down stairs and bring up that kettle. Oi'll do what needs to be done 'ere an' cut the cord, an' then Oi'll wash off the baby an' give 'er to the new mum."

The midwife noticed something strange. The little girl's feet were webbed between her second and third toes. She said nothing, washed her in the warm water and swaddled her in clean linens. She and her assistant helped Mary back into bed. She put the baby on Mary's chest, and the protests became gurgles of pleasure as the midwife helped the baby find Mary's nipple. Mary giggled as the baby took hold, and then she bent her head to watch her daughter feeding and smiled with pleasure.

"There she be then, all shipshape and Bristol fashion. What will you name 'er?" asked the midwife. She went to the door and called Willy up to the bedroom. He clambered up the stairs and came hesitantly across the room, the floorboards creaking as he moved. Slowly he approached Mary with the babe on her chest and leaned over for a look.

"Well Oi never, fancy that," was all he could manage to say. Then he beamed and bent over to kiss Mary on the forehead.

"Us be thinkin' of callin' 'er Catherine," answered Mary, and Willy nodded. "Mrs. Eliot is so koind to we, an' us would loike to name 'er after 'er. Oi 'ope she don't mind."

"Don't fret yourself, m'dear," said the midwife. "Now all you got to think of is the baby. Just rest awhile; she'll wake you soon enough when 'er gets 'ungry again. Oi'll just tidy up. Come along, missy."

"You 'old little Catherine a minute, Willy; 'er's a dear little mite."

"Oi must get off, Mary me luv," said Willy, looking nervous and slightly slurring his words. "It's high toime Oi got up to the estate office and met Mr. Polkinghorne. Us 'ave to walk over to the site fer the new quarry. Oi'll give them the good news."

"Now you take good care of yourself, Willy," said Mary Bunt, "Don' go fallin' about on no rocks. Remember you've got two of we to look out for now."

"Us'll need a godfather and another godmother too," said Willy, pausing by the door. "Oi could ask Mr. Polkinghorne."

"An' you could've asked my sister Nelly whilst you were in Liskeard."

"Oi could've," agreed Willy, "an mebbe there's someone else. Oi could ask someone from Lanhydrock. Oi 'ave to go over there soon. Lemme see first what Mr. Polkinghorne says."

It was still early in the morning and the tiny bedroom was lit by a candle. Willy was already dressed for the workday ahead. He leaned over to kiss his wife and new baby good-bye. Mary had a puzzled expression on her face, but he didn't think much of it. Willy at first had had a moment of disappointment at Mary not presenting him with a son, but he quickly got over it just as soon as he mistook the little thing's first burp as a loving smile at her father.

"Now you stay in your bed an hour or two Mary, me luv, and take good care of our Catherine. 'Er's a pretty little maid, make no mistake. Takes after 'er mum," said Willy with a big smile on his face. "Don't ye go tearin' about cleanin' an' cookin'. Oi'll fetch some bread and cheese for me breakfast. I've looked after the stove downstairs and put enough coal an' logs on to keep the cottage warm for a good while, and Oi filled up the kettle for more 'ot water. Seems 'er uses ever so much, dunno what 'er does with it all," he added, pointing his thumb at the midwife.

"Us can't lay about long, Willy," said Mary. "The midwife can't stay forever. She sent a message to Mrs. Eliot an' she be comin' to visit we soon to see 'ow the baby is and 'ow us be doin'. Oi hope she be pleased us be goin' to christen 'er Catherine after 'er. Oi'm afeared Mrs. Eliot might think we'm disrespectful loike. Oi wish you didn' 'ave to go back to Lanhydrock; you got to watch out for them people."

"Oi can take care of myself, me luv, don't you worry. Well, Oi be gettin' along then. 'Twouldn' do to keep Mr. Polkinghorne waitin'. He'd be sorry 'e asked we to work on the road stone project if us showed up late for work."

Little Catherine whimpered when her father left, disturbed by his slamming the door. She got back to the enjoyable task of suckling at her mother's breast, and as contentment overcame hunger she fell asleep. Mary leaned over and tucked her into the bed beside her, pleasantly surprised at how quickly she had gained confidence in handling the helpless little bundle. She vowed to watch over her for a while and then get dressed and get about her chores. After all, she was a robust working girl, and a minor event like childbirth could not justify the indulgence of keeping her bedridden for long. However, she too fell asleep, tired from lack of sleep and the stress and effort of the labor. It was an hour or so later when she rubbed the sleep from her eyes, awoken by a knock at the cottage door. The midwife answered. It was Mrs. Eliot.

"May I come up?" called Catherine Eliot, "I hope I didn't disturb you."

"Oh, us was just lookin' after the baby, mum," said Mary, propping herself up against the pillow and hoping her voice did not sound too sleepy. Who would want a servant who was lazy? "Come right on up."

Catherine entered the small room and approached the bed with a smile. "What an adorable little girl!" she said, pulling the covers back from the sleeping baby and touching her little cheek. "She looks so contented! What are you calling her? How are you in yourself, Mary? Recovered from the labor? Not too difficult, I trust?"

"Aw no, t'was easy," Mary smiled. "Willy and me wants to call 'er Catherine, mum, after you," said Mary, "that is if ye don' mind loike. Cuz you and Mr. Eliot 'ave been so kind to Willy and me."

"I would be honored, Mary!" said Catherine, her eyes sparkling with pleasure. "Mr. Eliot will be pleased, too. We take such an interest in you and Willy, you know. He is a promising young man, and Mr. Polkinghorne thinks he can go far. Just you encourage him to work hard. And, my dear you need to improve your education, so I have taken the liberty of asking the curate to work with you both to improve your English once a week after church."

"Oh, thank 'ee kindly, mum," said Mary, her face lighting up.

"You know," said Catherine, tapping the side of her head, "I do believe there is a christening robe of mine put away in the attic up at the house. Little Catherine will wear it for her baptism. Just take care of it, and one of the maids can launder it and put it away again for the next little one. And I will stand godmother if you'll have me. Now, nanny, have you had a good look at that baby and made sure she has all her fingers and toes?"

"Right you are, mum," said the midwife. "I haven't had a chance to mention it to Mary yet, but I did notice a funny thing when I was bathing her after she was born. She has webbed feet, just between her second and third toes. 'Ere you be, my darlin', let's unwrap you and see how ye be doin'. Is that there mum of yourn feedin' you proper?"

The old woman lifted little Catherine with the firm gentleness of long experience, but nevertheless the baby let out an indignant squall at being disturbed.

"Here, let me have a look," said Catherine, "My goodness, she has, indeed. Looks like a darling little duckling." Catherine knew where she had seen toes like that before, remembering little baby James Trenance. Knowing Mary and Willy's story, she thought it best to leave the subject aside in front of the midwife.

"My lands," said Mary, "Where did she get those? Will they be any bother?"

"Don't you worry, Mary," said Mrs. Eliot, "she'll just have to keep her stockings on when she gets older, and that'll do her nothing but good. You take good care of them both, nanny, and help Mary tidy up. I've got to go back up to the house, but I'll call in on the vicar and arrange about the christening. I'll also send some food over, so you don't have to cook for a few days."

Catherine walked off briskly, closing the door quietly behind her. On her way home she stopped by the vicarage to tell the vicar about the Bunts' new daughter and the name they had chosen for her.

"A new parishioner, God be praised, and a Catherine," said the vicar. "How fitting that she be named after her benefactor, my dear lady. There are two other new arrivals in the village, and I would, of course, be delighted to perform the Publick Baptism of Infants for them all. What a wonderful rite!" He beamed beatifically, clasped his hands upon his breast and intoned, "Forasmuch as all men are conceived and born in sin, none can enter into the kingdom of God, except she be regenerate and born anew of Water and of the Holy Ghost."

"Now, now vicar," said Catherine, "You don't have to go into the whole thing for me! Save it for the congregation next Sunday."

"Ah, but they are such comforting words, dear lady," said the vicar unperturbed. "After all, children are the fruit of the womb, an heritage and a gift that cometh from the Lord. Happy is the man that hath his quiver full of them."

"Vicar, you are getting quite carried away," teased Catherine. "I hope you realize that we women have our own role in this miraculous process!"

"Yes, indeed, Mrs. Eliot, and my duty is clear and my faith unchallengeable. In forty days we must bring Mary and the other young women into the priory for their churching. I will pray to Almighty God, and tell him that: 'we give thee humble thanks for that thou hast vouchsafed to deliver this woman thy servant from the great pain and peril of Child-birth; Grant, we beseech thee, most merciful Father, that she, through thy help, may both faithfully live, and walk according to thy will, in this life present; and also may be partaker of everlasting glory in the life to come'.'"

"You make it all sound quite terrifying, vicar," said Catherine gazing out the window and then back at the rapturous gentleman. "I wonder that we women ever willingly consent to provide you men with your heirs and heiresses. I can assure you that there would be far fewer new parishioners if you and your like had to give them birth!"

She left the vicar looking somewhat perturbed and headed for home pondering on the future of such a little girl. Webbed toes, indeed.

Chapter Twenty-two

Quarry

Willy Bunt hastened over to the estate office to meet Charles Polkinghorne as arranged. He was much aware that he was not walking as steadily as usual, but deep breaths of the brisk air soon blew the remaining unaccustomed fumes of gin from his brain. He cut a stout stick from a hazel bush to support himself as he walked, and with greater confidence, lengthened his stride. He knocked on the office door and went in.

"You're late; I expected you first thing," Polkinghorne greeted him. "You can't hold up my day by wandering about like a gentleman of leisure."

"Sorry, zir," Bunt said, "Oi was occupied like at 'ome."

"Work always comes first, my boy, and don't you forget it," chided Polkinghorne. "We need to get over to the quarry site and make arrangements for the workings."

"Sorry, Mr. Polkinghorne zir, but my Mary 'ad 'er baby last night, so Oi thought Oi should stay with 'er."

"Well, then I suppose congratulations are in order, well done. That does put a different light on it, but don't make a habit of it."

"Oi don't 'spect us'll 'ave a baby every day of the year, zir," said Bunt with a grin.

"That's enough impertinence, man! Well, you might as well tell me, boy or girl?"

"Girl, zir, an' us'd appreciate the honor of you standin' godfather, loike."

"Oh, well, in that case, doubly happy to hear the news," said Polkinghorne, hiding his pleasure to maintain his authority. "Mother and daughter both doing well, I trust? What are you calling her?"

"Catherine, zir, that's if Mrs. Eliot don't moind, loike."

Young Bunt might be getting above his station, mused Polkinghorne. He would have to have a word with him if this kind of self-promotion continued. But he was a promising lad, the Eliots wanted to encourage him, and after all he had connections at Lanhydrock that might be useful. He would just have to keep an eye on him.

In a formal tone, Polkinghorne added, "I would indeed be honored to act as godfather. Let me know about the christening." He might as well encourage the young man's looking to him as a mentor. Taking his coat off the hook, he added, "Well, at least you'll be free to get to Lanhydrock in the next few days. Right now we need to get on over to the quarry site. Mr. Eliot had to leave for London to attend the House, so he has left me in charge and instructed me to move ahead as rapidly as possible."

They left the office and walked across the park towards the bank of the River Tiddy and to the quay where boats loaded and unloaded their cargoes. It was used by the family when they traveled far afield and also for farm produce and supplies and goods for the village and the estate. Eliot had confidence that the facility could be expanded to handle the output from the quarry, and given the present absence of decent roads, transportation by water was the cheapest and most efficient.

"What do Mr. Eliot want we to do 'zactly?" Bunt asked Polkinghorne.

"He wants us to plan workings for the quarry on a modest scale that can be opened at low cost, using manual labor to supply the early needs of the Liskeard turnpike project, but laid out in such a way that the quarry can readily expand and made more efficient as demand grows. Don't forget we'll need a source of sand as well as rock."

Bunt nodded, which he hoped made it look as if he understood the need for sand as well as stone.

"Mr. Eliot is very progressive," continued Polkinghorne, "and he's not afraid to try new methods. He wants us to consult with an engineer to look at the whole plan for the future, not just blasting out the rock, but also shaping the larger pieces to use in building while crushing the smaller pieces to use for roadbeds. Then we must plan the most efficient layout for transporting the finished product right to the building sites."

"Us got plenty of men needin' work around 'ere and nearby," said Bunt, "and in the winter time some of the farm laborers ain't got that much to do. Them can 'andle a pick an' shovel well as any, even miners, and 'andle 'orses an' mules better'n most. Us can start with the 'ome farm."

Bunt had not learned even a modicum of reticence in expressing his opinion, thought Polkinghorne, even though he had been warned repeatedly.

"The present methods will do for now, Bunt," said Polkinghorne, "and what you may not know is that Mr. Eliot is a member of the Society for the Encouragement of Arts, Manufacture, and Commerce, and when he's in London he attends their meetings regularly and hears about the latest methods. You heard him say on the journey to Liskeard that he is a Commissioner of Trade and Plantations, and in that position his duty includes keeping abreast of methods and advances. He says that men are constantly inventing new ways that will revolutionize trade and manufactories, and agriculture, too. He wants to be in the forefront."

"Oi did 'ear tell when Oi was at Lanhydrock that them was doin' away with 'orses and puttin' steam engines in their place," said Bunt.

Polkinghorne stopped walking and turned to Bunt. "What details do you know?"

"Oi just overheard Mr. Clymo one day talkin' about it to one of the men what 'elps 'im," Bunt said, stopping also, a few paces along. "They was talkin' 'bout a Newcomen steam engine, for pumpin' out water down the mines. P'raps Oi could find out more when Oi goes over there. What 'zactly do 'ee need to know?"

"I'll discuss this with the engineer and get a list of questions," said Polkinghorne, picking up his pace again, "but I myself would want to know the price for purchasing such an engine and the cost of fuel and maintenance."

"Aargh," said Bunt moving fast to keep up with him, "an' 'ow many gallons of water it could pump per day, from what depth, whether it could pump sea water, and what kind of fuel would be best. Them people at Lanhydrock sell an almighty lot of fuel to the mines. Could we make charcoal ourselves from the woods round 'ere, to fuel the furnace to raise the steam? Do we 'ave enough 'ard woods to burn charcoal, or would it work better to ship in coal from up country, though it might cost more to buy? For the quarry, Oi'd want to know could we 'ook 'er up to a crusher, or some kind of big shovel, an' could we haul the crushed rock down to the quayside, maybe on a skid of some kind? An' 'ow many tons it could put out in a day? Stuff like that. What kind of men would we need to work it and repair it? That's what Oi'd want to know."

Talking this much had Bunt out of breath, so he slowed down.

"Quite," Polkinghorne said, and cleared his throat to gain a little time to think. Young Bunt actually was getting ahead of him. He raised questions that were beyond Polkinghorne's own sphere of knowledge. He needed to settle him down before things got out of hand. Polkinghorne got a stubby clay pipe out of his pocket, leisurely filled the bowl with tobacco, tamped it firmly with his thumb, topped it with tinder, struck a flint on a piece of iron and set about lighting it, sucking in his cheeks as he did so.

"For the time being, Bunt," Polkinghorne said, ending his silence, "we simply need to estimate how many men will be required, how many picks and shovels and wheelbarrows they will need, and how much will have to be spent. Unless I miss my guess, men will cost a lot less than steam engines."

"You would know best, Mr. Polkinghorne," said Willy deferentially.

"Right," said Polkinghorne, "you give some thought as to how to arrange things around the quay to handle the stone and let me know. Now let's walk across through the village and take a look at where we might site the workings."

Bunt thought a minute; he had a lot of ideas but resolved to keep his counsel for now. The two men walked around the prospective sites, identifying areas of the richest deposits of stone, with Polkinghorne raising questions about possible approaches to layout, manpower, tools, supplies and equipment. Forgetting his resolution of moments ago, Willy Bunt found himself overcome with enthusiasm and making one suggestion after another. Charles Polkinghorne became more and more fascinated with Bunt's ideas and his instinctive grasp of requirements and possibilities, despite his limited education. To make sure that he could remember the ideas, he wrote them down with a pencil in a notebook he had in his pocket. He would present them to Mr. Eliot upon his return, in a meeting that he would arrange while Bunt was in Lanhydrock. He was confident that his employer would be favorably impressed with him, he hoped.

"Where will Mr. Eliot get the money what us need?" asked Bunt.

"Mr. Eliot enjoys substantial investments," said Polkinghorne. "In addition, when he received his place in His Majesty's administration earlier this year, he became remunerated in accordance with the importance and burden of his duties; so, for now, also taking into account the estate's rents from the tenant farmers, there will be sufficient to get a small scale of workings started.

"Then he has in mind approaching adventurers to supply funds for a rapid expansion once the potential is certain," Polkinghorne continued. I have already presented to Mr. Eliot a schedule of tolls for the turnpike, and my expectation is that, once travelers experience the benefits of using the new road, the revenue will be sufficient to pay interest on loans and repay the principal over a very few years."

"Aargh," said Bunt, hoping he sounded wise but in turn being impressed with how Polkinghorne dealt with important matters. He had a grasp of what was required, and it would be no bad thing for Bunt to appreciate it.

"Now, of course," Polkinghorne continued, "next year's parliamentary elections will also require money to persuade voters in the boroughs of the virtue of our candidates, so we must assure adequate supplies of money. There are men in Cornwall who could be approached, and Mr. Eliot has friends in London who no doubt would find it beneficial to allow him to incur their favor."

"If Oi may be so bold as to inquire, zir, would one of those friends be Baron Trenance?" asked Bunt.

"That is not a matter for your concern, Bunt. These are matters where Mr. Eliot relies only on my advice on behalf of the estate. I am, of course, aware that during the negotiations at Port Eliot at which I was present, the baron, then Sir James, was prevailed upon to act as a guarantor of some financing. But I have my doubts whether our master would wish an intimate business relationship with the baron, and I also have some doubt as to whether the baron, in the end, will honor those guarantees."

"Loikely not. Then where would Mr. Eliot turn?" persisted Bunt.

"There are more honorable men in whom to entrust our fortunes," responded Polkinghorne, his desire to impress the young man with his importance outrunning his discretion. "No doubt, Mr. Bolitho would oblige, and I understand that Mr. William Pitt's elder brother, Thomas Pitt of Boconnoc, is one who seeks opportunities, indeed with some urgency. The Eliots also have close connections with the Earl of Chesterfield, whose son Philip Stanhope counts Mr. Eliot a friend and sits in parliament for Liskeard. Possibly our neighbor Lord Edgecumbe would have an interest. Many would welcome sharing opportunities for profit with Mr. Eliot."

"Oi see, zir," said Bunt as confidently as he could muster. Such concerns and arrangements were new to him.

Realizing the information he had placed in Bunt's corner, Polkinghorne added, "But these are matters you must keep under your hat. You keep your mind on the workings, and leave business matters to me."

"Aye, zir," Bunt said, "as you please. But it 'elps me know what to look out for when Oi goes to Lanhydrock."

"Indeed, Lanhydrock," said Polkinghorne. "I am sure Mr. Eliot would invest more than a few coppers to know what Baron Trenance is up to."

Bunt busied his mind, when not focused on the workings, with how to extract such information from the few he trusted at Lanhydrock.

Chapter Twenty-three

Drink

It was getting late and after looking in to the estate office to see if the clerk had any messages for them, Polkinghorne gave Bunt his instructions for the next few days and then sent him on his way home.

"We've done a good day's work, Bunt," said Polkinghorne, "well on the way to completing plans for the quarry. Just need to get some more details. You go into Liskeard tomorrow to the ironmonger and get a list of prices of tools and supplies that we'll need to get started. Don't order anything yet, not before I get a chance to show Mr. Eliot the whole plan. I dare say we'll set up an account for the turnpike trustees rather than paying out of estate funds. Keep everything separate and proper tidy, that will. Now you'd best get off home; you've got family to see to. Let the groom know you'll need a horse tomorrow."

"Right you are, zir, Oi'll take care of that," said Bunt, trying not to scowl. He would have thought by now that Mr. Polkinghorne would have trusted him to have some initiative, without having to give him instructions on every minute detail.

"Then in a few days make your way to Lanhydrock," continued Polkinghorne, oblivious to his underling's impatience. "You might need to stay a day or two to give yourself a chance to get all the information you can. Is that clear?"

Willy was glad to leave and walked across the park to the village. When he got to his cottage he kicked the mud off his boots before opening the door and going inside. The midwife was back again, and he could hear her voice upstairs as she took care of baby Catherine and gave instructions to Mary. He called a greeting.

"Don't you go comin' up them stairs!" shouted the midwife. "Us is doin' women's work an' you got no place 'ere for now. Oi'll come down in a minute an' give you some bread an' cheese for your supper."

"Oi don' need no bread an' cheese from you, old woman," shouted Willy angrily, "Oi come 'ome to see my wife and daughter, not you, ye bloody old witch!"

"Aw, don' 'e take on so, Willy," Mary called, "us'll soon be done with the baby an' all, and Oi want to see you bad."

But Willy stormed out into the evening, not sure where to go or why the scene upstairs had got his anger up, but he walked fast into the village. He was irritated with Polkinghorne and, truth be told, he was a might worried about his upcoming visit to the scene of the horror that had driven him and Mary out of Lanhydrock. Now he saw welcoming lighted windows in a substantial stone building just ahead. The signboard proclaimed it to be The Eliot Arms. He went in through the stout front door and followed another sign to the public bar. There he found a snug low-ceilinged room lit by candles, warmed by a smoky fire, and fuggy with tobacco smoke. There were settles and small tables strewn around the cozy room.

The publican welcomed him. "Evenin' zir, bit raw outside, set yoursel' down. What'll ye 'ave? We've rough cider made local, an' our own 'ome brewed bitter. Pint or 'alf?"

Willy pulled up a stool and sat at the bar. He looked around and saw a handful of men, mostly clutching mugs filled with a foaming brown liquid. Some of them were smoking as well as drinking. Not having ordered in a pub before, he did not want to make a fool of himself.

"Oi'll 'ave same as them."

"Pint o' bitter, comin' up," said the publican as he pulled on the pump handle behind the bar and filled a mug with beer for Willy from the keg down in the cool cellar. "New around 'ere?"

"Aargh," responded Willy. "Got anythin' to eat?"

"'Ow 'bout a nice piece of cheese with home baked bread and a pickled onion?"

When it was popped down in front of him, Willy ate it hungrily and washed it down with the unaccustomed beer. The publican put another hunk of cheese on his platter and refilled his mug.

One of the men in the settle opposite the bar addressed him. "You'm new around 'ere, work up at Port Eliot? Furriner?"

"Oi'm workin' on new quarry, been 'ere few months. From down Bodmin way," Bunt replied.

"Would'n' moind gettin' work over quarry meself, not much farmin' goin' on this toime o' year." The others nodded. The man continued. "Ye in a position to put in a good word?"

"Mebbe," Bunt replied, "assistant manager."

"Aargh. Any fambly?"

"Girl, just born."

"Whaddya call 'er?"

"Catherine."

"Aargh, fancy, loike Mrs. Eliot."

"Aargh," Bunt said, reluctant to expand on his and Mary's connection with the Eliots. He now knew the pitfalls of being perceived to act above his station.

"Better wet the nipper's 'ead, pints all round, eh mateys?"

Willy Bunt found himself surrounded by good cheer as the men charged and recharged his mug and their own, and drank toast after toast to his daughter's health and longevity, along with his own manhood and continued fecundity. Bunt felt increasingly relaxed and at home with his new friends. The village seemed a welcoming place. He and Mary were going to like living here, and maybe in forty years or so when their grandchildren were grown up and had children of their own, they would no longer be foreigners, especially since they were true Cornish.

When it came time to leave he found himself walking unsteadily, just like after sipping the midwife's gin. But it wasn't a bad feeling; in fact the world felt like a good place. He couldn't wait to get home to his loving wife. It had been too long since her protuberant belly had made it awkward for him to demonstrate his affection, or so she had said.

He fiddled with the latch to open the cottage door. There was light from a candle in the bedroom. Willy went to hang up his coat and cap on the peg on the wall. The task was beyond him. He stumbled as he bent to pick up the coat, and he needed a couple of attempts to make it stay in its place. He staggered up the stairs grabbing the rail. Mary and the baby were asleep.

"'Ullo me darlin'," announced Willy, startling Mary. "Oi bet you'm pleased to see us." He took off his jacket and threw it on the floor, and leaned over the bed to embrace her, staggering and falling on top of her. "Give us an 'ug then, it's been a long toime."

"Stop it, Willy," protested Mary, "you stink somethin' awful. Geroff, you're squashing me, and you'll 'urt the baby. Get off!" She tried to roll away, but he was too heavy. As Willy belched and fell asleep, Mary managed to wriggle out of his clumsy embrace. What had happened to her loving and considerate Willy, who had agreed to become her husband, to protect her, when she desperately needed him?

Chapter Twenty-four

Morwenna

A few days later it was time for Bunt to get about his errand to Lanhydrock, to find out what Baron Trenance and Clymo were up to in possibly competing with Port Eliot to supply road stone to the turnpike project. It was cold and drizzling, an insidious damp cold that went through everything, along with the misty rain that was characteristic of the Cornish climate at this time of year, and for that matter many other times of year, too.

Still aggravated and no closer to getting back to his and Mary's old ways of bed sport, Willy had got up early, dressed warmly, kissed a sleepy and reluctant Mary goodbye, broken his fast with a piece of home-baked bread, and stuffed the leftover crust in his pocket. He walked up the long graveled drive to the stables and borrowed a cape to protect from the weather. Mounting the cob that had been saddled for him, he set off on his own towards Bodmin. He kept up a steady pace in order to reach his destination in time for dinner.

The rough and rutted roads were muddy after the rain, so the best he could do was to walk up the hills and trot from time to time on the downhill and level parts unless they were too slippery. He was glad of an excuse not to trot very often. His thigh muscles had not yet got used to raising his body up and down in harmony with the gait of the horse, posting as the experienced riders called it, and the jerky motion made his head ache. He imagined how much better and faster the journey would be once the turnpike was built. A smoother surface without deep ruts and potholes would make a big difference to travelers in this part of Cornwall. He, Willy Bunt, would play an important part in bringing this to pass.

His headache went away after an hour or two. Perhaps Mr. Polkinghorne wasn't such a bad fellow to work for. After all, he and Mr. Eliot thought highly of him, enough to seek his opinion, give him responsibility, appoint him to a well-paying position, and now they had sent him off alone to accomplish a critical mission without their help or oversight.

Into the bargain they had given him an opportunity to get his own back on that bloody rascal Sir James Trenance, although nowadays he supposed he would have to call him Baron Trenance, not that there was much noble about the bastard. Bunt knew that he should be happy with all the good fortune that had befallen him, but something was missing. The coming of the baby was proving more frustrating than fulfilling. She was a dear little mite, and he loved Mary too. His wife was a pretty thing, or would be when she got her figure back, and cheerful and supportive and affectionate for the most part. But since the baby was born she paid much more attention to Catherine than to him, and he needed her affection too. It was only natural.

With his thoughts for company, Willy plodded on, arriving at the outskirts of Liskeard, intending to stop only to rest a few minutes and water his horse at Pipe Well, since he probably would not have time to look in on Mary's sister Nellie at Eliot House. There would be plenty of opportunity on his way back to give Nellie news of Mary and the baby and to talk about her standing as little Catherine's second godmother. But the sign for The Barleysheaf nearby caught his eye and he thought that a nice drop of beer would be more refreshing than water, and besides he'd grown to like its bitter taste and the warm glow it gave him. Now that he had a good job and coins in his pocket, what better way to spend them?

Willy tethered his steaming horse at the rail outside and went in through the door to the public bar. He took off his damp cloak, shook off the clinging beads of drizzle and hung it over the back of a chair near the fire to dry off. He ordered a pint of bitter and stayed longer than he had intended, talking with the few locals there at that time of day, and long enough to down another pint. Nellie would definitely have to wait until his return. The cob would be refreshed by its rest, so maybe he could make up time on the last leg of his journey. He climbed up the mounting block and set off.

In a few hours he saw the squat tower of St. Petroc's through the leafless trees and soon after stopped at the hunting lodge at the entrance to Lanhydrock. He tucked his muffler over his chin as the porter came out to ask his purpose. The porter, to his relief, confirmed that Baron Trenance was still not back from London and gave Willy directions to the house where Joseph Clymo and his daughter Morwenna now lived. He didn't think the porter recognized him, but it didn't really matter if he did. The rest soon would.

He rode through the park to the estate manager's house, dismounted stiffly and tethered the cob by the gate to the little garden. Mr. Clymo might not be at home at this time of day, and if not he would just ride over to the back of the big house and go into the servants quarters and see whom he could find to strike up a conversation. He knew he had been well liked and was sure he would find friends there. He knocked on the front door of the house and heard footsteps inside; he was in luck. But it was not Mr. Clymo who answered the door. It was Morwenna, and she smiled broadly when she saw who it was.

"Willy Bunt," she said, "as I live and breathe! What on earth are you doing here? We all thought you were lost and gone to heaven. I'm so pleased to see you. Where have you been? Come on in and sit down."

Willy was surprised at how glad he was to see her. He had always had a soft spot for the attractive Morwenna Clymo, and who knows how things might have turned out if she had known a year ago what an important man he would become. She had encouraged him at the servants' Boxing Day party last Christmas with a little canoodling in the empty butler's pantry.

"Pleased to see you likewise, miss," said Bunt, "Oi just popped in loike to see if your dad were 'ome."

"Well he's not now, but I expect him for supper. He's out and about looking after business. He's been doing a lot of traveling, down west and all. Take off your coat and make yourself comfortable by the fire."

"What be 'e doin' down them parts? Oi'd of thought 'e 'ad plenty to occupy 'imself at 'ome."

"Since the old baron died, the new one has been pressing Dad to provide him with more income, improving the mines. Did you hear that Sir James is now Baron Trenance? He's been up in London for the parliamentary sitting. He's taking quite an interest in the House of Lords. Lady Trenance has been with him lately, and they left the baby here at home with Nanny. They'll be coming back for Christmas soon."

Willy was impressed with how much Morwenna knew about the goings on in the Trenance family. She very likely could be as good a source of information as her father, perhaps of a different kind. But he would have to watch his step; she clearly was no fool. He mustn't give too much away.

"Would you like some tea?" Morwenna asked Bunt. "It is such a treat. Dad is able to get some from the baron. Milk and sugar, or lemon? I'll put a drop of brandy in to warm you up."

"Just the same as you," Bunt replied, since tea was quite new to him.

Morwenna rang for the maid and ordered the tea with toasted and buttered crumpets.

"Now you haven't told me about yourself, Willy. What's going on in your life? Where are you living? Have you got a sweetheart? Anyone you fancy, handsome lad like you? Y'know, I recall something about you and that pretty little upstairs maid, Mary Abbott. She's gone off somewhere too. Have you heard anything of her?"

"Well, miss, now you asks, us is married loike," said Willy, looking away from Morwenna.

"My stars, that was quick. Get her in the family way did you? You're a lively lad, and no mistake!"

"Not zackly, miss. Oi did'n' know if she were or weren't. 'Er did'n' tell us 'til a month or two ago, when 'er knew for sure like."

"When is the baby due then? How soon?"

"Little girl, born last week 'er was."

"That was quick work." Morwenna counted on her fingers. "So she must have got with child about the time you left Lanhydrock!"

Bunt was silent. He was right to be wary of Morwenna. She was quick, that was clear. But they could be friends. Maybe they could trust each other. Maybe they could have things in common. He would have to see.

"What are you calling her? Is she healthy?" persisted Morwenna. "Got all her fingers and toes? How is Mary doing?"

"She's a dear little mite," Willy responded, "although there is one thing. 'Er toes got webs between them, second and third. Midwife said 'twould do 'er no 'arm, not when 'er grows up."

"Webbed toes!" exclaimed Morwenna. "But that's just like the baron, and the Honorable James! What a surprise. They must be related. But how could that be?"

"But 'ow do you know?" asked Willy.

"Nanny told me," said Morwenna quickly, looking him right in the eyes, daring him to question her further. "P'r'aps I shouldn't have said anything."

"The baron as well as the baby?" pressed Willy. "'Ow would that be?"

"Can you keep a secret, Willy?" Morwenna demanded impetuously. Bunt nodded; she had not called him by his Christian name before. "I've got to tell somebody, can't keep it bottled up inside me any longer. We've always been friends since we were little nippers, haven't we? Used to have fun playing."

"Cross me 'eart and 'ope to die," said Willy, reaching for Morwenna's hand.

"You must swear to me to tell no one, or I'll make your life miserable, and don't doubt I can." Willy nodded, now all ears.

Morwenna continued, "Baron Trenance, Sir James as was, had his way with me, made me become his mistress, he forced me. Then he made me promise to keep my mouth shut or else he'd sack my dad and make sure we both starved. I'll wager the same thing happened to poor little Mary. When he took off his breeches and his stockings I couldn't help seeing his feet. There were webs between the second and third toes!"

"That bloody bastard!" yelled Willy, jumping to his feet. "He forced my Mary, too, up in the stable. 'E was too strong for 'er. Us knows for sure, I saw it with my own eyes. Mary were goin' to meet me there, and

Sir James followed 'er out. 'E'd 'ad 'is eyes on 'er for some time. Oi took 'er away with us. An' then she found she was 'avin' 'is baby, an she was so relieved when Oi said Oi'd marry 'er and take care of 'er. What Oi'd give to lay my hands on that bugger!"

"Me, too, Willy, now that I know him better. What am I going to do? He was kind and considerate at first, and very generous, and I liked being invited to ride to hounds with him. But then I found he has a vile temper and lots else that's ugly about him. At least he hasn't got me pregnant; well I don't think he has. If my father found out, I don't know what he'd do."

Morwenna put her head in her hands and rocked forward in her chair. "Oh, Willy, is there some way you can help me? I don't know what to do." She began to sob, and stood up and moved closer to Willy. He stood, too, and couldn't help allowing her to come into his arms. He could smell the scent of her hair. She really was a tantalizingly attractive woman, and apparently quite experienced, and Mary had been so unapproachable lately. Who would ever know?

At that moment there was a rattle as the front door opened. They sprang apart, and Willy quickly resumed his seat. Someone was moving about in the little entrance hall, then Joseph Clymo opened the door of the parlor and walked in.

"Father, you're early. How good to see you," Morwenna said, trying to slow her breathing. "Look, we have a surprise visitor. And you're arrived just in time. The maid has put the kettle on for a pot of tea. You must be thirsty after your long day. I'll ring the bell for her." She embraced her father and kissed him on the cheek. "You remember Willy Bunt, don't you?"

"Bunt," said Clymo, "thought we'd seen the back of you. What are you doing at Lanhydrock? Looking for your old place back? Not much chance of that; the baron's not one to forget and forgive."

"'Twasn't Oi what did no 'arm, zir, anyroad. You'd have to look elsewhere for that. Oi just came by to pick up some of my things what Oi left 'ere."

"Do you recall that Mary Abbott the upstairs maid left about the same time, father? Well, they are married now, just had a little girl," said Morwenna.

"Can't say I do remember her. Don't hold with servant gossip," said Clymo. "You need a job, Bunt, keep you out of mischief. You need to make a fresh start, act responsibly, likely lad like you. They're looking for more men down west, at the Poldice tin mine. You could make a decent wage; the baron hardly ever gets down there. You could support your family in time."

"That there's a long way, zir. Oi don't know nothin' about mining; don't know if Oi could do the work, not down those dark pits. What be goin' on that they need men?"

"You don't need to know, Bunt, all you need is a job. Anyway, it wouldn't actually be mining. We're opening up a new project. Something I suggested to Baron Trenance, making use of the tailings. He thinks well of it," said Clymo proudly.

Morwenna smiled to herself. She always learned more from listening to what her father told other men, even of lower class, than from what he ever told her directly. So her father had passed on her idea to crush the tailings that would otherwise be wasted to use for road stone, and he had of course taken credit for it. Just wait until she next had a private conversation with James! She'd let him know whose idea it had been. Maybe he would be nicer for a while.

"Doesn't sound much good to us, just a pile of old rocks," said Bunt, rubbing on the subject to see if more were to be got from Clymo.

"That's why you do what you do, and I do what I do," said Clymo, smoothing the back of his head and arching his neck. One has to have imagination and see possibilities to get ahead."

"Wish Oi'd 'ad your education, zir. Oi'm willin' to work as 'ard as the next man. Just 'aven't 'ad no opportunity. You'm very fortunate, zir."

Joseph Clymo had not intended to converse at length on the merits of his station with Bunt who had no importance in his life, but he warmed to his admiring audience. Morwenna observed her father squaring his shoulders and looking more complacent and self-important than usual, and she smiled to herself again. She realized that she must not underestimate Willy.

"It's more than good fortune, young man. I have applied myself, and I strive constantly to learn more about the world and affairs, so that I can bring opportunities to the baron. Likely you don't understand, but take these tailings as an example; if they're crushed and properly sized they will make excellent surfaces for the new turnpikes. And one must be farsighted as to methods. Do you know that up country they've been using steam engines for some time to drive pumping machines? Some folks say that in time they will do the work of a score of horses, and they need no fodder and not much rest. Invented by a Devon man, Thomas Newcomen, but we won't hold that against him, eh Bunt?"

"Don't sound to me no pumpin' engine would be much good for crushin' rocks, zir. Anyroad, they'd need somethin' to feed 'em if not 'ay. Besides, they must cost a pretty penny, more'n most men 'ave lyin' about."

"Oh don't you worry about such things, Bunt. Those are matters I understand, that's my job, to do the worrying, figuring things out. That's what the baron wants, you mark my words, pays me well, too. These engines are a marvel and can be adapted to drive crushing mills and stamps. Most people fuel the boilers with wood, or better charcoal, and Lanhydrock makes a lot of money supplying them. But for the mines we operate I'm going to improve on that. I have calculated that shipping in coal will be more efficient, probably bring it in to St. Agnes from the pits in south Wales. Might pay to get into the coal business. The harbor would need rebuilding, of course. The government just needed to end the tax on sea-borne coal. As for money, thanks to my persuasion and the baron's connections, we can lay our hands on plenty when we need it."

"Oi see, zir. Wish Oi knew about such things."

"Money is power, young fellow, when you understand how to make use of its influence, even if you don't part with a single guinea. Why, we have even convinced some simple bumpkins at Liskeard that we will stand behind their borrowings to build their turnpike. And that's with another man's store of gold put at our disposal because of the baron's position."

"Ow'd you do that?" asked an admiring Bunt.

A gleam came into Clymo's eye as he bent towards Bunt. "The fools believe they have a contract of guaranty, but it was drawn by our notary on my advice, and there is no power to enforce any claim they might have on us. Now, if they think we're contributing to the turnpike, and if you have a shred of imagination, whom do you fancy will be favored to supply the stone for the road bed?" He sat back and watched for Bunt's reaction, but Bunt just stared at him with feigned admiration and a look of dumb incomprehension.

"Is that why you have been spending so much time with Mr. Bolitho lately, father?" asked Morwenna.

Judging that it was futile to try and make Bunt understand, though he was relieved in a way, since he had said more than he should have, Joseph Clymo glanced at Morwenna. "We don't need to go into that now, my dear. Don't worry your pretty head about such things; leave them to me. Now where's that tea? Hurry it up. I have other important matters to attend to, and Bunt had better be going on his way."

The maid entered carrying a tray laden with a teapot and cups and saucers that she set before Morwenna and then withdrew. No one's attention was on Bunt while Morwenna went through the pouring ritual. He hid a smile as he reflected on the implications of what Mr. Clymo had let drop. This time he would keep his own counsel until he could tell not only Mr. Polkinghorne but also Mr. Eliot himself in person. They would be most interested to learn that their suspicions of Sir James bloody Baron Trenance's intentions to steal their turnpike business were well founded, and how he planned to undercut the price. Armed with this information, they could plan counter measures that ensured his failure.

As Morwenna passed Bunt his cup of tea she studied his face with a new awareness. He appeared serene, confident, half smiling, pleased with himself. No, she thought, Willy Bunt is quite attractive and furthermore he is nobody's fool. She had better watch herself or she would get into more trouble, and after all Willy was married now and with a fmily.

Chapter Twenty-five

Captain

A week or so before Christmas, a horse and cart drew up outside the cottage in Gwennap where Addis Penwarden and his family lived. Addis had been newly appointed mine captain at the Wheal Hykka mine, so the family was moving to Pendeen to be near his work. Jonathon Turner, a member of the Methodist congregation in Gwennap, had offered to lend them his horse and cart and give them a hand packing up their meager possessions and carrying them to their new home.

Things were looking up for Addis, Lizzie and their two boys. John Williams, the mine captain at Poldice who had recommended Addis to Joseph Clymo and the Trenance interests, was proving a good friend and mentor who sought Penwarden out as an ally.

Williams had seen to it that Addis would receive much higher wages in his new position, with bonus money if his management led to the mine being more profitable. Penwarden couldn't do much about the market price of tin and copper, but he could choose reliable tributers, encourage them to produce as much high-yield ore as possible below ground, see to it that supplies of powder and tools and candles were plentiful and of good quality yet not overstocked, and manage the hauling and stamping works above ground efficiently.

It appeared that Joseph Clymo was committed to making funds available to enable improvements to increase production and profits at the mine. Addis had some ideas about that. He was already secure in his leadership ability; he was willing to learn new skills; and he was confident that he could make a success of this opportunity.

"We'm goin' to 'ave a much better life, me luv," said Addis, putting his hand on Lizzie's shoulder and giving her a squeeze. "Big house, 'ave a seamstress run up a pretty dress for you, you won't 'ave to work no more at the mine, plenty of food. It'll be really nice for all of we."

Lizzie was a good trouper and had always supported her husband, like a good wife should, but as the time to leave approached she seemed reluctant. She did not respond to his affectionate gesture.

"What's goin' on with you now, Lizzie?" said Addis. "Oi'd've thought you'd be lookin' forward to this, new 'ome, better job. Good opportunity, better for the boys, you an' me together, 'tis an adventure. Oi'm just doin' me best to make things better for us."

"Oi know you be, Addis. It's goin' to be strange, that's all. Us've always lived in Gwennap, us an' our 'ole famblies, aunts an' uncles, cousins, nieces an' nephews, there's always been Penwardens in Gwennap as long as anyone can remember." Lizzie caught her breath and tears rolled down her reddened cheeks.

"Aw, come on, Lizzie, you'll love it. You'll quickly get to know people, 'ave new friends an' all. Reverend Perry won't be far away. An' Mr. Williams says there's three bedrooms in the house, Jemmy and Jedson can 'ave their own. An' maybe us'll 'ave a little girl one day, 'er can 'ave 'er own too, when 'er's big enough."

"That'd be lovely, Addis, Oi'd loike that. Us could find a carpenter to make some beds, you'll be too busy now in your new job. An' you said there's a back kitchen with a pump, so Oi won't 'ave to go out in the cold to fetch water from a well neither."

"There is, yes, Lizzie, and a parlor. Us could 'ave people in, company loike, treat 'em proper nice. Oi'll be Cap'n Penwarden from now on, people will look up to us. Us'll 'ave a position to keep up."

Lizzie looked up at him, raised her eyebrows. Whatever question or doubt she still harbored remained unasked. "Us'd better get on, Addis, or us'll never be ready in time," she said. Wiping her tears on her sleeve, Lizzie launched into packing up with her usual energy and good sense, throwing out the few accumulated things they would no longer need.

Their life at Pendeen would be good, thought Lizzie, once they got settled in. She had to make sure of that and Addis deserved nothing less. John Williams had promised them that the company would provide Addis with the use of a horse, so that he would not waste time walking from the village to the mine and back, even though it was quite close. He would also be expected from time to time to ride into Penzance to meet with suppliers and customers. Perhaps, eventually, they would get a cart as well, so that Lizzie and the boys could ride with Addis to chapel or into the shops in Penzance. Her husband was going to be an important man and people would look up to her, too.

As Lizzie and Jemmy helped Addis and Jonathon Turner stack the last of their belongings into the cart and cover them against the threatening rain, her daydreams were interrupted by a pony and cart coming from the village. Perhaps someone was delivering their own cart already. But no, it was the Reverend Perry driving with John Williams as his passenger. They were coming to wish them farewell.

"It's the entire Penwarden family hard at work!" called the Reverend Perry. "Gwennap is going to miss your industry, especially at the chapel, not to say your voices for the hymn singing. We've come to see how you are getting along, and to make sure we stay in touch. And, of course, to ensure that Brother Jonathon is doing his fair share."

"And I have come to give you some last-minute advice, because that is what I do," said John Williams, smiling broadly.

"Thank 'ee both," said Addis, taking out a big red kerchief and mopping at the sweat that had broken out on his brow despite the cool temperature. "Let's go inside and chat a while. Lizzie, be a dear an' get us some nice cold water. That's thirsty work." He ran the kerchief over his brow again.

Jonathon made sure his horse was tethered, then put on its nosebag with a couple of handfuls of oats. The horse would need all its energy when they set off with this load.

They all went into the cottage and settled down, Lizzie taking the baby to his crib at the back.

"Penwarden, we are all counting on you," said John Williams, taking the chair nearest the fire. "I know you will not let me down. Just count on me to help with any support and advice I can as you learn the ropes. I'll come over and spend some time with you once you've settled in. Now that I own a small part of the Trenance mining company, I have an even bigger interest in your success. Be clear that if you make a bigger profit at Wheal Hykka, you will be rewarded. That's how you will be judged. And consult with me on plans for the improvements, and I will in turn support you with Clymo."

"Thank 'ee, zir, Oi appreciate what you 'ave done for me, and Oi'm goin' to make sure that Oi continue to earn your regard. But Oi been thinkin'. What Oi must do, too, is make the mines safer for the miners. There's no two ways about it; us can't allow so many injuries and, worse, deaths."

"I praise the Almighty that you hold this determination in your heart," said the Reverend Perry. "The tinners of Wheal Hykka are blessed to have you as their new captain."

"I sympathize, Penwarden, Reverend, I really do," Williams said, "but I must emphasize that your job and, indeed, your personal well-being, depend on profits. I will support you in making gradual improvements for the workers as profits come to pay for them. Consult me closely on this though, as we do not want to offend Mr. Clymo, let alone the baron, with too much independent thinking, or your career will be short-lived and you will be in no position to do good for anybody, certainly not a bunch of raggletaggle miners, for that is how the mineral lords regard them, make no mistake."

Addis listened carefully, his jaw set, but he did not respond.

"Take heed of what I say, Penwarden," said John Williams, "or you will regret it. It'll take money as well as hard work to make Wheal Hykka profitable, and for that you'll need to be on Joseph Clymo's good side. Make money for the adventurers and they'll listen to you. Then you can bring up safety."

Lizzie came over to pass the water around. She had been listening to what the men were saying and spoke up. "Surely you know that my 'usband is a good man. Oi'm so proud of 'im. But a change come over 'im when his brother was killed down that mine. Oi 'spect the drink did'n' 'elp Jedson neither, God rest 'is soul. Addis loved 'im, us all did, our 'ole fambly, 'is friends, never a cross word passed 'is lips, 'e were cheerfulness itself, good for a laugh, always offerin' an 'elpin'. There were a 'uge congregation down chapel at 'is funeral, tinners, Gwennap village, you Reverend Perry, you Mr. Turner, and you, too, Mr. Williams."

"Lizzie, Lizzie, 'ush now," protested Addis.

"Oi 'aven't finished, Addis," Lizzie said, lifting her chin and shaking a finger. "Nary a one from Lanhydrock showed their faces, not Mr. Clymo let alone that bastard Sir James fancy boots Trenance. He took Jedson's work, 'e took 'is life, but them took no notice of 'im, them would'n' give tuppence for 'is soul. 'E were just a tinner to them, like all the tinners, just for them gettin' more rich, but 'e was fambly to we. 'E'll never 'ave 'is own fambly now, not now 'e's dead." She paused to brush away a tear but she kept going.

"How many tinners does it cost to get a ton of ore? 'Ow many famblies 'ave to grieve to pay for a great big 'ouse? Them took no notice of my dear brother-in-law, us never 'eard nothin' from they. But Oi'll tell you who took notice, my 'usband took notice. Them'll 'ear from my Addis, an' people listen to 'im, don't you make no mistake."

Tears streamed unchecked down Lizzie's red face. The men were silent and cast down their eyes. Then Reverend Perry spoke.

"My dear Mrs. Penwarden, I hardly know what to say. I had intended to call on you and your husband after you had settled in at Pendeen. But I have now with me a most compelling letter from Mr. Wesley after his recent visit to us in Cornwall. He told me of the new chapel being built in Redruth, a place that not so long ago reviled and rejected him. More than progress in the material realm, he wrote of his personal Savior, as you yourselves have heard him preach, of His comfort in times of trouble, but also of his own exhortations to raise ourselves up, by our own efforts. Allow me to read a paragraph to you."

"Please go ahead, Reverend," Penwarden said, "us all need much comfort and encouragement."

John Williams' face was impassive as Perry took the letter out of his coat pocket, unfolded it and read:

"Experience shows us that even they who are Christians indeed, who serve God with all their strength, may go on their way weeping, perhaps for many years, perhaps to

the end of this transitory life. They are followers of Him who was a man of sorrows and acquainted with grief; and if any man will come after him he must deny himself, and take up his cross; he must suffer with his master, to be made perfect through sufferings. For this very cause are these sufferings permitted, to lead them to higher perfection; they go on their way weeping, that the good seed they bear may yield them more fruit; and that good seed (even all those Christian virtues which are perfected by affliction) shall in due time grow up into a plenteous harvest of rest, and joy, and life eternal."

"Amen, Reverend," said Williams, relieved that the passage spoke of endurance rather than outright rebellion. "Did he say more?"

"That he did, Mr. Williams, that he did. He charged me as his exhorter, indeed as the messenger of our Savior himself, to lead our people to a better life not only in the world to come, but also in our world here on earth. And, above all, he charged me to inspire the help of all good men and women to pursue that aim with faith, energy, conviction and hard work."

"Us'll join ye, Reverend," said Addis and Lizzie Penwarden.

"I regard that as a holy commitment from you both," said Perry. "Mr. Williams, may I count on your wholehearted support of Mr. Penwarden to improve the safety of the miners at Wheal Hykka, and you yourself to do the same at Poldice?"

"Mr. Perry, you may," said Williams, clearly moved. "But I have laid out my cautions already. We must take this slowly, or Penwarden will lose his job, and any hope of improvements to conditions will be lost in the bargain."

"Mr. Penwarden, as I may count on your wholehearted support for that and more," said the Reverend, "there are important charges that I must add. Mr. Wesley calls on us to help our fellows cast out their demons, above all the demon drink. Drunkenness is a destroyer of men, of families, and it leads to riotous behavior, injury, sickness, poverty and vice. Drink is the curse of the laboring poor. We must lead our fellows to total abstinence through the love of our Savior, the only sure cure."

"Oh, Reverend," cried Lizzie, "indeed you can. Oi promise to show the way to as many as Oi can, to save them from what befell Addis' brother."

"There is more," Reverend Perry cleared his throat. "Mr. Wesley, above all, charges us all to get to the root of the improvement of our people, education. We must provide schools. We will start with Sunday schools to teach the children the Good News, to bring them up in virtue and faith. But we must, as well, provide learning to all the people, so that the lives of even the humble tinner and his family may be enriched with knowledge and understanding."

"On that, you may definitely count on me," said Williams, glad of a subject on which he did not have to advise caution. "If I may be more candid than you might wish, Penwarden, you could gain in your career through education, through a better knowledge of our rich English language and its grammar, and through a practical familiarity with arithmetic. Your voice will be heard clearly by our betters, and your influence will be increased if you think as they think and speak as they speak."

"Betters!" scoffed Lizzie. "Oi don't know about that, but Oi do know that if you will teach me, Mr. Perry, Oi will work 'ard to teach others, that you can count on."

It was time to stop talking and set off if Jonathon Turner was to get the Penwardens and their belongings settled in their new home in Pendeen before nightfall. Lizzie picked up little Jedson, wrapped him up warmly against the cold and looked around for her elder son. He was nowhere to be seen.

"Jemmy!" she called. "Where you'm to now? Us got to get off, hurry up." The back door opened and in came Jemmy, carrying a stout stick as tall as himself. "What you been up to, what you got there? There's no room to take that gurt long stick in the cart. Throw 'er away."

"Aw, Mum," said Jemmy, "Oi just been lookin' around, loike, one last time. Oi found this stick, 'er's a good un, might need it to protect us when us gets to Pendeen." He sniffed bravely and looked appealingly at his dad. "Besides, it's right from nearby, 'ere in Gwennap where Oi grew up."

"Let the boy keep it,' said Addis. "Lad's just doin' 'is bit." Addis led his family out into the cold and over to the cart. He and Lizzie waved their goodbyes to John Williams with lightened hearts and the promise of enlightened minds. Lizzie ran back into the cottage and took one last look around to make sure the fire was properly banked so that it could safely be left to die down and that nothing had been left behind. Jonathan Turner and the four Penwardens then piled into the wagon and headed for Pendeen and a new life.

It was a bumpy ride, and they had to stop along the way to tie on extra ropes to prevent their things from falling off. One wheel was cocked by a boulder that Jonathon Turner could not avoid and Lizzie took a tight hold on Jedson. Addis reached out for a too adventurous Jemmy so that he did not fall off.

The countryside they passed through this far west in Cornwall was quite unlike the patchwork of fertile fields and woods and high stone and earth hedges further northeast, the barren moors of the center, the rugged escarpments of the Atlantic coast or the softer cliffs and coves on the

Channel side. The winter day was grey and their surroundings looked bleak.

Mining hereabouts had turned this landscape into a wasteland, yet with an austere and evocative beauty of its own. The buildings were solid, industrial; they surely had not been constructed with architectural beauty in mind. The piled-up tips for the tailings and the scars of diggings would never be walled in for decorative parks of the great houses of the rich. Addis mused that this is probably what the surface of the moon looked like, although he was too much of a realist to think that any man would ever be a witness to that distant desolation.

They were on the road to Morvah when they caught sight of the ancient and mysterious Men-an-Tol, one of the many megalithic monuments still surviving in Cornwall. It comprised three great boulders each four- to five-feet tall. The one in the middle was like a letter "O" standing on edge, flanked a few feet apart by two standing stones. Jemmy's curiosity was aroused, which was not hard to do. He guessed that his parents would be unable to give him an answer, so he asked their driver. "What's them big ol' rocks then, Mr. Turner? What's them for? Who put 'em there?"

"I don't know how them got there, young feller, just that whoever 'twas must've done it 'undreds of years ago," said Jonathon Turner. He pulled back on the reins and stopped his horse to give it a rest while letting Jemmy jump off the cart and run over the short spongy turf to take a closer look.

"The old women 'ere abouts said if you passed a child through the 'ole in that there round boulder, it would never get rickets," said Jonathon Turner. Addis frowned and looked quizzically at him. Turner went on, "My old gran said 'er knew a woman who 'ad the ague, real bad. An old crone who dabbled in herbs an' such told 'er to crawl through that 'ole seven times against the sun. Well, 'er did and 'twasn't many months before 'er was cured. Mind, Oi never told Reverend Perry about that."

Addis snorted. "Old wives' tales. Come on, Jemmy, get back in the cart," he called, "us need to get on."

Jemmy did as he was told. Jonathon Turner did not reply, just flapped the reins against the horse's rump. The horse leaned into the collar and jerked the cart forward on its way.

Looking her husband in the eye Lizzie said quietly, "Reverend Perry says our ancestors were really wise and there's a lot in them tales from a long time ago. There be a lot of truth in 'em, that's what Oi think."

They plodded on in silence for a mile or two. A cold wind picked up, gusting from their right towards the north, the Atlantic Ocean. The passengers huddled together to keep warm and Lizzie pulled the shawl tighter over the baby. Then Jonathon Turner announced, "Soon be there now." Jemmy stood up in the cart to get a better view, grabbing the side rail to steady himself. "Look," he said, "a signpost pointin' straight ahead. That's a letter 'P,' like Mum showed us."

"You'm quite right, young man," said Jonathon Turner, "us'll soon be at Pendeen. 'Ave to ask someone where your new place is. Now, young nipper, you sit yourself down so you don't fall."

They passed a lone cottage, then a group of cottages in a row. They turned at a corner past an inn, The Trewellard Arms. The countryside was stark, windswept, gently rolling, sparse with few grazing animals and few trees, yet commanding a compelling kind of beauty to which Lizzie felt she would grow deeply attached in time. The road was stony, sloping to the north. They passed a two-story house on the right, bigger than most of the cottages. It appeared deserted, no smoke coming out of the chimneys and they saw no one they could ask.

"Stayin' indoors to keep warm on a day like this," said Lizzie.

Addis shook his head. "Workin' at the mines more likely," he said.

They passed several cottages close together and one or two bigger houses on the left and a big building that looked like a chapel or gathering place. They had reached the main part of the village of Pendeen.

The wind picked up, blew cold. Jemmy pulled his coat closer around him. He stood up again, holding on tight with one hand as the cart lurched along. As they crested a rise he waved his other arm and called out excitedly, "Oi see the sea, Oi see the sea! Look at them big waves. Oi thought the sea was blue, this 'ere's grey."

A few yards further on in an instant they all caught sight of the great expanse of ocean stretching out for miles to a distant horizon. Lizzie gasped and clutched Addis by the hand. She had never seen anything like this before. There were more buildings between them and the cliffs, some down right near the edge of the sea, and signs for mine workings. Addis did not see a sign for Wheal Hykka; it must be further along.

"The boy's right," said Jonathon Turner. "That there's the Atlantic Ocean, it be blue when the sun's shining. Us've come too far, Cap'n Penwarden, need to turn 'round. If us goes much farther us'll be at Lands End. Oi reckon that there empty 'ouse is what we'm lookin' for. Should've thought of that before."

"Wait, Mr. Turner," said Lizzie, "let's go on down an' get closer. If we'm goin' to live close to the sea Oi want to see what it's like."

Addis nodded and they drove on down a rough rutted track gently sloping towards the sea. Its stones were different colors, grey, brown, mottled, mostly red. They passed a lot of mine workings and buildings. Addis would have to find out how to get to Wheal Hykka before he set off for his first day of work there as captain. Right now he just wanted to find their house. They saw one or two men walking out of one of the buildings too far away to hail to ask directions. Most of the people working there must have been inside or down below in the shafts. They reached a point where they could look down a steep rise into a cove far below where waves smashed violently against rugged rocks and threw angry spray skyward.

"My," said Lizzie, leaning against Addis, "Oi wouldn't want to be stuck in a boat down there. You'd be smashed to pieces. Keep me on dry land where it's safe. Them poor fishermen what 'as to go out in all weathers, Oi wouldn't wish that on me worst enemy."

Addis patted her shoulder. "Don't you worry my love," he said, "stick by me, Oi'll always protect you, just you see." Lizzie leaned her head against his cheek. "Come on now," continued Addis, "time for us to find that new place of ours." He was silent as Jonathon Turner turned the cart around and headed back up towards the village. Addis took a last look towards the forbidding sea and the rocky landscape. Wheal Hykka must be close by, he mused. He would get to see it soon enough when he went there to take up his new job. So this was where they would be living now. The land was filled with rocks like Gwennap, but being so close to the Atlantic Ocean made it feel different. They would get used to it; anyroad, they had no choice. This was where they would live.

They soon reached the house they had spotted on their way down. Addis jumped down from the cart and went through its gate. The house stood alone behind a dry stone wall. It was sturdy, built of stone that harmonized with the landscape, no doubt hewn from a quarry nearby. There were four pots on two chimneystacks on the roof, one on each side. The roof was slate as was the cladding on the side walls. The ridge and edges of the roof were yellowed with lichen, flourishing in the damp climate.

There was a lone May tree, a hawthorn, growing between the house and the hedge by the road. It was gnarled and bent as if it could not grow upright against the force of the wind and the rain; it seemed lifeless. Addis said, "Oi'll go look an' see if this be the right place." He stopped by the tree and patted its trunk, almost as if he were encouraging it in its battle against the elements. Proper Cornish, he thought; it bends but it does not break. He turned up his coat collar and walked right up to the house. He found a note nailed to the front door. He brought it back to Jonathon Turner to read.

"Penwardens," Turner read, "key under stone to right of door." He drove the cart through a side entrance right up to the house. Addis found the key and unlocked and opened the door. He beckoned to the others to follow him. Lizzie was uncharacteristically silent, then smiled quietly. Stiffly climbing down from the cart and holding Jedson, she walked up the path to the red painted front door, noticing a path that continued around to the side past a fenced paddock. John Williams had told Addis that there was a big kitchen garden at the back, with currant bushes, gooseberries and fruit trees.

"Us could keep a cow," cried Lizzie, breaking into a wide grin, "get our own milk, keep chickens."

"An' Oi could 'ave me own pony!" enthused young Jemmy.

Lizzie brushed a tear from the corner of her eye. This would be her home? Why it was a castle compared with their old cottage. There were two white-framed windows on either side of the center door and four more upstairs. They went inside. Addis shut the door to keep the draught out. The house was indeed empty, cold and dimly lit but not forbidding. Lizzie gasped as she saw a parlor on each side of the center hall, each with its own fireplace, and thrilled as she went through to the separate kitchen with its iron stove and the utilitarian scullery with its own pump beyond.

"Oi think Oi can be very 'appy 'ere; Oi've almost forgot Gwennap already," Lizzie said, handing baby Jedson to Jemmy and clapping her hands. "Oi'm goin' to like bein' a captain's wife, an' Oi'm going into Penzance to buy meself a new dress and a nice 'at. Now all we 'ave to do is strive to 'elp others be as well off as we is, just like Reverend Perry told us."

"We'll do that, indeed we will," said Addis quietly as he hung his hat on a peg by the back door and looked around. He walked over to Lizzie and put his arm around her shoulders. "This be a proper place, our very own 'ome. Come on, my sweetheart, let's get a fire lit an' then get to work haulin' our things in."

"It'll be really lovely 'ere in Pendeen, us'll all be 'appy," said Lizzie. She would put down her family's roots in this place. She smiled warmly up at her husband, but then she frowned and her shoulders sagged. "You won't get too uppity now you're captain, eh me 'andsome? You'll still look out for the tinners, right, not be just on the side of them rich people?"

Chapter Twenty-six

Christmas Goose

In the new year, Lizzie Penwarden settled into their new home at Pendeen and her new life as a mine captain's wife. She told herself that she did not get out and about much because she was too busy setting up house and looking after little Jedson, but really she was not yet ready to reach out to strangers. She liked the house more and more and quickly realized that what at first she took as unaccustomed spaciousness was actually emptiness unfilled by their scanty possessions.

Lizzie thought she would someday like to have comfortable parlor chairs with arms, but for now even a few benches and stools would be welcome. The house had been cleaned before it had been turned over to them, but she nevertheless went to work with enthusiasm to bring it up to her newly rewarding standards of neatness and cleanliness. She reminded herself to clean the new tripod skillet Addis had given her for Christmas. She would now be able to cook smaller amounts than before without using the big crock pot.

The morning was bright and chill that first day Lizzie kissed Addis goodbye seeing him off to the Wheal Hykka mine. She realized she would have to become used to staying home. Her time as a bal maiden picking and sorting ore on the surface at the mine was over. Even after Baby Jedson became old enough to be left in someone else's care during the day, Lizzie would not go back to work at the mine. However, she was determined to keep her promise to Reverend Perry and spare some time to help him with the new school. She was equally determined that young Jemmy would be one of the first pupils.

Her main job for now was to take care of her husband and her children, do the housekeeping, and get them settled in. For the time being Jemmy would stay home with her. She welcomed his company and found it useful to have an extra pair of hands helping around the house.

She called to her son. "Come on over 'ere and help me tidy up in the kitchen. Then you can 'elp me throw out the Christmas decorations."

"Aw mum, Oi want to go out and explore," said Jemmy. "Besides I told my new friends that I'd meet them down the road."

Just like a boy, thought Lizzie. "You're twelve now," she said, "old enough to make yourself more useful. Come on, many 'ands make light work."

"My dad said once 'e gets settled in at Wheal Hykka, Oi could go to the mine with 'im, learn the ropes like. Do proper men's work. Besides, women and girls do 'ousework," Jemmy added, his hands on his hips.

"Plenty of women work at the mines, kids too, so turnabout is fair play," said Lizzie. "Oi did meself when us needed the money, until your dad got more wages in 'is new job. Anyroad, you won't be workin' at no mine no more, you'm goin' to school soon."

"Aw mum, Oi don't want to go to no school," said Jemmy. "What good's sums and spellin' an' stuff? Dad says I can learn from 'im an' be a mine captain when Oi grow up. Pick it up on the job. Them'll pay me a few coppers too. Oi'll 'ave me own pocket money."

Young Jemmy was a bright enough lad. Addis said he could go far, and if his father had anything to do with it, he would. Perhaps spending some days at the mine from time to time would do him good, but whatever happened Lizzie was going to see to it he could read and do his sums. However, it would be many weeks, if not months, before Mr. Perry could get the school started. He first needed to arrange a lot of support for his plan to educate the people.

Jemmy reluctantly joined his mother doing the house chores. He soon forgot his resistance and chattered away about his new friends, especially a boy his own age who lived four houses down the road. "He's got a pony," Jedson told Lizzie.

As they tidied away the decorations, Lizzie recalled the good time her little family had enjoyed at Christmas. This year, it was a bigger celebration than they could ever afford before. Their new-found comforts had their advantages, she thought. Lizzie had roasted a goose with sage and onion stuffing for Christmas dinner. She used some of the goose fat to make rich pastry for mince pies. Without much persuading, Jemmy had helped her make decorations for the house, boughs of greens they hung around the door frames. Jemmy was willing enough when what he was asked to do was fun, and he always wanted to learn.

He was an inquisitive boy, which Addis said was a sign of intelligence. But his questions sometimes hindered Lizzie as much as his hands helped her. There was a holly bush in a copse at the edge of the village, and Jemmy had helped her cut some branches to make a wreath to hang on the front door.

"Why do us put 'olly in the 'ouse at Christmastide, Mum?" Jemmy had asked.

"Us be remem'brin' the birth of the baby Jesus," explained Lizzie, " an' people say the spiky leaves be loike the crown of thorns, and the red berries be 'is drops of blood when 'e were crucified."

"But why do us put up stuff loike the crucifixion on 'is birthday?" Jemmy asked, "don't make sense. Wouldn't put a coffin on my birthday table."

"That's just what people say," said Lizzie.

"What people?" pressed Jemmy.

"Well, Oi 'spect it says so in the Bible," Lizzie tried.

"Where in the Bible?" Jemmy persisted.

"You'll 'ave to ask Reverend Perry when you see 'im down chapel; he'll know for sure," parried Lizzie.

Then they had found mistletoe in a nearby oak tree and picked a sprig to hang over the parlor door. The vicar had said that the white berries represented the purity of the Virgin Mary, but the old folk said it really celebrated the old goddess of fertility. Anyway that's what the Druids had used it for. Jemmy was a bit young to know about that. Perhaps he wouldn't ask her.

"So what do people say mistletoe be loike then, Mum?"

Lizzie sighed. "Jemmy, let me get on. Stop pussivantin'! Don't ask so many questions. It be just a custom. Oi 'spect people think 'tis pretty, and that be a fact."

Addis had cut a big dried log to burn in the fireplace in the parlor on Christmas Day. He had wanted to use a stick of charcoal to draw a picture of a man on the log, like the custom from olden days of remembering human sacrifice, but Lizzie wouldn't let him. She wanted no more questions from Jemmy. Anyway, what would Reverend Perry say?

She and Addis had filled a stocking for Jemmy with an apple, nuts and candied fruit and hung it over the mantelpiece in the parlor to find when he got up on Christmas morning.

On Christmas Day, though, Jemmy made his own toy. A day or so earlier, Addis had been experimenting with gunpowder, wrapping up small amounts in twists of paper, trying to work out a safe way of detonating it. Jemmy had found the almost empty tin, taken some of the quills plucked from the goose wing, cut off the tips and filled them with the powder. Then he threw them in the stove where they smoldered and sizzled and then burned with a satisfying whoosh, filling the kitchen with a dreadful smell of burning feathers. Addis to Lizzie's surprise did not scold Jemmy for his mischief. Rather, a look came over his face that signified that he had an idea.

"That lad will be a real somebody some day," Addis said to Lizzie, when they were out of earshot of Jemmy.

Whatever the men got up to, Lizzie had to get on with her work, she thought, especially now that, adding to her new pleasure of devoting full time to being a wife and mother, the Penwardens were looking forward to sharing their home with friends. Their first visitor would be the Reverend Perry, who was coming over from Perranporth on Sunday to preach in the chapel at Pendeen. They had invited him to join them to share their family midday dinner after the service.

Lizzie eyed the dying embers in the stove. "Jemmy," she called, "go outside to the wood pile and bring in some logs and get the fire goin' again." She herself made a fire of blackthorn in the cloam oven next to the fireplace. There was nothing like the clay brick lining for even baking. Then she sent Jemmy to fill the iron kettle from the pump in the scullery and put it on the trivet in the hearth to heat for washing the pine table-board. Addis had made the table, fashioning a frame from which the board could be detached. Lizzie used up her last but one cake of lye soap scrubbing the table and made a note to boil up a fresh supply.

When the table dried she went to the shelf on the side wall and got down the tin canister filled with oat meal that she had brought with her from the old cottage in Gwennap. When Addis got more of his new wages she could afford wheat flour already ground from the miller in the village, rather than having to pound oats or barley herself. Now that she could afford to keep more supplies on hand, she would ask Addis if he would make her a kitchen dresser like the better houses had, or perhaps hire the carpenter to make one.

Lizzie sieved the meal to get out the husks and emptied enough into her wooden mixing trough for two loaves of bread and a dozen buns. She had already stood a pint or so of her home brewed ale in a tin pitcher on the stove to warm it. She poured it in with the flour and added barm from her last brewing to make sure that the dough rose.

She wondered how much longer she would be brewing beer or making cider. Reverend Perry had been talking to them about setting a good example to the miners to persuade them to give up alcohol altogether. He said it was the only way to be sure to rescue them from drunkenness. Many of them seemed incapable of drinking in moderation, especially on Saturday nights. But how else were they going to relieve the monotony and misery of their lives?

"Jemmy, go get the sharp kitchen knife from the box," said Lizzie. "Here be the block of salt. Scrape some off, Oi need a good pinch for the dough."

Jemmy did as he was told, but spilled salt on the clean floor. Instinctively, Lizzie picked it up and threw it over her left shoulder for luck. That brought back unhappy memories. Her brother-in-law had been killed down the mine despite her doing just that on the day he died.

Lizzie separated out about a third of the dough mixture in her trough, chopped up some mixed fruit she had dried during the autumn and added saffron she had soaked in warm water, to give the dough its distinctive flavor and yellow color. Like her mum and grandmother and great-grandmother before her, Lizzie loved to bake with saffron. It came from Spain and was made from the dried stamens of a special crocus. It was said the Cornish had traded tin for saffron with the Phoenicians in the Mediterranean Sea donkeys years ago, centuries. Lizzie believed this, as you did not find saffron being used in the rest of England. She rolled up her sleeves and began to knead the mixture. When it was springy and shiny, she covered the dough with a cloth and laid it aside to rise.

Her saffron buns would taste delicious with the fruit and all. Now with the fruit trees and bushes in their garden, she could preserve enough fruit and make enough jam next year to keep their family fed as well as give some away to people less fortunate.

Finally, she went outside to fetch the milk can from the cool windowsill and poured some into a shallow pan. In a few hours when the cream had risen to the top, she would gently warm the pan, skim off the crust and they would have clotted cream.

Lizzie was interrupted by a demanding cry from the crib Addis had brought down from their bedroom upstairs to the kitchen so she could keep an eye on the baby. "Jemmy, go see what your little brother wants," she said.

Young Jedson was hungry and gave out a lusty howl. Jemmy lifted the toddler from his warm nest and carried him to their mother, holding him under his arms and dangling the rest. "Not like that, Jemmy. Here let me show you." Lizzie scooped up the baby, cradling him in her arms and sat down on her kitchen rocking chair to nurse him. She sent Jemmy to play outside and leave her in peace. Perhaps he would find his new friend.

Before long the baby was satisfied and dropped away from her breast, so she sang a lullaby to him and laid him back in his crib, where he fell asleep. He looked so contented. She was contented too; she took pride in being a mum who could feed her baby son; nowadays, even the upper classes were turning away from wet nurses who might carry diseases and were nursing their own babies. There would be a time when she had to think of weaning him, but before that, she would start giving him a little table food mashed up.

Time to get on with her baking. She saw that the cloam oven had got white hot. First she raked out the ashes and shoveled them into the old barrel she kept in the outhouse beside the back door. Addis had got the barrel from a fisherman down at the cove. She had scrubbed it out well to get rid of the fishy smell. The fresh batch of ashes filled the barrel so her next task would be to make lye to use for her new batch of soap. But first she would finish making the bread. Lizzie checked that the dough she had already kneaded had risen. It was time to form it into loaves and buns. She laid the loaves inside the oven and shut the clay door. Later when the bread was done, she would cook the buns as the oven cooled. They would be ready to eat, piping hot, with the clotted cream and her homemade blackberry and apple jam when Addis came home from the mine hungry.

Now she was ready to start making the soap. She would make more than she needed right away so that she could store the surplus and let it age for a few months. The baby was still asleep so he would be out of the way when she started; it could be dangerous. She got a bucket of water from the pump and set it on the fire to boil. Then she carefully poured the hot water into the barrel over the potash, standing back to avoid being splashed by the boiling hot mixture created by the chemical reaction. As the water soaked through the ashes the lye leached out through a spout that Adds had fixed at the bottom of the barrel and into a wooden tub. Lizzie knew that to make good soap the lye had to be just right. She fetched an egg and laid it with a long-handled spoon on top of the liquid. If it floated the lye would be ready to use. But the egg sank. She would have to wait to refill the barrel with fresh ashes and pour the lye from the tub through the ashes again.

It would be a day or two before she could make the soap. The clothes wash would just have to wait because she wanted to save the last of the remaining soap for their hands and their dishes. Anyroad, it would give her a chance to save up more fat and add to what she had left over from the goose after her baking, then she could make a bigger batch that would last longer.

Oh well, a woman's work is never done she thought to herself, as she fetched her brush and knelt on the kitchen floor to sweep up the remains of the salt that Jemmy had spilt. What will that boy be up to next, she wondered? He was so active, so inquisitive; she loved him with all her heart, Addis too. Standing up and looking around her, Lizzie felt a moment of peace and gratitude as the warm yeasty aroma of baking saffron cake filled the kitchen. Addis would be home before long. She would take great satisfaction in his enjoyment of his supper. Yes, she was proud of being a mine captain's wife and the Penwardens would lead a good life in Pendeen.

Chapter Twenty-seven

Safety

In the frosty morning of his first day of work, having left Lizzie at home to set up housekeeping and take care of the boys, Addis Penwarden had walked in darkness the mile or two along the rocky track to Wheal Hykka. He was used to walking, of course, the walk to Poldice had been longer than this, but he looked forward to the arrival of the promised horse to make his journey easy, indeed luxurious. The dawn was breaking as he arrived and he was overwhelmed by what he saw. What had possessed him to accept John Williams' offer to promote him to mine captain? How would he ever manage. Might he fail? Then what would he do? He knew he could command respect from the tinners, but there was so much more he had to know, so much new to learn.

Addis had stopped as he reached a rise in the track and saw that the mine was bounded to the north by the Atlantic Ocean and stretched from a headland away to the west, then over as far as the eye could see to a cove marking the eastern end of the site. There were workings and buildings scattered about, even right down at the edge of the sea where the jagged cliffs jutted out and bordered the cove. He looked down at the sea and counted the waves; every seventh wave or so was huge and the spray from the breakers drenched the rocks and the buildings standing on them. The roar of the sea was deafening. A ship swept onto those rocks wouldn't stand a chance.

He turned away and walked on to an imposing two-story building that looked more like a big house than a mine building. There was a sign by the front door announcing that it was the count house. He went in and introduced himself to the most senior looking of the men inside who were sitting at desks and laying out papers to start their day.

"My name is Addis Penwarden and Oi'm your new captain."

"Good day to you, zir, and welcome. Oi'm chief clerk. Cap'n Williams said you'd be comin'; e's got enough on 'is 'ands over at Poldice now that Wheal Hykka will be addin' on new workin's. Told me to show you around. He'll be over in a day or two to help you settle in and then us is to take our orders from you."

✢✢✢

In no time Addis was working just as hard as mine captain at Wheal Hykka as he had as tributer at Poldice. The work was different. He no longer had to exhaust his muscles with hammering and drilling, lifting and pulling, or keeping his senses at high alert to guard against danger. But he tired his brain with far more of the thinking and organizing and planning than he had been used to. True, for years he had directed his pare, but that was just a small group carrying out a few basic, if critical, tasks. Now he had not only to organize hundreds of men, tut workers digging new shafts and adits, as well as miners, women and children too, doing work he knew well down in the pit; but also he had to direct tasks he was unfamiliar with on the surface, including overseeing clerks and checking on accounts.

Fortunately nothing out of the ordinary came up, so he was not faced with having to make decisions while he was yet unprepared. He was relieved when John Williams showed up and wasted no time in briefing him. The first thing Williams told him was a surprise.

"Couple of things, Penwarden. First off, get yourself the proper clothes, right away. Start out the way you intend to carry on. Get a tall hat, black frock coat and pin-striped trousers, and wear them at all times you're at work."

"Oi never been much for fripperies, Mr. Williams," said Addis, "Oi'm a plain man, take me as you foind me. Got other things to spend me money on."

"Just do as I say, man," said Williams, "I know what I'm talking about. You're mine captain now; you've got to look like the captain as well as acting like the captain. Why do you think I moved you from Poldice? Because there the men looked at you as one of their mates. Here at Wheal Hykka they've only known you as the one set over them. Keep it that way. Keep yourself to yourself."

"Us don't want to disagree, Mr. Williams," Addis said, "but Oi never 'as no trouble gettin' folks to do as Oi say, natural loike."

"Of all men, Penwarden, you should know that you're dealing with Cornishmen, and we take pride in our independence. We don't take to being ordered about. But you are responsible for results; your job and their lives depend on that. And always remember that one of these days something might go wrong, and then it'll be following your orders without question that saves them."

Addis removed his cap and scratched his head. "Oi think I see what you mean, us'll do as you says," said Addis. "So what's the second thing Oi needs to watch out for?"

"Expect a visit from Joseph Clymo. He'll come every time there's a new quarter and new setts; make sure you're keeping up to the mark. He'll go easy on you for a month or two just maintaining production; he won't press you just yet. After that, more than likely he will be looking for more and more revenue. Joseph Clymo's not a bad sort, but I hear that young Baron Trenance got on his back when he came home to Lanhydrock from London for Christmas. His lordship wants results, now. Seems it's more than simple greed. My guess is the Baron needs money bad, lots of it and soon."

"But Oi came 'ere with promises there'd be money for improvements," said Addis.

"That promise was made to me too," responded Williams, "and now I am one of the owners of this mine, so what I say carries weight. Otherwise I would have told Mr. Clymo to manage on his own. I've got plenty of places I could go. He's got brains enough to know that they'll have to invest money to make money. He'll convince the Baron. And that Mr. Bolitho will make money himself out of lending funds to Lanhydrock, and he'll see to it that improvements are made to protect his own interests. Just you leave that part of it to me."

Addis put his cap back on and then scratched his chin and thought for a moment. He was putting a lot of trust in John Williams. What would he do with a fancy suit of clothes if he got the sack? Well, he would just have to make a go of it. It was better to take the risk or he'd never better himself, and then he'd be in no position to help the boys have a better future.

"Well, Oi'll just 'ave to rely on what you tells us, Mr. Williams. Oi do know what goes on down the mine an' can see to that, but it's the office work what's new to us."

"You'll catch on, besides you'll have help. Just you be sure to walk through the underground workings every day, show your face," advised Williams. "The tributers will see to it that they fetch up plenty of ore. Their livelihood depends on it. There's a lot you can do to avoid danger, without spending any money. Watch out for the men drilling in the stopes; those vertical shafts are more dangerous than the levels. Whenever you hand out supplies, remind the men to be careful. Be extra careful when they charge the drill holes for blasting; only give out enough black powder for the one shift, so that none is left behind in the workings. Tell the men over and over to warn the others, even in neighboring areas, when there's going to be fire in the hole. And make sure that any rungs on rickety ladders get fixed before anyone falls."

"Oi reckon Oi'd know 'bout that," said Addis. "Do you keep it all in your 'ead, Mr. Williams?" asked Addis. "There be a powerful lot to remember."

"I make a practice of not keeping it all in my head," Williams said, "I write things down, make lists, especially instructions."

Addis looked at his feet. Writing was not among his strong points, let alone spelling or grammar and composition. He had always worked with his hands.

"I don't have time to do it all myself," Williams went on, "that's what the clerks are for. Here, let me show you, see who you've got to work with."

He called the chief clerk over and asked him to send for the clerk of the works to join them. A young man came over, dressed in a worsted coat and breeches, wearing wire-framed spectacles. He nodded to them respectfully. "All right, young man, here's what Captain Penwarden wants you to do," said Williams. "Get your quill and some parchment and we'll make some lists. You write down what I say."

Williams verified the requirements for the surface workings, how the ore that was brought up should be spalled and bucked, what sizes the lumps should be broken down to, as well as the necessary amounts of sand. He confirmed with the clerk that he would see that the tributers were properly credited for the amounts due them and that the materials sent to the smelters were accurately assayed and weighed and accounted for.

"Those requirements all right with you, Captain Penwarden?" asked John Williams. Addis nodded his agreement, very relieved. His mentor was smoothing the path for him, setting him up as appearing to be in charge. He could learn a lot about leadership from Captain Williams. Then Williams turned to the chief clerk. He knew him to be experienced and reliable, hand picked by Joseph Clymo, able to make up the accounts. He acted as purser for the mine.

"Now then," said Williams, "Captain Penwarden here wants you to see to figuring wages and shares, purchasing routine supplies and checking stock levels. Can he count on you?"

"Aargh, Oi know 'ow to do all that right enough," the clerk said. "Oi've been doin' them things for some years. Then Oi send reports to Mr. Clymo as well as the captain."

"Do you keep a count of the dips, and make sure them's all paid for?" asked Addis. He knew from experience that a pound of tallow candles could easily disappear into a bal maiden's apron to light her family's cottage after she left the mine. John Williams smiled, glad to see Addis asserting himself, picking things up quickly.

"Aargh," said the chief clerk, "that Oi do an' all, 'tis easy for all manner of stuff to disappear if us don't watch out."

"Grand. Then that'll be all for now," said Addis, "Be sure to go over the figures with us at the end of the day. Now, Mr. Williams, we have somethin' else to talk about."

Like Addis, John Williams knew that one of the biggest safety problems came from blasting. The miners would tamp powder into the holes they had drilled in the rock, trying to avoid accidentally igniting with sparks. Then they would lay a long open trail of powder to a safe distance and light the end. Usually that worked. Sometimes an impatient miner would think that the spark had gone out and would go in to relight it. Once in a while the lit powder trail would reach the hole and explode just as he got close.

The open powder was dangerous and too often fatal. Addis thought that maybe young Jemmy had stumbled upon something that Christmas morning when he was fooling around with his goose quills, and he felt that Williams would be open to trying out a potentially more reliable and hence safer method.

"Me boy Jemmy gave us an idea that might make it less dangerous when us sets off charges for blastin'. Twouldn't cost much neither. Let us show you."

He got the goose quills he had brought from his house to the mine, long fat ones from the wing tips of the goose. Just as Jemmy had done, Addis cut off the pointed ends and carefully filled the hollow stems with gunpowder. He laid one on the hearth and made a touch-paper, which he lit from the fire, and ignited the feather tip.

It smoldered, and the flame spread slowly up the shaft and lit the powder. John Williams nodded as he grasped the significance of the demonstration.

"Oi reckon that if us cuts the ends off the quills and poke one inside the next one, us could make a long rod of quills that us could fill with powder and stuff down the drill 'ole. Then us could set a candle under it an' light it an' get clear out of the road before 'er sets off the charge," said Addis. "Us could get the quills same place the clerks do, or maybe use up the ends of them what they can't write with no more, too short to sharpen. 'Twouldn't cost much at all. Waste not, want not, that's what Oi say."

Williams thought a moment, going over the process in his mind, then smiled. "You may be on to something, Mr. Penwarden. Let's try it."

They cut both ends off half a dozen quills, keeping the feathers on the end of one quill, poked the tapered ends into the bottom ends, fitted them together into a long rod. They carefully poured in some powder. "Oi reckon if we bruise the powder," said Williams, "make the particles smaller, it would flow in easier and burn better. Let's try that way."

Addis Penwarden cut a square of parchment and rolled it into a funnel. He left a small hole at the pointed end, which he then poked into the cut end of a quill. He poured the powder into the funnel and the filling went faster with less spillage. Then he plugged the open end of the rod with the feathered quill.

Williams smiled again. They put on their top hats and coats and made their way down into the mine, climbing down the long ladders into the deep Gurnard's Shaft where blasting was to take place. Addis directed one of the miners to pierce a small hole down the length of the powder that he had tamped into the hole, using a tool called a needle. Then he carefully stuffed the rod of quills deep into the test hole. When everything was ready, they set a lit candle under the open end.

The candle flame ignited the feathered tip, which smoldered slowly and spread along the rod. They had ample time to take cover around a rock corner. After a few minutes there was an explosion. The rock face collapsed and they were unharmed. With the help of a small boy's imagination, they had discovered a safe method of detonating gunpowder, the simple rod of quills.

"Promising lad, that son of yours," said John Williams, beaming.

"Thank 'ee. Cap'n," said Addis. "Oi been thinkin', maybe Oi could bring young Jemmy along to the mine with me a couple of days a week. Oi could do with some 'elp in the office, runnin' errands, stuff like that, pay 'im a few coppers. He was a good worker down the mine alongside me, part of me own pare where Oi could keep an eye on 'im. Wouldn't want 'im doin' that for nobody else, not safe. Maybe Oi could learn 'im somethin' about the business aspects of mining. Lizzie wants 'im to go to school too, give 'im a chance at a better future."

"You're a man after my own heart, Cap'n Penwarden," said Williams. "That's what my father did for me, and now I'm a mine captain like he was. No reason the Penwarden family shouldn't make something of themselves, just like us Williamses. Wish more Cornishmen thought like you. Jemmy's a good boy, he can go far and when he does he can bring others along with him. You take the lead on this and I'll be right behind you, just don't rush your fences."

Chapter Twenty-eight

Superstition

By the time John Williams left the Wheal Hykka mine to return to Poldice, he was obviously pleased. As he and Addis parted, Williams advised once again that Addis keep a close eye on spending, the key to making profit. In particular, he warned, "Do not put much money into pet projects until you are well established and profits are consistent. For now, be satisfied with inexpensive initiatives that do not require approval from Clymo. Your rod of quills worked well, and is not costly."

Captain Williams would make sure that Penwarden got the credit for this idea. The miners accepted Addis as captain; they saw that he treated people fairly as well as firmly. There were the usual rumblings and resentments, but Addis well understood these from his own days of being the miners' spokesman at Poldice. After setting day, miners at Wheal Hykka had settled down and, for the moment, accepted the promises of John Williams and now himself that conditions would improve.

But then two miners reported something very strange, and fear as well as discontent infiltrated the mine. They told their tributer what they had seen, and he in turn insisted on an interview with Addis right away, who then agreed to see the men, despite being preoccupied by having just received report of an accident.

"Us was comin' to work, Cap'n Penwarden zir, on our way to night core, an' us was proper startled to see our mate, who was s'posed to still be on day shift, already upside walkin' on 'is way 'ome," the older of the miners recounted.

"Did you speak to 'im?" asked Addis.

"Us called out to 'im, but 'e took no notice loike. Course, 'e should've still been down shaft at that toime, could've got into trouble. So us carried on to report in, but everyone were solemn loike, so us wondered what 'ad 'appened."

"Who was it?" asked Penwarden.

"Thomas Richards."

"Thomas Richards!" Addis exclaimed. "Richards was reported to 'ave 'ad an accident not an hour ago. Them'd blasted an' 'e went back to clear the rubble, pulled out a big piece of rock, part of the roof fell on 'im. Poor man 'ad no chance, snuffed out." How could they've seen Thomas Richards?" An odd queasy feeling began to stir in Addis's gut. "Are you sure 'twas 'e?"

"Sure as us is standin' 'ere, zir," the miner answered.

There was a knock at Penwarden's office door. It was the chief clerk. "Sorry to trouble you, zir. They brought Richards' body up, 'alf an hour ago. He's dead. Them's put 'im in the store buildin', poor soul. Better let his missus know."

Addis took a few moments to compose himself. He was in turmoil, a miner dead on his watch in but a short time of his taking leadership at Wheal Hykka; but he needed to present a face of calm to the miners. "You tell the widow then, 'er'll want to see 'im, Oi dare say," Addis told the men. "Wheal Hykka'll pay for 'is burial, 'ave the carpenter make 'is coffin, let 'er know. Go on an' see to it."

Addis hoped his words and his concern would help settle the miners, but he could see by the stricken looks on the faces of those in his office that they were affected by more than grief for their fallen comrade. They thought they had seen the ghost of Thomas Richards on his way home.

Addis was enough steeped in Cornish lore not to dismiss their claims out of hand. There was much superstition in Cornwall, and Addis was a son of Cornwall, though also a practical man and a Christian who regularly attended chapel. He kept his thoughts to himself, in part because his thoughts were ajumble.

One of the miners spoke again. "Cap'n Penwarden, there be knackers in this 'ere mine," he asserted. Some of the older Cornish folk were convinced of the existence of "knackers", whom they described as wizened little creatures, believed to be the spirits of those who had crucified Jesus Christ. The knackers were condemned to work out their doom underground. Despite their fate, they were thought to represent good luck to miners, as they only appeared near rich metalliferous lodes.

The miner told his story earnestly, a taint of fear in his voice. "Us was workin' down lower shaft an' my mate 'eard clickin' noises t'other side of wall, so 'e took 'is boryer an' drilled away. Broke through into a vug, a 'ollow space in rock, stuck 'is lighted dip in the space an' saw 'twas filled with shiny crystals, tin an' copper an' all, roof an' sides. Then 'e looked closer an' saw three knackers, no bigger 'n' a sixpenny doll, yet in their faces an' clothes them looked like little ol' tinners. Middle one 'ad tiny 'ammer an' a boryer no bigger 'n' a darning needle, an' a tiddly little dip with a flame flickerin' in the draught."

This story of knackers at Wheal Hykka did not entirely surprise Addis Penwarden, nor did it please him. Mining was hard enough business, and now, dreadfully, a miner dead, without mixing in ghosts and knackers. Still, Addis respected what the men told him; he, too, had grown up listening to tales of knackers and such. These stories had moved and frightened him.

"What 'appened after?" he asked the miners. "Did ye speak to the little folk?"

"Me mate's light blew out, so I offers 'im a pound of me own candles, big enough to properly light where them was workin'. So Oi looks into the vug to see what was goin' on, and blow me down if them wasn't gone already, never did see 'ide nor 'air o' they. So me mate said us should leave they a piece of our croust so them'd 'ave somethin' to eat if they got 'ungry, so that's what us done, an' never 'eard nothin' more."

"Keep this to yourselves, no point gettin' folks riled up," warned Addis, hoping to contain the fears that this story might stir up. But the older of the miners spoke forcefully. "Ye'd better watch out, Cap'n, if Oi were you," said the old man. "Oi'd tell the others, just in case anyone should see 'em and take a fright and a fall. Them knackers should'n' do us no 'arm; just we be sure to leave 'em somethin' to 'eat an' them'll be no bother at all. Leastways, if we know where they're workin' us'll find rich tin."

"Prob'ly imagined the 'ole thing," said Penwarden, "just flickerin' shadows an' all from their candle flames and them crystals," more command and bravado in his voice than he felt.

The old miner was not reassured, so despite some misgivings, Addis agreed to put the word out. Again he kept his conflicting thoughts and jumbled feelings to himself, but as he made his way home from Wheal Hykka to Pendeen that evening, Addis was startled a couple of times when the wind howled through the trees and the clouds scudded across the face of the moon.

A ghost seen above ground, knackers seen below, what did this portend? How might he handle it as the new captain of Wheal Hykka mine?

Addis decided to have a quiet word with Reverend Perry when he came to dinner after the morning service. He hoped to untangle his own mind and to restore good Christian order to Wheal Hykka. Addis would suggest that it might be time for a sermon urging the people to fully embrace the teachings of the Good Word and set aside superstition and lingering beliefs in witchcraft. It would serve a dual purpose, to settle the miners and to quiet doubts that existed in Addis's own head.

The moment came the next Sunday after they had mopped up the last of the gravy with Lizzie's crusty bread, and Jemmy had gone outside to play. Addis did not want to discuss these matters in the hearing of his young son, who missed very little.

"Oi been thinkin', Reverend," said Addis, "about them schools you intend to start, to learn the children education an' Christian beliefs an' all." He told Mr. Perry about the tragedy of the dead miner at Wheal Hykka and the man's ghost believed to be seen above, and the knackers below; he suggested a sermon about superstition and its roots in old ideas and thereby bringing Cornwall into the modern era.

"That's all very well, Penwarden," said Reverend Perry, "and my training as a minister and the teachings of Mr. Wesley and my readings in the Bible all support what you are saying. But I myself can never forget that I am Cornish, part of a long Celtic tradition that even the saints did not succeed in putting out. Of course, I was born and bred in Perranporth, and I feel a strange connection to St. Piran and the legend of the Druids hurling him off the cliff into the stormy Celtic Sea bound to a millstone. It was a miracle, the storm calmed and he floated all the way to Cornwall and became the patron saint of the miners."

"Just a legend?" asked Lizzie Penwarden. "I thought that's 'ow it really 'appened."

"I think about it, and there are ways one could explain it, Mrs. Penwarden," replied Perry. "What is undoubtedly true is that St. Piran himself grew up under the teachings of the Druids. Today, we vilify the Druids as illiterate because they used no books. But they were extremely learned, required to study for the priesthood for twenty years, to memorize hundreds of ideas and stories and legends to preserve the oral traditions of the tribes. They were respected, their prestige only behind the king. They looked down on those who lacked their intellectual power and had to resort to the written word."

"Well Oi never," said Lizzie, "an' 'ere was Oi thinkin' Oi'd 'ave to read an' write better so Oi could learn the children at school!"

"You'll have to do that all right," said Perry. "It's the only way we do things now, and I'm counting on you, helping in the Sunday school to start with."

"P'raps Oi could learn them the ol' Cornish litany then," said Lizzie, "might do the nippers more good than just what's in the Bible! From ghoulies and ghosties and long leggity beasties, good Lord deliver us! That'll keep 'em safe when they're out on the moors at night!"

"My dear Mrs. Penwarden," chided the Reverend, "I do believe you would have joined your fellow Cornish in the Prayer Book Rebellion in 1549. You would rather keep the Latin than allow English to replace the Cornish language. I expect for two pins you'd still worship the moon goddess and dance on Midsummer Night's Eve!"

"You may jest, Reverend," said Penwarden, "but surely you believe it is your calling and our duty to bring the Christian religion to the people, and to set aside heathen ways?"

"Of course, I do," said Perry. "It's just that I understand that we aren't going to win the hearts of the people by being bull-headed about it. Don't you feel something special when you walk among the old stone circles, or visit the ancient monuments? I do."

Reverend Perry warmed to his subject: "The Venerable Bede recorded the advice of Pope Gregory to the early Christian missionaries not to destroy the places of pagan worship or to stamp out the ancient festivals. Rather, he urged sprinkling the temples with holy water and naming the traditional festivals after Christian saints, so that the people would frequent their familiar places and maintain the essence of their customs, while through pious usage coming to know the true God."

Addis Penwarden did not know what to say. His friend and mentor had surprised him. Would he ever understand this mix of ideas and beliefs, ever understand human nature well enough to be a truly good man, a man headed into the future, a mine captain?

After Reverend Perry took his leave, Lizzie asked Addis, "What did the reverend mean by ways to explain St. Piran's floating on a millstone?"

"You'll 'ave to ask 'im," replied Addis.

Chapter Twenty-nine

Port Eliot

As winter turned to spring, the sparse snow that had dusted the little valleys around Port Eliot surrendered to the mild Cornish climate, and the melt seeped down the hillsides to swell the lazy currents of the River Tiddy, thence to feed the Lynher and the Tamar as they paid their modest tribute to the busy waters of the English Channel. The tenant farmers and their laborers stirred, sharpened the ploughshares, greased the harnesses, groomed and shod the great shire horses as they prepared to cultivate the rich red brown loam to embrace the new season's seeds. Their labor would give rise to a flow of revenue that would swell the wealth of their squire even as he played his role in the busy doings of the English capital city.

The awakening of the new season at Port Eliot welcomed Edward Eliot home from London, where he attended the House of Commons and performed his lucrative duties as a Commissioner of Trade and Plantations. This parliament had come to the end of its seven-year life as provided by law and hence in March, 1761, was dissolved by the new king, George III. There would be a general election and places to be sought, but no doubt the Whig oligarchy would protect its position despite now receiving less support from the crown.

Edward Eliot and his wife Catherine traveled from London to St. Germans to prepare for the election. The roads near London were kept in reasonable repair but further west towards Cornwall they became rougher, narrower and more dangerous. Under Catherine's urging, Edward took advantage of the generosity of his friend and neighbor Lord Edgcumbe, who offered to lend them the sloop that he kept at Plymouth Dock. Of course, Edgcumbe's generosity may have been stirred by favors past and anticipated. So it was that the Eliot family and a few servants sailed from the Port of London along the south coast and landed conveniently at the quay at Port Eliot. The voyage proved vastly more comfortable than traveling by road and was faster. Furthermore, the hold in the sloop was capacious enough to accommodate all of their baggage, which had been augmented by Catherine's visits to London's shopkeepers.

The Eliots covered the distance to the house in short order, and Catherine whisked off to see about unpacking and to be reunited with young Edward, who had been left behind with his nurse. Before Eliot went to meet with his agents and supporters and arrange to canvass the voters in his boroughs, he wanted to see to matters at home, where the foundation of his wealth lay. He made his way to the estate office and had a long chat with his man of business, Charles Polkinghorne.

"How's the quarry coming along?" Eliot enquired. "Unearthing good deposits? What are the production figures? Bunt making out all right as manager?"

"Things are coming along fine, sir, I reckon," said Polkinghorne. "Mind you, I've got to keep an eye on Bunt. He's young and inexperienced. But he's got a knack for machinery. He's got the men digging out plenty of stone and getting it crushed and ready for the turnpike project. Keeping to the timetable, too."

"How are the farmers doing? Got through the winter without too many mishaps?" asked Eliot.

"We're lucky that agricultural prices are still firming, sir. It's the demand from the war," said Polkinghorne. "The sheep did well over the winter with them new fangled turnips we planted, even up on Bodmin Moor. Looks like we're going to fatten up some good mutton. Several of the tenants have gone along with trying out them Dorset tups you brought in. The shepherds say the ewes caught pretty well, and the new lambs are looking bonny."

"Well, I don't expect they would have tried new things without our help," said Eliot. "Farmers aren't the most progressive mortals, especially not in Cornwall. Glad to hear the estate is well found, because I've got work for you."

"What may that be then, sir?" asked Polkinghorne, intrigued.

"The election," said Eliot. "I have to make sure that our men get in. I promised Mr. Pitt. And while we are about it, we would be well advised to ensure our position with the turnpike. I want you to help me as my political agent; bring Bunt along."

That prospect sounded interesting to Polkinghorne, perhaps adding to his own importance, although he wasn't too sure of the idea of advancing Bunt yet again.

"I'd be glad to do what I can, sir," said Polkinghorne, "with your guidance of course."

Eliot knew that Pitt counted on him to guarantee the four seats in the Commons that he had in his pocket and others where he had growing influence. He also realized that while he could rely on the loyal support of the candidates he selected, he would have to make sure that the voters followed his wishes in supporting his candidates. Many voters were his tenants, who were clear where their interests lay. But persuading others could take favors and plenty of good ale, although, unlike some others, Eliot was unwilling to go so far as blatantly offering money.

Eliot, however, was always prepared to try new things in managing his estate and his business interests. Why not his boroughs? He was certainly winning the gratitude and probably the loyalty of the burgesses of Liskeard with his leadership of the turnpike project, which benefited the borough as well as the estate.

Edward headed back to the house, and as he walked an idea that he had been mulling over for some time came to him again. Elections were primarily men's business of course. After all, men were the ones who voted. Elections could be rough and the spoils were large. Politics was like business. Everyone knew that women did not have the temperament to be entrusted with the vote, even if they wanted it, which happily they never would. But his wife was different. She was not only beautiful and intelligent, but charming and beneath it all determined.

Catherine was proving to be a very capable helpmeet. Perhaps it would be to his advantage if she were to help him a bit more, around the edges of course. He decided to discuss his idea with her that evening as they took sherry in the library at Port Eliot before dining alone.

After changing for dinner, Edward found Catherine already seated in the library, singing a song with Edward James on her lap. Their son was happy to be with his mother, although it took a while for him to get used to her again after being parted from her for several weeks. A cozy fire was blazing in the grate. Edward picked up his son and carried him about the room for a while, talking to him, until Catherine summoned Nanny who took the boy off to his nursery. The butler placed a silver tray on the piecrust table between them, bearing a pair of the new goblets they had bought in London, into which he had decanted an exquisite fino. Then the butler too was dismissed, leaving the two of them alone together.

Edward stretched his legs and yawned. "Catherine, my dear, it is a pleasure to be back home in Cornwall and to sit and relax with you after long days of traveling, working and planning."

"I share your sentiments, Edward," said Catherine. "I have grown to love Port Eliot and am happy to be back. But there is much that I enjoy about London, and miss; it is lively and stimulating. You must admit that Cornwall is quite bucolic. I have much to keep me occupied, of course, but one's brain does not get much exercise."

"You don't do yourself justice. You have many pursuits that make use of your intellect as well as your physical energy. In fact, I have some ideas for you."

"I can't wait to hear about them, but first let me tell you of my reflections entertained while on our journey home. You must confess, Edward, that you men have advantages over women. My cousin Edward Gibbon, you yourself, your friends among the gentry, all enjoyed a superior education. You went to Oxford. That was denied to my sisters and me. We sat at home and did needlework, sang to entertain our families' friends, played the harpsichord, indeed played the hostess."

"Which you perform most charmingly, my dear."

"That is simply not enough, Edward. I insist on more. You must not patronize me. I am curious, and I intend to satisfy my curiosity. While you were engaged in matters of national importance in London, I was doing the social rounds with some fascinating people. Your friend Joshua Reynolds introduced me to a group of exceptionally intelligent and well-informed women. They call themselves the Blue Stockings Society and they have invited me to join them. I intend to do so. We will meet again when we go up to London, and in the meantime I will correspond with them and intend to invite some of my favorites to visit us here."

Catherine snapped open her fan, waved it vigorously to cool her face, which had been warmed by her enthusiasm, and took a deep draught of her sherry.

"Catherine, I am delighted," said Edward, looking more alarmed than his words suggested. "Be assured that I never underestimate your abilities, as you will see when you allow me to tell you my plans for you." Catherine smiled, leaned over and patted her husband's knee affectionately.

"Let me assure you that I will not neglect my wifely duties. I had a most rewarding conversation with the housekeeper, Edward. I showed her the bolts of Italian damasks we purchased in London. We thought the gold would look well on the cushions in the state room and chose the dark pink with leaf green figuring shot with a gold thread to make curtains for this room. It will warm up the room by day and look iridescent and quite beautiful in candlelight."

Catherine stood up and walked over to the widows to demonstrate where they would hang. "One of the brave young footmen climbed up a step ladder and measured these high windows from the ceiling to the floor. The seamstresses will start cutting out tomorrow."

"You seem to have bought an awful lot of fabric, my dear. I didn't want to say so at the time, but isn't that rather extravagant?" asked a slightly worried Edward, trying to keep up with his wife's ability to change the subject.

"Oh, we're hardly in a position where we have to pinch pennies, Edward. You tell me the estate is doing well, and nowadays your commissioner's salary is handsome. Besides, you have a position to keep up." She smiled at him. "You know, I am terribly proud of you, Edward my love, and you have to realize that we will be entertaining a lot of important people as befits your position. You surely don't want them coming to a shabby old country house, do you?"

Edward gazed at her, marveling at how easily she could get around him. Catherine continued, waving towards the windows. "While they're about it, they're going to line the new curtains with that fine woolen material the women in the village wove from those new sheep. You must remember that your beloved Cornish climate gets damp and cold in the winter, and the wind howls through those rattly great windows."

"Nothing like a little fresh air for the health, my dear," said Edward teasingly, knowing she would have her way regardless of what he said. "Besides, we usually have a fire when there's snow on the ground."

Catherine just shook her head and rejoined her husband, reaching for the glass of sherry he had refilled for her. "Just leave the domestic details to me, Edward," said Catherine. "You have much serious business to occupy you. You simply need to make sure that the estate's income keeps up with our ambitions. I have so many ideas for making your home more comfortable, and more fashionable."

"I imagine you have, Catherine. I imagine you have." He set his glass down and turned towards her. "Speaking of ideas, you do know how much I value your advice and how deeply I trust your judgment?" asked Edward.

"What would you like me to do for you now, husband?" Catherine replied. It was rarely necessary to explain the subtleties of a conversation to her. Edward smiled. He noticed that her never idle hands were now working a piece of petit point for a cushion cover that she had retrieved from the bag at her feet. "Woman's work," thought Edward, "but directed by a mind of which many a man would be proud, and one never to be underestimated." He sipped his sherry, enjoying the warmth of his wife's companionship, then spoke his thoughts aloud.

"My dear, you are shrewd as always. In fact, I want to try a different strategy in managing the elections. I want your help in wooing the voters. Not literally, of course, but I do believe the good citizens of my Cornish boroughs would respond warmly to being entertained by you."

"So," she laughed, "this proves my point regarding the fabric. I imagine my hospitality might also maintain your purse, my dearest," responded Catherine looking up with a needle poised in the air. "Tell me your plan and how you would like me to help you. There is a remote possibility that I might even be able to improve upon it, of course in modest ways."

Catherine did have a knack for hitting even the most tactfully positioned nail squarely on the head. Edward raised his fine new crystal goblet with the spiral stem, passed it beneath his nostrils and sniffed the subtle bouquet. He held it up to his eyes and admired the clear pale golden color, and as he looked through it to the windows and beyond he noticed the buds springing forth on the trees in the park and the setting sun tinting the clouds. He allowed himself to imagine how elegant the new curtains would look.

"Fulfilling one's public obligations can indeed strain one's purse, as our neighbor Thomas Pitt over at Boconnoc discovered to his cost," said Edward. "It was he who wrote that there are few Cornish boroughs where the common sort of people do not think they have as much right to sell themselves and their votes as they have to sell their corn and their cattle."

"I trust that you, my dear, will apply your masculine instincts for business to ensure that your investments on behalf of England yield adequate reward for Port Eliot."

"You may rely on me for that, Catherine, but I am coming to believe that your advice and assistance would not go amiss. I have told you, my dear, that I had planned to ask Anthony Champion to give up sitting alongside me at St. Germans and change his seat to Liskeard," continued Edward. "He has agreed; he seems satisfied that representing a larger borough will make him more important, and there are hints that he too may have opportunities to be more active in business. Moving Champion makes room for young Philip Stanhope to vacate Liskeard and move to St. Germans. We Eliots go back a long way with the Stanhopes, but his father the Earl of Chesterfield is a dyed-in-the-wool Whig, so he's likely to support the Duke of Newcastle.

"Too, I have promised Pitt I'd do my best to support his administration, and that means I must keep a close eye on young Stanhope. Of course, the old earl paid a pretty penny for Liskeard, twenty-five hundred pounds as I recall, but as long as the young feller gets an equally safe seat he shouldn't object. Besides, I might be able to put some opportunities his way. He's not likely to go far on his own limited merits. We'll have to see how he turns out."

"I'm sure you have your reasons, my dear," said Catherine, "and I have no doubt there are advantages to being the wife of a man of affairs who appreciates her assistance. However, I was wondering . . . but your glass is empty. Your eloquence has made you thirsty." She sat forward to pour another portion from the decanter into his glass.

Edward thanked her and sipped appreciatively from his recharged glass. It warmed his heart. The Jerez fino from that cask in the cellar he had imported from Portugal really was exceptionally fine. It compared well with anything Lord Trenance served, and he was confident it came from more respectable sources.

"Catherine, do join me in another glass," he said.

"It may not be wise in my condition," responded Catherine, modestly lowering her eyes.

"Are you sure, my dear? How wonderful!"

"The midwife from the village called in this morning after we arrived. She confirmed the reasons for my feeling queasy in the mornings and was quite sure that she could explain why my new clothes from London already seem a little tight."

"When can we expect the happy event?"

"Towards the end of September. That should be no surprise to you, my dear, after the rollicking way in which you so impetuously celebrated the arrival of the New Year with me. You can be quite the, ah, devoted husband, husband."

"My dear, you are full of surprises. What splendid news." said Edward, as he got up from his chair and leaned over to kiss her on the cheek. "Ah, uxorious! I well remember that glorious word from the days when Latin poetry was being flogged into me at Eton. Ovid I think, but was it Horace?"

"I did not realize that you learned how to treat a woman from your schoolmaster," said Catherine with a smile.

"Hardly, my dear. It was from my mother, full of joy and laughter she was. She was so young when my father married her, and her own mother was famous for charming and delighting her gentlemen friends. I was fortunate to grow up loved by and loving beautiful women. But none could be more delightful a wife than you, my dearest." Edward smiled warmly. He was delighted by this turn of events in his family life, but sentiment quickly turned back to the business at hand.

"You look as though your mind has turned to something else, Catherine. What could you possibly be wondering about?" Edward said. "You know you ought to leave the wondering to your husband. I simply need you at this point to help reaffirm the loyalty of the voters of Liskeard and St. Germans. Perhaps I could invite them to tea at Eliot House and Port Eliot, and you could act as my charming hostess. They would be most impressed with such a lavish refreshment."

"Edward, what I was wondering," said Catherine pursuing her own thoughts, "was whether your connections might benefit my family and consequently yours as well. My cousin Edward Gibbon is extremely talented. He will soon return to England from his Grand Tour and will be publishing his essay on literature. His intelligent counsel would make him invaluable as a Member of Parliament."

"We don't need more intelligent men in Cornwall, my dear," said Eliot; "we need men we can count on, good churchmen. Besides he is still young. Just make sure our established candidates are elected."

"You seem concerned, Edward."

"It's nothing, my dear. Although there is a fellow called Morshead who has been running around to the freemen in Liskeard offering to represent them. Fortunately he has found little support, although in all modesty I suppose I did see to it that there was more than mere fortune involved. After all, the good burgesses understand clearly the value of having a turnpike running through their market town, and they would never have obtained the parliamentary support without me."

"Ever the statesman and the man of affairs," said Catherine.

"H'mm, quite. But we can't have upstarts being encouraged. The place will go to the dogs if elections get out of hand, men deciding to stand wherever they choose whenever it comes into their own heads. It's bad enough dealing just with the burgesses in the towns and the freemen in the county."

"You'll determine how to ensure events follow your wishes, I know," said Catherine.

"It's settled, then, you will help me take care of St. Germans and Liskeard. I will vote as Mayor myself, and I am confident I can secure the votes of the three capital burgesses and the five other burgesses who make up the corporation of the borough. Altogether, with the non-resident voters I expect somewhere between thirty and forty votes must be accounted for."

"You do indeed keep your ear close to the ground, Edward."

"It is simply what one must do if one is to play one's part in affairs," said Edward. He continued, "For my part, I need to spend some time at Grampound. For years it's been quarrelsome. Our good friend William's elder brother Thomas Pitt never got on with Christopher Hawkins as his Vice Warden of the Stannaries, even though both of them supported the interest of the late Prince of Wales. And they couldn't see eye to eye with our good neighbor Lord Edgcumbe, who had thrown in his lot with the government."

"My instinct tells me they would have done better to agree and share their influence," observed Catherine.

"If they had followed your instinct they would have saved themselves a great deal of money, my dear," said Eliot. "At the last election my Lord Edgcumbe and his friends are said to have spent in excess of six thousand pounds, in no small part to thwart Mr. Thomas Pitt's scheme to disenfranchise fifty freemen. One can buy a seat outright for less than that, even though these days the borough jobbers are asking for more and more."

"That is a great deal of money," said Catherine. "All spent in bribes?"

"Hardly bribes, my dear," said Edward. "Well, at least I wouldn't say that publicly, and I myself would not countenance the payment of money in my boroughs. I do enough to earn their support in other ways, but Edgcumbe may see it differently. I can provide certain well-deserved emoluments; advances against the needs of certain freemen; some kitchen money to assist the mayor in carrying out his duties; a bullock to feed the poor; even things of lasting value like repairing the town hall and its clock."

"That sounds like a better idea in my opinion," said Catherine. "You might consider that for Liskeard to ensure that the good burgesses remember you whenever the hour is struck. It would keep Eliots close to their hearts, and indeed their polling places. But what I really want to know is, was the prize worth the price of the game for old Lord Edgcumbe? After all, he died not three years ago. What gained his interests then?"

"Astute comment, my dear; I like that you are increasingly conversant with the affairs of your adopted county. The Edgcumbes can well afford what they spend, and they increase their worth as they spend. They have bought political place and sold political influence. In his younger days old Richard sat here in St. Germans, until he was kicked upstairs twenty years ago. Do you know how he earned that promotion?"

"I expect I will learn soon enough," said Catherine.

"They say he knew too much about the king's minister Sir Robert Walpole and his expenditures of secret service money in the Cornish boroughs, so they made Edgecumbe a peer and thus ineligible to give evidence in a court of law. Soon after that he became Lord Lieutenant of Cornwall."

"Ah, how virtue is rewarded," said Catherine, barely troubling to hide a smile. "Sometimes I suspect you are too virtuous, my dear Edward. I look forward to your receiving greater rewards, in which procurement I would be glad to assist."

"I appreciate your loyalty, my dear. For myself, I do not wish the Edgcumbes nor any family ill through the death of their chief; but one must not stand idly by when the country's governance is at stake. After Edgcumbe died, I wrote to the Duke of Newcastle and advised him that the Mayor and magistrates of Grampound have prevailed upon me and my good colleague William Trevanion to accept the parliamentary interest of that borough. It is my duty to assist them in maintaining the influence of the government, but I pointed out to His Grace that I am loath to attack the reputation of Lord Edgcumbe. But I know that if Trevanion and I do not accept the burden, the good citizens will offer the opportunity to others."

"Ah, Mr. Trevanion, the Member for Tregony," said Catherine. "You have become good friends. Your own influence is also growing steadily, Edward. To build on that, you must not shirk your duty. You owe that to Port Eliot, and your son."

"Indeed, my dear, so very important. We build influence in many ways, political friendships, business connections, family relationships. My mother's father, James Craggs, was the member for Tregony forty years ago. We owe a great deal to the positions and wealth he acquired."

"I do enjoy learning about the world I entered when I married you. But tell me more about our neighbors the Edgcumbes, Edward. I love their former home at Cotehele."

"A charming place indeed," replied Edward, "good enough for a Tudor squire but not grand enough for a Georgian baron. Mount Edgecumbe is impressive, grander, more fit, and it has been improved with comforts in the modern fashion. You know it was Lord Edgcumbe who met Joshua Reynolds when he had a studio at Plymouth Dock, before he moved away to London. His lordship introduced Reynolds to my father and to several of our neighbors. That is how he got his start, and see where he is now.

"Mind you, Port Eliot is perfectly suited for us as it is," Edward added, always aware of Catherine's interest in improving their lot.

"Of course. However, it would behoove us to improve Port Eliot, lovely though it is," said Catherine, "add to its comforts, collect more fine paintings, retain architects to create fabulous rooms, make the grounds magnificent. If you please the Duke of Newcastle, Edward, you will gain not only influence but wealth to satisfy our loftiest ambitions."

"All in good time, my dear. I am on the whole satisfied with the part I play, although I confess I do wish to add to the Eliot fortunes. But I never forget that he who is one's patron today may be out of favor tomorrow. My increase is steady as my experience and friendships grow, and I like to maintain a firm foundation in the income of the estate that is less subject to the whims of others. We must keep our friends and interests at home in Cornwall as well as London."

"Ah, yes, that reminds me of something else that concerns me," said Catherine. "We have heard little from Lord Trenance of late. What might he be doing to meddle in your plans?"

"He is too preoccupied with his personal pursuits," said Edward. "He is more amused by games than occupied by business. He will dabble in his mines from time to time, or use the efforts of his friends to gain some advantage in a turnpike project or to invest in a maritime venture. But he appears to leave a great deal to his steward and Thomas Bolitho, or so young Bunt reports, just so long as they make him enough money to keep up with his expenses, which due to profligate gambling and basking expensively in the admiration of certain women, continue to mount.

"Besides, now that he has ascended to the upper house after the old baron died, he has no need of pursuing the votes of the common man. I have less to concern myself with him in politics than even in matters of business, and there we must simply convince him that he has our confidence."

"I trust you are right, Edward. You usually are, but do use caution where he is concerned. Now, pray explain to me before we leave the fascinating subject of politics, how on earth did Cornwall get so many members of parliament? It seems far too many for the number of inhabitants."

"The inhabitants have little to do with it, my dear, and indeed neither do politics. Fewer than fourteen hundred propertied men have the privilege of the vote throughout the entire county. The county itself returns two members to parliament, like the other shires in England, but in Cornwall there are also twenty-one boroughs that return two each. We must thank the Prince of Wales for many of those; remember that the king's eldest son has been the Duke of Cornwall, since Edward III bestowed the duchy on his son. When the Tudors held the throne they determined to add members who would support the crown in parliament by simply creating royal boroughs in their Duchy. Unfortunately for the prince, he did not reckon with the robust independence of the Cornish, so over the centuries few of the court nominees supported the royal party. That independence is a tradition I am privileged to uphold. And it never ceases to delight me that our forty-four members are only one member shy of the entire country of Scotland!"

"Such behavior may be privileged, Edward, but it does not seem fair to me. Is it right that the two members returned by our little village of St. Germans and by the small market town of Liskeard means that between them they have the same representation in parliament as the great city of London?"

"It may seem unfair to you, Catherine, but I assure you fairness has very little to do with it. And remember, as the wise William Pitt observes, our Cornish boroughs serve as an antechamber for rising men as well as a refuge for those on the downward path. Many an able London businessman resorts to a seat in the country that is not open to him in the city." He paused, looking at her engrossed expression.

"I suppose I will never be able to explain it all to your satisfaction, and indeed such oddities apply to many aspects of life throughout England. But I assure you that the system works, not least in enabling people like us to make a worthy contribution to the way of life of Cornishmen and thus the entire English people, and it leads to most enjoyable lives as we do so."

"Now that surely interests me," said Catherine. "If my wooing, as you phrase it, helps return your candidates, no doubt we will be able to curtain every window in Port Eliot in damask, and St. Germans and Liskeard as well! Do your friends in the gentry own all the boroughs in Cornwall?"

"This is serious business, my dear," said Edward, a little ruffled at being teased. "It is natural that our tenants feel an obligation to us, and of course they appreciate that we know what is best for them. In actuality, there are some boroughs we do not influence, although I fully intend to expand my own sphere. The admiralty sees to it that the interests of the Royal Navy and the ordnance are properly advanced. Old Admiral Clinton has sat for Saltash for years, and I hear that the Secretary of the Admiralty will be put up this year. Of course, Admiral Boscawen represented Truro, when he was not sailing to the American colonies, but his father Viscount Falmouth would see to it that he held that seat anyway. Course, he died in January, poor fellow, and now I have been reliably informed that his brothers John and George will take the seats, so the Boscawens hold on to Truro."

"His widow must miss him," said Catherine, "up to a point, I suppose, but she didn't see him for months on end when he was at sea." She sipped her sherry. "I would like to know Frances Boscawen better." She changed the subject back to what engaged her husband. "What about East and West Looe?" asked Catherine. "They are practically at the end of our park."

"Of that, I hear that John Frederick will not get West Looe again, but that the Duke of Newcastle will see he becomes a Commissioner of Customs. That's a place worth a thousand a year, and his father's a London merchant who's already wealthy. Meanwhile John Buller grows more influential and manages the government interest, despite casting votes in opposition to some measures. He'll try to get one of his family in, alongside young William Trelawney."

"Well, can't you at least make an effort, Edward?" asked Catherine.

"The Bullers are entrenched. It may be more politic to offer help than rivalry. At least Port Eliot must maintain influence sufficient to ensure that we supply the road stone when an extension of the turnpike is authorized. I may well send Polkinghorne and Bunt down to see how the land lies."

"It all still seems terribly complicated, as well as not being very fair," said Catherine, "but I suppose you know best and that I will learn."

"It is not up to us to question custom, my dear; we are obliged simply to observe it and follow it. We truly are well advised to give our attention to ensuring that the worthy Mr. Pitt enjoys support in parliament that enables him to pursue his aims, which ultimately are to our great benefit. That is what will serve our interests. I would urge you not to complain, as I certainly do not."

"My dear Edward," smiled Catherine, placing her needlework back in the bag at her feet, "I hope my curiosity and comment do not sound like complaint. Do not fret. You know you can count on my help. You have no idea how much I enjoy being the lady of this sleepy manor in the depths of the Cornish countryside. Now, allow me to perform my wifely duty and ring for dinner."

Chapter Thirty

Looe

Before the week was out, Edward Eliot met with Charles Polkinghorne and Willy Bunt in the estate office and briefed them on going down to the south coast to Looe to begin work on the elections. Catherine had made a good point. Looe was close enough to St. Germans to make it practical to explore extending Eliot political influence, or at least business interests. The electoral situation in the Looes was complicated and changeable. Even the redoubtable Lord Edgcumbe had given up trying to establish his own interests, since the Trelawnys and their relatives the Bullers had, over time, developed a strong hold locally.

Edward knew he might not possess the brilliance of some men with whom he rubbed shoulders in London, but one thing he had learned from observing them was that much could be gained from methodical and thorough administration. He summoned his clerk to lay out letters he had received from the Duke of Newcastle and his advisers regarding the forthcoming election in Cornwall, as well as copies of his own replies. As he stood at his desk he perused the sequential correspondence in order to discern patterns in the negotiations. Somewhere there could still be an opening for Eliot interests in the Looes, perhaps in alliance with others, especially if the burgesses were discontented and open to change.

The Trelawnys claimed control of six seats. Edward Trelawny had received places as a Commissioner of Customs and then Governor of Jamaica. His brother Sir John received an allowance of five hundred pounds a year from the government and a present of a thousand pounds at election time. Young William Trelawny had applied to the Duke of Newcastle's brother for one of the Looe seats back in '54, only to learn that it had already been settled on one of Governor Edward Trelawny's candidates.

William acquiesced in the arrangement. Not surprisingly considering how things were done, His Grace the Duke then saw fit to induce the Admiralty to give young Trelawny command of the sloop H.M.S. Peregrine, despite his not hitherto having demonstrated his skills as a mariner and a leader of men. Young William learned a lesson in the importance of representing the interests of his employer, and his reward duly came in being invited to take his place in the election this year.

Eliot noted that the Corporation of the Borough of West Looe, that is to say its town council, consisted of twelve burgesses, among whom two families simply took turns occupying the position of mayor for one year. Those twelve alone comprised the entire electorate. The burgesses gained their privileged positions through co-option, appointment by their peers, thus the Trelawnys and their friends did not have to face a popular election to maintain the borough as a family preserve. Everything went smoothly until a couple of years ago when James Buller, M.P., had seen to it that his man had been chosen Mayor.

Four new aldermen were installed who were not even residents of West Looe: James, John and Francis Buller and Charles Trelawny. Acting without a quorum they had nominated as freeman an opponent of the government, a stranger from Tiverton, which was not even in Cornwall, along with Charles Trelawny and the young son of James Buller, who was still a minor.

Edward Eliot had entertained Catherine's notion that there might be an opportunity for his candidate amidst this change. However, the Bullers were deeply entrenched. They and the Trelawnys were related and had been cementing their control over the borough for years, negotiating for lucrative government places into the bargain. Even the present Member of Parliament was not expected to be put up again for the seat. Running against these odds, the past winner of the Derby would come in last, or more likely not even finish. Eliot would await the reports of his men on the outcome of their visits to the Looes, but was not optimistic. If he sent anyone to West Looe it would be Bunt, for the experience. No point in wasting the time of Polkinghorne on such a futile journey.

East Looe on the other side of the river might be a different matter. The town council there comprised a mayor, recorder, eight aldermen, and an indefinite number of freemen or burgesses who possessed the right of election. The Trelawnys and the Bullers did not have the same grip. Perhaps Polkinghorne could find something worth pursuing there.

In any case, no election had been contested at the Looes for many years. But the government in London did not always receive the support it felt it had earned by its favors if not by its policies. The local families had increasingly pursued their own interests. After all, it was they who lived in Cornwall, not the king or the duke.

If Edward Eliot were in the Duke of Newcastle's shoes, he would seek a more loyal manager of these boroughs. Perhaps the government could be persuaded of the benefit of listening to suggestions of change. Yes, Catherine might be right; there could be an opportunity for the Eliot interests. Stacking the papers in order, Edward was ready to give his men their instructions. He summoned them.

"Polkinghorne," he said, as they came through the door, "you have been in my service long enough to understand sufficiently how things work at election time." Turning to Bunt, he added, "I don't suppose Lord Trenance ever used his valet to advance his public interests, am I correct?"

"You are, zir," said Bunt. "Oi never did nothin' loike that when us was down Lanhydrock way. Oi don't know nothin' about elections and such as that. Course, that Trenance wouldn't 'ardly trust nobody, can't be trusted 'imself. But Oi'm willin' to be teached, you might say."

"I want you both to go to East Looe, get yourselves a room at The Fisherman's Arms. Stay there for a day or two and use their excellent beer to cheer up the good burghers. Mr. Polkinghorne will show you the ropes, and you can stay and follow up with any laggards. Then you can ride over the river on your own to West Looe, Bunt, and meet with the voters over there. Keep in mind that each Looe has two members of parliament. The mayors of both towns will be expecting your visits; I've seen to that."

"Will us be able to meet all the voters that quick, zir? There must be 'undreds of 'em, both towns together."

"Good heavens no, man," chuckled Eliot. "There are fewer voters than there are in Liskeard, and we only have to deal with the mayor and corporation, and a few freemen who pay scot and lot."

"Gawd! What the 'ell's that?" sputtered Bunt. "Oi just thought Oi 'ad to deal with them inhabitants of Looe."

"It just refers to householders who qualify by having paid the full amount of their local property taxes," explained Eliot.

"Be thankful, Bunt," Polkinghorne interjected with a grin, "that Mr. Eliot does not want us to pursue sake and soke and infangentheof!"

Bunt's jaw dropped.

"I don't believe Polkinghorne intends you to take him seriously, Bunt," said Eliot, chuckling. "He is just referring to the rights of landholders to judge pleas and hold courts and to arrest a thief who is caught red-handed. Unlike the householder, the thief will not escape scot-free. But we've done away with such things since feudal times. Matters are more straightforward in modern times."

"If you say so, zir. Good job too, Oi reckon," said Bunt.

"Now then, young man, mind you don't go too far; it is important that we honor custom and usage," said Polkinghorne sternly, and then addressing Eliot respectfully asked for his instructions as to their mission in Looe.

They had all been standing, but now Eliot waved them to seats. Once settled, he explained. "Looe differs from our nearer boroughs of St. Germans, Liskeard and Callington. Port Eliot has few tenants in Looe, so they are less beholden to us, and the leading local families have been strongly allied with the Admiralty for years. Nevertheless, they have not always put the government's interests foremost. I want you to sound out the townsfolk and see whether there is any way we can persuade them that allying with the Eliot interests is to their advantage. Then I can find out from our friends in London how we might be of service.

"Remember, what benefits Port Eliot benefits both of you. Keep your counsel, and speak nothing of this conversation. The idea is to see which way the wind blows, so listening is the order of the day."

"I heard tell that last election the Trelawny and Buller men took the Looe folk along to The Fisherman's Arms," said Polkinghorne, "and by the time they drained their tankards a few times they were willing to vote any way they were told to. Only trouble was holding them upright long enough to tell the town clerk who they were voting for."

"You make a good point," said Eliot, "observe carefully, Bunt. I plan to use your services on Election Day in our own boroughs. Note that you must be sure you stand prominently in the polling place. Be sure to listen carefully and be seen to make note of the name of each voter and for whom they tell their vote. This will remind the voters that we know who they are, and know whom they support."

"Oi'll do my best, zir, but Oi dunno 'ow you keep all this stuff in your 'ead, Oi don't really. To my way of thinkin' us should just slip a guinea into their pockets," Bunt said, "that should do the trick, much less to think about."

"A guinea is too much, except perhaps for the mayor himself," said Polkinghorne; "half a crown should satisfy most of them. Anyway, Port Eliot has plenty of things to spend money on; shouldn't waste it on voters who ought to know their duty to respect their betters."

"I don't hold with outright bribery," said Eliot sternly. "Nevertheless, we must ensure our men get elected when the time comes. We owe that to Mr. Pitt, and his support continues to be of value to Port Eliot. But I wonder, perhaps, if there is something other than money we can offer that will benefit not only Mr. Pitt but also Port Eliot after the election is done and gone."

"If you want to know what Oi think, half a crown b'ain't enough to butter no parsnips," said Bunt, "not if us got to be certain sure like."

"Don't you be so free with Mr. Eliot's money, young man," Polkinghorne said.

"Do you have a better idea, Polkinghorne?" asked Eliot.

There was a pause. Then after hesitating briefly, Bunt chirped up. "What if we told 'em we were considerin' building the turnpike down past Duloe, going all the way to Looe? That would be good for their business. Them could send their fish to Liskeard market nice an' fresh, cheaper too, an' get top prices. Us could sell the road stone from Port Eliot, contract to build the road, and collect the tolls when 'er's finished. But us'd need to know that Looe was friendly to Port Eliot, like, to make it worthwhile troublin' with."

Polkinghorne appeared pensive. He reached into his pocket, took out his clay pipe, filled the bowl with tobacco, lit it, and thoughtfully puffed out a cloud of smoke.

"Capital idea, Bunt! That might indeed benefit all parties, don't you agree, Polkinghorne?" said Eliot. "Yes, that suggestion appeals to me a great deal. Keep this kind of thinking up, young man, and you'll go far."

The atmosphere in the office was filled with more clouds of smoke as Polkinghorne tried to screen his discomfort, but Eliot's pleasure at the imaginative idea remained clear. He and Bunt smiled.

"What if the voters won't shift, prefer to stay with the devils they know?" interjected Polkinghorne.

"A good argument, Polkinghorne," said Eliot, sensing the man's discomfort. "I knew I could rely on you for sound advice. Nothing like a good dose of experience. Let's keep in mind that the turnpike business is generally important to Port Eliot, and if there is no practical and affordable appeal to the voters of the Looe boroughs, let us not lose sight of other opportunities, turnpikes elsewhere, other fields of endeavor. Meanwhile, be sure to find out what exactly is going on with the voters."

"That's all very well, zir," said Bunt, "but as Oi told Mr. Polkinghorne when Oi got back from my visit to Lanhydrock, Mr. Clymo let slip they was plannin' to use mine tailin's for road stone, real cheap, undercut Port Eliot, just like that Mr. Ough let on."

"Then we must do everything in our power to beat them at their games," said Eliot, "while behaving with complete honesty, of course, and we'll have to make our own production and transport efficient. Well done, Bunt. We'll just see if we can get the burgers of Looe in our camp. Now you two get on with it."

Eliot assumed Polkinghorne's agreement and gave the men instructions to make arrangements for their ride to Looe the next day. Polkinghorne was to take some money from the heavy chest under Eliot's desk in the office and to be sure to bring back a list of the men they contacted in both towns. Bunt would tell the groom to saddle up two sound horses for early the next morning.

"I am counting on you both," said Eliot, "so do not fail me. By the way, Bunt, Mrs. Eliot is asking after Mary and little Catherine. Both well, I trust?"

"Thank 'ee, zir," said Bunt, "both fit as fiddles, zir." He respectfully stood and helped Eliot on with his coat for the walk back to the big house.

✛✛✛

Next morning dawned damp and cool. Polkinghorne and Bunt met at the stables, stepped up onto the leaping stone and mounted horses that the groom had saddled for them. The road through Polbathic and across to the Looe valley was foggy. However, they made good progress, stopping only for a quick pasty and pint of cider on the way and arriving at The Fisherman's Arms on Higher Market Street in East Looe by mid-afternoon. They made arrangements with the landlord for their beds, for a parlor for their meeting, and with the ostler to feed and water their horses. Then they walked over to the Guildhall in good time to call on the town clerk in the council chambers, to make arrangements to meet at the inn later that evening with the mayor and members of the corporation.

Their visit was expected. Eliot had prepared the way with a letter sent to the mayor several days earlier. The mayor had other business that afternoon, but they were welcomed warmly by his deputy and the town clerk and promised good attendance and a courteous reception that evening. Polkinghorne hinted that they bore good news for the citizens of East Looe and urged that all the aldermen and town councilors attend. They agreed to meet in the parlor at The Fisherman's Arms at seven o'clock for a few tankards of the landlord's best bitter, a smoke, and a discussion of affairs that might be of interest to the borough.

With nothing more to keep them for now, Polkinghorne took Bunt down to the quay to look at the fishing fleet in the harbor. The boats were lying with their sails furled, tied up alongside the quay or moored to buoys out in the stream. Polkinghorne thought that they might look around to see whether they could gather persuasive support for Bunt's idea of bringing the turnpike to Looe.

With the tide out, the estuary of the Looe River was too shallow to keep the bigger boats afloat, so they were resting on legs attached to their beams. All kinds of rubbish and detritus were revealed by the low water, and the smells were unmistakable reminders that Looe was a fishing port. Seagulls screamed and swooped greedily on to piles of fish scraps and entrails thrown into the river by the workers gutting and skinning and packing the fresh catch.

Although not at their best at low tide, the twin Looe towns were picturesque. Polkinghorne pointed out to Bunt the solid stone buildings of the fish market, the packing houses, the ship's chandlers, the sail lofts and the drying racks for the nets clustered around the harbor. Bunt looked up at the hills rising steeply on both sides of the river, with close set whitewashed stone houses and cob cottages clinging hither and yon to the slopes, their slate roofs glistening from the recent rain. The narrow winding streets were interspersed with small shops and inns and blessed by the occasional chapel.

As they walked along the quay, a bearded man in a navy blue fisherman's jersey with holes at its elbows came out of a large three story stone building. Polkinghorne hailed him.

"Halloa there! A word if you please. I'm Polkinghorne, from St. Germans. Tell me your name."

The man slowed, moved a chew of tobacco from under one cheek to the other. He had a pronounced limp, and a peg leg. "My name be Pengelly, zir. What's it to ye?"

"I manage business for the Port Eliot estate," said Polkinghorne, "and my man and I are in East Looe to meet with the mayor and corporation about the election and matters that will be of interest to the town. Tell me pray, what is that fine building used for?"

"Well, Oi dunno whether it's none of your business," growled Pengelly, "Oi don't 'old with elections any'ow, not when common folk 'as no say, not that them in parliament would take notice of we if us did say what was on our moinds."

"There's nothing to be done about that," replied Polkinghorne, "it's just the way things are ordered, whether we like it or not."

"Not me you should worry about, zir," said Pengelly, "my wife carries more clout nor Oi do."

"How come, my good man?" asked Polkinghorne, "surely you wear the trousers in your household?"

"My wife be the mayor's big sister, an' 'e do listen to 'er when 'er wants summat powerful bad," said Pengelly. "That's 'ow us got yon building for the pilchard packing, right on the quayside. 'Elps make sure fishermen 'ave powerful voice in what goes on in East Looe. An' 'tween you an' Oi, that might 'ave 'ad summat to do with 'ow Oi myself got to be foreman." Trousers, thought Bunt? Glancing surreptitiously at the man's peg leg, Bunt mused that Polkinghorne might have chosen a more diplomatic turn of phrase when addressing a one-legged man.

"Ah, the mayor, that'll be His Honor Richard Puddicombe, I dare say," said Polkinghorne trying to ingratiate himself. "Fine upstanding gentleman, I'm told. Tries to do what's best for Looe," he said, hoping his local knowledge would soften things.

"Beggin' yer pardon, zir," said Pengelly, tugging at his forelock, "Puddicombe's mayor for West Looe, was anyroad, goes turn and turn about with his brothers and the Hearles. Leastways, that's what they was doin' until Mr. Buller pushed his man in, and now is pushin' out Mr. Frederick as their M.P. But them goings on is across the bridge; Oi can 'ardly keep up with this side.'"

"Well, thanks for your information, Mr. Pengelly, but we can't stand here chin wagging all afternoon," said Polkinghorne, "we have an important meeting to prepare. But perhaps we could have a chat tomorrow and maybe you could show us around. Port Eliot is always interested in possible ventures. Come along, Bunt."

"Right you are, zir," said Pengelly more warmly, "mebbe Oi could, an' all. Us ain't busy this time o' year. Come 'round when it suits you. Oi'm usually found somewhere near the waterfront."

With that Polkinghorne and Bunt made their way back to The Fisherman's Arms. It was still early for their meeting so they went into the snug, where Polkinghorne ordered a pint of home brewed ale and a beef, potato and onion pasty for each of them. Bunt looked thoughtful as he took a deep pull on his pint.

After a moment Bunt said, "Oi been thinkin', zir, sounds to me as if this election business be fair mixed up. May be too much to 'andle, what with everythin' else Mr. Eliot got on 'is plate, like. Maybe us could keep an eye on things and dip our oar in later on. Mebbe us should worry about the turnpike first."

"I've been thinking the same, myself," said Polkinghorne, "although it's not as if I couldn't take care of everything myself. Mr. Eliot knows he can rely on me."

"Oi knows that, zir," said Bunt, "but if us be goin' to encourage the burgesses with a turnpike for getting' their goods to market, the fishery would be a big part of that. Oi knows that Pengelly feller ain't no gentry and ain't no voter. But 'e 'as the ear of the mayor through 'is wife, an' Oi 'spect the fishermen listen to 'im too, seein' as 'ow 'e manages the pilchard packin' 'ouse. Us should make sure 'e be on our side too."

"Of course, man," said Polkinghorne, "why do you think I gave him the time?" He tapped Bunt on the shoulder and smiled. "You're not the only one with a brain around here. Now drink up, we need to get our supper and then our guests will be here."

They went into the parlor after a hearty supper and were greeted by a cheerful fire and soon joined by the town council members. The landlord sent in his barmaid to serve them beer all around. Polkinghorne frowned as Bunt took yet another refill for his tankard and seemed to be paying more attention than was proper to the barmaid who was giving back as good as she got, with smiles and smart replies. However, he decided not to say anything. He noticed that the mayor ordered just a glass of water. Then after introducing himself and Bunt to their guests, Polkinghorne explained that they were here to see what might interest the town in switching allegiance to the Eliot interests.

Initially it seemed to go well. The townsfolk were friendly towards the Eliot family and knew of their benevolent influence over the generations, even though they had had few direct dealings. It was soon clear that with the election in a few weeks, they did not have time to make the effort it would take to put in a rival candidate, even if Mr. Eliot was inclined to meet the expense. Polkinghorne became concerned that they were making no headway. Mr. Eliot would be sorely disappointed if they failed to accomplish their mission.

Polkinghorne decided to change the conversation. He brought up the importance to East Looe of extending the turnpike and Eliot's willingness and ability to make it happen. There was a shuffling of feet, and the men sat up straighter. For the mayor, it was the first time he had heard of the idea at first hand, although the town clerk had advised him of the possibility. Polkinghorne felt it might be a good move to involve Bunt in the proceedings, since he would be working with them on the actual management of the project if it came to pass, and it would help if they got to know each other.

"Bunt, stand up! Would you please describe to His Worship and the good councilors the quality of the road stone from Port Eliot and how we could ensure reliable supply at a very good price."

Bunt looked up. His eyes were not focused. He had not been following the conversation. He appeared to be concentrating hard. He tried to stand, but slumped back down to his seat, knocking over his tankard, spilling the dregs that were left.

"Road shtone, zir?" Bunt said, recovering his balance. "Aargh, road shtone. Us 'as plen'y road shtone, us makes a proper job of road shtone, aargh, bloody road shtone." He burped, and his speech dwindled to a murmur as he stretched his legs and promptly closed his eyes.

"I apologize, gentlemen," interrupted Polkinghorne, "my man appears to be not himself. Said he wasn't feeling well on the way over. We will continue without him."

"We've heard enough, Mr. Polkinghorne," said the mayor firmly. "We thank you for your hospitality and bid you good night."

With that he got up, and the rest followed him out of the parlor. The last to leave was the town clerk, who whispered urgently.

"Come to the Guildhall in the morning, Mr. Polkinghorne, there are matters we must discuss."

Chapter Thirty-one

Voters

Charles Polkinghorne was furious. He was slow to anger, but nothing upset him more than seeing his carefully constructed schemes brought down by someone else through rash and intemperate behavior. After the meeting broke up, Polkinghorne summoned the landlord and the potboy and between them they dragged an unresisting Bunt into the stable yard behind the inn, pushed his head under the pump and doused him with bitterly cold water.

"There, that should sober you up, you foolish young pup! Wait until Mr. Eliot hears of your disgraceful behavior. I cannot allow you to meet with the voters of West Looe on your own. I'm going to keep a close eye on you from now on. You can't be trusted to behave like a proper representative of Port Eliot. You may have lost us the voters of East Looe, and for sure you won't be the Eliots' blue-eyed boy after this escapade."

They hauled Bunt upstairs and dropped him on his bed. Unlike Polkinghorne, who spent the night tossing and turning in anxiety and frustration, Willy Bunt slept the sleep of the just despite his transgression. Next morning, Polkinghorne enjoyed the landlord's hearty breakfast, with fried bread, bacon, sausage, lamb kidneys, fried eggs, potatoes and baked beans. Bunt looked over what was offered through bloodshot eyes and nibbled at a dry crust of bread.

"Look lively, my lad," boomed Polkinghorne, "we've got to get on to the Guildhall and see if we can mend the damage."

Bunt winced. "Aargh, zir," he whispered. Bunt dragged his heels as they walked over to meet the town clerk, who greeted them with surprising cheer.

"I'm sorry about last night," said Polkinghorne.

"Think no more of it," said the town clerk. "You must make allowances for the mayor; he's got a powerful bias against drinking. You see, his son was the apple of his eye, spoiled, consequently of weak moral fiber. The boy fell in with bad company, drinking, roistering, not attending chapel. This deeply troubled our mayor, who is a righteous man." The clerk's visage darkened. "One night the boy was out drinking with a bunch of fisher lads. They were in no condition to fight or flee when they were set upon by thugs of the press gang, looking for recruits for the king's navy. They were hauled off to serve in a sloop of the line, H.M.S. Peregrine, for

God knows how long. The mayor hasn't heard from his son in going on three years."

"Do you know where he got to?" asked Polkinghorne.

"There is news that a number of Cornishmen sailed with Admiral Boscawen to the Americas," said the town clerk, "went to Newfoundland and Canada. Boscawen has been in the thick of the fight with the French. We have not heard whether our boys still live or have been killed, even scalped by Indians."

"Boscawen? He was Member of Parliament for Truro, until he died a couple of months ago," Polkinghorne said. "We'll need to find a new man there, too. Mr. Eliot knows many men in high office, he'll probably be asked for his advice. Come to think of it, Mr. Eliot may be able to make inquiries and find out what has befallen the boys."

"Mr. Eliot would be a true friend of Looe if such a thing could be done, and better still if the boy could be returned to his family," said the town clerk.

"I will see what can be done," said Polkinghorne, "but I make no promises. Say nothing just yet. It would be an extreme favor, and Mr. Eliot can only do such things for close friends, or perhaps for those to whom he himself owes favors."

"The mayor is a man of rare integrity," said the town clerk, "and whatever personal benefit he may gain, he would always put the interests of Looe first. I am, however, in a position to advise him in his private as well as the public interest."

"Mr. Eliot will not forget to see that you are rewarded for your diligence in the citizens' interests," said Polkinghorne. "I will be sure he is reminded, won't I Bunt?"

"Aargh," said Bunt noncommitally. He seemed to have recovered his equilibrium, but wanted to pursue other topics. "Us saw a fisherman down on the quay yesterday, name of Pengelly. Said he'd show us around where they pack the pilchards."

"Ah, Pengelly," said the town clerk, stroking his chin. "Don't make the mistake of underestimating him. You need to keep on his right side. He doesn't qualify for the vote, but he has influence with the mayor. Their sons were good friends, got each other into mischief. Those boys were impressed at the same time. The press gang took Pengelly too, he's an experienced sailor, but they let him go when they saw his peg leg."

"Told us 'is wife be mayor's sister," said Bunt.

"That's true. She is a right tyrant," said the clerk. "She was from St. Keyne, and they were married in the church there. There's an old story that the water from the well has magical properties. The first spouse to drink from it after they're spliced gets to wear the trousers. Old Pengelly limped off to the well after the service as fast as he could go. But his bride had taken a bottle of the water to the church with her! She's been running his life, and most of East Looe's, ever since."

"Poor old Pengelly," chuckled Polkinghorne. "Perhaps I can quietly persuade Mr. Eliot to bring cheer into his life by freeing his son, too. But the lad might prefer to stay aboard ship rather than come home to a mother like that. No wonder he took to drink."

"Aargh, but what Oi wants to know is 'ow us can get Pengelly on our side," said Bunt, "so 'e persuades 'is wife to see to it that the mayor makes sure East Looe votes for Mr. Eliot's candidates."

"That sounds like a tall order," said Polkinghorne, glancing at the town clerk, "from what we know about the voters. What I'm thinking for now is that the mayor and corporation could at least be persuaded of the benefit from Port Eliot's support for a turnpike. One has to think ahead."

They both waited for a response from the town clerk but he was non-committal. "That would depend," said the town clerk, rubbing his chin. "What I'll do is take you down to the pilchard palace, as we call it, and make sure Pengelly gives you proper respect. He's a leader among the fishermen, and if he's your man, East Looe will listen to what you have to say for sure."

They walked on down to the quay and found Pengelly smoking his pipe at the doorway of the pilchard palace. His greeting was noticeably warmer than yesterday. Polkinghorne reminded Pengelly that he had agreed to show them around, which he promptly did.

"This 'ere buildin' is where us does the pilchards, brings in the catch, salts 'em down, packs 'em up, ships 'em out," said Pengelly. He limped ahead of them into the big stone-floored room inside. "This 'ere's where us brings the catch, does the curin', piles 'em up in big bulks with layers of salt, leaves 'em three weeks 'til they be 'fairmaids,' ready to be pressed an' packed."

"Then what? 'Ow do ye pack 'em? Where do ye ship 'em? Who do ye sell 'em to?" asked Bunt, his curiosity kindled.

"When they'm cured, the fish maids layer 'em in casks, all neat like in circles, 'eads out. Then us press 'em for two or three hours with the weight of that great pressin' stone over yonder, squash 'em down. Get oil out, used for lamps, greasin' engine bearings," replied Pengelly, warming to his story. "Then next day the maids fills up the casks with more pilchards. Then the cooper comes in an' 'eads up the cask. The buyer's agent comes in, checks casks, weighs 'em, stamps 'em. Then us be ready to put 'em on board ship."

"Where do you send them?" asked Polkinghorne. "How many?"

"Italy, usually," said Pengelly, "a few locally. 'Undreds and 'undreds, two thousand each cask."

"Why aren't you working now?" asked Polkinghorne.

"Tain't season. Pilchard schools come around the English Channel late summer. Before 'ere they goes down Atlantic coast, first Newquay, then St. Ives and Newlyn, then 'round Lands End an' up to Polperro, then 'ere. Huers up on top the cliffs calls out when they see 'em coming, so boats can go out and seine them in, millions of 'em."

"What do you catch at this time of year?" asked Polkinghorne.

"Wrasse, cod, hake, 'erring, bass, flounder, sometimes mackerel," said Pengelly. "Fish takes lot of work. Got to salt 'em down, otherwise they'd rot before them gets to market."

"Ah, could you sell more if you could deliver them fresh?" asked Bunt.

"Aargh, would taste better. Us would still 'ave to go as fast as pack 'orse could carry 'em," Pengelly said, "costs a pretty penny too, can't 'ardly take enough to make the trip worthwhile."

"Sounds like you need a good road that would take a wagon load," said Polkinghorne. "Maybe Port Eliot could make that happen. Now that's something we could work on, after the election. Let's see how that goes."

"That would be a wonderful thing for East Looe, wouldn't it Pengelly?" interjected the town clerk.

"Now ye're talkin'," said Pengelly, and ruminatively spat out a wad of juicy tobacco. "What's the catch?"

"There's a lot to such a project; it takes a lot of organizing, and not least an Act of Parliament," said Polkinghorne. "You can rest assured that any dealings East Looe has with Port Eliot will be fair and aboveboard. Mr. Eliot knows that a venture is only good if it benefits all parties. We will follow up our meeting with the mayor and corporation, and now we can tell them that the fishermen of Looe would welcome better roads to get their fish to market. All that's needed next is for Mr. Eliot to put his mind to it."

"Well, Oi s'pose no 'arm's done," said Pengelly, putting a fresh wad of tobacco into his mouth between gaps in his stained teeth. "Us'll 'ave to see what's what. Oi wouldn't moind much."

Polkinghorne and Bunt took their leave and headed back towards The Fishermans Arms, leaving Pengelly and the town clerk in earnest conversation.

Bunt felt better.

Chapter Thirty-two

Viscount

The indoor staff at Lanhydrock was bustling about, preparing for the imminent arrival of Lord Trenance. Her ladyship had received a letter from him some days ago announcing that he had completed his business in London and should be expected home shortly to take up the reins once again. She had spent only ten days with him in Town doing some shopping and catching up on social engagements with old friends, and then he had sent her back home. Her husband claimed he would have no further time to spend with her in view of the press of business brought about by his new responsibilities in the House of Lords, and besides, he reminded her, her duty lay with their son and with Lanhydrock.

As Lady Elianor reread the letter in her boudoir she had no doubt that he would be fully occupied in London but felt many doubts as to the nature of that business. In any event the likely outcome of it would be anxious meetings with Clymo upon his return and, as ever, the pressing need for funds would dominate their discussions. From the tone of the letter he would return with a greater sense of self-importance than ever, although to understand its basis she would have to wait until they met face to face.

Late in the afternoon she heard a commotion in the hall downstairs and the barking of the dogs outside as the butler opened the door. Footmen were waiting to carry in his trunks. Lord Trenance made a noisy arrival, and she went down to greet him.

"Blast your eyes man," he was shouting at the butler, who was trying to help him off with his coat, "can't you see I've been travelling over those damn roads in that damn wagon for day after day to get back to this godforsaken hole? Get those cursed dogs off me! Stop fussing with that coat and get me a tankard of warm sack. My arse is so bruised I'll have to drink it standing up. Where's her fancy ladyship? Oh, there you are, my beloved!"

Lady Elianor came down the stairs behind him and walked around in front of him. Despite exerting as much self-control as she could command, she wrinkled her nostrils. She spread her arms to embrace him, placing her chin on his shoulder to avoid his breath. "Welcome home to Lanhydrock, James. You appear travel-stained and weary. Cook has kettles of water on the fire ready for you if you wish to take a bath, and the maids have warmed towels. I'll send up your valet to prepare it."

"I'll send my valet to do my own bidding," snarled Trenance. "But now I would prefer a warm welcome from my wife over a warm towel. Where is my son? Been playing with all the knickknacks you bought him? Is he riding yet? Decent seat, what? Where's that rogue Clymo? I wrote him to expect me today. Probably been stealing while my back has been turned. I want to see him in the library in an hour, catch him out in his trickery. Probably needs a good flogging."

He studied Elianor, who wore a silk gown of the purest emerald green. "Welcome to Lanhydrock, indeed. Now, my dear, high time for you to do your wifely duty and give me a properly affectionate welcome. I expect you've always wanted to make love with a viscount, eh? I am now Dunbargan!"

Reddening and glancing around at the waiting servants, Lady Elianor pursued the least sensitive topic. "What do you mean, James?" she asked. "You have been raised to a viscountcy? How did that come about? Will a place come with it? Will there be emoluments?"

"More likely more damn expense," he replied. "Turns out Eliot and his friends are backing the wrong horse. The king is getting impatient with Pitt's damn arrogance, and the war's costing too much. Interesting goings-on in the Lords while I was in town. Newcastle had better watch out, too. Bute's the coming man, has the ear of the new king, quite the favorite. Splendid fellow. Approached me through a mutual friend, good old Buckingham. All I have to do is support the king's friends in the election, make sure they're elected in some of these boroughs as well as the county. Made me a viscount. Cost me a pretty penny though, ten thousand pounds. Need new robes too, and the old coronet won't do, need one with eighteen silver balls. Suppose you'll need one too, now that you're a viscountess. Worth it, though, should show these Cornish gentry how to make real money."

He stepped towards Elianor. "Well, come on, don't keep me waiting. Let's get on upstairs."

"My dear, there is nothing that would please me more," said Elianor, "but there's Clymo coming up the steps now." She smiled widely at him. "I know your business with him is urgent. And he has Mr. Bolitho with him. Imagine, Viscountess Trenance!"

"No, no my dear. The name's Dunbargan; it's an Irish peerage. Those heathen won't be needing it any more. Better put it into sound English hands with me."

Clymo approached them. "Welcome home, your lordship," he said, a little out of breath, bowing.

"Better show the proper respect," said James, swiveling around to face his man of business. "I'm Viscount Dunbargan now, or will be as soon as we get a few affairs in order. Glad you didn't forget my arrival. Well, well, Bolitho here too? Join me in the smoking-room, and we'll get down to business right away. Where's my damn sack?"

"My lord, I offer you my humble congratulations," said Clymo, narrowly refraining from tugging at his forelock. "Your father, the late Baron Trenance, would be proud."

"Huh, the old man would have to show me some respect at last," said James. "I outrank him. Of course, I won't stop at viscount. I'll be an earl before I'm done, perhaps even a marquess. Just have to make sure His Majesty appreciates my worth. Matter of time."

"And, of course, my congratulations also, my lord," said Thomas Bolitho. "Your elevation adds great prestige to Lanhydrock, and indeed to all of Cornwall. May we hope that in good time you may even receive the dukedom you deserve. It is my honor and privilege to be associated with you, and I am sure I speak for my partners at the firm as well."

"Wasn't expecting you, Bolitho," said James. "What are you here for? Anyway, appreciate your kind words. But we'll have a Duke of Cornwall when the king gets around to having a son. Wouldn't do for me to overdo things, keep everything in reasonable bounds, don't you know?"

"I asked Mr. Bolitho to join us," said Clymo, wiping his brow with a kerchief and gesturing at Bolitho, who had entered behind him. "I felt your lordship might require a thorough discussion of your affairs, and there is much that has transpired while you have been away."

"Honor and privilege are all very well," said Viscount Dunbargan; "these titles don't come cheap, so I hope you are here with splendid ideas for coming up with the money. And my stay in London didn't come cheap either; her ladyship's extravagance doesn't help; and there are one or two fellows pressing to be paid a few guineas for one thing and another. Ah, about damn time," he added as the butler came up with a tray carrying James's mug of hot sack. The butler offered drinks to the others and then withdrew.

"Now what's been going on here down among the savages?" asked the viscount, as he strode ahead of them into the smoking-room.

"You charged me with finding additional sources of income for Lanhydrock, my lord," said Clymo, positioning himself before a chair but waiting to sit until James was seated. "With Mr. Bolitho's advice and assistance I have been successful in meeting your needs in due course."

When they were all seated and the butler had provided Bolitho and Clymo with their sack, James resumed speaking. "My needs are greater than they were," he said. "I have gone up in the world, and my new position must be paid for and supported."

"How much do you estimate your requirements to be, in the near term and looking further into the future as things settle down?" asked Clymo.

"Well, including a few mandatory entertainment expenses while in London, my needs for the immediate future amount to some twenty thousand pounds," said James.

Clymo reddened, and Bolitho choked on his sack. Neither of them spoke for several moments. Clymo looked at Bolitho.

"That is a great deal of money even for Lanhydrock, my lord," ventured Bolitho, "although no doubt it could be managed in due course."

"I don't have time, and the Earl of Bute expects the money now, not in due course," stormed James. "That's why I have a money man, Bolitho. It's up to you."

"Is there any possibility that the earl could be patient for a few months?" asked Bolitho.

"Bute expects to be appreciated, of course," said James. "It's mainly a matter of whether His Majesty will be patient, and anyway I will not lose face with the court just because you shirk your duty. It seems I may have to find someone else to take care of my affairs, someone I can rely on. Anyway, the settlement of my, er, entertainment expenses cannot wait. They are a matter of the utmost urgency."

"Perhaps Mr. Bolitho could prevail upon his partners to make special arrangements, given the long established relationship with the Trenance family," Clymo said.

"There are investments required at the mines in order to increase their income," said Bolitho, "and preparing the tailings for road stone will require stamping mills. Using men with sledgehammers would be too slow and expensive. And besides, we should reserve funds for the guarantees to Mr. Eliot on the turnpike project."

"Damn Mr. Eliot," said James, "I thought I told you to make sure that our agreement was not binding."

"Indeed, my lord, and our notary was most discreet. But in light of some potential inclination to minimize obligations elsewhere, my partners would not look kindly on an agreement for further loans to Lanhydrock on the basis of a signature alone. They have made it clear to me that some sort of surety must be provided. I must be frank with you, in your own best interest," said Bolitho.

James brightened. "Notary?" he asked. "My damn father-in-law had a notary talk my father into signing some kind of agreement when he settled her dowry upon her. It's high time she paid for her own extravagances. What do you say to that, eh Bolitho? I should rightfully be able to lay my hands on that money. Why didn't you think of that?"

"I am afraid, my lord, that whatever portions of the dowry were available to Lanhydrock have already been put to good use. I negotiated with her ladyship's trustees at the time and more proved impossible to arrange." Bolitho thought for a moment and turned to Clymo for inspiration.

The steward shifted awkwardly in this chair. "Perhaps arrangements might be made in conjunction with Poldice," Clymo said, mopping his brow once again.

"What in God's name are you maundering about, man?" demanded James.

"Ah, yes. We had an interesting conversation with Mr. Williams, the mine captain at Poldice," said Bolitho. "We sounded out the possibility of increasing revenue for your lordship. He explained that this could be done, but would require machinery, possibly with water wheels, at best steam driven. All this would require capital. Mr. Clymo told him in no uncertain terms that if he wanted to keep his position he would have to put up the capital himself. After all, his father died recently and was probably able to leave young John something out of what the late baron paid him over the years, including bonuses for exceptional performance."

John Williams might not recall the conversation in quite these terms, but Bolitho realized that he and Clymo were in a difficult position, and it was in their own interests to persuade Viscount Dunbargan that they could bail him out of his difficulties.

"And what he stole, I dare say," said James. "Well done, Clymo. Anything that increases revenue for Lanhydrock we must pursue. What did young Williams have to say then? Needs must when the devil drives, I suppose, although I'll be damned before any artisan gets a piece of the Trenance estate."

"I am confident that we can come to some arrangement that will benefit Lanhydrock," said Bolitho. "You will continue to own all of the land surrounding your mines and the mineral rights below, including beneath the sea, subject of course to the usual privileges of the Duchy of Cornwall. Just leave it to Mr. Clymo and Bolithos. It is possible that we may arrange a financing facility with Mr. Williams to purchase an interest that will only increase his efforts on behalf of Poldice, with Lanhydrock receiving the proceeds for you to disburse as you wish, with our advice of course."

"As for Mr. Eliot," added Clymo, "he will be too busy with the election to pay much attention to the details of his turnpike project. He may find himself rabbit hunting with a dead ferret."

James looked up, startled. This conversation was bringing back memories he had long suppressed. What could Clymo know about rabbit hunting? He took a sip of his sack and gathered his thoughts. "Ah, the election," he said. "Now that I am to be a viscount perhaps I should pay more attention to Bodmin than my father did. I could put in my own men, have more influence with the king."

"If I may observe, my lord," said Clymo, with more confidence now that the conversation was going better, "electioneering is an expensive business."

"Indeed," said Bolitho, "you are in a position to sell your seats to the treasury. Leave it to the Duke of Newcastle to trouble about the bother and expense of electioneering. Lord Bute and His Majesty would be most pleased and perhaps could regard such kindness as part of the consideration for the viscountcy."

"Capital idea!" said James, somewhat cheered. "Just see to it, but seek the help of a borough broker to achieve the highest price. Gentlemen, you are excused. I will leave the details to you to accomplish as soon as possible."

"There is one more thing, my lord," said Clymo. "With Mr. Williams' help we were also able to take steps to improve production at your Wheal Hykka Mine down near Pendeen. We have appointed a new captain, name of Addis Penwarden. I trust you approve. You may wish to meet him and satisfy yourself."

"I don't need to meet a mine captain!" scoffed James, standing. "Viscounts don't mix with riffraff. Just you be sure that he works his miners hard and increases my income. And now I have my homecoming celebration to attend to. Good day, gentlemen. Be off with you. See yourselves out."

With that James settled gingerly back in his chair and reached for his tankard. He was still stiff and sore from the journey. As he swallowed more sack a thought came to him. Addis. That was an unusual name. Had he not once come across an Addis? Was not that the name of the boy in the woods down west, the one who showed him how to kill a rabbit, how to wrestle with a bully? If it were the same chap, now grown to manhood, he had better keep his mouth shut. Viscounts did not put up with being reminded of embarrassing happenings.

Anyway, he was more than a match for a mere tinner. And he would show those men of business who was master now. Bolitho did not even know all of his business, poor fool. He had not mentioned that he expected his financial circumstances to be further improved as a consequence of the delivery by his seafaring friends of several casks to the undercroft of St. Hydrock's church. Tomorrow he would have to talk to the vicar about it, in the strictest confidence of course.

Now he had pleasanter things to think about. He drained his tankard, left the room and strode upstairs in a better mood than before. His damned wife would pay for the privilege of her position in one way or another; he would make sure of that.

Chapter Thirty-three

Campaign

All across England, current and would-be members of parliament, their supporters, agents, burgesses and freemen with the privilege of the vote were engaged in the general election, the first for seven years. Voting began in some parts of the country as early as March 25th and ended in others as late as May 5th. As was typical in other matters, Cornwall was a laggard in elections. There was an old wives' saying that "procrastination is the thief of time," but it didn't make the Cornish hurry.

At Port Eliot, Edward and Catherine were fully engaged in the elections. After receiving the report from Charles Polkinghorne that things did not go as well as hoped during his and Bunt's visit to Looe, Edward Eliot was not counting on swiftly breaking the Buller family's electoral stranglehold there. At the same time, he was used to persevering and getting his way; he was reluctant to give up on Looe.

"Polkinghorne, surely with the influence of Port Eliot you could have prevailed," said Eliot. "Perhaps greater skill in persuasion, more determination. After all, our offer to extend the turnpike must mean a lot to Looe. Why would they not be grateful?"

"We did our best, sir," said Polkinghorne.

"Then you must do better," said Eliot. "Is there no other more persuasive reason, no influential individual whose support we could enlist?"

"I hadn't meant to say anything, sir," Polkinghorne hesitated, he hoped convincingly, "but Bunt was part of the problem. He took too much ale and couldn't hold it, he stumbled and made no sense. He mortally offended the mayor, who is a teetotaler."

"You mean Bunt got himself drunk? Silly young pup! Well, it won't be the first time such a thing has happened. When I first went out into the world, my father gave me very good advice. Told me to drink as much as I liked, but count how many glasses it took to get me drunk. After that he told me to always drink one less."

Polkinghorne chuckled obligingly, but it irked him that his master was not more inclined to reprimand Bunt. It was apparent that Bunt had gained much favor in the eyes of the Eliots. Even Mrs. Eliot took an interest in encouraging Willy and Mary and her little goddaughter Catherine.

Polkinghorne spent a moment filling and lighting his pipe. He blew rings of smoke into the air. "I have no doubt that you comport yourself with dignity whatever the circumstances, sir," he said. "However, Bunt's behavior damages the reputation of Port Eliot."

"Well, that cannot be tolerated," said Eliot. "I had high expectations of your visit to the Looes and they have been dashed. I trust that you gave Bunt what for, Polkinghorne. It seems that he cannot hold his drink. I will speak to him myself if you wish, but he is your responsibility and he needs to take his orders from you. It's a great pity; Mrs. Eliot takes much interest in the Bunts."

"Thank you, sir, but I believe I have dealt with the situation," said Polkinghorne, puffing on his pipe. "I made my displeasure clear to the young man." Polkinghorne saw Eliot frowning. He thought for a moment and added, "Nevertheless, Bunt has promise and I'm sure I can make the best of him. I must point out, sir, that the burgesses were taken with Bunt's idea of Port Eliot making possible the building of the turnpike south of Liskeard towards Looe. They understood right away how that would benefit the fishermen. Perhaps we could work on making that happen and, by the time of the election after this one, they would strongly support our candidates."

"You may be right, Polkinghorne. I'll rely on you to take care of the matter. For the present, let us put our energies into making sure that we win in Liskeard and St. Germans, and I do want to take on Grampound," said Eliot. "However, before we leave Looe to the Bullers and my lords of the admiralty, is there nothing more we can do to secure our influence?"

Polkinghorne took his cue, and told Eliot about the fate of the sons of the mayor and his brother-in-law, the old fisherman Pengelly, at the hands of the press gang. Seeing the opportunity, Eliot unhesitatingly promised to see what he could do on their behalf. He immediately called a clerk and dictated a letter to William Pitt, reminding him of their previous discussion on the matter of impressment of sailors. His message not only expressed the worthiness of helping those in distress who were not in a position to help themselves and their families, but also strongly put forth the political benefits of doing favors for influential citizens.

His employer was at heart a kind man, Polkinghorne thought, sometimes too kind; but he also had political wisdom.

The Eliots turned their attentions entirely to the election. In Liskeard, the mayor and governing corporation had commissioned the building of a husting at the Bull Ring, across from the White Horse in the center of town. The sturdy wooden platform was four feet high, so all could see the candidates, and about sixteen feet long by eight feet deep. It was smaller than at the last election since, after the withdrawal of Mr. Morshead due to his lack of support among the freemen, there were only two candidates. There was, however, room for the returning officer, his clerk and their table, with space for the voters to stand in front of it when they told their vote. The expense had been borne by Port Eliot, and Polkinghorne made sure that the citizenry was aware of this generosity.

The last possible day for polling, the fifth of May, was chosen for the great event. This was a practical decision since the day before was the first Monday of May, called Whit Monday, the day after the Christian feast of Pentecost and a popular time for baptisms. The custom was for participants to wear white garments to church on Sunday, and so the name Whitsun came into use. As everyone knew far and wide, Whitsuntide was a time of great thanksgiving and merrymaking in Liskeard.

The festival reputedly originated as a celebration of the relics of Liskeard's patron saint, St. Martin, to whom the parish church is dedicated, being brought to the church in 1001. The town council took advantage of the festivities coinciding with election time to draw the largest possible crowds. It would be good for business, and town elders would be more popular than ever with the brewers and publicans. Whitsunday itself was sober, but the next day the population broke out of its reverence with an enthusiasm that continued for several days thereafter.

Edward and Catherine Eliot traveled into Liskeard to their town house a day or two before polling day. The setback at Looe continued to discomfit Edward. He was determined to ensure there were no setbacks elsewhere. He took Polkinghorne and the Bunts with them, so that he could explain to them exactly what had to be done and how to comport themselves when they were left in place in Liskeard to manage the election. The Eliot children were left behind with the nanny at the big house.

The Eliots and their servants usually went to church at St. Germanus on the Port Eliot estate, but this Whitsunday the Eliots decided they should attend matins at St. Martin's in Liskeard, since Edward felt it would be an opportunity to make their presence and that of his servants known to the voters.

The travelers caught sight of the church tower as they neared Liskeard. The battlemented tower stood as a landmark in the highest part of town near the old castle. Catherine pointed it out to Polkinghorne and the Bunts. "Look," she said, "there's St. Martin's. Did you know it is the second largest church in Cornwall, after Bodmin? It goes back to Norman times, built to last of granite."

"Aargh," said Willy Bunt, "Them old timers knew 'ow to build, solid, not all airy-fairy loike these days. That gurt tower could stop a siege."

"Indeed," said Catherine, "although our churches are intended to defend our souls, Bunt, not our bodies." Edward smiled to himself as Catherine continued. "The tower was built in four stages and is fifty-seven feet high."

"What's that there church loike inside?" asked Mary Bunt.

Edward Eliot was about to respond, but as he drew breath Catherine answered Mary. "The interior is quite impressive, you'll see it when we attend the service tomorrow. There is a chancel and a long nave with lofty north and south arched aisles. There's a Lady Chapel by the south aisle, with a second floor of seating above, called the Ladies' Gallery. The townspeople of Liskeard are justifiably proud of St. Martin's."

Edward never ceased to be amazed by the energy and enthusiasm of his wife. There was a time early in their marriage when she lovingly chided him for his habit of teaching her about the history of his family and Port Eliot, of Cornwall and indeed the whole of England and much of the world. Now Catherine had become quite the pedagogue. Edward smiled affectionately to himself again.

Charles Polkinghorne was also observing this exchange. He would be wise, he thought, to be cautious in his criticism of Willy Bunt in front of Mrs. Eliot. It was clear that she was quite taken with the young man and was a champion of his value to Port Eliot. There would be occasions when Polkinghorne would keep his opinions to himself.

Meanwhile, the Bunts for their part were overawed once again by the ecclesiastical architecture, and as uncomfortable as ever with anticipation of Anglican ritual. They wished they could go to the Wesleyan chapel on Sunday instead, but Willy knew on which side their bread was buttered. Eliot had reminded them that only members of the Church of England could sit in parliament, and this election season was no time to display non-conformist leanings.

Catherine Eliot's enthusiasm extended to embracing her husband's request to support his election efforts. She planned to entertain the chief burgesses at a lavish tea at Eliot House on Whit Monday, the day before polling day. That morning, Catherine directed Mrs. Bartlett, the cook, to serve their guests in the dining room. Catherine surmised that the generous selection of cakes and sandwiches would be better accommodated on the large table than on the unpracticed laps of rustic citizens perching unsteadily on chairs in the reception room.

"So, we will have tea in the dining room, Bartlett," Catherine said. "Mr. Eliot wants to make a good impression on our guests, and we must make sure not to embarrass them since they are not used to surroundings such as these. They are fine fellows, and I am sure their manners are excellent, but I think they might be more comfortable sitting at the table."

"I'll see to it, ma'am," replied the cook.

"Let us use the tea service from Josiah Wedgwood's new manufactory. It is fine and pretty, and it is made in England. Tell the parlor maid to set the table with one of the embroidered white linen cloths.

And we must offer our guests both India and China tea, fresh bread and butter, some cakes and plenty of jam and cream."

"Yes, ma'am," said Annie Bartlett, "and shall we use the silver tea service with the spirit lamps to keep the two teapots nice and hot? And I can make my special saffron cake."

"Oh good, that will be perfect," Catherine replied. "Mr. Eliot and I were just talking about that, it's one of his favorites."

"Everything in the house was swept and polished ready for your arrival, ma'am, so the housemaid will just need to do a quick dusting at the last minute. If that is all, I'll start giving directions right away."

"Be sure to have Mary Bunt help in the kitchen," said Catherine, "it will do her good to learn more about cooking, and I am sure her husband would appreciate that, too."

Annie Bartlett set Mary to work alongside her sister Nellie and the kitchen maid. Mrs. Bartlett made two tins of scones with buttermilk and potash and cooked a batch of ginger fairings, thin ginger wafers that had become favorites of Catherine's. Cook baked extra bread to slice thinly and spread with butter, and to use for sandwiches. She showed Mary how to make chicken liver paté and fish paste for the sandwiches.

"Just wash those there chicken livers in salt and water, Mary me luv," the cook said, "then simmer them in a saucepan until them is cooked through. Then put 'em in this 'ere mortar and pestle, chop up a bay leaf and a clove of garlic and a sprig of thyme, add a pinch of salt and pepper. I'll get butler to let us 'ave some o' that brandy he's got 'id away, stir a drop or two in and pound it all nice and smooth. Them'll fancy that, but we don't want so much brandy that the teetotalers know what they be eatin'."

Nellie gently scalded milk brought in from the home farm and set it in a shallow pan in the cool larder. After the crust had formed she skimmed it off to make Cornish clotted cream. She brought up from the cellar crocks of jams made last autumn: strawberry, blackcurrant, blackberry and apple, to spread on the scones with the clotted cream.

Annie Bartlett did not trust her helpers with the most important treat of all, the saffron cake. That she made herself from a special family recipe. She mixed wheat flour and butter from the Port Eliot mill and dairy, with a pinch of salt cut off the block she kept in the pantry, and a little sugar. Then she added dried currants, sultanas and chopped candied lemon and orange peel. She had warmed up some milk into which she stirred brewer's barm to make the dough rise and in which she had then steeped a drachm of saffron, to give her cakes their distinctive flavor and bright yellow color. Finally, she kneaded the mixture into dough that she set aside to proof before putting it into greased tins to rise again and then to be baked in the cloam oven.

There was one more treat that could not be left out, pasties. Not the hearty dinner pasties with meat, potato, turnips and onions. For this occasion, the cook baked dainty little tea pasties, some sweet filled with jam or mincemeat or apple and raisins; some savory ones with bacon and chipples, tender spring onions finely chopped; all wrapped in their pastry cases and folded into half moon shapes with edges crimped to seal in the tasty contents.

Meanwhile, Eliot sent Polkinghorne and Bunt into the town to meet with voters, to see how the land lay with them and to make sure that preparations for the next day were in hand. With Catherine in charge, he was free himself to travel back to St. Germans for election day. He would stand on the hustings with young Philip Stanhope.

Edward was exceedingly well entrenched at St. Germans and would not have to ask for a poll to be taken. And he certainly wouldn't discuss his views with the voters. After all, there was little need, as he owned the houses they lived in. Eliot's oratory skills would not be tested. But young Philip Stanhope was a different matter. He was less well known, having recently moved from Liskeard, and he was still inexperienced and not likely to command a good impression. He would need support.

Willy Bunt looked into the kitchen to say good-bye to Mary. "You take care of yourself, me luv," she said kissing him on the cheek, "and don't you go into them taverns drinkin' that there beer with them voters. Off you go."

"Oi can take care of meself, Mary," said Willy. "You 'elp Cook like a good girl, and don't go worryin' your pretty little 'ead about us."

Bunt followed Polkinghorne's lead out of the side door as they walked down Pondbridge Hill, turned right to Pipe Well, left up Pike Street and to the Bull Ring.

It was a warm spring day. There were crowds of people about in the streets, with groups of country folk who had walked in from the surrounding farms. They were in celebratory mood, laughing and shouting, many clutching tankards of beer or rough cider, "scrumpy" as they called it. Shop windows were boarded up. It looked as if the shopkeepers were protecting their goods from danger of the customary revelries getting out of hand.

Bunt and Polkinghorne pushed on up the hill through the crowd.

"We'd better split up to cover more ground," said Polkinghorne, "but you watch how much you drink. I won't put up with any more shenanigans like you performed down in Looe, and Mr. Eliot won't neither, I'll see to that, you mark my words. You'd better go to the White Horse, it's nearby, and I'll head on down to The Albion. If you see any of the councillors, speak nice to them. Tell 'em you're from Port Eliot, buy them some ale, but not too much. Be sure to remind them that Mrs. Eliot is expecting them at Eliot House at four o'clock, not a minute later, and they'd better be on their best behavior."

"Right you are, Mr. Polkinghorne, you knows ye can rely on Oi." So saying Willy walked on to the White Horse where he entered the smoky snug, went up to the bar, ordered a pint of bitter, gratefully picked up the foaming pewter tankard and looked around to see who else might be there. Would not do for him to stand aside while the others had their ale, now would it? He knew better than to let it affect him.

He was surprised to see Joseph Clymo sitting at a table in the corner with a lively group. His daughter Morwenna was among them. She was chatting vivaciously with a couple of men he had not seen before, and one he thought he recognized. It looked like Edwin Ough, the Town Clerk of Liskeard. That Morwenna was a lively one Willy thought, but he was here on Mr. Eliot's business; better be on his best behavior and pay attention to that. What was Edwin Ough doing with Clymo, Willy wondered. The Town Clerk was counted to be one of Mr. Eliot's staunch supporters.

"What ho, Mr. Clymo!" Willy called cheerfully. "You up from Lanhydrock for the election? Thought ye'd stay around Bodmin."

"We aren't paying much bothering with the House of Commons this election, Bunt," said Clymo, affably enough. "His lordship's gone up in the world. He's a viscount now, or will be soon enough, when the 'i's' are dotted and the 't's' are crossed; Viscount Dunbargan it will be."

Willy was impressed. "Get on!"

"We're here for Whitsuntide, an' all, Willy," Morwenna said smiling warmly. "We've got more business in Liskeard than elections. I'm glad to see you again!" She winked at him, in a way that the others could not see, reminding him of their interrupted embrace when he was over Lanhydrock way.

"Oi'm pleased to see you again too, Miss Clymo," said Willy, as formally as he could, "and you gen'lemen too, of course." This was indeed an unexpected encounter, and it might become interesting, and even pleasurable, after all. He took another sip of his beer and returned Morwenna's wink.

Chapter Thirty-four

Sport

"Come sit here with us, young feller me lad," said Joseph Clymo jovially to Willy, then called to the barmaid. "Bring this handsome chap a pint."

"I'll have another one too, Dad," said Morwenna smiling broadly at Willy. "How about you, Mr. Ough?"

"I don't mind if I do," said Ough. "Drinks all round. Bitter, everyone? Let me get them. Give me a hand at the bar, young man. The barmaid's got her hands full with all these other customers. We mustn't let these folk go thirsty." They walked over to the bar together. "I know you," said Ough. "You're Bunt, work with Charlie Polkinghorne for Mr. Eliot. What are you doing here? How do you know these people?"

"Oi might ask you the same, Mr. Ough," said Bunt quietly. "What are you doing 'ere with these people? Oi thought you were a friend of Port Eliot. You told us about them Lanhydrock plans to undercut us by sellin' mine tailin's cheap for the turnpike. Mr. Eliot trusted you. Just you wait until I tell Mr. Polkinghorne what you're about."

"It's not what you think," said Ough. "Hold your fire. Anyroad, how do you know them? How are you so friendly with Miss Clymo? We'd better talk later. Mr. Clymo is looking at us funny."

They carried extra tankards and jugs of ale drawn from the casks at the bar over to the corner table, and with Morwenna's help poured more drinks for the men holding out their tankards, except for the two strangers sitting next to Joseph Clymo. One was wearing a black coat; he had taken off his tall hat and placed it on the table in front of him. He waved away the jug of ale proffered by Morwenna. He had an air of authority about him. The man appeared to be in his thirties, with black curly hair, stained teeth, broad shouldered, well built. His complexion was pale as if he had rarely seen the sun. He turned to cutting slivers of plug tobacco, sharing it with Joseph Clymo as they both filled their clay pipes.

The other man was also dressed in black, wearing a wide-brimmed hat with a round crown. He had white linen bands at his neck, the mark of a clergyman. His hands were resting on the table, smooth, white. He was stocky, black-haired, swarthy complexioned, appeared to be of medium height and about fortyish. He did not accept ale either.

"This here is Addis Penwarden," said Clymo to Bunt, turning toward the younger man, "captain at Wheal Hykka, one of the Trenance mines down west, works for me, came up to visit Lanhydrock, discuss some plans. We've got big things going on. Penwarden, this young feller is Willy Bunt; he used to be a servant in the house at Lanhydrock. Didn't stick to it, so came up St. Germans way, works at Port Eliot for Charlie Polkinghorne. You'll be running into him, I dare say."

"Aargh," said Bunt, not acknowledging the introduction. He was watching more merrymakers streaming into the White Horse.

"And this is Mr. Penwarden's friend, the Reverend Perry," Clymo said, poking Bunt in the arm. "They came up together. Mr. Perry lives down that way too, Wesleyan minister. Perranporth, he told me."

"I thank you for your hospitality," said Reverend Perry, "but I cannot abide strong drink. The harm it does grieves me."

Willy stared at both strangers. "Oh, Willy," said Morwenna, "shake their hands like a gentleman, they won't bite you."

"Aargh," Willy grunted, offering his hand.

"And this here is Ough, Edwin Ough, Town Clerk of Liskeard," continued Clymo, "but I expect you've run into him already."

"Aargh, mebbe," said Bunt. "There's hordes of people 'round 'ere. Liskeard is gettin' to look like Lunnon!"

A loud hallooing and the sounds of wind instruments came from outside.

"Come on, Willy!" exclaimed Morwenna, "they've started the games! Let's go on out and join in. Come on, everybody!"

"You young people go on, us old 'uns will finish our pipes and sup some more. We'll be out later," said Joseph Clymo. He thought to himself, so it's Willy now, is it? I had better keep my daughter close, and my eye on young Bunt.

A crowd was gathered in a roped-off area around the Bull Post. At the center of the crowd riding on a donkey sat a very drunken old man dressed in a white wig and black gown like a judge; two pages held up his train from either side. He was escorted by a sheriff's troop and javelin men, about thirty in all. Some were on horseback, carrying painted staffs, their harnesses decorated with flowers. Near the front of the procession a man dressed in women's clothing brandished a ladle and belabored his companion, who lewdly grimaced and gesticulated while hitting back with a broom. They all set off in procession around the town, marching and dancing and singing and fooling, with followers waving tankards and drinking as they went.

"Who's that pair?" Bunt asked a neighbor in the crowd.

"Them's Joan and John," came the reply. "Show up every Whitsuntide; get drunk as skunks and us all has a good laugh."

"Look over at the husting," said Morwenna, catching up with Willy, "there's two ruffians with quarterstaffs doing their best to break each other's heads."

"Just you wait," said their new acquaintance, "that'll be over quick, then us'll see proper wrasslin'."

Soon enough, straw was strewn over the roped-off area and two wrestlers came into the ring. One looked somewhat heavier than the other, but they were both big men with sinewy muscles, barefooted, wearing tight breeches and loose canvas jackets around their broad shoulders, the fronts tied across their bare chests with tapes.

The bigger one was introduced as a tinner from near Redruth who spent his days heaving kibbles of ore; he had the broad back to prove it. The tinner had the neck of a bull, was bald with dark curly sideboards, piercing eyes and a determined jaw. The other was a local farm laborer, taller and not as heavily built but wiry.

"Oi've seen 'im at The Eliot Arms," said Willy, "works on a farm near St. Germans. Looks loike 'e pitched plenty of sheaves of corn."

A loud roar went up as the contest began. A third man standing between them seemed to be in charge, the judge. He gave a signal and the wrestlers came into the center of the ring and shook hands. Each wrestler gathered his jacket into his left hand and then tucked the loose folds under his armpit, keeping the jacket tight around his torso so his opponent could not easily grasp it. They half crouched facing each other, a pace or two apart, then circled about, eyes darting, each looking for a chance to grasp the other.

The stockier one, the tinner, lunged. The crowd clapped, but the farm worker nimbly evaded the charge. The tinner charged again and this time succeeded in grappling with his opponent, wrapping his hands around the folds of the canvas jacket and heaving him to one side. His victim staggered but somehow regained his balance before the heavier man could throw him to the ground.

The tinner was enraged. He charged again, panting, like a bull. This time the farm worker retreated a pace, then rolled onto his back and pulled his opponent towards him, got him off balance, tripped the tinner over on top of him. The farmer went for a 'flying mare'; he caught hold of the strings of the tinner's jacket, swung him right off his feet and planted him on his back on the ground. Then the farmer wrapped the jacket tightly around the fallen tinner's arms so that he could not break the hold, and pinned both shoulders and one hip to the ground in triumph. The judge signaled a fall and raised the arm of the winner. The crowd roared in excitement and appreciation. The wrestlers paused to regain their breath, shook hands, and got set for another round.

"Willy, you should be a wrestler," said Morwenna, her face flushed with excitement, her eyes sparkling. "Big strong lad like you."

"Wouldn't moind wrasslin' with you and that be a fact," said Willy grinning foolishly.

"That would never do!" laughed Morwenna, "Anyway, where's Mary?"

"She be up at Eliot House, 'elpin' Cook and Nellie in the kitchen, gettin' Mrs. Eliot's tea party ready for this afternoon," said Bunt. "Come on, just give me one little kiss; 'er'll never know. What the eye don't see, the 'eart don't grieve over."

They snatched a quick embrace.

"Come on, Willy, stop that now," said Morwenna unconvincingly. Willy Bunt could be fun, especially after a few beers, but she had to be discreet around her father. "We'd better go back in. Dad will be wondering where I've got to. Anyway, watchin' that wrestling made me thirsty. Let's go fill up our tankards." It was the Whitsun fair after all.

They pushed their way into the seething crowd and back into the White Horse, Bunt staggering through the doorway. He was intercepted by Ough who was watching them arrive. Morwenna wondered what he might have seen. She went over to her father's table, where they all seemed in high spirits, except Penwarden and Perry, who remained sober.

"Bunt," said Ough, seizing him by the arm, "listen to me. Make no mistake, I am behind Port Eliot. Clymo came to the corporation offices and told me he wanted to discuss something of interest to Liskeard. I had a good notion what it was about: Lanhydrock furnishing mine tailings for the turnpike. I agreed to meet so I could find out exactly what they're up to: prices, what quantities they could supply, how far away, delivery methods. Then I was going to report to you and Mr. Polkinghorne. We know how much Mr. Eliot does for Liskeard."

"Oi don't know about that," Bunt said doubtfully. "Should 'ave nuthin' to do with they if you'm for we."

"Don't underestimate what I can do for Port Eliot, young man. And while you're about it, be sure you understand that you need me to keep my mouth shut about certain young ladies, if you get my meaning."

Bunt belched. "So let me tell you to be sure to vote for Mr. Eliot's candidates tomorrow. That's what Mr. Eliot said Oi should tell all the voters. An' Oi'll be standin' by the hustin', watchin', me an' Polkinghorne."

"You can count on it," said Ough, "Mr. Stephens and Mr. Champion. And this very afternoon I'm going up to Eliot House to have tea with Mrs. Eliot, me and the other burgesses. It's very kind of her. The Eliots are good to Liskeard, and we are grateful to be sure."

"Oi should think so, not like that bloody Trenance, viscount Oi s'pose us should call 'im now 'e's jumped up. 'E would'n' do nuthin' fer nobody. Who's that other feller you was talkin' to, strong lookin'? Would make a tidy wrassler Oi'd say."

"Addis Penwarden?" said Ough. "Seems like a nice enough feller. Mine captain, come up from down west, with his friend the minister. Knows what he's about, so Clymo tells. Men respect him, stands no nonsense. Not much for joining in the fun though, don't drink much. Wouldn't like to go up against him. He's supposed to meet with his lordship at Lanhydrock while he's up here. They're looking to make more money; my guess is his lordship's in a bit of a pickle. Got to make the mines pay more, or so he told Clymo. That's why they keep on about selling the tailings for the turnpike."

Just then there was a fanfare and beating of drums from the direction of the Bull Post. The noise startled a donkey standing nearby, which bucked and threw off its rider into a heap on the straw. He lay there, either hurt or drunk, and nobody took notice. The crowd was giving all their attention to a group of rough looking men, farm hands by their dress and muddy boots, dragging a bull by a rope tied through a ring in its nose.

The terrified beast was kicking its hind legs, tossing its head on its heavily muscled neck, snorting and bellowing as they pulled on it mercilessly. One of the men tied the other end of the rope to a ring in the boulder sunk into the ground.

Another cut the twine holding shut cages made of withies, willow twigs. Out bounded five or six bulldogs, two white, another brindle, one piebald, all with short smooth coats, short-legged, heavy and thick-set, all yelping and snorting and slavering with excitement. They rushed at the bull in a pack. The bull tossed its head again to fend them off.

"Them's strange lookin' buggers, make no mistake," said Willy, already fascinated by the spectacle, "bow-legged, big-chested, their jaws stick out past their muzzles, their chops hang down loike."

"They're bulldogs," said Ough, "specially bred for bull baiting. They've powerful jaws. Once they lock on to the bull they never let go. And their nostrils are set back out of the way, so they can still breathe. They're strong, ferocious, determined. Wouldn't like to be attacked by one myself."

"What's going on?" It was Morwenna. She had come back out of the White Horse, accompanied by Addis Penwarden and Reverend Perry. "What are they doing?"

Just then a bulldog came flying through the air towards them, tossed by the bull's horns. The crowd screamed, drew back. The dog landed at their feet, howling in pain. It couldn't get to its feet. Morwenna bent to pick it up.

"Don't!" said Penwarden, "it'll bite you. It's fierce, may be rabid."

Morwenna left the dog writhing and stepped back. Two dogs charged at the bull, then retreated as it lowered its head and its fearsome horns threatened them. Two others took the opportunity to sink their teeth into the bull's fetlocks, hanging on grimly, slavering, drool flying. They hampered the bull's movements as it tried vainly to kick them off. It turned its head back for a thrust with its horns, but couldn't reach its tormentors.

Seeing an opening, the other two dogs rushed for the head again, one going for its jaw and sinking its fangs into the bull's fleshy lip. The crowd roared, their blood lust aroused. The enraged bull circled violently, pulling on its rope, trying to dislodge his tormentors, their jaws locked tight, not giving way. The rope in his nose checked the bull's stride. He turned the other way, surprising the dogs, and gored one through its belly and tossed it into the air. Blood spurted from its wound, splashing the face of a screaming woman.

There was another disturbance as the two men dressed in black shouldered their way through the crowd, which parted as Penwarden demanded, "Out of our way!" Then Perry cried out angrily, "This has got to stop. It's cruel. It's inhuman. It's ungodly. You will all be cursed!"

Penwarden took a knife out of his pocket, sawed through the bull's tether and tried to drag it free through the crowd. It broke loose, knocked over a young lad and trampled him, then charged up the hill towards open country. Its handlers ran after it in vain. The bulldogs milled about, snarling, puzzled at the escape of their adversary. The crowd murmured angrily.

"We'd better get away," shouted Morwenna, "come with me. Where's Willy got to?"

"Down there," said Ough, pointing. Willy lay prone on the straw. He had passed out.

"Fetch him!" screamed Morwenna.

"Leave him," said Ough. "He's drunk, full as a goat."

Someone kicked Willy in the side.

The group made its escape as best they could. It was Whitsuntide at Liskeard.

Chapter Thirty-five

Election

St. Germans, like Liskeard, had chosen the last possible day for holding the parliamentary election, Tuesday May 5th. The husting had been set up in the square in front of The Eliot Arms.

Eliot decreed that his estate workers could have the day off to observe the goings on. He trusted that their behavior would be civilized. Eliot knew the vicar had performed several baptisms on Whitsunday and had urged his parishioners to introduce their infants to a godlier way of life than that led by their neighbors in the nearby town.

"Never," the vicar had intoned from the sanctuary of his pulpit in St. Germanus, "follow the frivolous example of the dissolute townsfolk of Liskeard and sully the glory of Whitsuntide with ungodly games and pastimes."

Eliot rode into the village with a groom, followed at heel by Bracken, his favorite Springer spaniel. He also took with him Philip Stanhope, who was staying at Port Eliot for the run-up to the election and a day or two afterwards. Catherine remained at the town house in Liskeard to "woo" the voters, in her husband's rather quaint term.

Edward was pleased to see a hundred or more people milling around the village, most of its inhabitants. Even those elderly and infirm living in the Almshouses who could manage the short walk had come along to watch. He thought for a moment that they were admirably fulfilling their civic duties, sufficiently interested to hear the speeches of the candidates and listen to their arguments, even though but a handful of the more substantial men could actually vote. Then he realized that, of course, they were more drawn by the free pasties and beer that he had arranged with the publican to provide at midday. Watching an election could be thirsty work.

Eliot had grown up among the villagers and now received a warm welcome. He encouraged young Philip Stanhope to make himself less of a stranger, to greet the voters, shake their hands, slap their backs, make himself agreeable to men he rather too obviously regarded as his inferiors. He had better succeed at the glad-handing because, in the light of his prior performance when he sat for Liskeard, his election speech could not be expected to turn many heads, let alone change many minds. Eliot's influence, however, should ensure that the right man would be elected and that support for his friends in the House would not be diminished by lack of management in St. Germans.

Seeing one of his more prosperous tenants, Eliot hailed the man who farmed Tregrill. "Morning, Hocking," Eliot called, "how is your new plough working out? I trust those new fangled iron coulters are turning over that loam of yours a lot better."

"Morning, sir," Reg Hocking replied, tugging at the peak of his cap. "We've had a wet spring and before with the old plough I'd've had to wait until now to get started in this mud. As it is, Stony Drill is already ploughed and harrowed, and I've got my oats sown. Young Colin could 'ardly keep up with Hector and Lysander, they draw so easy now. Ten acres all done in two days. Best investment I've made in years, should be able to get 'er paid off in no time."

"Good man," said Eliot, "got to be progressive to make farming pay these days. That's a fine pair of Shires you've got. You should take a look at those new Dorset sheep we're bringing in. Improve your wool yield, gain weight young and produce excellent mutton too."

"Aw, I'm used to my own sheep, sir; our shepherd knows how to tend them. We're blessed with good pastures and I'm satisfied with what they produce."

"Can't stand still, Hocking. Talk to Polkinghorne about them. You can buy some of our new lambs to get started, once they're weaned. We can tide you over; you don't have to pay for them until you start selling their wool."

As he got only a nod for a reply, Eliot continued, "Fine day for an election. Looking forward to my speech? What do you think of my chances, eh?"

"I wouldn't bother with a fancy speech, if I were you sir," said the farmer. "Speaking for myself, mind you, I'd vote for your dog if you set him up on the husting. From what I hear from the other voters over at The Eliot Arms, they're of the same mind. We get fair treatment from Port Eliot, and we like to keep things the way they are."

The insistent clanging of a hand bell got their attention. It was the returning officer announcing that the election had begun. He stood on the husting behind a table, with a leather-bound book in front of him. After several irritated attempts to silence the crowd, he waited as more streamed out of The Eliot Arms bringing their tankards with them to join those already milling about the square.

The villagers crowded close around the platform and eventually quieted down after the bell stopped ringing. The returning officer directed the candidates to come up on the platform and sit at the table on either side of him. Stanhope swept off his hat, bowed deeply, and invited Eliot to precede him up the steps. They took their seats. Stanhope held a lace-edged kerchief over his nose; evidently the aromas of a rural village were distasteful to him. The returning officer gave a couple of rings of his bell, called for nominations, and sat down.

Reg Hocking climbed up the steps and stood in front of the table. In a loud, clear voice he announced, "I hereby am proud to nominate our own Mr. Edward Eliot as Member of Parliament for the borough of St. Germans once again. He has served our borough well for many years. He is a good squire and an honest man. There is no finer for miles around." With that he moved to one side, and people cheered heartily.

One of the other big farmers, who was also a voter, seconded the nomination. The returning officer asked for further nominations. The vicar stepped up and nominated the Honorable Philip Stanhope, whom he prayed would soon become well known to them all, his practiced voice carrying his lengthy speech beyond the square and almost across the park to Port Eliot. The crowd muttered and stamped their feet and then resorted to cheering in an eventually successful effort to persuade the vicar to bring his oration to a close.

The butler from the big house seconded the nomination in a surprisingly graceful but mercifully brief tribute to a man whom he had never met. Neither contribution to the goings on surprised Eliot, who had put the vicar up to his task and written out a speech for his butler. Eliot was, however, warmed at the practical way in which Reg Hocking had expressed gratitude for his support.

It was the turn of the candidates. There were but two. There had been a fellow from somewhere up near London who had been put forward, probably by someone in opposition to the administration, Eliot guessed. But the only one who had approached Eliot himself to buy the seat, and he after all owned the borough of St. Germans, was the Eliots' old family friend the Earl of Chesterfield, who was a Whig, and he had bought it for his bastard son Philip Stanhope. After all, if Chesterfield couldn't offer the boy legitimacy he could at least provide a living and a career, and what better than membership in a prestigious body like the House of Commons?

At any rate, the threat of a possible rival from outside the Eliot connections had not materialized. Really, there was no need for a vote since Eliot himself was as usual unopposed. But the returning officer had not gone to all the trouble of making up his book and arranging for the husting to be erected not to make a day of it. He rang his bell again.

"Order, order! Good people of St. Germans hearken!" he declaimed, "the nominations are hereby closed. The candidates may now address us. Mr. Eliot?"

Eliot rose and with a wave of his hand said, "Kindly allow my good friend Mr. Stanhope to speak first." Stanhope rose. He was slight of figure, pale and stooped and glanced from side to side. He coughed from time to time into his handkerchief.

"Having come all the way from London at considerable inconvenience to visit your village," he began, "my stay will be brief. Although the amenities to which I am accustomed are absent, you seem like good folk." The crowd muttered and shuffled their feet.

"Why should us vote for you, your honor?" demanded a man at the back of the husting.

Stanhope straightened his spine. "Well, I am the son of an earl and thus ably equipped to do the job," he responded.

"But what have you yourself accomplished?" asked another.

"Damn your impudence!" hissed Stanhope under his breath, his face reddening. Eliot glowered and examined his feet.

"Answer the question!" shouted a third.

Stanhope cleared his throat and had another wipe at his nose. "I serve His Majesty in the diplomatic service," said Stanhope defiantly. "I have been the British Resident at Hamburg, a most important post."

The returning officer intervened. "Thank you, Mr. Stanhope, most interesting, and now, Mr. Eliot, perhaps you would say a few words, sir."

Eliot rose and took command of the situation. "Good people of St. Germans," he began, "it has been my privilege and good fortune to represent you in parliament, like my forefathers from time immemorial. I eagerly look forward to continuing to serve your interests. I also ask you, out of respect for Port Eliot, to support my good friend the Honorable Philip Stanhope. His father, the Earl of Chesterfield, and his father before him, have been good friends to St. Germans, and to Cornwall. As you get to know Mr. Stanhope better, I am confident you will find him a good friend and worthy of your trust."

The crowd applauded and he took his seat. The returning officer stood and rang his bell once more. "I now declare that the votes are to be told. The gentlemen of property who are members of the Church of England and who are qualified to vote know who you are. Please step forward as I call your names from the book and tell your vote for each candidate loud and clear, yea or nay."

A score or so of men made their way forward across the platform. The crowd murmured in anticipation although the outcome was in little doubt. After marking down the votes in the record the returning officer rang his bell again. "Order, order! I hereby declare the results. Mr. Edward Eliot is elected nemine contra dicente; the Honorable Philip Stanhope is also elected with one dissenting vote. May they ably serve St. Germans and England and do their duty with honor. God save the King!"

"Long may he reign over us," intoned the vicar, not to be ignored. "Three cheers for our Members of Parliament and our incomparable British democracy! Hip, hip . . ." The crowd responded lustily, some throwing their hats in the air, "Hooray! Hooray! Hooray!" Well satisfied that they had done their civic duty they began to disperse towards the pasties and beer.

Eliot grasped the returning officer by the shoulder. "Well done, an excellent job, for which I thank you. But a word if I may. Allow me to see who voted against Stanhope." A brief perusal turned up the voter, "Aha, Robert Tremayne." Eliot thought a moment. "Ah yes, he keeps the village shop. Rather unwise. Port Eliot has customarily bought supplies from him. He will be hearing from Polkinghorne. On second thoughts, he simply won't be hearing from Port Eliot for a long time to come."

A minor irritation, thought Eliot, otherwise a most satisfactory day. He called for his spaniel, Bracken, who was foraging for pasty crusts in the crowd, and headed for The Eliot Arms stable where the groom had secured their horses during the election proceedings. He called Stanhope to join him. They would ride home across the park and relax in the library with a few friends to celebrate their success over glasses of port. He looked forward to Catherine joining them before nightfall and to learning from her the election results in Liskeard. He trusted that they would be equally satisfactory for his candidates. Perhaps some more port.

But before Eliot had walked more than a few paces he heard his name called out. A rider drew up beside him at the edge of the departing crowd, his horse lathered and snorting. It was the footman from Eliot House.

"Sir, an urgent message from Mrs. Eliot. She prays that you come quickly to Liskeard. One of your men from Port Eliot has been locked in the stocks. She fears he may be kept overnight, and the crowd is in an ugly mood. He may come to harm. Only you as mayor can order his release before the magistrates meet at the quarter sessions."

"What's the damned fellow's name? What did he do to deserve this?" demanded Eliot.

"Bunt, sir. Drunk as an emperor and disorderly, sir."

"Oh, whatever can you expect of the working classes, eh?" the vicar intervened, smirking. "I daresay I wouldn't interfere if I were you, Eliot. Let the fellow take his punishment, might teach him a lesson."

"Mrs. Eliot said would you please be sure to come, sir, as quick as you can, sir," repeated the messenger.

Eliot nodded at the vicar and summoned his groom to bring the horses and some pasties for their journey. "Vicar, you come with me. We have a sinner on our hands. That's your department. You can ride Stanhope's horse. Stanhope, you go on back to the house without me. It's not far to walk, the exercise will do you good. The butler will take care of you. Have anything you want to eat or drink, you're due a celebration. I've got to go to Liskeard to clean up this mess and take care of Mrs. Eliot. We'll both see you tomorrow afternoon. Welcome to St. Germans, your new constituency."

Philip Stanhope stared at him in alarm, but Eliot was already riding off with the vicar bouncing along on Stanhope's horse in his wake, leaving the new Member of Parliament for St. Germans with no choice but to follow instructions with the promise that sufficient attention awaited him. Stanhope kicked a stone out of his path and started his walk.

Chapter Thirty-Six

Mining

For Joseph Clymo and his friends the Whitsuntide melee at Liskeard culminated in the constable threatening to call out the militia to restore order at the Bull Post. The bull was long gone over the hillside and someone had rescued the injured boy.

The constable dragged a soporific and unresisting Willy Bunt to his feet and hauled him off to the stocks. There the constable unceremoniously dumped a bucket of cold water over Bunt. This woke him up enough to be seated on the bench with his legs stretched out and his ankles padlocked into the holes between the top and bottom boards of the contraption. This example made of Willy persuaded the crowd to break up, only to continue their rowdy reveling in other unpatrolled parts of the town.

Meanwhile, Joseph Clymo had decided not to wait for the election and to leave Liskeard behind as quickly as possible. After all, it is not as if he were a voter there. Clymo had made arrangements for an important business meeting the next day at Lanhydrock with Viscount Dunbargan. If he was to meet the viscount's pressing demands for money both immediately and for the indefinite future Clymo had to obtain financing. As far as he could see the only solution was to secure investment in increasing production and revenue from the mines.

To prepare the way Clymo had sent a message to Thomas Bolitho to come to Lanhydrock and discuss possibilities with him and Viscount Dunbargan. He had also invited John Williams to join them. Clymo would have Addis Penwarden ride down with him as soon as they could get away from Liskeard. Thus he could rely on Bolitho to address financial matters and the two mine captains to provide practical details at the meeting.

Joseph Clymo knew from experience that his employer was impatient and lazy and resisted paying proper attention to business. Nevertheless, it was up to the steward to anticipate all questions or objections the viscount might raise since any one could be fatal to his case. If the viscount's demands were to be met and his exasperation assuaged, Clymo had to make him face up to major decisions, and to stick to them.

Clymo felt he had thought of everything, but then he had an idea. "Penwarden," he called, "if we are to reach Lanhydrock by nightfall we must leave post haste. Let us get something at a food stall to keep us going and then we'll mount up."

"Right you are, sir," said Penwarden. "I'll be ready when you are. Give me a few minutes to bid farewell to our friends."

"If you see Mr. Ough ask him to join us for a bite," said Clymo. "I have something pressing to ask him."

Addis Penwarden shortly rejoined Clymo, accompanied by Edwin Ough, the Town Clerk of Liskeard. Clymo greeted Ough warmly. He had two things on his mind. First, if Lanhydrock could unseat Port Eliot in its bid to supply crushed road stone for the Liskeard turnpike a great deal of unanticipated revenue would be found, albeit not immediately. Second, if this could be brought about, Clymo would gain not only gratitude from the viscount but influence with him, since the steward claimed the use of mine tailings for road stone as his idea. The viscount would particularly enjoy winning against his rival, Mr. Edward Eliot.

At the same time Joseph Clymo was not sure that he had persuaded Edwin Ough to lend his support to Lanhydrock rather than Port Eliot. He put it to him straight. "You're a man of influence in the town," he told Ough as he waited impatiently for food and a hot drink before setting off. "You could see to it that the Liskeard corporation made a decision that would benefit the burgesses. Ride with Penwarden and me now to Lanhydrock to meet the viscount and give him your promise, man to man. I'll make sure that you would be remembered, it would be worth your while."

Ough hesitated, but pointed out that Mr. Eliot, as Mayor of Liskeard, carried more weight than ever. "Besides, I have pressing engagements here in the town," Ough said, "and I am a voter. I must stay here to do my duty at the husting." But there seemed to be more to his reluctance than duty. Clymo remembered that Ough had hinted in an earlier conversation that Dunbargan, or Sir James Trenance as he was previously known, had personally insulted him. Clymo tried to get to the bottom of it. He had hoped for some time that Ough would play a part in his plans and did not want a misunderstanding to block his way.

"Out with it, man, something seems to be troubling you."

"Well, Mr. Clymo," said Ough, "I well remember when I was taken to Lanhydrock by Mr. Eliot last year when he and Mrs. Eliot were on their way there as guests. I was traveling to Bodmin on turnpike business and they rescued me after a highwayman robbed our stage wagon. Sir James rudely told me to walk from there to Liskeard, but Mr. Eliot was gentleman enough to have his own coachman take me on my journey."

Clymo sometimes felt that the Trenance family made it difficult for their servants to serve them to the best of their ability, and this was turning out to be one of those occasions. It was more important than ever that the viscount be made to understand the issues and commit to irrevocable decisions.

Joseph Clymo had another disappointment. Morwenna, to her father's surprise, also asked to be left behind in Liskeard. Morwenna was just as reluctant to reveal the real reason for wanting to stay, but in her case she was hoping to rescue Bunt from the stocks and perhaps earn his affections by dressing his hurts and comforting his pride. She had asked the Reverend Perry to stay, as well, hoping that he might minister to Willy's spiritual needs. Most of all she wished to persuade Willy to give up the drink and the terrible effect it had on his behavior. She could easily persuade the good reverend to continue with his journey later, if it turned out that she and Willy might enjoy some privacy. Not all of young Bunt's vices had to be cured just yet, and he was attractive even when misbehaving.

Clymo was eager to get moving and in no mood to argue; he reluctantly agreed to Morwenna's crying off. He and Penwarden had a long way to go. After a hard ride, tired and saddle-sore, they reached Lanhydrock as darkness fell. Clymo invited Penwarden to sleep at his house, gave him a quick supper and urged him to join him for breakfast.

Waking early the next morning, they took their time over breakfast. Afterwards, Clymo showed Penwarden around the grounds. At around ten o'clock, they headed back to the estate business room for the meeting. Thomas Bolitho and Captain John Williams were shown in shortly thereafter. Clymo sent a clerk to let the viscount know that they were ready.

The clerk later reported that Dunbargan was engaged in a discussion with his wife which, it appeared, he was relieved to have interrupted. However, the viscount made his way immediately to the business room appearing jovial and greeting the strangers with unaccustomed warmth. The reason soon became clear.

"So Bolitho, Clymo," he began, "you're going to make me a great deal more money. How much? How soon? Now who are these fellows?"

"You are quite right, my lord," Bolitho said. "It will however require expenditure of money, as well as effort. Clymo will discuss the former. These gentlemen are here to enlighten us on the latter."

"These are the mine captains from Poldice and Wheal Hykka, Williams and Penwarden, my lord," said Joseph Clymo. "I know that, like the late baron, you will insist on understanding why investment is required and what for. They are best able to answer your questions about mining operations."

"What I want to know is where the money will come from," declared the viscount. "Williams? Ah yes, I met your father when the baron took me down as a boy to show me around Poldice. My father thought highly of old Captain Williams; I thought he talked a lot of mumbo jumbo, couldn't understand half what he was saying, but I was a lad then." He turned to the other Captain, looking intently at him. "Penwarden, you say your name is?" The viscount studied Addis for a moment. "H'mm, you seem familiar. Have we met before?"

"Can't say for sure, sir, mebbe," replied Addis Penwarden, not looking the viscount in the eye. He had anticipated this moment with concern. He had been fairly sure that Viscount Dunbargan would turn out to be the former Honorable James Trenance whom he had met as a boy and who had caught him poaching rabbits on Poldice land. Addis had taught young James to defend himself against bullies and in the process knocked him down. Addis recalled that, at the time, there was something about the boy that he had distrusted. If that same boy, now a man grown powerful and important, truly recognized Addis, the viscount might bear resentment and that would not bode well.

Viscount Dunbargan peered hard at Penwarden. "What is your Christian name?"

"Addis, sir."

"Unusual name," said the viscount, "don't hear it very often. So you're captain at Wheal Hykka? Hope you're up to it."

Joseph Clymo did not like the direction the conversation was taking, although he could not put his finger on why. He decided to screw up his courage and intervene. After all, his job depended on keeping the viscount happy and that hinged on this meeting being successful. He had to make the case for investment in the mines since the opportunity to sell mine tailings for the Liskeard turnpike had receded. He needed the mine captains to be credible in helping to make the argument.

"As we have reviewed the prospects, my lord," began Clymo, "the opportunities to expand on Lanhydrock's existing holdings and greatly increase your revenues have high potential, particularly in your mining ventures. But as Mr. Bolitho has made clear, this will require a great deal of capital. We have concluded from our analysis of the businesses that it will pay you to share the investment more widely with others in order to gain the greater rewards created by the capital they would then provide."

"I'll never agree to that!" expostulated Dunbargan, sitting down at the table and waving at the others to do likewise. "There are enough hangers-on sucking at my hind tit already. I need money for my own expenses. I'm not funding any one else's luxuries. Make the investments out of profits. Or just get money from Bolitho and his wealthy friends. They have plenty to spare. They'll never miss it."

Bolitho sat back and folded his hands, leaving the floor to Clymo.

"At the same time, sir," persisted Clymo, "bear in mind that the adventurers who can be persuaded to join us would bear a greater share of risk. That means we can take on more projects, confident that if some disappoint there will be more that can accomplish our desires."

Bolitho now saw fit to interject. "My partners are not eager to advance more funds without security until they can see they are even on past obligations."

"Stuff and nonsense," said Dunbargan, "I am a viscount now."

"We are talking about a more modern method of doing business, my lord, in which you can become an admired leader," continued Bolitho. "We are seeing this happening in progressive parts of England. Men say that there is aborning a revolution in how things are done, how goods are made, how ventures are financed. There are clever men who are inventing new methods of making things, new materials, new machines. Those of us who embrace change will profit from it, especially right here in Cornwall in mining."

"Cheaper just to put more men down the mines," Dunbargan objected, "set their women and children to breaking and sorting ore, just like they always have. Besides that, we can always use more horses. No need for newfangled machines and all that tilly-tally."

Sensing an impenetrable wall, Bolitho turned to Williams. "What do you have to say for yourself, Williams, and your friend Penwarden? You mine captains see what is going on at close hand. What would you do to make more money?"

The newly minted viscount rose and paced about the room, his hands clasped behind his back. What could these uneducated men teach him?

"I have been closely observing the advantages gained by our competitors using the Newcomen steam engines," said Williams. "They've been improved and can pump water from greater depths. There are some twelve of them already at work around the county. With the tax on coal lifted, we can operate them more cheaply. Installing steam engines will, of course, take capital, but we can make them pay handsomely."

"Seems to me, sir," said Penwarden, rubbing his chin, "us could make greater returns spendin' a guinea on a machine than a shilling on a man, if you take my meanin'. A machine don't get tired, or 'urt, or poorly, and 'er do what 'er's told and don't give its minder no back talk. Besides, us needs more production. Us're findin' good quantities of tin, but us could sell more copper if us could just bring 'er up, 'igher price too, that is if us could get 'er smelted. Need to mine deeper for copper, so us needs better pumps. Us got plenty of call for copper from them brass manufacturers up Bristol way. Need zinc, too, if us could find some."

"You've said a mouthful, man," said Dunbargan, rounding on Penwarden, "more than you can chew, I'll wager."

"Penwarden knows what he's talking about, my lord," Williams said. "He's been a mine captain for but a few months on my recommendation, but he has had years down in the mines. He has learned a lot and is very observant. As for me, I learned from my father how to get the most out of miners and out of a mine. Between us we can get a great deal accomplished."

"Penwarden indeed spoke a mouthful, my lord," said Bolitho. "What he says is why Clymo and I believe it is wise to bring in more adventurers to provide far more capital than would be prudent for Lanhydrock to risk alone. We must lead. Believe me, steam power alone is going to revolutionize mining and manufactory. Opportunity will pass to those who embrace it."

"How would you go about it?" demanded Dunbargan, intrigued but sceptical. "Don't try to pull the wool over my eyes."

"Here is the approach I would suggest, my lord," Bolitho went on, "one already being used by others. We could divide ownership of each mine into thirty-two, or even sixty-four, shares. Clymo could take the advice of the mine captains, particularly Williams and Penwarden as to specific measures and also appoint trustworthy pursers. The pursers would take charge of the subscriptions, keep a cost book for each mine, collect the proceeds of sales, and distribute the surplus to the adventurers every quarter day."

"Sounds a lot of trouble for nothing," Dunbargan objected. "More spent, more produced, but will that increase profits?"

"Yes sir," said Clymo. "With capital in hand we would not need to hold back funds from revenues for supplies or repairs or improvements. You could receive all the money that accrues to your shares every quarter without delay."

"Now you're making sense at last," said Dunbargan, "although of course I would keep the biggest share for myself. Make it sixty-four shares so there is as much money raised as possible, but I will keep at least twenty."

"Perhaps you should keep thirty-three, my lord, one more than half," Bolitho said, "then you would also have the majority of the votes in controlling the venture. You would pledge the shares to Bolitho's as guaranty. Meanwhile, my partners and I at the firm would be willing to lend Lanhydrock cash for expansion. We would, of course, expect to make exclusive arrangements for our interests to do the smelting."

"Aargh, would you pay cash or shares, zir?" asked Penwarden.

"What the hell difference would that make?" said Dunbargan. "Just make sure I get as much money as possible."

"Penwarden's right," said Williams, "the difference is important. We get a better return at Poldice from the blowing houses who pay in tin bills. We just have to wait for the cash until next coinage, when the tin is assayed and the block gets the Duchy stamp."

"Bolitho's always takes shares and gives bills," said Thomas Bolitho firmly.

"I want my money now," said Dunbargan. "I'll wager the damn Duchy doesn't wait."

"We can always discount the bills and pay sooner," said Bolitho. "It's a risk for the firm; we generally wait for the assay. However, we could make an exception for an old client like Lanhydrock."

"No doubt you customarily offer the same facility to others, Mr. Bolitho," said Clymo, looking to Dunbargan for approval for providing his employer with support but getting none. His lordship was staring at Penwarden. Bolitho glared at Clymo, who tried to mollify his indignation before a breach developed.

"Perhaps, my lord, with Mr. Bolitho's help," said Clymo, "you would in turn consider investing in further mines, where I and my people could provide the overseeing. And of course in your position you would have the influence to induce others to support such an adventure, and you would no doubt urge them to use Bolitho's services."

Bolitho nodded approvingly. "Not forgetting what influence a man in your position could bring to bear on the Duchy of Cornwall," he said. "The Duchy owns important mineral rights and access to the foreshores. There is much ore to be found near the coasts and beneath the sea."

"Naturally, gentlemen," Dunbargan said, "after all, the point of traveling all the way up to London to attend the House of Lords is to make friends who can increase one's wealth and influence. And we must not leave out our old friends and neighbors. I will ensure that Mr. Eliot is induced to participate. We must bear in mind that he is the Registrar General of the Duchy, and as such will be able to see to it that ventures of which he is a beneficiary obtain all necessary privileges. And although Mr. Thomas Pitt over at Boconnoc is no longer Lord Warden of the Stannaries, he surely is still familiar with the ins and outs of regulation of the tin trade in Cornwall."

Bolitho smiled. Perhaps the young buck was finally grasping some of the finer points of business that he and Clymo had been trying to drum into him. "My lord, you are well positioned indeed to increase your holdings and expand their revenues. And the House of Bolitho is privileged to offer facilities for providing the necessary capital, assuming that the risk is modest and we can see our way clear to a fair return and repayment in good time."

"Enough talk, I have things to do, must see what the gamekeeper's up to. Make sure there's enough birds for good sport, shoot some poachers while we're about it," said Dunbargan, chuckling. He went on, "Perhaps trap some rabbits, knock 'em on the head." He glanced at Penwarden, who looked down at the table.

The viscount turned to his steward, "Just get to work, Clymo, prepare whatever documents are required, put them before me to be signed, and then, damn it, bring me money. Good day, gentlemen." And he started for the door.

"Before you go, my lord," said Penwarden, "there is one more matter."

"Hold your tongue, man," Clymo said. "Can't you see his lordship is leaving?"

"Beggin' your lordship's pardon, sir, but zummat needs to be said. 'Tis about the miners, sir, their safety. There's too many accidents, explosions, collapses, drownin's. . . ."

"Penwarden! Costs!" warned John Williams.

"But my own brother . . ." Addis persisted.

"There's many more fish in the sea as ever came out of it," said Dunbargan, then turned on his heel and left.

"And that one's a hungry shark if ever I saw one," Penwarden said, expectorating angrily into the brass spittoon on the table.

"Mind your manners, man," said Clymo. "Remember his position. And you would do well to bear in mind what Captain Williams has gained through combining diligence with patience and persuasion."

"Would you care to clarify that statement, Mr. Clymo?" asked Williams.

"Perhaps Mr. Bolitho would perform that pleasant duty for us both," Clymo said, "that is if you understand my meaning, sir?"

"I understand well enough what you are driving at, Mr. Clymo," said Bolitho. "It seems that the way has been paved for Mr. Williams to become an owner of the Poldice mine, in accordance with the wish he expressed during our meeting after the late Baron Trenance's death. Perhaps if you play your cards right for a few years, Penwarden, and serve Wheal Hykka patiently as well as diligently, you too will have an opportunity for a share in ownership. Furthermore, it may be at least as many years before his lordship may need to be consulted again on such arrangements. What do you say, Clymo?"

"With you as our ally, Mr. Bolitho, I would bank on it," Clymo said and smiled.

"I hope and pray you are proved right, gentlemen," said Captain Williams, "but I don't see his lordship leaving us to get on without keeping his finger in. It'll be a while before he shows the trust his father did, if ever. And I fear he has taken exception to Captain Penwarden for reasons I don't pretend to understand."

Chapter Thirty-seven

Stocks

Morwenna Clymo was more concerned about Willy Bunt than she chose to say, even to herself. She was still shocked after the melee at the Bull Post, and she could not get out of her mind the picture of Willy lying passed out on the straw, kicked by a stranger in the riotous crowd as he lay helpless. There was nothing she could do to stop the constable dragging him off. She was appalled at the humiliation to which he had been subjected, locked in the stocks for all to see and for any passer-by, even a complete stranger, to mock him and pelt him with rotten fruit or worse.

Willy had already been confined for hours and had braved that. She could not bear to think of him being locked up overnight. The spring day had been warm but after the sun went down the night would be cold. Willy would be unable to keep himself warm, let alone sleep, barely able to move to stretch his cramped joints.

Morwenna had grown fond of Willy Bunt. Willy was a bit of a rascal but not a bad fellow, intelligent and attractive in a rough way. She enjoyed flirtation and fun with him. Why should he be so misused now? After all, he had only had a bit too much to drink. He did no harm, not that she could see, did not get into a fight. Who did not, on special occasions like Whitsuntide enjoy their tankards? Willy just was not used to it, could not hold his beer.

Morwenna would need immediate help if she was to save Willy from a night in the stocks, she knew. The Reverend Perry seemed resourceful for a man of the cloth; the powers of persuasion that went with his calling would be more useful than physical force. She found the preacher in the crowd and did not hesitate.

"Reverend Perry, you must come at once. Do you know that they have locked poor Willy Bunt in the stocks? We can't leave him there. The crowd will torment him unmercifully. If he stays locked up overnight he'll catch his death of cold. You've got to help!"

Morwenna was taken aback by the reverend's severe response.

"He deserves his punishment," said Perry harshly. "He was drunk. His conduct was lewd and disorderly. He must learn his lesson."

"But Reverend, we can't let him suffer," she pleaded. "I'm sure Willy will learn. Didn't our Savior teach us to forgive sinners?"

"The price of forgiveness is repentance, my dear," Perry affirmed. "I do not know young Bunt well, but I see little hope of redemption of his soul."

"Be merciful, sir," begged Morwenna. "He is young, he lacks experience in the world. With encouragement he will lead a good life."

"Then someone else will have to be his teacher. I must return to Perranporth; my flock is demanding of my shepherding. We do what we can, but it is not always within our powers to lead an unwilling sheep to salvation."

Morwenna would not accept this dismissal of Willy Bunt. The preacher did not know Willy's good side, his potential for making something of himself.

"Mr. Perry, I beg of you. I know Willy Bunt from when he lived at Lanhydrock. He was Sir James Trenance's valet and a footman, before the old baron died and Sir James went up in the world. Willy was treated harshly. But he acted kindly. He loved little Mary Abbott the chambermaid. She was wronged by Sir James, something terrible, grabbed her in the stable one Sunday morning when Lady Trenance was still in bed with their newborn son. What would have become of Mary except for Willy?"

Perry's tone softened. "What did become of Mary, then?" he asked.

"Willy rescued her. They fled Lanhydrock together and ended up at St. Germans where he works for Mr. Edward Eliot. He has done well there. After Mary found she was pregnant, Willy married her and now they have a lovely baby girl. Willy has his weaknesses, but I know he has a heart of gold. Don't let his promise be destroyed."

Even after this tale of Willy's better nature, Perry seemed intractable. "There are other young men more worthy of Mr. Eliot's patronage than that foolish drunkard, young men not easily led into temptation."

Morwenna, however, in the manner of pretty girls, was used to getting her way. "I implore you, Reverend, think of Willy's wife and their little girl. If he is not given an opportunity to mend his ways, their lives will be ruined through no fault of their own."

"It is not in my hands, Miss Clymo. No doubt Mr. Eliot will have something to say about the matter."

"Then put it in the hands of God, Mr. Perry," Morwenna retorted. "Is that not what you men of the cloth preach to us poor sinners? Come with me, now, talk to poor Willy, see whether he might be persuaded to repent and forsake drink. Let us at least ask the constable to alleviate his suffering and release him from his horrible bondage."

Perry sighed, succumbing to Morwenna's importuning and they hurried off to the stocks. Revelers still clustered around, drunkenly mocking Willy and singing rude songs. His arms and legs pinioned, the miscreant was helpless to defend himself. None in this unruly crowd was a friend; Willy was a "furriner" to them. There was no sign of the constable.

Morwenna and Perry edged through the crowd to stand beside Willy. Morwenna put her arm around his shoulder comfortingly. At that moment, they heard cries and footsteps approaching behind and turned to see Edwin Ough, accompanied by a lady, a gentleman and a servant women.

Willy seemed near tears as he recognized the newcomers. "Aargh, Mary, Lady Eliot, Mr. Polkinghorne, I be shamed and sorry," he said pitiably.

Mary rushed to her husband's side, which Morwenna had quickly vacated.

"Oh Willy, me 'andsome," wailed Mary, are you 'urt bad?" She gave him a warm hug, awkwardly because of the obstacle presented by the stocks.

"Mostly 'urt where you squeezed us, me sweetheart," gasped Willy, grinning. Mary smiled despite her concern; she was, as ever, amused by her husband's incorrigible sense of humor.

Morwenna addressed Mary. "Your Willy has got himself into a bad fix," she said. "I pray we may get him out."

Mary scowled. "What are you doing in Liskeard?" she demanded, her eyes flashing. "Why are you mixin' up with my Willy?"

Morwenna felt her face go warm. "Just came up with my father on his business," she said, "and now I'm trying to help Mr. Perry get Willy released. Doesn't seem fair. He did nothing more than the rest of these rowdies, far as I saw."

Catherine Eliot interrupted. "Explain yourself, Bunt," she demanded angrily. "What trouble are you in and why, as a representative of Eliot interests, have you got yourself into trouble at all?"

"Well, ma'am, us was watchin' the goin's on with the Whitsuntide festivities loike," began a chastened Bunt, "an' the crowd got pretty rowdy, an' someone knocked me down and Oi passed out. Oi dunno much else. Then they threw a bucket of cold water over Oi, an' that woke us up, and they put us in the stocks. Oi wasn't doin' no 'arm."

Catherine waved her gloved hand in a gesture of annoyance and asked, "Where is the constable? Only he will have the keys to unlock this contraption. The first thing is to get Bunt freed, and then Mr. Eliot will deal with him. I sent a messenger to Port Eliot to fetch him a couple of hours ago, so he should be here soon."

"Bunt, you have really done it this time," Polkinghorne shouted at Willy. "How many times have I told you to stay away from strong drink? You're a disgrace to Port Eliot. You've had a lot of chances. Mr. Eliot will not put up with it this time."

"I think we can allow Mr. Eliot to decide that for himself, Polkinghorne," said Catherine firmly. "He will deal with his servants himself."

"But Ma'am, Mr. Eliot told me himself . . ." complained Polkinghorne.

"That's enough," said Catherine. She directed Mary Bunt to find the constable and bring back the keys to release Willy, though she had no great expectation the girl would be able to do so.

Edwin Ough had been standing by diffidently observing the goings on, and now found an opening in which formal introductions of Catherine and Polkinghorne might be made to Reverend Perry.

"It is a pleasure to make your acquaintance, ma'am, and sir," Perry said, "although we all could have wished for pleasanter circumstances. I am a preacher by calling and I have been visiting Liskeard with Mr. Joseph Clymo, steward of Viscount Dunbargan of Lanhydrock. This is Mr. Clymo's daughter, Miss Morwenna Clymo. She is acquainted with Bunt from his days at Lanhydrock."

"Well met, sir. Indeed, it appears that Bunt could do with the guidance and prayers of a preacher," said Catherine Eliot frostily, "although he will need more immediate help before that would do him much good."

Polkinghorne swept off his hat and bowed gallantly to Morwenna. "A pleasure young lady," he said. "I have made the acquaintance of your father."

Polkinghorne had spent much of the day at The Barleysheaf. His head was more seasoned than Bunt's in holding his liquor, but he was not as clear-headed as usual. His powers of observation, however, had sufficiently recovered for him to appreciate the attractiveness of Morwenna Clymo. He kept his eyes on her several moments before turning to address Reverend Perry.

"So you are a stranger in these parts," he said. "Are you from around Lanhydrock way, Bodmin perhaps?"

"No sir, I am from west Cornwall," replied Perry. "I hail from Perranporth. I travel far in serving those who need to find their Savior."

As conversation continued, Morwenna edged away from the group gathered at the stocks. This is the first time she had seen Mary and Willy Bunt together. The reality of their marriage, of their fondness for each other, struck her with a wave of guilt. Perhaps she was the one who needed saving, not Willy, she thought. She would have to stop fooling with him. It could wreck this precarious little family and spoil Willy's chances to better himself. And it was not fair to Mary. And Morwenna owned to other misdeeds.

Morwenna wondered if she might be in the stocks herself if it were known of her doings with James Trenance. The wrong was his for forcing himself on her, but she was to blame for finding their lusty encounters exciting. She an ordinary girl, no part of the gentry, was the mistress of a viscount. I must learn to curb my own wildness, she thought, or no respectable man, one such as that nice Mr. Polkinghorne, will ever have me as a wife.

Morwenna's thoughts were interrupted when three panting and lathered horses pulled to a halt in the street in front of the stocks. Eliot and the vicar dismounted and handed their reins to the third rider, a footman from Eliot House.

"Mr. Eliot, I'm so relieved you are here," said Catherine, going to greet him.

Eliot took in the situation swiftly and cut off Catherine before she could elaborate. His expression revealed fury at seeing a man of Port Eliot so publicly degraded.

"Water the horses at the trough up the street," Eliot directed the footman. "Then fetch the constable from the gaol at the double. Tell him I said so. Tell him to be sure to bring his key ring. Vicar, you stay here with me. Now, my dear, what in heaven's name is going on?"

Catherine's ire had abated, and she told her husband a version of the story that gave Willy some benefit of doubt. "Bunt got mixed up in the Whitsuntide goings-on," she said. "May have had too much to drink. May have got into a fight, got knocked over. Someone called the constable. He picked Bunt up and dragged him off, probably because he was the one least able to resist. Locked him in the stocks."

"Well, I can't have anyone in my employment sullying the name of Port Eliot or being seen in the stocks, mocked by all and sundry. As Mayor of Liskeard I will order the constable to release this miscreant. But you're not coming back to Port Eliot, Bunt. You should be horse-whipped. You will have to go, that's final."

Mary had returned without success in locating the constable. Hearing Mr. Eliot's words she wailed, "Oh, but sir, what about my baby? She won't 'ave a roof over 'er 'ead. Us'll all starve."

Bunt, eyes bleary and wet with unshed tears, cried, "Zir, Oi won't do it no more. Oi'll never touch another drop nor long as Oi live, Oi swear."

"You should have thought of that before," Eliot said icily. "You've had warnings. I cannot and will not have men in my service upon whose comportment I cannot rely. I had entrusted you with responsibility, and this is how you repay me."

"Perhaps I could take responsibility for him." The voice that intervened was firm but respectful.

"Who the devil are you, sir, and what do you mean by your insolence in interfering between a man and his servant?" demanded Eliot.

"This is the Reverend Perry, my dear," interceded Catherine, as the vicar pricked up his ears. "He has been visiting Liskeard with Clymo from Viscount Dunbargan's place, and this is Miss Clymo with him. Perhaps he can do something to help us all. Like you, I feel that Bunt deserves to be punished, but I wish there were some way in which his punishment would spare Mary and baby Catherine. After all, the little one is my goddaughter."

The vicar raised his eyebrows and inspected his fellow man of the cloth from head to toe. "Are you a properly ordained priest of the Church of England?" he demanded with his nose in the air. "Or are you one of these damned interfering dissenters?"

"Oh, Vicar," said Catherine, "do mind your manners. Reverend Perry is a visitor and as such we owe him courtesy." The vicar turned aside and said nothing but Polkinghorne observed that his expression was angry.

"I do not wish to interfere, sir," said Reverend Perry, acknowledging Catherine's intervention with a nod, "but I have seen much drunkenness among the Cornish, and I have seen all too often how many lives have been wrecked by strong drink, not only of the sinners themselves but also of their innocent families. If you would allow me I believe I could help."

As Morwenna listened and realized that the preacher had softened his heart toward Willy, she said a prayer of thanks and a promise to begin mending her own ways. She noticed as the missing constable had finally made his way to the stocks, looking, she thought, hardly more sober than Willy, but also seeming attentive to the preacher's entreaty.

"If I could persuade the young man to seek God's grace, with the greater help of his Son, I am full of hope that he could hew to the path of abstinence, mend his ways, and become not only a good provider to his family but also a good and loyal servant to you, sir. Let me try."

"Stuff and nonsense," expostulated the vicar. "Good works are the only way to salvation, and that young drunkard has as much chance of entering into the Kingdom of Heaven as the proverbial camel has of passing through the eye of the needle. It's no good giving the working classes a second chance. They don't understand. You'd be better off transporting him."

"Please sir, let him try," pleaded Morwenna.

"Aw, do let 'im try," echoed Mary.

"What do you think, Polkinghorne?" asked Eliot.

Polkinghorne was torn. He sometimes felt Bunt could be his rival for Eliot's trust and favor. At the same time, the young man was intelligent and talented, and his work made his superior look good. He would miss Bunt's insights and ideas and his inside knowledge of the people around Viscount Dunbargan.

"You say you are an acquaintance of Mr. Clymo, Reverend?" asked Polkinghorne, scratching his chin. "We have had business dealings with Clymo and Lanhydrock. What does he think of Bunt?"

"My father believes that Bunt has a lot of promise," offered Morwenna. "I know that if Bunt came to him looking for a job that he would employ him, especially after what he has learned at Port Eliot." Morwenna had no basis for such an assertion but no one here would know that.

"I feel that Miss Clymo may be right, Mr. Eliot," said Catherine. "If I may be frank, it would be a pity if Bunt reformed and his knowledge were placed at the disposal of rivals."

"I agree, sir," said Polkinghorne, his mind now focused on the imminence of losing Bunt's increasingly valuable services. Besides, Miss Clymo might be pleased if he were to help Bunt.

"Oh, all right, all right! In that case," said Eliot turning to the constable, "as Mayor I order you to unlock this man." He then addressed the preacher. "Mr. Perry, I will indeed hold you responsible for working a miracle on this sinner. You'd better get Mary Bunt firmly on your side. Vicar, whether you can or wish to help I am far from clear. I leave it up to you."

He took Catherine's arm. "Come my dear, we will walk back to Eliot House to spend the night and return to St. Germans in the morning."

The constable was reluctant but nodded his acquiescence and did as he was ordered. As Willy Bunt staggered to his feet off balance, Morwenna reached out to stop him from falling back, but Mary forestalled her and took her husband in her arms.

"Oh Willy, me 'andsome," she said, "you'll just 'ave to let me take care of you."

Charles Polkinghorne noticed Morwenna's action and felt that, indeed, he could win her favor by supporting Bunt, although he would have to mind that she and Bunt did not become more attached.

Catherine Eliot smiled briefly at her husband who nodded his satisfaction at the influence he wielded in even this small matter. Eliot led the way from the place of the now empty stocks. Edward was slow to anger, but once aroused was formidable in his determination to correct what wrong he perceived. Catherine shared his emotion, but realized that her husband also felt embarrassed at the misbehavior of one of his workmen.

✤✤✤

After a light supper back at Eliot House, Catherine and Edward prepared for bed. It had been a trying day, but on the whole it had ended up a satisfying one.

"My dear Edward," said Catherine, moving out from behind a screen in her white-laced nightdress, "I can hardly express my admiration for you and what you have decided to do for Bunt. It reflects well on the interest you take in our people on the estate. They are fortunate to have a good master, and I am blessed to have a kind and generous husband. I love you more than I can say."

"Thank you, my dear," said Edward. "I just wish I could be sure whether this admirable decision was mine or yours." He pulled back the fresh linen covers and climbed up onto the high mahogany bed. "And now I must go to sleep. It's been a long day. Before I do, is there anything else you wish to discuss?"

"Oh, Edward, yes, there is one more thing, in fact two. First, I must tell you that the burgesses quite enjoyed their tea and promised that they would vote for your candidates to a man. Rest assured that your Mr. Stephens and Mr. Champion will take their seats for Liskeard in the new parliament."

"Thank you, Catherine. You are quite the politician."

"And Edward."

"Yes, my dear?"

"I am rather curious. How did the election at St. Germans go?"

Edward sighed. "Catherine, my love, can it wait until morning? I'm exhausted, it has been a busy day. Now go to sleep," and he leaned over to give her a kiss.

Catherine turned her cheek away. Edward thought better of his mood and said, "Oh, if you must know now, I was elected more or less unanimously, thanks no doubt to the appreciation of my tenants; and young Stanhope made a fool of himself but was elected alongside me despite himself. No surprises, everything turned out according to plan. Now, goodnight."

With that, Edward rolled sideways and fell into an instant and deep sleep.

Chapter Thirty-eight

Steam

Addis Penwarden rode back down west from Lanhydrock with John Williams. He was glad to get home. He preferred being in his own bed with Lizzie to gadding about the countryside sleeping in noisy inns or strangers' homes. He enjoyed a warm welcome from his sons, who had missed their father during his absence on business.

They ate the warm milk and saffron buns for their supper ever so slowly despite their youthful hunger to put off being sent to bed so that they could spend as long as possible with their dad. But Lizzie was eager to pack them off so that she could be alone with Addis. She had pulled off his riding boots and put his supper on a tray before him while he sat in his favorite armchair by the fire she had lit against the chill of the spring evening. She urged him to eat up the bowl of hot leek and potato soup with the crust of her freshly baked bread.

The boys bade a noisy and reluctant good night to their parents and trundled up to the cold rooms above. When the creaking of their feet on the floor ceased and all was quiet, Lizzie took Addis by the hand and led him upstairs to their bedroom. The room was cold, so they undressed quickly, put on flannel nightshirts and clambered into the big four-poster bed beneath the cozy down comforter, the feather tie as the Cornish called it, where Lizzie earlier had put the copper warming pan filled with embers from the kitchen fire. They listened for the boys but there was no sound from their room. Whispering, Lizzie told him how much she had missed him while he was away and how glad she was to have him back. It took no guesswork for Addis to realize what pleasure his wife took in his being beside her once again.

"Ah, Lizzie," he mumbled as he reached for her, "any time away from you is too long." Her only answer was to place a kiss on his lips and lay her body atop his.

They woke early the next morning. Lizzie did not say anything, but she was disappointed that Addis was so soon thinking about the day ahead of him. He wanted to get right up, get washed and dressed, have a quick breakfast, saddle his horse, and get off to the mine. He crossed to the boys' room and woke up young Jemmy, telling him to get ready to come to work with him.

"Oi 'ad a good long chin wag with John Williams yesterday as we rode down from Lanhydrock," he told Lizzie over breakfast. "Us was glad

to 'ave the time to talk things over, make plans. Us've got to get 'oppin',
now that Clymo and Bolitho 'ave talked the Trenances into allowin' us to
put money into the mines, that's for sure. Course, Sir James became a lord
when the old baron died, but 'e weren't satisfied with that. Gone an' got
'imself made a viscount now; calls 'imself Dunbargan whatever that means.
It's s'posed to be Irish or somethin'."

"So our Sir James 'as gone even further up in the world, eh me
luv?" asked Lizzie. "All hoity-toity, proud and moighty, Oi 'spect! What'll
'e be like to work for then? What's 'e doin' for the tinners, that's what Oi
want to know?"

"All 'e thinks about is 'imself," said Addis, "worse than the old
baron. Wants more money, really impatient, seems 'e might be in some
trouble, but that's none of my business. Oi 'opes Oi can stay out of 'is way,
nasty piece of work, but Mr. Clymo says 'e'll be all right if us keeps the
money comin' so 'e can go an' spend it in Lunnon. Cap'n Williams an' Oi
can get Clymo and Bolitho to do what is right, least some ways, do
somethin' about safety one of these days, long as the viscount don't find
out."

Addis decided to say nothing to Lizzie about his deeper misgivings
about the viscount, his memories of the nasty, arrogant boy who had
caught him poaching rabbits. No point in worrying her, nothing she could
do about it.

"Don't you go gettin' yourself in no trouble, that's what Oi say,"
said Lizzie anxiously. "You've a growin' fambly to take care of. Us needs
them wages."

"Be growin' again within the twelvemonth if us don't take more
care than we did last night," whispered Addis with a twinkle in his eye.
"Anyroad, us can't stop 'ere yammerin'. Tell little Jedson good-bye from
me when 'e wakes up."

"But Addis," Lizzie implored, "us was 'opin' you'd get the
vegetable garden tilled and planted. 'Tis 'igh time and won't wait. Mustn't
leave 'er much longer. You've been away for days for that blessed mine.
Spring'll soon be over. Oi could 'elp you."

"Don't fret, Oi'll stay 'ome Saturday and do 'er then, if Oi' ave
time. Oi must be off. Come on, Jemmy."

Addis kissed Lizzie lightly on the cheek and hurried out of the back
door to the stable. It was becoming clear to his family that the greater
comforts brought by the importance of Addis' position as mine captain
would not entirely compensate for the increasing demands on his time and
attention. But Addis' ambition was not to be denied, not only for himself
but also for his sons, and he understood only too well that realizing his
goals would take sacrifice as well as hard work. He was prepared to make

the sacrifices. He just hoped that his wife and family would see it his way. Sometimes it was hard to keep a balance.

Alone, Lizzie lifted the hem of her apron and wiped a tear from her cheek. She was suddenly aware that most of what she had counted on Addis for would now be hers alone to do. True, the new place made work easier and living more comfortable, but at times like this she missed her relatives and old friends in Gwennap. There was some money she had hidden in the clock on the kitchen mantelpiece. She could just hire the young gardener who lived over in Pendeen village for a few hours. Her vegetable garden would not wait for her husband and neither would she.

By the time Addis and Jemmy arrived at Wheal Hykka, the day core was already there, the miners had climbed down the long ladders to the workings, the bal maidens were at the stamps and the ore sorting tables. He and Jemmy went straight into the count house and Addis called his chief clerk.

"Did you get any replies to them letters we sent off the week before last?" Addis asked him. "We 'ave to get a move on. The owners want to make more from the mine, and they're willing to put money in now. It's all arranged; Mr. Williams and Oi talked to the powers that be."

"The most important one 'as responded," said the ruddy-faced clerk, adjusting his spectacles on the bridge of his prominent nose. "I sent off an inquiry like you said to the Proprietors of the Invention for Raising Water by Fire. You know, them're the ones who 'ave a monopoly on arrangin' the manufacturin' and installin' of the engines designed by the late Thomas Newcomen."

"Yes, yes, Oi do know," said Penwarden, "get on with it. Oi told you we 'ave to get a move on. How soon can they get someone down to Wheal Hykka, lay out a proposal, provide some costs, get us in production? How well does it work for pumpin' out the lower levels? 'Ow deep? Where can us observe one in operation?"

"Oi can't go as fast as all that, zir," protested the clerk mildly. "Oi just 'as to take 'er a step at a toime. The first one they put in down this way was over at Wheal Vor, been there a while. Trouble is, 'tisn't cheap to run. Them tried peat fuel, but there's not much around this way. So it takes eighty mule loads of coal every day to raise the steam."

"Coal got cheaper with the duty taken off," said Addis. "Besides, us can ship it in right nearby from the pits in South Wales. How deep do 'er pump? How much water at a toime?"

"So 'ow do the engine work, Dad?" piped up young Jemmy.

"You tell 'im," Addis said to the clerk. "But tell me first 'ow deep down 'er can pump."

"Wheal Vor goes down a hundred and fifty feet, ten gallons every stroke. The beam does twelve strokes every minute," said the clerk, proud to display his knowledge. He turned to Jemmy. "Well, me lad, the way 'er works is there's a cylinder beneath the piston that them injects with steam. Then cold water from the tank above the cylinder goes into the piston and condenses the steam back into water. That creates a vacuum, so the outside air pressure pushes the piston down again, which pulls one end of the beam down. Next . . ."

"Yes, yes!" said Addis. "That's enough. You understand, Jemmy? Us 'umans 'ave work to do too. Now, just tell me what the bloody thing does for the mine, Oi don't 'ave time for my clerk to learn us no more science."

"But Dad, can Oi make a little engine, to play with?" persisted Jemmy. "Oi reckon Oi could, if 'e would show me."

"Oi'll see. Mebbe one day, when you're older," said Addis, impatient but proud of his endlessly inquisitive son. "Where was Oi? Right, one hundred and twenty gallons every minute, twenty-four hours every day, assuming no stoppages. That's a hundred and seventy thousand gallons a day, give or take a few 'undred. Sounds to me like us'll need more than one engine, and we'll have to gang the lifting beams if we go any deeper or mine further out under the sea. You get hold of a couple of the tributers and get me some reliable figures. Then we can calculate what us needs."

"Oi'll do that by tomorrow, zir. But us still needs to find out how much it'll cost to buy 'un. That'll be a pretty penny. Specially since these days those Lunnon fellers 'ave made the cylinders a lot bigger since Wheal Vor, and cast iron, not brass. More money, Oi'll be bound. And us'd 'ave to pay millwrights to put 'er in an' set 'er up. Us don't know 'ow to do them things."

"Sounds to me like cast iron should be stronger, less likely to blow up an 'urt people," said Addis.

"Still sounds dangerous to me," said the clerk, "lot worse than bein' kicked by an 'oss and that's bad enough."

"Mebbe us can rig up guards, but us can't stop makin' progress. What were the production figures last week? 'Ow much copper is we findin'? Us'll need all we can bring up. Are you getting good prices from the smelters? Looks like us'll 'ave to send most to Bolithos' now. That's what suits 'is lordship, an' us got to keep on 'is right side or there'll be hell to pay."

"Oi'll 'ave the latest figures on your desk in the mornin', zir. Us won't 'ave the cost book all up to date until quarter day."

"What about stamps? We've tried a water wheel, a lot faster than hammerin'. Can the steam engine drive them faster still, more efficiently?" asked Penwarden. "And how about whims? Oi see 'ow the beam goes up and down, but 'ow about round and round? Could we haul more ore up in less time? Maybe haul the men up and down too, get them workin' sooner?"

"Ye must ask them Lunnon gen'lemen, zir. Oi jus' does the figurin' and enterin' the records, loike, for the mine. Oi do know water wheel's not much good come summer time, not much rain. Oi dunno nothin' much about 'ow them great steam monstrosities work. And mind, us'll 'ave to figure in buildin' an' engine 'ouse, an' all. Cost a lot more than mules or 'orses, Oi reckon."

"It'll be worth it 'ere at Wheal Hykka," said Penwarden. "There's plenty more tin and copper deep down, under the sea, too. Wish us could just find some coal. Them Newcomen engines is 'ungry buggers, but they do the work of five horses, so they tell me. They don't stop work for feedin' neither, nor don't need much rest to catch their breath. Wheal Hykka be goin' forward. Where us leads, others will follow, you mark my words. Need to get there soon as us can."

Chapter Thirty-nine

Election

Bath was looking particularly beautiful as the wagon carrying William and Lady Hester Pitt lurched along the last miles of its journey on the road from London. The evening sky had cleared after rain, and the early setting sun enfolded the honey color of the city's distinctive Bath stone in warm gold. The occupants of the wagon were looking forward to breaking up their long journey to Cornwall and enjoying the hospitality of their friend and supporter Ralph Allen. The Pitts' coachman drove the sweating team up the last hill south of the city and into the grounds of Prior Park, the grand and luxurious house built for Allen by the architect John Wood.

As he looked tiredly back at the golden city, Pitt comforted himself that an additional benefit of their stay would be partaking of the healing waters and soaking in the baths at the spa, which would undoubtedly relieve his troublesome gout and perhaps his rheumatic afflictions, too. The Pitts were looking forward to the visit. Ralph Allen was a generous host and a valuable supporter. As it was later to transpire, he was an unstinting friend too, and left the princely sum of £1,000 to the Pitts in his will when he died a year or so later.

The Pitts went in through the magnificent entrance and were welcomed in the front hall by Ralph Allen himself. "Welcome, Lady Hester, Mr. Pitt. I am delighted to see you both," said Allen, shaking their hands. "Not too trying a journey I trust. I will have you shown to your rooms. Rest a while if you wish."

"It is indeed pleasant to leave the burdens of office behind me in London, and to visit good friends in Bath," responded Pitt. "I owe thanks to you and many of your friends who have supported me."

"Mr. Pitt plans to take the waters during our stay," said Lady Hester. "He strives so hard for England. He rarely accepts my advice when I urge him to rest more, and I welcome this opportunity for him to be truly refreshed."

"Meet me in the library later," said Allen. "I have asked my architect John Wood and a few select leaders of our city to join us for dinner. They are looking forward to conversation with you both."

"Bath's reputation as the most beautiful city in England is well deserved, Mr. Allen," said Lady Hester. "I do not know it as well as does my husband, and I look forward to learning more of its famous architecture from its distinguished creator."

During their journey William Pitt had informed his wife of the importance of their host and the evolution of his adopted city. She was also titillated to learn that, among its many distinctions, Bath was the home of Beau Nash, the celebrated arbiter of fashion and keeper of a multitude of mistresses. More seriously, she learned that Ralph Allen, as well as being a patron of architects, was a wealthy entrepreneur with connections with important friends.

The foundation of Allen's success, Pitt told Lady Hester, was his career in the post office. Some fifty years ago at the precocious age of nineteen he had become Postmaster of Bath. Within ten years he had contracted with the General Post Office to control the entire southwest of England, a position that he expanded throughout his life. What Pitt felt it prudent not tell his wife was that as postmaster Allen saw to it that he was privy to the most interesting communications that passed through his office.

Although officers of the post office were officially banned from elections, their network was widely used by the government as a source for gathering and disseminating information. Ralph Allen took the opportunity to become active in civic affairs and had served as mayor of the city some twenty years ago. His rivals in politics as well as in business were amazed by the accuracy of the insights that made Allen so successful and so sought as a colleague. By such means he remained a member of the Common Council and hence a voter. In this role he had become a valued friend and supporter of William Pitt as Member of Parliament for the City of Bath.

What William Pitt did not know was that his recent letter from London to his elder brother Thomas in Cornwall had been stayed as it passed through the post office in Bath. Pursuant to the postmaster's instructions, a loyal employee with practiced fingers aided by steam from a compliant kettle relieved the seal of its duties in such a way that no one would later notice, once he had reapplied it.

The letter was brought to the attention of Ralph Allen. In it, William Pitt wrote that, once parliament was in recess after a grueling and contentious session, he would travel to Boconnoc to visit Thomas. William would have preferred the meeting to be in London, but since his brother could not show his face in the capital without risking arrest for debt, he would for reasons of familial loyalty sacrifice the opportunity to rest and instead make the arduous journey to Cornwall.

It had been thanks to William's discreet intervention that Thomas had been able to return secretly to England, whence he had fled to escape his creditors. Further, though reluctant to be embroiled once again he was concerned to protect his own reputation, William would strive to rescue Thomas from financial ruin.

Ralph Allen gathered that Thomas Pitt's various schemes to replenish his fortune had only partially succeeded and now he had little recourse but to swallow his pride and turn once again to his influential, though not wealthy, younger brother for help. The schemes included mortgaging the Pitt family's boroughs. Allen learned that Thomas Pitt had sold the family's property in Okehampton, and speculated that William Pitt had given up his seat there and moved his constituency to Bath in order to help his brother raise money.

The letter alluded to a remaining hope, an opportunity to invest in a turnpike project with a neighboring member of the gentry, one Edward Eliot, M.P. William advised Thomas to arrange a party at Boconnoc during his visit to meet with the Eliots and any other acquaintances who yet might offer relief, especially those prospering in the Cornish mining industry.

Ralph Allen saw opportunity in this information. Perhaps he could participate in a lucrative private investment; at least he could enhance his position with the statesman by sharing his own influence. That was why he wrote William Pitt and Lady Hester and invited them to come to Bath and take the waters. Allen had assessed the situation correctly. Pitt was delighted to refresh his exhausted body and assuage his excruciating gout. Furthermore, by staying with Allen in his house he could thank the voters in person for his election and meet the inevitable requests for political favors.

At the general election Pitt had chosen not to stand on the Bath husting in person, publicly pleading the pressure of his ministerial duties but privately yielding to his ever-painful gout and exhaustion. His seat was safe enough given his prominence and his reputation for ability and integrity, admittedly with substantial help from Ralph Allen. Further, when he had originally accepted the seat, Pitt had the foresight to secure the privilege of nominating his own candidate for Bath's other seat. Pitt now simply arranged for his fellow member to deputize for him in absentia on the husting. After his re-election, he had written a diplomatic letter to the Bath city corporation paying tribute to "a city ranked among the most ancient and most considerable in the kingdom, and justly famed for its integrity, independence, and zeal for the public good."

"My dear," said William Pitt to his wife, "It is high time we join our host and his guests. I trust you are sufficiently refreshed to charm these good citizens of Bath who are such generous supporters of my position."

"Indeed, husband," said Lady Hester, "my energies are sufficient to persuade them that their continued dedication to you can only result in our enhancing not only their financial interests but more importantly their social positions. My family connections and your intellectual abilities are an irresistible combination."

William Pitt smiled, as he took up his cane and escorted his wife downstairs to the library to meet the guests who had been invited to Prior Park to greet them. As their host made the introductions, it became apparent that the party comprised the elite and the influential. As the city's Member of Parliament and the king's first minister Pitt needed little introduction, but Ralph Allen explained to the company that they were being graced with a visit from the great statesman and Lady Hester as they were on their way to his brother at Boconnoc in Cornwall.

The first guest to be introduced was the great architect. "Lady Hester, Mr. Pitt, may I introduce Mr. John Wood?" said Ralph Allen. "Not only does he follow in his father's footsteps as the leading architect of our city, but I am proud to say that he has carried out projects for me."

"Your father designed Prior Park, I understand," said Lady Hester. "It is an elegant house in a magnificent setting, a tribute to its occupant. I look forward to conversing with you at length, Mr. Wood."

The architect bowed, but before the conversation could develop along these lines, Pitt turned it towards his host, whose importance to him was paramount. "As a young man you made the journey in the other direction, Mr. Allen. I understand you are a Cornishman by birth?" Pitt asked.

"Yes, I am," said Allen. "I was baptized at St. Columb Major, where my grandmother was the postmistress. It was her example that led me to my chosen career and gave me the experience to become the postmaster here in Bath and thus, eventually, led to my contract with the General Post Office. I have over the years reformed and built up the system in the western parts of the country and beyond."

"One cannot fault you, Mr. Allen," said Lady Hester, "for escaping the wildness of Cornwall for the sophistication of Bath. My husband has spoken often about spending his retirement years among his family at Boconnoc, but perhaps you would join me in persuading him that residence in Bath would be more conducive to the health of his mind as well as his body."

"It will be many years before England will spare me from my duty, my dear," said Pitt. "Perhaps you could persuade Mr. Allen meantime to join us in London and apply his abilities to supplementing my own efforts."

He turned to Ralph Allen and they touched glasses. "Would that we had more men of your energy and initiative governing the departments of the administration. I myself would value such assistance. The details of policy are a burdensome component of making wise decisions and persuading others to follow where one wishes to proceed. There are those who constantly challenge my conduct of the war and those who wish to skimp on providing for its successful prosecution."

"May I ask, sir," asked Allen, "where His Majesty stands?"

A glass of sherry put William Pitt into a talkative mood. "I trust I am among friends and may rely on your discretion," he said. "In truth the new king is less supportive than I would wish. Maintaining pressure on the French in Europe lies at the core of my strategy for capturing her empire around the globe. Yet the king in his speech from the throne chose to emphasize his Englishness and clearly signaled that he was not advocating continuance of the subsidies for Hanover. I wish he would learn to take my advice rather than that of the foolish Scotsman Bute, who unfortunately has more influence than wisdom."

Pitt continued after a sip of sherry. "However, I must ignore those who nip at my heels, keep to my own counsel, and pursue my aims with vigor."

"My dear," said Lady Hester, "you have my fullest support. I so admire your wise precept of not wearing the mind to pieces by indecision but to take one's party as appears best and submit the rest to Providence."

Ralph Allen nodded approvingly. He observed, "Surely in the House of Lords the Duke of Newcastle wields great influence in your support?"

"The election has strengthened the king's support among the Tories," said Pitt, "as a Whig that makes the Duke of Newcastle even more nervous than usual. However, the moneyed men in the City trust him, and he remains of great value in raising funds for the administration."

"That must be of comfort to you too," observed Allen.

"We do not always see eye to eye," Pitt said, "although there is no gainsaying he has his worth. Unfortunately His Grace's concerns are petty. He preoccupies himself with favor and places and votes and seats. He lacks the vision to lend strength in policy. I would prefer that he not meddle, although I must confess without his workings I could not carry my views with speeches alone. And now with the management of the election behind him he is free to address his worries primarily to finance. He frets of farthings while I need copious supplies of guineas. But enough of my concerns. Tell me how matters stand in your fair city of Bath."

"My good friend John Wood has much to do with that," Allen said.

"Thanks to my equally good friends like Mr. Allen," said John Wood, "we are progressing well with the King's Circus, Mr. Pitt. We expect to complete another segment next year. Gay Street will link it to Queen Square, and our city will take on an even greater classical aspect."

"I understand that the Circus is inspired by the Roman Colosseum, Mr. Wood," Lady Hester said. "You and your father share a noble vision, but one that is not, if I may dare say, entirely original."

"Often the measure of true creativity, my lady, " replied Wood, "is the taste to discern that which is worthy of copying and indeed improving upon."

"Well said, sir," Lady Hester responded. "Now tell me, I learned from my husband that Mr. Allen's former town house is now serving as the post office. Surely he must have sacrificed considerable convenience?"

"Such is the price of progress, ma'am," Wood replied. "Some things must change as we bring our city into modern times."

"No doubt the price was much in your favor, Mr. Wood. Now another matter, my husband plans to take your miraculous waters during our stay," continued Lady Hester. "It occurs to me that an elegant building to house the springs would enhance the enjoyment of visitors seeking a cure."

"There is some talk of that," said John Wood. "I wish my father had completed a design. But I myself am fully occupied with present projects."

"I enjoy Bath well enough as it is," Pitt said, "and I appreciate the honor of representing you in the House these past five years. My brother's reversal of fortune caused us to give up control of our family boroughs, so I had to leave Okehampton, and Old Sarum was no longer available to me."

Ralph Allen nodded; his guess had not been wide of the mark.

"I am proud that Bath is in no man's pocket, by long tradition," said Ralph Allen. "The first King Edward called upon us to send two members to his Model Parliament in 1295. And to this day the right of election is vested firmly in the mayor, aldermen and Common Council, on which I am proud still to serve."

"I have no doubt that you are a man of honor, Mr. Allen," said Pitt, "as I indeed pride myself on being. But that does not diminish your influence as a man of wealth and position. When I found I was no longer able to enjoy one of our family boroughs, it was comforting to be offered a seat where the administration's wish for my election was fulfilled by men able to ensure the desired outcome."

"Gentlemen," said Allen, "I offer you a toast. Influence with honor!"

The company drained their glasses with gratitude and satisfaction. John Wood patted Ralph Allen on the shoulder, smiling.

Allen turned and leaned towards Pitt. "A word in your ear, sir, in complete discretion, of course. As you converse with your brother and his friends in Cornwall, if an opportunity to make an investment to the benefit of all should come up, please do me the honor of considering me as an adventurer. It would be a privilege to connect with my native county and a pleasure to be of service to my friends."

Pitt nodded and they shook hands.

The conversation, and indeed the wine, flowed unabated throughout the evening. The Pitts enjoyed the excellent company arranged by their host, and it was with some regret that a day or two later they put all that Bath had to offer behind them and continued, albeit refreshed and reinvigorated, on their journey to face the next challenge in Cornwall.

William Pitt left Bath feeling confident that his position in the city was well entrenched. He even had a sliver of hope that his brother's finances might yet be alleviated. He was less sanguine about the future of his leadership of the administration in the House of Commons. He worried about the ebbing confidence he commanded from the king. He regretted that the achievement of his vision depended as much on the machinations of the Duke of Newcastle as on his own oratory and the wisdom of his policies. Influence with honor, indeed. Let His Grace concern himself with influence; he would always be guided by honor, regardless of where it led.

Chapter Forty

House Party

Arriving at the entrance to the Boconnoc estate after a long and bumpy journey, the horses drawing the wagon carrying William Pitt and Lady Hester turned down the long drive, trotted past the expansive park, the Lawn, green and luxuriant in the May sunshine. Upon reaching the graveled courtyard they drew up to the center of the broad front of the house. The travelers were relieved to end their journey, but not entirely looking forward to their stay.

William Pitt was drawn to his brother more by familial obligation than fraternal devotion. William owed Thomas gratitude for providing the seats in Parliament that launched William's political career and enabled him to maintain the family tradition. But, in recent years, Thomas's financial misfortunes had brought nothing but trouble and scandal to England's greatest statesman. Their personal relationship did not ease matters since Thomas was disagreeable, arrogant, resentful and frequently litigious, even within his own family.

Thomas Pitt greeted his brother and sister-in-law in the entrance hall. "Welcome to Boconnoc," he said. He moved slowly and his welcome was lukewarm, partly because their relationship was not warm but also because his health was failing. In his early fifties, he was aging, losing vigor, and depressed by the financial pressures and disappointments of his life.

"I wish I could say it was a pleasure, brother," said William, "although it would have been more convenient if you had come to London. I do have important demands upon my time, you understand. However, since you cannot show your face in the capital I suppose you have to skulk down here in Cornwall."

Thomas Pitt offered Lady Hester his arm, less in gallantry towards his sister-in-law than for her support as he led them upstairs to the library. He called for port and, having dispensed with pleasantries, asked the question that underlay his motive for meeting his brother. Much hinged on the answer; if Thomas gained a seat in parliament, that privilege would spare him bankruptcy. "Have you persuaded the Duke of Newcastle to allow me to sit for Old Sarum, William? After all it is my own borough, and he listens to you."

"Was, Thomas," said William Pitt, "was, before you mortgaged it to the Treasury, along with your other boroughs. And I cannot forget that you inconvenienced me by obliging me to move from Okehampton to

Bath. And I have told you before, Newcastle may be an unavoidable colleague, but he is no friend of mine. I refuse to deal with his manipulations and maneuvers. You are more of his mind, not me."

"It is your duty to assist me; that is the obligation of one brother to another," said Thomas.

"If I may express myself with the candor that is my privilege as a relative," said Lady Hester, "you are an exceedingly difficult man to assist. Your self-importance has always exceeded your ability, let alone your industry, and your foolishness and extravagance have wasted a fortune that my husband and I could have put to much wiser use. You are importunate and offensive to those who might be willing to help you because of their regard for William. There are even some who fear you may not honor your obligations. There is none left in London who might be persuaded to come forward."

"No, my lady, you may not express yourself in my house in such an insulting way," said Thomas, red in the face. "I will not permit you to breach my hospitality."

"It may not be your house much longer, brother-in-law, if something or someone does not rescue you," said Lady Hester.

"Thomas, I insist that you treat my wife with courtesy," said William Pitt, "and bear in mind that we have traveled a long way to help if we can."

"Everyone blames me," said Thomas, "but you know bad luck played a part. I have been led astray by unsound advice and by fellow adventurers who failed to play their parts."

"Luck, perhaps, but I imagine arrogance and overconfidence played their part," said Lady Hester, "qualities that seem to have been inherited along with your grandfather's great fortune. Governor Pitt was an interloper, let us not forget; he succeeded in upsetting the East India Company before they finally admitted him."

William Pitt interposed before anger flared further between his wife and brother. "In my experience, making money is not easy and it requires more concentrated diligence than I, for one, am prepared to give it. Do you remember the stories of how our father ignored our grandfather's letters from India demanding reports on his progress in having the first diamond cut, and finding a buyer for it? The old man must have been apoplectic."

"Father had more enjoyable things on his mind," said Thomas, subdued and humored at the recounting of family lore. "He was besotted with our future mother." His mood then shifted to somber. "Thinking of our mother reminds me of my own wife. I still miss her. Perhaps it is not too late to marry again."

After a moment of quiet Lady Hester spoke up once again. "Your father Robert made his own contribution to your family when he married Lady Harriot Villiers," she said firmly. "She brought much-needed social position to the Pitts, and you were fortunate to acquire her birthplace, Old Sarum, into the bargain."

"Enough," said William Pitt. "I came all this way for more serious business. Thomas, have you arranged to entertain your wealthier neighbors as I suggested?"

"Naturally," said Thomas, "the best in the county. Some of them still consider it a privilege to dine with me at Boconnoc. There is no wealthier family in Cornwall than the Trenances. Since his father died, young James has acquired a viscountcy, Irish, Dunbargan; and a charming wife before that, Lady Elianor, from sound local stock. He has the wherewithal, if he may be persuaded to have the will. The Eliots from St. Germans have accepted, too. I received a letter the other day."

"Good," said William. "Eliot did you a favor taking over Grampound. Troublesome bunch of voters, expensive I understand. I had an interesting conversation with young Edward last time I was in Cornwall. It might come to something that would benefit us all. Who else has been invited?"

"Yes, I was interested to read about that conversation in your letter," said Thomas, nodding. He went on, "I thought it a good idea to include Thomas Bolitho and his wife; not exactly gentry, but plenty of money, up-and-coming. Between you and me, he has been helping out with running expenses here at Boconnoc; his partners are in smelting with spare money to lend. Being included socially will encourage him. Oh, and I invited the vicar to round out the numbers. They'll all be coming tomorrow evening."

"Your vicar is a pompous old fool," said Lady Hester. "Couldn't you do any better than he?"

"In fact I asked George Edgecumbe, but his brother died a few days ago I'm sorry to say, so he is occupied. Richard didn't live more than a couple of years to enjoy the barony after their father died. George will inherit, of course, since Richard had no legitimate offspring. Eight seats in the Commons come with it; your colleagues will pay attention to him, William. I would not be surprised if George succeeds as Lord Lieutenant of Cornwall, and he would be an excellent choice on his own merit, not that merit should be allowed to have too much to do with it."

"Pity about Richard," said William, "sorry to hear it. You might mention his seats to Newcastle, but he probably knows all about it already."

"I, for one, will welcome a little rest before they arrive," said Lady Hester. "I'm for an early bed tonight and perhaps tomorrow we can take a turn around the Deer Park."

"If you promise a gentle stroll, I will endeavor to join you," said William.

"For once I agree with you both," said Thomas.

The following evening the guests gathered in the large drawing room with glasses of sherry in hand. Thomas sensed that they were more interested in conversing with his relatives and each other than with him, their host. Viscount Dunbargan headed straight for Catherine Eliot, who was next to her husband, but she adroitly turned her attentions to William Pitt, who was standing with Lady Hester and his brother Thomas.

"How delightful to see you again, my dear," said William Pitt. "I look forward to yet another interesting conversation with your husband. He is proving a good friend. You have met my brother? Thomas, you have gathered a distinguished company for our entertainment."

"My pleasure, Mr. Pitt," Catherine said, "it is delightful to be amongst this distinguished company." Not hesitating, she continued, "I trust you will not consider me forward, sir, but I must compliment you on your elegant house. I often wonder how it is that the Cornish gentry came to their magnificent estates. Has your family lived here since time immemorial?"

Thomas Pitt smiled warmly enough, gratified to be the object of attention of a gracious woman. Lady Hester rolled her eyes, spread her fan and covered her mouth. "Not exactly, Mrs. Eliot," responded Thomas Pitt, "but nevertheless it is a fascinating story." He nodded towards William. "Our grandfather, Thomas, was the son of a poor clergyman. He was sent to India to make his fortune, which in due course he did, eventually becoming Governor of Madras."

"How impressive," said Catherine. "My father also was a member of the East India Company." Lady Hester cleared her throat and fanned vigorously.

"Well, not at first," said Thomas, "that came later."

"You know perfectly well that he was an interloper, Thomas," said Lady Hester, "and I dare say you inherited his lack of diplomacy."

"Come, come, my dear," sad William, "we must make allowances. After all, we owe a great deal to our grandfather. He left a great fortune."

Catherine raised her eyebrows. "Did he bring it home with him?" she asked. "All that gold must have been terribly heavy, and dangerous to carry with you."

"He was cleverer than that," said Thomas. "Governor Pitt purchased a huge diamond from an Indian trader. Then he hid it in the heel of his son Robert's boot who sailed home with it, charged with having it cut and sold for some wealthy sovereign's crown jewels."

Catherine laughed delightedly and turned to Edward. "That is indeed clever, husband, don't you agree? Perhaps you should do something like that."

"Not quite the kind of thing I might get up to, my dear," said Edward. "Bit too adventurous for me. But it brought Boconnoc into the Pitt family."

"Along with 18,000 acres," said Thomas Pitt, "and that was just one of ten properties he acquired."

"With several seats in parliament as well," said Edward Eliot. "I learned the importance of that from my father."

"As I remind my admirable husband," said Lady Hester, "success in politics requires money as well as brains. It is a pity his brother has not succeeded in keeping more of it."

William Pitt felt it was high time to change the subject. Addressing his brother, he said, "Knowing the gallantry of our Cornish sailors I had hoped some of them might join us, Thomas."

"You keep them too busy, sir," Thomas said. "And I told you Edgecumbe couldn't come, of course. And poor Edmund Boscawen left this mortal coil soon after the new year; the typhoid. Probably caught it from those damn French waters; not yet fifty, so much promise."

"I understand that Mr. Edgecumbe is engaged to Miss Emma Gilbert, the daughter of the Archbishop of York," said Catherine. "Our Cornish society will enjoy a cultured addition."

"I must say, Thomas," William Pitt said, smiling in Catherine's direction, "despite what circumstances may have contributed to a lack of male gallantry in attendance you have more than compensated for in female charm."

"Sir, you are too kind," said Catherine smiling in return and dropping an exaggerated curtsey. Edward Eliot bowed toward William Pitt. Across the room Dunbargan scowled and held out his glass to a footman for more sherry.

"Mr. Eliot, it is a pleasure to enjoy your company again," said William Pitt. "May I thank you for your successful efforts on our behalf at the election?"

"You are kind, sir," Eliot answered. "I am only too gratified to be of service, but I must point out that the assistance of my wife was invaluable. It appears that her charm works its magic on the voters of Cornwall almost as much as it does on the ministers of his majesty."

This brought a smile to Pitt's face.

"His Majesty must be pleased, Mr. Pitt," continued Eliot, "many more Tories elected and solid in Cornwall."

"The Duke hints that he cannot manage the country gentlemen as well as I can lead them," William Pitt said. "He has the sympathy of the large landowners, by and large, but new influence rests in some fifty merchants coming into the house. I dare say if they play their cards right they will enjoy profitable dealings with the government."

Catherine Eliot called across the room. "Speaking of cards, Lord Dunbargan, how do you expect to mend your fortunes at Mrs. White's Chocolate House now that Lord Edgecumbe will no longer be there to lose to you?" Once again she smiled sweetly.

Dunbargan appeared not to hear, and she did not repeat her question. There was an embarrassed pause, which her husband filled by again expressing his appreciation to William Pitt.

"I must repeat my thanks to you sir," said Edward Eliot, "for your assistance over the Turnpike Act for Liskeard. We are now soliciting subscriptions to assist with the funds the project will require, as much as five thousand pounds to complete the road to Tor Point, although it will take a few years yet. The farmers and merchants of Cornwall will be grateful for the convenience and prosperity the turnpike brings as much as they will complain of the tolls."

"Glad to hear it and glad to help," said William Pitt. He stepped closer to Eliot and spoke low in his ear. "I spoke to good friends at my seat in Bath on my way down; they are in a position to take up a subscription if you so wish. Let me know. And as I mentioned, it might be advisable to include my brother Thomas among your adventurers. He knows his way around Cornwall, especially where the Duchy is concerned. He might encourage Trenance too; help keep an eye on him. Dunbargan, I suppose we must call him now. And Thomas could certainly help with an extension to Lostwithiel. Have a word with him when you can."

"I will do what I can, Mr. Pitt, happy to oblige you. And by the way, I am hopeful that the road may be extended to the Looes. The fishermen will be equally grateful. I just pray that I could support their wishes through their representation in Parliament."

"That is more the business of the Duke of Newcastle than mine, Mr. Eliot," Pitt said, "although I do understand that the Admiralty has important interests to maintain. And for my purposes I must insist that the Royal Navy be well manned, maintained and supplied."

"Just do your best, sir," said Eliot, "to see that as few good Cornish mariners and fishermen are pressed into service as possible."

There was another awkward pause, and then Pitt spoke. "Manning our ships requires large numbers of men. The country's needs must be met, they come first. But I do not lack sympathy, Mr. Eliot. Indeed, even Admiral Vernon himself opposes the press gang. I recall his saying that our fleets are defrauded by injustice, marred by violence, and maintained by cruelty."

Eliot nodded his acknowledgement, but before he could say more his attention was caught by Lady Hester, who was seated a little apart from the group, beckoning him with her fan. He went over to her. "A word if I may, Mr. Eliot," she said.

"Lady Hester, at your service," Edward said, "it is a pleasure to be with you and your husband this evening."

"Pleasure indeed, Mr. Eliot, please join me," she said. Edward sat beside her. "But as usual among politicians," she continued, "pleasure is merely a venue for business. It pleases me that you are an admirer as well as a supporter of my husband, but I have no doubt that your admiration proceeds as much from your assessment of his value to you as from your appreciation of his policies for England."

"But Lady Hester," said Eliot.

"No, do not protest," said Lady Hester, "I prefer my truth unvarnished, whether received or delivered. Remember I grew up among politicians. I want to make clear to you that although Mr. Pitt may impress you as a man of integrity absorbed in affairs of the entire world, he also is a man of family loyalty. If you wish to enjoy his continued support, make no mistake that you must take care that Mr. Thomas Pitt enjoys opportunities to repair his and the Pitt family's wealth. Do I make myself clear?"

"You do indeed, my lady," said Eliot, "but let me assure you that my regard for the Pitt family alone suffices to persuade me to do what I can to help." He would have said more but was interrupted by the butler announcing dinner. He offered Lady Hester his arm and escorted her into the dining room. She raised her open fan and covered a smile. She disliked her brother-in-law but would not permit his disgrace to sully her husband's reputation further.

Edward Eliot's focus turned to the beautifully proportioned room. His wife's passion for improving Port Eliot was making him pay more attention to architecture and interior design. Boconnoc's dining room was decorated with beautiful plasterwork, an elaborate anaglyptic medallion in the center of the ceiling, dentil molding on the ceiling coves and friezes ornamented with flowers and leaves on the pilasters between the tall windows. A fire blazed in the handsome marble fireplace. He would no doubt hear all about it from Catherine once they were alone. She would have additional expensive inspirations for Port Eliot.

The twenty-four guests took their seats at the silver-laden and candlelit mahogany table. Thomas Pitt placed his brother William's wife, Lady Hester, in the position of honor at his right hand. The footmen plied them with quantities of soups and meats and fish and fruits, many of them from the estate. Thomas Pitt was especially proud of the wine served with the baron of beef.

"Sister-in-law, close your ears," he whispered to Lady Hester and shouted across to Dunbargan. "James, we owe this wine to your late father and his merry men. Bolitho, your pater was his partner in crime, too, as I recall." Thomas Bolitho looked shocked, then embarrassed. He did not respond. Dunbargan ignored the sally but took note; Bolitho had a guilty secret that could be used against him.

"Yes, it's a rare Cabernet Franc from Loire," said Thomas Pitt, twirling his glass and rolling a sip of the wine around his tongue. "Vinted from a black grape, fruity and robust. Hard to get these days, thanks to my dear brother locking up the French ports. Wouldn't be surprised if the Burgundians adopted it, started blending it with their Cabernet Sauvignons; it would add a little finesse, some subtlety to the palate. Tempted to keep it for myself but nothing better than sharing one's treasures with one's friends, what?"

"Thomas, you really should support my husband in all matters, large and small," huffed Lady Hester. "It is difficult enough for him to keep his colleagues in the House in support without being concerned that a scandal might break out within his own family."

"It's a splendid wine, Pitt," enthused Dunbargan, recovering his composure. "Wouldn't mind having a drop more. Mind you, I don't have much to do with that smuggling business. Got to look out for one's reputation, sitting in the Lords, don't you know?"

"Quite," said Catherine, and smiled. Dunbargan glared at her. The exchange was noted with curiosity by Elianor, Viscountess Dunbargan, who made a note to keep a sharper eye on her husband and Catherine Eliot.

"Oh, one simply must not get too close to the smugglers, y'know," said their host. "Leave it to one's steward to make the arrangements, deal with their distant relatives. But for some months now, I hear that the revenuers have been too busy running the crown's errands for the election to spend much time chasing after smugglers and wreckers. Don't know which is better for the country. Probably better for Cornwall to have those

Londoners spend their money on votes and give us a free hand for the business of living."

William Pitt pricked up his ears from the other end of the table. "Thomas, in confidence, I'll have you know that I heard it on good authority that your late friend Admiral Boscawen wrote to the Duke of Newcastle about his own seat. He wanted the duke to throw the support of the customs officers behind him. His Grace rules on their appointments and they carry great weight in elections in the Cornish seaports. It troubles me that even a gentleman of such accomplishment could not trust his election merely to his own reputation."

Perhaps trying to suggest that he was not alone in skirting the law, Thomas Bolitho added his own gossip. "I heard that one of our Cornish members even importuned His Grace to intervene in the punishment of some wreckers who were facing transportation to the penal colonies. He regarded showing such influence as vital to his electoral support."

Before the conversation could become more revealing, there was a discreet interruption. A footman came into the room, whispered in Thomas's ear, and gave him a sealed and beribboned parchment.

"William, here is a dispatch for you. About affairs of state, urgent," said Thomas. "Perhaps you should read it now."

"It can wait until we gentlemen are alone with the port," said William Pitt.

At a signal from the host, the footmen cleared the remaining dishes and the ladies withdrew from the dining room. The butler placed decanters on the table and passed around cigars. William Pitt broke the seal and read the dispatch intently. "This requires no reply or action by me, merely comment. It is great news, gentlemen. We are mere days away from capturing Belle Isle off the coast of Brittany from the French. They succumbed to our navy's bombardment, our foot soldiers stormed the redoubts, and they have been driven to take shelter in the Citadel."

"What does this mean to the war?" asked Edward Eliot.

"It crowns the strategy we embarked on when we defeated the French navy at Quiberon Bay. We will now have a base off the Normandy coast from which our blockade will prevent the French supplying America, Canada, India and the West Indies. And England is spared the threat of invasion."

"At last we can make peace and staunch your extravagant expenditures," said Dunbargan. "The king will be pleased, as will the Duke of Newcastle. And I look forward to peace and traveling on the continent again. It's such a bore only to visit one's friends in England."

"No doubt your lordship will receive a warmer welcome further from home," said Eliot. As soon as the words were out of his mouth it was on the tip of his tongue to apologize. However, he immediately forgave himself. Given the increasing distaste his wife Catherine was feeling for the viscount, it was a remark she might have enjoyed making. However, Mr. William Pitt returned to the weighty subject at hand.

"His Grace must use his cunning to continue to supply the funds," said Pitt. "I have always made clear that the path to peace is victory, and a greater prize is now within our grasp, in Europe too, at the heart of France's crumbling empire. I said that when Newcastle was prepared to give Louisbourg back to the French."

"Louisbourg!" scoffed Dunbargan. "We only get a few boatloads of cod from Newfoundland. It's not worth much."

"From a Cornishman that's almost treasonous!" expostulated Pitt. "Newfoundland has brought prosperity to many a Cornish fisherman and to the merchants backing them. The prosperity of our foreign traffic brought to us by our wars has excited the amazement of the world."

"Hear, hear!" shouted Edward Eliot and Thomas Bolitho.

The viscount glared at the latter.

"And don't forget it was our late good friend Edward Boscawen who commanded the fleet that captured Louisbourg," continued William Pitt. "That led to the capture of Canada and our victories in America. When I apply to other officers respecting any expedition I may chance to project, they always raise difficulties. Boscawen always found expedients. And by the way, I will point out that our friend George Edgecumbe was at Louisbourg, too; captain of the Lancaster. I'll tell you why else Edgecumbe was too occupied to take his ease here with you and drink my brother's fine French wine. He captained H.M.S. Hero with seventy-four guns; she fought at Belle Isle."

Dunbargan was not to be silenced. During his time in London he had evidently spent enough time in the House of Lords when he was not engaged at the hazard tables to hear snippets of the arguments about matters of the day.

"Undoubtedly, you will admit, sir, that the forces required to prosecute the war at Belle Isle were large and expensive."

"Certainly, but the best victory is a decisive one," said Pitt, "and Belle Isle is well worth it. The navy deployed over twenty sail of the line, more than ten frigates, fire ships, sloops and scores of transports and supply ships. We sent marines and regiments of foot, seven thousand men at first, and later three thousand reinforcements."

Eliot was once again amazed at Pitt's grasp of detail. The effort required of him to amass all the facts and keep them fresh in his head must be demanding, but it underlay his brilliance as a strategist and a statesman.

"Therein lies the expense, naturally," said Eliot. "As a landowner I see my taxes increased fourfold. But as a patriot I am privileged to pay them. I would suggest, however, that the administration might find increased sources of revenue from this trade overseas. As a Commissioner of Trade and Plantations, I see multiple opportunities for a greater share in the takings of the colonies."

"These high taxes have gone on long enough," persisted Dunbargan. "Now the administration is even taxing beer. The public won't stand for it. His Grace Newcastle is forced to raise more and more from annuities. They will come due; they will have to be repaid some day. Future generations will be burdened by this extravagance."

"You seem to have joined the pack that is nipping at my heels, my lord," said Pitt with a smile. "When events are in our favor and success comes easily, there are many who sing of glory. We have had to stay the course of late; now, some of the terriers have turned tail and profess to love peace. It's clear that most of them in their hearts are loathe to pay for victory and would say whatever might carry the argument to protect their personal treasure. However, I am convinced that the colonies won by my strategies will bring us lasting treasure that far exceeds transient glory. We shall see which view England ultimately takes, and the consequence of her decision."

Chapter Forty-one

Instability

It was not many months before William Pitt's worst misgivings about decreasing support from the king and increasing criticism from his opponents were borne out. Discontent and dispute flowered into disenchantment and disgust, and by the fifth day of October Pitt relinquished the seals of his office and resigned as secretary of state. Granted, the results of the war during 1761 had been mixed; but on balance, they were by no means unsuccessful nor in Pitt's view grounds for seeking peace at any price. In central Europe events were admittedly going badly. The Russians had invaded and occupied Pomerania; England's ally Frederic the Great was at his lowest point, and Prussia verged on extinction.

A brighter point for England had been the capture of Belle Isle off the coast of Normandy, and to Pitt this was more strategically productive than continuing to distract the French with adventures motivated by the connections of the Hanoverian kings and their attendant subsidies. The genius of Pitt's strategy lay in simultaneously conducting the war in multiple theaters and in his recognition that forcing the French to commit resources in Europe weakened their ability to defend their gains in America. As the great orator boasted, England "won Canada on the banks of the Rhine."

Prospects for colonial expansion around the world at the expense of the French were brighter than ever. In India, Pondicherry was captured, and that gave England control over the Bay of Bengal. In the West Indies, the island of Dominica with its valuable timber had also fallen into British hands. In America the Cherokee nation was forced to submit. With all, even Pitt was disposed to reopening peace negotiations with France and her allies, providing the outcome was complete victory.

However, his suspicions of the French were rekindled by reports from his agents of a secret Bourbon Family Compact, by which the Bourbon monarchs of France and of Spain agreed to an offensive alliance against Britain if the war was still going on by May the following year, 1762. Spain was concerned that Britain had become too powerful through her victories over France and optimistic that the fiscal strains imposed by global operations presented an opportunity. Pitt's reaction was characteristic, as were the responses of his colleagues in the cabinet.

Pitt proposed to neutralize the threat with a speedy and decisive pre-emptive strike against Spain by seizing its annual treasure fleet as it sailed from Manila. It would be a brilliant stroke from the mind of a strategic genius. Its effect would be to cripple Spain's navy, deter her from allying with the French and attacking Britain, and capture sufficient gold and silver to finance the continuance of the war on multiple fronts. But it was not to be. Newcastle, the master of political debts, favors and schemes, and Bute led the opposition.

Newcastle lacked the courage to take the military initiative. As ever, he worried about the ongoing financial demands, especially if the strike failed. He feared that by appearing as aggressor, Britain would provoke the opposition of nations that had, to date, remained neutral. Bute's position was typically political, as he simply saw an opportunity to reduce Pitt's power by supporting Newcastle on a critical issue.

George III lacked the insight of his predecessor, who perceived the value of partnership between statesmen of opposing philosophies. The king did not press for Pitt's dismissal. He simply did too little to save him, resenting Pitt's autocratic ways more than he appreciated his genius.

Pitt could not tolerate opposition on such a vital question. He offered his resignation. Those cabinet colleagues who did not strongly disagree with him were unwilling to support his continued dominance over them and, indeed, his popularity in the country. The king was able to appear magnanimous by arranging Pitt's retirement with honor.

When Edward Eliot got the news he was dismayed and then wondered about the possible effect on his own career and influence. He owed much to his friendship with the Pitt family, and he was too loyal to abandon it merely because of what he hoped would be a temporary setback in his leader's fortunes. However, he needed to reassess his situation, not least in Cornwall.

Edward called a meeting in the library at Port Eliot to inform his trusted lieutenants. There, Catherine made her first appearance since the birth of their new son, on the last day of September. They had named him John, like Edward's younger brother, after his famous ancestor who so nobly, and to his own and his family's detriment, supported the parliamentary cause against the tyranny of King Charles I, ending his life ignominiously in the Tower of London. The proud parents had high expectations of their new son and his future contribution to his family's fame and fortune.

"Mrs. Eliot," said Polkinghorne with a degree of unctuousness, "it is my pleasure and privilege to congratulate you on the birth of your son, and to wish him well for a long, happy and successful life."

"Aargh. Us likewise," said Bunt, with the rough charm that served him.

"You are both too kind," said Catherine, as she took a seat by the fire. "I trust he will be faithful in carrying on the fine traditions of Port Eliot." To the men who had stood when she entered the room she said, "Please gentlemen, be seated."

"Indeed, my dear," said Eliot, "and now there are pressing matters of great import of which I must inform you all. There has been more great change in London. Our good friend and compatriot Mr. Pitt has resigned, leaving Newcastle and Bute whispering in the king's ear."

"Did Mr. Pitt resign, or did the king dismiss him?" asked Polkinghorne. "What effect will it have on us in Cornwall?"

"The initiative was Pitt's, I am confident of that, despite the machinations of his many rivals," said Eliot. "The king arranged a fine pension, and his wife Lady Hester became Baroness Chatham in her own right. The king is not ungenerous."

"Does this mean Mr. Pitt will enter the House of Lords?" asked Catherine. "Perhaps, Mr. Eliot, you could do the same. I would not be opposed to being a baroness. The neighbors would be quite impressed by Lady Eliot."

"My dear, you are teasing I trust, or otherwise I would consider you blatantly ambitious. No, Mr. Pitt chose to remain the Great Commoner and to stay among his friends," replied Eliot. "Who knows, perhaps he has hopes that the king will once again appoint him to lead an administration in the Commons. What I do know is that he resigned over distinctly opposing views on the conduct of the war."

"How much was his pension?" asked Catherine.

"You are a stickler for the material details," Eliot answered, shaking a finger at her. "I hear it was three thousand pounds a year. William Pitt did not inherit great riches, and he has devoted his life to serving his country rather than to becoming wealthy. Such an amount will enable him to live in a manner appropriate to his standing."

"Many people do wish that the war would end," said Polkinghorne, "and they fear the burden of taxation. Would it not it be preferable to end the war and be content with our gains?"

"You are correct in your assessment of opinion, but wrong in your view of policy," said Eliot. "The Duke of Newcastle never fails to point out that the annual supplies have increased from four million pounds before the war to nineteen and a half million this year. He has raised the land tax and now has added a tax on beer of three shillings a barrel. He fears the people will bear no more and cannot bring himself to go on much longer increasing the national debt."

"Don't matter none to me, Oi reckon," said Bunt dolefully, "not since that Reverend Perry made us take the pledge. Oi'm a teetotaler now."

"Make sure you stay that way, young man," said Polkinghorne. "You stray once from total abstinence and you'll be gone from Port Eliot." Bunt looked down at his hands and said no more.

Eliot plunged on. "Mr. Pitt tells me that his agents reported on a secret compact whereby Spain bound themselves to France to join together to attack us. His response was to urge taking the initiative to the Spaniards in the West Indies and to send the Royal Navy to capture their treasure fleet as it sailed en route to Spain. At one bold blow we would possess the gold and silver to continue to prosecute the war around the world. Brilliant, I say."

"All very well for Mr. Pitt," grumbled Bunt, edging into the conversation again. "If our poor bloody Cornish smugglers did such a trick they'd be 'anged, or worse."

"Bunt," said Polkinghorne, "have more respect for your betters and the laws that bind us."

Eliot ignored them both, took a breath, and pressed on with his thought. "Mr. Pitt insisted that our victories give us the right to dictate the terms of peace. His conduct of the war has been brilliant. The man is a genius."

"I am sure you and Mr. Pitt are right, my dear," said Catherine. "Would that England simply placed her trust in you both."

"Hear, hear!" enthused Polkinghorne, and with less refinement Bunt added a tentative "Aargh."

"You are too kind and indubitably correct," said Eliot. "Pitt is a man of intellectual breadth, but his determination and abilities arouse jealousies. I could smooth his path, act behind the scenes to win men to his policy. He brooks no opposition and some find that tiresome. He depends on convincing even those who disagree with public argument, with reason, the people as well as Parliament. He is contemptuous of machination behind the scenes. He simply insists that we must persist to a decisive victory to avoid giving up our gains at the negotiating table. He accepts no other way. The important thing is that his vision for England's destiny is right. Above all he grasps better than anyone the potential of great riches from the American colonies. Trade will increase and outstrip agriculture in bringing wealth to England."

"But, sir, what of Cornwall?" asked Polkinghorne. "America is a long way from St. Germans."

"In good time, Polkinghorne," said Eliot. "As I was about to tell you, Bute and Newcastle refused to support Pitt, and they carried the majority of the cabinet and the king with them. They fear, at least in part, the growing expense of the war, and lack the vision to foresee the great prizes."

"It be 'ardly my place to say, zir," Bunt hesitated, "but what Oi reckon your honor be sayin' loike, is that Mr. Pitt and that duke gen'leman be a good team, leastways some of the toime. Us got plough 'orses that way at Port Eliot, one pulls strong some toimes, 'tother pulls strong another toime. Plough would'n' go straight none of the toime if ploughman didn't use 'is whip an' give 'em a tickle be'ind the ears now an' then. Mebbe that's what them gen'lemen needs."

"Bunt, don't trouble Mr. Eliot with nonsense," said Polkinghorne, "how ever do such fantastical ideas fill that head of yours?"

"Hold on a moment, Polkinghorne," said Catherine. "Go on, Bunt. What else would you say?"

"Well mum, Oi'd say that mebbe the king was the ploughman, loike. Give a jerk on the reins now an' then, keep the team pullin' together, steady, straight loike."

"So how would you suggest our team at Port Eliot could pull stronger and straighter?" pursued Catherine. Eliot sat back in his chair with a growing smile.

"If you don't moind me sayin' so, mum, us could do with a bit more of that duke gen'leman. Mr. Eliot acts more loike Mr. Pitt, if Oi understands it aright, honorable loike, straight, honest. Works all right with most people who are honest too. Seems to work with Liskeard people, far as Oi can tell. But Oi know for sure it'd never work with Viscount Dunbugger, or whatever 'e calls 'isself these days. Us got to watch out for 'e, keep one or two moves ahead."

Catherine nodded at Bunt's words. "So perhaps, Mr. Eliot, it would serve us well to keep a closer ear and eye on the viscount. I do not doubt that many of Dunbargan's schemes are nefarious and that Cornwall and we, ourselves, might thereby suffer losses. Might we not borrow a leaf from the Duke of Newcastle's book in employing subtler, more cunning, wider relationships with those less easy to convince by reason alone?"

"I do that already, my dear, to the necessary extent," said Edward, "always, of course, in accordance with my principles and the Christian faith."

Catherine demurred. "You perhaps are too much of a gentleman, Mr. Eliot. Indeed, that is desirable and proper for the most part, as Bunt says. But there are some people whom one has to watch more carefully to further one's interests, exploit one's advantages. It might do to be a little ruthless, not show one's hand, or at least keep a mailed fist clothed in the velvet glove. And to be ever vigilant of those who might do harm to Eliot interests, notably and near, the former James Trenance."

Catherine continued, warming to her subject. "We must think hard. What are Viscount Dunbargan's weaknesses; where are his vulnerabilities?"

"Getting through that list would take up the rest of the day," Eliot said and smiled.

"For the present toime, zir," said Bunt, scratching his chin, "Oi've 'eard 'e's desperate for money. Always pressing Mr. Clymo, in a big 'urry to make more money, specially from the mines, dig more shafts, even digging under the sea, get in more capital, work the tinners 'arder, find more ore."

"That's all very well," said Eliot, "but he can't just trot off and expand his workings without arranging permission with the Duchy of Cornwall. The Duchy controls most of the valuable mineral rights, especially along the foreshore."

"And, indeed, who influences the financial decisions for the Duchy?" asked Catherine.

"H'mm, I suppose I do," said Eliot. "I am the Receiver General of the Duchy after all. It is a pity our friend Mr. Thomas Pitt has gone from this world. He did not appear himself when he entertained us at Boconnoc but nevertheless his death seemed sudden. Pitt knew his way around Duchy affairs, although he lost much influence with his position in the Stannary Parliament. And now that his son has inherited Boconnoc, perhaps there are ears in which he could whisper when asked. I shall inquire whether he stands in need of my friendship."

"Exactly, my dear," said Catherine, and smiled. It was not obvious whether her smile was for her husband or for Bunt; perhaps both.

Chapter Forty-two

Reading

It was a fine clear morning and the landlord of The Eliot Arms greeted Polkinghorne and Bunt warmly when they came in to the bar and ordered sausage rolls and pickled onions for their elevenses. Polkinghorne ordered a pint of bitter; Bunt ordered apple juice. After serving them, the landlord reached under the bar counter and drew out a folded parchment, sealed with red wax. He passed it to Willy Bunt who took it, turned it over and looked at both sides with a puzzled look in his eyes.

"Oi say young feller me lad," the landlord said, "this 'ere came for ye. Seems like a letter. Postman brought it day before yesterday. Says it's fer Willy Bunt, care of the village inn, St. Germans. Not much of an address, but 'er got 'ere safe an' sound. Course, Oi'm well known around these parts. Been landlord of this fine establishment for nigh on twelve years."

Willy squinted at the package and tried to make the best of his embarrassment. "Writin's not very good, 'ard to make out. Can't make 'ead nor tail of 'er."

"Gimme, I'll tell you what it says easy enough," said Polkinghorne, grabbing at the letter. The handwriting was indeed not the most educated. He pulled out his pocketknife, broke the seal and sliced the letter open. "Who might be writing to you, anyroad? My word! Says on the front it's private. Do you have a lady love or something? Wait 'til I tell your Mary. She won't half give you what for."

"Give it back, it's moine," Willy said, blushing beneath the stubble on his ruddy cheeks. "It says that 'er's private."

The landlord chuckled, and the men loitering on the benches around the snug looked up to take in the fun.

"I was just joshing you, Willy," said Polkinghorne. "I'll read it to you if you like and I won't tell nobody what it says or who it's from, unless you say so. We can keep it between us. You can trust me."

"All right then," agreed Willy. "But let's go over to that there table in the corner. Us don't want every Tom, Dick and 'Arry knowin' our business."

"*Dear Willy,*" Polkinghorne read, and turned it over to look at the signature. "My God, it's from that there Morwenna Clymo. So you do have a lady love!" Polkinghorne felt a tinge of jealousy.

"Keep 'er quiet and just read the bloody letter," Willy said, elbowing him in the ribs. Polkinghorne ignored the sally and continued.

"Mary was done wrong at Lanhydrock, and so was you. I know for myself what that James Trenance is like. Someone ought to make up for it. Maybe I can help make things right. He shouldn't have it all his own way. He makes trouble for everyone, just thinks of himself. I was sorry you got into trouble at Whitsuntide at Liskeard and I wish I could have done more for you. I thought Mr. and Mrs. Eliot were so kind. You two are lucky to have places at Port Eliot. I don't want to get my Dad into no trouble but I hear things, some of them bad. I'm worried James might drag him into something awful and blame him for it. It's not my Dad's fault, he has to do what he's told or he would get the sack and then what would we do? No money, no house, no references neither. The viscount has it in for Port Eliot. He thinks Mr. Eliot can't do nothing back now that Mr. Pitt is out of office. I have an idea. Meet me somewheres soon. Bring that nice Mr. Polkinghorne if you want. Don't tell nobody. Hope Mary is fine. When are you having more family? Morwenna."

Polkinghorne dug in his pocket and pulled out his tobacco pouch and old clay pipe. Thoughtfully, he filled the pipe, tamped it down, lit a taper at the fireplace and drew in deeply, then blew out a great cloud of smoke. He poked Willy in his ribs. "Looks like she isn't your lady love, lad. More's the pity, eh? Now for business. The first thing we must do, Bunt, is show this to Mr. Eliot."

"Us can't do that. Morwenna said 'tis private, us shouldn't tell nobody."

"It's more than our jobs are worth if we do anything behind Mr. Eliot's back. This could be important, risky. Beside, we owe it to Mr. Eliot."

Bunt thought for a moment, took a drink of his juice, and said, "It's up to you then, Mr. Polkinghorne. Oi s'pose Mr. Eliot'd understand if us explained it nice like." He coughed, and squinted as the smoke got in his eyes. They finished their repast and set off through the park to the Port Eliot estate office. They asked the clerk the whereabouts of Mr. Eliot and learned that he had left some while ago to meet Mrs. Eliot. The Eliots were going off somewhere and would not be coming back for several days.

"Then you'd better take the initiative, Bunt," said Polkinghorne. "Write a letter to Miss Clymo and tell her we'd both like to meet her at a convenient place between here and Lanhydrock in five days. That should allow time for a letter to reach her at her father's house. How about The Globe in Lostwithiel?"

"You write it, Mr. Polkinghorne," said Bunt, "you're the boss. You can say Oi asked you to, and Oi agree with everything what you say. Oi can mark my name at the bottom, if you want."

Polkinghorne dictated a brief letter to the clerk, got a shilling out of the cash box, gave it to the office boy, and sent him up to the landlord at The Eliot Arms to hand over the letter to the postman when he next called.

A few days later a messenger from the landlord delivered the reply to the Bunts' cottage. Mary gave it to Willy as soon as he got home at the end of the day, before he had a chance to take off his hat and coat, or even give a kiss to her or baby Catherine.

"What's this then, me 'andsome? Who's it from?"

Willy took it from her, opened it and pretended to read it. "It's from Mr. Clymo at Lanhydrock. For Oi and Mr. Polkinghorne," he answered. "Wants we to meet him there as soon as us can on an important matter. Won't say 'zackly what it's about. Oi'd better go and show Mr. Polkinghorne. Oi'll be back in toime for supper."

Willy found Polkinghorne at his house in the village and showed him the letter.

"Mr. Eliot's not back yet," Polkinghorne told him. "We don't know when to expect him. I'll leave a note for him in the office. This can't wait. Morwenna will meet us tomorrow at The Globe in Lostwithiel. You call in at the stables and arrange for a couple of horses to be ready for us at daybreak. I'll see you then, and don't be late on any account."

Mary had baby Catherine in bed and supper on the table when Willy got back. This time he hung up his coat and hat, but when he tried to take Mary in his arms and kiss her she rebuffed him. She went silently to the stove, served up their supper, put their platters on the table and sat down.

"Now what's all this about then?" she demanded.

"It's private business, for Port Eliot. It's about that there Viscount Dunbugger. Mr. Clymo is warnin' us that he is tryin' to cheat Mr. Eliot. Me and Mr. Polkinghorne is ridin' to Lanhydrock early tomorrow to meet 'im and discuss it. 'E says 'e's got some ideas."

"Why would Mr. Clymo want to warn you? Why would 'e take that much trouble over you? What would he get out of it? He works for Lanhydrock. Trenance would sack him if he ever found out. Somethin' smells like a rotten pilchard. 'Ere, let me look at that letter, now."

Willy handed it over. After all, there'd be less of a problem in Mary looking at it than keeping it from her and arousing her suspicions further.

"'Ere! That's not from Mr. Joseph Clymo. That's from Morwenna. She's got awful friendly with you."

Willy was flustered. "'Ow'd you know that? You can't read."

"Oh yes Oi can. Mrs. Eliot's been learnin' me. Writin' and spellin' too. She wants to open up a village school, and 'er wants me to 'elp 'er. Says it would 'elp our fambly improve ourselves if you learn to read and write too, an' if Oi read Oi could 'elp you and you'd be more likely to want to. Oi was keepin' it as a surprise, to 'elp you. Oi knows Oi look after the cottage and cooks your meals an' looks after little Catherine, but Oi want to do more, be more useful like. Oi don't want to work at the big 'ouse neither while 'er's so tiny, an' anyroad Oi want to be more than a servant, loike you be." Mary paused for breath.

"Blimey! You surprised me all right," said Willy. "Oi didn't want to tell you it was from Morwenna in case you thought it was funny loike, got you upset. It's just that 'er thinks me and Mr. Polkinghorne needs to know what's goin' on that's not right. 'Er loikes us both, Mary, you an' me, an' she don't want no trouble for 'er dad an' she 'ates Trenance who done 'er wrong, just like you. Thinks 'e needs 'is comeuppance. Anyroad, she asked after you. She wants to know when us is 'avin' more fambly."

"She do, do 'er? Well, be you ready for another surprise? Mrs. Eliot better 'urry up with that school. 'Er little John will be needin' learnin' before you know it. An' besides 'im another little pupil will be arrivin' before Eastertide."

"Mary, me dear, that's lovely!" exclaimed Willy delightedly, and dashed around the table, drew Mary to her feet and gave her a big hug. Mary's response was tepid.

"You just watch out who you're 'uggin', you girt lummox you. You don't always act dependable, and just you remember you're gettin' more responsibilities whether you like it or no."

"Oi promise, Mary. Oi've give up strong drink after all, an' Oi've stuck to it. An' Mr. Polkinghorne will be comin' to Lanhydrock as well, don' 'e forget. Everythin's goin' to be all right, you mark my words. Now, let's eat up and make up, and get to bed. Oi've got an early start in the mornin'."

"All right then, me love," smiled Mary, softened by the explanations and Willy's response to the coming baby. "Oi can't never say no to you. An' Oi'm not worried about you getting' me in the fambly way, not now!"

Chapter Forty-three

Lostwithiel

Mary was woken just before sunrise by a cry from a hungry baby Catherine demanding to be fed. She satisfied her little one's immediate need and then went downstairs to get Willy a hearty breakfast of porridge with warm milk, homemade pork sausages, poached eggs and fried bread. While he ate she wrapped up enough bread and cheese for two in a big red handkerchief.

"Oi don't want you goin' 'ungry, my love, you'm a long way to ride all the way to Lostwithiel there and back."

"Us'll do our best, Mary, but this be an important meetin', may take a long time, and Mr. Polkinghorne don't like travelin' in the dark. Gets nervous about 'ighwaymen an' such. Us'll be at The Globe and Oi dare say 'e might decide to stay overnight. 'E'll be takin' some money just in case."

"Aw, Oi don' want ye stayin' away. The two of you'd be too much for any robber. Oi want you back 'ere with us in our very own bed, specially now with a new baby on the way."

Willy tried to reassure Mary with a hug but he could tell as he got ready to leave that she was unconvinced and far from happy.

"You dress up warm now, Willy, them early mornings gets cold now it's autumn. Don't want you catchin' nothin' and givin' it to little Catherine."

Day was breaking as Willy arrived at the stables. He was pleased to see that he had got there before Polkinghorne. Willy would probably get into some sort of trouble before the day was out, but at least it would not be for being late this morning. Willy was getting used to Mr. Polkinghorne's ways as he got to know him better, but he could be awfully particular. At least that made Willy try his best, which could only make him more useful.

The top half of the stable door was open. Willy looked in and greeted the groom and stable boys. The groom had picked out two good horses and they were already fed, watered, tacked up and ready to go. As the groom led the horses out to the mounting block, Polkinghorne strode up.

"Morning all. Don't stand there gossiping, Bunt. We have to get a move on. We have a long way to go. Here, take one of these." He handed Willy a pistol. Willy put the pistol and the bread and cheese in his saddlebag and without further ado they set off.

The weather for once was dry, so the potholes in the road were not filled with muddy puddles. The journey as far as Liskeard was uneventful. They stopped in at Eliot House and changed horses. The fresh horses champed at their bits, eager to break into a canter. They held them to a fast trot except when going down hill and still made good progress. They passed a train of pack mules slowly coming the other way, led by a farm laborer on horseback. The mules bore panniers laden with turnips, apparently fresh dug and on their way to the Liskeard market.

"That's a crop that's really catching on, turnips," said Polkinghorne. "Mr. Eliot did a good thing when he brought in the idea from up country. We've encouraged the farmers to sow them, feed them to their sheep. They're wintering over better, producing more mutton, better wool. They say more and more people are eating them too; they're cheap and getting plentiful. Mr. Eliot says Cornish people eat pretty well compared with up north, what with local vegetables and meat and plenty of fish."

"My Mary cuts up a swede and puts it in a pasty with some beef and onion, very tasty," said Bunt, licking his lips.

"You've got a proper wife there," Polkinghorne said, "cooking for you and keeping house, taking good care of your baby." Bunt nodded. After a few moments of rumination Polkinghorne spoke again. "Envy you sometimes, Bunt. Gets a bit lonely living on your own."

"Oi can't 'ardly keep up with my Mary some toimes," Willy said. "Don't know what 'er gets up to from one day to the next. Now she's learnin' to read an' write, or so 'er says. Wants little Catherine to go to school when she gets older so 'er can read an' write too."

"She'd be better off minding the cooking and housekeeping," said Polkinghorne. "You keep an eye on her. Village nippers reading and writing! Don't you two go getting big headed, milking the pigeon. Pride comes before a fall, that's what they say."

"Some new ideas are good. You said so yourself about the turnips. New ideas pay. Mr. Eliot will be tellin' you to raise the rents again soon. And I'd bet a few coppers, if Oi 'ad any to spare, that before long Port Eliot will 'ave steam engines workin' the quarries an' crushin' the road stone. And think of the turnpike, that's a good idea and that's new."

"You're right there," said Polkinghorne, "bringing about a lot of changes too, I'll be bound. We won't be seeing many pack trains much longer. Soon as we get that turnpike built the carriers will be using wagons. I've heard Mr. Eliot say that they're getting an act of parliament soon for another eighteen-mile stretch from Lostwithiel down to St. Austell. And then from St. Germans up towards the Tamar to Saltash."

"Was that Mr. Pitt's doings?" mused Bunt.

"I dare say he had something to do with it," said Polkinghorne. "He's an important man, got influence, least he did have. What Mr. Eliot gets up to in parliament is no concern of yours, mind. Course, he sometimes asks my advice, but you've got your own work cut out without sticking your nose in what me and Mr. Eliot do."

"Mr. Eliot'll be makin' a lot of money with the road stone from Port Eliot, won't 'e? Partly thanks to me workin' my arse off, that's what Oi say," said Bunt. "Do you reckon us'll be seein' our fair share of that?"

"Don't you get fancy ideas in your head, young feller. I've warned you that you'd get into trouble trying to get above your station. You just be grateful to be paid decent wages and have a dry roof over your heads, you and your family."

"Might need a bigger roof soon. My Mary's in the fambly way again."

"All the best to you, that's good news to be sure," said Polkinghorne. "I 'spect you had something to do with it; you're a lively one and no mistake. But a bigger family is all the more reason to keep your head down, do your job proper, and don't go making no trouble."

The horses ambled up a rise though a wooded area as they made steady progress. It had warmed up as noon approached and the sun rose higher. They stopped by a stream to let the horses drink and take a breather and to get a cool drink for themselves.

"Toime to pump ship," said Bunt, going off to relieve himself.

When he returned, Polkinghorne pointed at a lane that turned off to the left, a signpost at the fork.

"That way's to Couch's Mill," he said. "Lostwithiel is straight on, another three miles. Why don't we stop for a bite of croust?"

"All that talk of pasties back then made me 'ungry," agreed Bunt and burrowed into his saddlebag to get out the homemade bread and cheese that Mary had packed for them. "Should be at The Globe in an hour or so, then. Keep wonderin' what Morwenna will 'ave to say."

"If your lady love don't have something to make it worth our while riding all this way . . ." said Polkinghorne.

"Aw, don' carry on so," protested Bunt, "Oi told you, 'er is not my lady love, just a friend; to Mary as well."

They remounted, and sure enough in just over an hour they caught sight of the spire of St. Bartholomew's above the roofs of the town. They walked their tiring horses over the old stone bridge across the River Fowey and turned left towards North Street. They went into the stable yard of The Globe Inn and were greeted by the ostler. Their horses seemed to know that their journey was at an end and allowed themselves to be led by this reassuring stranger into the stalls where they were unsaddled, fed and watered.

The men were glad to dismount and stretch their stiff muscles. They unbuckled their saddlebags and carried them through the back entrance of the inn into a large room with a low-beamed ceiling where a cosy fire greeted them. Morwenna was already there.

"Willy, Mr. Polkinghorne, welcome to Lostwithiel." Morwenna stood as she greeted them. "I am glad to see you both again. Did you have a good journey?"

"Good enough, miss," said Polkinghorne, stretching. "As I was just saying to Bunt here, I trust what you have to tell us is worth the long ride." He kept his manner offhand, but he felt a warm pleasure at seeing her again.

"Knowin' Miss Clymo Oi trust she would never lead us on a wild goose chase," Bunt said. "Been waitin' long, 'ave 'e?"

"No," Morwenna replied. "I left right after midday dinner and walked from Lanhydrock past Restormel Castle, just a couple of miles. Didn't take long at all. You been to Lostwithiel before, Mr. Polkinghorne? I know Willy has; he used to live nearby."

"I've not spent much time here, miss," Polkinghorne said. "It's a fair piece from St. Germans. But I did come to a meeting at the stannary with Mr. Eliot a time or two. Lostwithiel used to be a lot busier at one time, so they tell me. Funny-looking church, though."

"My dad told me Lostwithiel was once a port for shipping the tin down the estuary and into the English Channel, but then this reach of the River Fowey got silted up with the tailings from the mining up on the moors."

"Well, no matter," said Polkinghorne, "you can always go down river to Fowey and ship from there. Do you know why the church looks so strange?"

Morwenna nodded. "My dad said it looked just like a normal English church in the olden days," she related, "then in the fourteenth century some men came over from Brittany and built a spire on top of the tower."

"Bloody furriners," said Bunt, largely for something to say, since he felt left out of the conversation and, anyway, Morwenna was his friend, not Polkinghorne's. But Morwenna flared up.

"You're ignorant, Willy. The Bretons are like the Cornish, Celtic too. Haven't you ever seen them when they come over to wrassle our lads? Same kind of wrasslin', with that there canvas jacket. Bring over their onions to sell too, in long strings. Sweet, tasty in a pasty. We Cornish got

Spanish blood too, traded with the Spaniards for saffron donkeys years ago and lots of them stayed here when they was wrecked after the Armada."

"Enough of this chattering," said Polkinghorne, "let's find somewhere to sit and get down to business. What have you got to tell us?" He hoped that he might have an opportunity in future to continue a more intimate conversation with Morwenna.

The men put their saddlebags on the floor under a table and sat.

"I don't want to get my dad in no trouble," Morwenna said anxiously. "If I say too much he could lose his job. The viscount isn't loyal to anyone. He's got to be stopped. My dad is a good man, truly, but I think he's afraid of the viscount, deep down. But if I don't do nothing and my dad does something wrong just because the viscount tells him and they get found out, my dad would get the blame and get in worse trouble. Maybe I should keep my mouth shut."

"Too late now, girl," said Polkinghorne, "not after dragging us all this way. Anyroad, you can trust us, and Mr. Eliot if it comes to that. We'll make sure nothing gets back that gets Mr. Clymo in trouble. We respect him. He's good at heart, just mixed up with the wrong people."

"Well, it's like this, according to my dad . . ." Morwenna hesitated, took a deep breath and straightened her shoulders. "He came back home after the Michaelmas cost book meeting at the end of September. Viscount Dunbargan wanted it held in the Guildhall here down on Quay Street, being that Lostwithiel was once a stannary town, and it would be more convenient for the venturers from east Cornwall than going all the way down to the mines practically at Land's End."

"I'm all ears, pray proceed with your story," said Polkinghorne.

"Well, there was a bit of a kerfuffle. Dunbargan had told my dad and Mr. Bolitho to get as much money for him as they could because he really needed it. The mine captains were there, John Williams and Addis Penwarden. They said they needed to spend some of the profits on expanding the mines and putting in steam engines and new equipment. Mr. Bolitho said that's why the venturers had been asked to put money in, and why they'd taken risks; they should get some of the money too."

"What did your dad say?" asked Bunt.

"Nothin' much at first," said Morwenna. "He wanted the others to do the talking. Then all of a sudden the viscount got red in the face and started screaming at them. He said he owned the leases and he had the first call on the profits. It was a privilege for the venturers to join in and they would just have to wait for their money and consider themselves lucky to get any. Then he yelled at Dad and the captains and said it was their fault because they weren't expanding the mines quick enough. Mr. Bolitho said they were doing the best they could with what they had. Then he said the viscount had to keep up his end of the business. He hadn't got the proper licenses to dig more shafts."

"What do you mean, licenses?" asked Polkinghorne. He reached into his pocket and dug out his old clay pipe, cut off some plug tobacco and stuffed it into the bowl. He got up and fetched an ember from the fire to light it and puffed thoughtfully.

"Well, my dad says mine owners are supposed to get permission from the Duchy of Cornwall, pay fees, coinage," continued Morwenna. "The viscount said there wasn't a Duke of Cornwall, 'cos he died, and the new king doesn't have a son, so it doesn't matter."

"We'll see about that," said Polkinghorne. "Mr. Eliot knows a thing or two about what's right with the workings of the Duchy."

"So who sees to them kind of matters?" asked Bunt, getting interested.

"I'd have to ask me dad to be sure," said Morwenna, "but I think some is done by the Duchy for all of Cornwall, and some by the stannators for each of the stannary areas, like Lostwithiel or Liskeard."

"I know the stannaries regulate the mining and the tin trade," said Polkinghorne, "and they see to it that a corner is cut off each ingot of smelted tin and turned over as coinage to the Duchy. Then the Duchy controls the leases of the mineral rights. But Mr. Eliot would know for sure."

"Sounds to me loike Mr. Eliot better be a stannator, or whatever them be called," said Bunt. "He's already Mayor of Liskeard as well as a Member of Parliament and a big noise in the Duchy. That would make old Dunbugger sit up and sing to 'is tune."

"That's what I wanted to talk to you about," said Morwenna. "After the meeting was over and the venturers left, Mr. Bolitho asked Dad and the captains to stay and talk to him and the viscount. He said they are going to have to raise more capital if the viscount wants to take out profits for himself right now. He suggested asking Mr. Eliot."

"Mr. Eliot is already investing in the turnpike and the quarries," said Polkinghorne. "In fact, he is holding the viscount to supporting him with it. They made a bargain."

"Mr. Bolitho talked to my dad later. He said Mr. Eliot could come in on very good terms, he'd see to that. The viscount needs money bad but he wants to hang on to the mines."

"Then maybe there is an opportunity for Port Eliot," Polkinghorne said. "Did Mr. Bolitho say whether his partners would make a loan to Mr. Eliot if necessary?"

"Wish 'e'd make a loan to me," said Bunt, "Oi could use a spot more."

"Don't interrupt, Bunt," said Polkinghorne.

"I dunno about that," Morwenna said, "you'd have to ask Mr. Bolitho. But there is one more thing. The other day when the viscount heard about Mr. Pitt giving up his office he was glad. He said that meant Mr. Eliot would lose his influence. He told Dad to press ahead with selling the tailings for the turnpike an' said if Lanhydrock played its cards right, he could take over the Liskeard project, and if Dad didn't get it done he couldn't promise that he would go on having a job, and we'd have to look for somewhere else to live."

"The viscount is a hard man," said Polkinghorne, "even to his own faithful servants." Morwenna looked him in the eye, hesitated, then spoke.

"There's more. The viscount got me alone and said he'd be prepared to discuss some arrangement with Dad if I'd be more cooperative. He's always after me for something." She covered her eyes with her hands and sobbed. "I wish I didn't need to have anything to do with him." She looked up, her eyes flashing. "If only I could make him leave us both alone."

"Gawd," said Bunt, "that bugger hasn't changed his spots since he got to be lord almighty. Oi'd loike to take 'im to the stable an' show 'im a thing or two."

"Thank you, Miss Clymo," said Polkinghorne. "It took no little courage for you to inform us and we're grateful. If I may be so bold, let me offer you my personal assistance if ever I can be of help in any difficulty."

"Me too, Morwenna," said Bunt. "You can count on me too, an' Mary."

Polkinghorne glowered. "No doubt Miss Clymo will have adequate support," he said. "Now, come along, Bunt. I don't mean to rush off, but unless you have something else to add, Miss Clymo, we need to be getting back. What you've told us is most interesting, it's important for me to report to Mr. Eliot as soon as possible. I'm sure he will have some ideas as to how best to proceed. I'll be in touch with you or your father in due course. Good day!"

"Well, Oi say thank you kindly to Morwenna," said Bunt. "Our journey was very worthwhile."

"Glad to be of service," Morwenna smiled at them both, her look resting on Polkinghorne. "But don't go just yet. Why don't you stay the night? It's a long way back to St. Germans, and it'll be dark before you get there. It could be dangerous traveling on these roads, don't know who might be about. Just make yourselves comfy here at The Globe, get a bite to eat and leave in the morning. I could keep you company. I'm sure my dad would want me to be hospitable seeing as how you'll be helping us out, getting to be partners like."

"That's not a bad idea now, is it?" said Bunt. "It is a long way to ride back, Mr. Polkinghorne."

"We'll ride as far as Liskeard and stay overnight at Eliot House, thank you Miss, that will suit us fine," Polkinghorne said firmly. He would like nothing more than spending time with Miss Clymo but not in Bunt's company. "It would be a pleasure to meet again on another occasion. Meanwhile I know Bunt would agree that we should be particular to keep any partnership, as you put it, strictly business."

Polkinghorne got up, smiled at Morwenna warmly, left a coin on the table for the maid, reached for his saddlebag, and took a step towards the rear entrance to go to the stable.

"Don't be in such a big rush, Mr. Polkinghorne," said Morwenna. "I haven't finished. There's more I can tell you, and I didn't hear it from my dad."

Polkinghorne turned back. "Go on, Miss Clymo," he said and sat down again. Morwenna blushed and looked down. "I don't quite know how to put it," she said, "but like I told you, the other day James, Lord Trenance, caught me when I was alone because he wanted to talk about things, how things were going. He's always taken an interest in my dad and me. Him and me's about the same age, we played together sometimes when we were nippers. He can be quite nice to me sometimes, although I've learned to watch out for him."

"Go on, Miss Clymo," said Polkinghorne again, leaning forward in his chair. "What else did he say?"

"Well, he told me that I could still call him James when we were alone together, even though he's a viscount now. He liked our little chats 'cause he didn't have to be stuffy around me, not like with her ladyship and their uppity friends. I said that was nice, and he sort of let slip that he wasn't quite officially a viscount yet, not all proper yet. He talked a bit more, and I put two and two together. He didn't say so as you couldn't make no mistake, but I think he still hasn't paid everybody what arranged it for him, and that's why he needs money so bad. Anyroad, partly. He loses at cards a good deal too."

Polkinghorne beamed. He added another coin to the one he had left on the table. "Thank you for everything, Miss Clymo, you've been a great help indeed," he said. "If that is all we must now take our leave. Do come along Bunt, we have a long way to ride."

Polkinghorne reflected that Morwenna Clymo was quite a resourceful young woman. Next time they met he planned to ensure it would not be in the company of the gallant Bunt. He did not notice Willy giving Morwenna a quick kiss on the cheek and a pat on her bottom as he reluctantly followed Polkinghorne towards the stable yard. Willy tried to behave in accordance with his rising station but sometimes he found old habits hard to break.

Chapter Forty-four

Education

After their rigorous and uneventful ride from Lostwithiel, Polkinghorne and Bunt slept soundly at Eliot House in Liskeard. When they got up the following morning they were treated to a nourishing breakfast to equip them for the rest of their journey back to Port Eliot. Willy made sure to have a chat in the kitchen with Nelly, his sister-in-law, and give her the good news that Mary was expecting.

"Oh Willy," Nelly said, "Oi'm so 'appy fer you both. Maybe this toime you'll be blessed with a little tacker."

"Oi do 'ope so," said Willy, "then 'e could carry on the fambly name."

"Get on, you are a card!" said Nelly. "But you'm goin' up in the world and no mistake."

Polkinghorne and Bunt had returned the borrowed horses to the Eliot House stable upon arriving the night before. After breakfast they found the Port Eliot horses well rested and fit for the last leg of their trip. They were anxious to get back to St. Germans and did not talk much on the way, each occupied with his own thoughts. Unbeknownst to the other, each was thinking of the woman closest to their hearts. They rode to their respective homes when they reached the village, agreeing to look into the estate office in the afternoon after their midday dinners and return the horses then.

Willy was relieved to be greeted warmly by Mary. "Oi'm glad to 'ave you back at last, safe an' sound. Oi was 'opin' you'd get back last night," she said. "So what 'appened? What did Morwenna 'ave to say?"

"Well, 'twas mostly business, me love," said Willy, "what 'er was tellin' us about was things 'er 'ad 'eard from 'er dad. Things about the mines, to do with Mr. Eliot an' all, really important like. Us is goin' to 'ave to 'ave another meetin' with Viscount Dunbugger, Oi expect. Get 'im sorted out proper. Oi got to go over to the office to see Mr. Polkinghorne and talk to Mr. Eliot about it after dinner. What've you got for us to eat? Oi'm starvin' after that long ride."

"Won't do you no good," said Mary, "Mr. and Mrs. Eliot is still away. Not comin' back until tomorrow."

"So 'ow do you know?" asked Willy, irritated that his wife was more aware of the Eliots' whereabouts than he was.

"Oi got a message from the office boy, sayin' Oi should go to the big 'ouse tomorrow mornin' first thing to talk to Mrs. Eliot when she be back," Mary said. "Prob'ly wants to tell me about the school an' all."

Willy distracted himself by playing with little Catherine while Mary bustled about the kitchen dishing up their meal. As soon as they had finished eating Bunt rode over to Polkinghorne's house and gave him the news of the Eliots' impending return tomorrow. Polkinghorne decided they would take it easy the rest of the day and wait until the morning to go into the estate office when they could tell Mr. Eliot of what they had learned from Morwenna.

Bunt dropped off their horses at the stables and then ambled back home. He suggested that he and Mary take the baby for a walk. "Got the afternoon off, Mary," he said. "Us might as well enjoy it." Together they bundled little Catherine in a warm coat Mrs. Eliot had given her. Mary took her in her arms and the three of them set out across the field behind their house.

"Things 'ave been really nice while us been at St. Germans and married an' all, 'aven't them, me 'andsome?" said Mary. "But 'earin' you talk about that Dunbugger reminds Oi of toimes when things wasn't as 'appy."

"That bugger'll get 'is comeuppance, Oi'll make sure of that," said Willy, giving his wife's expanding waist a comforting squeeze. "Leave it to me to take care of you; you just take care of me an' the little uns."

"Oi know the vicar tells us to forgive those who sin against us," said Mary thoughtfully, "but sometimes that's 'ard. Oi can't 'elp wantin' his 'igh an' mightiness bein' taught a lesson what 'e'll never forget, treat servant girls proper."

They walked companionably with their thoughts across to the quay, one of their favorite spots. A stiff breeze had picked up and there was chop on the surface of the river. The baby's cheeks were ruddy with the fresh air and she started to fret. "It's getting' chilly," said Mary, "us'd better take 'er on 'ome before she catches 'er death. Oi want to take 'er an' show 'er to Mrs. Eliot tomorrow, and 'er can't be snifflin' then."

The next morning dawned fine but brisk. Mary and Willy walked across the park, again carrying little Catherine well bundled up, this time to see her godmother. Mary went to the lower entrance of the big house to meet with Mrs. Eliot as arranged. She went into the kitchen to chat with the cook and waited while she was announced. Willy meanwhile went over to the quarries to check with his foreman on the progress of work, intending then to go on to the estate office.

When she was summoned by one of the footmen, Mary left little Catherine in the kitchen to be admired and fussed over by Cook and the kitchen maids. The footman showed her into the morning room, where the vicar was sitting with Mrs. Eliot drinking tea. Catherine greeted her.

"Mary, I'm glad to see you. Did you bring my goddaughter? Oh, I expect you left her with Cook. I'd love to see her after our meeting is concluded. We are bringing new villagers to St. Germans between us, aren't we?"

"Oh thank you, mum," said Mary, "she be growin' into a dear little mite. And Oi'm 'appy to 'ear that you and Mr. Eliot 'ave been blessed with a new little boy, mum. Oi'd love to see your young man if you 'ave toime. Getting' on for a month old, Oi reckon."

"Why, thank you, Mary," Catherine Eliot said. "We are delighted to add to our family. He's a dear little fellow, takes after his father. We'll have the babies brought in for inspection as soon as our business is concluded. Now do have some tea. I will pour. You know the vicar, of course? This is Mrs. Bunt, Vicar."

"Good morning, my dear," said the vicar, unctuous as ever, "I trust our Lord is smiling upon you and yours."

"Yes'm, mornin' Vicar," said Mary rather shyly.

Catherine continued. "It's about the children in the village that I wanted to talk to you, Mary, and why I asked our good vicar to join us. It's time to think ahead about starting a village school. It'll be no time before our little ones will be ready to begin their education, the way time flies."

The vicar coughed delicately. "Mrs. Eliot, I feel obliged to point out that the church has had a most satisfactory school for over a hundred years. I agree that education indeed has its place, but I see no compelling reason to rush into making any changes."

"Come now, Vicar," Catherine admonished him, "your little school is all well and good but you have boys only, you hardly encourage learning in the village at large, and you offer a limited range of subjects."

"Mrs. Eliot," said the vicar, wagging his finger, "we owe it to the established Church of England to ensure that all the children privileged enough to attend our school are from families that are true Anglicans and fit to be educated."

Catherine sat up very straight. "Vicar, my husband and I have quite made up our minds that the village needs a school for all children, and that it will come into being. It is simply a question of how soon we can make it happen and how quickly it can grow to meet all needs. I trust that you will cooperate, you have much to offer."

The vicar nodded and slouched in his chair.

"Now, Mary," Catherine went on, "I think it would be wonderful if you would agree to help with the teaching. We'll have to employ a schoolmaster in due course, naturally, but in the meantime we have to improve your own education. I know the vicar is busy, but I am sure he will support our little effort and will personally help to prepare you, won't you Vicar? The only question, Mary, is when can you start? There's no time to waste."

"Well, Oi 'ardly knows what to say, mum," Mary said, blushing. "Oi might be gettin' a lot more busy meself. Me an' Willy 'as another little pupil on the way, an' all."

"That is wonderful news!" said Catherine. "The more the merrier. We'll need a school more than ever. But we can't have a little matter like pregnancy and childbirth stop us. Just gather yourself together, my girl, and get down to it. That's what I do."

Indeed, thought Mary, and with scores of servants to help you do the gathering.

The vicar kept his counsel and concluded that he might as well acquiesce. After all, he enjoyed a comfortable living and he did not want to jeopardize it. "No doubt you'll be able to manage, strong girl like you," said the vicar, "and I'm sure some of the times that are convenient to me will suit you too. You can practice your lessons on your own while you're taking care of the children."

"My husband believes that education is the answer to making the Cornish better able to earn a living, and that will make them happier," said Catherine, looking the vicar straight in the eye. "With all the modern agricultural methods and the newfangled machines, ordinary workmen will have to know more in order to carry out their duties, even farm laborers and tinners. Port Eliot's prosperity will depend on it, especially with all of his new ideas."

"Port Eliot has always taken its charitable duties to heart," said the vicar, hoping to mollify her further. "This is no new turn of events. Why the Almshouses in the village are over two hundred years old, and for all of that time the family has given one shilling and a peck of wheat to each of the twelve poor widows living there every year on New Year's Day. All of us in St. Germans are eternally in debt to you and your admirable husband for carrying on this noble tradition. I was thinking just the other day . . . ."

"Yes indeed, Vicar," Catherine said, smiling patiently. "And that's quite enough for the time being, I'm sure you will agree. Now Mary, while we're about it, we must hammer some education into your husband's hard head, my dear. He is endowed with native wit but he needs to be able to read and write properly. He can't understand how to manage the quarries as they grow unless he can add and subtract. And he won't make a good impression on the people he does business with unless he learns to speak properly and gets rid of that atrocious accent."

"Yes, mum," said Mary, casting her eyes down and fiddling with her fingers.

"That's all very well, Mrs. Eliot," said the vicar, "but we mustn't rush our fences. We must not allow an undue sense of importance go the heads of the laboring classes. They must know their places and be kept in them or there's no knowing where such thoughts might lead."

"Don't you worry about that, Vicar," said Catherine. "Mr. Eliot can decide who suits which place, I am quite sure. We can't stand in the way of progress, and never forget that with progress comes profit, in this case profit to all."

"Perhaps we should start modestly and cautiously with a Sunday school," said the vicar. "I've heard such things are being tried in other parts of the country. The children could be taught to read and write by studying the Bible. They could absorb Christian teaching and be turned away from a life of sloth or worse, crime. Furthermore, the working classes would have the leisure to attend on Sundays, which they would not have during the week."

"Quite so, Vicar," Catherine said. "I can rely on you to think of everything."

"Mum, if you don't moind me sayin' so," said Mary hesitantly, "them down at Lanhydrock and them little ones down west in the minin' villages needs learnin' too. Perhaps Morwenna Clymo could 'elp get a school started as well, and them mine captains what Mr. Polkinghorne and my Willy met at Liskeard last Whitsun."

"Don't run off too fast in untried directions, my dear, or you'll trip over your ignorance," said the vicar, taking out a big handkerchief and mopping his brow. Mary stiffened but held her tongue. "Mrs. Eliot," he continued, "I fear that some of the compatriots of Mr. Bunt may dissent from our teachings. I gather that the Reverend Perry who visited Liskeard is unduly influenced by the sermons of Mr. Wesley. Such heresy we cannot allow in St. Germans."

"Reverend Perry has saved my Willy from the drink, Vicar," said Mary, her eyes flashing and unable to remain silent a moment longer, "and that's more than what you troubled to do!"

"Now Mary, calm yourself," said Catherine. "I quite understand your concern, Vicar. Rest assured that nothing will be done that cannot be put in place to the general satisfaction of all concerned. Now if you will excuse us, dear sir, Mrs. Bunt and I have some little ones to make a fuss of."

With that the vicar rose, bowed to Catherine, made a cursory nod in Mary's direction and stiffly walked to the door.

"E's a bit windy, ain't 'e?" whispered Mary as the door closed. "Thinks a lot of 'imself, 'e does."

"Now, Mary, don't mind him. It's more important that we keep our attention on the school. We need him to help and leave it to me to make sure that he does," said Catherine with a smile.

"Oi know you will, mum," said Mary, brushing away a tear. "But 'e's supposed to 'elp people but 'e don't take no notice of people like we. My Willy needs 'elp and it's kind of Reverend Perry to do what 'e can like a good Christian, but 'e's far away an' Vicar's right 'ere in St. Germans. Why can't 'e 'elp?"

"I suppose the vicar feels it's enough to officiate at Sunday services at the church," said Catherine. "He needs a push from time to time. But your Willy has to overcome his bad streak himself; he simply must not fall back. Reverend Perry will try to help. But you're his biggest support, he loves you, you must be strong. My husband has high hopes for him, but he will not keep him if Bunt is a drunkard. He's had his chances."

Tears welled up in Mary's eyes. "Oi do 'ope 'e pulls 'imself together. Oi love 'im so, an' 'e's been good to me. An' us 'as to think of the little ones, specially with another on the way."

"We do indeed, Mary," said Catherine. "Dry your eyes and pull yourself together. You'll both do well in the long run, I'm sure. Now, speaking of little ones I can't wait to see my goddaughter and show off my new son to you."

They both went off to fetch their babies and admire each other's cleverness in producing such gifted additions to the population of St. Germans.

Chapter Forty-five

Devious

Edward Eliot had come into the estate office just after nine o'clock, earlier than usual. He was eager to catch up with what had been going on in his absence. Polkinghorne had already come in and was equally eager to brief his employer and make a good impression of his diligence.

"Sir, I have interesting news from Lanhydrock," reported Polkinghorne, taking the opportunity for a private conversation. "It appears that the viscount is in even greater need of money than we had previously been informed. He has already quarreled with the new venturers at his mines, demanding a larger share of distributions of money at their expense. There is something else. He is secretly planning to take advantage of Mr. Pitt's loss of office. He perceives that this change will weaken your position, sir, and enable him to make matters worse for Port Eliot."

"That is preposterous!" said Eliot. "How did you come upon such information?"

"It comes through Clymo, Viscount Dunbargan's steward. I took it upon myself to discreetly ride over there a day or two ago to see the lay of the land for myself, in order to give you a reliable report."

"But how did you learn that Clymo had news that he was willing to share?" Eliot asked.

"There was a letter, sir."

"Where is the letter, let me see it," said Eliot.

At that moment the door opened and Bunt walked in. Polkinghorne was disappointed. He had hoped to minimize Bunt's role in obtaining the news from Lanhydrock and, in particular, to save for himself disclosure of the details of Trenance's embarrassment at completing arrangements for his viscountcy. Now Bunt would divulge everything and establish the importance of his role.

"Ah, Bunt," Polkinghorne said, "Mr. Eliot was asking about the letter from Lanhydrock."

"Mornin' zir, 'ow it 'appened were this. Oi got a letter from Mr. Clymo's daughter, Morwenna. She be a friend of Mary's from Lanhydrock days, and Oi know 'er too, loike, a little bit. If you don't mind me sayin' so, although per'aps Oi don't really need to remind you, you actually met Morwenna that time at Whitsuntide when Oi got into a little bit of trouble, an' 'er 'elped me out' when Oi got put in the stocks by mistake, and 'er 'ad come up to Liskeard with 'er dad, Mr. Clymo."

"Get to the point, man," said Polkinghorne. "Tell Mr. Eliot what the letter said." Eliot waved a hand at Polkinghorne as Willy Bunt started to speak, "Let him tell it his own way."

"'Er said 'er 'ad news of important things what 'er 'eard from her dad, loike I told Mr. Polkinghorne right off. So us rode over to Lostwithiel to meet 'er, so us could tell you what might affect Port Eliot."

Then Polkinghorne jumped in. "However, if we play our cards right, sir, what we learned in Lostwithiel might fall to our advantage."

"Would one of you get to the point!" said Eliot. "Tell me where the threat to Port Eliot arises and where you think the opportunities lie."

"Right you are, sir," said Polkinghorne. "According to Miss Clymo, who heard it from her father Mr. Clymo, whom she is most anxious to protect, there was a big row at the Michaelmas cost book meeting about the doings at their mines. It was in the Guildhall at Lostwithiel where the stannators meet."

"Yes, yes," Eliot said, "go on. Who else was there? What was said?"

Charles Polkinghorne fidgeted, got out his pipe, filled it, lit it and puffed out a cloud of smoke that Eliot waved away from his face. "Mr. Bolitho was there, sir. The viscount said that he should be paid first himself, because he owned the leases and what he says goes. Mr. Bolitho said that the new adventurers had put money in to expand the mines and to pay for the new-fangled steam engines, and they deserved to get paid too. When all the new investments get put to work, the viscount would be paid handsomely, he would just need to be patient and wait his turn."

"What Morwenna said too," Bunt added, "is that 'er dad said that them'll 'ave to get more adventurers to put in money to do what Dunbugger wants. So mebbe the terms could be good if Port Eliot was in a position to invest."

"That I would consider," said Eliot, "since tin and copper prices keep going up with the demand from the wars. But I would have to arrange to obtain the funds, and I hesitate to get deeper into a business arrangement with the viscount. I can't trust him."

"Anyroad," Polkinghorne said, "expanding the diggings might be held up, because the viscount hasn't got the proper permission from the Duchy of Cornwall to dig new shafts."

"He hasn't?" said Eliot. "How does he think he's going to get away with that?"

"Well, sir, he says since there's no Duke of Cornwall and won't be until the new king has a son, there's no one to stop him, and he'll do what he likes."

"We'll see about that. I'll have a word with my good friend Mr. Thomas Pitt. He might be of assistance now that he has inherited Boconnoc," said Eliot. "His late father was the Lord Warden of the Stannaries some years ago, so I imagine he picked up a lot about such matters. At least he would know whom I could consult. The elder Mr. Thomas Pitt headed the Stannary Parliament and was responsible for the regulation of mining in Cornwall and everything to do with it, including making sure the Duchy got its proper payment of coinage."

"Beggin' your pardon, zir," said Bunt, "but according to Morwenna, Miss Clymo that is, 'is lordship thinks you don't 'ave much influence no more, now that your Mr. William Pitt is out of office. Nor the 'ole Pitt fambly prob'ly."

"He does, does he?" said Eliot. "Then he must be shown that as Receiver-General of the Duchy I do have a say, and I will stop him until we can work out a fair and proper way to get everyone paid at the same time."

"An' 'e says that now that Mr. William Pitt's gone us won't keep the Liskeard turnpike, an' 'e'll just move in an' sell the tailin's from Lanhydrock, an' all, an' more besides prob'ly. Oi 'ope that don't mean Oi don't 'ave no job no more, managin' the road stone quarries. Oi got me own fambly to support."

"The man is preposterous!" declared Eliot. "Don't you worry Bunt, nor you Polkinghorne. What do you call the viscount, Bunt? Dunbugger? Not very genteel perhaps, but extremely fitting. I shall do the same from now on. I'll take care of Viscount Dunbugger and his nefarious plans; you can count on me."

"Sounds like a proper job to me, zir," said Bunt. Polkinghorne nodded.

"Then let's get to work," said Eliot. "Is there anything else? We have a lot to do. And I have no time to waste. I must soon return to London for the new session of parliament."

Polkinghorne fiddled with his pipe and kept his silence.

"Well zir," said Bunt, "there is one more thing that Morwenna, Miss Clymo Oi mean, told us that 'er wasn't quite sure of, 'cause 'er didn't 'ear from 'er dad but just 'eard 'erself like, so Oi dunno whether you'd want to know it or no."

"Of course Mr. Eliot would," said Polkinghorne retaking the initiative. "It could be very important."

"Would one of you please go on," said Eliot, slapping his hand on the table.

Bunt started to speak, but Polkinghorne interrupted him. "Apparently his lordship was indiscreet on one occasion at which Miss Clymo was present. She is not sure if she understood everything aright, but putting two and two together she drew the conclusion that the arrangements for the viscountcy might not be complete. His lordship appears to still owe money to influential parties who assisted in his latest ennoblement and who expect his appreciation to take tangible forms."

"Thank you for providing a complete account, gentlemen," said Eliot, "but such arrangements are not unusual, and I am sure any embarrassment will be only temporary. We have learned quite enough about the important business concerns to ensure advantage for Port Eliot. If you have no more, I will bid you adieu."

Eliot left the business room and returned to the house. Polkinghorne relit his pipe and studied Bunt. After a few puffs, he too left, and Bunt followed.

Later that afternoon as Edward and Catherine were dining alone together, he was pleased to observe that his ever-attentive wife had ensured that he would experience a gustatory treat. Catherine told Edward that she had instructed the cook to roast a leg of lamb from the home farm, with cloves of garlic inserted beneath the skin to infuse the succulent meat with flavor. Cook had brought up from her root cellar the young carrots and new potatoes she had saved from early summer. Catherine herself had taken a few moments to make his favorite sauce with chopped fresh mint and sweetened wine vinegar. To enhance it all she had ordered the butler to raid the cellar and decant two bottles of Edward's most cherished Burgundy.

The table was set with a fresh damask cloth and the candelabra lighted. After enjoying a creamy leek soup they were each served a cold smoked speckled trout from their own River Tiddy, with a pungent horseradish sauce. As the footman cleared away their dishes, the butler placed the leg of lamb on a platter in front of Edward and equipped him with a sharp steel carving knife and a two-pronged fork. As Edward cut deep slices across the center of the leg, red juices trickled into the grooves in the platter, and a rich aroma tantalized their palates. He placed a couple of slices on a plate, and the footman took it to Catherine at the other end of the table, served her the vegetables and spooned fresh mint sauce onto both the meat and roast potatoes.

The butler poured the wine for Edward to taste. Edward sniffed, sipped, rolled it around his tongue and held the glass up against a candle flame. "A magnificent Burgundy." he said. "One I put down a few years ago, I believe, but not among the darkest of reds. Rather a voluptuous bouquet. What is it?"

"It's the Pinot Noir from the Côte-d'Or that you laid down in 1757, sir," said the butler. "I believe it lives up to its reputation."

"Ah, an ancient vine," said Edward. "Popular with lovers. We must thank the Duc de Valois for its development, *n'est ce pas?*"

"Indubitably, sir," said the butler.

"*Mais oui, bien sur, mon cher,*" said Catherine, with an especially winning smile. As they ate, Catherine told Edward about her conversation with the vicar and Mary Bunt.

"I do believe my project to have a school in the village is poised to bear fruit. Oh that reminds me, Mrs. Bunt is expecting again, another little pupil on the way she told me. They are both delighted."

"Do pass on my good wishes to her," said Eliot. "I'll speak to Willy in the morning. The Bunts are certainly settling into village life. I'm pleased for them both. Young Bunt is turning out quite well. Giving old Polkinghorne a bit of a run for his money, loosening him up a bit. Bunt's the one who could benefit from education. What do you think?"

"I'm starting with the younger children, my dear," said Catherine, "but we must include older villagers too. You can't make your improvements for Port Eliot succeed unless you have people working for you who understand business and all of these new ideas you keep introducing. Not only the foremen and the apprentices, but also the common laborers must know how to read and write and follow written instructions. And you're quite right, Bunt needs to be educated up to managing his responsibilities. He's intelligent enough and has imagination but he lacks education."

"You are certainly shaking things up around Port Eliot," said Eliot fondly.

"You can leave it to me, my dearest," Catherine said, smiling.

"Not entirely," said Edward. "After all, I have done my bit for education at Liskeard. The town has had a school since the days of the Stuarts, although it runs out of money and has to close from time to time. I was able to help last year when my cousin St. John Eliot died. He left one fourth of the thirty-five pounds annual income from his Old South Sea Annuities for teaching poor children to read."

"I am glad that we are so much of one mind, Edward. You are a most wise and generous man."

"Well there is that, of course, my dear," he said, "but if you recall I happened at the time to be nominated by the corporation as Mayor of Liskeard. I confess that on occasion there is more than charity to my generosity. What does the vicar think of a village school?"

"Oh, he's more or less in favor," said Catherine. "He'll play his part, but he has a few misplaced ideas to get out of his head. I'll manage him."

"I'm sure you will, my dearest," Edward said. "Of that I have no doubt."

"Now tell me all about your day," said Catherine. "What was Polkinghorne bursting to tell you?"

Eliot told her what he had heard about the viscount's plotting against him, the business issues that had arisen and discussed the steps he was proposing to take.

"Oh, Edward," she said, "thankfully we are indeed seeing the viscount's true colors. I have stated my doubts about him ever since I first met him. It is clear now that we can no longer regard him as a good neighbor, let alone as a friend or a potential ally. I am relieved his stripes are shown. But there is no reason for you not to turn the tables on him. I know you value your integrity, as do I. But if you could create opportunities for Port Eliot, it is your duty to your position and your family to seize them."

"Then I will go forward with exploring the opportunity to become an adventurer with Lanhydrock on favorable terms."

"But where will you find the money?" asked Catherine. "You have been making vital improvements to the estate, and I have several more plans for the house that I would be deeply disappointed to postpone. Are you confident it would be wise?"

Edward carved more lamb, which Catherine refused. He put two more slices on his own plate. He took a tender mouthful, chewed delicately and washed it down with a sip of wine. "You are enjoying your meat, Edward," said Catherine, smiling. "I hoped you would; it is from your new sheep. I must say their mutton is especially delicious." She raised her glass and sipped. "But do tell me, where will the money for all this come from?"

"I shall seek the advice of Mr. Bolitho, of course," Edward replied, "and I may also seek a loan to facilitate the matter."

"But Mr. Bolitho and his partners are already furnishing financing to Dunbargan," objected Catherine.

"Indeed," Edward said, "but I have reason to believe that their trust in the viscount is ebbing, and they have a higher regard for me. Besides, such a connection will ensure that we are not dislodged from the Liskeard turnpike project, and there will be increasing opportunity for Bolithos to profit by backing Port Eliot."

"Tell me more about the implications of Lanhydrock's dealings with the Duchy of Cornwall," Catherine said, looking pensive.

"I have just sent a letter to young Thomas Pitt at Boconnoc asking his advice," Edward replied, "but I believe that Lanhydrock must have permission and a license from the Duchy before they can expand their mine shafts, particularly if they go out under the sea. I also believe that I have an indispensable role as Receiver-General in getting approval."

"Then I wonder, dearest," Catherine said, "whether you could be persuaded to assist, or at least guide Dunbargan in these matters in your official capacity. After all, expanding the mines would help provide employment for miners and work for the companies building the equipment and supplying the candles, explosives and tools. You have always told me how much you wish to help increase prosperity in Cornwall."

"You may be right, my own dearest," said Eliot, smiling.

"But it would only be prudent on behalf of the Duchy if you were an adviser to Lanhydrock to oversee matters directly," said Catherine. "Unless the Duchy would handsomely recompense you, I would think that your time could only be spent if you took a position as a adventurer in return for your trouble and advice."

"You mean without committing any funds?" asked Edward.

"Precisely, my love," said Catherine.

The footmen entered and removed their empty plates, the butler refilled their glasses, and a footman put dishes with syllabubs before them. At a signal from Eliot the servants then left the dining room.

"No funds from me? That would indeed solve the problem, my own special love," said Edward, smiling appreciatively. "But first I would have to be sure I could persuade the Duchy to grant the licenses and confirm that they are, indeed, a necessity."

"There will be no problem whatsoever," said Catherine. "Before anything else, the viscount would have to agree to your terms and complete all legal arrangements with Port Eliot in order for you then to agree to explore advancing his position with the Duchy. I am sure you could find additional ways to persuade Mr. Bolitho to support your argument, and for that matter Mr. Clymo too."

"Now that you mention it, my irreplaceable heart's desire," said Edward with a smile to acknowledge the humor of his excess of endearments.

"And my beloved," returned Catherine, "I am sure Mr. Polkinghorne would advise, no doubt reinforced with the good peasant business instincts of Bunt, that an additional condition would be that Dunbargan must agree that Port Eliot would have the sole contract for the agency to supply mine tailings for road stone throughout Cornwall, with Lanhydrock as one among several producers on acceptable terms to you."

"Aha, that too," exclaimed Edward. "I will dictate a letter to Dunbargan to arrange a meeting as soon as everything is in place," said Edward. "But it can wait until tomorrow. I'll do it first thing in the morning."

"I would be willing one last time," Catherine said, "to invite the Dunbargans to Port Eliot for such a meeting, on our home ground. Perhaps we could have it just before we leave for London for the new session of parliament. It would be a convenient stop for the viscount, assuming he intends to take his seat in the House of Lords. I am sure he could not fail to accept, and for my part I enjoy Elianor's company, although how she can put up with him is beyond imagining."

"There may be an additional snag for our wily neighbor. Polkinghorne says there could be a problem in completing arrangements for the viscountcy if Trenance doesn't come up with money soon. My guess is it's probably a generous token of appreciation for my Lord Bute. Only rumor, no doubt nothing more than a slight delay, probably nothing to it. Happens all the time, soon be sorted out."

"You are too much the gentleman," said Catherine. "We women would never underestimate the inherent social implications of such a situation. If this became widely known the embarrassment would completely undo a man of his vanity. Why, the king could renounce his title at a whim. My intuition is that beneath the bluster, James Trenance is none too sure of himself. Social disgrace would sully his reputation, such as it is, and hound him from the best drawing rooms. He could never stand up to Port Eliot after that."

"Then let us indeed invite the Dunbargans, or perhaps I should say Trenances, to visit. He has been known to be indiscreet when in his cups, and that is a state not difficult to bring about."

"Refill my cup, husband, and induce my own private indiscretions as we drink to a shining future for Port Eliot. I am sure that between us and the fecklessness of our rivals, we can bring that about."

"Indeed, I share your confidence, my own precious dove whose eyes are like emeralds," said Edward. "And now I think it is high time to bring this delicious and interminable dinner to a close and seek the privacy of our bedroom. Come my dear." He rose and held out his hand.

"Yes Edward, I cannot wait to conclude this most fruitful and delightful conversation and start a new one elsewhere," said Catherine smiling and taking his hand as she rose from her chair.

Chapter Forty-six

Schools

Mary could not get her conversation with Catherine Eliot out of her head. The notion of playing an important role in educating the children of St. Germans as well as her own children intrigued and excited her. She had come a long way from being a humble maid at Lanhydrock, worth no more than a plaything to satisfy the momentary lusts of a spoiled aristocrat. Mrs. Eliot was indeed good to her, and to Willy. Willy had his faults but he had shown signs of trying to improve himself. There was no doubt he had a head for the workings of Mr. Eliot's many business interests and made himself very useful. He should probably watch out not to get too useful and upset Mr. Polkinghorne who, after all, had worked for Mr. Eliot for a long time and belonged at Port Eliot.

She wondered how Willy would take to being taught reading and writing by his wife. Not well, she guessed. Mr. Eliot would just have to tell him that he must. She and Willy had their ups and downs, but he was good to her most of the time, at least when he was not misbehaving, and she was grateful for his marrying her when she was pregnant. At least Willy was trying to stay away from the drink that used to get him into awful trouble. Now, blessedly, they were going to have their own little one. Perhaps there were other grown-ups who would be willing to learn their lessons too; there were plenty who needed help.

Mary had given Willy a big hug and a kiss earlier that morning after feeding him a good breakfast and sending him off to work, and he hugged and kissed her back. He seemed happy enough. She still suffered intermittent worries about Morwenna Clymo. She felt she could probably manage her husband, and perhaps somehow she could make better friends with Morwenna herself. Then Morwenna might feel embarrassed about any more carrying on with Willy, if that was what was happening, and give him up. Anyroad, if Morwenna got really busy with a school at Lanhydrock, she would have her hands full. She would have to talk to Mrs. Eliot more as soon as she had finished feeding little Catherine and straightening up the kitchen.

Perhaps she should write a letter to Morwenna. That way she could decide herself what she wanted to offer. Mrs. Eliot would be sure to make suggestions, but at least Mary would be able to put her own ideas forward and let Morwenna know who was in charge. The more she considered it the more she thought that writing the letter was a good idea. As soon as she had tidied up she sat down at the kitchen table with a quill pen and her inkpot. For a while she stared at a blank piece of parchment. Writing a letter was surely difficult. But finally she got started.

Later that morning with her tasks completed, Mary presented herself at the big house, once again going in by the side door and leaving little Catherine with an admiring kitchen staff. She sent a message by a footman into Mrs. Eliot who soon replied that she would receive her in the morning room.

"Do sit down, Mary," said Catherine, "what do you have to talk about so soon after our conversation with the vicar?"

"Well mum, Oi've been thinkin' loike," Mary replied. "Oi really and truly want to 'elp you with startin' the school. Oi've got some learnin' meself, but of course Oi'd 'ave to improve, read and write better, and Oi'd loike to speak proper too. An' Oi'd loike to start soon, not wait until our own kids are old enough, get in practice loike."

"No doubt the vicar and I can help you as much as you want," Catherine said. "No time like the present. You mustn't drop your aitches. It's not 'elp, it's help, now try again."

Mary blushed, took a deep breath and breathed it out through her mouth as she tried again. "Help, mum," she said, and smiled.

"That's very good, Mary," Catherine said. "That wasn't so hard, was it? It's just a matter of getting out of your old bad habits and getting into good new ones. Just remember not to drop your aitches. Now, is there anything else on your mind?"

"Well, yes. If you don't moind, mum, Oi'd loike to send Morwenna Clymo a letter and tell 'er about our ideas and see if 'er is willin' to 'elp, Oi mean help Mum." Mary blushed again and grinned triumphantly.

"Good, Mary!" smiled Catherine. "Well done. And instead of saying 'er you must try and say her."

"Yes mum, her, mum," said Mary, "her, her. I think Oi've got it."

"Almost Mary, but it's not just how you pronounce the word," said Catherine, "it's using the correct word, the correct grammar. Her is a pronoun, so is she. We often use pronouns instead of nouns or proper names; they make a sentence flow more easily. Instead of repeating Morwenna's name you used a pronoun. But you must remember that when the pronoun is the subject of the verb you use she and when it's the object of the verb you use her. Do you understand?"

"Yes mum, sort of, mum," said Mary, looking puzzled. "Oi'll try to remember, but it's 'ard, Oi mean hard."

"It's just a matter of practice, Mary," said Catherine, "and I promise to help you, then you can help the village children and even Willy. Now, tell me about this letter."

"Loike Oi said, Oi think if us told Morwenna about our school 'er would, Oi mean she, would want to help. Oi've tried me best, but Oi wonder if you could look at it and correct it and see if you agree, loike?"

"Of course, Mary," Catherine readily agreed; she wanted to encourage Mary as her protégée. "As a matter of fact, Mr. Eliot has decided to invite the Dunbargans to visit Port Eliot on their way up to London next month, assuming the viscount plans to take his seat in the House of Lords at the start of the new session. Mr. Eliot and I are agreed to pursuing the idea of starting village schools with them, and their visit would be a good opportunity to discuss this project, among others. It would be beneficial if we could tell them that we already have a teacher in mind to start things off."

"Oh thank you, mum, that is good news. Oi 'ope us moight do somethin' down west for the miners while we'm about it."

"All in good time, Mary," said Catherine. She took the letter from Mary and read it, suggested some corrections and some changes and then sat Mary down at the writing table to rewrite it. "Don't dip your pen so far into the ink, Mary," she advised, "then you won't spoil the look of your letter with blots. And try and write more neatly, it'll make your letter easier to read. Here, use this blotting paper."

Mary concentrated hard to remember all the advice she was given and unconsciously the tip of her tongue stuck out through her lips. She was pleased with the result.

The finished letter was clear and much neater. It told Morwenna Clymo about Mrs. Eliot's plans for starting a village school for grown-ups as well as children and about Mary's keen interest in supporting her. It asked Morwenna to join the crusade, for crusade is what it amounted to. It mentioned the vicar's role and Mrs. Eliot's preference for working presently with the Church of England and also alluded to the possibility, if necessary, of getting support from the Reverend Perry. Perhaps he could enroll the mine captains and their wives to help, if their wives were suitable.

"Leave the vicar to me, Mary," said Mrs. Eliot. "I'll take care of any objections he might raise. And I'll write to Lady Dunbargan and see to it that she agrees with us. Her husband may be a peer but he is no gentleman. At least her ladyship seems to be developing a mind of her own."

It was only a few days until the two women heard back from their correspondents. The replies that they shared with each other starkly contrasted. Morwenna wrote:

Dear Mary, I would love to help. I'm lucky that my dad made sure I learned my lessons, so I can read and write and spell pretty well although grammar is a bit hard. I can do arithmetic, and with some help I think I could help others. My aunt thought I should stay home when I was a nipper and help out, cuz my mum was poorly, but my dad said I should go to school, and a girl from the estate came in to help. My dad sent me to the church school in Bodmin where he was taught too. It was a long walk in the winter but was worth it. Sometimes my dad arranged for me to ride with someone from Lanhydrock what had to go in for something. It would really do the village children good to go to school and the grownups too I think. The miners down west need it too. Tell me more. Perhaps I should talk to my dad about it. He'll know what to do. Maybe we should meet and make a plan. Say hullo to Willy for me, and tell him to stay away from the drink. Love, Morwenna.

The missive from Viscountess Dunbargan was less encouraging.

My dear Mrs. Eliot, What an extraordinary suggestion! I talked to my dear husband about it, and he is not only completely opposed but also indignant that you should meddle in his affairs by even bringing the subject up. He can't begin to understand why the lower classes should be improved, particularly at his expense. He said he will be damned before his son and heir mixes with illiterate louts from the village. He is down for Eton and until then will be tutored at home.

In the strictest confidence, I sometimes wish that Dunbargan were a little more open to new ideas. Times, after all, my dear Mrs. Eliot, are changing. But he is the way God made him, although I'm not entirely confident that God would wish to take credit. I will, however, as you, talk to our vicar; but I fear he may not be much more amenable, and it may be unwise to go forward in view of my husband's quite firm opposition.

We indeed plan to go up to Town for the new session. After all what is the point of going to all of the expense to get a more impressive title if one does not make full use of it? We are delighted to accept your most kind invitation and look forward to staying a day or so at Port Eliot on our way. Perhaps we could travel to London together. Faithfully yours, Elianor Dunbargan.

"It appears that you are a more successful persuader than I, Mary," said Catherine, obviously disappointed. "I thought my new friend Viscountess Dunbargan had more backbone. She's from an old Cornish family, after all."

"Oi wouldn't blame yourself, mum," said Mary. "Just seems that Morwenna was already willing, and Lady Dunbargan was a harder nut to crack. Got her husband to deal with. Us'll just 'ave to keep tryin, that's all."

"That's the spirit, my girl! After all, Rome wasn't built in a day!"

"What's Rome got to do with it, if Oi may be so bold as to ask?"

"Just a figure of speech, Mary. You'll get used to that kind of thing as your reading improves. Now let's just think where we go from here. I will consult with Mr. Eliot to see what ideas he may have to bring to bear on the viscount. Not that money should have anything to do with education or even doing some good in this world, but when one is short of it, money can be quite persuasive."

"My stars, mum," said Mary, "why would you consult with him exactly? Oi expect 'e'd do what you want if you just asked 'im, knowing you."

Catherine looked at Mary quizzically.

"Oh, Oi mean him, mum." Mary smiled.

"Excellent, Mary," Catherine said, smiling back. "I knew you would be a quick learner. Do go on."

"Well, mum, you look as if you be ready to go on a real tear. Oi wouldn't want to stop in your way if you had your 'eart set on summat, heart Oi mean, not if Oi was Mr. Eliot 'imself or even that old viscount, that Oi wouldn't."

Catherine laughed. "We must respect our husbands, Mary," she said, "and we must always let them think that whatever we suggest is really their own idea. But enough talking." She stood up and moved towards the door. Mary put on her hat and followed her. "We have much to do and little time in which to do it. You write to your Miss Clymo and tell her to make some excuse to come to Port Eliot with her father and the Dunbargans, and tell her too to be ready to meet with you and me and the vicar about getting a school started as soon as possible, now that the harvest has been brought in."

"Oi will, mum," said Mary, "Oi'll do it d'rec'ly."

"I will meet with Mr. Eliot and discuss what he must tell the Dunbargans," Catherine continued. "I will suggest that he invite not only Mr. Clymo, but also Mr. Bolitho, who carries much influence at Lanhydrock, and the Town Clerk of Liskeard as well. That should surround the viscount. And I must remember to ask my husband whether he has heard from Mr. Thomas Pitt about the powers of the Duchy of Cornwall concerning mineral rights. He must be well prepared to exert his influence and hammer out an agreement with our less than admirable neighbor once and for all."

Mary only half understood what Catherine was talking about, but she was satisfied that all these projects were in good hands. "Oh mum, will he really?" said Mary. "Mr. Eliot is a very important man an' 'e's awful busy. Will 'e bother?"

"I can promise you Mr. Eliot will ensure that we are successful," said Catherine. "I will speak to him as soon as he gets 'ome." Mary giggled, then covered her mouth with her hand and blushed.

"I mean as soon as he gets home," said Catherine, and giggled too."Oi hope Oi don't get you into no bad habits," laughed Mary, "that would never do. What would Mr. Eliot say?"

Chapter Forty-seven

Women

Typically in this rural part of Cornwall time moved at the pace of the ploughman plodding behind his team of great Shire horses. But when Catherine Eliot set her mind to something the pace accelerated, and the people responsible for making things happen around Port Eliot felt a whirlwind sweep through the place carrying them along with it. Edward Eliot himself was quickly persuaded that his wife's ideas and approaches made sense and agreed to pursue them vigorously on all fronts.

A week or two after Catherine and Mary became determined to establish a school, Viscount Dunbargan set off from Lanhydrock with the simple intent of stopping for a day or two at Port Eliot on his way up to London. Lady Elianor and a few servants accompanied him on his journey. Their party included Morwenna Clymo and her father Joseph, who had mumbled something about seeing Charles Polkinghorne on some business matter to do with the turnpike project.

Dunbargan's mind was on the forthcoming session at the House of Lords and the distracting joys of London. He had not bothered to grasp what lay beneath his steward's goings on. He couldn't wait to get to Town to seize the opportunity to recoup his gambling losses and enjoy some jolly company. At the same time he was dreading having to face the Earl of Bute to try to convince him to wait for his money. James's viscountcy was turning out to be more expensive than he had bargained for, but he deserved it and it would be worth it in the end. Upon their arrival at St. Germans, tired from their journey, he was glad of a light supper and an early bed, where his wife made it perfectly clear that she was similarly weary.

After a deep sleep and a good breakfast the next morning, the viscount was taken by surprise to find that this was more than a friendly social occasion among neighbors. He was immediately separated from his wife who was whisked off to the morning room by Catherine. What was going on?

As Elianor later reported, somewhat distraught, not only the vicar of St. Germans but also Morwenna Clymo and her former maid Mary Abbott (now Bunt), of all people, were there to greet her. They were sitting together drinking tea with their betters and looking determined. The purpose seemed to be to enlist Elianor, Viscountess Dunbargan, into the cause of education for the ordinary village people of Lanhydrock. Catherine firmly assured her that it mattered little whether the viscount opposed the notion or not.

The vicar, evidently irresistibly prompted by his formidable female companions, explained that Mrs. Eliot was not to be dissuaded from bringing education to the working classes in Cornwall and that it behooved the gentry to lead the way. Catherine added that she expected the Dunbargans to join her with enthusiasm in pursuing learning not only for the peasantry living on their country estate, but also for the miners and their families working on their mineral leases. The children would attend school on every weekday and their parents on Sundays, when they were not working.

"This is God's work, Lady Dunbargan," intoned the vicar, "which will be propitious in the saving of souls and the rescuing of the poor from lives of the sins of idleness, ignorance, and indeed crime."

"That's all very well, Vicar," said Elianor, "but would not we Cornish be well advised to await guidance from more civilized parts of the country?"

"I have learned, dear lady, that my brothers in the cloth elsewhere seem to agree on the merit of schools, though like you I sometimes wonder whether their zeal may be premature. In answer to my recent query I have just received a letter from the vicar of St. Mary Redcliffe in Bristol. He tells me that the Society for the Propagation of Christian Knowledge is widely supported in that fair city, by clergy and laity alike."

"Perhaps you are right," said Elianor. "I will have to ask our own vicar about it."

"I have no doubt that my colleague in holy orders at St. Petroc will join me and we hope your good self in this great work. You must ask him to make room in his church available. The project has the benefit of learning combined with furthering the teachings of the church."

"I shall have to ask the viscount," a somewhat flustered Elianor said.

"I should also point out, perhaps unnecessarily," continued the vicar, ignoring her comment, "that Mrs. Eliot is supported in her interest by her husband who, I may add, is becoming a personage of great influence in these parts and whose wishes should not be lightly crossed."

Catherine was delighted at the vicar's decreasing resistance to, indeed growing support for, her education project. She would like to attribute his change of heart to her own persuasiveness or even his innate wisdom, but felt it more likely to be a result of dear Edward's proprietary interest in the vicar's livelihood.

"You should all be aware," Catherine said, "that my husband has already played his part as a patron of the school in Castle Park for the pupils of Liskeard, including poor children."

"Our squire is a man of the highest virtue," responded the vicar. "One hopes that the viscount will heed his example. You know, our good Lord taught us to beat our swords into ploughshares, and doubtless He would also favor beating knowledge into the heads of poor children. It is fitting that the castle has been put to peaceful use. Indeed, I seem to recall the most fitting inscription on the wall, *Olim marti, nunc arti.*"

"St. Germans is fortunate to have a vicar of your erudition," Elianor said. "Pray what does it mean? My Latin was never bright and has become rusty."

"I construe it to mean that the place formerly used for war is now used for art," said the vicar smugly. "One can only pray that the little savages of the town will spend less time in fighting and rowdy behavior and more in pursuing their studies. The animalistic behavior that distresses us all can only improve when the lower classes are brought to our Lord. And we must not spare the rod, lest we spoil the child." He sat back with his arms crossed over his chest.

"The point too, Vicar, is that they be educated," said Catherine. "Educated; never forget that. It's not just about harsh discipline, vital though that may be. The children must be taught." She paused, composing herself. "But you strayed from your news of the Society for the Propagation of Christian Knowledge."

"Do tell us more, Vicar," Elianor said, ever so slightly warming to the ideas being put to her. "Would the Society members be willing to help in the work? That is, if it should be agreed that we pursue it?"

"It appears that they might. Indeed, such charitable work is their mission. The Society would advise us as to how to approach subscribers for financial support and how to find and train teachers. There are some schools with wealthy patrons whose teachers are actually paid, although naturally we should encourage volunteers. The Society even goes so far as to publish pamphlets imparting Christian teaching and the catechism. I myself favor sticking strictly to the teaching of Holy Writ."

"That is exactly what we need," enthused Catherine, "enlightening pamphlets. We will have our village children civilized and literate in no time."

"But my dear madam," said the vicar, "we must constantly bear in mind that the purpose of such Christian education is to condition the poor for their station as hewers of wood and drawers of water and to be content in the Lord."

"Good God, vicar," Elianor said with a snort, "you sound just like my husband. And here I was beginning to see the benefit of enlightening the rabble in order to bring them to more orderly and enlightened behavior in service of the Lord." She thought a moment and added, "Perhaps it would also serve to help those more able among them to improve their lives."

Mary and Morwenna had been keeping quiet, feeling that it was not their place to participate in the conversation among their betters unless asked. However, their deference could not mask their feelings. They exchanged glances, both of them rolling their eyeballs in disgust.

Mary, like Willy, had known Morwenna since they were children together at Lanhydrock and had always liked her and admired her free spirit. The time at Liskeard when Willy was locked in the stocks and she came upon Morwenna with her arm around him had made her jealous. However, Willy had assured her that there was nothing more than friendship between them. Now Mary welcomed Morwenna as a friend too, and enjoyed her as an ally.

Their glances turned into quiet smiles. Catherine, observant as ever, caught their expressions. The vicar caught her attention.

"As you wish, my lady," pressed the vicar. "We do seem to agree that the purpose of such schools must be to act as a shield and defense against the religious and social perils of our age. Dissent is abroad, even in our beloved Cornwall."

"Oh come now, Vicar," said Catherine, "you mustn't be so unbending. How can you possibly expect these young ladies to devote their energies as teachers to keeping members of their own class in their place? And how can you expect our husbands to support our efforts unless they can look forward to improvement in the skills of their workers? What do you girls think?"

"Oh yes, mum, thank you, mum," chorused Mary and Morwenna.

"And we must make quite sure that the children come to learn useful trades as well," continued Catherine. "We must see to it that the brighter boys go to apprenticeships, as Lady Elianor suggests. And the girls must be taught needlework and knitting, things that will make them better wives and mothers. What do you think, Lady Dunbargan? What would the viscount say to these arguments?"

Elianor shifted in her chair and tucked a wayward strand of hair back from her brow. She looked Catherine directly in the eye and said, "I suspect that if I could persuade my husband that supporting your efforts to a small degree could enable his workers to make more money for his mines, then he might not offer too strenuous an objection. I have heard the viscount say that the difficulties of making his ignorant louts operate the modern steam engines without breaking them is frustrating. Some of them can't even manage mules it seems."

"My own family has always valued education, especially for the boys," said Catherine. "My gifted young cousin, Edward Gibbon, attended Oxford at the age of fifteen, as a gentleman commoner, and enjoyed the Grand Tour. He has as a result been able to convey his scholarship to others through his writing."

"The universities are quite beyond our humble parishioners," said the vicar, raising his arms in protest. "It will be sufficiently difficult to pound a smattering of letters and numbers into their thick heads. Besides, we must not give them grandiose ideas. They must keep to their own class."

"I for one want my sons to attend the village school for part of their education," said Catherine. "We will of course employ a tutor as well to prepare them for Eton. But Mr. Eliot wishes them to take a leading part in the world, and with such rapid changes occurring in farming and engines and religion all over the country, indeed in the world, they must learn about the lives of those they will govern."

"I don't believe the viscount would go that far, Mrs. Eliot," said Elianor, fanning herself. "No doubt he would expect our son to learn what little was necessary about the lives of the peasantry and the miners from our steward and his minions. That's their duty, not ours. We employ them to keep those people at work, earning the money to keep Lanhydrock prosperous, and providing the wherewithal to support our needs. After all, a viscount has a certain position to keep up. He takes no interest in laborers or servants, and for my part I think few of them would care to add education to their skills."

"Oi don't know if Oi'd quite agree with 'im, my lady," said Mary, barely stifling her indignation. "Oi mean him."

"Nor I," said Morwenna. "I think there's also plenty of people around Lanhydrock who wouldn't quite agree with that, my lady."

Catherine cocked an eyebrow and looked quizzically at Elianor. The vicar maintained an impassive expression and folded his hands in his lap. Lady Dunbargan averted her gaze and did not pursue the conversation any further.

The vicar was shown out, leaving the ladies to themselves. "That will give the old bird something to think about for his next sermon, telling us all to be virtuous," said Catherine smiling. Mary smiled back. She patted her tummy affectionately; it was beginning to betray her condition. Morwenna leaned over, patted her friend on the arm encouragingly and looked over to the viscountess. Lady Elianor smiled too. This was a group of powerful women, of which she was looking forward to being a member.

Chapter Forty-eight

Influence

While the ladies and the vicar were having their discussion, the viscount was unwillingly engaged in a meeting in which his future and that of the Lanhydrock interests were being determined which, much to his astonishment, would include his support of a local school.

As Lady Dunbargan was being led away by Catherine Eliot, Edward Eliot linked his arm into Dunbargan's with what appeared to be the cordiality of a hospitable host and marched him over to the estate office. There in the business room several men were seated around a large table, looking serious. They rose to acknowledge his entrance. They were all familiar to Dunbargan, who was taken aback and paused at the door, disentangling his arm from Eliot's.

"Bolitho, what the hell are you doing here?" he demanded, blood starting to suffuse his face. "And Clymo, I didn't realize I would be seeing you so soon."

"You remember Mr. Edwin Ough?" said Eliot, smiling cordially at his guest. "In my position as Mayor he acts as my Town Clerk for the corporation of Liskeard. You may remember sending him away from Lanhydrock to walk to Bodmin when my wife and I visited, while your father was still alive. Polkinghorne of course is my man of business. And Bunt, as you will recall, was once your manservant. He is now a loyal and valued servant of Port Eliot. Bunt may have had his faults, but unkindness is not one of them. He is blessed to have married a most capable girl, Mary Abbott, who turned out to be pregnant at the time, in circumstances that had little to do with Bunt. You may understand why."

Eliot was now standing behind Dunbargan, blocking the door, and he waved the confused man to an empty seat at the far end of the table, taking his own at the head.

"Don't see what any of this has much to do with me," spluttered Dunbargan. "What's Bolitho doing here?"

"Given the importance of the matters that will be on our agenda, I felt Mr. Bolitho should witness our discussions and agreements. He is a man of affairs whose wisdom and integrity are respected by us both." As Dunbargan was still standing, running his hands over the back of the chair, Eliot repeated, "Please, please be seated."

Dunbargan nodded towards Clymo and sat. He had, of course, not realized that he would be taking part in this meeting and, despite the thinly veiled reference to Bunt's wretched little wife, he surmised that at least this self-righteous prig Eliot could know nothing about his troublesome affair with Morwenna Clymo, so her father would remain in ignorance.

Dunbargan's confusion gave way to indignation that in turn stifled rising embarrassment. "What is the damn meaning of this charade?" he demanded.

"Gentlemen, let me explain," said Edward Eliot, taking command. Charles Polkinghorne lit his old clay pipe. Joseph Clymo shuffled his feet and looked at the fireplace. Willy Bunt was frowning and trying to remain calm, gripping his hands beneath the table. Edwin Ough had a look of expectant satisfaction, proud to show himself to the viscount as part of such distinguished company. Thomas Bolitho sat with one eyebrow lifted, completely the observer and in command of himself.

"We have many important matters to discuss, matters that concern us all," continued Eliot, "and we must reach a conclusion before the morning is out. The subsequent arrangements will be undertaken in short order."

"I'm not putting up with this," spluttered Dunbargan, rising from his chair and glaring down at them. "I have my dignity. I am a viscount, you know. You can all go to hell. Is this some kind of damnable conspiracy? Clymo, you'll hear from me later."

"I'm here at the request of Mr. Bolitho to support your interests and those of Lanhydrock," said Joseph Clymo, "which I will do to the best of my ability. I did try to tell you, sir, before we left."

"My lord," said Bolitho, "you would be well advised to sit and listen to what Mr. Eliot has to say. The benefits to Lanhydrock should be a persuasive argument for that."

Once again, Dunbargan sat.

"I have learned from reliable sources," said Eliot firmly, "that the conspiring, as you call it, has been on your account. I take strong exception. There is much at stake for your future, and you will hear me out now."

With that, Edward Eliot outlined to Dunbargan the steps that he was planning to take and the requirements he would impose on the viscount. Eliot was well prepared. Every step took into account the considerations reported to him by his faithful aides, and he faithfully followed the suggestions that had been made to him by his wife. Every measure was reinforced by the advice of his influential friends.

"My lord," said Eliot, courteous as ever while suppressing anger, "you judged, quite erroneously, I assure you, that my influence would be severely curtailed upon the loss of office by Mr. William Pitt. I have been in regular correspondence with him and have no doubt that when the time is ripe the king will call upon his brilliant service once again. Meanwhile, he assures me in my position as Member of Parliament for St. Germans of his continued support for my projects benefiting Cornwall."

"Load of codswallop!" said Dunbargan.

"I have also heard from his nephew and my neighbor, Thomas Pitt of Boconnoc," continued Eliot smoothly. "You may observe that my influence is derived from more than one source. Mr. Thomas Pitt learned much from his late father who served as Lord Warden of the Stannaries and he has been kind enough to advise me of the powers of the Duchy of Cornwall regarding mineral leases. In my capacity as Receiver-General of the Duchy, I must now advise you that your expansion of mine workings on the foreshore and under the sea without proper license is forbidden, and I personally will ensure that you will be stopped unless and until such licensing is obtained."

"Damn you, Eliot," seethed Dunbargan, "you'll never get away with it. You can't stop me and neither can the Duchy. I have many powerful friends, and you're not even a member of the Lords. Besides, there is now no Duke of Cornwall; the king has no son."

"You are mistaken. The power of the Duchy always continues even though at times it awaits a new duke. And I have the power among Duchy officials to veto the actions of anyone who fails to receive the necessary licenses or pay the required coinage to the Duchy, including members of the House of Lords." He paused. "On the other hand, I am also in a unique position to help those who have failed to obtain licenses even after the work has commenced."

"I shall do just as I like," blustered Dunbargan.

"You would be well advised to heed Mr. Eliot," interposed Thomas Bolitho. "The Duchy's legal position is quite clear and do not doubt that it will be enforced. You have no choice but to comply. Further, not doing so would imperil the investments of your fellow adventurers in the work to date."

"They can all go to hell," Dunbargan said.

"And the miners would all be out of work," said Willy Bunt.

"They can all go to hell too," said Dunbargan.

"However, the furtherance of mining in Cornwall and the moneys due the adventurers and the miners are all considerations important to me," said Eliot. "For those reasons and especially if I were to join the adventurers myself, which I surmise is in your plans, I would be prepared to intercede with the Duchy to enable the work on your mines to continue."

"You join the adventurers?" asked Dunbargan, now preempted in his original scheme but interested. "How much are you prepared to invest?"

"In my judgment and that of my partners," said Bolitho, "it would be in the interests of the Duchy, and even more Lanhydrock, to have the benefits of Mr. Eliot's advice as a committed adventurer and to have him in regular attendance at the cost book meetings. I would advise that you urge him to participate on the basis of his undertaking that task alone."

"Pshaw!" said Dunbargan.

"What about the mine tailings?" asked Clymo.

"Perhaps I could respond to that," said Edwin Ough, who up until now had remained quiet. "As Mayor of Liskeard, Mr. Eliot serves as Chairman of the Liskeard Turnpike Commission. As such, the borough has sought his advice and appointed Port Eliot to be the sole supplier of road stone. I understand from Mr. Polkinghorne and Mr. Bunt that the supply could be supplemented by mine tailings from several sources. I have advised the corporation to simplify its dealings by insisting that Port Eliot be the sole agent for all such supplies."

"We would be happy to make the arrangements," said Charles Polkinghorne.

"I see," said Dunbargan. "You've got it all arranged behind my back, what? Well, just you wait. I have a few ideas myself."

"Your cooperation would be much appreciated," Eliot said. "I might mention that in my position as His Majesty's Commissioner for Trade and Plantations, I am advised that there will be profitable opportunities for investment in mining ventures in the American colonies. If the right conditions prevailed it might be arranged that Lanhydrock could participate in those future dealings."

"I see," Dunbargan said again, at a loss for further words.

"No doubt something could be arranged to the benefit of all parties," said Bolitho. "I have sounded out my partners and in general they have signaled their willingness to contribute financially."

"There is one more thing," said Eliot. "The education of the Cornish, children and their parents, is close to the heart of my dear wife. She is at the moment discussing her ideas with your wife and our vicar. I have every reason to believe that those discussions will proceed well. I would like to assure these good ladies that their husbands are in agreement. May I count on your full support?"

"Her ladyship wouldn't dare oppose my will," fumed Dunbargan, aroused to belligerence once again. "Well, if she does," he conceded, "at least it'll get her out of the bloody house I suppose, just as long as no children of mine are involved. I put my son down for Eton when he was born, and before he goes away he will be prepared at home. That is final. The curate can make himself useful, be his tutor, drum some intelligence into the boy."

"One step at a time," said Eliot. "My sons will join yours at Eton in due course, My Lord, but first they will learn something of the world at the church school. I advise you to consider something similar. But back to our business, eh? Now we have some papers to be signed. Mr. Bolitho?"

Bolitho laid a stack of documents on the table in front of the viscount, who glowered at him under raised eyebrows. Bolitho nodded. Eliot smiled slightly.

The others were impassive. Realizing that he had little choice and eager to reach London where he would now need more than ever to be smiled upon by Lady Luck at the gaming tables and by other ladies too when suitable arrangements could be made, Dunbargan picked up the quill pen, dipped it in the pot of ink, and signed each agreement in turn. Eliot signed too, and Bolitho. Clymo and Polkinghorne witnessed their signatures.

Eliot walked around to the far end of the table and put out his hand. The viscount had little choice but to accept the firm grasp proffered to him and shook the hand of the Member of Parliament for St. Germans, the Receiver-General of the Duchy of Cornwall, the Mayor of Liskeard, the Chairman of the Turnpike Commission and, not least, the Commissioner for Trade and Plantations. Reluctantly, he then shook the second hand offered him, that of his alleged supporter Thomas Bolitho. He ignored the others, giving Bunt an especially wide berth.

Edward Eliot beamed around the table at his firm allies. How did he feel about the day's good work? Well, it would be a long time before his neighbors and adversaries doubted the extent and depth of his influence or his determination. He had restored the influence of Port Eliot, and wealth would surely follow. Those generations of Eliots in their graves both here in St. Germans and that worthy Sir John who had met his fate in the Tower of London would be proud of what he had accomplished for his family and his descendants. Not only that, but his dearest family member, his beloved wife Catherine, would be delighted to learn that the projects closest to her heart would proceed without the opposition and perhaps even with the reluctant support of their noble neighbor, whom she no longer trusted but whom she had now managed almost as efficiently as she did her own loving husband.

"We are done, then," exclaimed Eliot, rising. "Let us celebrate with a special libation." He signaled to his clerk who brought a decanter of his finest French brandy from a nearby cabinet and dispensed generous measures to the assembled gentlemen.

Chapter Forty-nine

Management

The May Day cost book meeting held at Wheal Hykka in the spring of 1762 was the first attended by Edward Eliot after asserting his power in Cornwall. He had felt it important enough to leave his duties in London and travel down to Pendeen in the far western end of the Cornish peninsula. He was enjoying his work in the capital at the Commission of Trade and Plantations, but his parliamentary duties had been less satisfying since his friend William Pitt had left office. There was an atmosphere of instability in the government as His Majesty's new ministers spent as much energy pursuing personal rivalries and rearranging their posts as in settling national affairs.

The Duke of Newcastle was frustrated by his waning influence since the loss of Pitt's leadership in the Commons, and the king paid him less heed since the ascendancy of the insidious Earl of Bute. Even his grace's expert advice on financing the war was challenged. He had reached the point of resigning. Eliot was glad of an excuse, indeed a reason, to leave London and seek recreation and success in his beloved Cornwall.

The Eliots removed themselves and their entourage to Port Eliot and took up residence at their country seat. It was the turn of his agricultural and business affairs to command Edward's attention. With the ever reliable Polkinghorne he reviewed plans for the home farm and progress among the tenants. Rents from the agricultural activities of the estate were the foundation of his income. But he did not stay for long; he was eager to get down west to the mines. Profiting from his success in acquiring interests in the Lanhydrock mines was the next step in Eliot's plan to rebuild the family fortune.

Edward, at Catherine's insistence, spent the evening with her before he set off. There were matters she wanted to discuss with him before he became embroiled in the meetings with Dunbargan and the other mine adventurers. They were in their sitting room after dinner, and she poured him a goblet of tawny port.

"Edward, you know how much I love you, but I also want to impress on you how much I admire you and all you have accomplished for our family."

"I appreciate your words more than I can say, my dear," said Eliot. "What prompts them?"

"To start with, you are well regarded in the House. You hold an important position in His Majesty's administration, as you do also in the Duchy of Cornwall. On top of that you have been building up the rent rolls at Port Eliot, not by racking your tenants as some of our neighbors do, but by working with them to improve their methods of husbandry."

"I mustn't take all the credit you know," replied Edward, becoming a bit apprehensive at the flattery he knew from experience preceded another of Catherine's requests. "I enjoy excellent assistance. My London staff at Trade and Plantations is very experienced, and at home Polkinghorne is a devoted and capable fellow, and even young Bunt is making himself more and more useful."

"He should be settling down, behaving in a mature way, fulfilling his promise," said Catherine, "now that he's a father of two. And he'll want his son to look up to him."

"Calling him Charles, I hear," said Edward, "and even asking Polkinghorne to stand godfather for the boy. He's already godfather to their little Catherine. Might be overdoing things a bit, but on the whole it's rather diplomatic, that; perhaps it'll settle things down between them. Polkinghorne sometimes seems to resent the attention we pay to Bunt and his increasing responsibility, and I perceive that Bunt gets fed up with the overbearing way in which Polkinghorne so often treats him."

"Mary giving birth on Easter Sunday was quite a special occasion for the village," said Catherine. "Even the vicar allowed himself to express a mite of joy. I must say it gives me pleasure to preside over the lives of your tenants with you, Edward, and our servants. You are a good and kind squire and I gain much satisfaction from being Lady Bountiful."

"Quite, my dear," said Edward.

"Polkinghorne needs to take himself less seriously," said Catherine. "He's too settled in his bachelor ways. Time he got married, found a wife, added to the village's population himself."

"He's a very sound fellow," said Edward, "I appreciate that he takes his duties seriously. You must be careful not to take too much interest in the lives of the peasantry. You could care too much, and they could resent it as meddling. Better they keep their complaints beyond the doings of the lady of the manor."

There were a few moments of silence between them. Edward sipped his port. Catherine had been airing rather a lot of opinions. He sensed there was more advice coming on. He truly did appreciate his wife's counsel, but she had provided rather a lot of it of late, whether requested it or not. She had inherited exceptional intelligence and was energetic and curious enough to keep herself well informed of affairs affecting not only Port Eliot but also the country as a whole. He found her insights helpful and generally welcomed them, but he wished from time to time that she showed more self-effacement in respecting his role as head of the family. He was a man after all. But if a little patience was the price of peace between them, so be it.

After a moment Catherine looked up and said, a little petulantly, "I trust you find my advice and support of some value."

"I was saving that up until last, my dearest. I have indeed grown to look to you for advice and encouragement, more and more."

"Then perhaps I can speak frankly, Edward," she continued. "I am concerned about this mining venture."

So here it was. Edward sighed. "Oh, what troubles you? There are tremendous opportunities to make a great deal of money."

"You're involved with Dunbargan. He is not a sound or trustworthy man of business. I admit that you are managing him very well with the Liskeard Turnpike project where you are on your home ground. You have certainly asserted your influence of late and you see clearly that he is not only a rival but also a rogue. And I want you to think carefully about how to outmaneuver him; to sum up the strengths and weakness on both sides."

"At heart he is a playboy," said Eliot, standing up. "He is idle. He has more bluster than wisdom. His attention is limited: money, gambling, hunting, women." He took another deep sip of his port and refilled his glass from the decanter on the sofa table. "I on the other hand do pay attention. I work hard at what I judge is important. I did not inherit the kind of wealth that fell to Dunbargan, and I cannot afford his risks. I must take care to rebuild Eliot wealth, step by step." Edward resumed his seat.

"Frankly, my dear, you do not possess the temperament to take risks," said Catherine. She looked away, hoping she had not gone so far as to lose the ground she might have gained in influencing her husband. "You have other quite marvelous qualities. You take pride in attending painstakingly to detail. Far from despising your underlings because of their class, you respect them because of their ability and industry. They are loyal to you because they respect you, not because they fear you. Herein lies your opportunity, Edward."

"I don't quite understand, my dear." Now he was thoroughly puzzled.

"When you go to that meeting show a deep interest. Ask questions until you understand everything about making mining pay, how the work can be made more efficient. Demand explanations, facts and figures."

"Ah, I see. Then the captains, the pursers, the head clerks, the stewards, even Bolitho, will know that I am to be reckoned with. They will be obliged to manage their charges well because they will be accountable to me. Is that where you are leading? I believe I have already made it clear that I will not accept slackness or carelessness to gain favor."

"Yes, and more, Edward," Catherine pressed. "They will grow loyal to you as they see that you make the effort to understand their issues and show them respect, provided they perform their responsibilities conscientiously and well. I know, of course, that you will be courteous towards them, but also firm. They will follow you, instead of Dunbargan, because you are a good leader."

"I believe you may be right, my dear. You know, as I reflect upon it, this in part is what makes William Pitt such a great statesman. Behind the powerful oratory and the commanding presence lies a mind that studies the details to ensure that the facts support his brilliant insights. He works hard at leadership."

"Oh, exactly, Edward. I agree that Mr. Pitt is a master of all this. But also make sure that your underlings, the Polkinghornes and Bunts of your world, understand as well as you do. Then they will support your endeavors wisely and well, confident that they are doing their best to meet your desires and knowing that the results benefit them as well. You will be surrounded by good and loyal servants."

With that, Catherine held out her glass for a refill and abruptly changed the subject to the antics of their boys when she had walked with them that day.

Over the next two days Eliot was thoughtful as he rode down to Wheal Hykka with Polkinghorne and Bunt in attendance, to protect his person on the journey as well as his interests at the meeting. He would conduct himself in ways that would enhance the dominance and wealth of Port Eliot. He and Bolitho had both advised Viscount Dunbargan to attend. His lordship was secretly loathe to forsake the card tables and gambling clubs, less averse however to abandoning the debates of the House of Lords. As Eliot observed, the viscount preferred not to divert his attention from his pleasures to his business, and rather to simply trust the reliable and conscientious Joseph Clymo to keep an eye on the details.

The letter Dunbargan received from Thomas Bolitho stating his intention to attend contained an unwelcome message. In the old baron's days it would have gone without saying that the Bolitho firm would exclusively represent the Trenance family and Lanhydrock, but no longer. It seems now that Bolitho felt that his partners' profits depended more on acting impartially to protect the interests of all of the adventurers. It was due to that fellow Eliot's interfering ways no doubt. Not only dull but meddlesome. All work and no play. Never saw him at the gaming tables. Hardly ever had too much to drink with those good fellows at the club. However, he could hardly stop Bolitho from being there and having his say; had too much money tied up in the Lanhydrock affairs. He would have to get Clymo to speak up.

To Addis Penwarden's relief, Joseph Clymo had asked Mr. Bolitho to chair the Wheal Hykka cost book meeting. Addis felt that he had enough experience as mine captain by now to handle the responsibility, but he was nervous about dealing with the viscount. He'd been around enough to learn of his lordship's reputation for arrogance and anger, even cruelty. But it was more than that. The more he thought back to that encounter over the rabbiting with the youthful Honorable James Trenance, the more he was discomfited by the fact that the boy and the viscount were one and the same. He had not treated the Honorable with deference, and he had seen him at his weakest as a coward and a crybaby. The viscount would not like to be reminded of that.

Joseph Clymo's advice saved the day. "We'll be taking important decisions that will affect the whole future of Wheal Hykka, Cap'n Penwarden," he said. "And Mr. Eliot will be attending for the first time in his new position. We have to sound him out. I must warn you in confidence that the viscount can be difficult. You should avoid being seen taking sides between them. I have asked Mr. Bolitho to take the chair. He is diplomatic but firm, respected and widely experienced. We can count on him to guide the meeting towards wise decisions. His firm's money is indispensable to our employers and, what's more, his power does not depend on their favor."

"You're right, Mr. Clymo," agreed Penwarden. "Oi appreciate your advice."

Also John Williams was coming over from Poldice. There would be technical details as well as general business matters to discuss. Captain Williams had a quiet authority about him. He only spoke when he had something worthwhile to say. People listened to him. He knew mines and mining. And these days he had a small but influential ownership interest in the Lanhydrock mines. On the day following this meeting he would have his own cost book meeting with many of the same participants back at the Poldice mine. Like his protégé Penwarden, he was dressed formally in top hat and black morning coat and trousers, as befitted his position.

And then there was the man whose presence would make this meeting different from any that had come before. He was John Smeaton, one of those great geniuses who would change the face of mining in Cornwall. He had arrived last evening after riding down from Plymouth. He had stayed upstairs in one of the guest rooms above the count house, where he and Addis Penwarden had met for the first time. Addis had spent the night too so he could devote more time to picking his guest's brains. Addis knew that Lizzie didn't much like being left home alone, but she would just have to accept it. His job came first. He did think of his family anyroad and had brought young Jemmy to Wheal Hykka with him. Perhaps one day Jemmy would follow in his father's footsteps. He would gain more useful knowledge observing his father at work and meeting clever inventors than spending all his time at some school.

Jemmy had been thrilled to meet Mr. Smeaton. There were so many questions he wanted to ask that he hoped he too would get a chance to talk to him in the next few days. He had asked his father if he could listen to the goings on at the meeting. Addis told him he could sit quietly on a stool by the fireplace and bring out refreshments to the adventurers when they asked.

Once everyone had arrived at the count house from varying directions, Thomas Bolitho called the meeting to order. "Gentlemen, silence please, and take your seats at the board table. We have a long agenda to get through."

"What I want to know," said Dunbargan, "is how much money I will get out of this and how soon. That's what I bloody want to know. Took the trouble to come all the way down here when my presence in London on important matters is sorely needed."

Eliot just managed to stifle a snort.

"All in good time, My Lord," said Bolitho firmly rapping his gavel on the table. "The first order of business is to introduce our distinguished guest who is here to advise us on potential improvements that will increase the production of your mine."

"Profits too, I trust," grumbled the viscount under his breath.

"Indubitably, my lord," said Bolitho. "Now, if I may proceed. I have the honor to introduce the great mechanical engineer and eminent physicist, Mr. John Smeaton. He is a Yorkshireman, but we mustn't hold that against him." A polite laugh went around the Cornishmen seated at the table. "He is a Fellow of the Royal Society, which recommended him to the task that he completed here in Cornwall in 'fifty-nine, that of designing and building the new lighthouse on the Eddystone Reef, nine miles out in the English Channel off Rame Head."

"Indeed," said the viscount, "capital fellow. My father had an interest in ships plying the channel. One was saved from shipwreck on Eddystone during the big storm a couple of years ago. Valuable cargo from France."

"Despite the Royal Navy's blockade of the French ports?" asked Eliot, smiling slightly. "Pray what was the nature of that cargo?"

"Gentlemen, gentlemen, let us leave that topic to a more suitable occasion," said Bolitho. Dunbargan glared at Eliot.

"The former lighthouse Rudyard built saved many ships, many lives," said Smeaton, "and it lasted nigh on fifty years. But his mistake was making the outer shell of wood; it burned. I perceived that the structure that best stood up to stormy winds was the grand old English oak tree, so that's what I modeled my tower after, but constructed it of Cornish granite. Then I designed a method of dovetailing huge blocks of granite together for structural strength and durability. We shaped them on shore and ferried them out to the reef. I designed a hoist and tackle for erecting them."

"But how did you fasten the joints?" asked John Williams, fascinated. "You had the tidal waters of the Channel to contend with."

"I had to invent a new kind of cement," said Smeaton, warming to his subject. "I conducted hundreds of experiments, and eventually I discovered the components that would give to lime the property of hydraulicity, the ability to set hard and resist decomposition under water."

"Gentlemen, gentlemen," said Bolitho, rapping his gavel once again. "With apologies to Mr. Smeaton, while this is an interesting discussion we have much ground to cover. We have brought Mr. Smeaton here on an errand affecting the Lanhydrock mines. We will get to Mr. Smeaton's ideas in due course. He will join us for dinner later, and you can talk of other matters then. For now, we must provide the incomings and outgoings report to the adventurers. Mr. Penwarden?"

"At last, about bloody time," said Dunbargan.

"I'm pleased to report, gentlemen," said Addis Penwarden, avoiding the viscount's eye, "that the chief clerk has figured that the mine workings 'ave been satisfactory for the first quarter of 1762. A record quantity of tin stuff has been brought topside, and copper ore too." There were murmurs of approval around the table. Addis paused and nodded acknowledgement. They all looked pleased except the viscount who scowled. The captain continued. "Thanks to putting in a new buddle, we've separated more 'eavy sand from waste and sent more sacks of good ore to the smelter. Prices are strong and the market is growing. Us is ready to drive more shafts and mine more ore."

"Tell me, Captain Penwarden, what is a buddle?" asked Eliot. "What prices are we getting, and what are your costs exactly?"

"Some damn heathen contraption, Eliot," said Dunbargan. "No concern of yours or mine; let them worry about it. Let's get to the profits."

The mine captain turned to look at him, and the viscount stared Penwarden straight in the eye. Yes, by damn, it was the young poacher who had thrown him to the ground, seen him cry, knew the secrets of his weakness. So now he had been jumped up in the world? Penwarden had better understand where his orders came from, his livelihood. He himself was a man now, a viscount no less, and he would show the captain who was in charge, make no mistake.

Penwarden cleared his throat and continued. "After the boys and the bal maidens have crushed the ore with their hammers and picked it, us shovels it into the buddle to sort the heavy tin from the tailings. That way we don't pay to send waste to the smelters. Last quarter, Mr. Eliot sir, stamping and dressing cost three shillings and six pence per hundred sacks of tin stuff."

"You don't have to overdo it, Penwarden," said Bolitho. "As a smelter I don't mind charging you a little extra." There were appreciative chuckles around the table except for the viscount, who scowled again.

"I could design and build a mechanical stamp that would do it cheaper and faster," Smeaton said.

"Sounds expensive," said Dunbargan, "money better paid out to the adventurers." He would show that upstart new captain to pay attention to his concerns, not chase off after Eliot's ramblings, or that Smeaton fellow, thinks a lot of himself.

"We must take a long view, my lord," said Eliot; "we must be patient and look to tomorrow. I'm sure Mr. Bolitho would appreciate that."

"That's all very well for you to say, Eliot. I've got expenses to meet today," said Dunbargan.

"Indeed, my lord," said Eliot. "Captain, how much tin stuff is in a sack?" He had pulled an inkpot and pen towards him and was now making notes.

"Around Wheal Hykka, zir, 'tis eighteen gallons. That's our standard. One mule can carry two sacks. Some mines further away from the smelters send only eight gallons per sack, easier on the mules over distance. Course, smelters pay by the ton, depending what the assayer says the metal content is. They pay on twenty hundredweight to the ton. Mostly there's a hundred and twelve pounds to the hundredweight."

"Twenty hundredweight to the ton is just for tin, Mr. Eliot," said John Williams. "For copper we have to send twenty-one hundredweight. The price is set at the public Copper Ticketing, based on dry weight. The mining agent has to sample the ore a fortnight before. The smelters write their offer on a ticket and pass it to the chairman of the meeting, who by custom is the purser of the mine sending the biggest lot. Of course, the smelters take off the returning charges before paying."

"What are they for? How much? And how do you calculate the dry weight, Captain Penwarden?" asked Eliot. There was a brief silence. Addis gave a little cough and looked across at John Williams pleadingly. Jemmy felt sorry for his father, whom he had never before seen at a loss. Joseph Clymo jumped in to save embarrassment for the man who had become something of a protégé.

"I believe the returning charges recently amounted to two pounds and fifteen shillings per ton, right, Mr. Williams?"

"Right you are, sir, and that covers extracting the metal, carriage, agencies, interest on capital, and profit to the smelter."

"Bloody outrageous!" said Dunbargan. "We would be better off in the smelting business."

"One thing at a time, my lord," said Bolitho. "My partners would not be pleased if you went into business in competition with them."

"God in heaven!" interrupted Dunbargan. He wasn't going to put up with any more of this claptrap. "When are you going to get to the point? I did not come all this way to listen to endless blathering about sacks and mechanicals and sorcery, and how peasants pass their days. I'll leave you to it. Let me know when you get to the money. I'm going out to see what the bal maidens are up to. Got to study methods, you know," he added giving Eliot a smirk.

"My lord," said Eliot, "it is important that we understand what is going on. I for one have a lot at stake. Gentlemen, please continue."

"Gadzooks!" thundered Dunbargan, grabbed his hat and coat and stormed out of the room. "Conversation's enough to make a dog laugh," he muttered as he slammed the door.

Chapter Fifty

Inventor

" Gentlemen, please continue," pursued Eliot, "as adventurers we must pay attention to details. I for one have a lot at stake. We were discussing return charges. How do you arrive at the correct weights and measures?" He dipped his quill into the ink and prepared to resume making notes.

John Williams gathered up the thread. "For one thing, the smelter won't pay for wet tin stuff. So we accurately weigh out a sample of one pound of ore, then dry it over a fire and weigh it again. This gives us the neat weight, the percentage of reduction. Then we weigh the whole parcel wet in pounds and calculate the neat weight of the total by taking the percentage reduction."

"What would be the weight of the whole parcel of tin stuff that you send off?" asked Eliot.

"It varies. We'll give you a recent example. Look in your Assay Book, Penwarden, that'll tell you," said Williams.

"The last sample came from several kibbles, sir," Addis said, reaching into his desk, pulling out the leatherbound ledger and thumbing through the pages covered with his assistant clerk's neat copperplate penmanship. He was not very quick at reading words yet but he could readily discern figures. "'Yes, 'ere 'tis. This last lot was one ton, five 'undredweight, three quarters, seven pounds and eleven ounces."

"I see," said Eliot, raising his eyebrows.

John Williams warmed to his subject. "The rule of thumb is that every pennyweight of black tin produced from a sample of one gill of ore, wine measure, will give a hundred pounds avoirdupois in one hundred sacks. Of course, that would be eighteen-gallon sacks, beer measure. Did I say avoirdupois? That's tin. Copper produce is weighed in troy."

"I see," said Eliot again, scratching his chin. "At least I think I do. Wine measure, beer measure?"

"Oh yes, sir," said Williams. "There's thirty-two gills in a gallon, but a wine gill holds twenty-two percent more than a beer gill. Course, if you were asking about noggins, I'd say there are sixteen in a pint." Eliot put down his quill and stared at Williams.

Willy Bunt's jaw dropped. He was about to ask a question when Polkinghorne caught his eye and put a finger to his lips. Bunt kept his counsel but wondered whether someone clever enough could devise a simpler system. Bunt realized he must be educated, learn reading, arithmetic; he needed education to earn more responsibility in his job, get better wages. But how would he ever understand all the different standards and customs for different materials, even different parishes? Thomas Bolitho interrupted his musings.

"Now that you raise the question, Eliot, I must say that my own curiosity about some of the pertinent details is aroused. How exactly do the assayers know the value of the ingot when it comes back from the smelter?"

"Oh, nothing to it, Mr. Bolitho," said John Williams. "It just depends on the purity of the tin. The assayer needs experience, of course. He puts the ingot on a bending machine. As the tin flexes it makes an eerie sound from which he judges its value. They call it the cry of tin."

"Amazing," Eliot said, looking back at the notes he had been furiously penning, hoping that in time he would make sense of them. Penwarden looked relieved that he did not have to give the answer to that question. "Speaking of ingots," Eliot continued, "I trust all of the Lanhydrock mines are properly clipping the Duchy's coinage from each and every one?"

Joseph Clymo spoke in a loud voice. "Indeed, sir, I can personally assure you of that. I have taken the responsibility of informing all of the mine captains of their duty, to be ignored at their peril."

"The Duchy is anxious to receive its dues in return for granting licenses to mines," said Eliot. "I personally am gratified that Wheal Hykka's record-keeping seems to be in order."

"I may say you will find the same at Poldice," said John Williams.

"It's about time all this random way of taking measure was put on a scientific basis," said John Smeaton. "Weights and measures, testing methods, assay values. His Majesty's government should lay down national standards, eliminate this local variation and custom. Make it more efficient for everyone to do business."

Willy Bunt smiled quietly. Now that Smeaton was a clever gentleman. He had hit the nail on the head. Must be some kind of mind reader.

"No doubt Lord Dunbargan would want to keep the government out of it," said Bolitho. "Give them an inch and they'll be employing more revenuers to bother us. Ruin the smuggling trade," he added with a smile. "I must say I agree that Cornishmen can manage perfectly well without His Majesty interfering in private matters. Now, let us proceed without further delay to Mr. Smeaton's presentation. How can you help our captains mine and process more ore at the lowest cost?"

John Smeaton rose to his feet, clasped the lapels of his frock coat and rocked on the balls of his feet as he spoke. "Gentlemen, I have been studying the challenges of improving the workings of mines for some time, and I am an authority on the efficient design and use of mechanisms for generating power and replacing the horse. I have used mechanical power for pumping out water, tramming ore along the tunnels and raising it to the surface, and also stamping it to recover the precious metal. No doubt one day we will be able to carry the miners down the shafts and back up to the dry by mechanical means."

"What do you reckon will work best for Wheal Hykka?" asked Addis Penwarden. "Us fancies the Newcomen steam engine, but it's 'ungry for coal."

"Mr. Newcomen showed us the way, but I am greatly improving his design," said Smeaton. "What are the proprietors of his invention proposing?"

"Them'll license us to erect an engine at our own cost, we trust with your 'elp of course. For a rent of eight pounds a year for eight years, us can build an engine with a steam cylinder no longer than nine feet and a diameter of no more than twenty-eight inches. They can have the most difficult parts built and supplied to us: the cylinder, the regulator, the valves."

"What would their cylinder be made of?" asked Smeaton.

"Brass, Oi reckon," Penwarden said.

"Too expensive," Smeaton said. "Cast iron is cheaper, but it's been too hard to cut or bore, too slow to heat up or cool down. I've worked out how to make the walls thinner yet strong enough. And I've experimented with attaching a broad leather belt as a seal. Less steam leakage and altogether more efficient."

"The proprietors tell us their engine will do the work of five horses and be fed with eighty mule loads of coal a day," said Penwarden. "Reckon you can do much better than that?"

"I'll stake my reputation on it," said Smeaton, beaming.

"Good man," said Captain Williams. "How will you do that? Now we're getting somewhere. Is that a promise, for Poldice mine too?"

"I am confident that my experiments will double the efficiency of the Newcomen engine," said Smeaton, looking around the table at each of them in turn. "I am convinced that you can only efficiently manage that which you can measure. So I have developed a standard for measuring the performance of the steam engine."

"Interesting," said Captain Williams, "what is it? What exactly do you measure?"

"I have called it 'duty', and I define it as follows," said Smeaton. "It is the number of pounds of water which can be raised one foot by burning one bushel of coal." He smiled, pleased with himself.

"That seems to cover all important aspects," said Williams.

"As a farmer I am curious," said Eliot. "Does a bushel of coal weigh the same as bushel of corn?"

"Ninety-four pounds, sir," said Smeaton. Eliot nodded.

"You say you can double the Newcomen's efficiency?" challenged Penwarden.

"Maybe three or four times eventually," said Smeaton. "My experiments demonstrate that the chief impediments to performance are the poorly designed boiler, ill fitting pistons, and faulty valve gear."

"Three or four times, that's impressive," said Bolitho, "that will save on the cost of coal."

"Ah, but I will not rely on steam power alone," Smeaton said, and paused to take in the effect of his words on his attentive audience.

"You see," he continued, "I have been working with water power for some years, with excellent results. My clients in the Yorkshire coal mines have similar challenges to yours. But the Yorkshire fells are higher than the Cornish hills, so the burns develop more power than your streams. When I was brought in they were using wheels of only twelve to fifteen feet diameter, but I saw the possibility of linking them in series. At one mine there are as many as seven wheels, each one above another, so the total power generated was greatly multiplied. The size of the wheels was only limited by their construction. Fortunately, I happened to be able to design a superior axle out of cast iron. Now I can with confidence propose to you a more powerful wheel, with a diameter of thirty feet."

"Thirty feet!" exclaimed Addis Penwarden. "That be a powerful 'un indeed! Trouble be, Mr. Smeaton, it rains in Cornwall a lot, but 'bain't heavy. And in summer maybe 'er won't rain for days on end. What do us do then? Build bigger ponds to store water, more leats to channel the flow? That will cost a lot. Or go back to using whims with mules or 'orses?"

"I've already thought of all that, captain," said Smeaton, smiling. "I can build a way of linking an improved Newcomen steam engine to a big water wheel. That way, when there is plenty of water flow you will have plenty of cheap power. When there is too little water, you switch to steam power. Costs more, but it's more reliable and fills in the gaps in water supply. No interruptions to production."

Young Jemmy was doing as he was told, sitting quietly in the corner. But he was listening closely to every word. Mr. Smeaton knew so much about so many things. He wished he could be like the great man. Perhaps he would be after he had been working at the mine a few years, listening to what his father said and watching what he did. He should learn from Captain Williams as well.

"So that way we have the best of both worlds," said John Williams. "I like that idea, the power of steam as well as water. Production won't have to wait on weather."

"Steam engines don't get tired like mules," said Penwarden, "but them can be dangerous. Oi 'eard a miner got scalded bad over Botallack way. Them's afraid 'e might die."

"I can prevent some accidents," said Smeaton.

"At considerable expense, no doubt. We have to watch our pennies, Mr. Smeaton," said Joseph Clymo, "then the sovereigns will look after themselves."

"Quite," said Bolitho. "All very interesting, Mr. Smeaton. But you are going to have to advise us how much all this is going to cost. And now, gentlemen," he paused and looked around the board table, "it's time we asked Viscount Dunbargan to rejoin us. Captain Penwarden, would you send your boy out to fetch his lordship? Make himself useful."

During the break, Eliot wrote down a few more details. Presently, the viscount strode back into the room, slamming the door behind him. "Well, have you got through your nonsense and down to brass tacks? How much do I get?"

"My lord," said Bolitho, "we were just getting to that and thought you'd want to be here." Dunbargan sat down, and Bolitho turned to Smeaton and said, "We all have an interest in this quarter's returns. You were just explaining how you can help us make more profit in the future by investing wisely now. How much will your machinery cost, sir?"

"I can only venture a guess at this stage," Smeaton said, "until I study the lay of the land under question more closely. But the most recent steam engine I installed cost in the realm of two thousand pounds, with all its appurtenances. Adding safety devices would add to the cost."

"My god, man," expostulated the viscount, "that amount would keep me in comfort for several weeks. Pay off some damn creditors too."

"Indeed, Mr. Smeaton," said Eliot, "you certainly don't come cheap. Why, one can buy a seat in parliament for that kind of money." Dunbargan shifted in his seat and narrowed his eyes at Eliot.

"If I may be so bold, gentlemen," said Joseph Clymo, "the mines can repay such a cost many times over out of the bigger quantities of ore we can get out of the new deeper shafts."

"And there can be less danger to the miners," said Addis Penwarden.

"Work out the figures with the mine captains, Mr. Smeaton, and give me a detailed plan in writing," said Bolitho. "No doubt the adventurers would support my partners advancing an additional loan if they can be sure the investment will pay off."

"That is a sound approach, Mr. Bolitho," said Eliot. "I would be inclined to support it. I just need to understand the costs, the level of risk compared with the size of reward we might reasonably expect."

"All very well for you, Eliot," said the viscount. "You don't have to meet immediate needs. I have a position to keep up. But I must say, if Mr. Smeaton can guarantee to make us more profit in the near future, I suppose I would go along with you. But don't waste any of my hard-earned funds on fancy appurtenances to make sissies out of the miners. Mining's a dangerous game, but it pays well. That's what my father always said. He knew what he was talking about. You have to take risks to make money."

Willy Bunt had been listening intently to the discussion all along. He found it fascinating. He wished he could be as wise and inventive as John Smeaton. Perhaps he could some day; just needed the education. But, as usual, the viscount's arrogance had got under his skin. "Seems them what takes the biggest risks don't make the biggest money, that's what it seems to us. Sittin' back in some posh 'ouse countin' sovereigns ain't dangerous."

"Hold your tongue, Bunt," said Polkinghorne, "sit quiet and pay attention to your betters."

"You need a good whipping, young fellow, teach you manners," said the viscount. He turned back to Bolitho. "Now, once again, how much do I get?"

"My lord, the facts are," said Bolitho firmly, "your advisers have decided to withhold distributions for now and to use the monies for needed improvements for a more prosperous future. I have prior to this meeting discussed this approach with the other adventurers and my partners. They are sufficiently in agreement to proceed."

"That is preposterous!" Dunbargan protested. "I agreed to admit new adventurers in order to ensure my own payments."

"Be patient, my lord," Eliot said. "Mr. Bolitho and I have taken your interests into account. After our meeting at Port Eliot, I further approached the Duchy of Cornwall with my proposal to grant additional mining leases to Lanhydrock to permit driving shafts under the sea. As I have told you, the Duchy has confirmed its approval, subject to my taking a substantial position as an adventurer, to which you have already agreed in principle. Captain Penwarden informs us that preliminary borings are promising. Accordingly, Mr. Bolitho has agreed to advance funds to enable Wheal Hykka to proceed, with Mr. Smeaton's advice on mechanical enhancement of our workings."

"But I can't stand by . . . ."

"My lord," Bolitho said, "a sufficient amount to meet your needs may be included in the plan, in view of the agreements with which you concurred at the Port Eliot meeting."

"I see," said Dunbargan. "What do you think, Clymo?"

"Everything seems cut and dried, your lordship," said Clymo. "It will be to your advantage in the long run. I've seen to that."

"My lord, you have little choice but to agree," Bolitho whispered in Dunbargan's ear. He then announced, "Now gentlemen, shall we conclude our most satisfactory meeting? Captain Penwarden's staff has prepared a feast for us. We will eat from Wheal Hykka's beautiful new tin dinner service. We are adjourned."

Chapter Fifty-one

Gardener

Lizzie Penwarden's day had not started well. The old rooster had roused her as the sun was rising. She turned over to steal a little more sleep, but then little Jennifer woke her again, crying in evident pain. Lizzie rose and picked the baby up, laying her over her shoulder and patting her back in case she had wind. It was not yet fully light outside, but as she looked out, the hawthorn trees in the hedges seemed to be covered in May blossom. She walked closer to the window, breathed on the pane to clear the fog on the inside and looked again. It was not blossom, it was snow, a light dusting covering the garden and the surrounding hedges and fields. This was unusual; Cornwall rarely had snow, even in the depth of the winter. She hoped it would melt in time to allow the gardener to get on with his work.

Little Jennifer had been crotchety during the night, crying, waking her up every now and then. The new baby had been born in January, the happy result of her warm welcome home to Addis after he came back from the trip to Liskeard last Whitsun. What tales he had told, with the drunken goings-on ending up with one of Mr. Eliot's men in the stocks. They were glad to have a little girl after two boys. Boys were rambunctious, always into something. Addis was proud of his sons Jemmy and Jedson, and he tried to be a good dad. Now Jennifer was the apple of his eye, his little princess.

The baby appeared to have an upset tummy. She seemed to have a weak digestion. Usually Lizzie would have tried to keep her quiet so as not to disturb Addis. Her husband was the man of the house. He had to work to support the family, and he needed his rest, of course. But last night he was gone, spent the night at that blessed mine, and had taken Jemmy with him. Said an important visitor was coming to the May cost book meeting and he might have to stay and talk to him. It was all very well, but now Wheal Hykka always seemed to come before his wife. Lizzie too needed her sleep. So she had got up and brought Jennifer into bed with her. The little mite snuggled at her warm breast and quickly settled down. She was just hungry.

After the baby had taken her fill, Lizzie changed her nappy. No wonder the baby had been crying; she had loose stools. Lizzie brought up some warm water from the kettle on the kitchen stove and washed the baby. She dressed little Jedson and washed his face. She held Jennifer in one arm and held Jedson by his hand as she took them downstairs to the kitchen for breakfast. Jedson was walking now, but still unsteadily. She missed her eldest, even though he had only been away one night, and her husband, too.

Lizzie put some coal on the kitchen stove and opened the draft to get a good fire going to heat up the porridge that she had left warming overnight. One good thing about those dirty old clattering steam engines that the mines were putting in was that there was plenty of coal to be had around Pendeen. She told little Jedson to keep an eye on Jennifer while she put on her shawl and slipped outside to look for eggs in the chicken coop. She came back in and scrambled a couple for herself and spooned out some porridge with cream for herself and Jedson. She sat him down at the kitchen table, laid Jennifer over her shoulder, and ate her breakfast.

Today was going to be busy. Any time now the young gardener she had hired last year from Pendeen village would be coming over to help get the garden ready for spring. Truth to tell, he would be doing most of it. She had not fully recovered her strength from giving birth to Jennifer and would not be much help with the heavy work, the digging. But someone had to do it. Addis was too busy these days to take much care of family matters. The gardener was a handsome young man, seemed to take notice of her too. Addis had better look out; she was still quite attractive. Whatever would they think at the chapel if they knew her mind ran to such sinful thoughts?

Reverend Perry was coming over at midday to have a bite with her and chat about the village school. She was looking forward to it. Now, there was someone who paid attention to her and told her she could learn to do a lot of good in this world, help others. There was a knock at the back door. She opened it to the gardener. She was pleased to feel the early warmth of the sun, and to see the dusting of snow already melting.

"Mornin' mum. Be strange to see that snow, not like Cornwall. Soon be all gone though. Oi've brought boxes of plants with me to get the vegetable plot started like you said, cabbages, brussels sprouts, onions, kale, and seed potatoes."

"Glad to see you," said Lizzie. "Did you remember seeds? Us wants broad beans, runner beans, peas, turnips and carrots."

"Yes mum," said the gardener, "them's all in little paper twists in my pockets. Oi saved them myself from last year's crop. Oi needs to dig over the patch first. You got plenty of horse manure? Oi reckon 'tis better'n cow dung, specially mixed with straw. Do us need to get the manure merchant?"

"There be plenty in the heap over behind the stable. There's a barrow in the shed. You can borrow Mr. Penwarden's tools, go 'elp yourself. Oi'll be out in a minute, show you where Oi wants things."

Lizzie closed the door and went over to settle Jennifer in her crib where she would be safe. The baby was already sleepy. It was cool outside, so she dressed Jedson in the wooly long-sleeved sweater and cap that she had knitted for him. She had used the yarn from a worn-out old pullover she had made for Addis; saved buying new wool. "Now you come outside and help your mum in the garden. Your dad would be proud," she told her son.

The gardener raked off last year's leaves and pulled the few weeds from the vegetable patch. Lizzie had kept it trim and tidy this Spring, with a little help from Addis, when he had time. She got a fork from the shed and helped the gardener fill the barrow with horse manure, but she only managed two or three forkfuls before she got tired.

"Let's put the potatoes where the beans were last year, and put the beans where the cabbages and sprouts were. They'll get a nice lot of sun and do well," Lizzie said. She got out a long cord wrapped around two short sticks from the pocket of her apron and gave one to the gardener. "Now, you take one stick to the other side of the garden as I unwind the cord. Push it in the earth and we'll make a nice straight row. Come on, Jedson, you help the gardener, too." Jedson toddled along between them holding the cord.

They were using the newfangled method of planting crops in orderly rows rather than any old how across a patch of ground. The farmers had been taught that this allowed better cultivation, hoeing the weeds beside the rows, getting at the crops more easily to harvest them. Lizzie had convinced the gardener that he should change the old-fashioned ways that he had learned from his father.

The gardener took the long-handled Cornish shovel and dug a trench along the stretched string guide, setting a pile of earth along the side. The soil was only slightly damp and in good condition from years of cultivation, easy to work, friable. As Lizzie wheeled the barrow along beside the trench the gardener placed manure in the bottom and covered it with a layer of earth. In places where there was too much manure she bent over and spread it more evenly with her hands.

Lizzie sowed broad bean seeds in two rows a foot apart, each seed three or four inches apart. She gave Jedson a pocket full of seeds to plant. He tried to help, but Lizzie had to go after him and set his seeds straight. The gardener raked the piled-up earth to cover the seeds an inch or two deep, breaking up any lumps to make a fine tilth. Then he and Lizzie worked together to place stakes along both sides of the seedbed. They tied several strings the entire length of the row to support the bean stalks as they grew.

They repeated the procedure with runner beans, but this time they stuck long sticks the length of a man into the earth beside the trench every two or three feet, tying the tops together to form a kind of tent. They looped string up and down diagonally along the row to make a frame for the tendrils to cling on to as the bean plants grew to full height.

It was now the turn of the potatoes, one row for new potatoes and two for the main crop. Again, they dug trenches, shoveled manure along the bottom and covered this with fine earth. Lizzie gently placed the seed potatoes a foot apart and three or four inches deep, being careful not to knock the eyes off. The gardener raked the soil from the side in long heaps along each row. This would provide cover for the plants when they grew, and keep the sun from turning the growing potatoes green and poisonous. Potatoes were the same family as deadly nightshade.

Planting potatoes was heavy work, and the mid-morning sun was warm. They were both sweating. The gardener rested on his rake, pulled out a red kerchief and wiped his brow. "Gettin' a bit warmish," he said, "Oi could do with a nice cool drink."

Lizzie went into the kitchen to get him a mug. She checked on the baby. Little Jennifer was stirring. Lizzie gently put a finger in the baby's mouth to suck on to quieten her, without success. Lizzie was in a hurry to get back to the gardening, but she picked Jennifer up and fed her for a few minutes to settle her. She changed her baby's badly soiled nappy again and laid her back in her crib, where the baby soon slipped into an uneasy sleep.

Lizzie went outside to the pump by the back door and filled mugs with cold water. At one time she would have poured some of her home-brewed beer or cider, but since Reverend Perry preached against strong drink she kept to water. While she was indoors, the gardener had stripped off his shirt and hung it on a low branch of the apple tree, careful not to knock off the blossom. Lizzie could not help observing his muscular arms, trim waist and bare, well-developed chest. As she passed him his mug, she brushed against him, smelling his sweat. She felt a little susurration of excitement. Oh my, this would never do. She was a mother of three, wife of an important man. Must be that she was missing Addis more than she realized. Must not let that get to her.

"Wait," she said, "let me clean that mug off. Should've wiped me 'ands, you'll get a nasty taste in your mouth." She lifted the hem of her dress and wiped the smudge of earth and manure from her hands off the rim of the mug. She took her time, aware that she had revealed her legs. The gardener was diligently studying the far end of the garden. Lizzie stopped letting her imagination wander along forbidden paths.

"Let's get back to work," she said, "get this over with. Us got a guest comin' 'ere soon, Reverend Perry from the chapel."

"Oi put in the cabbage plants an' sprouts whilst you was inside, mum," said the gardener, "and little Jedson was a big 'elp, for a little tacker. Did a proper job."

"Good boy," Lizzie said. "Before long them'll get covered with caterpillars. Oi'll pay you a farthing a 'undred for pickin' 'em off, just loike Oi did Jemmy when 'e was your age. Then them little wrigglers won't eat the cabbages."

The only thing left to do was to sow the tiny seeds for the root vegetables, carrots, parsnips, and Addis's favorite swedes, the big yellow kind of turnips. The gardener carefully sieved the soil to cover them so the seedlings would not have to fight their way past lumps of soil.

"That's all done then, mum," he said, wiping his brow and putting on his shirt. "Just 'ave to wash off the tools and put them back in the shed."

"That was a good morning's work, Oi could do with a sit down," said Lizzie, smiling warmly.

"Oi'd best be on my way," said the gardener hastily. "You should be all right 'til next year. Tell Mr. Penwarden Oi said 'ullo."

"Wait a minute, an' Oi'll give you your wages," Lizzie said. Just then the clock in the church tower in the village struck twelve, its chimes ringing clear in the still air. "Oi must make 'aste, Reverend Perry should be 'ere any minute." She rushed inside and found the money and quickly paid out the wages.

After the gardener left, Lizzie went back inside to wash her face and hands, check on the baby, and give Jedson a snack. She heard a jingling of harness outside and hurried into the front hall. The Reverend Perry was getting out of his cart and tying a strap from his pony's bridle to the hitching post. He gave the pony his nosebag.

Lizzie opened the front door and welcomed him. "Glad to see you could come, Mr. Perry. I'm looking forward to our chat. You must tell me what us can do to 'elp. Come on in, and take off your coat and 'at. Oi'll give you some of my mutton an' vegetable stew. Did you 'ave a good journey over?"

"Glad to see you too, Mrs. Penwarden. I am a bit peckish; your stew smells tasty, but to tell you the truth one of the fishermen brought me some mackerel and we could have those instead. They're lovely and fresh. The road from Perranporth is pretty bad, but it hasn't rained for a few days so I had a decent drive, although there was a little bit of snow. That was a surprise. Now, I've got a lot to tell you. Look at little Jedson, my goodness how he's grown. And how is your precious little girl?"

"She's doin' well, right over there," said Lizzie gesturing towards the crib. "Let's sit at the kitchen table, Mr. Perry, it's cosy out here, and I won't have to disturb Jennifer. I'll boil up them mackerel, and we'll 'ave 'em with pepper and a nice dab of butter."

Lizzie went over to the stove and carefully set her iron cauldron of water on the embers to boil. The cauldron sat on three legs, so it was steady. She unwrapped the mackerel, sliced their bellies, drew out the guts, and cut off the heads and tails. She turned to Perry and asked, "I don't suppose you'd like a mug of cider, would you? It's made from our own apples, not strong like beer. But, I expect you'd prefer water."

"No thank you, Mrs. Penwarden. Since I took the pledge I haven't touched a drop of any alcoholic beverage, and we must remember that cider is alcoholic. In my position I have to set an example, and besides I took my pledge before God and that is a solemn oath."

"Oi respects that, Mr. Perry, really Oi do."

"Since we have mentioned it, Mrs. Penwarden, one young man I saved from the demon drink is married to a young woman with whom we may become involved. It's a long story, so I'll just give you the gist. I was in Liskeard with your Addis when we went up to meet the people from Port Eliot. It was Whitsuntide last year, and the people were celebrating in a most ungodly manner. The young man got into the drink that day, not for the first time, and was locked in the stocks for being drunk and disorderly. Mrs. Eliot came along and persuaded her husband to have him released."

"That don't sound like the way gentry folk be'ave usually, Mr. Perry. They'm usually uppity, don't care about us ordinary folk, even their own servants, no matter 'ow much trouble us gets into. Our Viscount Dunbargan wouldn't lift a finger to 'elp nobody. My 'usband says 'e won't spend a penny in the mines to keep them poor tinners from gettin' 'urt even; that's what my Addis says, and 'is little brother killed down the mine an' all. Viscount just says everyone knows it be dangerous work, but well paid. No wonder they call 'im Dunbugger."

"Now we must be charitable to our fellow man, Mrs. Penwarden," said Reverend Perry, "even though I appreciate that it is sometimes hard. But even those we think of as sinners can be brought to see the merit of good works, thanks to the mysterious ways of our blessed Lord."

"You'm too good sometimes, Reverend," said Lizzie. "Some of them sinners is past 'elpin'."

"Our Savior commands us to do our best, Mrs. Penwarden. We must try." Peter Perry continued. "Now, the young lady of whom I just spoke is Morwenna Clymo, daughter of the viscount's man of business. She was there when this fellow, young Willy Bunt, got put in the stocks, and she will probably become involved with the schools. I have received a most encouraging letter from her."

"Bunt's 'is name?" asked Lizzie, "do 'e work for Mr. Eliot?"

"Yes, he does," replied Reverend Perry. "Under Joseph Clymo. Promising young man by all accounts, but he can't hold his drink. Tried to stop, took the pledge, thought he could handle it, but turned out to be a backslider. Mr. Eliot asked me to see what I could do, and I said I would, although my own flock keeps me busy enough."

"That's really nice of you," said Lizzie.

"He came down west where I can keep an eye on him for a while," Reverend Perry went on. "He used to be at Lanhydrock. He was valet to the viscount, then he married one of the maids, Mary, and they left for St. Germans. However, Mr. Clymo agrees young Bunt is worth saving."

"That Mr. Clymo is a good man at heart, my Addis says. He 'as to manage the viscount though, 'as to do what 'e says, can't cross him. But as long as 'e provides plenty of money, the viscount don't ask too many questions."

"Well, it appears that the good Mrs. Eliot has got Lady Dunbargan to persuade her husband that he would make more money by not opposing education for our children, and even the miners. And money is what matters most to him."

"If you say so, Mr. Perry. 'Ow did 'er work that miracle then?"

"Morwenna didn't exactly say, but if my guess is good for anything, there's something going on that nobody's telling. I don't need to know as long as it helps our aims, provided of course it's not illegal or immoral. What it boils down to is that it suits these grand families to support education. I pray at least in part it's because they feel it is right and their duty."

"Never mind why, as long as them 'elps us get on with it." Lizzie rose and pulled the mackerel off the fire and served them to Reverend Perry and herself, with a helping of the stew for Jedson, who was still hungry.

When they had settled down to eating, Reverend Perry recounted Morwenna's telling how Mrs. Eliot planned to start a village school in the church at St. Germans, with more down west for the miners and their families. Perry wanted Lizzie Penwarden to be a teacher at the school in Pendeen, not least for the benefit of her husband and her children. However, he wanted the school to be at the chapel, in the meeting hall.

"Sounds lovely then," said Lizzie.

"Up to a point. While I respect our brethren in the Church of England, Mrs. Penwarden, I never forget that it is the established church. It is an extension of the monarchy. It supports, and is supported by, the aristocracy and the gentry. My old grandfather used to say that the Church of England is the Tory Party at prayer. He was joking of course, but it is the truth. The Church of England presently cares little at heart for the ordinary folk, the poor, the miners, the fishermen, the farm laborers."

"Us can't do much about they," said Lizzie. "Them's what's in charge, I reckon."

"We must have more of our own chapels, and our own schools," said the reverend. "One day Mr. Wesley himself will agree that we cannot reform the established church from within. We must completely separate."

"Oh, Mr. Perry, that means trouble," said Lizzie, shaking her head. "I want to 'elp you, but Oi don't want my Addis to get the sack because we'm troublemakers."

"If the ordinary people don't stand up for themselves, no one will. We must act together with determination but with courtesy, firmly and with little noise. We must choose our battles where our adversaries see little importance. We must allow them to underestimate us. They support education for now because they see it as furthering their own interests. But we know inside ourselves that education is the key to the enlightenment and emancipation of working people. In education lies the key to future power in parliament."

"Oi 'ope you'm right, Mr. Perry, bless us all and keep us in peace. But me an' mine'll be right with you, fightin' the good fight with all our might."

"Bless you, Lizzie! That's what I like to hear. Fighting spirit."

"Oi'll start with our Jemmy, an' drag 'im off to school an' out of that mine whether 'e likes it or not. An' Oi'll get Addis there to school Sundays. Oi knows 'e wants more learnin', and 'e's not too proud to show others the way. He may be mine captain, but 'e's not the Lord God almighty."

Chapter Fifty-two

Details

Following that awful time his beloved younger brother Jedson was killed down the mine, Addis had felt his bad luck turned to good. He was happy that he had been given an important job, captain at the big Wheal Hykka Mine, with greater responsibility and authority and, yes, more wages, all long before he had aspired to such an increase in his station. With it came the comfortable house in Pendeen to provide for his family, so much nicer than the cramped cottage at Gwennap.

He felt he was doing a good job as captain considering he had so much new to contend with. At least Mr. Clymo and Captain Williams had few criticisms to go with their copious advice, and as long as they were behind him the adventurers would not complain much. He was working hard to make improvements to increase production and profits. He had to be firm with the miners, especially the tributers, but he knew from experience that a fair captain could get more from his men than a harsh one. Nevertheless, they always had something to grumble about, some things that were justifiable, some that could not be helped. Addis was doing his best.

The tributers who were awarded setts down the new shaft won them with high bids, because few wanted to work there. It was hundreds of feet deep and they were digging the level further and further out under the Atlantic Ocean. The miners were used to dangerous conditions; dark, dirty, wet, confined. They were tinners, strong, tough men. They did what it took to win tin. However, they were not foolhardy, not seeking out danger, not taking risks to prove their courage. One of the old tinners confided to Addis that he got frightened.

"Don't tell anyone Oi told 'e, moind, Cap'n," he whispered one evening as he was leaving, "but us was drillin' down that new level when that last gurt storm were ragin'. As true as Oi'm standin' 'ere Oi 'eard boulders on the sea bed over my 'ead rollin' and thunderin' as the great breakers crashed above, pushin' 'em against the cliffs and pullin' 'em back again. What if one of 'em broke though the bloody roof above us? What would 'appen to we then?"

"That level's in hard rock," assured Addis, "you know how strong it be. Took 'e long enough to drill through 'er. You'll be all right, you was better off than them poor fishermen out in the thick of it, weren't 'e?"

The old tinner was not mollified. Neither was the young man who had been assigned to helping John Smeaton. "Calls 'isself an engineer!" he scoffed. "Nothin' but a bloody furriner. Couldn't tell 'is arse from 'is elbow. Can't even make out what 'e's talkin' about 'alf the time, talks funny. Bloody furriner, bad luck most likely."

"Mr. Smeaton's a clever man, indeed knows what he's talkin' about," said Penwarden. "He'll make all of our work easier, safer too later on, you mark my words."

At home, Lizzie seemed contented and was a staunch support, even though she complained from time to time that his job claimed too much of his attention. She could push him sometimes, but he didn't mind much; he admired her strength and independence. And now after having two wonderful sons, they had been blessed with a daughter, his darling little Jennifer. Could his good fortune go on forever? Did he really deserve it? He couldn't seem to shake a feeling of foreboding.

He had talked about his doubts with the Reverend Perry. The minister reassured him. "Mr. Penwarden, our good Lord looks with favor on those who faithfully love Him. Keep up regular attendance at the chapel and pray every day for His blessing, and indeed His forgiveness. Continue to do good works, as I trust you now do at the mine as well as in your home and village, and you will enjoy His grace."

"I trust you are right," said Addis, "but what if . . .?"

"Just keep to the straight and narrow, and all will be well. If some evil or sorrow should befall you, He will comfort you and lead you through the darkness and out to the other side."

Addis's misgivings were realized, although it was some time before he heard the news that troubles were brewing. He was working late at the mine. Back home, Lizzie was worried; she needed her husband's support. They were both aware that little Jennifer had a weak stomach, a poor digestion. She would wrinkle up her face with pain, draw up her little legs, and cry piteously if you pressed her tummy ever so gently. But usually nursing her, patting her back, and changing her dirty nappy would settle her down for a while. But now she seemed to be getting worse, and there was blood on her nappy. Her forehead felt hot to the touch and her lips were dry.

Lizzie realized it was no good trying to get hold of Addis. Even if she sent a message, he would say that he was too busy. There was no doctor in the village, so she called in the nurse from St. Just to help. The coarse and dirty old woman did not inspire confidence, but she was available. She had been put in Bodmin Gaol at one time for prostitution and thievery. Since she didn't have the money to pay for her keep in prison, she was made to help take care of the sick prisoners. There were plenty to care for, because conditions were terrible. The gaol was filthy. So were the prisoners; most were infested with lice. There was only foul water to drink, scarcely any for washing. The food was rotten, unless you could afford to buy some from the gaoler. After eventually completing her sentence, the old woman passed herself off as a nurse and earned a few coppers from time to time.

Lizzie let her into the house, averting her face to avoid the stench that came in with her, obliterating the strong scent of June flowers outside. After taking a cursory look at little Jennifer the woman made up her secret herbal remedy and tried to feed it to the baby in a spoon. But it smelled and tasted bitter, so Jennifer spat it out, and anyway she was too small to drink from a spoon. Lizzie tried too, but it was no good.

"It be the bloody flux, that's what the little maid's got," said the nurse. "Oi can always tell. 'Er's feverish, loose stool, blood in it. 'Tis the bloody flux. Er's really poorly, poor little mite. 'Er humors is all upset. Oi'll do what Oi can, but tain't much. 'Er won't take my potion. Not much else Oi can do." The nurse reached into the crib to pick the baby up.

"'Ere, you leave her be, Oi'll take care of 'er," Lizzie shouted, shooing the woman away. She then took a piece of cloth and soaked it with cold water at the pump, moistened Jennifer's parched lips, and laid it on the baby's baking brow. It seemed to soothe her, but only for a few moments. The baby drew her legs up again and whimpered. She needed changing again. There was more blood. All Lizzie could do now was let her lie in her crib and hope she would improve. The nurse was no help, so Lizzie gave her a couple of coppers and sent her packing.

Perhaps she could get hold of Reverend Perry and he could offer some comfort. He had said he was going to be at the chapel in Pendeen that day. She wished Addis would come. Perhaps she could get someone to take a message to him. Surely Addis would come if he knew the importance of it, though he was more than usually preoccupied at Wheal Hykka. John Smeaton had come down to stay at the count house again to supervise the installation of the Newcomen engine.

June was a lovely month to be in Cornwall. Joseph Clymo had come down from Lanhydrock to deliver gold to the contractors and generally to keep an eye on this big investment. The stonemasons had built an engine house near the cliff edge, with a deep foundation on solid rock to bear the weight. The axle for the great beam arm was set in granite lintels. There was a tall chimney for the smoke to escape and to keep a good draught on the furnace. The main cylinder had been put in place and the bearings connected. However, Joseph Clymo was unable to override the viscount and give permission to Smeaton to spend additional funds to install safety devices, pressure control valves, steam bleed taps, and guards over the moving parts.

Young Jemmy constantly followed the great man around, peppering him with questions. Smeaton was patient, seeing something of his own youth in the lad's insatiable curiosity. England needed ingenious and innovative men to design and install the machinery and devices that would bring her prosperity as new industries revolutionized the way her economy operated. This young man was worth encouraging. An opportunity came for them to spend time together when Smeaton discovered that the inexperienced mechanics at Wheal Hykka lacked the proper set of spanners to wrench the big nuts to the required degree of torque needed to secure the main cylinder firmly in place. He asked Addis Penwarden to suggest a solution so the work did not get delayed.

"Run over to the ironmonger's in St. Just, Mr. Smeaton," said Penwarden. "He keeps a good stock; see whether 'e can 'elp us. Jemmy can drive you over. He knows the way better'n you, and 'e's big enough now to 'andle the cob."

"I'll do that, Cap'n," nodded Smeaton. You could tell he was a Yorkshireman by the way he spoke, and he sounded out of place in Cornwall. "It'll give your lad summat to do. Wouldn't mind t' chance to chat with 'im. You've a bright one there, pay to encourage 'im. T' men have plenty to do while I'm gone. We need to run a test on yon cylinder before we can go much further. Should be back in a few hours, then I'll show them how to use those tools."

One of the ostlers in the mine stables tacked up the cob and hitched it up to a small four-wheeled cart. It wasn't fast but it was sturdy enough to carry the weight. They made good time, considering the hilly and winding stony track. They passed the Botallack mine on their way, leaving Cape Cornwall and the Atlantic Ocean to their right, a brisk offshore breeze throwing up big breakers in the incoming tide.

"What's them animals playin' in the sea, Mr. Smeaton?" asked Jemmy. "Look just like dogs with short coats, but flippers instead of legs."

"They're Atlantic grey seals, Jemmy, largest mammal in the whole country. They look like they're playing but they're fishing. The fishermen don't like them; think they can spoil a fishing ground. They kill a terrible lot of fish, and often will just take one bite and leave the rest. Awful wasteful."

"What can the fishermen do?"

"Not much. They'll kill them when they find them asleep on the rocks. But there are too many of them. Look over there; see the little white ones? They're pups. The sharks will get some of them. Course, the fishermen have to put up with a lot more than seals. Look at all those birds, diving down and catching fish. Mind you, they're useful too. By watching the birds, t' fishermen can see where the schools of fish are, mackerel, herring, catch hundreds of thousands of pilchards when they're running."

"Seagulls?" asked Jemmy.

"Some are. But there are lots of different types of birds. I can see fulmers, gannets, and look there's a kittiwake."

They saw a stream beside the track and stopped to let the cob have a drink and cool off for a few minutes. They got down and stretched their legs, Jemmy keeping hold of the reins so the cob wouldn't stray.

"Have you ever seen a Cornish Chough?" Smeaton asked. "I haven't, and I'd like to. It's unique to this part of the world."

"Me neither. So what's it like, then?" asked Jemmy.

"They're related to crows. Black, medium-sized, with red bills."

"How big zackly?"

"They can be almost a foot and a half long, three foot wings."

"I'd like to see one," said Jemmy.

"Are you interested in birds?" asked Smeaton, smiling.

"Oi'm in'erested in lots o' things," said Jemmy.

"I used to collect birds' eggs when I was a boy," the great man said, "that's a good way to learn a lot about birds. You find out how to identify all sorts, by t' size and shape of the egg, t' color of the shells, and the different markings."

"Don't them eggs stink after a toime?" asked Jemmy.

"You have to prick a hole in both ends of the shell, gently, being careful not to break it, and blow the insides out. Then you can keep them forever. It's a wonderful hobby, teaches you a lot too."

"Sounds really in'erestin', Mr. Smeaton," said Jemmy, "Oi think I'll try that if Oi 'ave the toime."

"We'd better get on, young feller me lad. We've still a ways to go, and we need those tools," said Smeaton, smiling at his young charge's enthusiasm. They climbed back into the cart. Jemmy picked up the reins and shook them across the cob's withers. He didn't like to use the whip unless he had to. The cob leaned into his collar and the cart moved forward. As they drove along the crooked track towards St. Just, they came across a large number of heavily laden mules in a train traveling towards them. They were carrying panniers strapped to their backs. The drovers gave them a cheerful wave.

"Look at all them mules, scores of them. What are they carrying?" asked Jemmy.

"Mining coals," said Smeaton. "Won't be long before we get more steam engines installed, and there'll be hundreds of them bringing coal from the Cornish ports, shipped by sea from south Wales. I've designed and built all kinds of contraptions for the coal mines, far away as Yorkshire. Coal's being used more and more. Lot of money being made from coal. Dirty stuff to handle; still, where there's muck there's brass. That's what we say in Yorkshire."

Jemmy had to listen carefully when Mr. Smeaton spoke. He was quite difficult to understand, not like the Cornish. It must be because he was a furriner, from way up north in Yorkshire. Jemmy noticed that when Mr. Smeaton said brass it sounded clipped, short, not like his dad who said brass with a long a, took more time over it. Odd, and instead of saying "the," Mr. Smeaton said "t", but Jemmy was too polite to say anything.

"Oi wish Oi could be an inventor like you, Mr. Smeaton," said Jemmy wistfully. "Must be very in'erestin', thinkin' up new things, tryin' things out, and seein' the world."

"You could be whatever you want, Jemmy," said Smeaton, "if you are determined enough and study hard. Course, you have to have the imagination, and most of all you have to be educated. You must look into t' details, and measure what you do, always measure. And just try things. Nobody succeeds t' first time. I've done experiments that didn't work, hundreds of times, until I got it right in the end. Have you tried inventing anything?"

"Yes sir, I did. My dad was really pleased; it's called the Rod of Quills. They use 'em down the mine at Wheal Hykka now, all the time. He says it saves miners' lives."

"That's good, Jemmy," said Smeaton. "How does it work?"

"Well, 'twas last Christmas. Mum had cooked a goose. Dad had been experimentin' with gunpowder at 'ome and I wanted to set a little bit off, see it burn, for fun. They didn't take no notice of me, just playin', so Oi got some of the big feathers, the quills, cut the tips off and filled the 'ollow stem part with gunpowder. Then Oi lit the feather ends in the kitchen fire. They sizzled slowly, awful stink, 'til the flames got to the 'ollow end and set off the gunpowder, whoosh! My dad gave a start, an' Oi thought I was goin' to get into trouble."

"What then?" asked Smeaton.

"Well, 'e didn't say much, but a look came over 'is face, all interested like. So later 'e took me down Wheal Hykka, tried it out down mine, stuck in one quill after another end to end with all the tips cut off, long enough to stuff down a long drill 'ole. Now they use my idea all the time, the Rod of Quills they call it. Gives the miners time to get safely away after lighting the feathers before the powder sets off the blast, like a safety fuse, them say. Nobody's been killed at Wheal Hykka in a blastin' accident since, like my uncle was."

"You are an inventor, Jemmy," said Smeaton, smiling broadly. "I'm going to talk to your dad about helping you. You know, when I was a young man in Yorkshire I started out in law, followed in my father's footsteps, before I decided on what I really wanted to do with my life. I call it being a civil engineer. What I learned from my father was that t' law could protect my ideas from being stolen, and make sure that the inventor could be paid. I learned how to write a proper specification and even how to apply for a letter patent from the king. You've got to learn about such things, otherwise you'll always be giving away inventions."

Jemmy was distracted, not paying attention to his driving. He did not notice another train of mules coming around a bend in the track.

"Watch out, Jemmy! Pull over," said Smeaton. Jemmy felt foolish. He stopped the cart while the train passed. He hoped that his new hero still thought well of him. He recovered his composure and said, "Oi'll never forget this day, Mr. Smeaton, never in my 'ole life. Oi'm goin' to be an inventor when Oi grow up, make things so minin' is better an' safer, an' get really rich."

"You will, Jemmy," said Smeaton, "but you will have to apply yourself. It's not just about having ideas, it's about working out all t' many details so that you can put them into practice. It's hard work." Smeaton smiled at his new protégé as the mule train passed and the cart started up again. "It is a lovely day, I like being in Cornwall and enjoying its beautiful scenery and its special people. Look at those rocky cliffs, and t' sea, and the birds, and the wildflowers. Perhaps I should come down here to live."

The cob ambled on as they absorbed the peace and beauty of the scene. Suddenly their reverie was shattered by a hideous noise, a loud explosion from behind them. The cob neighed and snorted, its nostrils flaring. Terrified it kicked his heels, almost turning the cart over. They instinctively leaned to one side and barely held the cart's balance. They looked around and saw a great pall of black smoke rising in the air, then another. They heard a second explosion. Beyond the headland they saw the mules had panicked, bucking and kicking, spilling the coals from their panniers.

"That must be at Wheal Hykka," said Smeaton. "Turn around and head back. We must go and see what's happened, see if we can help. Whip up, drive like Old Nick himself is after you!"

Chapter Fifty-three

Chaos

The cob was lathered up and panting heavily as the cart swerved and bounced over rocks and ruts, careening through smoke and dust down the last hundred yards of the track to Wheal Hykka. Smeaton was holding on for dear life. "Slow down! Slow down! You'll take us over the cliffs, right into t' sea!"

Jemmy hauled back on the reins. They screeched to a stop to avoid the knots of men milling about, others rushing in all directions. The mine alarm bell was clanging. Now they could see flames coming from the new engine house down near the cliff edge, right over the new shaft driven deep under the sea. They saw Addis Penwarden's top hat above the heads of the crowd by the main entrance; he was waving his arms, pointing, giving orders, yet seeming calm, in charge. Jemmy rushed to him, putting his arms around him.

"Penwarden, what t' hell's going on?" demanded Smeaton striding up behind Jemmy.

"Fire from the boiler 'ouse got to the powder store down the new shaft, seems loike, set off an explosion," Addis said, striving to control the shaking in his voice.

"Engine damaged?" asked Smeaton.

"Worse. Blew a hole in the shoreward stretch of the new underwater tunnel. Us was gettin' ready to blast a new section under the sea. Men trapped down there. Sea water flooded in."

"Was the engine damaged? How badly? How did it happen?"

"Can't stop 'ere talkin'," said Penwarden. "Get a bucket, both of ye. Mr. Clymo is down cliff top; 'e's organizin' formin' a chain. Us needs to get water on the fire up this end. Wish that steam engine of your'n was workin', could do with a big pump. Need to empty out shaft down bottom end, plug up the 'ole, get those men out. 'Urry!"

"But how did it happen?" Smeaton pressed. "What caused it?"

"Dunno yet. No more time. Gotta be off." Penwarden strode off, calling on more men, women and boys to get buckets, get over to where Clymo could set them up in a longer line. Smeaton called after him. "Penwarden, I could do more good at t' engine house. See what's up yonder. You carry on. Jemmy, you stay here with me. I may need your help."

They hurried over to the tall stone building where black smoke was streaming out. They tried to get in, coughing and spluttering, their eyes smarting and watering. Men with blackened faces holding wet cloths over their noses were just inside the entrance trying to pull out their mates still inside, overcome by fumes and in danger of succumbing. There was a loud hissing noise. Smeaton realized some of the clouds were steam.

"What's going on?" he shouted above the noise. "What happened? Where's the steam coming from?"

"Dunno zackly, Mr. Smeaton, zir," said the nearest one. "One of the young fellows set the fire goin' under the boiler."

"Why in the devil would he do that?" demanded Smeaton.

"Wanted to get it ready for when you got back for the test, surprise you loike."

"Surprise me? I'll say he did," said Smeaton. "Where is he? Who was it? I'll give him a piece of my mind, damned young fool. He should have known better, waited for me. They all knew I had more adjustments to make. Let me get in there."

"Wouldn't if Oi were you, zir. 'Tis powerful 'ot. 'Twas young Ben Trethewey, keen as mustard, poor lad. Wanted to 'elp, show 'is mettle. Oi tried to stop 'im. He'd got a good fire goin', raised steam, but the pressure got out of 'and, started blowin' out the top." The man paused, covered his eyes with a dirty hand, couldn't go on.

"What happened next? Come on man, spit it out," Smeaton pressed.

"Well, Oi stayed out the road, looked really dangerous. Then one of the tinners from down below came up askin' for a couple of buckets of live coals to take down shaft. Them wanted a brazier to heat up the boryer, them rods they drill with."

"Why in God's name would they do that?" demanded Smeaton.

"Them sometimes 'ave to dry out the 'oles in the wet rock before they tamp the powder in, in them quills. Otherwise won't go off proper."

"Then what?"

"Ben was trying to stop the steam blowin' off. So 'e shoveled some 'ot coals out of the furnace into the buckets, gave another one to the tinner. But that didn't do no good, just let air in, made the fire burn fiercer. So then 'e threw water in the fire. That just made more steam, scalded 'im, all over 'is face." The man took a deep breath, tried to control himself, wiped a tattered sleeve across his smoke grimed face. "He screamed, it 'urt so bad, poor lad. He staggered back, knocked over the other bucket that was sittin' on the floor behind 'im. Coals went all over the place, set the wood frame on fire. Tinner just went runnin' off, takin' 'is bucket with 'im."

"Where's young Trethewey? What's happened to him?" asked Smeaton.

"Fell over. Fire must've got to 'im. Us tried to save 'im, 'aven't got 'im out yet. 'Tis 'ot as 'ell inside, can't stick it long, too much smoke. But Oi reckon 'e's a goner." He choked back a sob. "Dunno what 'is old mum will do, 'er bein' a widow woman an' all. 'Tis a disgrace, should never've 'appened, if you ask us."

"What caused the explosion down the shaft?" asked Smeaton.

"Oi dunno, Oi weren't there, was Oi? Ye'll 'ave to ask the tinners, or mebbe Cap'n Penwarden. 'E knows pretty much what goes on around 'ere. Now 'e's got that there Clymo, owner's man, gettin' folks fetchin' water up in buckets. Then us can put the fire out. Look, 'ere 'e comes now."

"Stop!" Smeaton yelled at Clymo. "Where'd that water come from?"

"I assume it came from the flooded shaft," said Clymo. "They're trying to lower the level, rescue the men trapped down there."

"So it's sea water," said Smeaton, red in the face, blocking the entrance to the engine house. "You can't throw that on the steam engine. The salt will ruin it, corrode the cylinder, all the moving parts. Stop! Don't do it. Get fresh water."

"Out of my way, man," shouted Clymo. "There's no time. The whole building will burn if we don't get water on the fire."

"It's your fault," said Smeaton, "if you 'adn't been so damn cheap I could've put safety valves in t' engine; this would never've happened."

"Damn you, Smeaton," said Clymo, "you don't have to deal with the viscount. You don't know what it's like. Anyway, we've got to drain the mine, save those men."

"There's no hope for t' men," Smeaton said. "You can't bail the Atlantic Ocean with buckets, you damn fool. Even King Canute himself couldn't help. We must save t' engine while we can. It's a thing of beauty. At least next time we can pump out t' mine and save t' men. Get fresh water, to hell with salt water, you'll ruin everything, and then what will your precious viscount say?"

"At least we can throw the sea water on the burning timbers," said Clymo and then called out, "You men carry on, but be careful where you throw it, mind the engine."

"It's on your head, Clymo," said Smeaton, waving his arms in the air. "I've made my position clear. You'll find out I'm right, when the smoke clears." He turned and looked back towards the burning engine house. "Right, when t' furnace cools off, happen I can reduce the steam pressure, get some valves open, best I can. But I need those big spanners. Jemmy, we didn't get the spanners. Where's that boy got to? Ah, there you are. Jemmy, get back to St. Just and fetch those spanners as fast as you can drive."

Jemmy had appeared from behind the engine house where he had been helping direct the chain of bucket handlers. "Right you are, Mr. Smeaton. Oi'll do my best, but the old cob is wore out. 'Ow do Oi know what kind to get?"

"Use your whip, or get another horse," said Smeaton. "Here, I'll give you a note. I left the money in the cart. Give it to the ironmonger, this says exactly what we need. Now hurry." Jemmy put the note in his pocket and ran off to the stable.

Addis Penwarden could not be found to give the orders. But there was no argument from Wheal Hykka's ostler, who was caught up in the emergency and quickly got a fresh horse harnessed to the cart. Jemmy set off up the rocky track back towards St. Just at a rapid trot. He had to swerve sharply to avoid a pony and cart that was coming in to the mine at the same time. "Look out man! You nearly knocked us off the road," he shouted, but kept going. As he passed he recognized the Reverend Perry. What on earth was he doing here? He could not have chosen a worse time for a pastoral visit.

Perry was overwhelmed by the chaotic scene that he had stumbled upon. But his mission was urgent too. A distraught Lizzie had got hold of him at the chapel in Pendeen and told him that the Penwardens' beloved little Jennifer was deathly poorly. She pleaded with him to drive to Wheal Hykka and take a message to her husband. Only Addis would know what to do, whom to send to for help. Perhaps one of his important acquaintances could send a doctor. Perry hurried on his way to the counting house, not stopping to satisfy his curiosity about the fire at the engine house as he passed. He rushed in through the door without knocking, but no one was inside. They must have all left to help put out the fire. He came out again and caught sight of Clymo with a group of bustling men by the engine house. He hailed him.

"Mr. Clymo, where's Captain Penwarden? I must talk to him, now."

"He's busy, man. Can't you see we're dealing with a disaster? The engine house is on fire, men burned. An explosion has flooded the shaft, men drownded. Penwarden is in the thick of it; he's indispensable. You'll just have to wait. Maybe you'll see him at chapel next Sunday. He'll have plenty to pray about."

"What I have to say to Mr. Penwarden, and only him, can't wait. Don't stand there arguing. Fetch him right away."

Clymo registered the look on Perry's face and ordered a boy to get Penwarden. "Tell Cap'n he needs to get here, fast as he can. Mr. Perry has to speak to him." The boy left and quickly returned with a sweating and panting Penwarden.

"What's up, Mr. Perry?" said Penwarden. "Can't it wait? Can't you see I'm fierce busy?"

"I'm afraid not," Perry replied. "I have bad news for you. Lizzie sent me. She couldn't come herself. Your little Jennifer is mortally sick. There's nothing anyone in Pendeen can do for the poor little mite. Unless a proper doctor takes care of her right away, you will lose her. I am deeply sorry."

Penwarden gasped, his face ashen. "Good God!" he exclaimed.

"I indeed hope so," said Perry. "I pray that our Lord will be good to you and yours. I fear that nothing less than a miracle will do."

Chapter Fifty-four

Help

It was late in the morning two days later before an exhausted Joseph Clymo reached Lanhydrock, where he now sat in the entrance hall of the big house impatiently waiting for an audience with the viscount. At his suggestion, Addis Penwarden had ordered urgent messages addressed to Viscount Dunbargan to be sent by homing pigeons. They told the viscount briefly about the mine disaster and also begged him to send his personal doctor from Bodmin to attend to the Penwardens' sick child and try to save her life. Two pigeons were sent carrying identical messages in case one was blown off course or killed by a hawk.

They anxiously waited for a response, but nothing came.

As the afternoon drew on, Penwarden could endure waiting no longer and entreated the reluctant Clymo to deliver a message personally on horseback. It was a long, arduous and dangerous journey. His pistols in his saddlebag were loaded and primed. The day was hot; his horse was soon sweating and panting.

Clymo pressed ahead, galloping long stretches and changing horses at inns along the way. How would the viscount take the news? Clymo stayed in the saddle until he could no longer stop himself from dozing off and had to snatch a few hours sleep and rest his aching thighs. He was wakened at dawn and ate a quick breakfast before saddling up again. He would have preferred to sleep longer, but he had to get to Lanhydrock. Speed could be the difference between life and death.

When he reached his destination without mishap, he went in through the kitchen entrance and refreshed himself with a mug of cold water and a cold sausage from the cook. She told the butler of his arrival and his urgent need to see the viscount, who fortunately was at home. A footman was detailed to take Clymo up to the hall and announce him. The footman found the viscount in the library, but was sent packing with peremptory instructions for Clymo to wait until his lordship, who was otherwise engaged, would be prepared to see him in due course.

Clymo speculated that the books in the library were not engaging the viscount's attention and hoped that his employer's characteristic impatience would not keep him diverted for long. After some minutes they heard voices from the library raised in anger, the viscount's and a woman's. Sounded like her ladyship. Clymo glanced at the footman who said nothing and remained discreetly impassive. Then the bell in the butler's pantry sounded. The footman answered the summons and went into the library.

The viscount was standing with his back to the empty fireplace, a goblet of port within reach on the mantelpiece. Her ladyship was over by the windows looking at the flower gardens outside. She did not turn at the interruption. Dunbargan ordered the footman to send Clymo into the room.

"What the hell are you doing here, Clymo?" demanded the viscount. "I thought you were supposed to be at Wheal Hykka, working. Well, not proper work, lolling about supervising I expect, you lazy bugger. Did you at least bring me news of profits, I hope? Or do I have to wait until the next boring meeting with those adventurers?"

"No sir, well yes sir, not exactly any accounts, sir. That will be after quarter day," said Clymo, nervous now that the anticipated moment of giving the news had come. He shifted from one foot to another.

"No, yes, what do you mean? Did you get anything useful done in that godforsaken hole? Is the engine running? Pump installed? Production up? Exactly why are you back so soon?"

"W-well sir, it's like this. Not all the news is good."

"Don't come to me sniveling with bad news, Clymo. I won't stand for it. Cut to the chase now, out with it, whatever it is."

"Sir, there's been an accident, at Wheal Hykka, couple of days ago. Happened in the new engine house, and down the mine, in the new shaft. Captain Penwarden is doing his best, but it's pretty bad. Men killed, some burned, some drowned."

The viscount went red in the face, then purple. "How much is this going to cost me? What's happened to production? Whose fault was it? Someone is going to have to be punished."

"There was a fire in the engine house. Then somehow there was an explosion down the new shaft. Seems the powder store down below was set off. Blew a hole in the wall of the tunnel, the sea rushed in. Some of the miners were trapped. They couldn't get them out, most drownded."

At the news Elianor turned from her stance near the window. She snapped open a fan and held it in front of her face. Clymo saw that her eyes were troubled. She turned towards the window again. She did not speak. The viscount turned away and faced the fireplace. He slapped the mantelpiece with a thwack.

"Was the engine damaged?" he shouted. "This kind of thing is not supposed to happen. Where was that opinionated ass Smeaton? He was supposed to see nothing went wrong. He's the expert, costs enough to hire him. Why didn't he see to things the way he was paid to? Why didn't you keep me informed sooner?"

"We did try, sir," said Clymo, taking a kerchief from his pocket and mopping his forehead. "We sent messages by carrier pigeon a couple of days ago."

"Oh, that must have been the one I saw. I was out walking in the park the other evening, looking for pheasants. Saw a pigeon circling over the stables. Took a pot shot, winged it in one. Not worth giving it to cook, scraggly little thing. Wrung its neck and fed it to the cats. Thought I noticed something odd attached to its leg. But don't try and put me off the track, Clymo, you sly fox. What does that pompous braggart Smeaton have to say for himself? I'll make him pay."

"Begging your pardon, sir," said Clymo softly, "but Mr. Smeaton said that he wasn't permitted to make the proper safety arrangements, on account of the venturers not letting him spend anything on escape valves and guards and such. Said they were to blame."

"Arrant nonsense," said Dunbargan, "none of those fools knew what they were talking about. I'll have his guts for garters if he dares to try and drag me into it. Stuck-up ass. Send for Smeaton and Penwarden immediately. They'd better be prepared to explain themselves."

"If you don't mind me saying so, sir," said Clymo, "you may be better off for a few days leaving them down there to get the situation cleaned up, try and get production going again at full rate. We need to keep sending tin to market."

The viscountess turned again from the window, her face drawn and pale. Clymo could not help noticing that she was wearing a voluminous dress; her usually elegant figure was less slender than normal. Perhaps that explained why she had stayed facing the window. She was indeed angry, perhaps now more than before. "Good grief! What happened to those poor men, Mr. Clymo? Were there survivors? Are they badly hurt? Who is taking care of them? What about their families?"

"Oh, be quiet, Elianor," said the viscount. "Don't go all sentimental on us, for God's sake. Leave this to me, it's men's work. Penwarden will just have to find more miners, plenty where they came from, looking for work."

"I will not be quiet," said Lady Dunbargan, furious, her eyes flashing. "I refuse to be a party to such heartlessness. Is there anything we can do to help those poor people, Mr. Clymo?"

Clymo braced himself for a moment before responding. He would offend one or the other however he replied. He chose to speak from his heart. After all, he was clear why he had ridden so hard to deliver his message. "Well, your ladyship, now that you mention it, if you'd be willing, there is, if I might be so bold. There's no doctor near Pendeen, no surgeon. Perhaps if you could send the doctor from Bodmin, dress wounds, salve a few burns. I'd escort him, perhaps bring my daughter Morwenna to help out."

"No doubt that can be arranged," said Elianor. "Husband?" The viscount frowned, opened his lips as if to speak, appeared to think better of it and said nothing. Elianor glowered at him.

"There is one more thing," Clymo braved hesitantly, "having the doctor would be a godsend in more ways than one. Captain Penwarden's baby daughter is very poorly. The old nurse in Pendeen village has tried everything she knows, I'm told, and nothing works. There's nothing more she can do. Only a doctor can save the baby's life. She needs a miracle, with God's help. Penwarden is stricken with grief."

"Oh Dunbargan," cried Elianor, "you simply must help. Those poor people, the poor parents, they must be beside themselves. You must know how they feel, you are a father yourself."

The viscount appeared for a moment to soften. What if some tragedy befell young James, his son and heir? How would his own father deal with a situation like this? He straightened his shoulders. Enough, that damn woman is always interfering, making her opinions known. She must understand that I am master in this house.

"Those people should be made of sterner stuff," pronounced Dunbargan. "And that fellow Penwarden had better stick to his job. He's needed at the mine, clean up the mess he's got us all into, bringing in that ass Smeaton. He's got no time for his peasant brood, got to pay attention to his responsibilities. More babies where that one came from, I'll be bound. He's sailing close to the wind already, might be best to get rid of him," Dunbargan grumbled.

"Besides, I fancy I may've caught a bit of a chill out in the park the other day, bit damp for the time of year. That Bodmin quack is my doctor, and I may well need his attentions myself."

Chapter Fifty-five

Tragedy

The situation at Wheal Hykka had deteriorated by the time Joseph Clymo rode back there late on the following Monday. He had taken Morwenna with him, riding pinion since he did not want to ask permission to take another horse. Morwenna had a cool head in an emergency, and while she had no training as a nurse she had plenty of initiative and common sense. She could at least try to help take care of the injured, and possibly little Jennifer. Just before leaving, Morwenna dashed off a letter to Mary and Willy Bunt at Port Eliot, telling them the news of the baby's sickness, the dreadful events that had transpired at the mine, and their plans to go down west. Perhaps the Eliots would do something. After all, Port Eliot had an investment at stake.

By the time the Clymos got to Wheal Hykka the fire had been put out, but the superstructure of the engine house was a skeleton of charred joists and beams, stinking of smoke. The floor and the surrounding ground were scattered with ash and charred fragments of wood. The cylinder of the steam engine and the boiler were scorched black, but at first glance did not appear damaged beyond repair. There were not many people about, just a few men listlessly tidying up, looking distraught, sulky, grief-stricken. Two men and a boy in the carpenters shop were planing planks that looked to be about six foot long. Evidently there was no mining going on down the shafts. The whims were not working or bringing up kibbles loaded with ore; there were no bal maidens spalling and bucking the tin stuff to send to the smelters.

"It's awful quiet here, Dad," said Morwenna. "What's going on? Where's everybody? I don't like the feel of this."

"Just keep moving, my love," replied her father. "We'll go on to the count house, find Captain Penwarden; he'll know what's going on. There's nothing to worry about while he's in charge. The men trust him as well as respecting him."

They walked their horses to the stables, dismounted, and left them in charge of the ostler. They instructed him to leave them saddled in case they should need them again right away. They walked over to the count house but could not get in; the door was locked. Clymo knocked on the heavy door and called out. They heard someone moving about inside and demanding, "Who's there?" It was the chief clerk, who admitted them after Clymo announced his name. The clerk was alone.

"What's going on?" Clymo asked. "Where is everybody? Where's Captain Penwarden? Who's in charge?"

"Cap'n stayed 'ome, 'asn't come in yet. Sent young Jemmy with a message. 'E's stayin' with 'is missus today. Their little lass be really poorly. 'E's tryin' to find someone to tend 'er. Told me to set men to cleanin' up, them what's come in, that is."

"He should be here. He has no right to stay home. He needs to be here doing his duty," said Clymo. "Wheal Hykka needs him to be here, get the mine back in production. Where's Mr. Smeaton?"

"Smeaton went back up country. Said 'e 'ad to see about spares for that there steam engine. 'E's caused enough trouble with that bloody monster already, if you ask me. Don't need to cause no more. Us didn't 'ave no trouble when us just used 'orses an' mules; them buggers don't catch on fire. New-fangled contraptions put good men out of work, and women too. Now them kill our mates."

"You can't stand in the way of progress, my good man," said Clymo, "might as well make the best of it, that's what I say."

Morwenna was agitated. She interrupted her father before he could launch into a speech. "Dad, don't stop here yammering. Nothing you can do here. We'd better get along to the Penwardens' house. You need to see what the cap'n has to say. Perhaps I can help Lizzie with the baby."

"Hold on, Morwenna, we'll go in a minute. Now, you, tell me where the rest of the workers are? Why aren't they here?" The clerk looked away then spoke.

"Well zir, it be loike this. Reverend Perry arranged with the cap'n to move the bodies and them what was 'urt bad down to Pendeen, to the big room at the chapel. Oi 'eard tell the undertaker from Penzance be comin' tomorrow to get 'em ready. The carpenter 'ere be makin' coffins. Cheaper to borrow them what's kept at the church for poor people, that's what Oi say, but Cap'n Penwarden wouldn't 'ear of it. Said them deserved their own coffins, and the mine could pay for them. Proper wool shrouds too, can't use linen no more, 'tis against the law."

"What do you mean? Why are linen shrouds against the law? Why must you use wool?" demanded Morwenna. The chief clerk looked puzzled and shook his head. "Dunno, miss."

Joseph Clymo gestured impatiently to his daughter. "Nothing you can do about it, Morwenna. Anyroad, what's good for the wool trade is good for Port Eliot. Mr. Eliot might've had something to do with it in parliament. " He turned to the clerk. "When's the funeral?"

"Them's goin' to be buried Wednesday. Big funeral at the chapel, none at the church, all chapel people; 'ole village will be goin'."

"Big funeral? How many bodies? Wait, that doesn't explain it," persisted Clymo. "Why aren't the rest of them here at work? They just can't take off work whenever they feel like it. You make damn sure they don't get paid for this time."

"Well zir, Oi 'spect it 'as summat to do with the sermon Sunday."

"That Reverend Perry? What did he have to say?"

"Well, 'e said us 'ad to pay respect to the dead so them would be lifted up into 'eaven. If us didn't, nobody else would."

"Speaking for myself and my daughter," said Clymo, "we came back to Wheal Hykka to see what we could do to help. We have every intention of attending the funeral service; you can assure the tinners of that. I want you to send a message from me to Viscount Dunbargan and advise his lordship that I will take it upon myself to officially represent Lanhydrock as well."

"Aargh," said the clerk.

"Come, Morwenna," said Clymo, "we'll ride over to Pendeen. You see what you can do to help Mrs. Penwarden and I'll speak to the captain and get the mine back to work."

"In a minute, Dad," said Morwenna. "Tell me, how many men were hurt, how badly, how many killed? How are the families taking it?"

"Two men were burned to death, miss, young Trethewey and an oiler in the engine house," the chief clerk replied. "Six men were drownded down the shaft, and one boy. 'Twas two tributers and their pares. Some were saved, I dunno 'ow many. Two were scalded, four 'ave trouble breathin', four more 'ave broken bones and bad cuts an' bruises from rock falls from the explosion."

"And their families?" persisted Morwenna.

"There's not much them can do about it, is there Miss? Give the dead a good sendoff, mend the others as best they can and get over it. Trust in God and try to get by without 'em. 'Spect them'll do all right, in toime. Us Cornish be sturdy folk, used to gettin' up after a setback."

Morwenna wheeled around and strode to their horse. Clymo followed and they headed for Pendeen. Joseph Clymo dismounted upon their arrival at the Penwarden house and helped Morwenna jump down. They were greeted by the two boys, who were outside in the garden where they had been sent to pick caterpillars off the cabbages and stay out of the way of the grownups. The boys were glad to earn a copper to take care of the horses. The Clymos knocked on the back door and went into the kitchen. They walked in on a small group standing around a cradle on the table, looks of concern on their faces. The village nurse was speaking in hushed tones. There was a sour smell in the room, the stink of the bloody flux. Addis Penwarden turned as he heard them come in.

"Clymo! You've come in the nick of time. Did you bring the doctor with ye? When will 'e be 'ere? The old crone says 'er cannot do more. Little Jennifer is failin' fast."

"Oh Mr. Clymo, Oi'm so relieved to see you. And this must be Morwenna, good of you to come too," said Lizzie, giving them each a warm hug. "Us was prayin' you'd get 'ere soon, before it's too late."

Morwenna looked down at the floor, unable to meet their troubled searching glances. She covered her nose with a kerchief, wondered whether this was what death smelled like. Joseph Clymo took off his hat, ran his fingers through his hair, took a deep breath. "I'm afraid the doctor couldn't come," he said.

The other man in the group looked up aghast. It was the Reverend Perry. "What do you mean, he couldn't come? This is a matter of life and death. It is a doctor's God given calling, to save lives."

"He actually wasn't notified. It seems another patient needed his attention, one of his own, of long standing with the Trenance family, a generation or two. It was thought impossible for him to neglect his own patient for several days to come to Pendeen."

"But surely he would've done whatever the viscount asked of him," said Addis Penwarden, incredulous. "Nobody turns down a powerful man like 'im. An' you rode all that way to ask 'is lordship special."

"Who was this patient?" demanded Lizzie. "Who could be more in need than dear little Jenny, lying sufferin' at death's door."

"Well, I didn't exactly talk to the doctor myself," said Clymo.

"Oh come on, Dad," said Morwenna, stamping her foot. "It was Viscount Dunbargan himself; thought he had a chill coming on. That's what you told me. That man is spoiled and selfish, he's despicable. Never stops until he gets what he wants for himself."

"Hush girl, don't speak ill of your betters," Clymo scolded.

"With all due respect, Mr. Clymo," said Reverend Perry, "sometimes I wonder if those who consider themselves our betters truly are, in the eyes of our Lord."

"You don't know the half of it," said Morwenna, glowering.

Addis Penwarden could contain himself no longer. He rushed at Joseph Clymo, shook him by the shoulders like a rat, and reared back to punch him in the face. Perry pulled Penwarden off before he could strike. Morwenna with a cry placed herself between the struggling men. "Stop! You'll only end up in trouble yourself, Cap'n."

Breathlessly Perry said, "Don't be a fool, man. Control yourself. There are better ways of dealing with this." Clymo smoothed his jacket, stepped back, and sat down in a kitchen chair. Lizzie got a wet rag and dabbed Clymo's brow.

"Oi lost my temper, Mr. Clymo," said Addis, panting. "Oi don't quoite know what came over me, but Oi'm really angry, 'ave been for days, 'ardly slept a wink. All of those men killed, badly 'urt, a boy dead, buildings damaged. It was a terrible sight to see, and me in charge. An' Oi was countin' on you to 'elp them an' save little Jenny. Now there bain't nothin' us can do. Couldn't you 'ave really talked to the viscount, persuaded 'im loike, just made 'im see 'ow our fambly matters to us, our neighbors? But Oi s'pose oi'm only a tinner in 'is eyes though, plenty more where us come from."

"I'll do what I can to help, Lizzie," said Morwenna. She turned, "Come on, let's try and get the little mite to sup something from a spoon, give her a nice warm bath, freshen 'er up a bit, help her feel a bit better."

"Won't do no good, missy," said the old nurse, "but no 'arm tryin'."

Lizzie was in tears. "Just leave 'er be, nothin' will 'elp."

"I will ask the Lord for his mercy," said Perry, "and if needs must, to bring her safely into His kingdom, where she will be happier than she has been on this sorrowful earth. Will you be staying for the funeral in the village on Wednesday, Mr. Clymo?."

"I will indeed, Mr. Perry," said Clymo, "and I will be representing Lanhydrock."

"What, couldn't 'is jumped-up lordship bother to come hisself?" asked Lizzie, tears welling into her eyes.

"Now my dear, you must calm yourself," said Perry. "You shouldn't expect a man in his lordship's position to come himself. After all, he says he's poorly enough to keep his doctor nearby."

"Well Oi would," said Addis belligerently, "all those men killed and 'urt, and a little boy, for no good reason. A proper doctor could 'elp some of them get better, support their famblies. And Mr. Smeaton said that if the viscount 'ad agreed to spend the money on safety measures, none of those lives need've been lost. If Oi 'ad 'im in front of me, Oi'd punch 'im in the jaw same as you, Mr. Clymo, so 'elp me."

"Mr. Smeaton is only making trouble, saying things like that," said Clymo. "Keep such talk to yourself. It would only stir the men up. There's nothing we can do about it now. Mining is dangerous work, and that should be an end of it."

Morwenna looked at her father in alarm but said nothing.

"There are those who might disagree with you, Mr. Clymo," said Reverend Perry, angry, "strongly disagree with you. There are things that can be done, when someone cares enough. I am gratified that you will attend the funeral. You weren't here to hear me preach on Sunday, but

I've been thinking a lot about it since. I don't know how I could have been so restrained in the circumstances."

"I trust you will remain restrained, Mr. Perry," said Clymo. "It would be for the best. It would be folly to arouse feelings further."

"You may be surprised at what I will have to say in my sermon at the funeral, sir, and no one will stop me. You have come representing Lanhydrock. By the time you leave, I trust you will represent the Cornish tin miners and their families as well. Now, I must leave and comfort the injured, and see to it that the coffins will be ready to bury the dead.

Reverend Perry turned to go. The others said nothing in response to his outburst. What could they say that would make any difference?

The preacher had not finished. "You, Mr. Clymo, no doubt wish to return to Wheal Hykka and to seeing to business for the viscount," he concluded dryly.

Chapter Fifty-six

Funeral

The little chapel at Pendeen was packed. A few tethered horses and some dogs milled about the yard outside. It was a clear summer day and birds sang and darted amongst the wind-stunted trees. The entire village, men, women and children, as well as neighbors from the mining and fishing villages and farms in the surrounding countryside, had turned out in their Sunday best for the funeral service. They were mourning the dead and condoling survivors and the wounded. But there also could be sensed among them a fear that their own turns might come next. The men supported their families by earning meager livings in occupations that might at any unexpected moment destroy them through nature's counter-attack from the land or the sea, whose treasures they plundered to shelter themselves from poverty while they enriched their betters.

Six tinners had carried each plain pine coffin of their dead comrades in slow procession to the front of the chapel and laid them in a row beneath the simple stained glass window. The boy's coffin was short; it needed only four bearers. Sunrays through the window painted the coffins in blues, reds and greens. Some women laid wreaths of wildflowers and branches of twisted hawthorn picked from the windswept hedges of the village. Two young men brought up the rear with one tiny coffin that they reverently laid on a stool in front of the others. In it lay the precious body of baby Jennifer Penwarden.

Lizzie, Addis, Morwenna and their dearest friends had given little Jennifer all the loving care they could. Lizzie had held the baby in her arms and walked endlessly up and down trying to soothe her to sleep. She had fed her at her breast, but Jenny just cried louder, drawing up her little legs in pain and vomiting up what she had tried to take in. After an exhausted Lizzie had lain down to snatch a few minutes sleep, Morwenna took over the baby's care, cradling the mite in her arms. She had bathed little Jenny's forehead with a cool, damp cloth. She had brought a flask of gin with her from the viscount's private stock, having learned where he kept it during their close relationship. Putting a few drops on the tip of her finger she had given it to the baby to suck, but not even that had stilled her.

Addis had paced helplessly, distraught with grief but powerless to help with the work that the women kept to themselves. Reverend Perry had prayed fervently for divine intervention to cure her sickness and save her life. Sadly, without knowledge and skill none of their efforts had been enough to save Jennifer from the bloody flux, dysentery, one of the worst of the terrible diseases that ravaged so many babies in these parts. The reverend's prayer had turned reluctantly to the salvation of her soul.

On the day of the funeral, places in the front rows of the chapel had been saved for the bereaved families, including the Penwardens and their surviving boys, and also for Morwenna and Joseph Clymo representing Viscount Dunbargan and his lady. The harmonium was playing as the mourners and the choir reverently took their places. Addis had given up singing in the choir when they moved from Gwennap, since his new responsibilities left little time to attend rehearsals. Today he could not have faced the congregation anyway. He preferred to be with Lizzie and the boys and provide them with what comfort he could, although if truth be told, it was he who was most in need of comfort.

Reverend Perry stood before them in his black robe on the dais at the front of the chapel. His back was towards the congregation as he faced the window looking out. Dust motes were dancing in the sunbeam that seemed focused on the smallest coffin. In his mind's eye he saw angels come to carry Jennifer's soul to heaven. He announced the first hymn. The congregation joined with the choir with what little spirit they could summon, their voices growing louder as they sang.

My days are few, O fail not,
With thine immortal power,
To hold me that I quail not
In death's most fearful hour:
That I might fight befriended
And see in my last strife
To me thine arms extended
Upon the cross of life.

The congregation sat and the preacher bade them bow their heads in prayer. The chapel was filled with the soft sounds of shuffling feet and the shifting of bodies. Perry watched his congregation settle into silence. The morning sun streaming through the windows lighted their persons, but the light could not lift the gloom in their hearts.

The preacher had been deeply moved by the tragedies that had befallen the village and the Penwardens, the explosion, the drowning, the sickness. He had given a great deal of thought to the funeral service and to comforting and uplifting his flock. Like his mentor John Wesley and many of his colleagues in dissent, there was much that Reverend Perry admired in the 1662 Book of Common Prayer of the Church of England.

Of course, Reverend Perry mused, the Cornish were a stubborn and independent lot. They had rebelled against the imposition of that English prayer book, thousands killed in a lost cause. The score or so killed or injured at Wheal Hykka the other day were comparatively few. You would think they had learnt that opposing authority was not worth it. Not Cornishmen. How would he speak to his people now? What message would he give them? Should he counsel patient suffering, relying on God's love to assuage their grief over time? Or should he urge them to do something to prevent or at least reduce the misfortunes that constantly beset their lives?

Perry doubted that the anger that wrestled in his heart with grief was a good Christian emotion. He must strive to control it. John Wesley, however, taught that Christian ministers, while leading their flocks to a spiritual life, should deal with the terrible matters of social concern in a practical way, prisons, poverty, drunkenness, ignorance and sickness. But Wesley urged respect for authority, for the maintenance of public order. He held no truck with revolution, like some of the hotheads in other countries.

Reverend Perry decided that early in the service he would calm himself and comfort his people with the Book of Common Prayer. Men had fought over this book. Its words aroused strong emotions, but they represented a tradition, continuity, and their orderliness would serve his purpose. There would be time enough for strong words when he preached his sermon in his own words. He read now from the Order for the Burial of the Dead. His voice caught in his throat as he read.

I am the resurrection and the life, saith the Lord: he that believeth in me, though he were dead, yet shall he live: and whosoever liveth and believeth in me, shall never die. I know that my redeemer liveth, and that he shall stand at the latter day upon the earth: and though this body be destroyed, yet shall I see God.

Joseph Clymo found himself strangely moved by feelings of compassion for the grieving families. He had come back to Pendeen to attend the service more from a formal sense of duty and propriety than from pity or shared emotion. Indeed, he had come as the representative of the man whose wealth was created by common people, whose only interest was in the money he could make from their labors, but who had nothing in common with their lives.

Naturally, those who were destined to rule had to give orders to keep order, and had to keep themselves apart and never get familiar. But could they perhaps act in humanitarian ways without losing authority? Could he, Joseph Clymo, influence the viscount to the better? For one thing, maybe Penwarden and Smeaton were right; they should do something to make mining safer. No point, after all, in squandering laborers who had become skilled in their craft. His attention was drawn back to the present as the preacher read from the Burial of a Child.

O merciful Father, whose face the angels of thy little ones do always behold in heaven; Grant us steadfastly to believe that this thy child hath been taken into the safe keeping of thine eternal love.

Out of the corners of his eyes Joseph Clymo became aware of Addis Penwarden reaching across their two boys sitting between them to place his hand on his wife's back. He saw that Lizzie could not be comforted; her shoulders shook as she wept silently. He could only imagine the pain she must feel to have given birth, nourished and loved a child, only to lose her to a disease from which she might have been cured. Clymo felt a pricking in his eyes. He turned his attention to his feet.

The preacher asked them to stand and join together with him in saying the Twenty-third Psalm. As they spoke the words they knew by heart, many in the congregation wept.

He restoreth my soul . . . Yea, though I walk through the valley of the shadow of death, I will fear no evil, for thou art with me; thy rod and thy staff, they comfort me.

As he continued to pray for them, the preacher turned away from the book and spoke from his heart. He asked their Lord to comfort them in their loss, to give them patience in their grief, and to keep them from further harm. Then he urged their Savior to show them the way to maintain and deepen their trust and faith in Him, and to renew their covenant with their God. But he also prayed, with a fervor that they had not heard before, that they would join together in supporting and helping each other. They joined him in loud amens.

Addis listened expectantly when the time came for the Reverend Perry to preach his sermon. The preacher began with more words of comfort for the bereaved and of eulogy for the loved ones they had lost, although there was not much to say about the abbreviated lives of these simple people. Blessedly he said little of baby Jennifer; there had been enough weeping already in their own home.

Reverend Perry's voice took on the resonance, and the words took on the power that Addis had anticipated, with no little apprehension as well. He had been through this before. He was now unable to keep out of his mind that other occasion back at Gwennap when the Reverend had preached at the funeral of Addis' beloved younger brother Jedson, after he was killed in the accident down the Poldice mine.

Addis thought he had got over that grief; it was more than two years ago that there had been an explosion and a rock fall and his brother had fallen climbing down the ladder, buried by tons of rock and crushed to death. Addis had tried to bury the terrible memories and for some months now had succeeded. So much in his life had changed, so many new things to learn, so many people and actions to be responsible for. But now the memories rushed back with a vividness that brought more tears. He had sent his brother up to the dry for powder. He had warned him to be careful; the young fool had drunk cider with his croust, his pasty, must have gone to his head. Then he had heard the explosion. Addis had ignored the warnings he sensed, and he had killed his brother.

"My brothers and sisters in Our Lord," said Reverend Perry, "you in this village have suffered terrible losses. Here in our chapel today we are gathered together to offer each other comfort in our grief, but also much more. We have prayed for the souls of the departed and for the healing of those who were grievously hurt. But I want you to draw strength and with me to look forward. What can we gain from our loss? Can our grief inspire loving action?

"I urge that we sitting in this chapel today enter into a covenant blessed by God to befriend each other in a profound way. John Wesley has taught us of the importance of our personal faith, but he has also taught us that our faith must show us how to take good works into our community in practical ways. We must reach outside our own families, and ourselves to our neighbors and our fellow workers. Mr. Wesley has written that: *"The gospel of Christ knows of no religion but social; no holiness but social holiness."*

Joseph Clymo was discomfited. He glanced sideways at Morwenna, but she was staring straight ahead at the pulpit, enraptured by the words of the preacher.

Clymo had grown to like Reverend Perry, admiring his intelligence, his sincerity, and some of his ideas. Perry fought strongly against the evils of drink, and he had certainly turned Willy Bunt from the reckless behavior that had been destroying his promise. But Perry was liable to go too far. What was the preacher up to now?

"We must tend each other when we are sick; visit each other when we are lonely; feed each other when we are starving; give alms to each other when we are poor. Many of the rich are generous in their charity, when they are aware of the need, and when they sympathize with the plight of those in need. But we cannot depend upon occasional alms such as these. It is we who know what ails our neighbors, and we who are on hand to befriend them. Mr. Wesley has shown us how to organize to bring others to our Savior, how to spread the good news, how to support each other in community, and indeed how to build chapels such as this for our worship together. In that same spirit and with those same methods we can imbue our entire community with social holiness.

"And we must do more. These deaths and injuries at the mine occurred because the owners of the mine did not care sufficiently for the miners and their families to make their work safer. Yes, we all know that mining is dangerous work. But steps can be taken to make that work safer.

"We understand that owners have the right to profit; *mes yma an gwir dhe dus val ma na vydhons ledhys na pystigys pan wrons an ober kales dhe wul an budh na;* but miners have the right not to be killed or hurt when they do the hard work that makes that profit. The owners are willing to put in machines that take work away from men and that also kill men. *Res yw dhyn gul gorholeth dhe'n berghennow i dhe spena ynwedh rann a'ga budh may fydh salwa an jynnow ha'n lavur.* We must demand of the owners that they also spend part of their profit on making the machines and the work safer."

Joseph Clymo pricked up his ears. What was the preacher saying? He could not understand the words, but the villagers could. They still spoke Cornish in their everyday lives, in their homes, at the mines. Was the preacher speaking sedition? As the owners' representative Clymo must warn Reverend Perry to be more discreet, less confrontational. If he made trouble he would get into trouble.

Lizzie grew nervous. She had heard the preacher say things something like this before, but he had not gone as far then as he was going now. What about Addis? What about their family? When Addis was just a tributer he was persuaded by the preacher's words, at least in part, especially when his brother was killed. But now he was the mine captain. He was the owners' representative. It was his job to make the mines profitable, and their own livelihood depended on it. She didn't want to go back to living in a tiny cottage, having nobody to help in the garden, walking everywhere, not having a horse and cart.

Addis Penwarden was in a quandary. Whose side was he on? He wanted the mines made safer as much as any man, he had said so, again and again. But Clymo and John Williams had advised him to bide his time. When he eventually made Wheal Hykka more profitable and repaid more of the huge investment the owners had made, then he could make his case again.

He had tried to pave the way at the last cost book meeting, but the viscount had stormed at him, and he felt he had overstepped his bounds and set his cause back. He had tried his best. He had to feed his own family. He needed to get production up. John Smeaton's engine would help, once it was repaired. He could do no more for now. Anyway, he had his own grief to deal with. It was easy for the preacher to talk; he didn't have to support a family, or deal with the viscount. He turned his attention back to the pulpit.

"Perhaps in time we should press that more of our rightful needs should be met. You are bidding against each other for work. That is wrong. One eats while another starves. If you band together you can assure just wages for all. Tin cannot be wrested from the earth without your hands. And is it right that children work down the mine, that our women carry great burdens in addition to raising their families? The work of men should support the needs of families."

There was a murmuring in the congregation, people looking at each other, wondering what others were thinking.

"I can see that some of you are not comfortable with what I am saying," continued the preacher. "You are thinking that the owners are too powerful to take any notice of what we say, that we might be punished for expressing such thoughts, that it is not lawful, that we should keep in our appointed places.

"Indeed, Mr. Wesley believes that the authority of the king is derived from God, and it is our divine duty to obey his government. But he also believes that there are lawful ways in which the poor or downtrodden can fight for their betterment. And I promise you that, while none of us alone has the power to overcome oppression, all of us together can achieve the conditions that allow us happier and more fulfilling lives."

Clymo started in his seat. There he goes again challenging the accepted order of things, no matter how you looked at it. Why had the preacher lapsed into Cornish earlier if not because he did not want the owners' representative to understand what he was saying? Clymo had to admit that he had sympathy with much of what Mr. Perry advocated, and he knew Morwenna did. But there were limits and if he allowed the preacher to go too far it could cost him his own job.

Reverend Perry continued his sermon in English and while what he said was not entirely welcome it was hardly revolutionary. "I have one more thing to say, and then I will spare you to leave this place and pick up the pieces of your lives. To improve your lot, you and yours must be educated. You must read and write, study the Good Book, do sums, gain understanding; in short, become more worthy members of society, gain the respect of all men. I intend to start a school for the village here in this building, with your help. Some of you will be teachers. I want you to send your children, and come yourselves when you can.

"Now in closing, I pray that we may fight befriended, and join each and every one in strife, with our Savior's arms extended, to give all a better life. Amen."

He sat. The congregation echoed his amen and then sat in silence. After a few moments he announced the final hymn. He was at the door to greet them as they filed out at the end. Their faces showed wonder and a tinge of hope mingled with their grief, except for the Clymos and the Penwardens, who showed concern, as well.

Addis Penwarden paused as he shook the preacher's hand. "Thank you from the bottom of my heart, Mr. Perry, from me and Lizzie," he said quietly. "You mean much to my fambly, to Pendeen, to Wheal Hykka. You are a leader, you make us think. I must become a better leader to help you. I know Oi need education. Will you 'elp us? Oi can't wait for your school, Oi needs 'er d'rec'ly."

"I will do all I can, Cap'n," said Reverend Perry. "We will start as soon as can. Let's start with correcting your English, your grammar, your pronunciation, every time we are together. We'll do it quietly, privately, you need not fear embarrassment."

"Thank 'ee, Reverend, thank 'ee," said Addis, putting his hand on the preacher's shoulder. "Us'll do it, gradual like; people will listen to what Oi say, take notice." Addis smiled through tears as he led his little family, a tearful Lizzie and just two children, to their nearby home in Pendeen.

Meanwhile at Lanhydrock the viscount was also concerned. What was going on at that damned mine? Was it back in full production yet? His need for ready money was nearing urgent. The king had demanded full and immediate payment for his viscountcy, and he had not yet rewarded the powerful Earl of Bute for his part in making the title possible. Bute was no longer even being civil when their paths crossed.

Why had that idle fellow Clymo not given him more details? Perhaps he should consult Bolitho. He would know what to do. He felt it was high time to take strong measures. Show those bloody tinners who was in charge. It was not fair. Damned Smeaton engines, damned tinners, and more recently damned Elianor! All he asked from life was a little pleasure and the financial freedom to do whatever he wanted when he traveled to London. Why else did he pay Clymo, if not to make it possible? What good was a wife who refused him her bed by night and carped at him by day?

Chapter Fifty-seven

Patron

Later that summer Catherine received a letter from Joshua Reynolds, written from London. He had been extremely busy and planned at the end of the Season to leave Town for a few weeks and take the opportunity to visit clients in Cornwall and renew his Westcountry connections. He begged the favor of staying with his patrons the Eliots at Port Eliot and, if possible, visiting with Edward's widowed mother, his old friend Harriot Hamilton. She was previously married to the late Richard Eliot.

As a young man growing up in Plympton, Reynolds had been apprenticed at the age of seventeen to the well-known portrait painter Thomas Hudson of Exeter, studying at his studio in London. He quickly became one of the artist's assistants, painting in landscape backgrounds and draperies while the great man concentrated on faces. The arrangement had not gone to their mutual satisfaction. Reynolds left and took what he had learned with him, and then after his father died, had set up his own studio at Plymouth Dock. There he made the acquaintance of officers at the naval base and many of the Cornish gentry, who would become important to his career.

The Eliots were delighted to welcome Reynolds, who had perfected the art not only of painting but also of developing and keeping up with his connections. He arrived in early August and was happy to learn that, as he had hoped, Mrs. Harriot Hamilton was also at Port Eliot.

It had been raining hard during the last stages of Reynolds' journey, and his traveling clothes were wet. After the butler showed him to his suite, he changed into dry clothes and settled in. Presently, Reynolds joined his hosts in the salon.

"Welcome to Port Eliot, Mr. Reynolds," said Catherine. "We are so pleased you could get away from London and visit us. We're looking forward to catching up with your news and the goings on in the capital of arts and culture."

Joshua Reynolds was slight of build, of modest height, with dark brown curls above a florid complexion. He spoke with traces of a rustic burr; his origins in Devonshire were readily deduced. He was of an amiable disposition, and there was no doubting his creative drive. A lifelong bachelor, he enjoyed conversation and the company of his wide circle of friends.

"Mr. Reynolds, how charming to see you again," said Harriot, still vivacious and youthful-looking in her late forties. "I suggested to Catherine that we meet in this room. I thought you might enjoy gazing once again upon the splendid portrait you did of my family."

"My dear lady, it is indeed a pleasure," Reynolds replied with a smile, "and not least because you appear as youthful and beautiful as the day I painted you." Harriot was not easily moved by flattery, but she nodded and smiled broadly at him.

"Mr. Eliot was very proud of that painting, standing there in the bosom of his family," she said. "I often rejoice that my marriage to him brought to Port Eliot the wherewithal to enjoy such excellent pleasures," she added with a twinkling eye, "although late in his life we did go through some rather diminishing circumstances."

"It was all in a good cause, Mater," said Edward. "You both enjoyed a prominent position in the Prince of Wales' household, but that is a way of life that comes at a high price, as our neighbors the Pitts also learned to their cost. Luxury among the royal family is expensive, but I observe that at least we Eliots have enjoyed lucrative places as a consequence."

The artist was not to be diverted from his blandishments. "I have no doubt," he said, smiling at Harriot, "that your royal favor stemmed considerably more from your beauty and charm, dear lady, than it did from your wealth."

Edward enjoyed having the famous artist as a visitor to his country house; he brought a touch of sophistication and urbanity. "Reynolds, my dear friend," he responded, aspiring to add his own contribution to the repartee, "You have become as much an artist as a diplomatist, as you have always been a diplomatist as an artist!"

Edward smiled in a self-congratulatory manner, pleased with what he considered his polished and amusing compliment. His smile turned to a frown as Catherine's blank look revealed that she did not share his assessment, perhaps saw it as derogatory, portraying the artist as a shallow flatterer. Their visitor ignored the gaffe and smiled.

"How pleased I am to see you again, Eliot," replied Reynolds, striding across the room to shake his hand. "I am relieved I cannot say you still look as youthful as you did when I painted you as a callow youth. But I see that the pure Cornish air has preserved you well despite the cares of office."

"And for my part, I am happy that my office has served you almost as well as it does his majesty," said Edward, smiling. "My Mr. Sedgwick tells me that he and his family are well pleased with the portrait you painted of him a year or two ago. I told him he is fortunate that you obliged him when you did; you are far too much in demand these days to trouble with the likes of him."

"I remind myself that the guineas of those in the professions are as welcome to my creditors as the guineas of those in the gentry," he said with a laugh. "While my commissions continue to grow with my reputation, I confess my ambition remains far from satisfied."

"Pray, husband, who is Mr. Sedgwick?" asked Catherine.

"A solicitor in London who now serves me at the Commission of Trade and Plantations," said Edward. "Sedgwick enjoys his position and had no objection to helping me do a favor then for my good friend, Reynolds, at least so he expressed. Tell me, how much do you extract from your fortunate clients these days?"

"I hardly like to speak about such mundane things," said Reynolds.

"Do tell," said Harriot. "More than you charged my late lamented husband so long ago, I'll be bound."

"I am consumed by curiosity myself," said Catherine, "and I also want to know how many paintings you produce. But first, you must need refreshment after your journey. Edward, do send for port, and Mr. Reynolds, pray sit down." Reynolds nodded to Catherine as he took a chair. He spoke to Harriot.

"Madam, I am eternally grateful to both of your husbands for encouraging me in my career. Mr. Eliot was one of my earliest and most prolific patrons. But it was my portrait of Captain Hamilton that was the first to achieve fashionable notice. As you remember, I had just left Plymouth Dock and set myself up in London. He was already a hero of the Royal Navy, but I painted him in the uniform of the Hungarian Hussars: those magnificent furs, fit for such a heroic and handsome adventurer."

"How could I resist him?" said Harriot, her eyes shining. "A handsome hero indeed, not to mention the son of an earl, old Abercorn. Ah, Captain the Honorable John Hamilton, Royal Navy. Mr. Eliot took me to the showing at your studio in London, and I'm afraid it was love at first sight, but love unrequited for many years, of course." She turned towards her son; "I adored your dear father, Edward; and, after all, that dreadful consumption had taken him from me for a whole year before I married Captain Hamilton, so propriety was observed."

Edward glanced at his mother with a fond look born of long familiarity with her playful nature.

"They were both charming men, dear lady, worthy of your hand," said Reynolds. "I was privileged to regard them both as good friends. It was a joy to paint Captain Hamilton a second time after your marriage, in his naval uniform. His drowning was such a tragedy, a loss for us all."

"The sea gave him to me, and then the sea took him away," said Harriot. She dabbed a lace-trimmed handkerchief to her eye. "I grieve the loss of two husbands, but I am blessed with my children, especially my son Edward, and with the gain of a beautiful daughter," she added, smiling at Catherine.

"We all have our crosses to bear, dear lady," said Reynolds, "but indeed we have blessings to count as well, including the acquaintanceship and affection of the friends we have met throughout our lives.

"I do look back fondly on those early days, so fruitful for me," he continued. "I gained a wealth of knowledge and many friends among the Royal Navy and the Cornish gentry: Lord Edgcumbe, Captain Keppel, Carews, Poles, St. Aubyns, Molesworths, Trenances, as well as, of course, Richard Eliot and Captain Hamilton. I would just wish for more royal patronage, but no doubt that will come in due time."

"That may be something I could help you with, Reynolds," said Edward. "What are friends for, after all? And a title would not come amiss. Clients would flock to you more eagerly than ever."

"Always thinking of others, my dear," said Catherine, "but it would be well to think more of your own preferment from time to time," she tossed in.

"Quite right, my dear," said Harriot, "I fancy myself as a dowager of some grandeur, Edward. You simply must see to it." She crossed her arms under her breast and grinned at Reynolds.

"All in good time," Edward said. "If one serves one's friends in all walks of life, someone will doubtless seek to return the favor. Just be patient."

"Silly boy, you certainly did not learn patience at your mother's knee," said Harriot.

"Nor does your wife consider patience a virtue," added Catherine.

"You were telling us about your early days at Plymouth Dock, Reynolds," said Edward, in an effort to divert the feminine chorus, "do tell more."

"This conversation brings back joyful memories as well as sad ones," said Reynolds. "You know, Captain Keppel was kind enough to take me with him on H.M.S. Centurion on his voyage to the Mediterranean. It was a voyage of discovery for me."

"You left us for some considerable time, Reynolds," said Edward. "I remember those were eventful years for me too; going down from Oxford, taking the Tour myself a little before you, losing my father and succeeding him, my mother remarrying."

"Come now, Edward," said Harriot, "you make it sound so glum. I recall you had a grand time on the Tour. Philip Stanhope was a pleasant companion, and when Lord Charlemont took you to France you met all manner of interesting people."

"Indeed, Mater," said Edward. "We went to Bordeaux and stayed at the Château de Brède with the Baron de Montesquieu the year before he died. Brilliant fellow. Thought himself an expert on our British constitution after spending a mere eighteen months living among us. Talked some sort of claptrap about the separation of powers. Couldn't have noticed that half the members of the government are related to each other and the other half spend much of their time in and out of each other's wives' bedrooms!"

"Oh Edward, really!" said Catherine, not amused. Edward looked rather crestfallen.

"Indeed, Eliot," continued Reynolds. "I was blessed to spend two years in Rome, time well spent. I found great inspiration among the Italian Mannerists, and I learned much about how diligent they were in their methods and how they achieved such depth of color, the pigments they used. I had met Canaletto during the years he spent in London and was especially impressed with his architectural landscapes; such detail, such accuracy. I visited him in Venice to find out more of his methods. What was his secret? Do you know he started his career as a theatrical scene painter?

"It was an invaluable experience. I learned not to depend upon one's own genius. If you have great talents, industry will never fail to improve them; if you have but moderate abilities, industry will go some distance in compensating for their deficiency."

"Talent and industry indeed may lead to achievement, especially if you possess other advantages. It all came right for you, Edward, when I married you," said Catherine with such a winning smile that Edward could not take amiss the underlying reference to the fortune she brought with her. "But as for you, Mr. Reynolds, I do believe you may have succeeded in changing the subject, and I shall not allow it. I insist you tell us the amount of your fee, and also the quantity of paintings you produce."

"You will have to speak up, my dear," said Reynolds. "Unfortunately one of the things I brought back from Rome is a touch of deafness."

"Then use your ear trumpet, my dear man," said Harriot. "You can't get away with that with either of us. We are not fools to be fobbed off so easily, and we demand to know."

"Ladies, you are terriers digging me out when I thought I had gone safely to earth. I surrender. I promise I will tell you in a few moments. But first let me finish my story about my Italian experience. In all modesty, what I learned I have been able to apply to my rather unusual style, and it's why my work is in gratifying demand."

"Really, Reynolds?" asked Edward. "You are extremely dexterous with the brush, and you paint a good likeness. But you imply there is much more to it. Do tell us, did you practice with the masters?"

"I did little painting, but a great deal of studying. I visited palaces and cathedrals; churches and monasteries; buildings where the great classical works of the old masters could be seen. I spent hours studying and observing them. You were fortunate, Mr. Eliot, to study the classics in literature. You can draw on the writings of the Greek and Roman poets and historians, leaders and lawyers, when you speak in the House or converse with your learned friends. This is what makes you and your kind civilized and eloquent gentlemen." Edward bowed his head appreciatively.

"So you see," the artist continued, "I felt the need to learn in the same way in the field of art. I gazed upon the faces and the forms, the landscapes, and the scenes of glory or of historical or religious significance. I memorized the compositions, how the figures were arranged, how they were enhanced by the background, by the light and shade."

"So much to keep in your head, Mr. Reynolds," said Harriot.

"I kept journals. It is a habit my father taught me. He was my schoolmaster as a boy, of course. I keep detailed journals to this day. I learn from studying methods I have used before and discarding or improving on them."

"How exactly have you been able to make use of your studies, Mr. Reynolds?" inquired Catherine, always the practical one. The artist put his ear trumpet in position, and asked her to repeat the question before he could respond.

"That is very interesting, Mrs. Eliot. You see, I came to realize that if English artists were ever to be recognized for their true worth, they not only had to master a painterly technique; they also had to treat their subjects in distinctive ways. English collectors buy subjects dealing with religion and ancient history from the Italians. What remained for us aspiring painters in England was to become portraitists. I dreamed of enhancing my portraits with the heroic scenes that I observed in Italy, using their methods of applying their wonderful pigments to achieve rich colors."

"How fascinating, Mr. Reynolds," said Catherine. "How did you achieve your dream?"

"My first success was with a portrait of Captain Keppel. It was my way of thanking him for introducing me to Italy. I painted him against a background of a stormy sea beneath dark lowering clouds with a watery sun shining through to illuminate the spot where he stood on the shore. I posed him like a statue of Apollo I had seen on my travels; very heroic, in the grand style. After all, invention, strictly speaking, is little more than a new combination of those images which have been previously gathered and deposited in the memory; nothing can come of nothing."

"A dramatic composition, I'm sure," said Harriot. "Now you have enthralled us quite enough. I see you have your little trumpet, so you have no more defenses. Satisfy our curiosity without delay: now that you are famous, how much injury do you do to your clients' purses?"

Reynolds smiled a little, and turned to Edward with a pleading look. Getting no respite from that quarter, he held out his glass to be refilled. He took a sip of port. He put down his glass on the candle stand beside his chair. He looked at Harriot and Catherine. "I must confess, ladies, that my generous clients grace me with a fee of eighty guineas for a full-length portrait. But I do believe that before long they will be obliged to pay a hundred. This war you know, prices go up. Costs a lot to keep an army in America, they tell me, let alone supporting Hanover. Surely, I can keep pace with the economic drift."

"At last, Mr. Reynolds," persisted Catherine, "although I can't see how the war would affect your supplies. Now tell us how many you produce?"

"You are asking me to delve into my memory," said Reynolds. "In my busiest year so far, I believe I was privileged to please one hundred and twenty clients, and that entailed some six hundred or more sittings."

"Good heavens, man," said Eliot, "that's sounds like more work than my most ambitious tenant farmer undertakes, and he doesn't have to spend his time flattering clients or using his imagination. And this year their sorry reward is a poor harvest; so much rain. Tell me, how do you manage to accomplish so much?"

"Perhaps that is a secret I should keep," said Reynolds. "It would not do for my rivals to learn the details of my methods. That fellow Gainsborough gives me enough trouble, with his advertisements for the demi-monde."

"Oh pish, Mr. Reynolds," said Harriot, "You are unrivalled. You are original, you have nothing to fear from the copyist. And, furthermore, you say that you wish to improve the regard in which English painters are held, so you must tell. How else will your compatriots learn and improve?"

"You are quite right, madam, as always," said Reynolds. "A mere copier of nature can never produce anything great, can never raise and enlarge the perceptions, or warm the heart of a spectator."

"Go on, Mr. Reynolds," Catherine said. "This is fascinating. I have heard that some artists make extensive use of an ingenious contrivance that produces an image for them to copy in every detail. It doesn't seem quite fair to me."

Reynolds raised his eyebrows. "Your intelligence knows no bounds, dear lady," he said. "You have learned of a secret I once kept to myself. You speak of the camera obscura. I discovered this from Canaletto. It is a darkened chamber with a pinhole in one wall through which light from the subject projects an image in reverse on a reduced scale onto the opposite inside wall. Vermeer used one as well; this explains the brilliant reality of his interiors."

"Why, dear Mr. Reynolds," said Harriot. "You are as cunning as you are creative. No wonder those who would emulate you never outdo you. But surely such a device is large and can only be used in your studio."

"There are more ways to use one's imagination than with canvass and pigment, Mrs. Hamilton. I persuaded a fine craftsman to make such a contrivance for me that folds up like a book and can be carried with me when I visit valued clients such as yourself.

"Unfortunately, many more observers see me at work and the secret is no longer mine."

"I have no doubt, Mr. Reynolds," said Harriot, "that while many may learn of your methods few can match your skills."

"What other secrets may we prize from you, Mr. Reynolds?" pressed Catherine. "Surely you have other methods that depend on the human hand."

"I have in my studio a man who is not only talented but practiced in the painting of landscapes, of backgrounds," said the artist. "I have another who is equally adept in the painting of fabrics, of dress, folds and textures and colors and shadows.

"Now, my dear ladies, that is the sum of my secrets, or at least those that I am prepared to divulge today."

Reynolds sipped his port and then continued.

"I, of course, do equally well, if not better, and I keep a close eye on all they do. Unlike the portrayal of faces, or indeed the eloquent composition of a great painting, their skills are not unique."

"Your likenesses are quite remarkable," said Catherine.

"It's a good deal more than that, Mrs. Eliot," said Reynolds, putting his fingertips together in a steeple. "Many an ordinary painter can represent a face. But it is not the eye, it is the mind that the painter of genius desires to address, to achieve his great design of speaking to the heart."

"I believe it is time for a worthy portrait of my husband, Mr. Reynolds," Catherine said. "He is a man not only of integrity and worth, but also one of accomplishment and position. He should be remembered by his family and friends for all time."

"I trust you would not look so intensely into my eyes that you found some deeply secreted fault, Reynolds," said Edward with a chuckle.

"Oh nonsense, Edward," said Harriot, "such false modesty is silly and does not become you. An excellent idea, my dear Catherine; it should have pride of place in the lower lobby, as our guests mount the broad stairs." Harriot smiled warmly at Catherine and was puzzled when her warmth was not reflected in Catherine's eyes and her smile was not returned. She looked down at the fan she was holding in her lap. Something was amiss.

Harriot turned back to the artist. "I have an idea, Mr. Reynolds. Indeed you are right, with this war going on and those dreadful taxes one must economize where one can. I shall commission you, but you must include his wife as well as my son in your portrait; they make such a handsome pair. I fear I shall afford considerably less than eighty guineas, and we can dispense with the ministrations of your costly assistants."

Catherine looked up and the women exchanged understanding glances.

"Mother, that is kind of you. I accept with delight," said Edward. "You do agree, Catherine my dear? Then it is settled."

Edward continued, "You know, Reynolds, a thought has come to me. You wish to further English painting; I have an idea that may assist you in accomplishing your goal." He paused.

For a moment Reynolds did not take the bait. He was contemplating how to do business with Harriot. He glanced at her with a mock scowl. "You drive a hard bargain, dear lady, one that may bear further discussion," he said. "But thank you, regardless, Mrs. Hamilton, it would be a privilege to paint your son and your daughter-in-law. Let me begin with sketches while I am here."

"Perhaps, Reynolds, you could learn something from our Cornish tinners, of all people. Hear me out," said Edward. "I have been informed that they are joining together to press us for better conditions, egged on by those damn Wesleyans. I don't like it, but it seems to be having effect. I have in mind some sort of organization that would encourage painters," said Edward, "provide a forum for discussion where they could learn to improve their skills, where they could exhibit their works to clients and collectors, bring notice to English art."

"You know, Eliot, you suggest what might be a beneficial step," Reynolds replied. "I am contemplating starting a Literary Club in London. Such societies are becoming quite the thing, as people seek to improve themselves. My friend Samuel Johnson is urging me to proceed. We share interests, and we could have most learned and stimulating gatherings. Boswell would come in, of course, and Sheridan and Goldsmith have expressed interest. I believe David Garrick might join us too. No doubt I would meet prospective clients."

"You must watch out for these actors," advised Harriot with a smile, "they love to command the floor."

"You might invite my cousin Edward Gibbon," Catherine said. "He is highly regarded by the leading luminaries in thought and letters. It could perhaps be some kind of academy, open only to the very best," Catherine added, "chosen by an august committee."

"Let me give consideration to your ideas," said Reynolds. "I wonder if such an institution might attract the notice of the king? And while I think of it, I must mention something that might be of interest to you, Mrs. Eliot, as a lady of cultivated learning."

"What might that be, Mr. Reynolds? Do go on," said Catherine.

"There are some ladies who are entertaining quite learned gatherings," said Reynolds, "with more and more erudite discussions."

"Come now, Mr. Reynolds, you seem surprised that members of my sex could be learned," Harriot chided their guest.

"Not at all, Mrs. Hamilton," replied Reynolds, "indeed I so admire the intelligence and culture of yourself and your daughter-in-law that I suggest you consider honoring them with your presence."

"Not for me I fear," said Harriot, "I prefer my gatherings to be for amusement. But perhaps Catherine?"

"I would be delighted," said Catherine. "Who are members? What do they call themselves?"

"Some wit named them the Blue Stockings Society," said Reynolds, "disrespectfully at first, but now they are much admired and proud of their name. Elizabeth Montagu is their founder; her husband is older than she but wealthy, coal mines in Northumberland I believe."

"Mining?" said Edward. "Coal, eh? Lot dirtier than the stuff we deal with in Cornwall. Quite profitable though, I hear."

"Are there any members from Cornwall, Mr. Reynolds?" asked Catherine.

"Admiral Boscawen's widow, Frances, is a member, much admired. There are several Westcountry members; the More sisters are from Bristol, well educated, writers. Hanna is a teacher as well as a fine poet and playwright."

"Teacher?" said Catherine. "Perhaps you would introduce us one day. She could help me in my efforts to encourage education here in Cornwall, especially among the poor mining families."

"My wife has such wide interests, Reynolds," said Edward. "I'm sure she would appreciate your assistance in engaging them still further afield." His encouragement was rewarded with a warm smile from Catherine.

"Oh, I am so enjoying your visit, dear Mr. Reynolds," interrupted Harriot, clapping her hands. "I rarely have the opportunity for such an interesting conversation. Imagine amusing oneself so much in the wilds of Cornwall!" Reynolds beamed.

At that moment a footman entered the room, carrying a note on a round silver tray. He walked to Edward's chair and leaned over to give it to him.

"What's this?" Edward asked. "You're interrupting us. Is it important?"

"It's a note from Mr. Polkinghorne, sir," said the footman. "He told me it was very urgent, and to give it to you right away."

Edward broke the seal and unfolded the note. "Good God," he said, "there's trouble at Wheal Hykka. There was a terrible accident a few days ago, people have been injured, some killed. The miners are angry, looking for someone to blame. This could get very serious. Someone has to maintain calm, keep order. I'm urgently needed at the mine. Reynolds, ladies, excuse me. Enjoy your visit without me. The sketches for the portrait will have to wait." He started out of the room.

"Remember me to the viscount," said Joshua Reynolds, always alert to the possibility of inviting a commission. Catherine rose and embraced her husband. "Be careful, my dear," she said. Edward impatiently pulled away and turned his attention back to the footman.

"Tell Polkinghorne to prepare horses. Ask him if he knows what Dunbargan is up to, and tell him to send a message to Bolitho. Fetch Bunt. Bring pistols. We need to get down there, post haste." He hurried out.

Chapter Fifty-eight

Hunger

There was trouble indeed at Wheal Hykka, serious trouble. The miners were angry. Certainly, many had been discontented before the disaster. The work was always dangerous and difficult. They knew that, it was an inescapable part of life. And they could not count on getting any pay; that was just the way things were. It all depended on the bid their tributer put in on setting day. Some tributers were experienced and wise and sensed how much to bid to win a sett and still be adequately paid for the work. But if the bid was too high they did not get work, and some had to go to other mines to seek employment. If the bid was low enough to win they might not get paid enough to support their families. The method of payment, as well as the rigors of the work, made hard rock mining in Cornwall a risky way of living. So, indeed, were fishing and even farming, where the seasons ruled.

And now mining at Wheal Hykka had become harder. To get to work down the new shaft to the new level under the sea meant climbing down the dark ladders scores of fathoms and then back up again to the dry. It took them over an hour each way, and the miners were not paid for that time. They had heard that the newfangled steam engines could some day be used to bring men as well as ore to the surface. Most likely though it would take work away from the trammers who hauled the tin stuff from the blasting site to the shaft. Some said before long an engine would be used for crushing ore, stamping. Then bal maidens and boys would lose work as well. Dangerous monsters, those engines.

None of that made any difference right now. While the repairs were being made and the damage cleaned up, the mine could only work at limited capacity. As a result, most of them had no work at all. They had become more discontented. Things only got worse, and that angered them. They chose leaders among themselves to go to the count house and complain to Captain Penwarden. He at least listened to what they had to say, even though he told them there was little he could do to help.

"My 'ands are tied so far at Wheal Hykka," he said. "Us would like to do more, but no adventurer has ever agreed to pay out money for compensation. They got their 'ands full payin' for improvements that will get you back to work in due time."

"Them of us what's still alive, not 'urt," growled an old tinner.

"Accidents 'appen," said Penwarden in a tired voice. "One day us'll try to make things a bit safer. Why don't you talk to Revcrend Perry? Mebbe 'e'll 'ave some ideas about organizin' 'elp in the village. Oi'll do what Oi can, but ain't much 'ere at the mine, Oi'm afraid."

They had already tried appealing to Mr. Clymo. "You must be mad if you think I would suggest to the viscount that families who lost loved ones should get compensation," he told their leaders. "It was an accident. You know to expect accidents in mining, and to demand that you should be provided enough for food while there is no work is preposterous. It's nothing to do with the viscount. It's up to you. You were paid what you demanded when there was work; you should have put something by."

Clymo's job was to be the viscount's representative after all, and he had to take a strong line. But they sensed that he was not at ease with what he was saying. For his part, he wanted to take his daughter Morwenna safely back with him to Lanhydrock, but he had felt it was his duty to stay in Pendeen and support Penwarden if things at Wheal Hykka got any worse.

Things did get worse. On top of everything else, food had got scarce and prices went up. Cornwall did not have enough fertile land for its small farms to grow enough grain for its population in the best of times. And this year with so much rain, the harvest of wheat and oats and barley had been disappointing. Furthermore, the war had increased the demand for food to be exported from Britain to the armies and the navy around the world. The millers up country had raised the price of flour. Some towns were buying up scarce supplies and stockpiling to fend off hunger for their people.

Reverend Perry had told the tinners at the funeral service to befriend each other, to band together, and to demand help from the mine adventurers. This did not come easy to them; they were used to bidding their labor against each other, competing. But now maybe it was worth trying; they had few other options. Some of them considered following Captain Penwarden's advice and calling on Mr. Perry at the chapel, if he was there, at least see what he had to say.

A ringleader named Tom Kegwyn had emerged. He was a tough wiry man of middle height, his broad shoulders, black hair and penetrating brown eyes added a touch of menace to his already intimidating presence. He was in his early thirties, married with two small children. His father and grandfather before him were miners, and he had married a miner's daughter. He had a reputation of being a malcontent, inclined to spend too much of his time when he was not at work drinking cider with his mates.

"*Ny vydh travyth anodho,*" Kegwyn said to his cronies as they gathered at The Trewellard Arms discussing what steps they might take next. "Won't come to nothin'."

"Aw, come on, Tom, can but try," said one of them, "ain't got nothin' else to do, nothin' to lose."

"All very well Cap'n tellin' we to go talk to reverend," replied Kegwyn. *"Da lowr yw, Kapten ni dhe gewsel orth an pronter. Flows yw heb ken. Oll an bregowthoryon yw an keth, geryow teg mollethys heb gul travyth.* All 'tis is talk. Preachers be all the same, fancy bloody words and do nothin'.'"

He took a swallow of his cider and spat. It would not be easy for them. They weren't much for talking, preferred doing. Among themselves they spoke their own language, Cornish. With the preacher they would speak English. One of the tinners reached across the table, patted Kegwyn on the shoulder.

Tom Kegwyn would do his best, hoped at least to make him listen. "All right, but you'll see; nothing'll come of it." Tom put down his cider, and a small band of miners walked over to the chapel at Pendeen. The door was unlocked. They found Reverend Perry in the vestry with Lizzie Penwarden and three other women from the village, sitting round a table making notes.

"There you be, Reverend," said Kegwyn, "just who us be lookin' for. Cap'n said you'd find a way to give us food enough to feed our famblies."

"I'm doing what I can," Perry replied, "with the help of these good ladies. We've collected a few vegetables that you're welcome to take, over there on that table."

"Nyns yw lowr dhe voesa hwannen," Kegwyn said scowling. "Bain't enough to feed a flea."

"It's the best we've been able to do so far," Perry said. "People in the village don't have so much as a turnip to spare. And we have to get more helpers organized to go further afield asking and collecting whatever folks are in a position to give. Then we'll get word out so everybody knows to come here to fetch it. It'll take a day or two. Be patient."

"You're an ungrateful good for nothin', Tom Kegwyn," said Lizzie Penwarden, rising out of her chair. "Reverend's doin' the best 'e can, an' we'm 'elpin 'im out of the goodness of our 'earts. Us got plenty else to do. If you don't like it you can lump it."

"Aw, don't take on so, Mrs. Penwarden," said Kegwyn, "Oi'm just upset, worried about what's goin' to 'appen to my fambly if us don't get work soon."

"You're angry, Kegwyn," said the preacher. "I understand, but I'm going to tell you something. Getting angry won't get you anything but trouble. If you or your friends breach the peace or do damage to property you'll be severely punished. That won't help your families, now will it?"

"You can't tell us what to do, Mr. Perry," Kegwyn said truculently. "Us'll take matters into our own 'ands if us 'ave to, make them buggers take notice."

"Listen to me, Tom," Perry said, "don't be a fool. Befriend each other, ask your neighbors to help. And by all means band together, persuade the mine owners to do what is right. But don't put yourselves in the wrong. Don't break the law."

"Us'll provide vittles as soon as us can," Lizzie said.

"You can go to the parishes too," said Perry, "or the towns. Penzance might help; they sometimes provide relief to those in need. The Town Council meets tomorrow afternoon, try them."

"That's a fair piece, good couple of leagues," grumbled Kegwyn. "Us'll 'ave to get up before the cock crows to get there in time."

"Needs must when the Devil drives," said Lizzie.

"Fine for you to say, if you don't mind my sayin' so," said the ringleader to her. He turned to the little group behind him, "Right boys, reckon that's what us'll 'ave to do."

"Aargh," agreed his mates.

Going to the parishes for poor relief was a blow to their pride, their independent spirit. Tinners were different from other people. They kept to themselves, they spoke differently, they were tribal even if they were in competition, had different folkways. They worshipped in different ways; they were now Wesleyans, dissenters. But now it was desperation that drove them to walk to the nearby market town demanding food, lower prices, and relief. They were disappointed but not surprised to be met with a wall of distrust.

That week's issue of The Cornish Chronicle had pronounced: *"Their conduct did not win them the good will or any attention of relief officials or the winter charities, as they are always considered a lawless set of people who are much to be feared but little pitied."*

Before they even met with the Town Council, the tinners were seething with anger and resentment as they walked through the Penzance harbor on their way to the chamber. They passed St. Michael's Mount in the background, a fortress of the wealthy, with Battery Rocks in the foreground. When they reached the quay they saw a merchant ship tied up alongside. A stevedore told them they were loading a cargo of barley to be sent up country, a discouragingly big share of the sparse early harvest.

"Give us bread, for our famblies," shouted Tom Kegwyn. "Us be starvin'."

The bos'n berated them from the safety of his deck, "Get off, you lazy buggers, go an' work for a livin', or Oi'll send for the justices. This cargo be bought and paid for with honest sovereigns."

"Well then, us'll just come take'n fer ourselves," shouted another tinner. The bos'n did not say anything, as he calmly took a pistol from a sash at his waist and waved it at them menacingly.

"Don't shoot," cried a tinner, "us bain't armed." Another shouted, scowling, "Us will be the next time, make no mistake." They retreated, disconsolate and dissatisfied, and continued walking on towards the council chamber. "Us'll be back," cried Kegwyn over his shoulder, shaking his fist.

A lot of people were watching as, in the end, the tinners left peacefully. The onlookers were afraid and wondered what would happen next.

Reports of the incident had already reached the Town Council by the time they arrived for the meeting. There was muted concern about such an incident being repeated or deteriorating into actual violence. The tinners' obvious determination to seek satisfaction at least got them admission to the council chamber. They were promised a hearing, and Tom Kegwyn tried to make their case, but as it turned out the councilors did most of the talking. When he left to wait outside as requested, with the others following, the councilors debated the issue.

The senior alderman was all for forming a corps of local home defense volunteers and arming them with clubs and pitchforks. "That's the only thing these barbarians will understand, brute force. We must stand firm, protect our property. We owe that to the townspeople." The youngest councilor suggested a different approach. "These people are in need. They have suffered a dreadful tragedy, many of them have no work and little prospect of wages for some time. And now food prices have gone up too. Of course they're angry. We have to help them. Give them provenance, that's what parish relief is for."

"That's all very well," said the Town Clerk, "but who's going to pay for it? The citizens won't stand for it. These bloody tinners don't even live in Penzance, and we don't want them coming here for relief. They're not settled, move from mine to mine, they don't belong here. They can't expect the good citizens of Penzance to look after them. We have to take care of our own first."

The youngest councilor disagreed. "It'll cost less to provide a little food than repair the damage if they take things into their own hands. I know tinners, they can be a rough lot."

The Town Clerk suggested, "We should ask the mine owners to pay. The tinners work at their mines, after all, and the owners get the profits. They should pay. They can afford it."

"Why should they?" demanded the oldest alderman. "Anyroad, they wouldn't. Them's gentry."

"What I think," said the Mayor, as all eyes turned to the head of the council table, "is that we should use both repression and relief. Form up volunteers and discourage rioting in Penzance. There's not much militia in Cornwall, but we can at least ensure we've got what there is standing by. At the same time, let us show some Christian charity, so the tinners will feel gratitude to Penzance, not hatred. We should pay part, the parish council must pay part, and we will ask the gentry and those who can afford it to take up a subscription for the rest. Keeping the peace is in their interests too." Most of the councilors nodded. "That's settled then," concluded the mayor.

"Once them think they've prevailed them'll be back," grumbled the senior alderman, with a contemptuous sneer. "That's what Oi say. Bloody tinners. There'll be no end."

The mayor went outside and addressed the group milling about near the door. "Leave peacefully," said the Mayor, "and we'll let you know whether we can help in a few days. That's your best chance, I give you my word. There's nothing we can do right away anyhow. It'll take time."

Grumbling, they followed Tom Kegwyn's example and headed out of the council building. Hours later they got home to Pendeen disgruntled and exhausted. They found that a handful of their fellows had gone down to some of the fishing boats seeking work, any kind of work. There was really nothing for them to do, but a skipper who was brother-in-law to one of the tinners had just landed a good catch of mackerel and pollock.

"'Ere, my son," he said, "Oi could do with an 'and landin' them there fish and hangin' up my nets and sluicin' out my boat. Oi can't pay you but Oi can give you a passel of fish, enough to feed a few famblies. Oi got too many to sell before they go off, so you might as well take some as watch me throw 'em back in the sea."

Reverend Perry and his helpers had scrounged up some vegetables as well. There wasn't much, but at least with one thing and another a few of them did not go hungry that night. However, the village's problem was far from solved. They would have to try harder.

"Us might need sterner steps," said Tom Kegwyn, "it's about survival."

Before separating to go home to their cottages they agreed they would all march up to Wheal Hykka the next morning and try again to make Captain Penwarden not only hear their pleas for help but do something about them. They left still frustrated and angry. Tomorrow they would see to it that something was done one way or another, come what may.

Chapter Fifty-nine

Riot

Next day found Captain Penwarden in the counting house arguing with Joseph Clymo and the Reverend Perry. They were all sympathetic to the plight of the miners, but Penwarden and especially Clymo were adamant in defending their position as representatives of the owners. Any minute now they would have to open the door and answer the demands of the impatient tinners milling about outside.

"Now just you listen to me, Reverend Perry," said Clymo, "I appreciate that you are doing your best to help the villagers and get some food together, and that in itself will calm things down. But you've got to watch your words in the pulpit, don't go stirring up more anger. It can only lead to violence. I must say that I admire you personally, but you'll only get into trouble if you get on the wrong side of the viscount and the other adventurers. We all need their cooperation, not to antagonize them."

"I believe you are a decent man, Mr. Clymo," replied the preacher, "and I am a patient man. But there comes a time when injury outstrips our ability to suffer in silence, especially when it could be avoided. If I don't speak up for the miners, encourage them to band together peacefully to right their wrongs, then they will listen to more violent men than me."

"Preacher's right, Mr. Clymo," said Penwarden. "What you say sometimes worries me, preacher, but it's going to be said and it could be worse if 'twere left to others. First us've got to get through this mess without more injury to men and property. Oi've got to go outside and talk to the tinners as their captain right soon or them'll batter the door down."

"You must be firm, Penwarden," said Clymo. "They respect firmness, and the viscount won't stand for it if you let them force you to make concessions."

"They also need compassion, man," said Perry, "and they deserve it. They're in terrible straits through no fault of their own. Our Savior spoke of the power of charity."

"You're a man of God, Reverend," said Clymo, "don't meddle in what doesn't concern you, and stay on the side of law and order like your Mr. Wesley."

"As a man of God, gentlemen, my part is to do my best to bring understanding and order to the affairs of men and to improve the bodily as well as the spiritual welfare of my flock. I refuse to let the viscount or anyone else stand between me and my God-appointed duty."

Addis Penwarden had enough of this kind of talk. He put on his top hat and strode to the door and opened it. He held up his arms for quiet and spoke in a loud voice to the seething crowd. "Listen to me, all you good people, Oi'm doin' what Oi can. You'll just 'ave to be patient until us gets the mine back to work. It'll take a little more time."

"Listen to us, Cap'n," one of the leaders shouted at him, "we mean it." He was desperate, angry. *"Res yw dhis gul neppyth ragon-ni. Nyns eus ober dhyn, nyns eus arghans ow tos, travyth dhe brena boes.* You've got to do something for us. Us've got no work, no money comin' in, nothin' to buy food with."

"Oi be luckier'n some," shouted another. "Oi got a little garden, grow some beans and tedders, but nothin' fer bread. My little tacker is 'ungry all the time. Ain't got enough to 'elp me mates much."

"I've told you before, there just ain't much us can do," Penwarden replied. "Ain't much use tryin'. Oi've done me best. Just ask Mr. Clymo 'ere."

"What about that bloody Viscount Dunbugger then?" demanded another.

"It's not up to him, nor the other owners," said Clymo, coming out of the door to stand next to Penwarden. "Besides they've spent a lot of money improving the mine, can't afford any more. You'll benefit eventually; there'll be more work when everything's repaired, back in working order, more productive."

"Just go on home quietly now," pleaded Captain Penwarden, "there'll be awful trouble if you don't. Us'll let you know soon as there's work."

Reverend Perry joined them outside. "I'm seeing what I can do," he called out. "I've put the word out; people are trying to gather up what food they can; and I'll go back to the chapel in Pendeen and get some good souls to help make some nourishing soup and some bread in the next few days." He waved to the crowd and headed towards his pony and cart, relieved to be leaving the mine. A few of the men, members of his flock, slapped him on the back as he passed, but the majority scowled and shook their fists.

"Yeah, bloody Christmas is comin' too," growled a tinner angrily. "Us needs relief now. Us can't wait no longer."

"You mark my words, cap'n," yelled another, "you'm a good man, but us needs 'elp now. Us don't 'ave more time."

The crowd began to break up and reluctantly left the area in front of the counting house, muttering and grumbling. Knots of miners were hanging around in the yard outside; some of them were supping mugs of cider. The mood of most was heavy; some at the back of the crowd seemed hopeful, expectant. But they knew the worst when they caught the way their leaders left the group clustered around Addis Penwarden, faces averted, heads bent, shoulders downcast. It appeared hopeless. Then Tom Kegwyn shouted, seething, "It's that there bloody steam engine! That's the cause of all the trouble. Blew up and killed our mates, made the shaft collapse, set the powder off, let the sea in, tinners drownded."

The cry was picked up, swelled by the crowd, "It's the steam engine. *Yth yw an jynn-ethenn mollethys!* It's the bloody steam engine!" Tom was red in the face with fury. He stood up on a boulder and yelled, "Us knows 'ow to break rock, that's what us do for a living, when them'll 'ave us. Us can break a bloody steam engine easy. Come on. Us'll show 'em us means what we says."

He jumped down off the boulder and led the way to the tool shed, followed by angry tinners shouting, *"Yth yw an jynn-ethenn mollethys.* It's the bloody steam engine. *Torr an jynn mollethys!* Break the bloody engine!"

They broke open the latch on the sturdy door of the tool shed and burst inside. They grabbed sledgehammers, cold chisels and boryers, the long steel rods used to drill holes in the rock. Others ran to the storehouse, broke open the locked cupboard where the black powder was stored.

Tom Kegwyn led them to the engine house. They were chanting a furious chorus, "Break the engine, break the bloody engine." There was a handful of men inside working on repairs. They scattered as their maddened mates surged in. "Gerrout of our way," shouted Kegwyn, "you'm no business workin' while us can't."

Their foreman yelled back, "Nothin' us can do about it, cap'n gave we orders. Us got to do what we'm told. Anyroad, mine can't start up again 'til us got done with repairs. Don't act like bloody fools, you'll only bring trouble on all our heads."

Penwarden and Clymo hurried towards them, following the crowd to the engine house. "Put them tools back where they belong!" bellowed Penwarden.

"You're stealing; we'll set the justices on you!" yelled Clymo. The crowd took no notice. The stragglers jostled them. Clymo staggered, and Penwarden reached out an arm to hold him up. Some of the miners turned towards them with threatening gestures. "Come back," said Clymo, pulling on Penwarden's arm, and as they ran and barred themselves inside the counting house, they were left to themselves and not pursued.

Tom Kegwyn took a boryer and laid its point at a seam at the bottom side of the main boiler of the engine. The fire had not been relit since it had gone out on the day of the accident, and the engine was cold. "Someone bring a sledge over 'ere," he ordered, "'elp us pry open this boiler. Let the water out." Two men brought heavy sledge hammers and took it in turns in rhythm to hit the top end of the boryer as Tom guided the chisel against the big rivets that sealed the main seam of the big boiler. It took several blows but first one and then more rivets popped. Kegwyn guided the chisel into a gap between the heavy plates, and as they hammered the gap wider, water began to trickle out. "Come on you lazy buggers, what are you waiting for," shouted Tom. "You two, come on 'ere an' work on the other side. You two, go t'other end, make a proper job of it now."

Quickly the trickle became a stream. The seam buckled and the water emptied out as the monster bled to death. The tinners cheered. Others joined in the dreadful game, smashing couplers, dislodging linkages, breaking chains, destroying valves. There wasn't room for them all to attack other parts of the machine, so they rushed into other parts of the engine house and broke pipes, smashed gauges, knocked down walls, tipped over containers of supplies.

Some men in the repair crew tried to block them and stop them from undoing their painstaking work, but the angry crowd was determined to undo the repairs that had been done. Their excitement exploded in an orgy of destruction as they spread through the building smashing and spilling and overturning.

Addis Penwarden watched in horror through a window in the counting house, helpless, helpless to stop the riot. He saw one of the young repair crew running to the counting house, unlocked the door to let him in and locked and barred it again after him. He was breathless, frightened. "Cap'n, cap'n, they'm tearin' the place up, all the stuff what us already repaired, all that work wasted. Oi dunno what them'll get up to next. It's terrible. I 'ope they don't come after we, them're madder than a bunch of squalling cats."

"Listen carefully," said Penwarden, getting a grip on himself. "Us've got to get messages to the viscount and Mr. Eliot, so them can send 'elp. Wait, Oi'll write to Mr. Eliot; Clymo you do the same for the viscount. You take 'em to the post office in Penzance and send them off, my son, quick as you can. Can you ride an 'oss?"

"Oi dunno cap'n, Oi can try like. But won't they stop me? An' Oi don't want them to get in no trouble. Them're me mates."

"They'm in trouble already, and you will be too if you don't follow my orders. Anyroad, my letters are askin' for 'elp and relief. Oi'm not askin' for trouble; these are my neighbors, my friends too. They're decent folk at heart; they're just angry because them can't look after their famblies. But some of 'em 'ave put their foot right in it. No tellin' what will 'appen now."

"You've got to restore order, man," said Clymo as he scribbled a note; "you've got to assert your authority, or you'll be for it when the viscount hears about this. You'd better call in the justices, and don't delay."

"Oi know what's best, Clymo," said Penwarden. "These are my people and they trust me. Oi'll deal with 'em, once them've blown off their anger." He finished his letter, picked up Clymo's, folded them both, sealed them and handed them to the reluctant messenger.

"Take these, scoot out the back door, run to the stable as quick as you can and ride to Penzance as if Old Nick 'imself was after you. There'll be a sovereign for you when you get back. Now 'urry!"

The slamming of the door attracted the attention of the rioters. A knot broke away from the engine house. "What are you up to now, cap'n?" shouted an angry tinner. Penwarden looked out of the window beside the door to see what was happening. He ducked just in time to avoid a brickbat that shattered the glass and narrowly missed his head. In the confusion the terrified messenger made his escape.

"Just you deal with that however you want," said Clymo, at the end of his tether. "I'll do it my way." He reached for into his saddlebag for his pistol and started priming it.

Penwarden saw a crowd of rioters streaming out of the engine house, running, scattering. There was an explosion. The roof of the building blew off, hurling debris around the yard. In the chaos men screamed, cursed. More trouble. Things were completely out of hand.

Chapter Sixty

Order

When Edward Eliot and his companions reached Wheal Hykka a day or so later, tired from the journey and apprehensive about the news they had received by way of Morwenna's letter to the Bunts, they found that matters had grown far worse than they expected. They had feared discontent among the idle miners, but they certainly were not prepared for the extreme effects of anger, hunger and desperation upon the behavior of folk who could generally be held in check by vague promises and their own incessant needs and dependency. However, as they approached the main entrance of the mine they came upon a crowd of hundreds of miners, running in all directions, shouting, armed with cudgels and pitchforks and the tools of their trade, hurling stones and rocks at the engine house. Rioting.

"Come on," shouted Bunt, "let's go round the back way before they catch sight of us and attack us."

"They wouldn't dare," said Eliot.

"I wouldn't count on it," said Polkinghorne, pulling on his horse's rein and turning back to the road. "I'm with Bunt. You too, sir. Time enough for bravery later."

They trotted their horses along the road that led to the back entrance to the mine, looking over their shoulders at the chaos behind them. "There's smoke coming up from a big pile of timbers," said Polkinghorne. "They're setting fire to it. Look, the roof's off the engine house. Keep going, sir, hurry!"

The horses whinnied, snorted as the acrid smoke reached their nostrils, pulled on their bits, resisted going any further. Bunt's horse reared up and nearly threw him.

The riders spurred their way on and dismounted at the back of the counting house, which lay between them and the crowd around the fire at the engine house. They tethered the horses and collected their saddlebags. The ostler was nowhere in sight, so Bunt unsaddled their horses and tethered them to a post. He knocked on the back door and announced their arrival. They heard voices from inside, a key being turned in the lock and heavy bolts being drawn back. The door was cautiously opened, and Addis Penwarden appeared.

"Gentlemen, I am relieved to see you," Penwarden welcomed them. "Come in. Things is goin' from bad to worse. Did you see that smoke? There's no reasonin' with 'em. They think Oi can do somethin' about this mess."

Joseph Clymo stood up as they went inside. "Glad to see you, Mr. Eliot. What are we going to do? Have you heard anything from the viscount? Now that you're here, tell 'em they've got to quiet down and go home. They're all riled up, maddened with anger, frustrated, but maybe they'll listen to you."

"Oi hope Reverend Perry will come back soon," said Penwarden. "Some of the women in the village are makin' up some food, soup, maybe they can scrape together some bread, fish. That'll at least feed some of the famblies, show them that us is tryin' to 'elp."

"The first thing you have to do, Penwarden," said Eliot, "is restore order. You've lost control, man. It's your job to reassert your authority, maintain order. If you can't do it I'll find someone who can. Clymo, can you reach Captain Williams?"

"There won't be no need for that sir," said Penwarden. "I know what needs to be done, I'll do my job. But a firm word from you would 'elp. Them is accustomed to payin' attention to the gentry."

"I'll try and find someone to send to Poldice to fetch Williams," said Clymo, "but it'll be at least tomorrow until he could get here. Fact is we've done what can be done, sent word to the justices, the constable. It's a matter of time. Course, once Penwarden gets Wheal Hykka repaired and they go back to work, earning money, things will settle down."

"When the food arrives that'll 'elp," said Penwarden.

"Them's their own worst enemies. Need to be shown who's boss, that's what Oi think," said Bunt. "Lot of them're drinkin' too."

"That'll do, Bunt," said Charles Polkinghorne. "Mr. Eliot will decide; he doesn't need your help."

Bunt did not reply. Eliot observed that his expression was set, without animation. Bunt seemed to be growing increasingly resentful of Polkinghorne's overbearing manner towards him. He would take an opportunity to have a word with his man of business. Young Bunt still had much to learn, but it would not do to have his keenness and imagination stifled.

Eliot turned towards Polkinghorne, but before he could speak they heard a commotion outside. Penwarden walked over to the window and peered out. He saw a horse and cart and a cluster of people, men and women, walking down the entrance drive, carrying bundles and baskets.

"It's Reverend Perry," said Penwarden. "Them're bringin' the food. Look, my wife Lizzie is with them, so's Morwenna, Mr. Clymo."

Hearing Morwenna's name, Polkinghorne looked out. She had a lot of strength, that young woman; he was coming to admire her more and more.

One of the tinners caught sight of the approaching group and called out a warning. A knot of tinners moved up towards the entrance and took up position across the drive, blocking passage.

"Oi'm going out," Penwarden said, grabbing his top hat, "see those people ain't 'armed. Who's comin' with us?" Eliot and Bunt followed him without hesitation. Clymo stayed behind for a moment to pick up his pistol and put it in his pocket before joining them. He would protect them all if necessary, but one thing for certain was that he would protect his daughter.

"Let 'em through!" shouted Penwarden. "Them're bringin' food. It's for you and your famblies." He tried to walk around the obstructing tinners, stumbling as he shouldered aside one who reached out to stop him from passing. Clymo held onto Penwarden's arm, prevented him from falling. The ringleader Tom Kegwyn stepped in front of them.

"That bain't enough grub, don't look like much to Oi." One of the bal maidens shook her fist. "You tell 'im, Tom, us needs food for the 'ole bloody village," she screamed.

"Now see here my good man," said Eliot, "just tell your fellows to settle down and go home, there's a good chap."

"Now who are you then, lord 'igh an' mighty?" demanded Kegwyn belligerently.

"This is Mr. Eliot of Port Eliot," said Clymo, putting his right hand into his coat pocket. "He's one of the mine's owners. You'd better do what he says, or it'll be the worse for you."

The Reverend Perry was herding his party together, encouraging them to press with their cart through the crowd. "Make way, we're here to help you," he cried. Lizzie Penwarden grabbed Kegwyn by the front of his shirt. "Come on Tom, gerroff it," she said, "Mr. Perry is tryin' to get more 'elp, find more food, let 'im get started with this lot, and us'll go back for more."

"Get out of 'ere, Lizzie," said Kegwyn, giving her a rough push, "you're on their side, just like your 'usband. Ye used to be one of us, but no more, 'e's 'igh an' mighty too." He grabbed the food bundle out of her hands and threw it on the bonfire. The flames were leaping higher now, gaining purchase, crackling. There was a stink of burning fish.

Then the crackling sounded different, regular, rhythmic. Bunt looked towards the mine entrance to see what the noise was. "Look who's comin' down the road," he shouted, "soldiers!"

Fifteen or twenty soldiers with muskets at the shoulder were marching in file two abreast towards the mine, a drummer boy beating the cadence and an officer on a black charger leading the way. As they got close the officer turned in his saddle, leaned back and said something to his serjeant. "Platoon, halt!" barked the serjeant. The soldiers were smart in their uniforms of long skirted red coats with black facings, buff leather belts, white breeches with black gaiters above the knee, black tricorn cocked hats on their heads. The officer and serjeant stood out in their distinctive scarlet coats.

Edward Eliot strode forward and addressed the young officer. "Who are you, what are you doing here and who sent you?"

The officer dismounted and saluted. "Maitland, sir, here to restore order under the orders of the Lord Lieutenant of the county."

Eliot nodded. "Who requested action from the Lord Lieutenant, and when?"

The officer replied, "I'm afraid I am not at liberty to disclose . . . "

The crowd edged closer to the soldiers, muttering, threatening. The soldiers stood their ground, staring straight ahead. Eliot looked the officer in the eye and then scanned the faces of the men standing at attention. With the exception of the serjeant and a couple of grizzled veterans they all looked awfully young, raw, probably inexperienced.

"Nonsense man, I'm Eliot of Port Eliot, Registrar-General of the Duchy of Cornwall. I am entitled to the information and I demand to know."

The ensign rested his hand on the hilt of the sword at his belt. "I understand the request came from Mr. Thomas Bolitho, sir."

Joseph Clymo looked at Penwarden and said, "He must have been instructed by the viscount after they got our message."

Penwarden glowered and replied, "Must've been after you went and told 'im what was goin' on, Clymo, before things really got out of 'and. No time for your letter from a day or two ago to reach 'im yet. Us never asked for soldiers, 'e jumped the gun, made the decision on 'is own loike. Now what?"

"Just keep everything calm, Mr. Maitland," said Eliot. "You take charge, but make sure everyone keeps the peace."

"I have my orders sir," said the officer. "Restore order whatever it takes. There's destruction here, arson, civil disobedience; this is a riot. I came fully prepared." He handed the bridle of his horse to the drummer boy who walked it to the rear of the platoon. He turned towards his men. "Serjeant, you know what to do."

The serjeant turned to face the men. "Platoon, forming rank of fours, march!" The soldiers performed the complicated maneuver flawlessly. The serjeant barked out more orders. "Fix bayonets. Load!"

The crowd quieted, watched in awe as they carried out the order with speed and dexterity. Each man took a paper cartridge from the pouch at his belt, bit off the end, sprinkled a little powder into the pan of his musket, pushed the steel back to cover the pan, poured the rest of the powder down the barrel, then inserted the paper cartridge and a ball into the muzzle. Then each man removed his ramrod from its position under the barrel, rammed the charge and ball down the barrel, returned the ramrod to its stowage position, and finally pulled the cock back to the "full cock" position.

"Phew!" muttered Addis Penwarden. "No more than fifteen seconds!"

The soldiers were ready for another order. The serjeant shouted again. "Front rank, kneel!"

Tom Kegwyn was undaunted. "You got no business 'ere. This be our place, be off with you. Us'll settle this ourselves." He took a swig from his mug and threw the dregs towards a soldier, wetting the front of his coat. The crowd murmured again.

"Stop it, Tom," said Reverend Perry, "give over," and he tried to urge him back among his mates.

Lizzie pulled on his arm, "Don't be such a fool, Tom, you'll get us all in awful trouble."

The ensign signaled the boy, who beat a tattoo on his side drum, silencing the crowd. The young officer addressed Eliot. "Sir, I advise you and your companions to stand aside in case there is trouble." Then he took a document from the pocket of his tunic, unfolded it, and said in a loud clear voice: "Under the authority duly given to me by the Lord Lieutenant of Cornwall I hereby give notice as follows." He read, *"Our Sovereign Lord the King chargeth and commandeth all persons, being assembled, immediately to disperse themselves and peaceably to depart to their habitations, or to their lawful business, upon the pains contained in the act made in the first year of King George, for preventing tumults and riotous assemblies. God Save the King!"*

He looked round the faces in front of him to see what effect he was having. Some appeared cowed. Others, like Tom Kegwyn, were defiant.

The officer continued to speak. "The Riot Act makes it a felony punishable by death without benefit of clergy for any persons unlawfully, riotously and tumultuously assembled together to cause, or begin to cause, serious damage to places of religious worship, houses, barns, and stables." He looked up and added in his own words, "That undoubtedly includes buildings such as this mine or places of manufactory."

"Go home, for God's sake, go home!" shouted Penwarden, turning towards the mob.

Some of the crowd moved back, including all the men who had worked on repairing the damage of the past days. Reverend Perry and his group urged those around them to move back and leave.

Tom Kegwyn didn't move, but stood his ground, his chin lifted. He picked up pieces of wood, threw one on the fire, and kept another as a cudgel. "Oi'd rather swing than starve!" he yelled. "Come on, arm yourselves, there's more of we than they." He started towards the soldiers.

Lizzie tugged at his arm to stop him charging. Tom broke into a run. He ignored an order to halt. The young ensign nodded to the serjeant.

"Platoon, present, fire!" A volley of shots cracked out and echoed from the walls of the engine house. The crowd groaned. Three bodies slumped to the ground. Two were tinners who had been at the side of Tom Kegwyn. One was the woman who had been trying to save him from himself.

Addis Penwarden screamed. "My God, Lizzie!" He rushed towards her, knelt and took her in his arms. Blood had soaked the front of her dress. "Oh Dunbugger, what under the name of God have you done now? Don't you dare ever show your face 'ere again or Oi'll strangle you with me own 'ands, Oi swear Oi will!"

"I warned you, reverend, I warned you," shouted Clymo, pulling at Perry's arm, "now see what you've done!"

"Oh my God, look what them've done now," said Willy Bunt, distraught. He felt he should help but did not know what to do.

Edward Eliot covered his mouth with one hand but did not speak.

Chapter Sixty-one

Sail

A week or so later and after considerable hesitation, Catherine responded to an urgent plea from Viscountess Dunbargan for the Eliots to take her and her husband to Wheal Hykka by sea. Elianor did not want to risk travel by road. Catherine had already looked at a recent letter from Addis Penwarden addressed to Edward. The head clerk in the estate office had brought it to her since Edward had already departed for Wheal Hykka.

This latest letter from Penwarden contained news that the situation at the mine had become tense, that the miners were discontented and angry, that Joseph Clymo and Morwenna were there, and that Clymo and Penwarden requested support from the viscount and Mr. Eliot to reinforce their authority.

When Edward had set off with Polkinghorne and Bunt, he had felt that Catherine could add little but distraction to the situation by accompanying him, and besides she had Joshua Reynolds and Harriot there. But now Catherine, not only reading more closely between the lines of Penwarden's letter, but also seeing what Elianor had added, sensed that the situation could potentially grow yet more serious.

Elianor Dunbargan stressed her husband's view that the owners should deal with the situation personally and not leave it to their lieutenants. Catherine realized that for the viscount to be distracted from more amusing pursuits implied that matters were indeed serious. Unfortunately, according to Elianor, he was in a furious mood, and Catherine felt he might exacerbate the situation instead of calming it. The viscount had consulted with Thomas Bolitho, who had advised that firm steps should be taken, so it appeared that he could not wait to get down to Wheal Hykka and show everyone how a man in his position could exert authority.

"Someone's got to be flogged," Dunbargan, purple in the face, told his wife. "That'll show those barbarians how to behave."

Elianor feared that he would only bring things to a boiling point and make matters much worse. She hoped that Edward Eliot's steadier temperament and presence would restrain Dunbargan.

However, she suggested that both women together could exert a calming influence on their husbands. They shared an interest in improving the lot of the miners, not least because it would be in the long term best interests of the owners to make them more skilled and productive workers. That, of course, required education. Besides, once they reached Wheal Hykka, Catherine and Elianor could take the opportunity to meet Reverend Perry, together with Lizzie Penwarden and Morwenna Clymo and any other potential helpers, to make progress in starting the school at the chapel in Pendeen.

Elianor's letter concluded by suggesting a rendezvous. *"Perhaps you would be kind enough to meet us at The Ferry Inn at Bodinnick, where we would be delighted to entertain you both to luncheon. In closing, I must confess that my traveling on these awful roads is precluded by my finding myself in a rather delicate condition. I would be eternally grateful if I could prevail on your husband's connection with Lord Edgcumbe in arranging the use of the sloop to allow us the luxury of being transported on the more hospitable surface of the English Channel. No doubt we can rely upon gentle breezes at this time of year."*

The letter was signed with affection. Always thinking about possibilities, Catherine observed that an additional benefit of this arrangement once they reached their destination would be sleeping aboard the sloop in safe isolation, rather than exposing themselves to the risk of disturbance or even danger at the hands of angry miners if they were accommodated on land at the mine or at a nearby inn.

Catherine dashed off a message to Elianor agreeing to meet them for lunch at Bodinnick down river from Lanhydrock and take them with her by boat to Wheal Hykka. She asked to borrow Lord Edgcumbe's private sloop once again, to which he readily agreed. Edward's star must indeed be on the rise. After an early breakfast at dawn, Catherine went down to board the sloop moored at the Port Eliot quay. Her maid and a footman had already embarked and stowed clothes and provisions for a coastal voyage and an extended stay.

Patches of fog floated on the surface of the river. The dawn sky was tinged with pink.

"Top o' the mornin' to you, Mrs. Eliot," the Edgcumbe skipper greeted her as he gave the order to the two-man crew to prepare to cast off. "'Spect you know yer way around to find the two cabins and the crown-office."

Catherine stifled a smile at his reference to the tiny head astern.

"Us'll go down the Lhyner with the tide," he continued. "Once we get into the Tamar estuary us'll pick up a nice sou'-westerly. Have to tack 'er way out at first, but then once we'm at sea us can sail abaft the wind most of the way to Fowey. Should get you there a little after noon."

"What's the weather going to be like?" asked Catherine. "Will we have a calm trip?"

"Well, you know what they say, me lady," said the skipper, "red sky in the mornin', sailors take warnin'. Weather seems all right for now, but 'er may pick up later. But 'ave no fear, this ere's a sturdy enough craft."

"I'm afraid I am not an experienced sailor," said Catherine, "but I expect I will manage. I've gained plenty of Cornish grit since living at Port Eliot. For now I'll stay above decks in the cockpit with you, skipper, if I won't be in your way." Catherine smiled: "Might as well enjoy the weather and admire the scenery. It'll be new to me." She tied a silk scarf over her hat to stop it blowing away and settled herself down.

The captain beamed at her. "Well then, ma'am, ye'll be interested to see the Eddystone Reef on the horizon to the south of us. Take my spyglass. See it? Right treacherous them rocks is, can't see 'em at high tide, they'm covered up by the sea. Used to be 'undreds of wrecks all the time at night before they built the lighthouse."

"My husband met the man who designed the Eddystone Light and built it," said Catherine. "Clever fellow he says, Mr. John Smeaton. Thinks a lot of himself, but he's quite an inventor and has accomplished a lot. He's working with Mr. Eliot on machines for the mines."

The captain nodded but said nothing. What landlubbers got up to did not interest him.

The weather stayed fair with a steady light to moderate breeze. The skipper felt no need to hug the shelter of the coast. The sloop was gaff-rigged and fifty feet long with a capacious hold. Once in the English Channel it got choppy, but they made good speed, four or five knots. They cut across Whitsand Bay and left Looe Island to their starboard. After a few hours they rounded Pencarrow Head and the skipper altered course northward to enter the estuary of the River Fowey, with Bodinnick half a mile or so up from the mouth on the east bank. The crew lowered the sails and they drifted to the mooring alongside The Ferry Inn.

The skipper handed Catherine ashore and she made her way towards the entrance. She staggered a little at first as she accustomed herself to walking on terra firma after having adjusted her balance to the rocking of the boat.

The innkeeper announced her arrival, and the waiting Dunbargans came out of the dining room to greet her. "Catherine, my dear," said Elianor, "how kind of you to take us with you."

Dunbargan added, "Delighted to see you, Mrs. Eliot, but where is your husband?" He looked around expectantly.

"He rode to Wheal Hykka with two of his men some days ago," replied Catherine. "He should have things well in hand by now."

Dunbargan paused as he took the information in. "Ah," he said at last. "I wouldn't be too sure of that; your husband's too mild to deal with rabble. He should've waited for me. One has to be firm, show them who's master, put 'em in their place. Someone needs to be flogged, made an example of. I've been discussing the matter with Bolitho; he's a man of the world and agrees with me."

Catherine turned and looked him directly in the eye. "Lord Dunbargan, I would remind you that even though he is absent, you are my husband's guest on this voyage. Pray take note of that and do not insult him."

"Come now, let us take lunch and be on our way," said Elianor soothingly, taking her husband's arm. "Really, James, the wiser course may prove to avoid stirring up further trouble." Dunbargan stared at her, saying nothing but nodding in what might be seen as an apologetic manner in Catherine's direction then following the ladies to their table. Conversation over lunch was at first tactfully kept to weather and asking after each other's families until more interesting but still neutral topics were broached.

"There was a time when you could have sailed right up the river to Lostwithiel," said Dunbargan. "Saved us no end of trouble, no need for my man to bring us down to Bodinnick. But the lower reach got silted up. Damn shame, spoiled the fishin' too."

"What happened?" asked Catherine. "What caused the silting?"

"Tailings from the mines upstream on Bodmin Moor," the viscount replied. "Those damn tinners don't care what kind of mess they make."

"Shouldn't it be the responsibility of the owners to see that things are properly managed?" pressed Catherine, her eyes sparkling.

"Course not," said Dunbargan, "we have enough trouble making ends meet paying all those heathens the outrageous amounts of money they demand, just for doing a little digging and a little hammering. It's contemptible!"

Catherine was relieved when the meal was over. The viscount at least had the grace to pay the innkeeper as they left. They walked down the steep hill, with Dunbargan striding ahead. The captain welcomed them aboard and reported that the Dunbargans' things had been safely stowed.

"I'll see the truth of that for myself," said the viscount and shouldered past the skipper to the gangway down to the hold. After a few moments he reappeared and joined the women in the saloon. "Seems in order. H'mm, plenty of room in that hold," he said. "I dare say the owner of this leaky tub puts it to more profitable use than a few ladies' trunks from time to time. I know I would."

"What on earth do you mean?" asked Catherine, but Elianor interrupted before her question could be pursued. "James, do be more discreet," she said. "You never know who's listening or whom they might tell. Now, why don't you go up on deck and instruct the captain how to sail his ship? I'm sure he would be grateful. Mrs. Eliot and I have things to discuss that are only of interest to women."

Dunbargan was taken aback and for once did as he was told without question. He hoped that Mrs. Eliot was not having a bad influence on Elianor. He preferred his wife to love, honor and obey, which seemed an increasing challenge. As for mistresses, that was a different kettle of fish. In their case a little spirit spiced things up, could lead to showing who was in charge.

The captain acknowledged him with a nod but did not speak as the viscount joined him in the cockpit. The tide had turned and was now coming in, so they made slow progress going back out to sea. However, once in open water the wind freshened, and the sloop picked up speed.

In the saloon the women conversed earnestly. "Catherine," began Elianor, "I know that it is properly none of my business since I am a woman, but I can't help but be concerned about what is going on at the mine. We haven't heard the last of it, and if James goes blundering in it'll only get worse, and a lot of people will suffer. You have convinced me that it is our duty as women to see that our fortunes can only benefit if we improve the lot of the mining families, especially through education. We are just about to start, and these foolish men can ruin it all."

"I quite agree," said Catherine. "Edward is steadier, and he does listen to what I say. I sense this is not yet the case in your marriage, and I want to be sure that there is enough influence on hand that is wise and for the good. I do not want Edward alone with your husband. We must pull together; then they cannot refuse to heed us. If I may be frank, I feel compassion for your having to deal with the viscount all the time."

"Out of loyalty I do not wish to pursue that subject," said Elianor, "although I know you mean well; perhaps at another time. Meanwhile, I will support you on these matters, and we both can ensure that our husbands listen to the good men who understand the miners, Captain Penwarden and Reverend Perry."

Up in the cockpit the viscount tried to engage the captain in conversation. "How far do you think we'll get this afternoon, skipper?" Dunbargan asked.

"Oi was just thinkin' about that, sir," the captain replied. The sun was high and the air grew hotter and sultry as it often did in late August. The sky had grown a little cloudy. "Us can make Falmouth by evenin', and us could lay up for the night in the shelter of Pendennis Castle. Or if you wish, we can light up and sail through the night. There'll be plenty of wind. Judgin' by the smell in the air there might be one of them summer storms acomin', but it shouldn't be too bad."

"Well, as long as you know what you're doing," said the viscount. "We should press on. We need to get to that hole in the ground as soon as possible. I'll inform the ladies." He poked his head into the saloon and delivered his message.

"Perhaps, my lord," said Catherine, raising her eyebrows, "since I am your hostess, you will allow me to make the decisions. I will tell the captain that he may proceed, if he is sure we will be safe." She stood and stepped from the saloon out into the cockpit where she delivered her own instructions.

"Aye aye, ma'am," responded the captain. "Us'll 'ave to keep a weather eye out, but bain't the first toime Oi been at sea."

"In that case, Mrs. Eliot," said the viscount, trying to preserve some dignity, "I presume you can at least provide us with a civilized meal on board, and something to drink? I'm parched."

"Of course, my lord," said Catherine frostily, "I have already told my footman to serve us in one hour."

They sailed steadily on. Catherine picked up some needlework she had brought aboard, and Elianor sat quietly. The viscount fidgeted and paced about the saloon, going into the cockpit from time to time. As evening drew on, the footman served a bottle of white wine, a Sauternes, with the cold roast chicken supper that the Port Eliot cook had packed for them. "Not a bad drop of plonk, my dear," said Dunbargan, "a bit sweet for my taste. All right for you ladies."

Catherine suppressed an urge to kick him under the cabin table. "It's a fine Chateau d'Yquem, my lord. Those cunning French vintners make it with a secret process using nobly rotted grapes. I thought it might quite suit you." She smiled sweetly. He said nothing but swallowed deeply; she was a spirited filly, make no mistake. He signaled the footman to refill his glass.

With their supper over they prepared to retire for the night. Catherine had offered the Dunbargans the comfort and privacy of the main forward cabin while she settled into the guest cabin between it and the saloon. She sent her maid to make the best of the sail locker in the bow, while the footman joined the crew to sleep under oilskins in hammocks under the stars.

Catherine couldn't get to sleep. The boat was rolling and pitching. Her stomach felt queasy. She did not undress but lay restlessly on the bunk. She rose on an elbow periodically and looked out of the porthole. Rain was pelting against it. It was dark, but there was enough moonlight between the scudding clouds to see that the waves had got bigger. The wind was blowing harder and howling in the rigging. The sloop heeled over, its bow banging into the valleys between every seventh wave or so. Sheet lightning flashed across the sky. She heard retching from the forward cabin. Elianor in her condition was not coping well with the deep swell and the roughness of the waves.

A figure stumbled through the dark from the door of the Dunbargans' cabin. Catherine couldn't see a face but knew it had to be the viscount. She sat up. He lurched towards her, reaching in front of him for something to grasp as they hit another wave. His hand hit her shoulder pushing her down again, and he fell on top of her. "Terrible sea," he mumbled into her neck. Don't worry, I've come to look after you, my dear." He raised his head and whispered, "But now that we're here, I've got an idea that you might find more than a little fun. "

She tried to scream, but he covered her mouth with his hand. She reached out to the table trying to find something to hit him with, perhaps a candlestick. A gust of wind made the boat heel again. He rolled sideways towards the edge of the bunk, and she took advantage of his lost balance and brought her knee up onto his chest and pushed. He fell off the bunk onto the floor with a clatter, as a candlestick fell beside him.

Someone knocked on the cabin door. She jumped up and opened it. "You all right, ma'am?" the captain asked. She was relieved to see that he was at the helm, leaning in to call to her. "I will be when this storm abates," she said. "It's got one of my guests quite beside himself."

By the light of the moon coming through the door, the captain saw the viscount trying to scramble up from the floor behind her and looked at her quizzically. "Oi've got the crew taking in a reef on the mains'l. That'll steady 'er. P'r'aps us could all do with a bit of steadyin'," he said, smiling at the sight of the viscount still rolling about on the floor.

Dunbargan screamed at the captain, "Turn this tub around, damn your eyes, take us to safety! You'll drown us all!"

Elianor came through into the saloon towards the captain, stopped and reached out for her husband, evidently more in fear than affection. Catherine grabbed her cloak, not wishing to miss the excitement. "You should stay inside, ma'am," said the captain, "you'll get soaked. This is just a little squall, nothing much."

The viscount was not mollified. "What the devil's going on?" he demanded. "You said the weather would be fair, that we'd be completely safe."

"Us'll just ride it out sir," said the captain. "Oi'm goin' in closer to the shore and get some shelter, then we'll keep movin' on our way west."

"It's too dark to see a damn thing," said the viscount, "you'll put us on the rocks. Call yourself a sailor? You couldn't paddle a dinghy across a mill pond on a calm day."

"Your eyes get used to it sir, there's some moon," the captain reassured them. "Besides, there's a light over yonder, movin' in the same direction as us, bit higher than our masthead light, probably a sloop a bit bigger than we."

"You're a bloody fool," shouted Dunbargan. "I know what these damn Cornish wreckers do. There'll be a party over on the cliff path with a donkey I'll be bound, with a lantern under its belly, trying to lure bloody fools like you onto the rocks. Watch out man!" He had caught sight in the moonlight of a line of white tops breaking just ahead of them.

"Hold tight!" yelled the skipper, and heaved on the wheel. The sloop heeled again as it swerved violently to avoid the partially submerged reef right ahead. The viscount staggered across the cabin. There was a crunching noise as the hull scraped on the edge of the rocks. The sloop lurched, lost way for a moment, its keel caught on the reef. The viscount lost his footing, fell to the floor. The keel broke free as a swell lifted the hull and a gust of wind swung the boom across and caught the flapping sails and dragged the sloop into clear seas.

There was a scream from the fo'c'stle and a thump as the maid fell out of her bunk. The bulkhead to the cabin was whipped open by the wind. The women hung on to handholds inside the cabin for dear life. Catherine saw naked fear on the viscount's face as he scrambled to his feet.

The viscount yelled, "Turn man, turn, goddam your eyes."

"Hold on, sir, we'm better off in the open sea," the skipper called, raising his voice against the noise. "Less danger of bein' 'it by another boat, runnin' aground. Oi've been through worse. She be already blowin' 'erself out. These summer squalls don't last long, you mark my words. Anyroad, with respect sir, O'im cap'n 'ere, an' my crew takes orders from me."

The viscount finally realized he was powerless. The three huddled together in the cabin, holding on. After an hour or so the wind indeed abated and the waves got smaller. They dozed off where they were in the cabin, Elianor leaning against her husband's shoulder. Catherine awoke to the sound of the captain's voice ordering his crew to bail out the seawater that was sloshing about in the scuppers.

After what seemed an interminable time, they saw the grey dawn through a porthole. Great cliffs loomed a quarter of a mile away to starboard. The motion of the boat was smoother. Catherine opened the cabin door and saw the captain still at the wheel. "Where are we, skipper?" she asked.

"We've crossed Mount's Bay and've just turned north around Land's End," he replied. "The wind's dropped, and blowing from behind us. It'll be a nice sail to Cape Cornwall."

"How long?" she asked. "Not more than an hour, ma'am," the captain said. "Thank heavens," said Catherine, "and thanks to you too, captain."

They dropped anchor in a sheltered rocky cove near Wheal Hykka and lowered the sails. The Dunbargans came in to the cockpit bleary eyed and dispirited. Catherine sent one of the sailors to row the footman in the dinghy to a little beach and set him ashore to walk to the mine and announce their arrival.

It was full light as the dinghy bumped against the rocks at the base of the cliff. The sailor wedged the painter into a crack between the rocks and stayed in the dinghy. The footman scrambled out, got a foothold on the lowest rock and scrambled up a yard or two until he reached a steep cliff path. As he climbed up he noticed the burned-out shell of a building. Further along he saw a substantial building that looked as if it might be the count house and made his way towards it. He tried the sturdy door but it was locked. He knocked three times. He heard a shuffling inside, a rattle of bolts, and the clanking of the lock.

An old man sleepily opened the door and growled, "What do 'e want? Who be 'e?"

The footman explained that he had come in the sloop lying at anchor below the cliff and had been sent by Mrs. Eliot to give a message to her husband. The door keeper pondered a moment and said, "Bain't 'ere."

"Where can Oi find 'im then?" asked the footman.

"Down Pendeen. Cap'n Penwarden's place," said the doorkeeper.

"How do I get there?" asked the footman.

"If Oi was ye Oi wouldn' start from 'ere," grunted the doorkeeper. The footman was having trouble following the conversation, but he put that down to the fact that the Cornish down west spoke differently. He couldn't think what to say next, so he just looked appealingly. After a moment or two the doorkeeper chuckled and pointed. "Can't miss it, m'dear," he said. The footman waved to the sailor in the dinghy below and set off. As he neared the village he asked a passerby for directions to the Penwardens' house and found it only a few yards further on. He knocked on the back door and announced himself to the boy of fifteen or so who opened it and took him into the living room.

Edward Eliot was sitting in a chair by the fireplace. He was deep in conversation with a powerfully built man who appeared to be in his thirties and another in clerical garb who seemed a little older. Eliot looked up. "What are you doing here?"

The footman replied, "Mrs. Eliot sent me. Said to fetch you. 'Er's in the sloop down in the cove below that there mine. Us sailed through a nasty storm. Wanted to stay on board safe loike, until 'er knowed where you was."

"Mrs. Eliot would be welcome in my house, sir," said the younger man. "P'r'aps Morwenna could leave the nurse to manage things upstairs and come down to arrange something for 'er to eat, unless she's eaten already on the boat."

"Is she all right? What's she doing here? Is there anyone with her?" asked Eliot. "There was a hell of a storm last night."

The footman responded, "Us survived, bit weary. 'Er came down west to see you and 'ow things was goin' at the mine. There's the crew and 'er maid, sir, and a lady and gen'leman what us picked up at Bodinnick, down the river from Fowey."

Eliot stroked his chin. "Names?" The footman looked puzzled. "Oi don't rightly know, zir, but Oi think them called 'im viscount, dung or some such."

"Dunbargan!" exclaimed the younger man, springing to his feet. "That devil will never cross my threshold!"

The preacher spoke urgently. "Control yourself, Penwarden, this is a time for seeking reconciliation, not further strife."

Chapter Sixty-two

Healing

Reverend Perry knew there were times he had to be a peacemaker. "Penwarden, swallow your pride, contain your anger. This is not just about you and your wife. It's about Wheal Hykka, Pendeen, all of Cornwall. You are their leader here. Right now many of the tinners are angry at you as well as at the adventurers and the authorities. But you are their best hope; they will come to see that. Remember, we have no choice but to struggle, but we must not fight. We can influence, but we cannot overcome; they have too much power. Be sensible, be wise."

"All very well for you to say, Reverend," said Addis Penwarden, "Your wife ain't been shot, lyin' at death's door, me worried stiff, all because of that arrogant bloody Dunbugger. Thinks 'e's lord god almighty, can do what 'e likes."

"Come now, Penwarden, there's a good chap," said Eliot, "the good reverend is right. I sympathize with what you are suffering; indeed I fear that my own wife has put herself in danger. But we all have to stay calm, get the situation under control." He turned to his footman. "You make haste, get back down to the sloop. Tell Mrs. Eliot to stay where she is. Make sure she understands that. Don't let the viscount or anyone else talk her out of it. They should all stay fast until I give a signal, you understand? Make sure the viscount understands that as well. I'll be at the mine within the hour, and I'll wave from the cliff top if it's safe to come up."

After the footman left, Reverend Perry slumped in his chair with his eyes closing. He rubbed his forehead, made himself alert and sat up. "Mr. Eliot, Mr. Eliot," he said, "now what do we do? No sooner have matters calmed down a bit than the viscount arrives on the scene. With respect, sir, and with all due regard for his position, we must ask you to see to it that he doesn't anger the people further and get things stirred up again."

"He's not comin' in my house, never," said Penwarden, thumping the arm of his chair with his fist. "If Dunbugger hadn't sent the soldiers us'd 'ave got through this on our own selves, without no blood bein' shed. 'E made it worse than what 'twere, an' now 'e's comin' stickin' 'is nose in, stirrin' it up all over again."

There was a clattering on the stairs. The door to the room opened and Morwenna came in, looking concerned. "Mr. Penwarden, your wife is very poorly. The old village nurse is back, doing what she can but that's not much. There's no one else to ask to help who knows any better. Lizzie's sweating; she's hot all over. I bathe her forehead with cold water and give her a sip to drink every now and then, but she's feverish. She's asking for you. I know you're busy, but you'd better come."

Penwarden jumped to his feet, and so did Reverend Perry. "I'll see what I can do, Penwarden," said the preacher. "You know, I grew up hearing stories about the wonderful works our forefathers performed, long before our Savior was born on this earth. I believe I am blessed with their gift of healing. My people have lived in Cornwall for generations. I know I too can lift a person's spirit. And often that does wonders for their bodily health."

"I don't know that I understand that kind of thing," said Eliot, "I'll leave you to it. I'll go over to the chapel and see how our men are getting on with the tinners. Join me as soon as you can. We'd better get over to the mine then, and see to the party on the sloop." He paused and looked with concern at Perry. "Perhaps you'd better stay here, Reverend. You look all in. Rest a while, refresh your energy."

"I'm in good hands, Mr. Eliot. My energy comes from our Lord. And through me he will send energy to Mrs. Penwarden and bring her to complete recovery, I promise you."

"You've been through a lot, man," persisted Eliot, "the village needs your support. Now is no time to collapse from overwork."

"See what you can do for Lizzie, reverend," said Penwarden, "'er thinks a lot of you, and your touch would give 'er comfort. But Mr. Eliot is right, you've been a tower of strength, but you've 'ad a powerful lot cast your way, one funeral after another seems like, an' that's not the least of it."

"Leave me be, I know my limitations and my strength," said Perry. "You stay with me, Penwarden, and we'll see to Lizzie. Then we'll do our duty and join the others."

Eliot left the house, waving to the Penwarden boys who were playing outside, and walked over to look in on the meeting at the chapel. The other men went upstairs to the bedroom where Lizzie was lying. They stood on either side of her bed. She was looking terrible, wan and with bright red spots on her cheeks. Addis bent over and kissed her gently on her damp forehead. She was frowning but smiled feebly. The nurse stood at the foot of the bed with Morwenna who said, "We've tried all we know, Reverend. Can you do something for her?"

"I'll do my best," said the preacher, "but it won't be me, it'll be our Savior." He knelt by the bed and reached across with his hands. He laid one on Lizzie's feverish forehead. He laid the other ever so gently on her bandaged shoulder, the one struck by the musket ball.

Reverend Perry knelt silently and slightly adjusted the position of his hands. He closed his eyes and his lips moved in silent prayer. After several minutes they saw the tension on Lizzie's face relax. Except for his lips, Perry did not move or open his eyes. Lizzie let out a shuddering breath. Morwenna dipped a cloth in the pan of cold water and moved toward her, but Addis put up his hand to stop her. "Leave 'er be," he muttered. Morwenna hung a sheet over the window to dim the sunlight in the room. Lizzie closed her eyes. They waited.

Reverend Perry opened his eyes and stood up. He held his forefinger to his lips, motioned to them to follow him quietly out of the room, and shut the bedroom door behind them. "Let her sleep," he whispered, "her soul is filled with hope, now give her body a chance to heal." The nurse remained sitting in a chair outside the bedroom, and the rest of them tiptoed down the stairs.

"You men go about your business," said Morwenna. "I'll take care of Lizzie." She set to work after they left to go to the chapel. She tidied up the living room, washed and dried the dirty dishes in the kitchen sink and filled the basin with fresh cold water from the pump for Lizzie. She carried it upstairs and quietly reentered the bedroom with the nurse behind her.

Morwenna gently felt Lizzie's forehead, trying not to disturb her. It was cool to her touch. Lizzie's eyes opened and she smiled. "It's dark in 'ere," she said. "Take that sheet off the window so Oi can see proper. Oi feel ever so much better. Oi'll be myself again in no toime, just you wait."

"You look better, brighter color, no fever," said Morwenna. "Whatever happened?"

"Oi don't rightly know," said Lizzie. "Oi started feelin' different. Then I realized Mr. Perry 'ad laid is 'ands on me. Oi felt all warm, all through my body, from the top of my 'ead right down to my toes, an sort of tremblin' loike. Never felt nothin' loike that before. Felt wonderful."

"It's a miracle," said Morwenna.

The old nurse shook her head. "Oi think 'twas me ointment, often works that way, least that's what people tell me."

Lizzie tried to sit up, then fell back on her pillows. "Oi knew Oi was goin' to get better," she said. "Oi knew Oi wasn't goin' to die, wasn't afraid no more. Oi sort of let go and slept. Now Oi've woke up, Oi almost feel as if Oi could get up right away. Where's Addis, where are the boys?"

"You stay right where you are," said Morwenna. "If you try to get up too soon it'll just take longer to heal. Nurse will stay with you while I make you some nice hot soup."

✥✥✥

Meanwhile in the fellowship room at the chapel, Reverend Perry attempted another miracle, although he was too modest to think of his efforts in that way. The two stewards, Clymo and Polkinghorne, with the eager but inexperienced aid of Bunt, had been talking to the ringleaders of the miners. They tried to get them to promise to act peacefully and with goodwill and patience while all concerned did their best to work things out and get the mine back to work. But they had made no progress. The tinners felt that the adventurers and their agents were more concerned with their own selfish reasons for getting repairs accomplished than with the welfare of miners.

When Addis Penwarden and Reverend Perry joined them, Edward Eliot and the stewards were on the point of giving up on reaching the slightest agreement. The miners were convinced they would have to fight to get anything but had little idea what the implications might be for themselves and their families. They were suspicious of any olive branch that was proffered. They were impatient. They were stuck in the stubbornness born of desperation.

Edward Eliot was reluctant to agree to fundamental changes in the way things were. The other adventurers had a voice, and Dunbargan's was loud. While he had received his share on favorable terms Eliot had a great deal at stake, not least his reputation and his influence, and he expected a commensurate return. Plenty of past optimists had spent their fortunes on digging exploratory shafts only at best to find meager deposits not worth extracting. Even with his important position with the Duchy of Cornwall, he could not, on his own, change the cost book system, or the auctioning of setts, or incur expenses for safety devices, or introduce compensation for injured miners. Every man had to look after himself; that is what toughened the breed, made Britain great. And when all was said and done, order had to be maintained. Being lenient with these people only encouraged further demands, even more riots.

Reverend Perry stood to speak. "I have nothing to do with managing the mines," he said thoughtfully, "but I have responsibility for my flock, socially and physically as well as spiritually, as far as it is in my power to influence things. It seems to me you must do first things first. Forgiveness can be a powerful force for change."

"The captain's job is to run the mine, tell the men what to do," said Penwarden. "If Oi forgave them for all the damage they done, causin' the soldiers to be sent for, so that my Lizzie got wounded so bad Oi might lose 'er, they wouldn't respect me no more. Oi couldn't go on as captain."

"Perhaps the owners might forgive them on certain terms," said Reverend Perry, "while still supporting your authority."

Eliot perked up, saying, "Go on, Mr. Perry." The tinners stayed quiet, ready to listen to what the preacher had to say. He was respected as a man of fairness and compassion.

"Perhaps Tom Kegwyn could get the men to agree to work on repairing the damage, especially the biggest troublemakers, maybe for a modest payment. They couldn't all be employed right away, so perhaps they could take turns, each earning enough to keep their families fed."

"They couldn't do no good with the steam engine," Penwarden said. "That takes skill."

"Perhaps repairing the buildings, with direction, cleaning up the place," said Reverend Perry. "One more thing. Perhaps the adventurers could subscribe to a fund to purchase additional food, pay for burials, even help with care for the injured. We could let that be known; bring good will."

"What about it, Kegwyn?" asked Eliot.

"Well zir," the ringleader replied, scratching his chin, "Oi think Oi might be able to talk them into somethin' loike that there." Eliot looked around the table at his men. Polkinghorne and Bunt nodded; so did Penwarden. They all looked at Joseph Clymo.

"I can't speak for the viscount, sir," said Clymo, "but I dare say you could persuade him to see things your way. You'd have to talk to him first, before he meets the men; prepare him." Reverend Perry leaned forward, put his elbows on the table, and rested his head in his hands. No one spoke.

Eliot thought fast. His instinct was to make no concessions, insist on order and discipline. That was the way things were done, the way his class maintained their position and authority. But was that the best way to get the men back to work, start the mine making money again? That, after all, was the important thing. Would they work well if they were driven back against their wills? What would Catherine think? Being a woman, she would probably feel compassion for the families and advise compromise, understanding. Typical feminine approach, but not without merit. Perhaps Reverend Perry was right; there could be a middle way, one that worked for the best for all. He got to his feet.

"That's settled then," said Eliot. "Penwarden, you and Kegwyn talk to the men and tell them the plan. I'll go up to the mine with the others. We'll need time to get his lordship's cooperation and rescue the ladies from that sloop. Perhaps they could be persuaded to help you, Mr. Perry, while they're here. No doubt you wish to get on with your organizing tasks."

"Indeed sir," said the preacher, "I must go about my duties and leave you to yours. Their help would be welcome and would not go unnoticed." As the others left the room Peter Perry stayed behind at the chapel to do what he could.

Eliot walked on up to the cliff path overlooking the cove. He felt confident that the situation would be brought under control, provided the viscount did not stir things up again. He waved at the sloop at anchor below. A sailor saw him and knocked on the door of the cabin. Catherine came out on deck and waved back. He signaled to her for them to come ashore and he scrambled down the rocky cliff path to meet her at the landing place. A sailor held a dinghy alongside the sloop. Catherine and the Dunbargans stepped down into it, and the sailor rowed them ashore.

Eliot gave his hand to the ladies as they debarked. "Welcome to Wheal Hykka all of you!" he said, embracing Catherine. "Things still in a tangle?" boomed Dunbargan, a little off balance as he clambered out of the dinghy and gave a disgusted glance at his wet boots. "I got here in the nick of time I expect. I'll soon sort these barbarians out."

Eliot restrained himself from the temptation to push Dunbargan back into the sea. "In fact things show signs of settling down," Eliot said. "I believe we have a plan, and your cooperation in furthering peace will be much appreciated, indeed essential. But, now, let's go up to the count house for a full report. Our men are waiting for us. Perhaps you ladies would like to go on into Pendeen village. See if you could lend a hand to Reverend Perry. He's arranging food with the village women. It's not far to walk, the sailor could escort you, and Perry will be looking for you."

"In due time," said Catherine. "Lady Dunbargan and I would prefer to attend your meeting, learn what has been going on at first hand. Am I correct, Elianor?"

Both men stared at them.

"Indeed," said Elianor, "most definitely. We would of course not expect to say anything, but we could later give you our views as detached observers, if we had anything worthy of imparting. And we might even be of some use to you."

"Oh, good God, this is serious business," spluttered the viscount, "no place for well-bred ladies like yourselves. No knowing what might come about."

"We appreciate your concern, my lord, but rest assured we are well able to take care of ourselves," said Catherine. She looked at her husband. "Don't you agree, my dear?"

Eliot hesitated for only a moment. "Well, of course," he said. "Advice from the fair sex is often invaluable and always irresistible."

They started up the path with the gentlemen helping the ladies and the sailor taking up the rear. They were not a quarter of the way before the viscount stopped, breathing heavily and mopping his brow. He turned to face the sea. "Lovely view," he panted. "You ladies should pause a while to enjoy it to the full. Atlantic Ocean, if I'm not mistaken."

Catherine hid a smile. "You are too courteous, my lord," she said, "but we must not allow our frailties to detain our husbands from attending to their important business with the greatest urgency possible."

The viscount glared and they resumed their climb, albeit at a slower pace. When they reached the counting house, Eliot posted the sailor to keep an eye on the dinghy and ushered the others inside. The group already sitting around the table stood up as they entered. In addition to Clymo, Polkinghorne, Bunt and Penwarden there were three other men at the table, shabbily dressed and none too clean.

"Who are these fellows and what are they doing here?" demanded Dunbargan.

"Morning, sirs, ladies," said Penwarden, ill at ease at the viscount's arrival and the sight of the ladies, but knowing he had to speak up, say his piece. "Them's tinners, work at Wheal Hykka."

The viscount scowled and said, "They can leave, can't stay here." What was Penwarden up to? Laborers had to be kept in their places.

"Perhaps you should learn what has been talked about before you act too hastily, my lord," said Eliot. "I understand these are the unofficial leaders of the miners; the others look up to them, take notice of what they say. They may be persuaded to help settle things down, and that is necessary to be sure."

"We don't need help," said Dunbargan, "we need discipline. Someone needs to be flogged. That's what I say, show who's in charge. Bolitho agrees with me. No time like the present. Let's start with these rascals. What have they been up to, eh?"

"Penwarden," said Eliot wearily, "send these men outside, but keep them around. We'll talk later. Bunt, go with them, keep an eye on things."

"But zir, p'raps Oi can 'elp make plans," said Bunt.

Polkinghorne jumped in, "Do as Mr. Eliot says, look sharp now." Reluctantly, Bunt left with the others.

"My lord, much has occurred since you last heard of goings on at Wheal Hykka," said Eliot, "serious goings on. The accidents, the deaths and the injuries, made the miners angry."

"Them thought them accidents could've been prevented with proper safety measures," said Penwarden. Clymo spoke in a low voice. "Later man, this is not the time."

"Without work and with no pay the miners can't feed their families," continued Eliot. "Things got further out of hand, no fault of Penwarden's. He did his best. Someone, we're not entirely sure at whose behest, called out the soldiery, a sore and tragic mistake. A detachment came down from Penzance. In my view, they made matters worse, antagonized the miners. Not to mince words, there has been a riot, tempers out of control, a lot of damage done to property."

"I see I was wrong about the flogging," said the viscount. "Flogging's too good for them. We need a good hanging around here, that's what would settle things down. Show them the halter, hang the ringleaders, flog the rest. And make them all pay for the damage, the repairs."

Penwarden could not control himself. "Bloody 'ell, that be 'alf the trouble; them don't 'ave the money to take care of their families, let alone pay for damage. I know. Them's my neighbors."

"Then take it from their pay when they start back to work," said Dunbargan, "those you let back. Your trouble is you're too soft, Penwarden, maybe too soft for your position."

Eliot was about to speak when there was a knock at the door, and Bunt came into the room, with a stranger at his side. "Pardon me interruptin', yer honors, but Oi thought as 'ow you might want to 'ear what this gen'leman 'ad to say."

The newcomer was portly, broad-shouldered and sturdy, with a florid complexion. He took off his hat and bowed. Then he addressed them. "Oi am the constable at Penzance, sent by authority of the magistrates on official business. Me an' my men is 'ere to effect the arrest of Tom Kegwyn and two of 'is companions. Them is to be 'eld in the town gaol until them can be sent to Bodmin to go to the assizes to be tried."

"On what charge my good man?" demanded Eliot.

"Breach of the king's peace, wanton damage to chattels, destruction of real property, and raisin' a riot, sir."

"What will happen to them?" asked Catherine.

"It's usually a hangin' matter, ma'am."

"Exactly what they deserve," said Dunbargan, sitting back in his chair and folding his arms over his chest, "the sooner the better."

Penwarden put both hands into his pockets, then clenched his fists. He took a deep breath, struggled to control his temper, then leapt to his feet, waving his arms. "When that steam engine blew up, it caused ructions. But that won't be the biggest explosion around these parts, not by a long shot!"

Chapter Sixty-three

Ringleaders

"Where them got to?" demanded the constable.

"Where are they, Bunt?" asked Eliot.

"Oi dunno, zir," said Bunt, "outside Oi 'spect. Oi kept an eye on 'em like you said, but they said them needed to go around the corner for a minute. Oi didn't ask why, if you know what Oi mean."

Dunbargan looked daggers at him. "You'd better find them, you idiot," he said, "or I'll have you flogged too. Should have seen to that years ago."

Eliot laid a hand on the viscount's arm. "He's my man now, Dunbargan: I'll see to whatever needs doing. Now, Bunt, hurry up and find them. You men help him, and be quick about it."

After the others left Catherine Eliot stepped forward and spoke to her husband. "This is going much too far. This is a matter for the mine, you and the viscount can deal with it. You must order the constable to leave. What will happen to their families if these men are hanged? What will ever happen to the mine? No one in this village will work willingly again."

"They'll have no choice," said the viscount, "or the village will die too. Good riddance, I say. We'll just bring in other miners; they must do what they're told."

Elianor Dunbargan frowned at her husband but said nothing.

"There's nothin' Oi can do, gentlemen," said the constable. "Oi don't make the laws, Oi just enforce them. That's my job, enforce the law. Now that them're in the 'ands of the law, you'll 'ave to speak to the judge when the time comes. Beggin' your pardon, Oi'll go look too."

Penwarden was leading the group of missing men from the back of a storage shed to the door of the counting house. Tom Kegwyn and the other ringleaders looked dumbfounded. Kegwyn was defiant, the others frightened.

"No good tryin' to run," said the constable, "would be worse for you." He gave an order to his men. "Put 'em in irons."

One of the men reached into a sack at his feet, took out a chain and manacles and hinged rings. The other grabbed Kegwyn who tried to pull free.

"Lay off me," said Kegwyn angrily, "or it'll be worse for you when me mates 'ear of it."

The constable said, "Shut your gob, you'm takin' orders from us now."

The assistant constable strengthened his grip on Kegwyn's arms, fitted manacles around both of his wrists, pulled his arms behind him and locked the manacles securely. Next he fastened the ring around Kegwyn's neck with a chain looped to the manacles. The other assistants treated the other two miscreants in the same way, none too gently. Then they linked them all together with chains fastened at the neck rings, connected with another length to lead them by.

They dragged their prisoners to the side of the count house where the horses were tethered. One fastened the end of the chain to a pommel on his saddle. The constable and his men set off, leading their prisoners roughly behind them, stumbling. One lost his balance and fell and was dragged along the stony track by the horse. Penwarden rushed forward, tugged on the horse's bridle, halted it, helped the man to his feet. His breeches were torn, his knee bleeding.

"Tell my missus what's 'appened to us," called Tom Kegwyn.

"Those poor men," said Elianor Dunbargan, shocked. She was surprised at her own reaction.

"Elianor, control yourself. They're getting what they deserve," said the viscount.

"Nothing we can do at this stage," Edward Eliot said.

Catherine was not mollified. "That is simply not acceptable," she said, her eyes flashing.

"What an outrageous statement you make, Madam," barked the viscount, rounding on Catherine. "We should never have allowed you women to join us. Done nothing but interfere and make trouble where you're not wanted and in affairs about which you know nothing."

Elianor was grim when she whirled to face Dunbargan. "Nothing like the trouble you have caused, husband," she hissed. "You alone have made things go from bad to worse. Do you have no decent feelings for anybody?"

The viscount took a pace back. "Wife," he said "control your tongue. I will have respect. Kindly have the decency not to demean yourself in front of servants. We will speak further in private."

Elianor threw her hands in the air, turned her back on her husband, and stormed out of the building, shouting over her shoulder, "Speak we will indeed, but not for long."

The Eliots hurried outside to join her. "Calm down, my dear, do calm down," said Eliot.

"Why on earth should she?" demanded Catherine. "The man is a brute. I don't know why she puts up with him. And don't talk to me about wifely duty."

Eliot looked over his shoulder to see if anyone was around. "It's important for us all to behave with propriety. Perhaps it is time that we took our leave. I could sail back with you ladies and suggest to his lordship that he travel to Lanhydrock with the Clymos at a time of his choosing."

"That will not do," said Catherine. "It is imperative that you stay here; it is your duty. You certainly can't leave Dunbargan here alone. You must see to it that Kegwyn and his friends are properly treated. It's not just a question of mercy, God knows. It is also a practical matter. If no end is put to this quarrelling the mine will never get back to making money. That's a matter of hard cash."

Eliot moved away from them to watch the receding backs of the constables and their prisoners.

"Oh, I'm sick of the mine, and all of Dunbargan's doings, his conniving, his gambling, and his smuggling," declared Lady Dunbargan, putting her hands over her face. "Yes, I know about that. He thinks it's a secret, but things get about, I have loyal servants at Lanhydrock. I keep my eyes and ears open, little is kept from me. What he gets into is nothing but quarrelling, and bullying, and anger and cheating. I can't even be confident that he remains faithful to me; sometimes I hope he doesn't." She stopped and looked at them. "Oh, forgive me for blurting out my worries, but I do consider you both good friends. Why can't I just be rich on my own account and be done with it?"

"My God, Elianor, I can quite see why you are upset," said Catherine, putting an arm around the lady's shoulders.

"Speaking for myself," replied Elianor, "if I may be candid, I would be only too happy to sail with you and leave my husband on the shore. But now that we have come all this way, Catherine, we must go to Reverend Perry. We have to be persistent and help him and the women gather food for the miners and then to get started with the school. We must at least make lists of what they need so that we can procure their requirements."

Eliot moved back to Catherine's side as she replied to Elianor, "If I may be equally frank, my dear, I'm glad to hear you say that, as I need you to stay here to help me persuade my own husband. You and I must personally concern ourselves with the village's welfare. We can't leave it to our husbands to do what is right, let alone wise. It's not their nature, not the way they were brought up. As women, we look at things differently. We are naturally more caring." She smiled sweetly at Edward. "You do understand, don't you, my dear husband? After all, it's just Christian charity, isn't it?" She put her hand in his arm.

"Ladies, you are incorrigible," said Edward, "but there may be some truth in what you say. For now, take one of the servants to escort you to the chapel. Talk to Reverend Perry. He seems to have a level head on his shoulders, up to a point, but don't get carried away. Don't make any promises without consulting me, and remember, we all have a position to keep up. If we lose that we also lose the ability to do anything positive. I'll go and see what's going on inside."

The ladies nodded, gathered themselves and prepared to leave. Eliot squared his shoulders, took a deep breath and turned to reenter the counting house.

"Wait," said Elianor, "I am not leaving here without talking to my husband. I have quite made up my mind. I shall walk to the cliff top. Please ask him to join me as a matter of urgency."

"But Lady Dunbargan," Eliot began. Elianor interrupted, "Mr. Eliot, please just do as I say."

Catherine was startled; her friend evidently had more determination than she had perceived hitherto. "Do or say nothing rash that you may live to regret, my dear," said Catherine.

"Have no fear on my account," Elianor replied, "I will do nothing that I have not already pondered over for months. And keep in mind that my family was landed gentry when my husband's ancestors were upstart merchants, no doubt making their fortunes in ways that would not have borne examination from that day to this. Oh no, Mrs. Eliot, I have no more respect for the title my husband purchased, like the tradesman he is, than I do for his behavior. Both are beneath contempt, and believe me I have only just begun to say and do exactly what I please." With that she lifted her skirts out of the dust and swept up the path.

The Eliots looked at each other. Catherine smiled with a twinkle in her eye. "I am not leaving now, my dear," said Catherine. "I would not miss this for the world. I can scarcely imagine the difficulty of the position you find yourself in, but I have every confidence in your ability to deal with it."

Edward grinned at her ruefully. "Perhaps I can rely not only on your continued presence but also the support that I have come to count on from you, my dear," he said.

"My dear Edward," she replied, "we women know that our proper place is to defer to our brave and wise husbands when it comes to dealing with situations of great difficulty." She patted his cheek.

Edward glanced up the path and saw that Lady Dunbargan had almost reached the top. He might as well proceed with his duty. Nothing would be gained by procrastination, even if the wife he loved would permit such a thing. He squared his shoulders once again and opened the door to the count house to admit himself and Catherine.

"Ah, there you are at last, Eliot," said the viscount, "been dallying with the ladies? Far more important things to do here. I've been telling Captain Penwarden that he needs to find a dozen more rioters to hang. Got to put one's foot down. Clymo agrees, naturally. Hope you don't intend to go milksop on me, eh?"

"My lord," said Eliot, "there is a bit of difficulty. Your wife wishes you to go to her as a matter of urgency to discuss something she has on her mind."

"Urgency, discuss?" Dunbargan asked, "What now? Why now? I have business matters to attend to. Where has she got herself to?"

"She took a walk to the cliff top, my lord," said Eliot.

The viscount harrumphed, "Why on earth would she do that?"

Eliot said, "I imagine she may be enjoying the view, but she said that it was imperative she speak with you."

"Might as well get it over with, I suppose, see what the hell she wants now. I'll be back to arrange the hangings shortly."

The viscount brushed past Edward, ignored Catherine, left the counting house door open behind him and strode up the path to the top of the cliff. The others crowded in the doorway and watched, not sure what to anticipate but not wanting to forego the possible spectacle.

Dunbargan reached his wife. She received him with arms stiffly at her sides. They heard her shouting at him above the distant crashing of the breakers on the rocks below, but the wind from the sea blew away her words. He waved his arms at her, and she turned her back to him. He seized her shoulders and turned her to face him again, shaking his finger in her face. She stamped her foot. He was bellowing and waving his arms again. She slapped his cheek. They saw him draw back, throw his arms in the air, turn on his heel and stride back down the path, leaving Lady Dunbargan weeping.

They scurried back inside the count house and were sitting around the big table by the time Viscount Dunbargan stormed in through the front door. "Clymo, give me your horse and get it saddled up immediately," he scowled. "Something has come up at Lanhydrock. I am going back now to deal with it firmly, and you will escort me." He crossed his arms over his chest and rolled back on the balls of his feet, facing Eliot. "Now Eliot, be sure you don't let things slide in my absence. Send me news of hangings, and get this damned mine ticking again."

"But my l-lord," spluttered Joseph Clymo, "how do you expect me to go? I can hardly walk. It's much too far. And what about Morwenna? I need to take her with me; she can't travel those roads on her own. She rode down pinion with me. How will she get back to Lanhydrock?"

"She's resourceful enough," said Dunbargan. "She'll manage somehow, trust me, I know. If not, she'll either have to walk or live among the tinners. Nothing to do with me. Stop blathering man, we must leave, now."

"Polkinghorne, lend Clymo your horse," said Eliot, "you can pick it up on your way back to Port Eliot later. Get one for yourself from the ostler at the inn."

Polkinghorne readily agreed. He was thoughtful for a moment, then said, "Mr. Clymo, just leave it to me. I'll personally see that Miss Clymo is apprised of your departure and help her make some suitable arrangement."

"Don't you worry, Clymo," interjected Catherine, "I'll see that your daughter is taken care of, and in fact I'll be glad for her to stay and help me while she is here."

Clymo looked relieved. Polkinghorne looked disappointed. Bunt thought of suggesting that Morwenna could borrow his horse, which he would be glad of an excuse to collect from her later, but resisted the temptation to intrude on the conversation. Besides, Polkinghorne's was a superior mount.

"What about her ladyship?" inquired Clymo.

"I've instructed her to remain here," said Dunbargan, "and to await my return in due course. Now then, can't wait around. Clymo, get your necessities together and prepare to leave. Bring money, we can buy food and stay at an inn on the way. Eliot, kindly instruct your captain to have my stuff sent from the sloop as soon as possible."

Quickly completing their preparations, it was only a few minutes before the pair mounted and departed. Clymo waved farewell. Dunbargan spurred his horse viciously and headed up the track at a sharp canter without a glance backward.

"Well, well, that's that for now. Now we can get down to business," said Eliot. "Penwarden, give me a detailed plan on how you will settle the men down and get the mine back to work. I need to see a list of repairs, costs, materials you require, helpers you need, how long it will take. Perhaps we should get Smeaton back here."

"I'm going to see to Lady Dunbargan," said Catherine. "I admire her spirit but she could no doubt do with some comfort right now. I'll get her to come down to the village with me to help Reverend Perry. Take her mind off her own troubles. It's no good you men expecting the tinners to go back to work if you haven't looked after food for their families. And while I'm about it, I'll see to those who were injured, help with dressing their wounds, nursing."

"I'd be glad to escort you, Mrs. Eliot," said Polkinghorne, "then I could look in at the Penwardens and give Mr. Clymo's message to his daughter."

"Oi could 'elp if you want," said Bunt, "give the message to Morwenna, see she's not upset loike."

"I expect you would, Bunt," said Polkinghorne, "but that won't be necessary; I can manage without you." He opened the door for Mrs. Eliot, who beckoned to Lady Dunbargan who had made her way down from the cliff and appeared to be lost in thought just outside the count house. Catherine caught her attention and they walked towards each other. They had a whispered conversation and embraced. Elianor dabbed at her eyes and smiled bravely. Catherine collected the footman and they set off together towards Pendeen.

Chapter Sixty-four

Love

Charles Polkinghorne walked from Wheal Hykka down to the village. With a spring in his step and a smile on his face he was more than ordinarily aware of the sea air in his lungs, of the rhythmic crashing of the Atlantic surf against the craggy cliffs behind him, the singing of the birds in the hedges, the scent of the wildflowers beside the track, and the rolling beauty of the wild Cornish countryside. He would have whistled if he had ever learned as a boy, but at the time it had seemed like a frivolous pursuit. He had to content himself with puffing white smoke rings from his old clay pipe towards the brilliant blue sky.

Usually he would have taken notice of the people he was walking with and been particularly solicitous of Mrs. Eliot and Lady Dunbargan, conscious of his responsibility for escorting them. However, today Polkinghorne's mind was on other things than business, and as it happened, the ladies were also preoccupied and talking between themselves, leaving him to his own thoughts.

Polkinghorne realized that his private contemplation for many weeks now had an unaccustomed focus. He had grown to wish that his life as a bachelor might come to an end and had finally admitted to himself that his admiration and respect for Morwenna Clymo had flowered into love. He had been eagerly looking forward to his role as the trusted messenger from Joseph Clymo to his beloved daughter and hoped that Mrs. Eliot would forget her offer and become involved in other issues. He would be glad of an opportunity to speak with Morwenna alone.

They arrived at the chapel to find a span of mules standing outside. The mules' handlers were unloading panniers of fresh vegetables and fruits with the help of a crowd of men, women and children. Inside Reverend Perry bustled about, his coat off, working with yet more villagers. They laid out baskets of all shapes and sizes on long tables and were filling the baskets with piles of produce of a size to feed a family: potatoes, cabbages, beans, turnips, apples, berries.

Two women were cutting off the outside leaves of the cabbages and the tops of the turnips and brushing earth off the potatoes. At another table women and children equipped with knives were reaching into buckets and putting slippery morsels into a cauldron.

"What is going on here?" asked Catherine.

"The children went down to the beach at low tide," said Reverend Perry, "knocked limpets off the rocks, now they're digging them out of their shells to make a stew."

"Goodness me," said Lady Dunbargan, "are they tasty? They don't sound very appetizing." She bent over the cauldron and sniffed the aroma. She wrinkled her nose.

"They're good eating, my lady," said the preacher, "and we don't have the money to buy beef or mutton. We make do with what Mother Nature provides us."

As Charles Polkinghorne had hoped, Catherine became absorbed with the activity in the room. "Our husbands will subscribe to a fund to purchase fish and meat," said Catherine Eliot, "you can count on us. They will talk to the other adventurers, in other mines as well as Wheal Hykka. We will take charge of organizing that. Now tell me, who are those poor people sitting at the side of the room?"

"They got injured or burned in the riot," said Reverend Perry. "Captain Penwarden sent the old nurse who was looking after Mrs. Penwarden to care for them, as best she can. She has made up some salves, but I worry about some who are badly hurt."

"I give you my word, Mr. Perry," said Lady Dunbargan, "that I will send Lanhydrock's doctor from Bodmin to help you. These people must be made well."

"If you ladies will excuse me," said Polkinghorne, "I had better get on to the Penwardens' house and let Miss Clymo know about her father's departure."

"Do ask after Mrs. Penwarden while you're about it," said Catherine, glancing at him, as she joined the others in parceling out the food.

"She is recovering, ma'am," said Reverend Perry, "on that you can count."

As Polkinghorne approached the house he saw the Penwarden boys playing in the front. The older one had climbed into an apple tree and was throwing apples at his little brother. "Hey, stop that, you'll hurt him," shouted Polkinghorne. "Naw, no fear of that, maister," said Jemmy, "Oi'm not tryin' to 'it 'im. Oi could if Oi wanted to, just keepin' 'im busy and collecting them for the Reverend."

"You're the one that needs to be kept busy," said Polkinghorne, "time you went back to work at the mine with your dad. I'm going in to see how your mum's getting along."

Polkinghorne knocked at the front door. Morwenna answered. He smiled warmly and raised his hat. "May I come in, Miss Clymo? I have a message for you from your father."

"Nice to see you, Mr. Polkinghorne," Morwenna said, with an answering smile. "I hope nothing is wrong."

"Nothing could be more right, Miss Clymo," Polkinghorne beamed. "It's a pleasure to see you again. Your father had to leave in a hurry in order to take the viscount back to Lanhydrock on an urgent matter. He asked me to see that you are all right while he is gone. He does not know whether he can come back to collect you himself, in which case he asked me to ensure that you get home safely."

"How kind of you, Mr. Polkinghorne," said Morwenna. "Have I done something special to earn your consideration?" She backed away from the door, waving him in. She turned to the parlor, glancing back at him over her shoulder to see that he followed.

"How is Mrs. Penwarden?" Polkinghorne asked.

"She seems not to be so poorly," said Morwenna. "She's better since Reverend Perry tended to her, I must say. I felt her brow half an hour ago and it was cool. I gave her a sip of cold water, but she was not parched, and since I left her she has been sleeping softly. I feel sure she will get completely well in time."

"Miss Clymo, ahem, if I may be presumptuous," said Polkinghorne, holding his hat by its brim and turning it around in his fingers, "there is something that has been in my mind to say to you for some time."

"Oh, Mr. Polkinghorne," Morwenna smiled, "would you like to sit down, and may I take your hat?"

He gave Morwenna his hat with relief and sat down in a chair. Morwenna took another just across from his. After a moment he put an idle hand into his pocket, thought better of the effect his old clay pipe might have on Morwenna, took his hand out again and folded both hands in his lap.

"Mr. Polkinghorne," said Morwenna, "do tell me what has been in your mind."

Charles Polkinghorne hesitated for a moment. What if Miss Clymo took offense? Well, nothing ventured and all that. He decided to plunge ahead.

"The fact is, Miss Clymo, over the months that we have had the opportunity to make each other's acquaintance, I have grown to admire you considerably. I find that you possess estimable qualities not often found in women. For example, you appear calm and efficient, practical and intelligent."

"You make me sound as if I am far too mannish, Mr. Polkinghorne."

"On the contrary, I could not fail to have noticed your feminine attributes. I'm sure you are aware that I am a bachelor, Miss Clymo, and I must confess that I am unused to conversing with young and attractive ladies, but . . . ."

"I may be young, Mr. Clymo, but I assure you that I am wise beyond my years, or at least so my father assures me, and he is not one to exaggerate. I can tell you that one gets used to things by doing them."

"In which case I will persist, Miss Clymo. Then I would add to your perceived virtues, charm and grace. I wish . . ."

"What is it that you wish, Mr. Polkinghorne?"

"I wish . . . Miss Clymo, I wish to make your closer acquaintance. Indeed, I wish to be of service to you. It has occurred to me that while duty requires us both to remain in Pendeen we could take the opportunity to get to know each other better, perhaps take some walks along the cliff paths, enjoy the beautiful scenery."

"With what in mind exactly, Mr. Polkinghorne?"

"That remains to be seen, Miss Clymo."

"Oh, do be frank, Mr. Polkinghorne, I become quite impatient when people skirt the issue, especially gentlemen." She tossed her head.

Polkinghorne thought again about lighting up his pipe, but once more decided against it. "I trust you will not consider me forward if I am too frank, Miss Clymo, but I assure you my intentions are honorable." He reached across and took her hand in his, his jaw set. He looked into her eyes. "Miss Clymo, as I have said, I am a bachelor. Let me now tell you frankly that I have grown discontented with that state. I cherish the notion that one day I may change that condition for a happier one."

"Why, Mr. Polkinghorne, that is good news indeed." She smiled winsomely and left her hand in his.

"This is not easy for me, Miss Clymo, and you are making it no easier."

"My father tells me that nothing that is worthwhile comes easily, Mr. Polkinghorne."

"It is not difficult to see from whom you gained your wisdom, Miss Clymo. I have grown to respect your father, although I cannot say the same of his employer. Mr. Clymo must sometimes find himself in a difficult position. How do you yourself regard the viscount?"

"I do not know him in the same way that my father does, naturally, but I have had opportunities to observe his behavior at close hand, living as we do nearby at Lanhydrock. I would say that he tends to be quite forceful in taking what he wants, although I have learned that it is best not to discuss one's opinions of one's betters. Now tell me, do you live on the Port Eliot estate?"

"Nearby, Miss Clymo. Mr. Eliot has been kind enough to provide me as his man of business with a comfortable house in his village of St. Germans. It is within easy walking distance of the estate business room at Port Eliot. It occurs to me that my house would be more than adequate for a wife and indeed a family. Perhaps you would like to see it if ever you have the opportunity to join your father on one of his visits to Port Eliot."

He felt Morwenna give his hand an almost imperceptible squeeze.

"I will make a point of it, Mr. Polkinghorne. Now, may I offer you something to eat or drink?"

"Thank you, but no. Duty calls. I wish to look in on the chapel and see how the ladies are getting on. And then I must get back to the mine. Mr. Eliot has more matters to deal with and desires my advice."

"I am sure he puts much reliance on you; he is fortunate. I look forward to seeing you again soon, but I too must do my duty and stay here with Mrs. Penwarden and the boys. Next time perhaps you could put pleasure before duty and stay with me longer . . . Charles."

"Perhaps I will . . . Morwenna. I already feel pleasure calling loudly."

They released their hands and stood, only to grasp them again more closely before wishing each other goodbye.

Chapter Sixty-five

Wrecking

A few days later, conditions at Wheal Hykka had changed little. A handful of men were working on repairs to get the mine back in order and operating again, but at the rate things were going that would not do much good, because most of the tinners, their women and the older children were nowhere to be seen. Addis Penwarden had sent messengers around their cottages to offer turns at temporary laboring work helping with the repairs, but there were few takers.

Willy Bunt had come up with another idea for setting some to work, if they showed up. "Us could start them sortin' the tailin's for the turnpikes," he said. "Now that Liskeard is done, us needs to build more, an us'll need plenty of stone. Wouldn't do no 'arm getting' it in place while 'tis cheap."

"You're not short of ideas, Bunt," Eliot said, "but first things first. We have to get the equipment and buildings repaired, the mine back at work. No point in spending money on what doesn't have to be done yet."

Edward Eliot had decided to stay at Wheal Hykka a few more days to see that things got back on the right track in ways that could last into the future, especially while Viscount Dunbargan was out of the way. He also wanted to keep an eye on what happened to the ringleaders of the riot at the hands of the magistrates.

"Aargh," observed Bunt, "but what Oi think is that a few men and some bal maidens could get back to work right away sortin' and crushin' and shippin' the tailin's from the dump. Wouldn't take no learnin', just beef. Could start pickin' out the pieces of the right size, puttin' 'em in panniers to load on mules for haulin' away."

"That'd be slow haulin' to Liskeard," said Penwarden.

"Just down to the sea," said Bunt, "some place where us could load 'er on a boat, sail d'rec'ly to Port Eliot Quay, pile 'em up there. Once us gets goin', mebbe that Smeaton feller could invent somethin', speed the work up, do it cheaper. Stamp the tailin's, shake 'em through a great big sieve, use an engine to carry 'em down to the cove."

"Won't 'elp," said Penwarden, "no one to work. Them's all gone off, who knows where. Lookin' for food mebbe."

"Them'll be back sooner or later, Oi reckon," said Bunt, "them'll need work. Now, if Oi were you, Mr. Eliot, and beggin' yer pardon, I'd tell the other adventurers that Port Eliot quarry would be willin' to 'elp out, while minin's at a standstill, an' buy the tailin's at a reasonable price. But Oi reckon you'd require an extra fortieth to make it worth your while, loike."

"H'mm, I see Bunt," Eliot mused, "That sort of thing is usually what I rely on Polkinghorne for. I'll be sure to discuss it with him, and perhaps Bolitho, but all in good time. Speaking of Polkinghorne, where is he? He would normally be here by this hour. Ah, that'll be him now, at the door."

But the person who came through the door of the count house was an unexpected visitor. Penwarden greeted him. "Cap'n Williams! It's good to see you. What are you doing here?"

"Penwarden, it is indeed a pleasure to see you again, but I fear you may not be pleased to see me," said John Williams, removing his tall hat.

"We have not had the pleasure of meeting," said Edward Eliot, "although your name is familiar to me and is well regarded. What is the purpose of your visit?"

"Meet Mr. Eliot of Port Eliot, St. Germans, Cap'n Williams," said Penwarden. "He is one of the adventurers most connected with affairs at Wheal Hykka. He is here because there have been troubles of late."

Eliot and Williams shook hands. "Gentlemen," said Williams solemnly, "my mission is not one that I sought out, believe me. I am here at the direction of Viscount Dunbargan in his capacity as chief among the adventurers at Wheal Hykka. He has ordered me to take charge immediately."

"Dunbargan left," said Eliot. "Penwarden is in charge with my support."

"Mr. Eliot," said Williams, "his lordship's letter advised me of some of the details of the goings on and his displeasure at how events have been managed. He has lost confidence in you, Penwarden, and you are to be replaced. I will be taking over. I'm sorry and, indeed, disappointed."

"Wait one bloody minute," said Penwarden. "Oi thought Oi've done the best Oi could in the circumstances, Mr. Williams. Until this latest kerfuffle, you seemed pleased. This'll blow over. Before this, us got the steam engine workin', pumpin' out the new shaft under the sea, bringin' up more ore, gettin' the tinstuff dressed and to the smelters, makin' money for the adventurers."

"Penwarden is right, Captain," said Eliot, "and he is too modest to mention how much he has done to get everything working, and better. The men look up to him as being one of their own. That counts for a lot."

"That's all well and good, Mr. Eliot," said Williams, "but his lordship's instructions are clear. I have to take over at Wheal Hykka immediately, today. I understand the viscount is going to Penzance with

Mr. Bolitho to speak to the magistrates about hanging the rioters. Then he's coming back here to make sure his instructions are carried out here at the mine."

"No doubt your intentions are honorable, and your loyalty to the viscount is commendable," said Eliot, "but I must put you straight. His lordship is indeed an important member of the adventurers here, but as a result of certain agreements that he entered into, I have the governing interest at Wheal Hykka, on behalf of not only myself but also the Duchy of Cornwall. And I will have my say with the Penzance magistrates too, of that you can be quite assured."

"You must answer us this, Mr. Williams," said Penwarden. "Oi am wonderin', how can you be spared for Wheal Hykka from a busy mine like Poldice?"

"It's because of the storm the other day, Penwarden. There was a wreck at Hell's Mouth, up Port Isaac way," said Williams. "Don't know the name of the ship but she was a big one, carrying a rich cargo from the West Indies, rounding Land's End on her way up to Bristol, blown off course at night out of the main channel. The word spread like wildfire, tinners for miles around been tearing her apart and carrying off her cargo, hundreds of them."

"Any of our Wheal Hykka folk among 'em?" asked Penwarden.

"You can count on it," said Williams. "I came from there a couple of days ago. Tried to get my tinners back to Poldice, men, women and children. They wouldn't listen, crazed with taking whatever they can lay their hands on. They've pretty well got her stripped, so it won't take much longer. They should all be back looking for work any day now, but Pendeen will not be starving for weeks."

"That must've been the storm Mrs. Eliot sailed through last week," said Eliot. "We were fortunate to escape."

"There's never a storm but brings Cornwall some good," said Penwarden, to the chagrin of Edward Eliot.

"Come now, Penwarden," Eliot said, "there must have been huge losses. I just hope that her owners sold off plenty of shares in that voyage and didn't bear all the risk themselves. What was she carrying?"

"Sugar, molasses, and tobacco mainly," said Williams.

"Rum?" asked Penwarden.

"I'm afraid so," said Williams, "scores and scores of hogsheads. They're selling most of 'em, but there's plenty left over to drink. Lot of tales of drunkenness. One poor fellow was staggering up the cliff path with a load of his ill-gotten gains, lost his footing, fell down to the rocks below, hit his head and rolled on into the sea. Don't know whether he bled to death or was drownded."

"No more than he deserved," said Eliot. "I don't mean to be harsh, but more needs to be done to protect English merchants from being ravaged in this way. It is their right to bring their goods from our colonies with no more danger than providence delivers them in the normal course of affairs. The American trade is the key to England's future growth and power and the source of the taxes to pay for the wars. It will vindicate everything Mr. Pitt stands for."

"How did the crew fare?" asked Bunt, who had been trying to keep his counsel but could no longer stifle his curiosity.

"I can't say for sure," said Williams, "but I saw nothing of any strangers. It was a bad storm, the wind was high, and the waves were rough. I fear our tinners do not go out of their way to save shipwrecked sailors."

"We'm told that our Savior teaches us to love our fellow men," Addis Penwarden said gloomily, "but I fear few of us take that lesson far beyond the door of the chapel. Perhaps you're right, Mr. Williams, I'm not fit to be captain at Wheal Hykka. Oi'm losin' heart. I know that mining be dangerous, but Oi've long wanted to make it safer. Oi'm blocked at every turn. The owners won't let me spend a penny to prevent injury, let alone save lives. Much as Oi respect you, Mr. Eliot, even you do not lift a finger."

"Come now, Penwarden," said Eliot.

"Let me finish," Addis persisted. "Good men was killed at Wheal Hykka, and a boy. It seems there's barely a month goes by but there's a funeral at Pendeen. Them accidents needn't've 'appened. And that bloody viscount of your'n, callin' in the soldiers; my God, that was downright cruel!"

"Enough, Penwarden," said Eliot, raising his hand, "control yourself. I can no longer support you if you insult the viscount. He is after all a member of the House of Lords."

"Mr. Eliot, Mr. Eliot," cried Penwarden, thumping his fist on the table, "Oi've tried to control meself these many weeks and months. But 'tisn't long since Oi were a tinner meself, a tributer riskin' life an' limb to feed my fambly and make fortunes for the adventurers, me own boy workin' beside me down the mine, me own brother killed, me own neighbors burned and broken an' killed an' starved."

"Steady on, Penwarden," said Williams, "watch what you're saying."

"Oi'm sick of watchin', sick of waitin' for things to get better," cried Penwarden, clenching his fist until the knuckle showed white. "Why, Oi watched me own wife shot by them soldiers ordered by bloody Viscount Dunbugger, nearly killed the mother of my children. An' she just watched our own precious baby girl die, when a doctor could've saved 'er, an' no one would 'elp, let alone 'is 'igh an' mighty lordship. No, Oi'm done watchin', Oi can tell you."

"Get a grip on yourself, man" said Eliot.

"Steady on, Mr. Penwarden," said Bunt, "at least things can't get no worse, that's what Oi say."

Before Addis Penwarden could burst out an angry response he was interrupted by a commotion as the door burst open and in strode three unwelcome visitors.

Chapter Sixty-six

Order

Viscount Dunbargan burst through the door of the count house with Thomas Bolitho and Joseph Clymo following hard on his heels. He was sweating, red in the face and panting with exertion. He brandished a riding crop that he slammed on the table, sending a neatly stacked pile of papers flying.

"Where is my bitch of a wife?" he yelled. "Goddamn you, Eliot, if you're hiding her, in league against me, I'll ruin you, I swear. You've given me nothing but trouble since I allowed you to do business with me. I thought you were a gentleman and I could count on you as a friend."

Edward Eliot got to his feet and put out his hand to restrain the seething viscount. His own temper was already stretched taut after his contretemps with Addis Penwarden. "Calm yourself, Dunbargan; she went into the village with Mrs. Eliot to meet with the Reverend Perry to make arrangements to succor the miners and their families and talk about the school. I thought you were going back to Lanhydrock."

"What's she doing helping those damned savages? What they need is discipline, not pampering. Anyway, I changed my mind. It came to me that I needed to take charge down here; much of my wealth is at stake. Can't leave it all to others. What's that fellow doing here?"

"Begging your pardon, I'm Captain Williams, my lord. Came here to take charge on your instructions."

"Ah, we've met before, I never forget a face. What's Penwarden still hanging about for? I ordered you to replace him."

"Let's take one thing at a time, my lord," said Eliot. "Bunt, you go into Pendeen and tell Lady Dunbargan that her husband is here and wishes to see her. And ask Mrs. Eliot and Mr. Polkinghorne to come with her. There are several matters we need to iron out all together. Be off with you, look sharp about it."

"Right you are, Mr. Eliot," said Willy Bunt, "Oi'll be sure to find 'em down the chapel. What about Mr. Perry?"

"Oi could go if you loike, Mr. Eliot," said Penwarden. "The preacher is a good friend to Pendeen and Wheal Hykka, to me too."

"No, Penwarden, you stay here," said Eliot. "You're still in charge at Wheal Hykka as far as I am concerned, although no doubt Mr. Williams' experience will be valuable at this time. Bunt, yes, you might as well ask Reverend Perry to join us too. He is wise and knows his flock and can help us settle the villagers down."

Willy Bunt took his leave and Eliot turned to the viscount. "Now, my lord, why else are you here, and Mr. Bolitho?"

"Lord Dunbargan requested my help in dealing with the rioters, Mr. Eliot," said Bolitho. "I know all the leaders of Penzance society personally, do business with many of them, including the magistrates. They may deal with the culprits locally, or decide to send them to Bodmin for the next assizes. Be that as it may, his lordship wished me to use my influence to settle any trial as favorably as possible."

"Trial!" expostulated Dunbargan. "We should simply do it the way they do in Devon. Hang 'em first and try 'em afterwards. If they're not guilty, pay a priest to pray for their souls. That would soon make things shipshape around these damn tinners."

"That's diabolical," protested Penwarden.

"Keep a civil tongue in your head," said the viscount, "you've caused enough trouble already. As for you, Eliot, we will discuss the future in private later on. Meanwhile, I will collect Lady Dunbargan and then we will go to Penzance. I will meet with the court officials with Bolitho and Clymo and arrange that the rioters are dealt with severely."

"There is one thing I should mention, my lord," said Bolitho, "something which you all should hear. The clerk of the court has told me in confidence that no witnesses have come forward. That means that it is most unlikely that any judge would pass a sentence of death."

"What do you mean, no witnesses?" demanded Dunbargan. "There must be severe punishment for their disrespectful behavior; they disobeyed orders and they damaged property."

"For one thing, my lord, that young Ensign Maitland has been posted to America along with his regiment. They've already left. He was the principal witness to the proper reading of the Riot Act, and he gave the order to fire. The constable was sent to summon the miners, but they've all disappeared, and who knows if they would bear witness against their fellows even if they can be found."

Bolitho paused and looked Dunbargan in the eye. "That leaves the Penwardens, my lord. Your gallant soldiers shot Mrs. Penwarden, and she will be in no state to appear in court for many weeks as she struggles for her life. I doubt if she will feel kindly disposed to your cause. As for Captain Penwarden, he has heard today that he has been dismissed from his position of responsibility at your order."

The viscount raised up his crop and smacked it on the table, then scythed off the mugs sitting on it and smashed them to the floor. "There must be some decent law-abiding creature we can prevail upon. Weren't you there, Clymo? You'll stand by me. And how about you, Eliot? You're bound to do your civic duty."

Joseph Clymo looked at Eliot and Penwarden. "Possibly, my lord," he muttered, "I could cast my mind back and see what I recall."

"Dunbargan, as I consider the matter, it is a question as to what I could swear under oath," said Eliot. "I would be loathe to weaken the case by being uncertain under questioning. The situation was most confusing, and the events happened so fast. My attention was diverted by trying to calm things elsewhere."

"I am determined to speak to the court officials in Penzance and pursue the matter to the fullest extent of the law," said the viscount. "You will all accompany me and I expect your full support. That includes you, Penwarden, or you'll suffer for it."

At that moment the door opened to admit new arrivals. Silence fell as Charles Polkinghorne and Reverend Peter Perry entered, allowing Morwenna Clymo and Catherine Eliot to precede them. "Excuse me, gentlemen, we appear to be interrupting. I have escorted the ladies here as you requested, my lord, to the extent that they were willing, and Reverend Perry has joined us."

"Where is my damned wife?" demanded Dunbargan, "and where is that rascal Bunt?"

"Bunt said he had an errand to complete, and then he would come along shortly," said Polkinghorne, glancing at Eliot. "I believe Lady Dunbargan may have asked him to escort her."

"Where the hell has she gone?" asked the viscount.

"Bunt said something about her ladyship wishing to go down to the cove to visit the sloop and see to her things," said Polkinghorne. Eliot hid a smile.

"Damn that blasted Bunt," said Dunbargan. "My instructions were perfectly clear. I demand to see her ladyship, and as soon as possible."

"It is conceivable, my lord," said Catherine Eliot pressing through the knot of people at the door and facing him, "that her ladyship may have other ideas."

The door opened again and in came Bunt. "What have you done with my wife, damn you?" demanded the viscount.

"Oi just followed 'er ladyship's orders, zir," said Bunt. "Took 'er down cove an hailed the cap'n to send the dinghy an' ferry 'er out to the ship. She's gone aboard an' is waitin' for Mr. and Mrs. Eliot to come too."

"You go back right this minute and fetch her to me," said the viscount.

"Beggin' yer pardon, zir, but Oi can't swim. An' 'er ladyship told the cap'n firm like to keep the dinghy alongside that there sloop until 'er gave 'im instructions otherwise."

"I'll see to her safety, you can be assured of that, Dunbargan," said Eliot. "She can sail with us to Penzance; it would be more comfortable than riding with you, I'm sure you will agree."

"Penzance? Why Penzance?" asked Catherine. "We interrupted you when we arrived. What have we missed? I would like to know."

"We just discussed various business matters among us men, my dear," said Eliot. "I can tell you later."

"I would like to know now what is so urgent about going to Penzance," insisted Catherine.

"Just a few details we need to discuss with the magistrates about dealing with the rioters, my dear," said the viscount, putting his hand on her arm. Catherine drew back.

"Ooh aargh," said Penwarden, "just about stretchin' the necks of Tom Kegwyn and his mates. Just a minor matter."

"Then I will accompany you and we will certainly discuss the matter later," said Catherine. "Now I have some other worries to consider while I have you all here, proposals with which Reverend Perry and Mr. Polkinghorne here are in complete agreement. Reverend, why don't you explain?"

They gathered around, except for the viscount, who started pacing near the door, swinging his riding crop, peering out of the windows. The preacher cleared his throat, grasped his lapels, and spoke firmly.

"Gentlemen, as you are aware the underlying cause of the discontent of the miners and their families is that they are out of work and are hungry. And they've felt for years that they are harshly treated, despite working faithfully in dangerous conditions. We have succeeded with the help of kindly neighbors and subscriptions from generous members of the gentry in procuring supplies of food. But I am puzzled to report that most of the villagers are nowhere to be found."

Captain Williams interrupted and stepped forward. "Mrs. Eliot, Mr. Perry and I are acquainted, but let me introduce myself. I am John Williams, mine captain over at Poldice, as was my father before me. There's a wreck from last week's storm up at Port Isaac, with a rich cargo. Leastways there was, but hundreds of tinners from miles around have been at the wreck. They'll have it stripped bare by now."

"My heavens," said Catherine, "desperate behavior by desperate people. All the more reason for us to forge ahead with our plans to improve their lot so they have no need to resort to crime."

"Nonsense. They've helped themselves to what they need, like they always do. I'm not going to put up with this. They deserve no help," said Dunbargan striding back to them, "just encourages the worst elements to robbery and rioting. Only thing to do is to put one's foot down, show 'em who's master and who's servant. I'm off to Penzance. To hell with Lady Dunbargan!"

"Wait, my lord," said Eliot, "you need to hear Mrs. Eliot and the good preacher out. They may be right; we have to get to the bottom of these troubles if we are ever to get the mines working properly and seeing any profits. What else do you have in mind, Mrs. Eliot?"

"Too many tinners get hurt, badly hurt. It's up to the captains to make the mines safer and prevent injury," said Catherine. "But we need to take care of them when they are injured, get them fit for work again. And, besides, their families need care when they are poorly."

"Damned if I'd ever send my doctor down to these ruffians," said Dunbargan.

"They can't afford to pay doctors," said Eliot.

"Where there's a will there's a way, with God's help," said Reverend Perry. "I believe there are enough families of substance in the towns and villages around to use a doctor's services perhaps half of his time. Only a handful of the miners are in need of a doctor's services at any one time. The purser could take a penny or two a week from each one's pay, note it down in the cost book, pay the doctor something on account to retain his services, pay for his services when rendered."

"I'll not put up with my purser's time being spent accounting for a nursemaid," said the viscount. "He'll stick to counting what is due me."

"Pardon me, gentlemen," said Williams, "but in my judgment what Mrs. Eliot and Mr. Perry suggest makes sense. I've fought trouble in the mines man and boy, and my father before me. The same problems arise over and over, and we need to look at the underlying causes. We need willing workers. I would be disposed myself to keep the accounts to try out this idea; count the doctor's pence myself."

"I'm afraid it won't work," said Bolitho, "no doctor worth his salt will rely for his living on the coppers of tinners. He'd never go for it."

"Oh, Mr. Bolitho, a businessman of your experience could make it work," said Catherine. "I am confident you can imagine a solution. What if my husband were to promise the doctor that his bills would be paid?"

"I perceive that your own imagination is not lacking, my dear," said Eliot. "However, I would see it as in the interests of all the adventurers to support such a program, and I would be willing to take the first step. Of course, I trust that Captain Williams would ensure that the need to call in my pledge would not arise. Perhaps he could look into a proper village nurse too. H'mm, doctor's pence, I rather like the sound of that."

Eliot quietly moved closer to Thomas Bolitho and the two whispered together for a few moments. "You must make the viscount see sense, Bolitho. His high-handed methods can only lead to more discontent. Frankly, there are thousands of tinners and only a few of us. If this riot becomes a hanging matter, there's no knowing what trouble there will be. You are a man of affairs; what can you suggest?"

"I must agree with you, Eliot," said Bolitho. "The first thing to do is to forestall any hanging; it would set us back. I took the liberty of making some preliminary arrangements. Give me a letter to the clerk of the court stating your support, and I will pass it to him before our meeting tomorrow."

They returned to their seats and Eliot scratched out a note while the others were distracted by their continuing conversation.

"Bless you, Mr. Williams," Addis Penwarden was saying, "the tinners will be grateful, Oi'm sure of that."

"Nothing to do with you, Penwarden," said Dunbargan. "I've had enough of this nonsense. I'm off to Penzance. Come Clymo, we'll leave now; you too, Bolitho. I'll see you tomorrow, Eliot. My compliments, Mrs. Eliot," he said with an exaggerated bow, "and you tell that wife of mine that I'm not finished with her. She's gone a length too far this time."

Joseph Clymo kissed his daughter goodbye and went out. No one noticed Eliot slip a note to Bolitho as he shook his hand in farewell. The relief in the room after Dunbargan left could be felt. Penwarden sat at the table with his head in his hands. Polkinghorne reached in his pocket for his old clay pipe and set about packing the bowl with tobacco. Williams reached for his tall hat.

Eliot looked at his wife. "My dear," said Catherine, "there is one more proposal to put before you and Mr. Penwarden publicly, although I have other notions to discuss with you in private." Penwarden raised his head.

"What now, Mrs. Eliot?" asked Edward.

"Bunt brought young Jemmy Penwarden with us. I visited Mrs. Penwarden with Miss Clymo. She seems to be regaining her strength, but she still needs to rest. I urged her to allow Jemmy to come to Port Eliot, so she can be free of that responsibility and he can be a pupil in our new school. It will prepare him to help his schoolmates when they get started in Pendeen. Besides, he is a promising young man. Mrs. Penwarden is agreeable provided you give your permission," she said, addressing Penwarden.

Edward nodded but otherwise did not respond. Catherine continued, "I invited Lady Dunbargan to come and help us at the school and to bring young James with her. She is inclined to accept. It would be good for all of our children to learn from each other and good for her to get a spell of peace."

"Thank you, Mrs. Eliot," said Penwarden. "It'd be good for Jemmy, broaden his outlook. We all need education, myself included; I understand that. I know that's what Lizzie wants too. But Oi'll miss him, that's for sure. Where would he live, who would look after him?"

"Mr. Eliot, with your approval, I though we might make available one of the cottages in the village," said Catherine. "There is an elderly widow of one of the farm laborers who might be more comfortable in the almshouses. Miss Clymo is willing to come and live with the boys and take care of them, at least for a few months."

"I'm rather surprised your father would let you go," said Edward, turning to Morwenna. "Don't you keep house for him, Miss Clymo?"

"I would ask his permission, of course, sir," said Morwenna, "but I believe he could be persuaded. It would be an opportunity for me, and I want to learn to be a teacher."

Polkinghorne closely examined his pipe and tamped the tobacco rather unnecessarily.

"As you wish my dear," said Edward, "as you wish." He had a lot more on his mind right now than children, schools, and the viscount's wife.

"Then everyone can be on their way," said Catherine. "Miss Clymo, you can sail with us and talk to your father in Penzance."

They all got up to leave. Eliot motioned to Williams, Penwarden and Perry to stay and told Polkinghorne to escort Morwenna down to the cove and call for the dinghy to ferry them all out to the sloop. After they left Eliot spoke to the men remaining in the room with Catherine.

"There are some matters I wish to clear up between ourselves," he said. "Naturally, I trust Polkinghorne completely, but I did not wish to risk Miss Clymo passing on what I have to say to her father. Williams, from what I know of you, you are a fine fellow and a good mine captain. The viscount has put you in a difficult position. I intend to keep Penwarden as captain at Wheal Hykka, but I must consult with my fellow adventurers before confronting Lord Dunbargan on this matter. I will support adding to your responsibilities at Poldice and our other mines. But I want you to support my position with the magistrates. Will you give me your word?"

"Indeed, sir," replied Williams, "but what exactly will that entail?"

"Oh, thank you sir," said Penwarden, "it would break my heart to be sent away from Wheal Hykka in disgrace. An' Oi would like to be with you at the court if you'll permit it."

"As long as you promise to keep a civil tongue in your head, whatever the viscount may do," said Eliot. "Now I see that my wife has something to say. I know that look."

"It is a matter that I have discussed with Reverend Perry," said Catherine. "It's about the ringleaders of the riot. They did wrong, they were foolish and they let their anger rule them. But they were sorely provoked. Tom Kegwyn's family has lived in Pendeen for generations; he has a wife and children. The others are decent fellows. Hanging is too harsh a punishment for their misdeeds. Is there nothing you can do?"

"Can you all promise secrecy about this matter?" asked Eliot. They nodded and he continued. "You must not say a word. This must not get out to Viscount Dunbargan, but I sent word to the commander of the militia and gave him excellent reason to send young Ensign Maitland to America. That's why he will not be able to stand witness to the riot."

"Well done, husband," said Catherine, "you are a generous man and a fine leader."

"Thank 'ee, sir. Thank 'ee," said Penwarden, as the other men nodded their agreement. "But will the tinners still be punished?"

"They attend the chapel in Pendeen, sir," said Reverend Perry. "They are not without sin, but they strive to improve themselves, and I would urge mercy and forgiveness."

"They aren't bad men, sir, fambly men, Oi'll vouch for 'em. Good workers too," said Penwarden.

"Mercy I can support," said Eliot thoughtfully, "but forgiveness is going too far. They damaged property, they were disorderly, and by their example they put their comrades in danger too. Order must be maintained, or the country will go to the dogs. They must be punished."

"They must take the consequences of their actions," said John Williams, "or we will never be able to assert our authority."

"But not hanged surely?" said Catherine. "Something less severe, I pray."

"Just leave it to me, all of you," said Eliot. "I will give the matter some thought before I talk with the magistrate tomorrow. I may have an opportunity to consult further with Bolitho, and I must of course take into account what Lord Dunbargan has to say."

Catherine beamed. There were smiles and nods around the table, and murmurs of approbation.

"I merely said that I would give the matter some thought," Eliot said sternly.

"We all understand, my dear," said Catherine, "and we trust you to be not only thoughtful, but fair and just as well."

"Upon consideration," said Eliot, "I would indeed like some of you gentlemen to join us in Penzance. I understand it will be an informal hearing, and I am sure your attendance can be arranged. Perry, you sail with us; it'll give us an opportunity to talk further. Penwarden, you ride over with Polkinghorne early in the morning. Let him know, would you? Williams, you can stay here as the viscount wished for now and keep an eye on Wheal Hykka. This is temporary, mind you, until Penwarden gets back."

"I would be happy to oblige for a day or two, sir," said Williams, "but I must then get back home to Poldice. There is an important meeting I promised to attend at Gwennap." He exchanged a glance with Reverend Perry and then continued speaking to Eliot. "I trust you will succeed in making things right with Viscount Dunbargan, sir." There were nods of agreement all around, and they prepared to set off.

Reverend Perry took Addis on one side before going out. "A word with you, Captain Penwarden, on a matter I assure you is more important than it may first seem. I commend you for trying to improve your speech, you are not dropping as many aitches as you used to. Now try to add the "g" to words ending in "–ing". It may seem a small thing, but I notice Mr. Eliot taking more notice of what you say, and I believe a more educated manner of speech plays its part."

"I appreciate your help, Reverend," said Addis. "It's hard to break old habits, especially when things get heated, but Oi know it matters in my position. Oi want to learn, and Oi know Oi need to get the clerk to pay attention to what Oi say when we get to that court in Penzance. Oi'll do my best."

Meanwhile, Morwenna and Polkinghorne were in no hurry to reach the cove. They had just arrived at the shelter of the engine house where they could not be seen by anyone who might happen to glance out of the windows of the count house. They looked around and stopped. They were alone.

"Oh, Charles," said Morwenna, turning to him and drawing him into an embrace, "if I come to Port Eliot to help at the school we can do as you wished and get to know each other better. I hope father allows me. I cannot wait."

"Morwenna," breathed Polkinghorne and kissed her warmly and at length. He wished that they could find even greater privacy to enjoy the warmth of the moment longer. They were engrossed in each other and unaware of the approach of young Jemmy Penwarden scrambling up the path from the cove, followed by Willy Bunt.

"Morwenna!" Willy screamed, waving his arms. "Mr. Polkinghorne! What the 'ell is goin' on?" He rushed up the path towards them, leaving Jemmy behind gaping. Charles and Morwenna sprang apart, startled. Bunt seized Polkinghorne by the lapels of his coat.

"Leave 'er alone, you brute," yelled Willy. "Don't you go grabbin' at Morwenna."

He felt Morwenna tugging at his arm and turned towards her, fraught with concern. "Morwenna, are you all right? Did 'e 'urt you?"

Morwenna laughed at him.

"Course he didn't, you gurt chump," she said. "He was hugging me, giving me a kiss. I think he really likes me. You should be pleased for me."

Willy took a step back, looked them both in the eyes in turn, put his hand to his forehead. What a blind fool I've been, he thought, never saw what was going on under my own nose.

"You wanted 'im too, Morwenna?" said Bunt. "But Oi thought . . . "

"Oh Willy, me 'andsome," said Morwenna, putting her hand on his arm again, gently this time. "What were you thinking about?"

"You be careful who you're laying your hands on, you young fool," said Polkinghorne angrily. "If I didn't know you better you could have got yourself into serious trouble with the law. Who do you think I am to suggest I might force my attentions on a young woman? I think you should know that Miss Clymo has given me permission to call upon her."

Polkinghorne straightened his coat and offered his arm to Morwenna, who put her hand in the crook of his elbow and smiled up into his eyes.

"Now don't you go getting cross with Willy, Charles," she said. "He just thought he was acting for the best, coming to the aid of a lady. You must understand, me an' Willy have been friends at Lanhydrock since we were kids, his Mary too, known each other for donkey's years."

Charles? Charles, thought Willy. Since when? Imagine, his own dear friend Morwenna, right under his nose. Surely she had always had a soft spot for him, Willy. For a moment he could not speak, coughed to hide a sob.

"Sorry, Morwenna," he said, "Beg your pardon, Mr. Polkinghorne." He looked around back at the path to the cove. "Come on, Jemmy, let's get goin'. Us can't do no more good 'ere."

Chapter Sixty-seven

Justice

After a blessedly uneventful sail from the cove below Wheal Hykka, the sloop was tied fore and aft to moor overnight in Penzance harbor. The next day dawned bright but with an autumn chill. Catherine Eliot wore a heavy woolen cloak for the short walk from the harbor to the magistrates court. Much as she, too, wished to be present at the proceedings at court, Lady Dunbargan was anxious not to encounter her husband; she stayed safely aboard the sloop under the protection of the crew.

Young Jemmy Penwarden also stayed behind, left in the charge of Morwenna Clymo. The captain was given instructions to help amuse the boy by showing him the sights while keeping a close eye on him to make sure that he did not stray and get into trouble. Jemmy, ever inquisitive, wasted no time in extracting a promise from the captain to be shown how to use his spyglass to take a closer look at St. Michael's Mount.

During the voyage the previous day, the Eliots and their guests had taken the opportunity to converse frankly among themselves, at leisure and without the presence of Viscount Dunbargan and his allies. Despite some hesitation on Edward Eliot's part as he considered the implications, they had largely agreed that it was indeed important to push the mine's owners to provide better treatment of the miners and their families as a means of encouraging loyalty and willing work. Reverend Perry had invited them to take the opportunity of being nearby to attend a meeting where John Wesley would preach.

"I have come to greatly admire Reverend Wesley," Perry said earnestly. "I appreciate that his message is not always pleasing to the gentry or the leaders of the Church of England, of which however he remains a member. But what he has to say will help you appreciate the troubles facing the ordinary people of England. By understanding those troubles you may be more able to help deal with them, and thus bring some peace to Cornwall."

"But is not the man a rabble rouser?" objected Eliot. "We must do nothing to encourage disrespect for authority, or worse."

"On the contrary, sir, with respect," said Reverend Perry, "while you may wish not to hear some of the truths he will express, in his heart he believes in the law of the land and the divine right of kings. He is a force for order and respect among the common people."

"When will this event take place?" asked Eliot. "I cannot spend much longer down here. It's September already. In no time I must return to London to attend the House, and there is much to deal with at Port Eliot before I leave."

"He will preach on Sunday afternoon," said Reverend Perry, "and it will not be too far, now that you are in Penzance, no more than a day's sail around Land's End to Portreath."

"Will he preach at the church there?" asked Eliot.

"Unfortunately, Mr. Wesley is rarely welcome in the pulpits of the Church of England, sir," replied Perry, "and no chapel would be big enough to accommodate his congregation. He will preach in the open air at Gwennap, just beyond Redruth. There are scores of mines nearby; some call it the richest square mile in England. We're expecting hundreds, maybe thousands of the faithful and the curious."

"It would be wise to make the effort, my dear," said Catherine, squeezing her husband's hand, "what you learn could inform your deliberations in parliament. We won't have to leave that soon, especially if we take the sloop straight to the Port of London and have what we require sent up from home. Besides, I would like to hear Mr. Wesley preach. One hears so much about him."

And so the matter was settled. As they disembarked and gathered on the quay that morning to set off to the magistrates court, Catherine Eliot gazed out to sea and took in the sight of St. Michael's Mount across its causeway. Often inquisitive and always practical she asked her husband about its history. "That is magnificent, Mr. Eliot," she observed, "but the scale seems extraordinary on such a small island; a fortress and an imposing church. Can't have many parishioners. Why was such a big church built there?"

Edward Eliot was unable to satisfy his wife's curiosity. He turned to the cleric. "Reverend Perry, you are the churchman among us. Can you enlighten us?"

"In my experience," Perry said smiling, "there is usually a simple explanation to such things. Many centuries ago the Archangel Michael appeared in a vision to some fishermen sheltering on the island. The Benedictines built a monastery and dedicated it to St. Michael, who became much beloved of the Cornish."

"Well, that explains everything!" said Catherine. "But I would not have expected a modern apostle of John Wesley to take an interest in such ancient customs."

"My interest goes to customs more ancient than our forebears in the Roman church, ma'am," said Reverend Perry, "although I confess this is not something I discuss with Mr. Wesley. If I may share a confidence, I feel a close connection to our Celtic ancestors here in Cornwall."

"Really, Perry," said Eliot, "tell us more. I would like to learn more of our Cornish traditions."

"I will tell you of our Christian pilgrims hereabouts. Over the centuries the mariners here in Penzance enjoyed a profitable trade carrying pilgrims across to northern Spain as they traveled on their pilgrimage to Santiago de Compostela."

"I heard of that when I took my Grand Tour on the continent," said Edward. "El Camino, they call it in Spanish, The Way. It draws thousands of the devout."

"Indeed," replied Perry. "Here in Britain our pilgrims walk the Michael Way. Starting at the Mount they follow the course of churches dedicated to St. Michael, which in turn follows an ancient ley line, a line of spiritual energy that flows all up through Cornwall and beyond to England, through the holy site of Glastonbury all the way east to Bury St. Edmunds."

"Where in east Cornwall?" asked Eliot.

"Not far from Port Eliot, sir, across Bodmin Moor past the ancient circle of the Hurlers and the great megalith of the Cheesewring."

"H'mm," said Eliot, "I've been told that country could be promising for tin. Perhaps Port Eliot could share in the blessings."

"Oh, Mr. Eliot," said Catherine, "ever the practical man of business."

"It's time to remember that we are here on business," said Eliot, "very serious business. We must hasten to the magistrates court."

"Those poor men," said Catherine, but contented herself with that comment. She had already urged her husband to be lenient towards the ringleaders of the riot at the mine. While Eliot seemed non-committal as to exactly what he was prepared to do, if anything, she was optimistic that she had persuaded him at least of the need for mercy if not forgiveness. She was quite aware that he took his responsibilities as a landed gentleman and Member of Parliament very seriously. What he said next revealed the growing extent of her husband's generosity of spirit, and even her benign influence upon him.

"My dear Catherine," Edward said after a moment, "it is all very well for you to urge that the tinners be spared. You are a kind and considerate woman, and such sentiments I have learned to expect from you. But I have a position of leadership, and it behooves the upper classes to preserve the order that is the stabilizing root of English society. However, I will tell you all in the strictest confidence that I have sent a letter to the magistrate asking that all aspects of the case be considered. It is up to him to determine whether the accused will be remanded to the assize court. That is where matters of capital punishment must be decided. For now we must just be patient in awaiting the turn of events."

"You have been a busy correspondent, my dear," said Catherine, "and I trust a persuasive one; first a letter to the commander of the militia and now one to the magistrate. I admire your compassion, despite your reluctance to admit your zeal."

As the Eliot party approached the courthouse they saw Polkinghorne and Penwarden waiting for them. "Mornin', sir, Mrs. Eliot ma'am," said Polkinghorne. "Still no sign of Willy Bunt. He's nowhere to be found. I have no idea what could have got into him."

"Oh, I expect he will turn up," said Eliot. "Something at Wheal Hykka yesterday seemed to have upset Bunt very badly. As we approached to board the sloop, we saw him run off in the direction of Pendeen, shouting and waving his arms. However, we can certainly manage this business without him," continued Eliot. "We'd better go on in and see if the viscount and Bolitho have arrived. Probably got Clymo with them too."

Eliot said nothing about his concern that whatever had troubled Bunt might drive him back to drink.

The Lanhydrock party was indeed in the entrance hall where, after perfunctory greetings, they all were ushered into the magistrates' courtroom. The viscount frowned at Penwarden but said nothing when he caught the determined expression on Eliot's face.

Catherine perceived Dunbargan raising an eyebrow when he caught sight of her. Probably thought a meeting in a courtroom concerning legal matters was no place for a lady. What a pompous and supercilious cad, she thought. She wondered whether he was pleased or sorry that his wife was not present. Catherine was quite sure of her own place here and equally certain that she would not hesitate to speak if she had something of importance to add.

Bolitho distracted the viscount by greeting the magistrate, to whom he was known, and making the introductions. Then the viscount took charge and addressed the magistrate. "You know what we are here about," he said. "That rabble from Wheal Hykka must be dealt with severely. Otherwise things in Cornwall will go to hell in a wheelbarrow. I intend to see that they are sent to the assize court and that the judge is aware of my requirement that they wear the halter. Nothing less will be acceptable."

"Indeed, my lord," said the magistrate, looking down from his bench, "Mr. Bolitho here has made me aware of your position, with which the court naturally sympathizes. No doubt when the time comes the crown will press for sentences appropriate to the offences. Quite reprehensible, quite. We are of course too late for the summer assize in Bodmin and we must unavoidably wait until the next assize in Launceston in Lent. However, there is a little difficulty."

"What difficulty?" asked the viscount. "The case is perfectly clear. They damaged property; they threatened the persons of His Majesty's subjects; they disobeyed orders from those in authority; they ignored warnings; and the Riot Act was quite properly read."

"Unfortunately, my lord, no matter how hard we have tried, we have been unable to persuade anyone to come forward and testify, which testimony the assize judge would insist upon and the law requires for a capital sentence," said the magistrate. "As I told Mr. Bolitho, the soldiers have been sent to America and cannot bear witness, and their officer was our likeliest witness. I'm afraid the judge's hands will be tied, and of course in your position you would surely insist that the law of the realm be strictly upheld."

"What about Penwarden here?" demanded the viscount. "He saw everything. He was in charge. He will bear witness, and he will tell the truth, or I'll see that he never works again."

Addis Penwarden sat without saying a word, his jaw set and his fists clenched. Eliot spoke for him. "My lord, there is no use. I have done what I can to persuade Captain Penwarden to do what is right in the circumstances." Addis rose from his seat. Eliot put a restraining hand on his shoulder, and he sat down again. The magistrate rapped his gavel on his desk and called for order.

"That is a travesty of justice!" shouted the viscount. "Plenty of people saw what they did. They acted in a crowd in broad daylight. The miscreants must be punished severely." Addressing the magistrate directly he demanded, "Am I not correct?"

"Indeed you may be, my lord, but as you see we have no witnesses to support your assertions," replied the magistrate. "I will of course do what I can to urge the judge to pass a sentence of hanging. But at the very least, lacking, as I said, any witnesses, the miscreants would be sentenced to transportation. Then they would be deprived of living in England for ever, and indeed the voyage itself would be under harsh conditions."

Catherine spoke. "This is barbaric, but I suppose we must be thankful even for small mercies," she said. "But what about their wives and children?"

"I would be remiss not to remind you, madam," said the magistrate with dignity, "that the assize court may not be willing even to hear the case."

"They must be punished," said Dunbargan, red in the face. "Should be hanged, but lacking that, transportation is no more than the treatment they deserve. They should have thought of the consequences before they rioted." He turned to Catherine, standing over her and wagging his finger in her face. "As for you, madam, meddling in the affairs of gentlemen! It's your ridiculous schemes that are half the trouble, tolerating ruffians, putting ideas above their stations into their heads. Bloody schools and safety measures indeed!"

This time Edward Eliot was too slow to restrain Penwarden, who leapt to his feet seething with anger, grabbed the viscount and pulled him violently away from Catherine. "You leave Mrs. Eliot alone, Dunbugger," Penwarden shouted. "'Twas you what caused the trouble, always has been. Throwin' your weight around, threatening, bullying, sendin' for the soldiers, almost getting my Lizzie killed. You'm the trouble, never did learn, now did you?"

To Catherine's delight, the viscount backed away from the advancing Penwarden and in so doing lost his balance and had to grab for a chair to steady himself.

The magistrate banged his gavel to no avail. "Constable, constable!" he shouted. Two beefy men in uniform rushed into the room, sized up the scene and pulled Penwarden off the viscount. "Seize him," ordered the magistrate, "take him to the cells. This session is adjourned." He banged his gavel again. The constables roughly bound Penwarden and dragged him out of the room, off balance and stumbling. Those sitting near him stood to get out of the way.

Catherine gasped, putting her hand to her mouth. "Leave him be, you're hurting him," she said in a whisper that came out as a shout in the shocked silence. Those remaining in the room got to their feet, exchanged looks ranging from shock to triumph and silently filed out. None of them for varying reasons was pleased with the outcomes of the session.

"Now what will transpire?" Catherine asked her husband, reaching for his hand. "Surely there is something you can do?"

"Now please, Mrs. Eliot, we are sorely tried, but we must indeed act with patience," he said. "We will have nothing further to do with the viscount at this juncture, except to ensure that he gets nowhere near the sloop and Lady Dunbargan. He and his minions will depart Penzance for Lanhydrock."

As they walked outside, he drew her close and said, "Catherine, I assure you that I will make every effort to assure that justice be done, but in due course. For now we will all depart Penzance going in opposite directions. I suggest that we follow the advice of Reverend Perry. Let us ask our guests to sail with us to Portreath and thence make our way to Gwennap. I'll tell Polkinghorne to join us. It might well do them all good to listen to the preaching of the Reverend John Wesley on Sunday. I trust that he may calm our souls, and even inspire in us the path to take next."

Chapter Sixty-eight

Gwennap

Fair weather on Sunday carried the sloop and the Eliot party uneventfully around Land's End whence the captain set a northeasterly course. They were headed toward the meeting at which John Wesley would preach. With a steady following wind and no danger in sight, Edward Eliot took the helm himself for an hour or two, enjoying the distraction from the troubles of recent days. Presently clouds signaled a change in the weather, whitecaps blew up, the wind turned squally, and the sloop tossed in the waves heeling over in the wind. The captain took command to the relief of the ladies and guided them to shelter at Portreath.

After making landfall Polkinghorne hired an open wagon to take them inland to the meeting place. The wind picked up more, and the ladies held on to their hats. They drove past the mining town of Redruth and some two and a half miles beyond to the village of Gwennap, arriving by midafternoon.

The Reverend Peter Perry took them to the cottage of a staunch Methodist family where John Wesley and his traveling companions were staying. Perry knocked at the door. The man who opened it was of middle height, well proportioned and fit looking, with a bright eye and an inquiring look on his face. In his sixties, Reverend John Wesley wore a broad-brimmed hat, black garb, with the white linen bands of a clergyman under his chin. Seeing the little group with Perry amongst them, he smiled a warm greeting.

"Mr. Wesley," Reverend Perry happily hailed him, "allow me to introduce my companions." He presented the Eliots and Lady Dunbargan, Miss Clymo and Master Jemmy Penwarden, and Mr. Charles Polkinghorne.

As the introductions were made Wesley's observant eyes took in his new acquaintances' fine clothes and surmised that some of them were wealthy, not that this would be deter him from preaching vigorously about the difficulties facing the camel trying to pass through the eye of the needle.

"It is a pleasure see you again my friend and to meet you all," John Wesley said. "Are you expecting a large crowd this afternoon?"

"We are indeed, Mr. Wesley," said Perry. "I and others have spoken of your coming in the towns and villages around. And they have heard of your preaching in the last few days in Polperro, Grampound, St.

Austell and yesterday in Truro. Your fame spreads, they want to be uplifted by your message."

"Ah, you are one of my most effective exhorters, Mr. Perry." He glanced beyond them at the trees bending in the stiff breeze. "I hope they will be able to hear my message in this wind," he said. "It seems we must meet in the open air to accommodate the crowd; let us seek somewhere sheltered."

"Indeed, sir," said Reverend Perry, "let us go to Gwennap Pit, where you and I have both addressed the faithful. There is room for thousands."

"Gwennap Pit?" inquired Catherine. "What is that? It sounds dangerous."

"It is a large round depression in the ground nearby, ma'am," replied Perry. "They say it formed long ago from the collapse of an abandoned mine. It's a big oval some two hundred feet across one way, three hundred the other and all of fifty feet from top to bottom, with a gently shelving grassy slope. It is a natural amphitheater, the people will hear Mr. Wesley's every word."

"I remember it well," said Wesley with a smile. "It as if Gwennap Pit was created for our use. I first preached there almost exactly two years ago. I recall the weather then was even worse, pouring rain. Let us immediately spread the word that we shall meet there. Please take your friends and lead the way. I plan to open the meeting at five o'clock."

People were already gathering in Gwennap village, murmuring with expectation as they awaited the arrival of the great preacher John Wesley. As the word of the venue spread further, the crowds walked towards Gwennap Pit. The Eliot party mingled with the crowd and then took their places near the top of the circle crowning the pit. Several people greeted the Reverend Perry, the women smiling warmly and the men shaking him by the hand or clapping him on the back.

Perry caught sight of a tall imposing man on the opposite rim of the pit. He had his back to them. He was wearing a top hat and a black coat, and he seemed familiar. The Reverend Perry cupped his hands to his mouth and called out, "Captain!" The man turned and waved and started circling his way around the rim of the pit through groups of people towards them.

"Captain Williams," Eliot greeted him, "so this is the meeting that took you from your duty at Wheal Hykka?"

"I confess I too am surprised to see you, Cap'n," said Reverend Perry. "I had the impression that you disapproved of the preaching of John Wesley."

"Ladies, gentlemen, good day," said Williams, doffing his hat. "My surprise is equal to yours. I am in fact pursuing my duty as mine captain and honoring the responsibility entrusted to me by the owners. As I have been frank to inform you, Mr. Perry, I have been concerned that Mr. Wesley arouses discontent among the tinners by encouraging them to improve themselves above their natural stations and to seek better conditions of work. I felt it my duty to hear what he has to say."

"But surely nothing will change if they themselves don't push for those improvements," said Catherine. "Of course they must be advised to pursue these ends through peaceful means."

Eliot took her hand. "Captain Williams is very experienced, my dear, and I am sure he knows what is best."

"These are not easy matters to deal with, ma'am," Williams said, gazing down at her. "I am often torn as to the best approach. But the system of tribute makes the tinners independent, not slaves to a fixed wage. The system works to encourage high production at a low cost, and I wouldn't change that. And you know, Mr. Perry, your John Wesley has grown in influence over his years of visiting Cornwall, and I need to keep abreast of what he has to say."

Williams looked around the group and asked, "But where is Captain Penwarden? I should have thought he too would wish to hear the words of Mr. Wesley. Indeed, Mr. Perry, is he not a devoted member of your flock?"

Charles Polkinghorne took it upon himself to explain the fate of Addis Penwarden, now in captivity in Penzance gaol for who knew how long. Jemmy Penwarden brushed away a tear and reached for Morwenna's hand. Williams looked deeply concerned and remained silent. Before he could muster a response, Catherine Eliot exclaimed, "Look at all of these people, and so orderly. This is an amazing place! So big, there must be hundreds of people here already and room for hundreds more. Look at them all streaming in."

Crowds of men, women and children continued to file into the great pit, taking their places around it, standing packed together, gathering to see the great man and to be inspired by his words. A chattering arose from the crowd, a susurration, a happy sound, a welcoming noise. They had spotted the arrival of a group of somberly dressed men walking up the path from the direction of the village.

The Reverend John Wesley was unmistakable. He was vested in cassock and surplice, imposing looking, commanding. He took his place on one side of the great oval near the top. He raised his arms to get the attention of the people, who fell into a hush as he began to speak. Despite the wind his voice projected throughout the natural auditorium so that the crowd heard his every word distinctly without straining.

He preached a wide-ranging sermon for over an hour, taking as his text a passage from the Gospel according to Saint Luke, "Blessed are the eyes which see the things that ye see, and hear the things that ye hear." He wove a passionate discourse on the seven areas of social responsibility that he had come to emphasize as his philosophy evolved: the poor and poverty, slavery, prisons and prisoners, the abuse of hard liquor, politics, war, and education.

He reminded his audience of his practical attitude towards money: *"Earn all you can, save all you can, give all you can."* He observed that most of his followers had learned the first, some had learned the second, but chided them that few had learned the third, let alone applied it. Edward Eliot felt that the preacher's eyes were upon him as he made his third point. While Edward felt his duty to his family was to increase his heritage, his conscience was clear. He gave quite enough; he supported his wife's good works, and he treated his tenants and his workers generously.

The preacher then spoke eloquently of the evils of slavery, of which he had learned so much when he lived and preached in America. He rebutted the assertion that slavery was justified by the need to amass wealth. "First, wealth is not necessary to the glory of any nation; but wisdom, virtue, justice, mercy, generosity, public spirit, love of our country. These are necessary to the real glory of a nation; but abundance of wealth is not." He spoke of the false characterization of the captured Africans. "Upon the whole, far from being the stupid, senseless, brutish, lazy barbarians, the fierce, cruel, perfidious savages they have been described, on the contrary, they are more remarkably sensible, industrious to the highest degree, fair, just, and honest in all their dealings, friendly, and kind to strangers, than any of our forefathers were."

Edward mused that this was not an issue that had touched his life and wondered at its introduction by Wesley at this time. Unlike some of his friends who profited from their ships transporting the captured Negroes, Dunbargan for one it was rumored, he had no direct benefit from the trade. He recalled that it was a good west country man who started the whole thing, two hundred years ago: Sir John Hawkins, sea captain, hero, victor over the Spanish Armada, made a profit on every leg of the triangular trade. These mariners captured slaves in West Africa, sold them in the West Indies, scrubbed out the ships and bought rum and sugar in the islands, sold the cargo in Bristol, refitted and sailed again.

Given his responsibilities as a Commissioner of Trade and Plantations, Edward quickly realized that this was indeed an issue he might not be able to ignore much longer. However, as a conscientious servant of the Crown, he wished troublemakers like Wesley would leave him in peace.

The vicar at St. Germans merely expected him not to fall asleep during his sermons, not to do anything about them. He attended the parish church regularly. Should not be this hard to be a good Christian. Anyway, how did the slavers manage to capture so many Negroes? Ah, John Wesley had the answer.

"It was some time before the Europeans found a more compendious way of procuring African slaves, by prevailing upon them to make war upon each other, and to sell their prisoners. Till then they seldom had any wars; but were in general quiet and peaceable. But the white men first taught them drunkenness and avarice, and then hired them to sell one another. Nay, by this means, even their Kings are induced to sell their own subjects. So Mr. Moore, factor of the African Company in 1730, informs us: 'When the King of Barsalli wants goods or brandy, he sends to the English Governor at James's Fort, who immediately sends a sloop. Against the time it arrives, he plunders some of his neighbours' towns, selling the people for the goods he wants. At other times he falls upon one of his own towns, and makes bold to sell his own subjects.'"

The fellow preaches strongly against slavery, thought Edward; keeps bringing up the evils of alcohol too. May have a point for poor wretches who cannot control themselves. Brought young Bunt to mind. Why did this Wesley fellow seem to be looking him in the eye so often? Edward felt he himself could manage how much he drank; enjoyed a good French wine, a fine brandy. Now what was he on about? Prisons, ah yes, Edward had heard that conditions could be dreadful. He wondered how Penwarden was coping. Most of the prisoners deserved harsh treatment, worked wonders to discourage a life of crime. But perhaps there should be exceptions, but who would see to that? Wouldn't be him.

And now the man was talking about education. He could see that this piqued Catherine's interest, and he agreed with her that it was in his interests as a landowner and mining adventurer that his farm laborers and tinners knew enough to be more productive. He would have a word with Wesley to encourage his wife in her worthy efforts, perhaps give her a few pointers, some help. Let Wesley know Eliot was doing his bit. For some odd reason, he wanted Wesley to think well of him.

Now the preacher was droning on about the evils of strong drink again. Portions of the crowd were growing restless, and the quiet attention of the majority became distracted by a group of tinners who had edged their way into the bottom of the pit at the far side. They were drunk, muttering, staggering, getting noisier by the minute. Wesley's followers grew concerned, alarmed, then fearful. Wesley himself was not unused to facing violent challenges. He addressed the unruly group with authority in a firm voice, seeking to calm them and bring them to order and turn them from their sinful ways.

"My brothers, you come here possessed of the demon drink, you are ready for the devil to do his work. You have given yourselves over to temptation. You have stripped yourselves of all goodness and virtue, and filled your heart with all that is evil, mundane, sensual and demonic. You have forced God's Spirit to depart from you, because you are not disposed to tolerate a reprimand, and you have given yourselves like blind persons into the hands of the devil, permitting him to guide you according to his will."

The tinners quieted down; some sat down on the grass with their heads in their hands, persuaded by the power of Wesley's words and the force of his personality, or perhaps it was simply the effects of the alcohol making them lethargic.

Catherine Eliot was nervous and asked Reverend Perry what was going on.

"Mr. Wesley has experienced such disturbances at his prayer meetings on many occasions, ma'am, although less often in recent years as his message has become better known, and he has earned the respect of those who once resented his teaching."

Catherine nodded as Reverend Perry continued. "But he still has enemies. There are those who profit from the sale of spirituous liquors, and they have been known to give away beer to our rougher brethren to make them drunk and create a disturbance to distract from Mr. Wesley's preaching."

"I cannot imagine such a thing," said Viscountess Dunbargan, "it is quite unthinkable."

"Indeed, my dear," Catherine said, "but see how Mr. Wesley is dealing with them with patience and dignity. I am impressed by his strength."

The Eliot men reassured the ladies that they were in no danger, but gathered closer around them nevertheless.

The preacher attempted to bring his sermon to a conclusion, speaking with emphasis and deliberation as he moved into his peroration. But he was again interrupted by a disturbance down in the pit on the far side, to the renewed consternation of the crowd. A disheveled man among the tinners was angrily shouting and swearing, remonstrating against the words of the sermon, protesting against Wesley's call for decent living, forswearing profanity and drunkenness. "You'm a bloody prig, preacher," he yelled. "Ye dunno whereof you speak, us can't 'elp takin' a drop from toime to toime, us needs cheerin' up in this miserable life."

The man staggered as his neighbors roughly held him up by the arms to restrain him and stop him from falling. He wrenched himself free and swung his bunched fist at his would-be captor, punching him squarely on the jaw, knocking him to the ground. Women screamed. Stewards who had accompanied the preacher came down to help restore order. The Eliot women recognized him first. Morwenna Clymo put her hand to her mouth. Catherine Eliot reached for her husband's arm. "My God, it's Bunt," she gasped. "So this is where he got to. Somebody get him away from those men."

John Williams shouldered his way forcefully through the crowd, leading the way and followed by Polkinghorne and the Reverend Perry. As they picked Willy Bunt up off the ground, he opened his eyes and saw Polkinghorne. He yelled, "You bloody traitor, you've ruined my life. She'm my friend, could've been moine. 'Er's too good for the bloody loikes of you."

A man standing nearby called out indignantly, "Call the constable, he's drunk!"

John Williams said, "We know this man, we'll deal with him, you can all rely on that." Reverend Perry caught the preacher's eye and said to his companions, "Let's take him over to Mr. Wesley; he needs to deal with this."

John Wesley called for silence and the crowd quickly fell still. He announced that the meeting was concluded, asked for a blessing upon them and this poor drunken sinner. He then instructed them to depart quietly, which they did. Turning to Reverend Perry he asked, "Who is this man, what do you know about him?"

"His name is Willy Bunt. He lives at St. Germans and is in the employ of Mr. and Mrs. Eliot," replied Perry. "Allow me to invite them to join us." When the Eliots and their party were gathered together Perry continued, "Bunt is a disappointment. However, there is good in him. He fled a harsh master who employed him as a footman and valet. He took with him a maid whose virtue had been breached by the same rascal, and he married her. They now have two little ones."

"We took them in," said Catherine, "and saw much promise in them. We provided a cottage in the village, and my husband employed him on the estate and advanced him."

"I have seen diligence and intelligence in Bunt," said Edward, "and he has a gift for new ideas, but he has a fatal flaw. He cannot hold his drink, and when drunk he is violent and abusive. I thought he had reformed and given it up, but I appear mistaken. I cannot tolerate such behavior."

"I have prayed with Bunt and persuaded him to take the pledge of total abstinence," said Reverend Peter Perry. "He seemed to repent and expressed good intentions, but he has slipped back into his sinful ways."

"More than you realize, reverend," said Polkinghorne, "more than any of you realize. I have been obliged to rescue him from excessive indulgence several times."

"Why did you not tell me?" demanded Eliot. "I can no longer tolerate such ingratitude. Bunt must go."

"But what about Mary? What about the children?" asked Catherine.

"Oh please, zir, give us another chance," pleaded Bunt, sobering up at the dilemma he faced. "Oi'll really try. Oi just got upset and forgot myself."

"Do give him another chance," said Morwenna. "I knew him at Lanhydrock since he was a lad, he's good at heart."

"The young fool has already been given many chances," said Eliot.

"Do not judge too hastily, brothers and sisters," said the Reverend Wesley. "Who among us is free of blemish? Leave him with me for a day or two, and I will counsel with him myself."

"Mr. Wesley, I am happy to leave Bunt with you. Pray do what you can with him, but I hold out little hope," said Edward Eliot. "I must add that much of what you expressed in your eloquent sermon I find strangely persuasive, but in candor I must also say there is more with which I disagree. The social order is the foundation of a stable England, and I fear that many of your Methodist opinions may lead the lower classes and the ignorant into discontent to their own detriment."

"I do not foster discontent, Mr. Eliot," replied Wesley. "Discontent lies in the conditions under which these people live. And you may call me a Methodist, Mr. Eliot, as many dub my compatriots, and I confess that I am one of those who prefer not to regard the Church of England as the Tory party at prayer. However, I remain a minister of the established church like my father before me. I draw my teachings from my reflections upon the gospel of our Lord. I do not ask you to agree with everything I preach. I simply ask that you see with a clear vision and listen with an open mind, and I hope that in due time you may further discuss our views with myself or the good Reverend Perry."

"For myself, Mr. Wesley," said Catherine, "I hear the words of the gospel week after week in our own parish church from our worthy vicar, but I must confess the message as interpreted by you sounds vastly different. I feel that much of what you say applies directly to me and to the way I lead my own life, not just to other people. And you have provoked me to think about people in far off lands, the dreadful plight of the slaves in America, as well as the poor and ignorant here in England."

Wesley beamed. Catherine continued, addressing her husband, "Mr. Eliot, there are matters we should discuss in the short time we have with Mr. Wesley. May I have a private word with you?"

While the Eliots drew apart for a few moments of earnest conversation, Wesley and Perry put their heads together. "May I compliment you on a fine sermon, Mr. Wesley," said Reverend Perry, "one of your very best, moving and persuasive."

"Thank you, my friend," said Wesley. "Could the good people at the back of the crowd hear me well enough? There were thousands of them, commodiously placed row upon row, some far away, and the wind was strong."

"Your voice was as strong and clear as your message, Mr. Wesley," said Perry. "You must come back to Gwennap Pit again. It is conducive to hearing the words of the speaker. We shall make it our own meeting place." He glanced towards Willy Bunt who was still in the grasp of John Williams. "Can you truly help poor Bunt?" Perry asked John Wesley. "I have tried and thought I had saved him, but I'm humbled by my failure."

"You may have failed for now, Mr. Perry," said Wesley, "but with my help and that of the Eliots also, Willy Bunt must be shown how to trust in his Savior, and then he will succeed."

The Eliots rejoined the group. Edward Eliot spoke. "Mr. Wesley, I have some difficulties with men in my employ whom I have respected but who find themselves in straitened circumstances. I happen to be a Commissioner of Trade and Plantations, so I have a particular interest in America." John Wesley nodded, paying close attention. Eliot continued, "I understand you learned much about conditions in America from your own sojourn there." Wesley nodded.

"There is little I can do in the way of reform in general at present," said Eliot, "but in my own interest I have observed that there may be lucrative opportunities for Port Eliot in the colonies. Indeed, there is mineral wealth that His Majesty's government must control. We can't let the colonists go around the mother country's interests. Wars have to be paid for, debts have to be dealt with, taxes have to be raised."

"What do you have in mind, Mr. Eliot?" asked John Wesley.

"I am facing an immediate concern," Eliot said. "You may not be aware of the details as yet, but as a result of a riot at the Wheal Hykka mine the ring leaders are in Penzance gaol, doubtless awaiting trial and sentencing. I have intervened and hope to save them from hanging, but they may not escape transportation. In that case, I shall urge the judge to send them to America. He will impose a term of years when they will have to work out their sentences, but after that they will be free men. England needs colonists who will work hard, skilled miners too."

"You mean you could find them employment, sir?" asked Wesley. "I find that where good works are matched with self-interest, faith finds a powerful ally."

"Perhaps in due course it may be worth my while to consider such a possibility," said Eliot. "I strive to keep up with the times. There's the matter of dealing with the mine captain Penwarden too. He is a good man but he is in serious trouble, and it may be prudent to get him far beyond the reach of Viscount Dunbargan, the principal owner. Perhaps Bunt should join them all in America. He appears to be beyond redemption at Port Eliot."

"Your kindness is beyond praise, Mr. Eliot," said Wesley, "but I would nevertheless urge caution." Reverend Perry joined with a fervent amen.

"I will consult with Polkinghorne and Williams in due course," said Eliot. "Matters will not be rushed. However, your power to improve the lot of sinners, together with your connections in America and my own influence, may prove a telling combination."

The reverends Wesley and Perry both smiled, and Eliot started to leave, but Catherine pulled him back. "I have heard, Mr. Wesley, of your success in bringing poor sinners into the fold," said Catherine. "However, I never imagined your skill in persuading gentlemen to practice what you preach, let alone to reach with their enterprises beyond the ocean."

Chapter Sixty-nine

Unity

Following their attendance at the meeting of Reverend Wesley at Gwennap Pit, the Eliot party embarked at Portreath where they spent the night on the sloop waiting for the weather to improve before setting sail early the next morning. They rounded Lands End and sailed easterly up the English Channel past Falmouth and Looe, eventually arriving safe and sound at the quay at Port Eliot late that evening.

Upon arrival, the captain organized the crew to help the passengers get themselves and their baggage to their respective homes. Edward gave the captain a generous tip and a letter to take to Lord Edgecumbe thanking him for the loan of the sloop. The Eliots were grateful to return to the comforts and tranquility of their own home after their adventures down west. Their guests looked forward to being in a safe haven and enjoying the hospitality of their welcoming hosts. None of them expected respite from labor. There would be plenty to occupy them all.

Viscountess Dunbargan had sent her footman ahead to Lanhydrock with messages to the servants arranging for her son, the Honorable James Trenance, to join her; and for additional clothes and personal supplies for an indefinite stay to be packed and sent, ready for her upon her arrival at Port Eliot. She had instructed the footman to watch out for the viscount and to be careful not to encounter him or let him forestall her plans. She was thus relieved to be greeted upon docking at the quayside by a delighted son and an equally relieved nanny.

Never one to shirk her duty, after seeing to the settling of her guests and getting bathed and changed, Catherine Eliot made it her first order of business before retiring to send a note to Mary Bunt summoning her to a meeting in the morning room at the big house the next day. Catherine's first duty would be to inform Mary of her husband Willy's latest misdeeds. However, there would be happier matters to discuss. She invited Mary to bring her children with her. Catherine took an interest in her goddaughter Catherine Bunt and also wanted to see how her little brother Charles was coming along. She would see to it that the Bunt children would be pupils at her school as they grew older.

The following morning, Catherine was busying herself with accumulated correspondence and household lists left by the cook for her approval when the butler ushered Mary and the children into the morning room.

"Mary, I am delighted to see you," Catherine said, rising from her writing table. "And the children, they are growing so. You must be feeding them well."

"You'm all back from Wheal Hykka, then mum?" said Mary. "Where's my Willy? Oi 'aven't seen 'ide nor 'air of 'im. Oi 'spect Mr. Polkinghorne's got 'im workin' somewhere or 'nother. 'E's always got somethin' to do, but Oi would've 'oped Mr. Polkinghorne weren't too busy just to pop in at our cottage an' tell me when Willy's comin' 'ome. Oi mean home."

"Mary, I'm afraid I have some bad news for you on that score," said Catherine. "Please, sit down."

"Oh Lor', is 'e hurt? Is 'e hurt bad? Oi 'ope 'e'll be all right."

"He's not hurt, he's in trouble Mary, again," said Catherine. "We're seeing that he's being taken care of, and I hope he'll be all right soon. But you must be brave. He's staying down west for a week or two with Reverend Perry and his preacher friend Mr. John Wesley."

"What's 'e been an' done now, that gurt lummox?"

"To be frank, I'm afraid he's started drinking again," said Catherine, "and it just gets the better of him. He can't control himself once he starts, then he gets angry, fighting mad, and gets into trouble."

"Oi've told 'im over an' over to stay away from the drink," said Mary, rubbing a knuckle into her eyes and putting little Charles over her shoulder as he started to whimper. "He'm been doin' ever so much better. Somethin' must've got into him."

"I think you're right," said Catherine, "but he didn't say what it was." She decided to say nothing to Mary of Willy's outburst about Miss Clymo and Polkinghorne having fallen in love. With luck and sound advice from the reverends she hoped that potential tempest would be contained within the proverbial teacup.

Little Catherine looked up from the doll she was playing with on the floor and climbed up into her mother's lap. "The preachers are going to try and talk sense into him and get him to give up alcohol for good. Perhaps they will succeed this time. I hope so for your sake, indeed for all of our sakes. I don't quite know at this stage what will occur. You're going to have to be brave."

Mary sobbed and could not speak. Catherine stood up and walked over to put a consoling hand on Mary's shoulder. "Now pull yourself together, Mary, let's hope for the best. I need your help. We've got work to do, important work, so you must be strong. Wipe away those tears."

Catherine explained to Mary that Elianor Viscountess Dunbargan was staying at Port Eliot with her son the Honorable James Trenance and also Morwenna Clymo, who had brought young Jemmy Penwarden.

"They are good women, capable and industrious," said Catherine. "They will be helping you and me set up the village school. I have prevailed upon our dear vicar to lend guidance if not active assistance."

Mary looked downcast. "Although p'r'aps Oi say it as shouldn't, the vicar's a bit old-fashioned, mum," she said.

"I must agree he is not the most progressive of clerics," said Catherine, "but given his position we can't leave him out. However, Reverend Perry has agreed to help, down west if not here, and his brilliant friend Reverend John Wesley will also lend advice. They'll keep the vicar on his toes."

Mary looked doubtful but offered no contradiction as Catherine forged onward. "Now, getting down to business, I'm sure that all of our own children, at least those of an age to walk, will be the first pupils. Naturally, they will be very young to be at school, but their presence will set an example for the village children. I imagine they will start after their fifth birthdays, if their parents will allow them."

Catherine Eliot was not the sort to wait patiently before taking action. With so much to do the months and years seemed to go by faster now than they did when she was younger. Mary Bunt felt quite consumed by this torrent of energy, to the point where she almost forgot her own troubles, which may have been part of what Catherine had in mind. However, Mary greeted all of this news with less enthusiasm than Catherine expected.

After hesitating, Mary's question provided an explanation. "Will her ladyship be here alone?" she asked. Mary's thoughts had momentarily revisited the assault the viscount had made upon her in the stable at Lanhydrock, a terrible thing, but which also had given her Willy and her darling little daughter.

Catherine set her mind at rest. "The Viscount will not be accompanying her," she said, "and it may be a while before they see each other again."

"Why's that then, mum?"

"I expect it's simply a matter of convenience at the moment," said Catherine. "Now, off you go. My husband needs my assistance on something or other, business or politics no doubt. And I have to look after my guests. I'll let you know when I need you."

Meanwhile, Edward Eliot had met in the business room with Charles Polkinghorne to review estate management matters and to read his correspondence. Polkinghorne was pleased to report that as far as he could tell, after quickly looking over the figures from the home farm, that it had been a good harvest. News from the tenant farmers confirmed that yields of barley and oats in particular were excellent. The weather had been glorious during the crucial period of reaping and threshing.

"So there should be no difficulty in collecting rents the next few quarters," commented Eliot, "and with no shortages that will mean no food riots among the poor and especially the miners. Now, how about the turnips? Have they been dug and clamped? How many of the tenants have come around? Will they winter over more beasts than they used to?"

"I haven't heard yet, sir," said Polkinghorne. "Give me a day or two to settle in now that we're back, and I'll ask around and get some news. Now I've got something to ask, sir. What am I to do about managing the quarries? How long are we going to be without Bunt?"

"I haven't decided yet," said Eliot. "Bunt may be coming back or may not. It depends on how he gets on with the preachers and then sticks to whatever promises they extract from him. Keep an eye out for someone else you could bring along, and speak to me before you make any selection. Have you given me all of the post?"

Eliot sorted through the pile of letters on his desk. One from Boconnoc caught his eye, and he broke the seal and opened it. It was from William Pitt, sent from Lostwithiel. He started reading eagerly.

Polkinghorne saw that Eliot was preoccupied. "If that will be all, sir," he said, "I'll get on up to the house. There are one or two things I have to see to there." Eliot, not looking up, waved him away, and Polkinghorne took his leave. If fortune smiled on him he would run into Morwenna Clymo, and they would be able to arrange to spend some time together.

Pitt had written to tell Eliot that he had gone to Bath to take the waters, trying to ease his abominable gout. Having traveled that far west from London, he had arranged to go with Lady Hester and their children down to visit his nephew Thomas Pitt at Boconnoc. Pitt said that they planned in a few days to head up to Town to prepare for the next session of the House and asked if they might make a stop at St. Germans on their way.

The great statesman had gone on to write that he hoped the visit might encompass politics as well as pleasure. He had become more frustrated than ever since departing the government, followed a few months later by his old partner and nemesis, the Duke of Newcastle, leaving as well. The king's administration was marked by more discord than ever and, in his view, less ability and judgment. He feared that much of what had been won during the course of seven years of war would be given up in the race to settle for peace and avoid expenditure.

Eliot shuffled through the rest of the post and then walked to the house where he told Catherine the news from William Pitt and they agreed not only to welcome the Pitt family to Port Eliot on their way up to London, but also to invite some friends and neighbors to dine with them. The visit and a great banquet were accordingly arranged for the following week.

Catherine would be in her element. Edward marveled at her energy and enthusiasm. There was no longer any question that he could relax at Port Eliot for a few weeks before taking up his duties in London. His wife was indeed a marvelous woman, a helpmeet, a support and an inspiration. Every now and then, however, he was dismayed at the challenge of keeping up with the force of her arguments and the energy of her constant activity; but her charm and the felicity of their marriage kept any reservations on that score at bay.

Chapter Seventy

Entertainment

Catherine Eliot summoned the Port Eliot butler and housekeeper to marshal their army of underlings to select the wines, prepare the foods, clean the house, polish the furniture, make the beds and trim the gardens. She insisted that every detail be reviewed, including rehearsing a relay team of footmen to carry chafing dishes with hot coals to keep the food warm during its hundred-yard journey from the kitchens to the dining room. Finally she was ready to review the guest list with her husband.

"Edward, I have invited Lord and Lady Edgecumbe to dine with the Pitts," said Catherine, "and Frances Boscawen; she has been alone since her husband died last year. Mrs. Boscawen is bringing her young friends, Mary More and her younger sister, Hannah More, who are down here from Bristol staying with relatives of Mrs. Edward Gwatkin. The More girls started a very successful boarding school there four years ago with the help of Ann Gwatkin." Catherine's voice rang with enthusiasm; she was indeed in her element as she smiled broadly at her husband. "You remember the Lovell family in Falmouth? Ann is their daughter. They're all part of the group of intellectuals in London that we were discussing with Joshua Reynolds, the Blue Stockings Society. They'd be valuable advisors with the school, if they will consent. I understand young Hannah is only about seventeen, but she is reputed to be a brilliant writer and works at the school as well."

Edward found an opening to respond. "Then let us include my brother John. He is the youngest Captain in the Royal Navy; they may enjoy each other. He's stationed at home at the moment and it would do his career no harm to dine with a senior officer like Lord Edgcumbe. Now I trust the Misses More ladies are amusing as well as intelligent," continued Edward. "Our guests would not warm to overbearing women. If you think they would add to the party then by all means invite them."

"We can rely on Mrs. Boscawen's good sense, Edward, " said Catherine, "and don't forget that Mr. Reynolds spoke highly of Miss Hannah More, and he is one who appreciates charm as well as intelligence. In fact, we should ask him to join us in welcoming them and the Pitts."

"If Mr. Reynolds comes I would like to invite my mother," said Edward. "They enjoy each other's company, and she is always a lively addition."

"We'll still be a bit short of men," said Catherine, "what about the vicar? He's rather earnest, I know. Nice but dull, but at least he is male. We can seat him with Elianor; she'll liven him up. What about Polkinghorne or Miss Clymo?"

"Hardly appropriate guests for such company," said Edward. "You'll be wanting the tenant farmers and the entire town council of Liskeard next."

"But surely it would affirm your importance to the voters if they had an opportunity to see you in the company of the great man?" persisted Catherine.

"Then arrange a garden party and include the hoi polloi," said Edward. "The weather is often quite mild at this time of year, and we can put out some braziers if it looks like being chilly."

So as the appointed day approached, Port Eliot garnered its harvests, put on its festive garb and entertained the great and the good on one evening, and the people and the peasantry on the following fine autumn day. Indoors, the dining room gleamed with polished mahogany and sparkling glass under the soft light of dozens of beeswax candles and glowed in the warmth of blazing fires against the coolness of the evening, as the bejeweled and bewigged guests were shown to their places.

William Pitt was placed at one end of the great dining table where he could preside over the company, with his hostess Catherine Eliot seated at his right hand. Edward Eliot's vibrant and still youthful mother, Harriot Hamilton, was at his left. She could be counted on to be a stimulating companion. Edward Eliot took his customary place at the opposite end. The guest of honor's wife Hester, Lady Chatham, was to Edward's right. Elianor, Viscountess Dunbargan, was seated to his left, next to the vicar where her determined charm could squash his more boring interjections. To the vicar's other side were seated Mary and Hannah More, whose intelligence would possibly stifle his ramblings. Next to Hannah was seated her friend Joshua Reynolds, flanked to his left by Catherine Eliot. The famous portraitist was well pleased to be the artistic rose between the thorns of two piercing female intellects.

The Royal Navy was well represented on the opposite side of the table. The Edgecumbes were also important guests, so his lordship was seated close to William Pitt, with whose views he did not always agree, but separated from him by Harriot Hamilton who could be diplomatic when the need arose. To Lord Edgecumbe's left was Frances Boscawen, recent widow of the gallant Cornish admiral Edmund Boscawen and a friend of Mary and Hannah More and fellow member of the Blue Stockings.

At the other end of the table the new Lady Edgecumbe was seated next to Edward Eliot. A reputation for worldly charm preceded her, so

Edward hoped that her presence would compensate for the vicar's penchant for adding non-sequiturs and platitudes to the conversation. Between the ladies was seated young Captain John Eliot, who was delighted to further his acquaintance with his commanding officer's wife and a hero's widow.

Edward's mother Harriot launched the ship of conversation. "It is delightful to have you and Lady Hester here, Mr. Pitt. What brings you to Cornwall on this occasion?"

"We have been staying with my nephew Thomas at Boconnoc, Mrs. Hamilton," said Pitt. "He sits for the family's borough at Old Sarum. You know, my brother had mortgaged the seat in the Commons to the Treasury to settle his debts. It's only been a year this summer since he died, but young Thomas has wasted no time in ignoring that arrangement and choosing himself as Member of Parliament. At least for now I can count on his support in the House. I don't know how long he'll stay. He needs more money. Looking for a place in the Admiralty I gather. He's quite capable, honest enough too."

"I trust you enjoyed a good journey," said Catherine Eliot, "no broken wheels, no encounters with highwaymen?"

"Our journey was quite comfortable, so much better than it used to be," said Lady Hester. "My husband tells me that we have Mr. Eliot's turnpike to thank for that. We were blessed with fair autumn weather too, and we always enjoy the beautiful Cornish countryside."

"We have to commend you, Eliot," said Pitt, "your turnpikes have much improved the journey from Lostwithiel. The driver commented on the absence of ruts and hazards. We made good speed and changed horses only once. The tolls were a nuisance but a good exchange for the improvements. We look forward to further sections being completed."

"The turnpike is thanks in large part to you, Mr. Pitt," said Eliot. "Your support in parliament enabled the passage of the Liskeard Turnpike Act, so we could form the trust and raise the capital and now keep the highway in repair. Our farmers and fishermen get their products to market faster and fresher, and goods are carried cheaper. Our travelers are more comfortable and safer."

The conversation quickly turned to politics. With this company there was little inhibition about such a discussion; it was the blood in their veins and the oxygen in their lungs. Catherine Eliot addressed an observation to her chief guest.

"England has seen great changes in administration in recent months, Mr. Pitt. I'm sure I speak for all of us when I say that we wish you and the Duke of Newcastle were still leading us. It would be a shame indeed if the new men threw away in the months of peace what you gained in seven years of war. Would they not be receptive to your wisdom and experience?"

"Dear lady, while his majesty might encourage such a thing," said Pitt, "it is not in me to join the men who thwarted me simply to patch up a peace that they would botch."

"The pusillanimity of your opponents regarding the provision of expenditures has made them too willing to treat with our enemies whom we have severely thrashed in oceans around the globe," said Lord Edgecumbe.

"Spoken like a true sailor," said Pitt. "For my own part, I have always held that the best way to have peace is to prepare for war."

"My late husband agreed with you," said Frances Boscawen. "The admiral believed in strength and preparedness, always preparedness."

"If you ask my opinion," the vicar began, but Edward Eliot interrupted before he could continue.

"I would prefer that you had stayed in office, sir," he said. "Do you sometimes wish that you had followed a different path?"

"I think deeply before taking action," replied Pitt, "and once I take a decision, I am unlikely ever to go back on it."

"As I have always advised my dear husband," said Lady Hester, "stick to your wise precept of not wearing the mind to pieces by indecision, but to take one's part, as appears best, and submit the rest to Providence."

"I am glad to take my wife's advice," said Pitt. "I only wish her brother had done the same. But he chose to stay in office when I resigned. George Grenville cannot now expect me to come to his aid in pressing for a more righteous peace."

"Far be it for me to say," ventured the vicar, not noticing Elianor Dunbargan's expression as she turned aside and rolled her eyes to the amusement of Harriot Hamilton.

"Indeed," Edgcumbe cut in, "if I may be blunt, the indecisiveness of the king's present first minister is only exceeded by his ineptitude."

"Lord Bute is a sorry example of a man who aspires to an office for which he is not fitted," said Pitt. "He lacks the firmness of character and steadfastness, let alone the judgment, the requisite knowledge and experience of affairs to meet his self-appointed task. It is a disaster for the man himself as well as for the country. The king should never have allowed his personal affection for him to have outweighed a sober consideration of his fitness."

"Dear Mr. Pitt, you are making us all too solemn," said Harriot Hamilton. "Tell us something to make us smile. I know you too well to expect you to make us laugh," she added with a twinkle.

"Well then, dear lady, since we are amongst a seagoing band, I can in the deepest confidence tell you that there will soon be another admiral among us," Pitt said, smiling in the direction of Lord Edgecumbe."

"George!" exclaimed Lady Edgecumbe.

"How splendid!" said Catherine Eliot, putting her table napkin to her mouth and smiling bravely. When would her own husband reap honors like these? He was worthy and loyal. How long before he would join those of the first importance? On one thing at least she was determined: he would enter the House of Lords before he went to his grave. The flow of the conversation paused as the servants passed more food and poured more wine.

"If you were to make your appointments according to how handsome your men were, you would have promoted My Lord Edgcumbe long ago," said Joshua Reynolds.

"Oh, Mr. Reynolds!" said Harriot Hamilton, "you say that just because his lordship commissioned you to paint his portrait. Do you expect that more clients will come rushing forward?"

"Dear Mrs. Hamilton," said the artist, "believe me, if my use of flattery were to be measured against your leveling remarks, I would be the loser."

"Lord Edgecumbe is more handsome in the flesh today than you portrayed him in pigment many years ago," said Viscountess Dunbargan.

"Since I married," said Edgecumbe, "I now have less to envy our host for his marital good fortune than I do for his collection of your paintings, Mr. Reynolds." He bowed his head towards Catherine, who blushed prettily and smiled.

Edward Eliot was a little embarrassed by the whole interchange. "We have not yet heard from my younger brother, John," said Edward, turning toward the young man. "You were of great assistance to him, Mr. Pitt. We were grateful for your efforts in securing his freedom after his capture by the French. He is enjoying a brilliant career."

"You had your revenge on the French, Captain Eliot," said Lord Edgecumbe, "captured that privateer in the Baltic, rich prizes since. Glad to have you aboard."

"Good show," said Pitt, "we need young officers like you. You've learned good tactical skills and shown the daring to go with them."

"I look forward to greater success, sir," said John Eliot, "and I'm eager to see the world."

"The future lies with the young," said Lady Hester. "We have brought our children with us: John, Harriot and young William. He is three and a half and still a little delicate."

"Do at least leave the older ones here with us for a while," said Catherine. "We are starting our little school and will have a form for the younger children. Such a good example for the village."

"Well, perhaps if I left their nurse here too, then William could stay as well. They would have someone familiar to look after them," said Lady Hester, "not that they see much of me and their father at the best of times. Our lives are fully occupied."

"Do William good, make a man of him," said William Pitt.

"Yes, do leave them," said Hannah More. "I am convinced that schooling is the making of children, and the younger they start the better. And so much better for them than learning alone at home with governesses."

"They'll be in good hands with these ladies, Lady Hester," said Joshua Reynolds; "they study the writings of the most enlightened modern philosophers. If the smallest particle of their learning rubs off on these children, they will be the best educated in the kingdom. My good friend Samuel Johnson and I are among the few gentlemen allowed on sufferance to join the deliberations of their Blue Stockings Society, and I confess we often acquire more knowledge than we impart."

"I remember the advice my late father gave to me when I was seeking my calling," said the vicar, pausing to give a polite cough before completing his speech, which again lost him the opportunity to make his mark on the conversation.

"Ah, if only I had remembered the advice my late husbands gave to me," Harriot Hamilton slipped in with a smile, "I would have been twice as virtuous as I am today and would need to spend half as much time on my knees in your congregation saying the General Confession." Her companions laughed with her, but the vicar merely looked puzzled. Edward Eliot glanced at his mother with a mixture of affection and disapproval.

Giving a sigh of resignation, the Vicar turned to Lady Dunbargan, "And where is your charming husband?" he asked.

Edward rushed into the exchange before Elianor could answer and asked, "How much longer before the peace negotiations are brought to a satisfactory conclusion, Mr. Pitt? Also, I must enquire, what rewards can England expect for her expenditures?"

"I cannot forget that I am a landowner as well as a navy man," interposed Lord Edgecumbe, "and though I believe England should press her advantage in victory, I personally will welcome a reduction in the land tax to its former levels."

"The beer tax requires others to share the burden with us country gentlemen," said Eliot. "That is welcome relief."

"Indeed," said Pitt, "and that is encouraging Bute to advocate a cider tax."

"That is a horse of an entirely different color," said Eliot. "It'll never run in Cornwall. How can it be collected from the myriad of small apple growers and pressers? It is an absurd notion, and I for one will oppose it."

"I shall join you, Eliot," said Edgcumbe. "My man has recently planted hundreds more apple and pear trees at Mount Edgcumbe. I didn't make that investment merely to write couplets extolling the blossoms."

"You were enlightening us, Mr. Pitt, on the negotiations for the peace," said Harriot soothingly.

"I trust, Mrs. Hamilton, that your son will receive a summons to come to the House for a vote before the end of the year," Pitt responded, "and I foresee that a treaty will be signed early in 1763, probably in Paris. There is no excuse for my colleagues dithering much longer."

"That is good news indeed," said Lady Dunbargan.

"I am determined that we should hold Canada," said Pitt, "but some of my colleagues don't have the stomach for it."

Lord Edgecumbe raised his eyebrows. "But surely allowing the French to remain in Canada would render the American colonists less troublesome by making them more dependent on us to protect their northern frontier," he argued.

This was an issue that was close to the sensitivities of the guest of honor, never one to brook opposition gracefully to causes that he had espoused. "I have never heard such nonsense in my life," stated Pitt, red in the face. "Canada will play an important part in English trade, of that you can be sure. It seems that you make a better sailor than you do a statesman, my lord. You may hope that I do not regain influence with Grenville before your promotion is confirmed by the king."

"Make no mistake that I value your brilliant service to our country, Mr. Pitt," said Edgcumbe, "but I am one of those who believe that it is high time to cease war expenditures and reduce the debt."

"The French are in far worse straits than we are," said Pitt. "A portion of our victory is that, with the help of our friends the Dutch in Amsterdam, London now controls the world's financial markets."

A general quiet had fallen over the rest of the group at the great man's indignation as his views were challenged. "Dear Mr. Pitt," said Mrs. Hamilton finally, "do tell us what riches your statesmanship has gained for us in America and the sugar islands."

"I anticipate some moving of the pieces on the board in the West Indies," said Pitt, recovering his equanimity. He took a large draft from his wine glass and grimaced at a twinge of pain from his gout. "We also anticipate great strides in the southern parts of America." He composed his features and took another sip before continuing. "France will cede Louisiana to Spain, and Spain will cede Louisiana and the Alabama country and Florida to us. We will form a new colony of West Florida. The potential for plantations and trade will be great."

"A very profitable demand for slaves, no doubt," observed Edgcumbe, looking rather complacent at changing the conversation.

"Quite," said Edward Eliot, not wishing to pursue the topic. Slavery was a trade that he was thinking about in different ways since hearing the sermon preached by John Wesley at Gwennap Pit. Thank heavens Catherine had not insisted on inviting the Reverend Wesley to join their table. Lord Edgcumbe would have struck more sparks with the preacher than he had with the statesman.

Come to think of it, Edward had just received an official report to the Commissioners of Trade and Plantations. He was about to tell his guests about it but thought better of imparting information that put the rather disreputable trade in an attractive light. However, he mused, the slave trade was doing well. Last year one hundred and ninety-five British ships employed more than thirteen thousand seamen, brought home over two million pounds. England now completely outstripped the pesky Portuguese. The profit would be greater if the number who died on the voyage could be reduced, fifteen per centum the report said. But that attrition had to be weighed against the cost of adequate food. Ah, his brother had something to say.

"What an exciting prospect, a new colony, West Florida." said John Eliot. "I joined the navy to serve England and expand her empire, to see as much of the world as I can, and I trust that opportunities in those parts will arise."

"England constantly needs reliable and forceful men to govern its growing empire," said Pitt.

"And to make their fortunes too," said Harriot Hamilton. "Why is it that the younger sons are always the adventurers in the family?"

"My husband is an exception," said Elianor Dunbargan. "While he is the eldest among the Trenances, it is precisely adventuring that is responsible for his absence." The Vicar looked up from his sleepy contemplation of his plate.

"That may be a different kind of adventuring than I had in mind," said Harriot. Catherine hid a smile.

"I don't know why that phenomenon prevails, but for my part I agree with you, Mrs. Hamilton," said Edgcumbe, determined to regain some control of the conversation. "Until my brother died I enjoyed the excitement and he bore the family responsibilities, but there are privileges that accompany them. Of course, I could have gone into the church but decided against it."

"Praise be to God," muttered the vicar, but under his breath so that he would not suffer rebuff once again.

"My husband was certainly the adventurer," agreed Frances Boscawen, "but then my brother-in-law inherited the viscountcy and the estate is entailed. Without land Edmund had little choice but to go to sea."

Catherine stood to suggest that the ladies withdraw. The vicar looked relieved. Edward looked pensive. Young John Eliot's face was shining as he stood and looked into his mother's eyes. With the aid of his family connections he had seized the opportunity of impressing important men. His naval career would assuredly continue on the rise.

Chapter Seventy-one

School

Catherine Eliot wasted no time in organizing her little school in a room in the undercroft of the church. There would be classes for girls as well as boys, starting with the younger ones. She encouraged families of all denominations to send their little ones, despite the vicar being quite put out at her insistence that even Methodists be allowed on Church of England property. He would continue his own church school exclusively for boys from Anglican homes.

Catherine's school began with the children staying at Port Eliot as pupils. In addition, with Mary Bunt's help, a handful of children aged five and under were recruited from the village. Mary was happy to help the mums by taking the children off their hands while they went about their work to put bread on their families' tables. With her own children, Mary walked them all from the village to the church, which was a fair piece. Catherine Eliot said the exercise would be good for them.

Catherine went to the schoolroom herself to supervise. Edward Eliot had directed Charles Polkinghorne to see that the estate carpenter made little desks with benches for the school, that each pupil was provided a slate to write on, and that teachers had a blackboard and chalk. Catherine told Mary Bunt that she would be in charge, assisted by Morwenna Clymo; but both would be under the temporary instruction of Mary and Hannah More, who had succumbed to Catherine's persuasion and were delighted to stay on for a few days after the dinner party to guide initial efforts.

Catherine told young Edward James Eliot to do what the teachers told him and had brought along a nursemaid to look after him and little Charles Bunt. The Pitts' nurse was encouraging John and Harriot Pitt to find their places and had taken young William Pitt to join the younger John Eliot and Charles Bunt in the care of the Eliots' nursemaid. Elianor Dunbargan looked on as her nurse handed her son, the Honorable James Trenance, over to the charge of their new teachers, along with Catherine Bunt and Jemmy Penwarden.

Hannah More, wearing a simple dress and sturdy shoes, soon had the older children sitting at their desks and paying attention, while Mary More conferred with Mary Bunt and Morwenna Clymo. Mary More explained that although the children were too young for real lessons, Hannah would get them started on playing together, learning songs, memorizing the alphabet and writing capital letters. In no time the children were singing nursery rhymes together, chanting the words and keeping more or less in tune. Then Hannah More introduced them to an action song, teaching them "Oranges and Lemons." But when they got to the bit about chopping off their heads, James Trenance got too rough with Catherine Bunt, and she pushed him back, sending him over the back of a bench.

Hannah More scolded the little girl, and she ended up in tears. Catherine ran to her mother for comfort complaining, "But 'e pushed me first, an' Oi don't loike 'im; 'e's a nasty boy. Tell 'im to stop 'ittin' me."

"She talks common," said James Trenance. "Pater says I shouldn't play with common children. I didn't really hurt her. She's a crybaby and I hate her." He stuck his nose in the air and turned his back. Mary Bunt was crestfallen. She lifted Catherine on to her lap and comforted her.

Lady Dunbargan stood up, walked over to her son and grabbed him by his arm. "You are being very rude," she scolded. "I saw you push Catherine, so don't bother to lie to me. Now you go over and say you are sorry, and behave like a gentleman. I am ashamed of you."

James stamped his foot and crossed his arms and scowled. He did not move.

"Come along, Master James," said the nursemaid, "do as your mother tells 'e, there's a good boy. I'm so sorry, Lady Dunbargan, 'e's not usually like this, 'e's a good boy really."

"Oh, let's all just settle down," said Hannah More, "we'll play another game in a little while. Now let's sit on the floor in a circle and you can all have a drink of milk."

"I don't like milk," said James, "I won't drink it."

"You will drink it and you will like it," said Elianor, "or I will tell your father to give you a good whipping when he gets home."

"Pater says I don't have to do what you tell me; I just have to obey him," said James, sticking out his tongue at his mother.

"You leave 'er alone," said Jemmy Penwarden. "You'm bein' a bully, may be richer nor us but Oi'm bigger'n you, so you'd better shut yer gob."

"Right then, that's it," said Hannah More firmly. "It will soon be time for recess, and those that don't sit down right now will have to stay here while the others play outside."

After everyone but James, who stood resolutely aside, was sitting in a circle, they were given milk. Then Hannah More said, "Mrs. Bunt, Miss Clymo, gather up the children, put on their coats and out we go, girls first and then the boys. Fetch the little ones and take them along as well."

They all trotted out, with Edward James Eliot shyly holding Harriot Pitt by the hand. "I think you're nice," said Edward James. Harriot blushed but did not reply.

James Trenance sat down on a bench and sulked. His mother went over to him. "Do you think you can behave now?" she asked. He looked at her and gave a small nod of his head. "Well then, you can go outside and join the others."

Mary More had hung back to see what became of James. She stepped forward and tried to take his hand to lead him out to the others, but he shook her off and ran through the door.

After the teachers and the children left, Catherine Eliot and Elianor Dunbargan were alone together for a moment. The viscountess was near tears, but she stiffened up. "His father spoils him," she said; "Nanny can't do a thing with him. I can hardly endure until Dunbargan is out of my life, and his son and heir is off to Eton and gets regular discipline from the masters. His father has turned my little boy into a monster."

"Oh, Elianor, my dear, I do sympathize," said Catherine. "Perhaps while he is here the Mores will encourage him to share with the other children and keep his temper. And perhaps we should let the Penwarden boy put him in his place, teach him a lesson. He seems like a fine little fellow, won't stand for any nonsense either. Young James can't go through life acting the bully."

"Unfortunately he can," said Elianor, "and my husband won't lift a finger to stop him. Like father, like son. The viscount would be furious that he is playing with a miner's son, let alone taking orders from him. And my husband seems to have taken a special dislike to Captain Penwarden with no provocation that I can see."

"Your lot is not a happy one for now," said Catherine consolingly, "but perhaps the viscount will act more kindly when your new baby is born. Far be it from me to say, but it may persuade him to take his responsibilities as a family man more seriously."

Elianor looked at her. "Catherine, my dear, you are too good, and you have a lovely husband. It must be impossible for you to understand how futile any hope of James' reform is. Nothing in his behavior, from the moment we were married, would persuade me that you are right. Now," she added with a forced smile, "we'd better go along and join the others."

The teachers had taken the children for a walk through the park towards the fishpond. Jemmy Penwarden had broken a hazel stick from a hedge and made a fishing rod with a length of string and a bent pin from his pocket. He dug up a worm from under a stone and stuck it on the hook for bait; the girls screamed when it wriggled. Harriot Pitt clung tightly to Edward James Eliot's hand, and he smiled at her.

Morwenna Clymo had succeeded in holding James Trenance by the hand to keep him under control, but as they neared the pond he jerked away. Little Catherine Bunt was standing by the bank watching Jemmy as he cast his line. James ran up behind her, catching her unawares and pushed her in with a splash. She cried out in fright as she sank under the water, then quick as a flash Jemmy jumped in after her.

The pond was shallow near the edge and Jemmy was able to find a footing. He bent over and grasped her and pulled her, spluttering and thrashing, above the water but couldn't manage to lift her out. Realizing what a foolish thing he had done, and despite his bravado not wanting to get in more trouble, James Trenance took off his coat and pulled off his boots and socks and waded in after them. The two boys together lifted her out and laid her on the bank, shivering.

Mary Bunt took off her daughter's coat and dress and her boots and stockings, then took off her own shawl and wrapped little Catherine in it to dry her off and keep her from getting chilled. James ducked away from his mother, afraid that this time she would be really cross. His nanny followed Mary's example, taking off her own shawl, wrapping James in it and drying his feet and legs.

"Why, look at them," whispered Catherine to Elianor. "See, they both have feet like little frogs." Having observed Catherine Bunt at birth and suddenly realizing the obvious paternal connection, she regretted her mistake in mentioning it and added, "I suppose they are quite fortunate really; make them excellent swimmers."

"I've seen that before," muttered Morwenna, wandering over and staring. So what Willy Bunt had told her all those months ago was unquestionably true. That nasty Dunbugger, Sir James Trenance as was, had forced himself on Mary in the stable at Lanhydrock. Morwenna knew full well the voraciousness of Sir James' appetites, although she could have been less flattered by him and more virtuous in resisting his advances. And if her father had not arrived home when he did, Morwenna might have had her way with Willy. However, she had vowed to mend her ways, and these thoughts made her appreciate the attentions of Charles Polkinghorne all the more.

Lady Dunbargan overheard Morwenna and looked at her in alarm. "And, where, may I ask was it that you saw such toes?" she demanded frostily. Morwenna blushed and did not reply. "Where have you seen that strange sight before? Tell me," persisted the viscountess. "Speak up, I insist on knowing."

"I don't rightly remember," said Morwenna, looking away. "Maybe when I was little, one of my playmates, maybe," she stammered. The viscountess seized Morwenna by the shoulders, turned her to face her, stared straight into her eyes and asked, "Was it at Lanhydrock? Have you ever seen my husband in his bare feet?"

No one said anything for several moments. Mary Bunt looked puzzled. Then Catherine Eliot spoke to the nursemaids. "Now you girls take the children straight back to the house. Get these wet ones into dry clothes and in front of a fire. Make haste, or they'll catch their deaths."

"I suppose school is closed for the day?" said Hannah More coming up to them. She got no answer.

Morwenna found her tongue. "I didn't mean it, ma'am, I couldn't help it. He made me. He was too strong for me. I didn't mean no harm. Please don't tell my dad, and whatever you do don't let Mr. Polkinghorne find out."

"What ever does Polkinghorne have to do with this?" asked Catherine.

"Well Oi never," said Mary Bunt.

"Was there more than once?" shouted Lady Dunbargan.

Morwenna swiftly put her hand to her throat and looked at the ground.

Elianor pulled Morwenna's hand away. "Where did you get that cameo?" she demanded, now furious.

"Wait 'til my Willy hears about this," said Mary. "That Dunbugger better stay out of his way."

Before she could be stopped, Morwenna ran off crying after the children, towards the big house. She did not see the horseman cantering down the drive towards the gatehouse and out to the Liskeard road.

Chapter Seventy-two

Gaol

As he pulled on the right rein to head towards Liskeard, the rider spurred his horse to a steady canter. Charles Polkinghorne took to heart his employer's order to get to Penzance with his letter and his precious burden with all possible haste. He had a brace of pistols in holsters strapped to his saddle; an ambitious highwayman would have a fight on his hands. Perhaps more important, if he had to negotiate with someone it would be from strength.

Edward Eliot had received a letter from Reverend Peter Perry and after reading it had given Polkinghorne only a few moments notice of his departure. Eliot told him to spare no expense in changing horses as often as necessary to keep up a fast pace; it was imperative to fulfill his mission as quickly as possible.

Polkinghorne had hoped that Morwenna's presence at Port Eliot would give them opportunities to spend time getting to know each other and even moving towards the possibility of marriage. But Mrs. Eliot had immediately pressed Morwenna into service for her new school, and now Mr. Eliot was sending him off on an urgent mission for days at a time. He had not even had an opportunity to speak to Morwenna to let her know the reason for his sudden departure, at least not without being too obvious to the others.

They had to be discreet. Now as he left he had seen her hurrying across the park to the house after a group of children, but it did not look as if she noticed him. No doubt she was being kept fully occupied. He was beginning to think that it might not be so bad having Bunt back so that he could be spared some of these duties, at least if Willy could stay away from the drink, and Morwenna.

The weather stayed fine and Polkinghorne pressed on at a good pace without incident, reaching Penzance by late the following afternoon. He made for the Turk's Head Inn near the harbor where he was to meet the reverends Perry and Wesley. He asked the landlord where he might find them. The landlord was a rough-looking fellow, surly and stricken with a bad cold. Somewhat reluctantly he called his ostler to stable Polkinghorne's horse and then took him to the dining room where the preachers were waiting for him. Polkinghorne kept his saddlebag with him. Before dismissing the landlord, he asked him to have an extra horse saddled for when he left.

The room was made noisy by a group of sailors gathered around a table in the back of the room. They were drinking, talking loudly and laughing uproariously. "Ah, Polkinghorne," Reverend Perry raised his voice above the din to greet him, "I see you made good time. Welcome to Penzance and the Turk's Head."

Polkinghorne shook their hands and looked around him. "I am pleased to see you both," he said, "but this seems like an unsuitable place to be frequented by gentlemen of the cloth who profess total abstinence."

"Indeed, yes," said Reverend Wesley. "It pains me to see these young fellows abusing themselves. If I were not meeting you on a more important mission, I would take them to task. But their lives are hard. They're from his majesty's ship lying in the harbor, preparing to sail into danger and no doubt under harsh discipline, in all probability pressed into service. They will be escorting hulks carrying prisoners and slaves to America."

"Penwarden is imprisoned nearby?" asked Polkinghorne.

"He is, and in horrible conditions, in a cell right here in this inn," said Reverend Perry. "We have visited him when permitted, taken him food from time to time, and assured him that Mr. Eliot would arrange his release before he came to trial."

"What of Tom Kegwyn and the ringleaders of the riot? Have they been tried? Were they hanged? It hadn't been decided by the time of the hearing in Penzance."

"The trial is over," said Perry, "and as we all hoped, no witnesses came forward. They were sentenced to being transported to America. They may be in servitude for no more than seven years, or they may be sold as laborers. They escaped lightly thanks to Mr. Eliot's influence. They are even now in chains in the harbor awaiting a fair wind to set sail."

"And the viscount?" enquired Polkinghorne.

"We've seen or heard nothing of him," answered Reverend Perry, "but we can't trust him to leave well enough alone."

"You say that Penwarden is here at the Turk's Head?" asked Polkinghorne. "That seems strange, why here?"

"This is an old building, and the constables use the cell as the town gaol," said Perry. "It's the first inn in England to be called the Turk's Head you know; it's used for many purposes. It was built over five hundred years ago. They say that a party of Turks from Jerusalem invaded Penzance back then when they were excommunicated during the Sixth Crusade. Imagine that! Might be a bit of a tall yarn, more likely Barbary corsairs. Anyroad, there are still priests' holes upstairs. And the floor above that is a fisherman's loft used to store nets."

"You'll be telling me it's a smugglers' haunt next," chuckled Polkinghorne. He changed the subject to what really mattered to him. "Has Clymo been here lately?"

John Wesley smiled, but wryly.

"Careful what you say," said Reverend Perry, ignoring Polkinghorne's lead. "Smuggling is a serious business around here, enough to get people killed. In fact, there is a tunnel that runs under the inn down to the harbor; it comes into the back of the dining room and up a shaft upstairs. I wouldn't mention it to the landlord if I were you; he's an ugly customer. He wouldn't like it if you knew too many secrets."

"We should summon the man now," said Reverend Wesley, appreciating Polkinghorne's concern. "He is not only the landlord, he is also the town gaoler. Did you bring the letter and gold from Mr. Eliot?"

Polkinghorne nodded and unbuckled the strap to his saddlebag. He reached in and pulled out a folded parchment and a leather bag tied at the neck and put them on the floor beside his chair. He left his pistols inside the saddlebag, but within easy reach.

Reverend Wesley called over the landlord and pulled out a chair for him. The landlord stood and looked at each of the men in turn and then flopped down in the chair.

"Is the prisoner ready for us to take into custody?" the Reverend Wesley asked the landlord. The landlord hawked, spat on the floor, and wiped his mouth with the back of his hand. "Aargh," he said, "where's my money?"

"All in good time, my good man," said Polkinghorne, "first you must sign this conveyance, or make your mark if that is the best you can do."

"Don't make no mind to we," said the landlord, "that be for the mayor and the sergeants at arms. Oi just needs my money."

"This here is an official paper from Mr. Edward Eliot, Registrar of the Duchy of Cornwall, His Majesty's Commissioner of Trade and Plantations, Member of Parliament, former Mayor and Magistrate of the Borough of Liskeard, gentleman of Port Eliot in the Borough of St. Germans in the County of Cornwall. This document requires and charges you to transfer your prisoner Addis Penwarden of Pendeen to the custody of his duly sworn deputies, myself and these two gentlemen, upon payment of twenty pounds in gold sovereigns to the duly appointed representative of the Corporation of Penzance, namely your good self. Is that clear?"

Polkinghorne turned the paper around and put it on the table between them so that the landlord could read it. He asked the clerk at the inn's entrance to bring a quill and ink. The landlord glanced at the paper briefly, spat, looked as wise as was in his power to do and said, "Aargh, Oi reckon."

Polkinghorne continued, "Then all that is required is for you to affix your sign and seal and for these gentlemen to witness the proper execution of this, and then we can complete our transaction."

The landlord said, "Where's my twenty sovereigns?"

Polkinghorne sat back and laid both hands on the table. "Where's the prisoner?" he asked.

"Us'll go fetch 'im when Oi see the money," the landlord responded.

John Wesley spoke firmly. "First I will come with you and see the prisoner," he said. "I will assure myself that he is unharmed, and you will strike his fetters from him."

Charles Polkinghorne bent down and picked up the bag of money. He counted out twenty sovereigns on the table and placed them before him. The landlord reached across for them. Polkinghorne smacked his hand away. The landlord leapt to his feet. Two of the sailors stood up to see what the disturbance was about.

"You keep your noses out of this," yelled the landlord at them, "or you'll end up in that cell. That's where us puts tars what can't 'old their beer. Mind your own bloody business."

Reverend Wesley put a restraining hand on his arm. "Come, show me where the prisoner is. We do not need a disturbance." They left together, and the sailors sat down and resumed drinking. Polkinghorne reached down to his saddlebag, took out one of his pistols, primed it and loaded it before laying it carefully on the floor beside him.

The landlord came back carrying a blacksmith's hammer and pincers and gripping Penwarden's arm as the prisoner stumbled after him. Penwarden represented little threat since he was manacled.

"He's lost weight but he's in good health," said Wesley, coming into the room and struggling to control his anger. Penwarden slowly followed him in, staggering, reaching out for support. He was emaciated, filthy, smelly and in rags. He had obviously been kept in foul conditions without exercise and barely fed.

"You owes us five sovereigns for 'is keep," said the landlord. "Like 'e promised when us gave 'im food. Pay us that, then us strikes 'is irons."

"That's outrageous," said Reverend Perry, no doubt thinking how many poor families such an amount would feed. "Five shillings at most."

"Sovereigns," said the landlord. "Shillings," said Polkinghorne, bending down and picking up his pistol and putting it on the table.

The landlord grunted, took a long look at the weapon and then quickly signed the document. He picked up his tools, broke the fastening, and released Addis Penwarden from his manacles. Penwarden stretched out his freed right arm and shook each of his rescuers warmly by the hand. Then with both hands he scratched his head and under his arms. He stumbled, evidently weakened, but Perry held on to him and steadied him and helped him sit down.

Perry looked closely at Penwarden's hair, and saw tiny creatures crawling. "The first thing we do is put your head under the pump," he said, moving away from the disheveled man's side, turning his head and holding his breath.

Polkinghorne turned over the twenty gold sovereigns and five silver shillings to the landlord and put the signed document in his saddlebag. He kept his pistol in his hand as he picked up his saddlebag. They all left through the door to the stable yard and collected the horses.

"Mr. Eliot has instructed me to take you to Port Eliot," Polkinghorne said to Penwarden. "He thinks it is too dangerous for you to go back to Wheal Hykka for the time being until Viscount Dunbargan has been dealt with. Your Jemmy is already there with Mr. and Mrs. Eliot, quite safe."

"All right. But what about Lizzie and little Jedson?" said Penwarden. "Us must fetch them. And who will take care of our house?"

"He's right," said Reverend Perry. "Let us go back to Pendeen and collect the others, and get you clean clothes, Penwarden. Perhaps we'll stay overnight to prepare for our journey."

"We need to leave, fast," said Polkinghorne. "That landlord can't be trusted. He's likely to call the constables and they might very well try and stop us."

They wasted no time in mounting and looked back over their shoulders. The landlord had come out into the yard. He was in earnest conversation with the tap man. He shook his fist when he saw them leaving. They looked back, but to their relief he made no attempt to mount up and follow as they trotted off.

"Where is Bunt?" said Polkinghorne, once they were safely on their way. "Mr. and Mrs. Eliot asked after him. If he is reformed I am to bring him back too."

"Bunt is in Pendeen in good hands with members of our flock," said John Wesley. "They can look after your house, Penwarden. Willy Bunt has clearly seen the error of his ways and has taken the pledge again. I believe he has truly put his trust in our Savior, as I have counseled him, and I pray that he will never slide back again, ever. I trust that he will stay sober for the rest of his life, and indeed faithful to the vows of his marriage. I would urge the Eliots and all of you to forgive him."

"There is some talk of sending the Bunt family to America, perhaps the Penwarden family too," said Polkinghorne. "Mr. Eliot has ideas of using his connections as a Commissioner of Trade and Plantations to enter commerce across the Atlantic, perhaps found a town."

"Perhaps Mr. Eliot could in time arrange the release of Tom Kegwyn and his friends too," said Reverend Perry. "They could be of assistance to any venture."

Charles Polkinghorne observed that the preacher was more ready to intervene on behalf of members of his own flock than he had been a stranger like Willy Bunt. However, he kept his thoughts to himself; they all needed to work together. As they got to the edge of the town Polkinghorne urged his horse into a canter. As the others followed suit, it was not easy to keep talking. "We can not settle the eventual fate of the rioters; it's up to Mr. Eliot," he called over the clatter. "If we are to get to Pendeen by dark we must hurry."

It was late when they reached the Penwarden home in Pendeen. The downstairs was dark, but a light glowed in the front upstairs bedroom. Addis knocked on his front door, opened it and went in calling, "Anybody home?" An excited child's voice cried out, "Daddy, daddy!" Little Jedson almost tumbled down the stairs and jumped into his father's arms. "You'm 'ome!"

Addison tousled his son's hair affectionately. The little boy drew back. "Ugh, you stink somethin' awful." He wriggled down hurriedly.

"Where's your Mum then, me 'andsome?" Jedson hesitated. "Go on, tell us. Be she upstairs?" pressed Addison. Jedson nodded. Addison went up the stairs by the light of a candle on the landing, leaving the others to wait at the foot. Addison went into their dimly lit bedroom. The village nurse was sitting by the bed. Lizzie was lying in the bed propped up against pillows, her long curly black hair spread out and her arms resting on the eiderdown. She looked pale. Her eyes were closed.

Addison was thrilled to be reunited with her. "Lizzie, me luv," he said softly. She opened her eyes and looked through him, not recognizing him. One side of her face was pulled down, distorted. She worked her mouth, trying to say something. She drooled. Her jaw struggled; she opened her lips a little. What came out was incomprehensible, something between a moan and a groan or a scream.

Addis threw his hands in the air, clutching the top of his head. He cried out with a horrible cry, "Bloody Dunbugger, damn your soul, may you rot in hell, you bastard!" Then he knelt at the side of the bed and wept.

The men waiting downstairs looked at each other aghast at the sound. None of them spoke nor moved. The sobbing did not stop.

Chapter Seventy-three

Travel

Charles Polkinghorne was the first to recover his presence of mind. He led them all up the stairs into the bedroom to see what had caused Addis to scream with such anger and despair. They feared the worst. Polkinghorne took in the situation at a glance. Lizzie was deathly pale and odd looking, twisted. Addis seemed out of control, almost mad with grief and anger.

Polkinghorne took charge. "Penwarden, we need to look after your wife. It seems she has been struck with a palsy. No doubt the village nurse is doing her best but she can't cope. We need to get a doctor to come as soon as we can. Is there someone nearby?"

"Not in Pendeen," said Penwarden catching his breath, "us'll 'ave to take 'er to Penzance."

"We can't risk that," said Polkinghorne. "The constables will not be pleased when they learn you have been freed. And I don't trust that innkeeper, we should stay clear of him and his friends."

"I'm sure I speak for my friend Mr. Perry when I say that we will pray for Mrs. Penwarden's recovery, and for your peace of mind, Penwarden," said John Wesley, "I have learned from experience not to underestimate the power of prayer."

"Yes, indeed," said Reverend Perry, "and perhaps I could ride to Penzance and bring a doctor back here. Then Mrs. Penwarden wouldn't have to be moved."

"No, no," said Polkinghorne, "the constables may come here looking for Penwarden. He won't be safe here. We must leave as soon as possible, tomorrow at the latest. We need a litter to carry her, perhaps slung between two horses. Penwarden, would the ostler at the inn have such a thing we could use, for a small consideration? Or could you get the carpenter in the village to rig something up?"

"I'll go see the carpenter right now; 'e owes me a favor, I'm sure 'e'd work all night if 'e 'ad to. I've never 'eard of such a thing as a horse litter in the village. It's getting dark; I'll be as quick as I can. While I'm about it I'll ask anyone I see to let us know if they notice any strangers around."

"We'll stay in your house overnight," said Polkinghorne. "We can bolt and bar the doors and windows and I have pistols. I think our best plan is to make for Port Eliot tomorrow. Mr. and Mrs. Eliot will be glad to take you in, and I know they'll see to it that the doctor in Liskeard will do his best. We must try to leave first thing in the morning."

"I fear I will be unable to join you," said Reverend Wesley. "I must continue with my preaching journey, my good people in several more towns and villages are expecting me at a quarterly meeting I am obliged to attend."

"Don't trouble about it, Mister Wesley," said Polkinghorne; "We'll manage fine."

"Be on your way as you must, sir," said Reverend Perry. "You have taught me well, and with God's help our friends will be in good hands with me."

Before Penwarden went off to the village to find the carpenter, he left little Jedson in the care of the old nurse and asked her to get a simple supper together for them all. They went downstairs and went outside to see to the horses and then fetched in their things for the night.

"Let's not forget poor Willy Bunt," said Reverend Wesley, as they took their places at the kitchen table. "Before I leave I will visit the cottage where he's staying and see if he is fit to come with you back to Port Eliot."

"I'll come with you, Reverend Wesley," said Peter Perry. "We must make sure that this time his pledge to give up the demon drink is fixed and firm. There will be no second chances."

"He's had more than two already," said Polkinghorne. "If it were up to me I would say that he's had enough. Fortunately for him, the Eliots want to give him one more, but this is the last."

Penwarden came back from his mission as they were finishing their meal of cold mutton and fresh bread. "Carpenter sketched out his idea and asked the saddler in to help," Penwarden said. "They're in his workshop now, and they'll stay until they'm done. They're riggin' up a litter that'll be carried between two horses, one in front and one behind. It'll be slow going, but it'll get Lizzie there."

"We'll need more horses," said Polkinghorne.

"I stopped in at The Trewellard Arms and they'll have two horses ready in the morning," said Penwarden. "They're both used to working between the shafts, as well as being ridden, so me and Willy could ride them and you could ride separate. Then us could leave the extra riding horses here. Give the landlord at The Trewellard Arms some money and he can return them to the ostler in Penzance after we're well clear. Jedson could ride in the litter with Lizzie."

"We can't count on Bunt; we'll have to hope. Mr. Perry, we'll have to ask you to come with us if Bunt can't. But you've thought of everything, Penwarden," said Polkinghorne, "like a good mine captain should. I'll pay them all in the morning. Maybe you'll get back to Wheal Hykka yet, but right now, you need a good bath, fresh clothes, and we've left some supper for you."

"Aargh. Just need to pay for the wood and the leather for the litter," said Addis. "Carpenter and saddler said them'll work for nothin'. My Lizzie is much loved in Pendeen."

Exhaustion brought sleep for all of them, but Penwarden roused them at dawn. After a hurried breakfast the two preachers went into the village to have a serious talk with Bunt and see if he was fit to resume his life in St. Germans. Penwarden and Polkinghorne rode to the carpenter's shop to see if the litter was ready. The ostler from the inn in the village was already there harnessing up his horses.

The saddler had fitted the carrying straps with buckles and helped adjust them to make a snug fit over the horses' withers and around their saddles. The saddler also attached straps to collars to support the litter from the horses' necks, with its handles suspended from loops fore and aft.

"That's a proper job," said Polkinghorne, "Mr. Eliot will be pleased." He counted out some sovereigns into the carpenter's outstretched and grateful hand.

"Oi didn't want nothin' for 'elpin' that good woman," he said, but his smile was warm as he glanced at the coins.

Polkinghorne made arrangements with the ostler and exchanged horses. He and Penwarden mounted the harness horses carrying the litter and headed back to the Penwarden house. At first the horses' gaits were out of rhythm, but they soon settled into a walk that steadied the motion of the litter. Encouraged, Polkinghorne urged his leading horse into a trot and called to Penwarden to do the same. But the litter bounced and swayed and they couldn't settle the horses into a matching smooth stride.

"Lizzie will shake out her guts if us tries to go faster'n a walk," said Addis. "Us'll take more'n a week to make it to Port Eliot at that rate."

"Nothing else for it," said Polkinghorne. "We'd be better off leaving her here with the old nurse, I can't dawdle. But we've got to get you out of Pendeen and away from Penzance. And Mrs. Penwarden needs a doctor. Best thing is for you and Bunt to take her to Port Eliot if she can stand the journey. I'll go with you until we're clear of Penzance then ride ahead. I just hope Bunt can get away from Pendeen and help. "

When they arrived they found the others all there including a smiling Willy Bunt, standing by the front door with a saddlebag by his feet. "That's a fine-looking contraption you've got there," said John Wesley, "and I am pleased to say that this young man will be helping you get it and Mrs. Penwarden back to St. Germans. I will be leaving you in good and sober hands."

"And I will be able to stay here with my flock," said Reverend Perry.

"Our thanks for all of the support from the both of you," said Polkinghorne, nodding first at Wesley and then at Perry.

"Mornin' all," said Willy Bunt, his complexion clear and face a little thinner. "Oi'll be glad to 'elp."

"Good morning to you too, Bunt," said Polkinghorne. Bunt put out his hand but Polkinghorne did not take it. "I trust you have learned your lesson once and for all, young man. There'll be no more chances if you haven't."

"Oi 'ave, Mr. Polkinghorne, you can rely on that," said Bunt. "Oi may find it 'ard some times. Temptation can be a terrible thing but Oi know who to turn to. Mr. Wesley an' Mr. Perry an' their friends 'ave been good to us, an' them'll be there if needed, so they've assured us."

"Not forgetting your Savior, Bunt," said Reverend Perry, "you must take that lesson to heart too."

"Well then, come and lend a hand, Bunt," said Charles Polkinghorne. "We have a long journey ahead, just like you, and we can use your help." He reached out his hand and the two men shook firmly.

There was a commotion at the door of the house and they turned to see the nurse had brought Lizzie downstairs. "Lizzie, me dear," said Addis, striding to her side. "How're you feeling? You'm goin' to be all right, I promise." Tears came into his eyes as he spoke.

Lizzie grunted incomprehensibly, her mouth pulled down to one side. She had been dressed in warm clothes. She stood slackly with the old nurse and Reverend Perry supporting her, one under each arm. As Bunt held the bridle of one horse and Polkinghorne the other, with Addis Penwarden and Jedson helping, they laid Lizzie onto the litter. The old nurse had grown fond of Lizzie during the time she looked after her. She tucked blankets around her and put cushions under her head as gently as she could. Lizzie lurched and let out a scream that subsided into a low moan. Jedson climbed in next to her and stroked her forehead, murmuring to her.

They set off with warm good-byes from the preachers and the old nurse. After a bumpy start the litter horses, with Penwarden and Bunt in the saddles, settled into a swaying walk. Polkinghorne mounted up and followed them. Seeing them going well, he said, "I have business I need to attend to on the way and must get back to Port Eliot as soon as possible, make arrangements for your arrival. We'll give Penzance a wide berth. Let's stay towards the north coast, but we can get on the new turnpikes to Camborne and up to Redruth. I'll leave you there with a pistol and a purse and go on ahead alone. I have to make a stop to do some business for Mr. Eliot in Grampound."

"Thanks, Mr. Polkinghorne," said Penwarden, "I hope us won't need to use no pistol. Anyroad, I've got my boryer with me; that'll flatten any rascal that comes near causing trouble."

"Oi would'n' want to tangle with that thing, Mr. Penwarden," said Willy Bunt; "it could make a hole in my head a lot easier than it could a rock." He chuckled, then asked, "Why Grampound, Mr. Polkinghorne?"

"The borough of Grampound attached itself to Mr. Eliot some five years ago," said Polkinghorne. "He commanded two thousand pounds from strangers for each seat in parliament last time, but he wants three thousand at the next election. I will meet with the agents and ensure we keep the voters. Perhaps if you behave yourself you can help next time."

"Oi've learned my lesson," said Bunt, "never fear. Oi promised Oi'll never touch another drop; it just don't do me no good. Oi promise that to you, and Oi'll promise my Mary."

They reached the tollhouse at the entrance to the turnpike, and the keeper came out to collect their money. "That be tuppence for the horse and rider, but I dunno what them call that there contraption," he said, scratching his head.

"Just charge us for two horses and riders," said Addis Penwarden, "us'll give you fourpence. This here's a sick woman travelin' to a doctor." The toll keeper shook his head and stood his ground.

Polkinghorne made a suggestion, drawing on his experience. "Liskeard turnpike would say it's a wagon, charge us a tanner, so here's eightpence altogether." The toll keeper looked doubtful, bit the silver sixpence, seemed satisfied and raised the tollgate to let them through.

They pressed on slowly but steadily. Polkinghorne was anxious to move faster, but he kept his promise to stay with them until the danger from the Penzance innkeeper or constables was well past. He was eager to forge on to Bodmin to get to Lanhydrock after Grampound, but his reasons were personal, and he had not told his companions what they were.

"Right you are then," said Polkinghorne as they got to the other side of Redruth, "I'll be on my way. You'll be all right. You can stay on turnpikes most of the way. I'd take the St. Austell to Lostwithiel if I were you and then on to the Liskeard pike and all the way to St. Germans. That pike's thanks in no small part to you, Bunt."

Willy Bunt smiled appreciatively; it seemed he really was getting another chance to make good. Polkinghorne continued, "Take good care of Mrs. Penwarden both of you. I'll see you at Port Eliot."

Charles Polkinghorne hastened on his way to Grampound, leaving the others to their slow progress. Once there, he sought out the Eliot electoral agents as swiftly as possible and reviewed their plans to maintain the loyalty of voters until the next election. He gave them gold to reimburse them for their properly accounted expenses. Informing them of what he presented as Mr. Eliot's personal views of the government's policies, particularly mentioning the negotiation for the peace, he quickly dispatched his duties. He did not disclose that, in fact, Mr. Eliot had received letters from ministers pressing him to support the government's version of the peace rather than backing the more demanding views of Mr. Pitt. Satisfied he had done all he could, he remounted his horse and took off at a canter to Lanhydrock.

Dusk was falling as he approached the steward's house on the estate, and he was grateful for the shelter it provided from prying eyes. "What a surprise to see you, Polkinghorne," said Joseph Clymo, opening his door and inviting him inside. "Where are you headed? You're welcome to stay the night. It's getting chilly at this time of year, and it's dangerous to be abroad after dark."

They settled in to the cozy parlor in front of a blazing fire. Polkinghorne got out his old clay pipe and Clymo offered him tobacco as he reached for his own churchwarden. Clymo poured them each a mug of home-brewed ale. He called for his housekeeper and instructed her to cook some more supper and make up a bed for his guest.

"You can have Morwenna's bed," he said, launching a conversation that promised to be as if it were between two old friends. "And speaking of her, how is my daughter doing at Port Eliot? Behaving herself I trust, and making herself useful?"

Polkinghorne hesitated. Morwenna's bed! This was even better than the opening he had been agitating over since leaving Grampound, presented to him on a platter. However, he decided to restrain himself from asking his beloved's father for her hand in marriage, not just yet. After all, he had not yet had the opportunity to sound it out fully with Morwenna herself, although she had given every indication that his suit would be welcome. Enough for now that he seemed to be getting on famously with his prospective father-in-law.

If things went well tonight, he might bring the matter up in the morning, seize the bull by the horns and at the very least seek permission to court his host's daughter.

Charles Polkinghorne sucked on his pipe and blew a cloud of smoke towards the mantel over the fire. They lapsed in to conversing over agricultural matters and presently repaired to bed.

Over breakfast next morning Joseph Clymo told his guest of his own plans. "I will be following you to Port Eliot myself in a day or so. I have business there. Perhaps if you could delay a while, we could ride together; there is safety in numbers after all."

Polkinghorne had been preoccupied with a large plate of bacon and eggs with fried bread and fried potatoes, but now he turned his full attention to his host. Perhaps he should wait to raise his question until they had journeyed in each other's company a while.

"Yes, indeed," continued Clymo, "the viscount has commanded me to accompany him to Port Eliot. He is going up to demand the return of Lady Dunbargan and the Honorable James Trenance. I will escort them back to Lanhydrock with him."

Polkinghorne choked on a mouthful of sausage. He put his hand to his mouth and coughed. This changed everything. Somehow he was going to have to get a message to the Penwardens and then ride ahead to tell the Eliots and warn Lady Dunbargan and Morwenna that the viscount would soon be upon them. Now he had to leave as soon as possible. It was fortunate that last evening his host had been preoccupied with his own stories and had not troubled to ask him where he had been and why he had been there.

Joseph Clymo did not notice Polkinghorne's distress. He smiled warmly. "I look forward to seeing the Eliots again, and Bunt too. That lad has done well for himself."

Clymo's remark did nothing to comfort his guest who, while willing to acquiesce in giving Bunt a second chance, was far from an enthusiastic supporter of his underling whom he considered a potential rival in affairs of the heart as well as the counting house.

Polkinghorne composed himself and said, "Mr. Clymo, I wish from the bottom of my heart that I could stay and ride with you, but Mr. Eliot has expressed the need for me to be in Port Eliot today, so I have no time to lose. It just remains for me to thank you for your hospitality and to be on my way."

Regretfully, he left the remainder of his breakfast on his plate, gathered up his things and in no time was cantering down the Lanhydrock drive. Then he stopped to think. If he rode back towards St. Austell to try and encounter the Penwardens and Bunt, he had no way of knowing where they might have stopped on the way or which way they were travelling. It would be easy to miss them and then he would lose time that he could no longer waste. He turned his horse's head in the other direction towards Liskeard.

At the entrance to the turnpike he dismounted and spoke to the toll keeper. "If you will do me a service, my good man, you will earn more than your customary tuppence. If I can trust you to give a message to my fellow travelers I will give you a silver shilling. Tell them that Viscount

Dunbargan and his steward are on their way to Port Eliot and to be sure to serve them well."

"Oh aargh," said the man, "his lordship, eh? Oi dunno about that. Anyroad, 'ow will Oi know who to give the message to?"

"You can't miss them, they're with a sick woman in a litter carried by two horses. Here's half a crown. And I'll be back this way, so if you fail me it'll be the worse for you." The man nodded, took the coin and touched his forelock. Polkinghorne remounted and headed off.

When finally he passed through the gate to Port Eliot, he turned over his panting and lathered-up horse to the groom and walked to the business office as fast as his aching thighs would allow. He was relieved that Edward Eliot was at his desk.

"Ah, Polkinghorne, I'm glad to see you," he said. "I'm putting my affairs in order before leaving for Town. I'm needed at the House for the debate on this infernal peace. How were things at Penzance? Are you alone?"

"Sir," said Polkinghorne, a little short of breath, "serious news. I stopped at Lanhydrock on my way back to rest my horse. Clymo told me that Viscount Dunbargan will be here any day."

"Dunbargan, here?" demanded Eliot, frowning. "He has received no invitation from me, nor has he requested my hospitality."

"His lordship is determined to fetch her ladyship and their son back home to Lanhydrock as soon as possible," replied the steward. "Knowing his lordship as I do, I assure you he will brook no disagreement. Clymo is coming with them, and they will probably insist that Miss Clymo accompany them too. Mrs. Eliot will be upset. I thought you should know as soon as possible."

Eliot rose to his feet and pounded his desk. "Coming to my house and demanding that my guests leave at his pleasure? They are in my protection after all. That man has gone too far. The peace agreement will have to wait. I will stay here. Polkinghorne, you are a good and loyal servant. How could I ever do without you?"

"I do my best to serve your interests, sir," said Polkinghorne, and bowed. "Now if you will excuse me, I have personal matters to attend to."

Chapter Seventy-four

Challenges

Edward Eliot was glad to have Charles Polkinghorne safely back. There was always an element of danger to traveling in Cornwall, and he relied on his man of business; but right now he was glad to see Polkinghorne leave the business room. There were some matters that he wished to attend to in privacy, at least until he had made up his mind about them.

First he needed to see to getting a message to Catherine. He called in his clerk and instructed him to seek her out either in the house or quite possibly over at the schoolroom, where much of her indefatigable enthusiasm resided these days, and to give her the message that the arrival of Viscount Dunbargan could be expected at any day. His capable wife would understand and would make up her mind what to do.

He then pondered the problem of Viscount Dunbargan. He found the man increasingly impossible to deal with. He was going to have to face up to it sooner or later. Now Polkinghorne informed him the preposterous fellow was about to foist himself on Port Eliot without a by your leave and drag away Lady Elianor and the Honorable James. At least he would have an opportunity to deal with the man face to face and on his own ground. No wonder Lady Dunbargan wanted to be rid of him.

There was no escaping the viscount's importance, and not solely in Cornwall. He was rich, despite appearing to be always in need of ready money, and he was a member of the House of Lords. This made him hard to ignore socially; and he was influential, although his reluctance to work hard made his influence much less than it might have been.

Imagine, for example, if he were to use his position as diligently as did the Duke of Newcastle. Certainly the viscount's time in London seemed to be spent far more on enjoying himself with gambling and his many other vices than on politics. Indeed, if the hints that Catherine dropped were to be believed, he treated his wife in a most disgraceful fashion, not that this made him unique among gentlemen of Edward's acquaintance.

There were also problems closer to hand. Dunbargan unceasingly wanted too much for himself. As Edward gained in business experience and confidence, he not only felt the need to be more selective in his fellow adventurers, but found he enjoyed making money, that he was good at it, and wanted more of it. Catherine enjoyed the finer things of life and her tastes never ran to the ordinary. She had ideas of making further improvements to the house and grounds, and she constantly urged him to pursue more important places and a title. And while his boroughs brought him influence as well as wealth, they were expensive to support. He felt he could make better use of wealth than that cad Dunbargan.

Eliot had been glad to take advantage of Dunbargan's backing to arrange the financing for the Liskeard Turnpike project and the development of the quarry, and of the Trenance family's relationships with Bolithos. But Dunbargan was ever insatiable. He wanted to develop other turnpikes on his own, wanted to sell the tailings from his mines to compete with the road stone from the Port Eliot quarry. Wanted to bully and control everyone he encountered including Edward himself, although Edward felt that he had put a stop to that. But take Penwarden, for example; Dunbargan seemed to have a grudge against him for some reason and rarely missed an opportunity to get a dig in. It seemed as if the viscount wanted to prove himself to his dead father, stand up for himself, never be taken advantage of.

Edward, however, had got himself into a position as a leading adventurer in the mines and he had brought in his own people. He had been able to use his place with the Duchy to exploit the vulnerability that Dunbargan had opened up when he failed to follow the mining rules. Typical. Did not think the rules applied to him. Furthermore, Edward had gained considerable support from Bolitho, weaning his loyalty away from Dunbargan.

The viscount remained a confounded nuisance. The question was how to get rid of him. Was he enough of a nuisance for Mr. Pitt to want to be rid of him? Probably not. He was too idle and ill informed to be a political nuisance, although he was dabbling in boroughs. He imagined it could be feasible to embroil him in a public scandal and disgrace him. He would not wish to be involved directly of course, but he did have people he could ask, from constables and tax collectors to Duchy officials and revenuers.

And there were Dunbargan's questionable business dealings: how the viscount and his father before him managed to keep such a superlative and rare wine cellar, for instance, and why were they on surprisingly friendly terms with humble fishermen? Hardly their social equals. Indeed, the whispers spread that Dunbargan invested in slaving ships, a practice that Eliot now deemed despicable.

Dunbargan was simply a mountain of difficulties. He did not yet want to discuss it with Polkinghorne; one had to be discreet. One never knew what the risks of getting too involved might be. The question was, who would rid him of this troublesome viscount? He would sound out Catherine. She often had more deviously effective ideas than he, not that she should be involved herself, naturally.

He got up from his desk and stretched. Thinking over all the twisted factors involving the viscount was exhausting. He would take a turn around the park while he mulled over the second matter that commanded his attention. He might even run into Catherine, and he could turn to leisure for the rest of the day while she amused him and suggested imaginative ways of spending his money. No, that would not do. He must address his responsibilities as a Member of Parliament.

That day he had received a letter from London over the signature of Henry Fox, M.P., P.C., advising him that it was his duty to attend the House and support the government over the debate on the peace that was being negotiated to end the Seven Years War, the interminable conflict that the Americans dubbed the French and Indian War. Eliot was self aware enough to realize that Fox did not seek his oratorical skills, simply the votes of his six boroughs, which could not be counted on without him.

Henry Fox was the leader of the court party in the House of Commons and a member of the Privy Council. Eliot aspired to a similarly important place for himself, although in truth he envied Fox more for holding on to his lucrative post as paymaster. The man had built himself a castle with the proceeds.

Eliot, however, had heard from a London correspondent that he himself had been put down by Bute, the king's favorite, on a list as supporting the government. He was, after all, an officeholder, albeit minor. Edward Eliot felt that he owed it to his sense of his own importance that he should consider the merits of the arguments as well as his personal advantages. He had heard from William Pitt at first hand the doubts that the great statesman felt about the peace terms, which doubts had caused him to leave the administration.

On the other hand, Edward Eliot's first duty was to his heritage and to his family. He had an estate to oversee, investments to watch over, tenants and agents to supervise and provide for, important business ventures to hold to account and difficult challenges to meet, let alone occasionally showing his face in the House and at the Commission of Trade and Plantations. Not, however, that he felt an obligation to be more conscientious than most of his friends.

He had walked almost around the park and was approaching the business office with no sign of Catherine; he would make the decision without her. He made up his mind as to his next steps. He would take charge. He would go up to Town, play his role on the stage of history, attend to his duties at the Commission, and while there talk to his friend William Pitt and decide how he would vote. He would persuade Catherine to stay and look after Port Eliot rather than traveling with him and enriching the expensive London merchants. He was sure he could convince her that her duty lay with her school. It was so new that the school could not yet do without her.

Meanwhile, he would go to the big house after he let Polkinghorne know his travel plans and discuss with him and Catherine arrangements for dealing with the viscount in his absence.

Where had Polkinghorne got to when he needed him? Annoyed, Eliot sent a clerk to the village to find him. The clerk reported that Charles Polkinghorne would come as soon as he could but was delayed by plans of his own. What the clerk promised not to tell Eliot was that Polkinghorne was inside his house with Morwenna Clymo and was reluctant to leave her side again so soon.

Polkinghorne meanwhile, comfortably settled by his fire, was relieved to find that not only his own feelings for Morwenna remained as strong as ever, but also that she seemed if anything more affectionate towards him. However, there was a niggling doubt. She had returned his welcoming embrace warmly. She had asked about his journey and what he had done. But when he told her the good news that her father was coming to visit Port Eliot in a day or two, her initial delight cooled rapidly after he explained that the occasion of the visit was to accompany Viscount Dunbargan.

That in itself was understandable; the man would be a damper on any situation. But when Polkinghorne questioned her about what she had been about during his absence, she seemed reluctant to go into details. There surely could have been nothing for her to hide. It was probably just the shyness of an innocent young girl. He had to admit that he was inexperienced and did not understand women very well. There was not much more he could say now. He would just have to be patient.

For now it was a matter of first things first, and clearly his duty lay with Mr. Eliot. He bade Morwenna goodbye with a kiss on the cheek that was more chaste than he would have chosen and dutifully prepared to set off for the business room.

Was Morwenna relieved to see him go? Patience, indeed; ah, well. As he reached for his hat and coat there was a knock at the door. What now? He opened the door to see who his caller was.

Chapter Seventy-five

Villain

Edward ran into Catherine in the hallway as he entered the big house. "Just the person I need to see," he said. Catherine looked up at him, "Edward, you look worried. Just let me give this list to Cook, and I'll meet you in the library." She hurried back and found her husband awaiting her. "Whatever is troubling you?"

"Several problems," he announced as he sat down. She took a chair opposite him. "First of all I need to be in London for the vote. I've received a letter from Mr. Fox. He needs me there for the vote on the peace."

"Well, of course you must go. Your views are valued. But am I not to accompany you? I have so many things I need to . . ."

He interrupted her. "Wait until you've heard it all, please, Catherine."

She folded her hands and waited.

"The second thing," he continued, "is that Polkinghorne has arrived with the news that at any moment the viscount and Clymo are to arrive with the intention of taking Lady Dunbargan and young James back with him to Lanhydrock. He's apparently in no mood for an argument on that score."

"Oh, Edward, how horrible! We'll have to put off our trip for a few days and shore up our defenses."

"That's just the problem, Catherine. I can't," he replied. "I'm sorely needed in London; my votes count, as do those of my boroughs; and my loyalty to Mr. Pitt demands it. Besides, you'll be needed at your school. You will just have to remain behind and deal with matters; I have every confidence that you will manage without me. Polkinghorne is aware and will help you send the viscount on his way and protect Lady Dunbargan and young James. I know it's not what either of us would prefer, but there's nothing for it."

"No, Edward. Aside from the fact that your duty now lies here with your family and estate, I fully intend to be in London with you when you go." She rose and paced about the room.

Eliot rose too and put his hand on her shoulder, forcing her to face him. "Catherine, for once I am telling you what to do. I am not asking your counsel!"

She looked at him in alarm. "But . . ."

"No, Catherine, you must understand. Just do as I say; you are my wife." He let her go and strode out of the room.

Catherine stood for some while trying to absorb his unaccustomed stern insistence. Finally, she left the room and mounted the stairs to their bedroom, where she found Edward giving orders to his valet to prepare for departure on the day after next. She did not speak to him, turned and left the room. An hour later, there was a flurry of gravel and a clatter of horseshoes in front of the main entrance at Port Eliot as a rider galloping through the park at breakneck speed pulled his exhausted stallion to its haunches. The stallion's hindquarters were lathered, sides bloodied and gouged by spurs. The rider dropped his reins and leapt off. He raced to the big door. He thundered on it with the handle of his riding crop.

When the old butler opened the door to enquire whom he wished to see and the purpose of his arrival, the man shoved him aside. He demanded admission. He bellowed, "Where the hell is Eliot? I'm Dunbargan. I want to talk to him, now."

He burst into the entrance.

Another rider followed not far behind at a more moderate pace. He had ridden his horse with more consideration; it was panting but not lathered. He dismounted and collected the reins of the other man's horse with his own. He waved to the gardeners tidying up the flower borders for the autumn. "I'm Clymo, from Lanhydrock," he called, "we're expected. I'll just take the horses around to the stables and go and find Mr. Polkinghorne."

At the stables, he called to a groom. "I'm Clymo from Lanhydrock, here with Viscount Dunbargan to see Mr. Eliot. See to these horses, get them unsaddled and put away. Feed and water them, not too much at first. We've ridden a long way. Take care of the stallion, he needs salve in those cuts."

Joseph Clymo was in no hurry to rejoin the viscount; it had been a trying journey from Lanhydrock in his company. Clymo also knew he had to face what promised to be an unpleasant duty. The viscount had come to Port Eliot to confront his wife and demand that she come home with him, bringing their son James with her. He had insisted that Clymo should attend the interview.

Dunbargan knew the viscountess well enough to anticipate that her temper could rival his own when he attempted to assert his authority over her or make her do anything she was set against. Clymo understood that he was to act as a calming influence; she was unlikely to release her deepest anger in front of a man like himself who was not a member of her own class. The viscount also made clear that he felt it would do no harm to have a witness who could testify to the reasonableness of his position should things ever come to that.

Clymo wanted to see his daughter Morwenna and catch up with how she was getting on, but that would have to wait until the dreaded interview was over. Meanwhile, he would seize the opportunity to go over to the business room to see Charles Polkinghorne. He had grown to like the younger man and felt that they were becoming friends despite the rivalry of their employers. Looking back on Polkinghorne's visit to him at Lanhydrock, Joseph Clymo felt that the man had wanted to confide something, but had not seized the opportunity.

However, the clerk in the business room told Clymo that Polkinghorne had gone back to his house in the village to fetch something. Anticipating having little time to himself, Clymo elected to walk over to the estate manager's house rather than wait for his return. He heard footsteps coming to the front door responding to his knock.

"Mr. Clymo! You've arrived," Charles Polkinghorne said rather loudly, seeming taken aback. "How nice to see you. Come on in, I have a surprise for you." When Clymo walked in he was startled to see his daughter in the parlor.

"Hullo, Dad," said Morwenna, catching her breath and blushing slightly as she smoothed her hair. "I was just helping Mr. Polkinghorne tidy his kitchen; you know how helpless these bachelors are. I try to make myself useful at Port Eliot." Bit far from the kitchen, thought Clymo, but perhaps she was about to get started. "Mr. Polkinghorne," she continued, "shall I put the kettle on the hob and make us all a nice spot of tea?"

Charles Polkinghorne collected himself and said, "Why thank you, Miss Clymo, that would be most kind. No doubt your father would enjoy a spot of refreshment after his ride."

"I hope I can stay long enough to enjoy it," said Clymo, "but I expect his lordship will be sending for me at any moment. I'm here because he needs my attendance at a delicate meeting."

No sooner had he spoken than there was another knock at the door. It was one of the Eliot footmen with a note for Joseph Clymo. "As I expected," he said, reading it, "I cannot stay a moment longer. Morwenna, why don't you walk back to the house with me?"

"I'll catch up with you later, Dad," she said, "then we can have a good old chin wag. I need to stay here a while; I like to finish what I've started. You always told me I should do that."

Clymo fleetingly sensed that his daughter was avoiding him but pushed that thought from his mind and followed the footman to the house. He was directed to the library where the Dunbargans were already waiting alone, seated on either side of the fireplace. The viscount was tapping his foot on the floor and staring at the fire. The viscountess stared at her knotted hands.

"Ah Clymo, I've been waiting for you. Where've you been?" said Viscount Dunbargan, looking up. "Kindly sit over there so that we can get started. I just need you to note what goes on and witness what is agreed. Shouldn't take too long. Her ladyship will need to instruct her maid to collect her things and the boy, and everything should soon be settled. Eliot has arranged for us to spend the night in the inn in the village. Not enough room in the house at short notice apparently, seems hard to understand. At least I trust Mrs. Eliot will find us a bite to eat. We'll get off in the morning."

"You'll get off without me," said Elianor Dunbargan firmly, glancing first at her husband and then at Clymo. "I will never return to Lanhydrock with you, and James stays with me."

"What nonsense! I'm your husband and you will do as I say. It's time you got over your ridiculous tantrum and settled down."

Elianor straightened her back and took a deep breath. "My lord, I have obeyed you for the last time. From now on I will do what I think is right."

"But where the hell do you think you will go? What will you do? You can't leave in your condition, quite unthinkable. What if it's a boy? Besides, you will be ruined. No one will receive you. I will see to it that no decent person will speak to you again, simply destroy your reputation."

Lady Dunbargan did not reply. She stood up, walked over to her husband and looked directly into his eyes. "Sir, you are an indecent and despicable person; you are a bully, a cheat, a cad and a rapist. Your reputation is one I would disassociate myself from as far as possible."

Clymo was taken aback; he lurched to his feet and moved towards the window to put himself some distance from them.

"What in hell do you mean? You have no right; I am a member of the House of Lords. As for whatever twaddle you refer to, you can't prove . . . ."

"My lord," said Elianor with emphasis, keeping her self-control, "the part of your reputation that disgusts me most is as a rapist."

Clymo looked aghast.

"There's no . . ." protested Dunbargan.

"Then how do you explain that your son James and little Catherine Bunt both have most unusual webs between their second and third toes?"

"Bunt? Bunt? My former valet? What's he got to do with it? Must be some kind of coincidence. Nothing to do with me."

Clymo rolled his eyes.

"Bunt's got everything to do with it. He had the decency to make an honest woman of the chambermaid you raped in the stable at Lanhydrock. You think you could keep that from me? I know that Catherine Bunt is your daughter. She is the goddaughter of Mrs. Eliot. She and Mr. Eliot were kind enough after your maid Mary Abbott and Bunt fled Lanhydrock to take them in and give them employment at Port Eliot. Willy Bunt married Mary before she gave birth. Now they live in one of the Eliots' cottages in the village. There are some decent people in this world, although you are certainly not among them."

"Must be some kind of mistake, people jumping to the wrong conclusions. That swine Eliot, taking them in. He betrayed me! They were my servants, should have been returned to me to deal with as I saw fit. Eliot's no gentleman; I will not hesitate to make that known."

Clymo coughed to avoid choking.

"There's no mistake," pressed Elianor. "Mr. Clymo's daughter Morwenna saw both the children in their bare feet. She recognized the webbed toes immediately, and she knew whom they came from. Attempt to explain that one too."

"How the devil would she know? Oh, now I see. Treacherous little trollop. Your own damn fault, Elianor. You've been a total bore in my bed ever since James came along. Well, at least with Morwenna it was no rape. Game little filly, quite handsome too, for a peasant. What do you think of that, eh Clymo?"

Clymo grew purple in the face, the blood vessel at his brow throbbing. He tried to control his anger. He turned from the window and crossed to Dunbargan's chair, his fist raised. "My Morwenna!" he fumed.

"You strike me and I'll have you in irons and in gaol like those rioters and that Penwarden fellow down at Wheal Hykka. How dare you? Now that I consider it, I've no more use for you. Get out!"

"James, you can't do that to Clymo," said Elianor heatedly. "He's been loyal to you all his life, and his father before him. That you did that to Morwenna is horrible, but Clymo has done nothing to you."

"Too late for that, he threatened me. I insist on respect and complete loyalty from all of my servants, and that includes you, wife. Since that now appears to be impossible, I no longer consider you to be my wife; you can get out too. You are not fit to be the lady of Lanhydrock."

With that Dunbargan picked up his riding crop, slammed it with a thwack on the table next to Elianor and stormed out.

Elianor regained her composure. "Well then, that's that, finally. I'm sorry you had to hear it, Clymo, sorry indeed, but it's all true. Truly, I am extremely sorry too for the effect of all of this on your employment, but we must hope it is for the best. Stay in St. Germans tonight and I will speak to you in the morning. Now, I must go to my son and keep him safe. I will inform the Eliots of what has transpired. Mrs. Eliot may have some ideas about dealing with this whole sorry mess." She raised her head and flicked a tear from the corner of her eye and left.

Joseph Clymo was too stunned to speak. He stood there for several moments, trying to collect his thoughts. The door opened and Catherine Eliot came into the room. Seeing Clymo's condition, she motioned him to a seat.

"I heard the shouting and came as soon as I was told the viscount had arrived," she said. "Please Mr. Clymo, tell me what has transpired. Where is Lady Dunbargan?"

He related the conversation between the viscount and his wife, how each left in a rage, telling of his dismissal, stumbling over his words; but when he got to the part about Morwenna he could not go on. He just sat there with his head in his hands.

"Take heart, Mr. Clymo, I will speak to Mr. Eliot and he will ensure that you come to no harm. I must confess I was expecting such an outcome. For the moment I think it best that you do not encounter the viscount. Go to the village and lie low. Now I must go and see to Lady Dunbargan."

Clymo left the room without saying a word. Keeping an eye out for Dunbargan as he went, he stole out through the kitchen to the stable and got his horse. He might as well claim it before Dunbargan took it. He made for the village and tethered it outside The Eliot Arms. He went into the taproom and ordered a pint of bitter ale. He looked around the room and saw Polkinghorne sitting at a table in the corner with Bunt and Penwarden. Polkinghorne saw him as he picked up his mug and waved him over.

"What's the matter?" asked Polkinghorne. "You look as if you'd seen Old Nick himself."

"I have, that devil Dunbargan," Clymo replied, sitting down and taking a deep swallow from his pewter tankard. "The old baron begged me to take good care of his son, and I promised him that I would. No good came of it."

"Glad to see you in St. Germans, Mr. Clymo, but you'm all in a twist," said Willy Bunt. "You, of all people, callin' Dunbugger a devil. What's 'e been up to now?"

"I served the viscount to the best of my ability, though I have never been blind to his faults. I never dreamed he would turn on me. What a fool I've been, a blind fool." He put his head in his hands.

"You should never've trusted him, as long as you've known him," said Penwarden, "you've known what he's really like."

"Come now, cheer up, it can't be that bad," said Polkinghorne. "Tell us about it and perhaps we can help."

"It's nothing to do with you," said Clymo, "I've got to deal with it myself, although Bunt here is in the middle of it too. Turns out that his lordship took advantage of Mrs. Bunt when she was a maid at Lanhydrock, and now Lady Dunbargan has found out about it. Bunt, is Lord Dunbargan the father of your daughter Catherine?"

Bunt grunted and took a sip of his drink, which fortunately was only apple juice.

"My God!" said Polkinghorne, "You didn't tell me about that, Bunt. I'm your daughter's godfather after all. And young Charles, what about him? Is this news to you, did you know when you married her?"

"Aargh, Oi couldn't 'ardly 'elp knowin', could Oi?" said Bunt. "Oi was waitin' in the loft right above the stable when 'e done it. 'Er was bringin' us food so Oi could run away, Oi 'ad to leave Lanhydrock, get away from 'un. Oi would'n' say 'e zackly took advantage loike. Bloody brute forced 'er, overpowered 'er, that's what Oi'd say. Poor mite, Oi felt sorry for 'er, Oi love 'er. 'Er's a brave girl, brave. Don't go tellin' everybody now, it's our business, just 'er and me, personal loike. An' little Charles is ours, all ours, Mr. Clymo."

"Won't be the first time such a thing's happened," said Polkinghorne, "the gentry take their privileges. You just have to make the best of it in your position, Bunt, that's what I say." He took a puff at his old clay pipe.

"Makes me fair 'oppin'," said Bunt. "Mr. Wesley taught me about repentance. That Dunbugger's not repentin', he's boastin'. Wait 'til Oi tells my Mary. 'Er won't be 'alf mad."

"That's not all," said Clymo, looking down and turning his mug around in his hands. He sighed and took a deep breath. "It appears that his lordship made my beloved his mistress too." He sunk his head in his hands again.

"Look what he did to my Lizzie," said Addis Penwarden, "she almost died. She might never get better. I really don't have a wife no more, and my boys don't have a real mum."

"Oi remember Mrs. Clymo when Oi was a boy," said Bunt. "She was awful good to me before she died. That Dunbugger 'ad 'is way with 'er, too?"

"No, no, not my wife, my dear daughter, my Morwenna," said Joseph Clymo, "that's who."

Charles Polkinghorne staggered to his feet, knocked over the chair behind him, slammed his hand on the table knocking over his tankard. "My Morwenna! My God, that Dunbargan, he's the cause of everyone's troubles," he fumed. "He's got to be taught a lesson, viscount or no. He's got to be made to pay!"

"You're right there, Mr. Polkinghorne," said Clymo, "I couldn't agree with you more." He drained his mug and slammed it on the table, calling to the landlord for more ale.

"That there viscount's had a nasty streak ever since he was a nipper," exclaimed Addis Penwarden. He held out his mug to be refilled as well.

Bunt looked wistfully at the landlord, but decided he had better stick to apple juice. "Aargh," said Willy, "Bloody 'ell!"

They sat there drinking and venting their anger and planning revenge until darkness fell, frustrated in their impotence. They reached no satisfactory conclusion and settled on meeting again later.

As Charles Polkinghorne walked home alone under a bright moon, he wondered now how willing he would be to marry old boots, as men termed marrying another man's mistress. He'd have to get some assurances from Morwenna that she had been a victim. He did not think he could bear it if she had been willing.

Chapter Seventy-six

Plot

Catherine Eliot returned to her boudoir to continue writing the letters she had begun earlier, and to seek some moments alone for contemplation. Clymo's report of the contretemps between her friend Elianor Trenance and the viscount had been disturbing but, all in all, doubtless for the best. She would speak to Elianor soon and offer advice and consolation. Furthermore, Catherine herself had been taken aback by her own husband's firmness with her, but chose to attribute it to his being overburdened and not by any real disregard for her feelings.

However, she quickly regained her spirits; a woman these days needed self-respect and had to be resourceful. She would cope. She enjoyed having a house full of guests and was loving starting up her school. There was plenty to keep her mind on positive thoughts. It all required energy, however, and right now she needed a respite.

The More sisters had returned to their busy lives in Bristol. Catherine wrote to thank them not only for sharing their experience and ideas for the school, but also for making possible her inclusion in the meetings of the Blue Stockings Society during her visit to London, which she regretfully now had to decline. Catherine was appreciative that their discussions while at Port Eliot had enabled her to get to know the growing intellectual side of Elianor Dunbargan and also to understand Frances Boscawen more intimately.

Catherine began another letter, this one to Joshua Reynolds, explaining that while she would not be coming up to London soon she wished to arrange to visit his studio next time the Eliots were together in London. But no sooner had she settled into her first paragraph than there was a gentle knock at her door. It was her maid.

"Excuse me, ma'am, but it's Lady Dunbargan. I told her you were busy and didn't want to be disturbed, but she insisted. If I may say so, ma'am, she seems a bit wrought up. I think she badly needs to talk to you. I heard some shouting from the morning room earlier when she was talking to her husband."

"Yes, I learned that the viscount has arrived already," said Catherine. "I am not surprised that Lady Dunbargan is upset. Please ask her to come up right away. Bring us a pot of tea, and then see to it that no one else disturbs us."

Catherine composed herself. She sanded her letter, wiped her quill, and tidied her desk. Little wonder that the viscount's behavior had upset dear Elianor. Perhaps matters would come to such a pass that Edward would reconsider his plan to go to London after all. Catherine was sitting in her chair by the window when her maid brought in the tea, preceded by Viscountess Dunbargan who hurried into the room and sat across from her.

"Oh, Catherine, my friend, I am beside myself with anger," Elianor said as soon as the maid left the boudoir. She fanned her face. "Candidly, I need your calming advice."

"My dear, I should have ordered something stronger than tea," said Catherine; "I don't often see you this distressed. How can I help? I saw Clymo and he told me that after he and the viscount arrived your husband demanded to see you and there was a colossal argument. Have you finally decided to leave him?"

"I have, thank God, and don't try to persuade me otherwise. I have been tempted by thoughts of duty and propriety ever since that awful scene on the cliff top at Wheal Hykka, but I no longer care about such trivial concerns. The man is quite impossible. He is a treacherous, selfish, evil brute. Anyway, after what I said to him today, I don't think he'd take me back if I begged him, which I never will. All that matters now is that I protect little James from him."

"All very distressing, of course," said Catherine "I must say I am delighted. But you must protect yourself as well as your son, my dear. You will have to be careful. Like all selfish men, he's dangerous. Where will you go? Where will you and young James live? What will you do?"

"My family is near Bodmin, where we have lived for generations. I'm sure they will take me in for the time being. I am not going back to Lanhydrock. I never want to set eyes on that horrible place again. I will send for my things; perhaps when that awful man is with his strumpets in London. Dunbugger, that's what they call him, you know; I think it's quite amusing, if a little coarse. I never ever want to see him again. Frankly, I agree with you; I am afraid of what he might do. Oh, I wish he would just disappear. I should have pushed him off the cliff when I had the chance."

"It is hard for a woman to live alone, without a man's protection," said Catherine. "You know I sympathize, but I am also trying to be practical."

"I have learned to be strong in a very short while and can look after myself," said Elianor. "I have had to, married to that monster. Truly, I'm not afraid to rely on myself. And while Dunbargan stole a generous dowry from my father, I am still far from penniless. But who knows, perhaps at some time in the future there will be a man who is kind and gentle who will love me and James and the new baby, and whom I can love in return. In my heart there is nothing that would please me more."

"Quite so, my dear," said Catherine, "but you may be getting ahead of reality. At this moment you must think about dealing with Dunbargan and protecting yourself and your son. We will consult Mr. Eliot before he leaves and seek his advice. He will know what to do. Meanwhile, stay here with us as long as you need to."

"Is your husband leaving? I suppose he has to go up to Town to attend the House. I know there has been mention of an important vote about the peace. I do wish he could stay at Port Eliot and keep us safe. I am afraid of what the viscount would do if Mr. Eliot were not here to restrain him, especially if he got into his cups. Might you persuade him to stay?"

"I will see what I can do," said Catherine. "I agree that it would be wise for him to stay and guard the fort. He will surely be concerned about your safety when he hears what has transpired. If necessary, I will get Mr. Polkinghorne to put in a word, as well, about the advisability of watching out for Port Eliot's business interests while the viscount is on a rampage. You stay here in my boudoir where even that dreadful man would fear to tread, and I will seek out my husband right away before his preparations to leave are complete."

As it happened, it was not difficult for Catherine to persuade Edward Eliot of the wisdom of remaining at home once she informed him of the outrageousness of the viscount's behavior and Elianor's decision to finally rid herself of him and seek divorce. Furthermore, Edward formed the impression that Catherine and Elianor would regard him as a gallant knight at arms protecting his damsels from dangers that they were too delicate to resist without him. He would have preferred to avoid conflict altogether, but was faced with a choice between arguments either in the House of Commons or in Port Eliot. In either place he would be besieged with people pressing him to do something for them regardless of his personal inconvenience.

In London the new men besought his votes with even less respect for his views than Pitt and Newcastle, whom they replaced. In Cornwall he would have to contain the machinations and anger of a neighbor whom he disliked and despised. Upon reflection he elected to fight the battle on his home ground, surrounded by his allies and admired by his wife.

Eliot had suffered an excess of distress at the hands of Dunbargan and his unscrupulous behavior, certainly in affairs of commerce and likely more than he knew in politics. At bottom he would like to be rid of the man, as much as Lady Dunbargan did. However, he recognized the importance of being discreet. Edward was not seeking more trouble than could be avoided. He had his reputation and his position to keep up, so he offered the ladies sound advice. They should take one step at a time and talk to the vicar without delay and see what he thought. After all, marriage and all that surrounded it lay firmly within the purview of the church. One could not interfere with that; it was the very foundation of society.

The vicar responded to Catherine's subsequent message within the hour and met the ladies in the morning room. It would hardly have been proper for him to enter the boudoir. "My dear Lady Dunbargan," said the vicar in response to their inquiry, "it is my solemn duty to advise you that there is nothing that can be done. In the eyes of the church the joining together of man and woman in the honorable estate of matrimony in the fear of God is a solemn covenant. My lady, you swore a holy vow to cleave unto your wedded husband for better for worse, until death do you part. Those whom God have joined together no man may put asunder."

"Come now, Vicar," said Catherine, "Cardinal Wolsey managed it for Henry VIII. Surely you or the vicar of St. Petroc's can do the same for dear Lady Dunbargan?"

"Since there is a son it would not be possible to plead that the marriage was never consummated," said the vicar pensively, placing his finger delicately aside his mouth and avoiding looking at her expanding midriff. "The simple fact is that a woman owes obedience to her husband; that is only natural. Now, rarely, divorce can be permitted in cases of impotence, insanity or incest. But if that succeeded, your children would be rendered illegitimate. They could never inherit."

"That is entirely unacceptable," said Elianor. "What about adultery?" The vicar looked shocked.

"I can hardly imagine such a possibility," he said.

"Oh, that is nonsense, Vicar, and you know it. You can hardly be that naive," laughed Catherine.

"There is proof," added Elianor.

"Well," replied the vicar, "I don't say it's likely, but if it could be proven, or indeed sodomy or physical violence, a separation might be possible. But there would be no possibility of remarriage."

"One step at a time, vicar," said Elianor. "Could I not petition Parliament?"

"It is possible, but such a process takes a very long time and is extremely expensive. One must discourage the lower classes from breaking their vows or behaving in unseemly ways."

Catherine was regretting having taken her husband's advice and seeking the vicar's counsel. What she really wanted was his support, but she should have known he would be unimaginative, stick to the letter of the canon law, be pompous and downright stodgy.

520 ✣ The Miner & the Viscount

"After all Mr. Eliot and I have done for you," she said, "I do think you might make more effort to cooperate. Is there nothing you can do? What might the bishop suggest?"

"I regret that there is nothing either he nor I can do, ma'am." the vicar replied, stiffening. "The laws of the church are clear. After all, it is the church's desire to promote morality and the permanence of marriage. That is the foundation of our society. If that order ever changed, England would crumble into chaos."

"Vicar, you disappoint me, but you do not surprise me," said Catherine. "However, my dear friend Lady Dunbargan is a very determined woman. I am not lacking in that quality myself, and I will not abandon my friend to a fate she has done nothing to deserve. You may leave."

Her attitude concerned the vicar, but he said no more, bowed and left the room to the two disgruntled ladies.

"Well, that's that," said Elianor. "I don't suppose I would fare any better with our vicar at Lanhydrock, worse if anything; his living is in the gift of the estate, so he's in Dunbargan's pocket. Men think they can tell us what to do with our persons, our opinions, our children and our property."

"Unfortunately the law is completely on their side," said Catherine. Elianor stood up and swept to the center of the room.

"Well then, I shall just have to take the law into my own hands," she said. "I'm going to have to get rid of him. All I need is some help. Can I count on you and your husband, Catherine?"

"Goodness gracious, Elianor," said Catherine, "what do you have in mind? Of course you can count on me and possibly Mr. Eliot, but only up to a point. He is a stickler for propriety and he certainly would not stand for violence. I have my own reasons to help you all I can, of course. And your charming husband has offended other people we can both think of."

"You too? We have learned about Miss Clymo and poor Mrs. Bunt."

Catherine looked at her in alarm. "What of Miss Clymo?" she asked. So Elianor related that part of the story to an increasingly disturbed Catherine.

"That is horrid," she said. "He made the most unwelcome advances to me when my husband and I visited Lanhydrock, while you were still in childbed of all times. I succeeded in rebuffing him, but I had to be quite firm."

"He was positively violent with poor little Mary," said the viscountess, "forced himself upon her. There's no telling what lengths he might have gone to next. She is fortunate that Bunt took her away and that you and your husband gave them shelter."

"And then there is Penwarden," said Catherine. "He treated him and his friends vilely and is the cause of the fearful injury to Mrs. Penwarden, which she yet may not survive. And he did nothing to save their baby when she was deathly ill."

"I can understand having to be firm with the rioters at the mine," said Elianor, "but hanging is going too far. Penwarden seems quite a decent sort of chap; Dunbargan provoked him beyond reason. I don't understand it."

"There are sure to be others of whom we are unaware," said Catherine. "My own husband is discreet to a fault, but I know he despises Dunbargan too. His lordship tried to cheat Edward more than once. He'd give a lot to be rid of him in business."

"I know," exclaimed Elianor. "We must follow the example of the wise Mr. Pitt. We must form an alliance and think up a strategy to ensure that he never shows his face in these parts again."

"My dear, that is a brilliant idea," said Catherine. "There is strength in numbers, and even the viscount is not powerful enough to stand against us all. We must seize the opportunity while he is still here at Port Eliot. We must be careful Clymo doesn't find out though, he always takes his part."

"Not anymore, I imagine," said Elianor. "He was dreadful to Clymo during my interview with him, after all those years of loyal service to the family. The viscount even had the temerity to boast to Clymo about what he did to his daughter. Clymo usually maintains detachment, but I could tell he was simply furious. It must have been an awful shock. I have no doubt he would join our alliance."

"My mind is moving along lines I would only share with my best friends," said Catherine. "Perhaps the stolidly reliable Mr. Clymo could be a secret agent. Let me think." She smiled wickedly.

Later that evening, when Catherine and Edward were alone in their bedroom, he pulled her to him. "I am sorry we quarreled when I thought it imperative to go to London. I was beside myself with worries on all fronts, and you must admit, you were being a bit stubborn. Am I forgiven?"

She smiled up at him. "You are forgiven," she said, "but only if I can further my plans for the house the next time we go to London." He pinched her cheek and gave her a kiss. "I've no doubt that my defenses will not prove sufficient to the task of restraining you."

As he climbed into bed, he said, "I realize how much I am needed home at Port Eliot; my duty is first and foremost to protect you and Elianor. Now I must tell you the latest from London. No, don't look long-suffering; this is not about politics."

She climbed in beside him and laid back, turning her head attentively while he continued. "As good fortune would have it, I went to the business room after speaking to you to find another letter from my clerk at the Commission. Apparently Dunbargan has really blotted his career this time. He has never paid Bute for procuring the title for him, and his gambling debts have reached astronomical proportions. He's rich, of course, but it's all tied up in land and leases, and mortgages; he can't lay his hands on enough ready money and he doesn't want to liquidate. The lawyers are being called in on both counts, and it will be a miracle if he'll be able to show his face in his club or at the House of Lords again. All London is abuzz with the gossip."

"Does he know this?" asked Catherine?

"He has learned," said Edward. "A messenger was sent from London to warn him. In all likelihood, this is the reason he has been so anxious to be reunited with his wife. She still has money in her control, and he'll want to get his hands on it."

"Well, it seems he hasn't a prayer of that now," said Catherine. "We'll need to be wary as long as he is in the vicinity. And now," she whispered, moving closer to Edward, "I'm very, very glad you made up your mind to stay home."

✣✣✣

The next day the ladies put their heads together. They were delighted with the imaginative ideas that they created to deal with the hated Viscount Dunbargan. Having heard Catherine out on the news imparted by Edward the night before, Elianor was more determined than ever to be shed of her husband and deliver him a blow. Plotting was becoming quite exciting. From time to time they had to pull themselves back from the brink of a plan that was downright criminal. They wanted to deal with the enemy, not get themselves or any of their friends or fellow conspirators into trouble.

Lady Dunbargan suggested again consulting Edward Eliot. Catherine was reluctant to do so, fearing that he would be too cautious, even if it transpired that his help were essential. But then, Edward would himself benefit from what the others were prepared to put into action, so why shouldn't he participate? She would have to think about that.

They decided to call a council of war without further delay. Catherine thought of summoning people to the business room but preferred not to tell her husband until after a plan had been made, so she chose the schoolroom by the church. She sent out servants with messages to the Clymos, the Bunts and Penwarden to meet them there in one hour, and to tell no one where they were going. Lizzie Penwarden would be unable to come or to say anything, but she would be in all of their minds.

They considered asking Charles Polkinghorne, but concluded that while he undoubtedly disliked dealing with Dunbargan, to their knowledge he had no personal reason to hate him. They settled on Catherine agreeing to mention the possibility of including Polkinghorne when she talked to her husband.

The meeting succeeded even better than they had hoped. The ladies stated their wishes and the others added their suggestions. Morwenna Clymo had some excellent ideas. Her father was so angry at the viscount that despite his lifetime habit of loyalty he was happy to take revenge on him. Mary Bunt was nervous but agreed to play her part once her husband Willy persuaded her that he would keep her safe.

Addis Penwarden cautioned that he would ensure that the viscount would be unable to do any of them physical harm. Elianor thought to herself that the mine captain seemed to be admirable, strong, staunch, steady, despite the tragedy lurking in his life.

The conspirators arrived at a plan they were sure would succeed. It was simple. They would exploit his weaknesses to lure him into an ambush where they would punish him for his evil deeds and frighten him into leaving them all in peace. What doubts lingered were silenced when Catherine said it was all settled, so it was agreed they were unanimous. Catherine Eliot would inform her husband of the plan and make sure that he would be on their side, and perhaps even join in.

His influence could be important if anything went wrong. Elianor enjoyed a sense of freedom knowing that she felt no obligation to consult with her husband about anything. She wondered if Catherine's resolve would be weakened after she had talked to Edward, who was not imbued with a similar spirit of adventure.

Every one of them felt much better about their chances of righting their own wrongs than they had earlier in the day. They each swore a solemn oath to keep the plan a secret from anyone else. Morwenna seemed a little reluctant to join in the oath, but said nothing as to why. The men exchanged conspiratorial glances, which seemed natural in the circumstances. Finally, they all committed to proceed with the plan to meet in the stables as soon as darkness fell.

It was an odd assortment of allies, gentry and common folk, who left the churchyard in mid-afternoon, all of them suspended somewhere between elation and anxiety. Catherine took Elianor's hand and said, "Let us take a turn around the park in this beautiful sunshine. It will calm us." They broke away from the others with lengthening strides.

Chapter Seventy-seven

Revenge

Edward Eliot was in a turmoil. He liked things to proceed on an even keel, but now the place was still full of people, most of whom were upset. Catherine was distressed, and when that occurred, Edward was inevitably affected. Dunbargan was causing trouble again, and Catherine's good friend Lady Elianor was seething. Not only had the viscount failed to persuade his wife to come home to Lanhydrock, but also they had another blazing row, and their split was irreparable. Dunbargan had lost patience with Clymo into the bargain and dismissed him, so the faithful retainer would no longer be in a position to act as a buffer between his lordship and the civilized world.

Edward's clerk at the Commission of Trade and Plantations in London had confirmed that Dunbargan was in serious trouble: he had not yet remunerated the Earl of Bute for procuring his viscountcy. It was not that the man lacked wealth; it was that his extravagance and his indebtedness to importunate characters of dubious reputation left him in persistent need of copious supplies of gold that he could lay his hands on immediately. Edward did not feel sorry for the viscount, whose actions alone were the cause of his troubles, but one could understand that the exploding pressures led him to more and more irresponsible and reprehensible behavior.

It was after the vicar came to call that Edward felt something approaching alarm. Whenever the vicar visited his business room without being summoned it was to solicit something, usually money. This time was different. He was offering something: a warning. He had met with Mrs. Eliot and Lady Dunbargan as Mr. Eliot had requested and given them the counsel that was appropriate to his cloth. While he was used to his advice being taken without demur, in this case he had a nagging suspicion that the dear ladies had minds of their own. He felt it his duty, without betraying their trust, to warn his patron that they may have in mind behavior that bordered on folly regarding Lady Dunbargan's relationship with the viscount, in connection with which he had felt constrained to remind the ladies of the strictness of the church's teachings concerning the commitment embodied in Holy Matrimony. Mr. Eliot might be wise to consider whether his masculine authority required assertion.

Exhausted by the effort of comprehending what the vicar was saying, Edward took a deep breath. He usually shared his wife's view that the vicar was a pompous fool whose insights into the human condition were gleaned more from Holy Writ than experience with the lives of his flock. However, reading between the several lengthy and ponderous lines intoned by the vicar, and peering past the veils, Edward guessed that Elianor was planning to divorce her husband.

This was a monstrous step for a lady of her class and one that could only give rise to conflict, expense and scandal, and to which it would be imprudent for Catherine to lend her support. He owed it to Lady Dunbargan to put a stop to any such radical notion. But before risking her ire and perhaps making an unwarranted accusation, Edward concluded that he should heed the vicar's warning and find out precisely what the ladies were up to. He knew they were up to something, but while he could only advise Lady Dunbargan, he could instruct his own wife. However, upon reflection he had to admit that Elianor was more likely to follow his advice than Catherine his instruction.

To make matters worse, Dunbargan had come barging into his business room just as he was about to end his labors for the day; although, if he were to be honest with himself, he had not been working very hard after the vicar left. Having already sent the clerks off to their homes, he was alone. Polkinghorne had taken himself off somewhere earlier, and Edward preferred to leave most tasks to his loyal and usually dependable man of business. Where the devil had Polkinghorne got to?

Edward felt it would be unwise not to hear Dunbargan out, much as he would have preferred to avoid unpleasantness. He had heard enough from Catherine to know the interview would be difficult. He would just listen, nod, say as little as possible, and content himself with finding out exactly how much of a threat the viscount posed.

Dunbargan had evidently started drinking early in the day; he was even more bellicose than usual. He demanded wine, which Eliot reluctantly supplied. Then the viscount started off loudly complaining about Elianor, his perfidious and treacherous wife with whom, despite his habitually tolerant and sensitive nature, he had finally lost patience. He had ordered her never to return to Lanhydrock. He would provide her out of his exceptional generosity with one maidservant, who would pack her things and which he would have delivered to her wherever she might take herself.

Of course the viscountess, as she would continue most unfairly to be called, could not expect her Trenance family jewels to be included. The viscount had not mentioned this to her yet, he confided, but given her insatiable greed, he would no doubt have to deal with her indignation as soon as she discovered this perfectly reasonable arrangement.

And then there was of course his son. Dunbargan slapped his hand on the table. The Honorable James Trenance was in his mother's care at the moment, but as soon as a proper settlement had been imposed, his heir would be removed to Lanhydrock, as was only proper. He would normally have left such a matter to his steward Clymo, particularly if the details became ticklish. But the damn fellow had proven unreliable after all these years of being in a privileged position with the family. It is what came of not treating people firmly enough, he told Edward. He could no longer put up with disloyalty, had to get rid of him.

Probably have to turn to Thomas Bolitho; now there is a man who knew how to get things done. And to top it off, the damn woman had another child about to enter the world. That might be one more nuisance, but with any luck it would only be a girl.

Edward Eliot found all of this embarrassing. The fellow really should not pour out personal matters, let alone give vent to his feelings. It simply was not done among gentlemen, and it was not as if they were friends after all. Quite the contrary. They were just acquaintances, because they were both Old Etonians and happened to be neighbors in the county and in recent years had done business together and were involved in politics.

Edward's own father had rarely seen old Baron Trenance; the man had been a damned moneylender. The viscount was going to be more difficult and less useful than ever. His reputation was now tainted in London, as well as in Cornwall, and it would only get worse. It would not do to be associated with him. All dealings between Port Eliot and Lanhydrock must now come to an end.

To top it off, the dreadful fellow had asked him for a loan. He complained that he had not been receiving his share of profits from Wheal Hykka. But surely his other mines were still paying handsomely. The prices of tin and copper were firm. No doubt he kept up the family money-lending business and was no less ruthless than his father in collecting what he felt was his due. Agriculture was doing well, so presumably his rents were coming in every quarter day. Edward had no idea how much money Dunbargan took in from the smugglers and did not want to know. And he had long suspected that he was embroiled in the slave trade. All added up to plenty of revenue, although apparently he could not lay his hands on enough ready money to suit his creditors; not only Lord Bute but doubtless all manner of debts arising from his extravagance, cards and ladies of questionable reputation.

Edward felt, all in all, that Dunbargan's tirade confirmed the wisdom of his own decision to sever all ties, although now was clearly not the opportune time for a rational discussion. Perhaps it would be wiser for Polkinghorne to have a word with Bolitho in due course, and they could deal with the matter. Eliot would stay clear of the whole thing.

At last he sent Dunbargan packing after convincing him that he had no ready cash to spare, and there was still no possibility of his staying at the house. It simply would not be appropriate in the circumstances. The viscount would have to go back to the inn in the village and then be on his way back to Lanhydrock tomorrow. He was certainly not in any condition to travel this evening. Perhaps they would meet in a few weeks in London, although Edward took care not to make a specific arrangement and bade him good night as he watched him stumble out of the door.

Edward put on his hat and coat, blew out the lamps and prepared to leave. He went to open the door, but before he could go out, Catherine came in.

"Edward, I am so glad I caught you before you left," she said. "I wanted to talk to you here rather than in the house. This is more private and we need to be discreet. Are you alone?"

"Yes. Come, come, you appear quite troubled, my dear," he said.

"As do you, dear husband."

He nodded. "I have a matter of urgency that I wish to discuss. But, first, tell me what is agitating you so?" Edward stepped aside to allow his wife to enter and then relit a lamp.

"I'm so angry," Catherine said, her voice shaking. "You know that Dunbargan has overstepped the bounds. He has not only dreadfully mistreated his wife but several others as well, Clymo, Miss Clymo, the Bunts, the Penwardens, you too my dear. Elianor is determined to leave him and we have decided to take matters into our own hands, all of us. He must be stopped."

Edward held her by her shoulders and steered her to a chair. "One thing at a time. Tell me exactly what you have in mind. You must take care. The man is not without power; he is a peer after all."

Catherine laid out the scheme that she and her fellow plotters had concocted, after first reciting a litany of the viscount's grievous bodily assaults and other wrongs inflicted upon others.

"My God, Catherine, the man is an even worse villain than I'd realized," Eliot exclaimed. "He is disgraceful, and no gentleman. I have just been through an impossible interview with him. Came pestering me for money of all things, drunk. Complaining about his wife. Wanting to stay here. I told him in no uncertain manner that he would have to find a room at the inn."

"It is clear there is no alternative but to get rid of him and put him in his place once and for all, for all of our sakes," Catherine replied. "Can we count on your support then, dear Edward?" she asked.

Edward took Catherine's hand and, somewhat reluctantly, shook his head. "No, no, my dear, not possibly. Your scheme is much too risky. You must think of your position, mine too. Something may go wrong. I can have nothing to do with it, and I forbid you to take any part. Bear in mind that I am a magistrate, and as such I am responsible for upholding the law. I cannot be seen to be part of what may be perceived as a criminal enterprise and neither can you. And, I will assuredly advise Lady Dunbargan to remain aloof as well. It won't do, not at all."

"That is the whole point, Edward. Nothing could possibly go wrong. We have planned every detail. No one can know, we are all sworn to secrecy, and I will ensure that the servants hear and see nothing. If by any remote mischance some minor detail goes amiss, your position as a magistrate will ensure that no one will get into trouble. You are our safeguard."

Edward dropped her hand. "Catherine, the vicar came and spoke to me; hard to make sense of what he was trying to say, meandering all over the place without wanting to betray any confidences. If I understood him aright he was concerned that your friend Lady Dunbargan is determined to pursue divorce. The vicar, of course, maintains that her clear duty lies with her husband. Given the circumstances, you must not get entangled with any impetuous actions on her part. Divorce alone would cause a great scandal."

"Duty? Scandal? Dunbargan's appalling behavior absolves her of all duty towards him. I will stand by my friend, no matter what, and it is your duty to help rid us all of an evil man."

"My dear Catherine, I most strenuously forbid you, I insist. And I know my duty. I have to think of my career, my position, nor can I leave for London harboring any fear that you will disregard my wishes."

"You, Edward, cannot leave, you have to think of your own wife. I need you here, and so do our sons. Anyway, the conspirators have taken their places in the stables by now, and I must join them. The die is cast."

Edward was displeased with his wife, and Catherine with her husband. He had agreed to lend his moral support to Elianor in her dilemma, but now he and Catherine were being embroiled as conspirators no less.

Edward prevailed in arguing that the plot could succeed without Catherine's presence, and insisted that she return to the house with him. Under no circumstances would he lend his own actions to such folly as was to occur in the stable. Catherine eventually, though reluctantly, accepted that she had no choice but to follow her husband in what she began to see as his wisdom and care for the family's reputation and safety. Silence prevailed as they walked the short distance.

Meanwhile, the absent Polkinghorne had made straight for Morwenna Clymo, whom he found conferring with her father in the garden of his house nearby in the village. Joseph Clymo saw the stricken look on the younger man's face and broke off his conversation with his daughter, which appeared to be heated.

"Sir," said Polkinghorne, "if I may have a word with Miss Clymo, I would be grateful." Morwenna stepped back, clapping her hand over her mouth. Clymo sized up the scene and coming to his own conclusions, stepped away and headed off.

Tears were welling up in Morwenna's eyes as she looked up at Charles Polkinghorne and saw all her hopes dashed on the rocks of her own foolishness. "Oh, Charles, you've heard the gossip. You must hate me."

Polkinghorne drew in a deep breath and said, "Gossip? Is that all it is? Gossip? No, Morwenna, I don't hate you. Therein lies the problem. You simply need to explain to me the circumstances of your liaison with the viscount. I need to know. Forgive me if I'm not doing this gracefully, but did he force himself on you?"

At this, Morwenna's tears gave way to loud sobs, unabated. Polkinghorne struggled not to comfort and embrace her, waiting. Finally, he said, "Morwenna, you must tell me." She moved over to a low wall and sat down, her sobs slowing. She took Polkinghorne's proffered handkerchief and dried her face and looked up at him.

"Yes," she said. "He did force himself on me, and I will spare you the details; but after it was over, he came after me again and again. He began showering me with favors." She pulled the locket forward to show him, heaving a shuddering sob. "You see, after a while I began to enjoy the favors and endure the ambushes. It was awful, but I didn't know how to get away from him, because he threatened my father's job, and then where would we have been? Out in the cold with no roof over our heads, bad references and no money."

Polkinghorne heard her out and then moved across the lawn, pulling out his pipe, lighting it, and watching the smoke rise into the darkening sky. Morwenna remained motionless. Finally he walked back towards her, putting his now extinguished pipe into his pocket.

"You must know," Polkinghorne began, breathing deeply, "that I was on the verge of proposing marriage, asking your father for the hand of a young woman whom I thought innocent. And now . . . "

"And now?" asked Morwenna.

"This is exceedingly difficult for me," said Polkinghorne in return. "I am not experienced in such matters, for which I am thankful."

She nodded but did not speak.

He looked at her a long while, drew another deep breath and plunged on. "I love you, Morwenna. I do, more the fool I. But I do. Give me some time, I've got to take all this in." He squeezed her hand, then turned and went into his house, leaving a crestfallen Morwenna to go to her father for comfort.

Inside the stables the plotters were taking up their assigned positions. Elianor Dunbargan was concerned that Catherine Eliot had not yet arrived to play her part. She did not risk sending a messenger to the big house for fear of revealing their positions, and was relieved to see Catherine's maid stealing into the stable with a note. She was disheartened to read that Edward had forbidden Catherine to participate, but was determined to carry on without her. Too much was at stake. She sent the maid away by a route that could not be seen from the drive.

As dusk fell, two men walked down the drive from the village to the stables behind the Eliot house. One of them was noticeably staggering. It was Viscount Dunbargan, accompanied by Joseph Clymo. Earlier, Clymo had carried out a mission in St. Germans for Lady Dunbargan, delivering letters to the postmaster. Then he had waited in the taproom at The Eliot Arms for Dunbargan to return from his meeting with Edward Eliot.

Clymo had expected after their earlier quarrel that Dunbargan would rebuff any approach from him, so he had concocted a story, that he was abjectly seeking forgiveness. When Dunbargan arrived, such a deception proved unnecessary since his lordship was not only preoccupied with his own sorrows but also too drunk to recall much about their earlier altercation. After swallowing another drink, the viscount rambled on about the ingratitude of Lady Dunbargan after all the care and comfort he had showered upon her.

By now, Joseph Clymo knew that the trap would have been baited with Mary Bunt and his daughter Morwenna taking their places in the stable. Clymo plied Dunbargan with more wine and after a while broadly hinted that Mary Bunt had made him promise to keep a secret, how surprised she was at her excitement at seeing her first lover again. Life as a married woman and mother had become dull, and although Willy was still handsome, he lacked his rival's aristocratic dash. Furthermore, on his modest wages, her husband kept her too short of money to afford the little treats that a woman enjoys.

The viscount followed the story with difficulty. He tried to pull himself together and to call out to the innkeeper to demand another bottle of wine but he had grown incoherent. Instead he waved his glass. The innkeeper was busy winding the clock on the wall. Dunbargan banged his glass on the table to attract the man's attention, too hard. The glass shattered. The innkeeper glowered but brought more wine as ordered.

Clymo noted the time. He had to make sure that the viscount swallowed the bait and then get him to the stable without delay.

Clymo leaned over confidentially and laid a forefinger by the side of his nose. "My lord, perhaps I am remiss in betraying a confidence from a member of the fair sex, but I know my duty. I must tell you that Mary Bunt then winked at me in an unmistakable manner and said she might be going alone on an errand to the stables this evening, but exactly for what she did not say."

Dunbargan guffawed and slapped his thigh. "Ooh," he muttered. "Ahah! Where, I mean to shay, why, who . . ." Clymo stood up and offered an arm to the viscount as he lurched to his feet, puffing, red in the face.

"Let me show you the way to the stables, sir," said Clymo, "Come with me, it isn't far to walk." Clymo put a sovereign on the table, elbowed their way through the crowd in the smoky taproom, pushed through the door to the outside, and led the viscount up the hill to the road into Port Eliot. The chilly air did nothing to improve the viscount's sobriety and, despite his eagerness, their progress was labored. Dunbargan grew visibly excited as the house loomed against the night sky and they approached the turning to the stables.

Neither of them noticed the figure stealthily following them from The Eliot Arms, lurking at the edges of the drive, keeping in the shadows of trees and shrubbery.

At the stables, Joseph Clymo opened the heavy outer door. "You go ahead into the first stall on the right, my lord," he said. "You'll get a nice surprise. I'll leave you here."

As the viscount made his way inside the stable, the horses seemed nervous, whinnying, stamping their hooves. Joseph Clymo climbed the end stair to the loft above where he joined Willy Bunt and Addis Penwarden already hiding among the sacks of oats and stacks of hay. He expected to see Mrs. Eliot; she was to give the signal to spring the trap. She must be hiding downstairs instead. No matter, they all knew what to do, all was in place now.

Bunt put a finger to his lips and quietly gave Clymo a pitchfork to arm himself with. Bunt had a quarryman's pickaxe. Penwarden brandished his miner's boryer. There was a hatch in the floor above each stall through which feed could be dropped to the manger below. Bunt stationed himself above the first stall, Clymo above the second, and Penwarden above the third.

Addis Penwarden wished he could have got Dunbargan down the mine. That would have been rough justice. But Willy Bunt insisted on dealing with him in a stable. Young Bunt had reasons of his own and that would be justice enough. They all had their reasons, could be counted on to play their parts.

Dunbargan went into the first stall and pushed aside the horse standing there. He caught sight of Mary's face by the light of the hanging lantern. Her eyes were shining, her cheeks flushed. By God, she was a pretty little thing! Wish she had never got away from Lanhydrock. Put on a few pounds, effect of child bearing most likely. Made her more voluptuous if anything, more desirable. He put out his arms and stumbled towards her. He did not notice Willy Bunt peering down from the hatch to the loft above, his pickaxe at the ready.

"Oh, my lord, Oi'm glad to see you, it's been a long toime," said Mary, clasping him to her, holding him upright. She put her face up to his. He kissed her hard on her lips and to his surprise she did not pull away but responded warmly. "Wait, let's not spoil it, don't go too fast," cajoled Mary. "Let's go next door, there's more straw in there, it'll be more comfy loike. Besides, Oi've got a surprise for you."

Supporting him by the arm she led him into the neighboring loose box. His own stallion was there, still recovering after the hard ride from Lanhydrock. The cuts on his flank from his spurs had scabbed over, but he still tired easily. The horse recognized him and whinnied nervously. Dunbargan slapped his rump, and as he moved over the viscount saw Morwenna Clymo smiling at him and fluttering her eyelashes. Once again he failed to notice the hatch above; at this one Joseph Clymo crouched clutching his pitchfork, with Willy Bunt now beside him.

"Surprised?" Morwenna asked, reaching out to him, taking his other arm and drawing him back into the loose box to her. "I couldn't be in Port Eliot without seeing you, not after all we've meant to each other."

In the next stall over, Elianor was standing in wait, surprised at herself playing such a daring role in the plot, but angry enough to abandon discretion. She would boldly seize her opportunity to escape the bullying and the insults of the madman who had tricked her into marrying him. She wished Catherine were here to lend her support, but at least her friend could be counted on to keep the secret. Now it was up to Elianor to make sure the plot succeeded. She signaled silently to Addis Penwarden in the loft above to come down.

Penwarden climbed down the ladder bringing his boryer and a leather satchel. In the dim light he missed his footing on the bottom rung and stumbled. She caught him just in time to prevent him falling. "Hush!" she whispered, "do you have the letters? Dunbargan is with Miss Clymo and Mrs. Bunt now."

Penwarden nodded and handed her the satchel. They listened as Dunbargan spoke in the next stall. "Morwenna, what are you doing here? You're the last person I expected to see after you betrayed me," he said.

"You neglected me, lover," chided Morwenna. "I would never betray you, not my Jamie." She winked at him and tossed her hair.

Dunbargan lost control of his emotions. He lurched across the loose box and seized her. He threw her down in the straw and grappled with her. There was a sound of fabric ripping. Her shoulders were bared. Her lower lip was bleeding.

"Stop!"

The angry shout surprised them all. A man rushed into the loose box and with one hand pulled the viscount off Morwenna and threw him to the ground. In his other hand he brandished a pistol. His face was distorted with fury. Elianor was taken aback. This was not part of the plan. By the dim light of the lantern she recognized the man: Charles Polkinghorne.

"Dunbugger, you get off my darling!" he shouted. "You've gone too far this time. Someone's got to stop you, and I'm going to do it." The viscount rolled onto his back and put his open hands in front of his face, beseeching the man not to fire the pistol that was aimed directly at his head.

"Don't shoot," sobbed Morwenna, "don't shoot!"

"Don't shoot!" echoed Penwarden and Bunt rushing into the stall, with Clymo half falling down the ladder hard on their heels. Penwarden lunged at the pistol and knocked it up with his boryer just as it fired; the ball flew harmlessly through the ceiling into the loft. The pistol fell onto the straw.

The stallion reared up, whinnying in fear. Mary quickly ducked out of the way. The other horses in the stable snorted, pawed at the straw, tossed their heads.

Willy Bunt rushed to his wife cowering in the back corner and took her in his arms. "Mary, my brave girl, you'm all right, 'e can't 'urt you now."

Joseph Clymo gave his hand to his daughter and helped her to her feet. She pulled up the torn sleeve of her dress and covered her naked shoulder. He held out his arms to her but she stepped past him and embraced Charles Polkinghorne.

"Charles, they'd've put you in gaol, they could've hanged you," she said. "He's not worth it. He'll get his comeuppance. Oh, Charles!" She buried her face in his shoulder as Polkinghorne wrapped his arms around her.

Penwarden stood over the viscount, holding the boryer against his chest. "Don't you dare move, Dunbugger," he said. "You stay right there." Clymo stood with his pitchfork and Bunt with his pickaxe over either side of him, threatening him.

Dunbargan whimpered, "Please don't hurt me, please."

"You always were a little sniveler," shouted Addis Penwarden, brandishing the boryer. "I should have hit you on the head when I had the chance years ago in them there woods, just like a rabbit. No one was about, no one would ever've known."

Elianor strode forward into the loose box waving the satchel in her husband's face. She bent over him and hissed, "You miserable coward, you bully. The shoe's on the other foot now; you're the victim and you don't like it one bit. I should let them finish you off now."

There was a commotion at the entrance. The Eliots appeared. "What was that shot?" demanded Edward. "Was anyone hurt?"

"Mrs. Eliot, Mr. Eliot, you've shown up," said Elianor. "Things got out of hand. Your man Polkinghorne turned up with a pistol. Shot at the viscount but fortunately missed."

"That was not the plan," said Catherine, "not to hurt him, just to frighten him and humiliate him."

"I will make an official complaint, then you'll all be sorry," said Dunbargan, sitting up and trying to reassert his dignity, but without success since there was straw in his mouth and a boryer poking into his chest. Penwarden prodded him and he fell back. "Us don't need to hear anything from you, Dunbugger," he said.

"Quite agree. No need to go any further, old man," said Eliot. "I am the official, I am the magistrate in these parts," and, taking in the scene before him, he suddenly laughed in an uncharacteristically triumphant way. Catherine reached for his hand.

"Then let us proceed," said Elianor Dunbargan, handing her husband letters from her satchel. "These are official letters addressed to leaders of the government in London, seeking my divorce from you. They demand immediate redress of my grievances and contain affidavits from those you have wronged, including these people standing around you now. Your behavior is described in detail. The scandal will ruin you. Your rank will not protect you. Your failure to pay your debts for your viscountcy has been revealed. You will lose your preferment. You'll never be able to show your face in London again."

"How did you know about the viscountcy?" snarled Dunbargan. "You couldn't have known; nobody knew."

"Oh yes, Clymo knew, and he told me after our delightful conversation earlier," said Elianor.

"Clymo would never betray me," said Dunbargan.

"You betrayed him after years of faithful service," said Elianor. "What can you expect?"

"All of London knows, Dunbargan," said Eliot; "I received a letter from my clerk."

Catherine tried not to gloat but could not help smiling as she looked at her husband. Edward Eliot continued, "I advise you to go abroad, my lord; England will be much too hot for you. Furthermore, I suggest you stay clear of any places where transported criminals might be sent. The news of your debts is all over London and my Lord Bute himself is highly displeased. No doubt His Majesty has been apprised by now."

Dunbargan scowled as he perused the letters with difficulty, peering in the light shed by the lantern, still lying on his back, the boyrer suspended over him, ringed by the pitchfork, the quarryman's pickaxe and the pistol. The names of the men to whom the letters were addressed were impressive, men of influence: the Honorable William Pitt, Esq.; Pitt's brother-in-law George Grenville, Leader of the Commons; the Earl of Bute, the king's favorite. He would be finished if the letters reached them. There was only one thing to do. Dunbargan laughed in his wife's face and tore them into shreds.

"Fool," she said, "those are copies."

"I took the originals to the post office this afternoon, my lord," said Clymo, for once permitting himself to sneer. "They are well on their way to London by now."

Morwenna and Mary each spat in the viscount's face. Bunt and Penwarden stood over him still and threatened him with their weapons.

"You should have been taught to treat your women better, my lord," chimed in Polkinghorne. "Her ladyship is more than a match for you, I am glad to see, and for that matter, so is Miss Clymo."

"Leave him be," said Eliot, "leave him be. It no longer matters whether or not he has learned his lesson. He's certainly not worth hanging for. He will trouble us no more."

As they made their way out of the stables Elianor, Viscountess Dunbargan, paused and went back alone for a last look. She saw the stallion prancing above the viscount, straddling him as he cowered in the straw, then settle, lift his tail and drench him with a long stream of piss, as Dunbargan struggled on all fours to rise. The horse whinnied, threw up his head, twitched his tail and stamped his hooves, barely avoiding the viscount's head.

Elianor blew out the lantern and threw her husband a mocking kiss, leaving him in darkness, sunk into the straw, his hands covering his wet hair, alone and weeping.

Chapter Seventy-eight

Cornwall

After a good deal of back slapping and hand shaking and hugging and emotion, Lady Dunbargan and the Eliots bade their fellow conspirators good night, walked back to the house and sat in the library, weary and enjoying Edward's favorite fino sherry. Edward instructed the butler that any wine or spirit supplied by any shipper or merchant connected with the Viscount Dunbargan should be opened tomorrow and emptied into the River Lyhner, with not a word to anyone who might try to make off with it before it reached its destination. The butler was quite taken aback, and had to recover his composure before he could take in Catherine's request that they be served a light supper at the small dining table.

They each had expected to feel triumphant, but their mood was somber. Edward reflected on the day's tumultuous events as he opened the conversation. "I had thought I would propose a toast to your health and happiness, Lady Dunbargan, but I was thinking as we walked back from the stables that all of our lives are changing in important ways, some welcome, some less so. We owe much to the support we have given each other, but I realize also how much we owe to the loyalty of those who serve us. We've seen that especially today. It's something that I am guilty of having taken for granted. So I ask you ladies to join me also in a toast to friendship and loyalty."

"Friendship and loyalty!" said the viscountess. She raised her glass and sipped her sherry. "I am awkward at expressing my emotions, but I truly value your friendship, Catherine and Edward."

"Elianor, your friendship means much to me, especially as a woman," said Catherine. "We have come through difficult times together, but also exciting and good times. I have admired your courage and appreciate your spirit. We will achieve much that is worthwhile together, and we have many good times ahead."

"There are things I avoid expressing too, Elianor," said Edward, "but I must confess, no that's not it, I must boast, that I have learned much from you ladies. My brethren and I are not used to such admissions. But I vow to devote myself to doing as much good as my abilities allow and to battle evil. The vicar may not always agree with how I view good and evil, but so be it."

"Edward, then I will boast too," said Catherine, "unashamedly in front of my friend. I am proud to have you as my husband, and I wish for Elianor that her future will include a husband with qualities as admirable as yours." She raised her glass and they all drank to each other.

"Hear, hear," said Elianor, "now tell me, Edward, how will you put your good intentions into practice?"

"How refreshing it is for me, dear lady," teased Edward, "to have you hold me to the mark rather than my admirable wife, whose standards are always high." Catherine's lip twitched in an expression that slowly became a smile after Edward reached over and squeezed her hand affectionately. He continued. "First, I will pay more attention to Cornwall. I have decided not to go up to London for this session. I will stay here. Politics can wait. Others can well see to affairs in London. I alone can attend to the business that must be done in Cornwall and, to be candid, I am not confident that we have heard the last of the viscount."

"Ugh, the viscount; he is so undeserving of his title," said Elianor, curling her lip. "I hope and pray that he is never able to pay all he owes and is stripped of his title."

"Now it's time for my confession," said Catherine. "I so wish a title for you, Edward, you deserve it for your service to our country."

"Hah! I am more likely to satisfy your ambition through my boroughs than my service," said Edward ruefully, and then added with a smile, "My dear, are your ambitions entirely altruistic?"

"Ambitious only for you, Edward," said Catherine without the hint of a smile. "But enough of that; tell us what you will do with your stay here. I must confess that I have some ideas that I would like to suggest."

"Allow me," said Edward. "I look forward to hearing your suggestions, but later. Before our guests leave us I have things I want to say to them. Tomorrow I will call them to the business room for a meeting. First, I will tell our good servants how much we value what they do for us and announce that I will increase their wages immediately."

"Oh, how wonderful, Edward," said Catherine, clapping her hands. "I admire your noble thoughtfulness, but can you afford it? There is so much that needs doing in the house."

"Thanks to their efforts, I can. And with increased rewards they will increase their effort and my profits, and I have ideas as to how they might apply themselves."

"Do tell us more, Edward. You're a sly one! You've been planning," said Elianor.

"I will," said Edward, "tomorrow, be patient. I want to sleep on it. But I plan to increase their responsibilities too. And I have sent a message to my brother John to join us."

There was a discreet knock at the door and the butler entered. "Your supper is served, madam," he announced and stood aside as Catherine led them out and Edward gave his arm to Elianor.

An air of jollity lay over the crowd in the taproom at The Eliot Arms, mingled with the sobriety that accompanies a sudden release of tension after long periods of worry, anger and conflict. Morwenna Clymo and Mary Bunt were the toasts of the party. Willy Bunt had lifted his wife up onto a table where she was smiling and blowing kisses to her friends and to the villagers who had joined their celebration. One of the villagers was playing a jig on his fiddle.

Morwenna Clymo started moving to the music, and Willy called out to her, "You jump up too, m'dear, we've all earned a bit of fun." Morwenna reached for his hand but drew back when she saw Charles Polkinghorne looking disapprovingly at her. She got on the table without help.

Joseph Clymo observed the glance between them. His beloved daughter had indeed been behaving differently of late. She was paying more and more attention to Charles Polkinghorne, and they were acting quite fondly towards each other.

Addis Penwarden had brought Lizzie along. She was still too poorly to join in, but she waved a hand more or less in time to the music. Addis was determined to enjoy himself, despite the afflictions of his beloved Lizzie. "Come on, everyone, this round's on me," he called.

The landlord and his barmaid filled the proffered tankards with their potent home brew. Polkinghorne was keeping an eye on Bunt. "Watch what you're drinking, Willy, don't go getting carried away."

"That's all right, Mr. Polkinghorne," Willy said, "Oi can look after meself, 'tis just apple juice; Oi'm stickin' to me pledge."

Even Joseph Clymo was loosening up, rather to his daughter's surprise, and called across to the fiddler, "Come on then, we've got something to celebrate, give us a song. How about Come, all ye jolly Tinner boys, then, eh?" There were shouts of approval and they all joined heartily in the chorus:

> *Hurray for tin and copper, boys, and fisheries likewise!*
> *Hurray for Cornish maidens, Oh bless their pretty eyes!*
> *Hurray for our old gentry, and may they never fail!*
> *Hurray, hurray for Cornwall! Hurray, boys, one and ale!*

Addis Penwarden noticed that one man did not join in the singing. He was standing somewhat apart, quiet, preoccupied. He slapped him on the back and said, "Come on, Mr. Polkinghorne, get your chin up! What's the matter? You're our hero, you gave that Dunbugger quite a fright tonight, no more than he deserved, and you did nothing the constables will complain about. You can count on Mr. Eliot to see to that. Landlord, fill 'em up again."

"It's not that, Mr. Penwarden," said Polkinghorne, "it's just that I've got something on my mind, something important."

"Well out with it, man," said Penwarden, "don't keep us wondering."

"Yeah, tell us," chimed in Bunt, "blurt it out."

"Well, I'm not sure," he said, glancing over at Morwenna who was still on the table and singing along with the fiddler. "Oh, in for a penny in for a pound, as my old mum used to say, and we are among friends," said Polkinghorne, pushing himself back from the table and getting to his feet.

"My own mum always said 'look before you leap'," said Willy Bunt.

"You didn't take much notice of 'er then, did you Willy boy, me 'andsome?" chuckled Mary. "Not that Oi noticed anyroad."

"You mind your lip, my boy," said Polkinghorne. "You're going to have to come back to work tomorrow don't you forget." He grinned good-naturedly, took a swallow of his beer, squared his shoulders and walked over to where Joseph Clymo was sitting and chatting. He took off his hat, held it over his breast and interrupted the conversation. "Mr. Clymo, a word if I may."

Clymo smiled expectantly. "Please proceed, Mr. Polkinghorne."

After taking a deep breath, Polkinghorne said without preamble, "I'd like to ask for your daughter's hand in marriage."

While not entirely unexpected after the encounter he had witnessed earlier in the garden of Polkinghorne's house, Clymo had not dreamed the matter would be brought to a head so soon. He faced Polkinghorne sternly. "You asking my permission to marry my daughter? That's a bit sudden."

Then he could carry it off no longer and broke into a grin. He clapped Polkinghorne on the back and said, "Don't think I haven't noticed the looks you give her, and yes, how nice you've been to me lately. Right? Well, it's about time."

"I tried to ask before, Mr. Clymo, I tried," said Polkinghorne, "but you didn't give me a chance."

"Didn't want to make it too easy on an old bachelor. Quite enjoyed watching you, I did. Anyway, you'll make a good enough son-in-law, I reckon, so I'll not make an issue of it. You'll have to ask her, of course, and for all I know she may refuse you."

Polkinghorne leapt over to the table where Morwenna was singing, her back to him. He tugged at the hem of her skirt to attract her attention. He knelt on a chair and looked up at her, again holding his hat at his breast.

Morwenna stopped singing in the middle of a high note and turned to look at the man kneeling before her. Startled, she said, "Mr. Polkinghorne! Good Lord! What are you up to?"

"I am proposing marriage, Miss Clymo, I am asking you to be my wife."

Morwenna's jaw dropped. "What, in front of all these people? What will my dad say?"

"Your father has given his permission," said Polkinghorne, "and these people are our friends."

"When? Where?" asked Morwenna, surprised. "I've been wondering how long it would take you to ask my father."

"Just now, here, while you were having a good time singing. You should pay more attention to what I am up to in future."

Morwenna recovered herself and cocked her head as a smile spread across her face. "Oh, Charles, you know I will, you silly chump, of course I will! I can't wait."

Polkinghorne stood up, pulled her to him, gave her a big hug and swung her down to stand beside him, laughing happily.

Willy Bunt's jaw dropped. "Well, Mr. Polkinghorne, you've given us all something to think about, an' no mistake," he said.

Mary Bunt chimed in with, "Full of surprises, Mr. Polkinghorne, decided to take your mum's advice and not Willy's, eh? In for a penny, in for a pound."

"I had to think about it a bit, but then with everything happening so fast I just made up my mind," said Polkinghorne. He let go of Morwenna to shake Clymo's hand as she went over and gave her father a big hug.

"I'm happy for you, my dear," said Clymo. "How about it landlord? Another round? And fiddler, give us another tune!" He turned back to Polkinghorne, "I'll miss my dear daughter of course; but, yes, I want her to be happy and trust you to take good care of her."

"It won't be half bad, Dad," chortled Morwenna. "You'll be a grandfather in no time, end up with a proper family."

"Not too fast my girl," said Joseph Clymo, "you're staying here in the inn tonight where I can keep an eye on you. Then I'm taking you back to Lanhydrock and having a word with the vicar."

"Don't be such a spoil-sport, Dad," said Morwenna, "we're all due a bit of fun after everything we've been through."

"If you don't mind, Mr. Clymo," said Polkinghorne, "and if Miss Clymo, er, Morwenna, agrees, I'd just as soon be married by Mr. Perry. He's been a good friend to all of us, and it would be a lot less fusty. Perhaps you'd be kind enough to give away your daughter."

Penwarden shook Clymo by the hand. "All the best to you, my friend," he said. "Let's all raise our tankards and toast the happy couple!" There were hugs and back slaps and kisses all round. The evening festivities showed no signs of winding down, with one sad exception. Lizzie sat mute in her corner, mouth agape, eyes closed, not taking it in. Addis Penwarden put on a good face, but he couldn't help wishing for the good old days when they were newly married, happy, in love, and full of hope for a future where nothing could go wrong.

Chapter Seventy-nine

Change

Morwenna Clymo, soon to be Morwenna Polkinghorne and none too soon for her, could hardly contain herself as she sat next to her fiancé in the business room at Port Eliot the next morning. Her father Joseph Clymo was there too, and the Bunts and Penwardens, although poor Lizzie was in a chair by the window looking out at who knows what. The children had been packed off to the schoolroom over at the church; this was grown-ups only. Charles Polkinghorne had tried to calm Morwenna and promised he would announce the news of their engagement to the gentry after Mr. Eliot had finished what he had to say.

They all stood expectantly as Mr. and Mrs. Eliot came into the room, together with Lady Dunbargan and a young man whom Charles Polkinghorne recognized as Mr. Eliot's brother John. Viscount Dunbargan was nowhere to be seen, thank the Lord. Edward Eliot took his place at the head of the table and signaled them to be seated.

"Good morning," he greeted them, nodding in turn at each. "We have been through turbulent times," he said, "and we have been through them together. I know that I speak for Lady Dunbargan as well as for Mrs. Eliot when I say that I am grateful to you all for the parts that you have played. Without you we could not have accomplished what we have. I know I can trust the discretion of each of you, because what happened here last night is not without hazard. A peer of the realm, after all, commands much power, whether he be a questionable viscount or merely a lowly baron. Thank you, all of you, for your courage, as well as your continued discretion." They clapped politely, but Eliot held up his hand for silence and continued.

"I have given much thought as to the consequences of our individual and collective actions, and if we remain discreet we can look to advantageous outcomes. Frankly, through much trouble, opportunities have been opened that otherwise would have been closed to us, despite the risk that the future may be clouded by new uncertainties. I have decided to do what lies within my power to reduce such uncertainties. Here's what I intend, and I will be brief, because some of you have to leave Port Eliot soon.

"Firstly, Lady Dunbargan found herself in a most unfortunate position and was obliged to do things that are frowned upon by society in order to extricate herself. Mrs. Eliot and I pledge to support her and ask you to do so as well. She will live with her own family for the time being, together with her son, as far as that is in her power. I trust I am not being indiscreet in observing that there may be an additional member of her family in the near future, also to be cared for."

The ladies exchanged knowing glances. The men pretended not to have noticed anything to be remarked upon.

"Next," he said, "there is news from London." He looked at Lady Dunbargan. "My sources inform me that the viscount's immediate financial and legal problems have reached insurmountable proportions and that he has apparently made a hasty decision to leave the country. For how long, we do not know, it may be just long enough for this storm to blow over. However, it is said he will be embarking for the American colonies within the month. His family apparently owns a plantation there, and that is where he will go."

Elianor clapped her hands and smiled. She glanced at Edward Eliot and said, "Perhaps abandonment added to his other failures will make my suit against my husband for divorce all the smoother."

Eliot nodded and proceeded, turning to acknowledge Joseph Clymo. "Mr. Clymo has served the Trenance family faithfully, but as a result of recent events finds himself without employment. With Lady Dunbargan's permission, I will employ him. I will put him in charge of the added responsibilities that have recently accrued to Port Eliot in the mining industry, not only down west, but also in finding new opportunities in east Cornwall. Polkinghorne and Bunt can't handle it all. When the Honorable James Trenance succeeds to the Lanhydrock estate, Mr. Clymo will be free to resume his employment there if that is desired."

There were murmurs of surprise and pleasure among the crowd, and Joseph Clymo expressed it. "Mr. Eliot, that is most kind and a relief to me, I must say, if her ladyship will agree. Now I should also add that it will be a special pleasure being a colleague of my son-in-law."

"Son-in-law, Mr. Clymo?" said Catherine Eliot. "What do you mean?"

"I am proud and happy to announce that my daughter Morwenna and your steward Charles Polkinghorne are engaged to be married."

Eliot looked surprised and turned to Polkinghorne. "Congratulations to you, sir, and our best wishes to the happy couple. We must have toasts all around after business is concluded."

Elianor Dunbargan added her felicitations. "Another alliance," she said, "and one that draws the ties between Lanhydrock and Port Eliot closer. I pray that the next generation will draw even closer." She smiled at Addis Penwarden.

Morwenna Clymo blushed prettily and Charles Polkinghorne beamed with pride and a little embarrassment as all eyes turned on them.

After a short pause, Edward Eliot returned to business. "Hear, hear! But if I may have your attention, I have further announcements, and I will continue to be brief. Mr. Penwarden has also endured travails and shown his sterling character. He is reaffirmed as captain at Wheal Hykka, but I have also informed Captain Williams that each of them will be charged with supervising three mines in which I am adventurer. I will support the doctors' pence plan to pay for care of sick and injured miners and their families, and we will start a search for a willing medical man right away.

"Captain Penwarden, I also want you to get hold of Mr. Smeaton and put him to work designing and installing engines to improve the hauling and stamping of ore at the mines under your charge."

Addis Penwarden was overcome. "Thank you sir, thank you; I will do my level best to deserve your kindness."

"You've already earned it, Penwarden," said Eliot. "But I am not finished. I also want you to instruct Mr. Smeaton to survey the workings and do what he can to make them safer, within reasonable levels of expenditure."

"Mr. Eliot, I hardly know what to say," said Penwarden. He glanced lovingly over at Lizzie by the window and then back at Eliot, beaming with gratitude.

"Bunt," said Eliot, "you're next, and I don't have to mention what the conditions are, but you have shown your worth. You will be in charge of all the quarries and all road construction for Port Eliot throughout Cornwall. I will see to it that we get our share of work on new turnpikes."

Bunt grinned, gave Mary's hand a squeeze. "Proper job! Thank 'ee, zir," he said.

"That leaves my man of business. I imagine, Polkinghorne, that you will not wish to travel far and wide in the near future for obvious reasons. I have been corresponding with my friends up country about further improvements in agricultural methods. I want them introduced not only to the home farms but also to all of my tenants. You will be in charge, and you will work with Mr. Bolitho to ensure that ample funds are available for investment, for the tenants as well as the home farms."

Catherine Eliot beamed approval at her husband. Leaders in thought and culture, political economy and government in England and Scotland were taking up the new ideas, trying new ways of thinking. Catherine recognized that she and her Blue Stockings friends were part of this growing enlightenment. She was pleased that their ideas seemed to be influencing her worthy but sometimes conservative husband.

"Which brings me to my last item," Edward continued. "I have asked my brother John to join us today so that you can all meet each other. He is a fine young officer in the Royal Navy, and his career promises to take him far and wide." John Eliot stood and bowed to the group.

"As you know," went on Edward, "I am Commissioner of Trade and Plantations, and in this position I have learned much about the potential for England in America. I must say, as an aside, I hope that our leaders do not spoil this opportunity for us. Be that as it may, my instinct tells me that Port Eliot will play an important part across the Atlantic. I cannot tell you what the future brings, but I know in my heart that we must be prepared to seize opportunity, and I believe that with John's help the Eliot family will play an important part.

"That is all I have to say. Let the rejoicing begin!"

Charles Polkinghorne got to his feet. "Just a minute, before ending this meeting, I want to say from the bottom of my heart to Mr. Eliot, and to Mrs. Eliot too, that they are jolly good fellows; and so say all of us. Three cheers for the Eliots, hip, hip, hooray!"

As the others joined in with enthusiasm, Edward Eliot held up his hand. "Enough," he said, "I am just doing what you all deserve. Well earned. Enjoy yourselves."

He signaled to a clerk standing at the back of the room, who opened the door to the inner office to reveal that the nursemaids had brought the children up from the schoolroom to join them. They were followed by servants who came out bringing drinks and hot food from the kitchen at the big house. There was cider from apples, and perry from pears, and beer brewed from malted barley, all produced on the estate. With all eyes on him, Willy Bunt joined the children in asking for apple juice, and both Eliot and Polkinghorne smiled. There were cottage loaves of bread hot from the ovens with cheese and blackberry and apple jam and, best of all, hot pasties.

"Enjoy that cider while we can afford it," said Eliot, ever the politician despite his protestations of renewed local interest. "Ending the war won't end the national debt. The brewers won't suffer alone. I have word a cider tax will be proposed, four shillings the hogshead, so drink up."

Spirits were generally high. But the children were sad at seeing their new friends prepare to leave. The Penwarden boys, Jemmy and Jedson, stood apart near their mother, one holding each of her hands as their father Addis looked on fondly but with a hint of despair in his expression. The Honorable James Trenance had made up with Catherine Bunt whose smile suggested that she had more than forgiven him for pushing her into the fishpond. Edward James Eliot solemnly shook hands with the younger William Pitt, but his eyes were on William's older sister

Harriot as he promised to be her friend for life and to be sure to stay with them next year.

Catherine Eliot overheard Morwenna pleading with her father to let her stay in Port Eliot, but he would have none of it. "It is only proper, my dear, that you come with me. You will have plenty of opportunity to be with Mr. Polkinghorne after you are married."

"Oh please, Mr. Clymo," interrupted Catherine, "I need Miss Clymo here. She is a vital part of my school. I have every confidence that she and her fiancé will comport themselves with propriety. Anyway, I will see to it myself that she is properly chaperoned." With characteristic finality, she added, "That's settled then."

Joseph Clymo nodded in defeat, recognizing that his odds of resisting two determined women were small. Edward Eliot joined them and said, "Mr. Clymo, in fact I want you to stay a day or so that we can discuss your new duties. Please postpone your departure."

Catherine Eliot went to stand close to her husband and raised her glass to him. "Oh Edward," she said, "my heart is filled with joy. What you have dreamed, what you have promised, what we will accomplish together! And the children, look at them, to think what parts they may come to play in all of our futures."

"That reminds me, my dear," said Edward, "but how could I forget?" He tapped his glass and called for attention. "My friends, there is one more thing that must be said. A wise man never takes his wife for granted. It is my duty, rather my proud joy, to pay tribute before you all to Mrs. Eliot and all that she does for me and for you, in more ways than I can enumerate. But to single out one way, which is destined to spread far beyond the bounds of Port Eliot, it is in her dedication to education. Our children and children in many other places in Cornwall will live fuller and more enriched lives because of her."

"Mrs. Eliot!" they responded, clinking glasses, sharing admiration and gratitude.

Catherine turned her attention to Elianor. "Lady Dunbargan, what I may achieve will be greater with your help," she said. "But you must stay too, since Mr. Clymo will not leave just yet to escort you."

"I must get to my family home in Bodmin as soon as possible," replied Elianor. "In my condition if I don't leave right away you may have me here for several months."

"But you must have an escort," said Catherine.

"Yes, indeed. I wonder," Elianor said, "I wonder whether you might permit me to join your party, Captain Penwarden?"

"It would be a privilege, my lady," said Addis Penwarden. "Us managed pretty well with Lizzie in the horse litter on the way up. Jemmy is big enough to ride one of the horses, and with them new turnpikes us should make fair time, if the weather holds off."

"Oh, thank you! My maid and James and his nursemaid will travel with us; I do trust you can manage us all," said Elianor.

"You must ride in my wagon, Lady Dunbargan, I insist," said Edward Eliot. "I will send my coachman with you as far as Bodmin, and then he can bring the wagon back. He can take you first thing in the morning. Penwarden, you can carry on from there."

Everything seemed to be settled and the party wound down as they expressed their thanks to each other for their friendship and support, enjoyed letting down after the stress of the last few days, wished each other well, and reluctantly said their good-byes.

But an event occurred to upset the well-laid plans and prevent the timely departure of Lady Dunbargan. That night her waters broke; she sent her maid to waken Mrs. Eliot who sent a messenger to fetch the village midwife to come as quickly as possible.

Chapter Eighty

Mission

Port Eliot was quieter after the departure of the guests, but it was not restful. While of a different order than the last few days, drama continued. In response to her urgent condition, Lady Dunbargan was attended by the village midwife and delivered in less than three hours of a beautiful and healthy baby girl. The infant had inherited her mother's distinctive coloring: porcelain skin, thick copper hair and what her proud mother discerned as blue-green eyes, although to the objective observer it required imagination to see anything distinctive about her eye color.

Only webs between her second and third toes marred her beauty, but at least that meant there was no question of her ladyship's fidelity to her husband during her troubled marriage. Revulsion at the child's paternity was overcome by maternal delight in bringing a new treasure into the world, and as soon as her baby was bathed and dressed sufficiently to make her debut, her proud mother asked her good friend Catherine Eliot to stand godmother, adding her to little Catherine Bunt as well as her own sons to love and advise.

She would be christened Gwenifer, the traditional Celtic name of Elianor's maternal grandmother and thus have no name connection with the Trenances. Elianor's whole being trembled when she thought of that family, even though the Baron had in the end, despite his obvious wish to encourage her in breeding heirs, been kindly towards her and given her that lovely necklace. She would no doubt never see it again.

There was much to plan, much to do. It was decided that Lady Dunbargan would remain with her servants at Port Eliot until she had fully recovered from the travails of childbirth and that, accordingly, the christening would take place in St. Germanus church. This would have the additional advantage of avoiding traveling to the church at Lanhydrock for the ceremony, which would have entailed risking an encounter with the viscount before his departure for America.

Another of the guests remained at Port Eliot. Morwenna Clymo's plans included marrying Charles Polkinghorne and becoming a permanent resident in St. Germans. Polkinghorne had little energy left to plan for himself and barely enough to do his job, what with his fiancée's energetic ideas for their future together and the additional tasks given to him by Edward Eliot as his responsibilities increased commensurate with his increased wages. Polkinghorne would have to discuss Morwenna's ideas with his employer when an opportune moment arose. They were manifold.

Edward Eliot kept his promise not to go up to London just yet but to fulfill his mission in Cornwall. He stayed vigilant to see to it that if Viscount Dunbargan did reappear, he would be in no position to cause trouble. He summoned his gatekeeper and ordered him to stay alert and to keep his mastiffs on short rations for the next week.

Eliot became more and more immersed in all that he had decided to do. As a result he encouraged the people who worked for him to be keep pace. As so often happens, Eliot observed, when work increases, enthusiasm and friendliness do as well, and that is a recipe for great accomplishment and the rapid passing of time.

Edward took it upon himself to speak to Catherine and ask her to help Morwenna Clymo organize her wedding, although knowing his wife he surmised that Miss Clymo would in fact find herself in the role of helper. Polkinghorne had reported that his fiancée would prefer the wedding to be at her home in Lanhydrock, but Eliot stated firmly that it would be most unwise to run the risk of the viscount interfering, so it must be held at Port Eliot. Furthermore, he would like to honor his valued employee by assuming the expenses. He had already taken the liberty of asking Mrs. Eliot to speak to the vicar about a date for the ceremony in the church.

"That is most kind of you, sir," said Polkinghorne, "but Miss Clymo is quite insistent that Reverend Perry should officiate, and I imagine the vicar would not permit him to do so in St. Germanus."

In the old days there is no doubt that Polkinghorne would have acceded to his master's wishes without demur, but since his betrothal, times had changed, and his beloved's wishes had become his commands. In the frenzy of activity he found himself largely out of the picture. At least it transpired that Mrs. Eliot's suggestions that Willy Bunt should be best man and little Catherine Bunt a flower girl at the wedding were warmly accepted, which was a welcome token of harmony prevailing between those families. The vicar's self importance was somewhat assuaged by getting an unexpected christening from a more socially acceptable quarter, and he would have to be content with presiding over the rite for little Gwenifer Trenance. Mrs. Eliot would make sure that Viscountess Dunbargan would not have to share the church with any other baptisms in the village.

Of course, Eliot could not resist keeping in touch with affairs in London, both in the House and at the Commission of Trade and Plantations. He maintained an active correspondence. He was not surprised, and happy to learn, that the cider tax was in trouble. His fellow squires resented the way that the government was meddling in their business as it tried everything it could to raise revenues to pay off the war debt.

Unlike the beer tax that inconvenienced a relatively small number of quite large brewers, the collection of the cider tax would be cumbersome and would put a heavy burden on thousands of small apple growers and cider makers. Though played out in the shires rather than on the world stage this was an issue that aroused passions, and Eliot determined that he would make the journey up to Town to exert his influence when it came to a vote. Nevertheless, he mused, someone had to pay for the war. Why not the American colonies? Much of it had been fought for their benefit. Pushing the French out of control in Canada would leave the colonists free to dominate trade with the Indians, tend to their farms and plantations, and exploit the natural resources.

He had heard that they had found deposits of iron, but the Americans had better not infringe on the mother country's monopoly. One of these days there would be opportunity to send some Cornish miners over, something he could arrange. They would fit right in with those unruly colonials, always agitating about their rights, complaining about infringements of their privileges, real or imagined, not wanting to pay their fair share. Perhaps he could arrange a place for young John. The new colony of West Florida sounded promising, although on second thoughts it would be better for him to go to the West Indies; their trade was more important.

He thought Mr. Pitt was quite right that the terms of the peace were too lenient. England always gave away too many of the hard-won fruits of victory. Too many nervous politicians wanted to skimp on war funds rather than finishing off the French when the English army and navy had them by the throat. At least, he consoled himself, he wouldn't have to pay exorbitant land taxes forever. The Cornish fishermen would do well in the Newfoundland fishing grounds, and the government should encourage them, not to settle there, but to use it as a secure base. Cornishmen should live in Cornwall. Settlement meant having to get tangled up in administration, and there was no need for that.

Eliot was all for the deep blue sea foreign policy. After all, he thought, the main point of all these wars was to dominate the world's shipping. He'd heard that England's merchant marine had grown to over five hundred thousand tons. That meant a lot of shipbuilding. Those new three-decker merchantmen on the India run only lasted three round trips, what with the ravages of the shipworm, and had to be replaced. The new copper bottoms helped, and provided another good market for the Cornish mines.

Damn foreigners had to be kept in line, too. The government should clamp down on those greedy American smugglers as well. Then the government could collect the proper duties, especially on molasses for the rum trade. And there should be stronger laws to make sure that goods were shipped in English bottoms, especially to and from the American colonies. Keep the Royal Navy busy after the war is over, and keep Cornish mariners employed, those that hadn't been pressed into the navy, poor devils.

Meanwhile, Eliot worked energetically with Polkinghorne at improving his agricultural interests, getting the rents up. Many of his tenants had followed his lead in introducing better breeds of sheep, but too many still clung to the scrawny half-wild Cornish native breeds. Conservative lot these farmers, but they had to be made to understand that investing in quality stock, albeit at a higher price, would improve yields. They complained about the increased cost of winter feed, but progressive landowners upcountry were getting good results with oil seed cake. He urged Polkinghorne to persist in encouraging them to try new things.

Eliot talked to Bunt about expanding the quarries and following up on the new turnpikes that were being built. There was still work required in making arrangements for the St. Austell and Lostwithiel roads, twenty more miles at Saltash and thirty-four at Callington. Bunt was a clever chap. Why could they not make more use of the steam engines, maybe for crushing the road stone, as Bunt had suggested? He kept in touch with Penwarden and Williams about developing the mines. They generally did a good job underground, but as he looked at the cost book figures, there were costs to be saved on the grass, preparing and shipping the tinstuff.

Catherine kept telling Edward about new ideas of natural philosophy which she had been discussing with her bookish women friends. She pressed him to consult further with John Smeaton. He was another clever chap, and Eliot would encourage him with the help of Penwarden and Williams to invent machines to do the work cheaper and faster, at the quarries as well as the mines.

Edward Eliot diligently interspersed these efforts with correspondence with his colleagues in London. He was more and more interested in America and the opportunities it might offer him, and he wanted to keep an eye on developments. As an official of the crown it was partly up to him to administer the policies of the king and his senior ministers. It was all very complicated. Nine of the thirteen colonies fell under the royal prerogative but two elected their own governors and two were proprietary. It did not seem to make much difference to how quarrelsome they were.

None of the colonies shared a sense of obligation to help pay for the war. To the contrary, Mr. Pitt had agreed to pay them for their modest military support. England had paid to get the French out. The colonists had better help pay to keep them out.

Eliot was not willing to continue paying high land taxes on Port Eliot to keep the farmers and merchants of New York, Massachusetts and

New Hampshire safe in their beds. Of course, if he had investments in the colonies himself, he would have more sympathy with their point of view.

Eliot did feel compelled to leave Port Eliot with Catherine in February long enough to attend the House and vote against the cider tax, but he might as well have stayed home. Lord Bute was determined to push it through, and he succeeded regardless of the opposition. He said that despite all the other measures that had been adopted, the government needed to raise the excise. He miscalculated. The tax and Bute himself had become so unpopular that people in the country rioted; even the Londoners went into the streets. Bute lacked the fortitude to withstand the pressure. He lost his nerve and resigned.

The king knew it was no good asking William Pitt to serve again, so he appointed Pitt's brother-in-law, George Grenville. He was another clever fellow, but arrogant. He was determined to get the government's finances under control. He was cheese-paring in the extreme. He would put things into proper order. Good for him.

Since the argument for the expense of the war was that it would bring about increased trade once the French were thrown out, then he would put an end to the lax enforcement of duties and make the colonials pay their share. He had ideas about new taxes in America too, something about imposing a fee on official documents and newspapers, a stamp duty it would be called. It was only just, not that the colonists would agree. Eliot was concerned that Grenville could press too far.

Later in the year, the Eliots were glad to get home again to Port Eliot. Edward was relieved that he had escaped Catherine's spending too much on new clothes or furnishings for the house; she found little that pleased her. What she did bring back were still more progressive ideas from her meetings with her Blue Stockings friends. Edward quickly got back into the swing of things and was pleased to hear from his increasingly trusted lieutenants that his farming and business interests were progressing well.

Catherine received a letter from Lady Dunbargan. The good news was that young James and little Gwenifer were both with her and in good health, doing well and even more importantly that the viscount had finally taken himself off to America. It was unclear how long his stay would last. While he had prevailed upon the Bolitho firm to oversee matters during his absence, he had made no permanent arrangements as to the disposal of his property. She was perfectly prepared to wait until his death, which she prayed might come soon, no doubt at the hands of someone that he gratuitously insulted or seriously injured.

"America should suit him well," commented Edward, as he and Catherine enjoyed their time before dinner in the library. "He'll find himself among kindred spirits, the heathens, not the gentlemen, and we are well rid of him."

The sad news from Elianor was that Lizzie Penwarden had made no improvement and was not expected to survive into the new year. Catherine was a little surprised that her friend would take such an interest in the Penwarden family. After all, they were hardly of her class, but of course they had all participated together in Dunbargan's downfall. Edward felt that Addis Penwarden was a valued employee and, as such, he and Catherine should also express their interest and sympathy and accordingly wrote a letter to Captain Penwarden.

The following February they received another letter from Elianor Dunbargan. They read, *"I have been advised that poor Mrs. Penwarden is dying. I know that you hold her husband in high esteem and indeed he has shown great kindness to me. I feel sure that you would wish to join me in extending sympathy to the soon to be bereaved family and attend their funeral. May I impose upon your friendship and request that you escort me upon the journey?"*

While the Eliots had a high regard for Captain Penwarden they did not know Lizzie well; Catherine was not inclined to comply. However, Edward felt it only proper to express their condolences in person to a valued employee in his great loss. Anyway, it was high time that he made a visit to his mining interests and thought that they should go. He decided to have Joseph Clymo come with them since he assisted in overseeing the mining interests. He would suggest that Miss Clymo came too, give Polkinghorne a week or two of breathing space from her energetic ministrations to his house.

They arrived near the end of the month to be greeted by the Reverend Peter Perry with the announcement that they were too late to say their farewells to Lizzie but just in time for her funeral. "Mrs. Penwarden was much loved in the village and the villages around," said the preacher. "Her husband is much admired. There are crowds among the farmers and the fishermen as well as the miners who wish to pay their respects. The chapel would be filled to overflowing, so with Mr. Penwarden's agreement I am going to hold the funeral in Gwennap Pit."

"How soon will that be?" asked Eliot.

"I'm going to wait a day or two, the weather in February is always cold, so there is no need to hurry," said Reverend Perry. "It's Leap Year, as you know, so the funeral will be on the twenty-ninth. That is a very significant date in these parts, and to me personally. I hear a comet is expected, altogether a most auspicious time. I am pleased and honored that you, your wife and Lady Dunbargan will be with us; Mr. Clymo and his daughter too."

"We are privileged to be here, Reverend," said Catherine, "and while we are here, I imagine Miss Clymo has something to request from you about a more joyful occasion."

"She already has," said the preacher. "Miss Clymo does not let grass grow under her feet. With your approval and assuming your vicar does not object, I would be delighted to marry them in St. Germans."

"Leave the vicar to me," said Catherine, "all it takes is to set the date."

Addis Penwarden joined them with his sons holding his hands, biting their lips, trying to hold back tears. Eliot shook his hand. "It is kind of you all to come, sir," said Addis. Elianor Dunbargan smiled warmly at him as he said to Eliot, "Perhaps you'd like to see what we've been doing at Wheal Hykka, sir, now that you're here?"

"All in good time, Captain," said Eliot, "All in good time." Joseph Clymo nodded his agreement.

A day or two later the Eliot party joined the crowds streaming into Gwennap Pit. For once at this time of year in west Cornwall there was no rain, little cloud and the sky was clear. The air was chilly that afternoon and the grass ringing the Pit was still damp from the frost that had been melted earlier by the watery sun.

Catherine Eliot tucked her hand into her husband's arm. "This place has a strange atmosphere," she said. "I don't think I'll get used to it no matter how many times I come."

A big crowd gathered to pay their last respects to Lizzie Penwarden, expectant, murmuring among themselves. The congregation hushed as the Reverend Perry entered at the top of the circle, ushering in Addis Penwarden followed by Jemmy and Jedson. Bearers quietly laid a coffin by the granite posts marking the entrance to the Pit. The choir from the Pendeen chapel sang a hymn composed by the Reverend Wesley, one they had grown to love. Reverend Perry held up his arms and the crowd bowed their heads in silence.

"We are here to wish God speed to our beloved Lizzie Penwarden, whom we took into our arms when she and her family came to live among us in Pendeen. She has set in her too short life a fine example of love and service and the courage to rise above tribulation and tragedy. She has been taken from us before she could do for our community all that she wished, but she in herself and in her support for her husband helped bring about change in Cornwall, change for the good."

Reverend Perry paused and looked around the men and women and children ranked around the great pit. He looked intently into the eyes of Addis Penwarden and the Eliots and their party. These were good people who still lived to do good, bring change. They exchanged warm glances, nods of mutual appreciation.

Addis Penwarden squared his shoulders; he had attended too many funerals with Reverend Perry. Perhaps with Mr. Eliot's help there would be fewer in future, at least among the tinners. Elianor Dunbargan, Catherine Eliot and Morwenna Clymo each brushed back a tear. Captain Williams stood near them having ridden over to pay his respects.

"There has been much change in Cornwall, and there is still much to come," said the preacher, his words heard clearly across the pit.

Edward Eliot looked at Joseph Clymo standing beside him and whispered, "You will be a big part of that change, Mr. Clymo."

Clymo took off his hat. "Thanks to you, sir, thanks to you from all of us."

When the funeral service ended the late afternoon light was fading. The people climbed out of the Pit and walked their separate ways. The visitors to Pendeen shook the hand of Reverend Perry and bade him and each other farewell. Those who could afford it went to their rooms at The Trewellard Arms to sleep before setting off the next day on their long journeys home. The other visitors went to the homes of friends in the village who were only too pleased to offer them hospitality.

Unbeknownst to each other they shared many of the same thoughts as they prepared to take their beds. They thought of those who died, of the conflicts and sicknesses that brought about their deaths. They wondered what change their deaths would bring to the lives of those who still lived. They thought about their own futures, those of their children, and the loved ones with whom those futures would be spent. They wondered what would happen to Cornwall, to America, and where they would live out their lives.

As darkness fell, those who looked out of their windows before blowing out their candles saw stars shining in the clear night sky. And some saw a comet, leaving its trail as it traversed the sky towards Lands End. It was February 29th 1764, leap year, a sign. Great change was coming to their lives, to Cornwall.

Acknowledgements

In the over five years of writing The Miner & the Viscount, I received bountiful help. Heartfelt thanks to those whose invaluable input expanded the scope and shed light on the context of this book.

Some I must single out, including my editors: my wife Cynthia Osborne Hoskin (also my designer and graphics and computer guru) and Maureen (Mo) Conlan (of the Monday Morning Writers Group), who both, as professional writers and editors, enormously enriched, enlivened and clarified my story.

For enlightening visits to the places where my story takes place, I especially thank:

The Earl of St. Germans and his staff at Port Eliot for their generous access to the house, artworks and grounds;

Mr. and Mrs. A. D. G. Fortescue of Boconnoc who took time from their busy restoration and planning to add vital Pitt family lore and provide a Cornish pasty lunch;

Paul Holden of Lanhydrock, curator and architectural historian, National Trust for Historic Preservation and Natural Beauty, author of *Lanhydrock*, (published by History Press, available from Lanhydrock Shop, Lanhydrock, Cornwall, PL30 5AD), whose erudite guided tour through the property added crucial details;

The guides to the mining museums in Redruth and Pendean for sharing their knowledge and dedication;

Thanks also to Maj. Hugo White, Maj. Trevor Stipwell and Ms. Rhonda Seymour of the Regimental Museum in Bodmin for contributing authenticity to the description of musket drill and the history of the predecessors of the Duke of Cornwall's Light Infantry.

I also thank Maureen Fuller, Grand Bard of the Cornish Gorsedh who, in the midst of worldwide travels and the demands of her office, gave insight and scholarly translation of dialog among the tinners into the ancient language Kernewek. Gratitude to my daughter, Sarah Hoskin Clymer, for her love of Cornwall, encouragement and social marketing support throughout. For her rigorously professional reading of the almost finished manuscript, I thank Carol Cartaino of White Oak Editions. For the impressive clues and access to sources, I thank Wikipedia and its many contributors.

And, lastly, my thanks to Cornish photographer Michael Saunders for the magnificent cover photograph of St. Michael's Mount. (See more photos at www.viewbug.com/member/Mick66ey)

There were many, many more whose advice and reinforcement spurred me on; they know who they are, and they know my appreciation.

✤✤✤

For information on visiting the properties featured in The Miner & the Viscount, please visit the following:
http://www.porteliot.co.uk/
http://www.boconnoc.com/
http://www.nationaltrust.org.uk/lanhydrock/
http://www.nationaltrust.org.uk/levant-mine/
http://www.gwennappit.co.uk/
http://www.visitcornwall.com/

Richard Hoskin
Kentucky, 2014